THE WISHING GAME

VERONICA LANCET

PREFACE

Dear Reader,

The Wishing Game is the first book in a trilogy. This will end on a cliffhanger. While this is not as dark as my other books, the hero is still a *villain*. You may know him from his appearances in the House of Cryos, where he is the main villain. If you like redemption arcs, then this will be for you.

This trilogy is a slow burn.

Trigger Warnings:
Dubious consent situations
Death of a loved one
Mentions of human slavery

Aperion
Aperionia
House of Cryos
House of Psyche
House of Moirae
House of Chronos
House of Gaia
House of Phaos
House of Ananke
House of Flora
House of Bronte
House of Arke
House of Skia
House of Polemos
House of Anemo
House of Pyros
House of Hydros

House of
Chronos
Aperio
Aperion
House of

House of
Cryos
House of
Psyche
House of
Moirae
House of
Gaia
House of
Phaos

House of Ananke
House of Arke
House of Skia
House of Pyros

House of Flora
House of Bronte
House of lemos
House of Anemo
House of Hydros
N
S
E
W

ONE

My lids are sluggish as I try to pry my eyes open. In the distance, I hear a beeping sound that seems to become louder and louder.

"Doctor, she's coming around," someone calls out—a voice I vaguely recognize.

"Please wait outside," someone else speaks.

A bright light probes at my eyes before an elderly woman's face appears before me.

"Mrs. Archibald, can you hear me?"

I open my mouth to answer, but my throat feels as if it's on fire. A ragged sound makes it past my lips as I mumble a barely intelligible request for water. A nurse seems to understand me, and she brings me a glass, then helps me take a few sips.

God, what happened? Every sip is as if something sharp is raking down my throat.

"You might feel some discomfort since we had to intubate you," the doctor explains.

My eyes flash at her before I frown.

"W-what happened?" I croak.

"You were in a car accident," she tells me in a matter-of-fact voice. "You broke your arm and bruised your ribs from the impact. But there was an explosion and you were hit in the back of your head by flying debris. We've had to perform a craniotomy to reduce swelling."

Looking down at myself, I note the cast around my left arm, and raising my good hand to my head, I feel the bandage that surrounds my entire head. My torso is tender, and discomfort accompanies every breath.

The events of the accident are fuzzy, but I remember the truck that almost hit us. Nikki veered to the side to avoid it, but it had been too late.

"My husband. I want to see my husband."

The doctor gives me a strained look, and panic swells in my chest.

"My husband, Doctor. Where is my husband?" I repeat more forcefully. My chest contracts with every word spoken, the pain intensifying.

"You've been out for a week, Mrs. Archibald," she continues, swallowing hard. "Your condition is still precarious and—"

"My husband," I grit out. "Where is Nikki?"

She blinks at me before she clears her throat.

"Your friend is here to see you," she says briskly before excusing herself.

I stare wide-eyed after her, shocked at her dismissive attitude. Yet that can only mean one thing... My lips tremble as all sorts of scenarios build inside my mind, but I quickly squash down those thoughts.

Nikki is fine. I nod to myself.

The moment the doctor is out, Noelle breezes through the open door, running toward me.

"Oh, Lulu! You're awake," she exclaims as she barely stops herself from giving me a hug. Her arms extend forward before she draws them back.

Her joy is genuine, although there's a wariness behind her eyes, something in the way her eyes glisten with a mix of tears of happiness and sorrow.

I gulp down against the wave of anguish that threatens to batter my very being.

"Noelle, where is Nikki?" I ask her directly.

She falters, taking a step back. Her body language screams distress.

A hollowness develops in my stomach.

"Lulu, you just woke up..." she stammers, fighting to keep the smile on her face.

"Where's my husband?" I repeat, my voice breaking as the meaning of their prevarication sinks in. "Please tell me where my Nikki is," I add in a pained whisper.

She bites her lip and, coming closer, she takes my hand in hers, squeezing tightly.

A flash appears in my mind and I see Nikki on the ground, covered in blood. His hand is on my hand, giving me a comforting squeeze right before he...

"He died at the scene," Noelle finally says. "There was nothing the doctors could do for him."

"No." I shake my head. "That's not possible. My husband can't be dead."

"I'm sorry, Lulu. I'm so, so sorry," she whispers, tears swimming in her eyes.

"It's not true. It can't be true. I need to see him," I mumble incoherently.

He's not dead. How can he be dead? No, I refuse to believe that.

Shaking off her hold, I rip the IV from my arm and swing my legs over the bed.

My eyes close just as I inhale deeply, a sharp pain pricking my side.

Everything hurts.

"Lulu, you can't..."

"I need to see him. I won't believe it until I see him. My Nikki is *not* dead."

He would never leave me. That day we met again, five years ago, he promised me he would never leave me—that I would be his just as he would be mine.

Forever.

He wouldn't break his word to me.

"Lulu, I know it must be hard to believe and I realize you must be feeling as if the entire world is about to end—I would feel the same—but you need to take care of yourself first," Noelle pleads with me as she tries to grab my arm.

I slap it aside as I put one foot in front of the other, almost as if learning to walk again. The pain is just as intense on the second step—maybe even more. But despite this excruciating physical agony I find myself in, I cannot bring myself to stop until I see him with my own eyes.

He's not dead. He *can't* be dead.

Just the other day he promised he would leave his mark on my skin—sear his words of love into my flesh so I'd never be ashamed of my scars again. Just the other day we planned a future—one far, far away from all the chaos of the city. Far from vengeance and greed. A future in which we'd be free.

Just the two of us.

Free...

"Lulu!"

I reach the door of the salon, wrench it open, and come face to face with the doctor and a couple of nurses.

"You can't be out of bed," the doctor says, instructing the nurses to take me back.

I shake my head, evading them. I'm not in control of my limbs at this point—my desperation is. "I need to see my husband," I mumble as I wobble down the corridor.

One of the nurses catches my right arm, trying to hold me back without hurting me.

"You need to go back, Mrs. Archibald. You'll hurt yourself."

"No," I spit out, and with a force I didn't know I was capable of, I dislodge her hand from my arm, continuing forward. "Just tell me where my husband is. I need to see my husband."

"He's dead, Lulu... You have to believe me. I wouldn't lie to you," Noelle calls from behind.

"No. I won't believe that until I see him. Take me to my husband, please."

"Lulu..."

"Mrs. Archibald, I'm afraid that won't be possible," the other nurse intervenes just as I spot from the corner of my eye a couple of security guards heading my way. "You've been asleep for a week. Someone had to decide what to do with his body, and his family decided they would cremate him."

"What?" I stop, pivoting to look at her. "What family? *I* am his family." I point to myself. Panic rises in my chest, and my vision starts to swim.

"Since you could not make that decision, the next of kin was consulted. I can find out who it was for you..."

"Who was it?" I turn to Noelle, walking around her in a circle, a harsh clamor laying siege over my mind.

She gives me an apologetic look. She knows enough of Nikki's family to realize why this should have never happened.

"His aunt. Ophelia."

I swallow hard, pressing my lips together.

"Why? Why would she cremate him?"

"She said it was what he would have wanted, and no one objected to it."

I close my eyes for a moment, stepping back until my back hits the wall. Even that small impact makes me reel in pain.

"He can't be dead," I whisper, anguish lacing my voice.

"I'm so sorry, Luce..."

I don't answer. I can no longer answer. My body moves at some point, either on its own or being led by others.

I'm put to bed.

There's a dull prick of a needle as an IV is inserted in my arm.

I stare at the ceiling. Numb.

No tears come out of my eyes. None.

I simply stare at the ceiling, counting all the little imperfections until my brain shuts off.

For the next few days, everything is a haze as I come in and out of consciousness. At some point, I realize they've decided to sedate me because I was a *danger to myself.*

I don't talk.

I don't speak to anyone.

I just stare at the ceiling, waiting for the next IV to be plugged in so I can burrow away into nothingness—so I can stop myself from *feeling*.

Yet even the sedative they give me cannot take that away.

Locked behind a wall of fog, I cannot form any conscious thought. But the pain is there. Oh, it's *always* there.

Yet I don't cry. Somehow, at one moment or another, I'd stopped being able to cry.

I think of Nikki—my sweet husband—and no tears come.

There's only this emptiness that becomes larger and larger with each passing moment—a void that threatens to swallow me whole. Oh, but I'd let it. In fact, I'm welcoming it.

Please swallow me. Please take me away from the meaninglessness of it all.

It doesn't.

It's simply there, torturing me, beckoning me, tricking me.

And I can do nothing but let it on the off chance that tomorrow might come and I won't open my eyes again—that I'll meet him again.

But that never happens.

It's at the end of the week when the nurses take the bandage off my head that I'm informed the police want to speak with me and take my statement.

For the first time since learning that the love of my life is no longer in this world, I feel a light jolt of awareness. He might be dead, but the person responsible for all of this is still out there, and according to Noelle, he's still alive.

"Officer," I nod at two men who enter my room.

"Mrs. Archibald. Thank you for agreeing to speak with us. I understand you're going to make a full recovery?"

"That is correct," I answer blankly. "I'd like to know what you're going to charge the man who crashed into us with," I say, cutting straight to the chase.

Both men frown.

"We're not going to charge him with anything."

"What do you mean?" My eyes widen as I shuffle into a sitting position.

"Ma'am, they didn't tell you?"

"What?" I frown.

"Your husband was the one who caused the accident."

"What?" I burst out in surprise. "No, that's not true. The truck was coming toward us and my husband tried to veer to the side to avoid it, but it still crashed into us."

"Ma'am." The policeman clears his throat. "Your husband's toxicological report came back positive for opioids. We know he was on drugs at the time of the accident. You don't have to hide it from us."

I stare at them, utterly befuddled.

"No." I shake my head. "Absolutely not. My husband only took anxiety medication. Nothing else. I'm sure of it. He's never done drugs in his life. Even when he got shot in the leg, he never took any opioids for the pain."

The two policemen share a look.

"We've checked with his therapist, and his toxicological report didn't match with the pills he was prescribed," one of them says. "He must have obtained the drugs illegally and disguised them as anxiety medication."

My face falls at what they're implying. My mouth hangs open in shock as I cannot find the words to refute their accusation—how could I when it's simply outrageous? Nikki would have *never* bought illegal drugs, nor would he have lied to me.

The other looks contrite as he adds, "I'm sorry to be the one to break it to you, Mrs. Archibald, but your husband had a very high percentage of opioids in his blood. If he was already taking other medication, he could have easily hidden the opioids from you."

The memory of Nikki taking that medicine right before the accident flashes in my head, but I dismiss it.

"No. You're wrong. He would have never done that, Officer.

He would have never taken a risk with my life," I tell them staunchly.

If there's anything that I'm sure of, it's that Nikki would have *never* done anything that could result in me being harmed. To hear that he had taken drugs while driving? With me by his side? Preposterous.

"The lab results don't lie, Mrs. Archibald. I know it's hard to believe, but it's the truth."

"So that's it? You're just going to make him the one guilty for the accident? Just like that? The other driver crashed into *us*."

"We've checked everything thoroughly, ma'am, and there's nothing to confirm your story. If anything, it's the reverse. The other truck has marks that show your RV crashed into it."

"You might be misremembering because of your head injury," the other one continues. "But back to the purpose of our visit. We wanted to let you know that the injured party will not press charges and has decided to settle with your family lawyer for the damages."

I stare at them, flabbergasted.

They say a few more things, but I tune them out.

"We wish you a speedy recovery, Mrs. Archibald," the words barely register in my brain. I don't reply, staring at their retreating figures until the door snaps shut.

Am I remembering it wrong?

That can't be, can it?

Did my injury change my perception of the events?

But no, I can remember everything clearly up to the moment of collision. I know what I saw and what I felt. The truck hit *us*, and we were both catapulted out of the cockpit.

My brows furrow as I try to focus on the events of that day. Had Nikki seemed weird? Had he behaved out of the ordinary?

Well, he'd certainly surprised me with our outing, but could that be the effect of heavy drugs?

I bite my lip in uncertainty, but I quickly shake myself.

He's my Nikki. I *know* him.

Coincidentally, not long after the policemen are gone, the new phone Noelle had gotten for me rings—it's our lawyer.

"Hello, Mr. Daniels. I understand you've settled with the *victim?*" I add sarcastically.

"Always straight to the point, Mrs. Archibald. Yes, indeed. We've given him enough to cover all the damages, both material and emotional."

"Is that so..."

"But that is not what I wanted to discuss with you," he continues blithely. "I've been told you will be discharged from the hospital tomorrow."

"That is correct," I speak slowly, alarm bells going off in my brain.

"I will have a car waiting for you to take you to the penthouse. The entire family will be present for the reading of the will."

"What?" I ask in a clipped tone. "I don't want *any* of those people in my home."

"Then perhaps you'd be amenable to coming to our office?"

"Why would they be needed there anyway? Nikki assured me they weren't included in the will."

"I cannot say, I'm afraid. This is the protocol."

"I'll meet you at the office," I add dryly.

"Three o'clock," he says in a sing-song voice, and before I utter any profanities, I hang up.

Oh, Nikki, what the hell happened?

I'm slow to react due to my brain injury and the sedatives that have kept me in a state of drowsiness. My mind is starting to awaken and ask all sorts of questions.

Nothing makes sense. Absolutely nothing.

But practical as I always am, I force myself not to dwell on my husband's death—if I did, I doubt I'd ever be able to get out of this goddamn bed—and focus on the matter at hand. The suspicious accident. Nikki's supposed drug use. My alleged faulty memory...

Could any of this be possible?

Yes, I admit that it *could* happen. Logically, things *make* sense. But I don't trust logic as much as I trust Nikki, and because of that, I'm certain he would *never* take opioids. On top of that, with his family's presence at the reading of the will, my senses are telling me something is definitely off.

How many times had they tried to kill him before? How many times had they tried to get their hands on his money, only to fail?

Experience tells me they are the most likely culprit. Why else would they cremate him so quickly? Why else would they make it all seem his fault?

"They won't get away with this, Nikki," I whisper, the chasm inside my heart deepening even more. "I won't let them."

I won't rest until I get justice for you. And then... Then... I smile, closing my eyes and thinking back to our happy times.

Then we'll be happy again—together.

TWO

One week ago

My palms are clammy, my breathing accelerating with each passing second. The elevator doors open again and Nikki takes my hand, leading me out.

We walk for a couple of minutes before we suddenly stop.

Nikki reaches behind my back to untie my blindfold. I blink a couple of times as I look around. We're in the garage, but I don't know what I'm supposed to look for. I don't drive, and though Nikki has a license, he doesn't drive either.

"I don't get—" I stop as it dawns on me what he's pointing toward.

It's an RV, a really big one by the sight of it. It's almost the size of a truck.

"Is that..." I clear my throat, barely able to form any coherent thoughts. "Is that ours?"

"Remember what you told me a year ago when we moved to New York and you saw a motorhome for the first time?"

I nod absentmindedly. How could I not remember that?

"You said how freeing it would be to live in one of those, not tied to any place but at the same time belonging to all? You said you'd love to travel around and see all the places you'd only seen in movies or read about in books. And when you realized that you might never be able to do that because of my condition, you apologized and said it was just wishful thinking. That it didn't matter where we lived as long as we are together."

"And you remembered." I swallow hard as my heart rate picks up.

"Of course I remember. It was more than wishful thinking, Luce. I could tell how much you wanted it, but you settled for less because of me. That was when I realized I couldn't go on like this. I couldn't..." he trails off, his Adam's apple bobbing up and down in discomfort. "You should *never* settle for less, sweetheart."

I watch the warring emotions on his face and realize how much thought he put into this. Now it makes sense why he'd suddenly decided to switch therapists and why he'd gone through a few before finding a good fit. He was doing it all for me.

Tears of happiness slide down my cheeks as I look into his dark eyes. The magnitude of his love for me floors me, and not for the first time, I thank the fates for bringing this man into my life.

I first met Nikki when I was sixteen. I was living in a remote area of Mexico that was under the control of Sergio Villanueva—a self-proclaimed god who dabbled in various illegal avenues. I'd been given to him as tribute when I was thirteen, and because I rebelled against what that entailed, I was sent to waste away working in tunnels of his temple—a grand, ostentatious display of Sergio's wealth and his divine providence. It was in the darkness of that tunnel that I met Nikki, the only flicker of light in my hopeless life.

I knew right away that he didn't belong there, and I did my best to help him escape, never thinking he would actually come back for me. Yet he did. A little over two years later, he showed up for me—to save *me*. And the only reason why he'd taken so long had been because he'd been in an accident that had put him in a coma for two years.

Nikki, or by his full name Nicholas Archibald, had been born to unimaginable riches. His family owned almost half the United States, and he was the heir of a dynasty. But with so much power comes so much danger. He survived seeing his parents brutally murdered in front of him at the age of ten, five successful kidnappings, and over sixteen attempts on his life, including one that resulted in brain damage that put him into a coma and a shooting gone wrong that gave him a permanent limp for which he requires a cane to this day. But despite still being alive, some scars can never heal.

A few years back, he was formally diagnosed with PTSD, social anxiety, and agoraphobia. And while the meds he was on did their job for a while, after he got shot in the knee during our honeymoon, his anxiety skyrocketed to the extent that he barely left our home anymore.

We lived in Texas for a while, in a home with security features specifically designed for his paranoid mind. But after I reconnected with an old friend, he made the effort to move with me to New York so I could be near her. Still, it hasn't been easy on him, and although we go out once every couple of months or so, it usually causes him great distress. So to hear that he's made such strides in his mental health journey makes me overflow with hope. I can't stop myself from crying, tears of joy spilling down my cheeks.

"You're so brave, Nikki." I smile as I take a step forward.

Molding my palm to his cheek, I stroke him lightly, all the while not taking my gaze off his. He swallows hard, and in his eyes, I see mirrored all the pain and struggles he's had to overcome to get to this point.

"You deserve nothing less," he replies in a low voice. Clearing his throat, he grabs my hand, laying a sweet kiss on the inside of my wrist before he invites me to check out the inside of the RV.

My cheeks heat as I realize I've already forgotten about the RV.

"I've already loaded it up with all necessities, but I wanted to wait for you to pick out some clothes and items for the road."

"Wait? The road? When are we leaving?"

"I didn't buy this to sit in the garage." He laughs. "We leave the moment you're ready. I have a few locations picked out upstate so we can slowly get used to it, but after that, you can decide our itinerary."

I stare at him, flabbergasted. Although I was sure I'd love his present, I never imagined it to be something like this.

"We leave tomorrow," I declare suddenly.

He doesn't object, his lips merely pulling up in a knowing smile.

"The fridge is already stocked," he whispers in my ear.

Oh, the rogue! He knew I'd want to leave as soon as possible.

Nikki steps in front of the RV door and places his thumb on the exterior pad. The door slides open just as a staircase unfolds in front of us.

Shaking my head at him, I go up the steps until we're both inside the RV. Nikki closes the door behind us and waits tensely for me to react to what I'm seeing.

"Nikki..." I murmur in awe.

I take a step forward, simply marveling at the inside. It's about forty feet long.

"You had this custom-made," I state. The entire RV is decorated in a mix of pastels, lilac being the predominant one—and also my favorite color.

"Of course," he replies, almost offended I'd think otherwise.

As we step inside, there's the driver's seat in black leather and next to it another purple seat, which I assume is for me. My lips tug up at the level of detail of the RV, but this is just the beginning.

Turning, I notice a small sitting area with a leather love seat in a deep purple color and a black table in front of it. Right next to it is a full-sized kitchen.

"This was one of the things I wouldn't compromise on. I know how much you love to cook, so I told them to add all your favorite appliances."

The counters and the furniture are a light lilac color, while the appliances are a deep violet. To say I'm impressed would be an understatement.

Curious, I go over to the fridge and open it to find it fully stocked with fruits, vegetables, yogurt, and a variety of meats.

"You really went all out," I praise him.

He merely smiles, showing me all the compartments the kitchen has. Even though the space is limited, it has a lot of storage, all cleverly designed to blend in with the background.

As we walk further into the RV, there is a sliding door that leads to a narrow path. On one side, there's a bathroom, fully equipped with a sizable shower and toilet, while on the other side, there's a double study space. One desk is black while the other is a pastel mauve, each with matching chairs. There's also an iMac on each desk—of course, mine is the purple one.

"And here's the pièce de résistance." He points toward the door at the end of the hallway.

I follow him as he slides the door open to reveal our bedroom.

A king-sized bed is in the middle of the room and a wardrobe right behind it. On each side of the bed, there are huge windows that light up the entire room.

"These are tinted and bulletproof," Nikki comments as he knocks on one window, pride evident in his voice. "No one on the outside can see us."

Giving him a wide grin, I throw myself on the bed to test the mattress. A giggle escapes me when it bounces as Nikki joins me. He tackles me, rolling with me as he showers me with kisses. I wrap my arms around him, out of breath but incredibly full of happiness.

"Scratch that. I can go up and pack a few things, and we can leave at dawn. What do you think?"

"You just have to say the word, Luce." He smiles and lays a kiss on my nose.

It doesn't take us long to pack our stuff. I only grab a few of my favorite clothes, my Kindle, a few makeup items, and a couple of perfumes. I noticed that the bathroom was fully stocked with soap, shampoo, and conditioner. At this point, what had Nikki *not* thought of? I'm still in awe at his surprise, and I don't think I would have ever guessed it—not in a million years.

How could I, when I've known about his struggles for years, and at one point, instead of getting better, he'd only gotten worse? Yet because I loved him so much, I didn't care. I would have been satisfied with being with him in our home—without ever going out if that was what he needed.

————————

It's almost dawn when we both take the elevator down to the garage, each carrying a bag and nothing more.

"This feels like the start of an adventure, Nikki. I can't wait." I squeal when the elevator stops and run out toward the RV.

Nikki opens the door, making sure to add my fingerprint to the system before we climb in. It takes us less than half an hour to organize our stuff, and once we're done, Nikki takes his place behind the wheel and I sit next to him on my purple seat.

"You're sure you're good with driving this?"

"I took some extra lessons," he assures me with a wink.

My cheeks redden, and I put on my seat belt as he leads the car out of the garage and onto the freeway.

The entire RV is inundated with natural sunlight, and that only increases my good mood as I put on a cheery song on the radio.

Nikki is focused on the road, but I'm quick to realize I shouldn't have worried at all. He's a very smooth driver, making it seem almost effortless.

"I want to get my license, too," I tell him.

"Anytime, sweetheart. I can teach you the basics first and then we'll look into booking you an exam."

I nod vigorously.

"God, Nikki. I can't tell you how excited I am for this. It's the best surprise ever, and it's not even my birthday yet!" I gush, my eyes sparkling with excitement as I glance at him.

"Oh, just you wait for it. I have another little surprise for you. Later," he says with a languid grin.

My brows shoot up in curiosity, and I barely stop myself from badgering him about it since I know he needs to keep his attention on the road.

Since this is my first road trip—*ever*—I can't help but be in utter awe of my surroundings. Especially as we exit the city and there's nature everywhere. Compared to the area I grew up in Mexico, this is so green and lush and so inviting. I'm close to sticking my face to the window as I try to take in the scenery. Nikki chuckles at my expense, but I can tell he's equally intrigued by what he's seeing. If to me this feels absolutely freeing, then I can't imagine what it must be like for him.

"How are you feeling?" I ask him a while later when we decide to stop for the night.

We drove for about six hours upstate, and it's already taken a toll on Nikki since he's not used to driving for such long periods of time.

"Tired but otherwise good," he says as he pops a pill in his mouth before chasing it with water.

I make us a quick dinner, and Nikki helps me set the table for us to eat. Since I don't want to waste any of these precious moments, I decide to go with an easy stir-fry with vegetables and chicken.

"How's your anxiety?" I ask as I take a bite.

"Just a little hum. I'm fine, Luce. You don't need to worry about me." He gives me a tight smile.

I purse my lips.

"This is our first real outing. Of course I'll worry."

He waves me off, but I'm not deterred.

We chat casually as we eat, but my eyes are on him, and I'll be watching him like a hawk for any sign that he might be feeling off—and if he does, then we return home immediately. I don't want him to suffer in silence just to please me.

After we load the dishes into the dishwasher and set the timer, Nikki pours both of us a glass of red wine.

"Your family won't like it," I note quietly as I take a sip of wine.

"I know." He sighs. "I hope to avoid them finding out for as long as possible. But considering they have spies everywhere..."

"There should be something we can do."

"What? I've thought of everything over the years, Luce, but I don't have any proof. Not for the accident, not for the shooting, not for any of the other attempts on my life."

"Shouldn't the fact that they have the most to win if you die count?"

"Not anymore." He smiles.

I tilt my head, frowning.

"What do you mean?"

"You're the sole beneficiary of my fortune. I changed my will as soon as we got married. I would have changed it sooner, but because of my head injury, I had to pass some tests before they declared me mentally fit to make any such decisions."

I blink in surprise.

"You..."

"Of course, a part will go to Malia, too," he mentions our goddaughter with a smile.

"That's... I don't know what to say, Nikki."

"You don't have to say anything. All my life I've been hunted down for this cursed money. They've taken almost everything from me, Luce. Almost everything." He takes a deep breath. "But I won't let them take it all."

Although he'd been born to generational wealth, his parents

had more than increased the family fortune, becoming one of the richest couples in the world before their gruesome deaths. From the beginning, Nikki had suspected that it had been his kin who'd done it in an attempt to gain control over his parents' company and fortune. He has one aunt, two uncles, and a slew of cousins, all of whom are rich in their own right. But one thing I've learned, regardless of whether you're from Mexico or the U.S., even if you have money, you'll always want more of it. And how could anyone turn their noses up at the billions of dollars under Nikki's name?

Unfortunately, Nikki has never been able to enjoy his fortune—not with how bad his mental health had become as a result of other people's greed.

"Enough of this morbid talk." I wave my hand.

"Don't worry about it. I have a security team on standby if anything happens. They're always behind us, but they'll keep a distance so they don't interfere with us."

I raise a brow at him. Now, he hadn't mentioned that before. But I should have realized that someone who's come to call paranoia his closest friend could never go somewhere without a full security detail.

"Well, I guess it's all right as long as we don't notice them," I grumble.

He gives me a wide grin and, coming to my side, he pulls me into his arms, leading me to the bedroom.

After throwing me on the bed, he takes a step back and starts unbuttoning his shirt.

I bite my lip as I watch him toss it aside, my eyes feasting on his naked chest. Like me, he bears the scars of his past. There are a myriad of scars all over the surface of his chest, some deeper and gnarlier than others.

Raising my leg, I trail my foot down his torso, feeling the ridges of his muscles. Despite his agoraphobia, Nikki has always taken care of his physique, installing a gym in our home and using it on a daily basis. In his own words, it helped him to clear his head when his anxiety was at its worst.

"I have one more surprise for you," he murmurs suggestively, catching my leg and kissing the arch of my foot.

"Is that so?" I challenge, grabbing the hem of my shirt and taking it off before doing the same with my bra and underwear.

His eyes darken, his pupils expanding as he takes in my naked body. His gaze moves from my face to my chest where most of my marks are clustered together, going all the way down to my thighs. There are different shapes littering my flesh, a haunting black against my lighter skin. I'm still not sure what they are, and no doctor has been able to tell us for sure if it's a tattoo, or if someone had branded my skin. I only know what they represent—years of servitude that almost erased who I was. Because of that, I've always been ashamed of them.

"You're beautiful, Luce," Nikki whispers reverently. "All of you is beautiful."

His intense scrutiny makes me blush, and I look away.

"Don't," he rasps. "Don't take those beautiful eyes off me."

A tremulous smile tugs at my lips as I slowly meet his gaze. After all this time, I still get self-conscious about the marks on my skin. I don't like them. Why should anyone else like them?

He kisses his way up my leg. When he reaches my marks, he pays special attention to them, kissing each one in turn, lingering on the larger ones. He moves slowly, trailing his tongue up my chest until his mouth is on mine. Wrapping my arms and legs around him, I pull him closer as I give myself to his embrace. He's slow but thorough, worshipping my body with his and bringing me to the brink, time and time again.

My skin is slick with perspiration as he spoons me from behind, his body still joined with mine. He trails light kisses over my neck, small touches that ignite me all over again.

"I think you'll like this last surprise even more," he murmurs in my ear as he trails his fingers down the valley of my breasts.

"I don't think anything can top today, Nikki." I smile languidly.

"Oh, I'll let you be the judge of that." He smiles as he pulls himself from me. I whimper at the sudden loss of his warmth, my arms still reaching for him. Going to the storage area, he pulls open one of the drawers and takes out a small box.

"What's that?" I ask as I pull myself into a sitting position. My skin is covered in goosebumps, and I wrap my arms around myself in an attempt to preserve heat.

He places the box on the bed, then opens it and lays the contents in the open.

I shuffle closer to get a better look, but I still don't know what it is.

"It's a tattoo kit," he explains.

"Tattoo kit?" I repeat, confused. "Why would you need a tattoo kit?"

"Because you're going to use it on me."

Now I'm even more confused.

"I don't follow," I frown.

"I know you're self-conscious about your marks, Luce. This way, we'll both have etchings on our skin."

I stare at him, flabbergasted. He... he wants me to tattoo him so I won't be the only one with marks on my skin?

"Nikki... I..."

I don't know what to say. I simply stare at him, my mouth half-open as I try to come to terms with the enormity of what he just proposed.

"I'm guessing that means this tops the other surprises?" he asks playfully.

"You'll let me ink your skin? Just like that?"

He nods solemnly.

"Just like that, Luce. Anything you want. I'll be your canvas." He winks at me.

He sets about assembling the tattoo gun, and it soon becomes clear that this isn't his first time handling it—he'd studied it before.

My heart beats erratically in my chest as I imagine him at night, poring over the instruction manual to figure out how to install it—all so he could surprise me.

How many nights has he spent just like this? Focusing on my happiness rather than his?

His regard touches me in a way nothing else ever has, and my entire being becomes so full of love for him that I can't stop myself from reaching out, framing his face between my hands and kissing him deeply. In that one kiss, I channel all the emotion that's surging through my veins and that threatens to overwhelm me—all this love that's infiltrated every cell of my body.

"I love you, too, Luce," he whispers, almost as if he can read my mind.

My lips tug up. "Okay, I'll do it."

He smiles at me, and when he's done assembling the kit, he sanitizes the area and places some paper towels on the bed. He then demonstrates briefly how to use it before lying on his back and pointing to his naked chest.

"My chest is your canvas. Do whatever you like with it."

"Whatever?" I raise my brows. "You know I'm not very good at drawing."

"But you have superb penmanship. So write me something. Write me a love letter."

My mouth parts in wonder at the trust I see reflected in his gaze. Knowing I can't fail him, I grab the tattoo pen, getting used to the feel of it in my hand.

Without dwelling too much on it, I bring the tip to his skin. The machine vibrates slightly in my hand, releasing a humming sound as the tip penetrates his skin. I take my time, making sure each stroke is perfect.

"Does it hurt?" I suddenly ask when I feel him wince.

"No, keep going," he assures me.

I take a deep breath as I concentrate on my design, letting the letters curl in a beautiful ornament. I'm so focused on what I'm doing that I lose track of time.

Line after line, stroke after stroke, I only know that I can't afford to make even one small error. And after what seems like an eternity, I lean back, wiping my forehead with the back of my hand.

"I think I'm done." I smile as I regard my masterpiece.

His skin is red all around the new tattoo, and I grab the soothing gel, gently applying it to the sensitive area.

Nikki releases a big breath, and despite his assurances, I'm convinced it wasn't all that comfortable for him.

"So what did you write?"

"Go see for yourself." I point to the bathroom.

He gets up and, grabbing his cane, goes straight for the big mirror in the bathroom.

"Fucking hell," he mutters in awe.

At the top of his collarbone, I wrote:

Lucero's Lover

Underneath it, I put the first lines of my favorite poem by Pablo Neruda:

Cuántas veces, amor, te amé sin verte y tal vez sin recuerdo, sin reconocer tu mirada, sin mirarte.

"You like it?" I ask sheepishly as I lay my head on his back.

"I love it, Luce. This is... It's absolutely perfect." He swallows hard, his throat clogging with emotion.

I smile as I nuzzle my cheek against his skin.

"How many times, my love, I loved you without seeing and maybe without memory, without recognizing your gaze, without even looking," I whisper the words in English.

Meeting his gaze in the mirror, I notice the moisture clinging to his lashes and the heartfelt *I love you* that he softly mouths to me.

We start our morning with a hearty breakfast. Nikki takes his medicine while I tend to his tattoo, applying more cream and some foil on top of it so it won't get irritated by his clothes. Once that's done, we're back on the road.

"Tonight, I want you to tattoo something on me too," I tell him once we're back on the highway.

He looks at me in surprise.

"I know there isn't much space, but I'd love to have your words on me, too."

"Of course," he readily agrees, something akin to a blush creeping on his cheeks. "I'd be honored."

With that settled, I bring out the map on one of the screens, thinking about where we could go, feeling a little intimidated by all these options. Like that English saying, the world is our oyster, and I aim to truly take advantage of it.

"What if we went to Niagara Falls?" I suddenly say. "It's not too far from here."

"That's a good idea. If we go west, it's less than a couple of hours."

"Oh my God, Nikki. I can't wait to see it. I've only seen it in movies, and I'm so curious if it's as huge as it seems on the screen."

"It is." He smiles fondly. "I went there once with my parents, and it was breathtaking."

"You rarely talk about them."

"It's hard to talk about them and not miss them." He sighs. "They were the best parents anyone could have asked for. Even though they were running a billion-dollar enterprise, they always made time for me."

"I'm happy to hear that. I wish I had that too, but I don't even know who my father is." I give a bitter laugh.

My mother had only told me he was a *gringo* and that he'd left after I was conceived, never to be heard from again.

"Do you want to know who he is?" Nikki suddenly asks. "I'm sure if we hire the right people, we might be able to find out."

"No." I shake my head. "That part of my past is better left alone."

I don't tell him, however, that I'm pretty sure he'd been one of my mother's clients. After all, I'd never told anyone that she used to sell her body for money, and that was how she managed to bring me up until I was thirteen, when she couldn't afford to feed two mouths anymore and decided to sell me to Sergio.

I'm not sure why I haven't shared much of my past life with Nikki when I've shared everything else with him. Maybe it's the fact that I'm a little ashamed of where I came from and how different our upbringings were. Or maybe, it's just my own failing and the fact that I don't think I ever forgave my mother for selling me.

And to divert his attention from this topic, I play some music, inviting him to sing along with me.

He shakes his head at me initially, but eventually, he relents and joins me in an impromptu karaoke session. Quite fittingly, we're singing Bon Jovi's "It's My Life", and for the first time, there's actual meaning behind the words.

We're finally taking charge of our lives.

"I thought you said our security detail is keeping a distance," I say suddenly as I notice a car trailing behind us.

"They are." He frowns, pulling up the rear camera on the screen. "That's not our security detail."

"They've been following us for a while," I add, worry gnawing at me.

"Let's see." Nikki mutters a few curses under his breath, and at the first opportunity, he turns the RV around. The other car, however, breezes right past us.

I breathe out a sigh of relief.

"Have we become a little too paranoid?" I attempt to make light of the situation.

Nikki doesn't find it funny, though. Turning the car around so we're back en route, he rummages through one of the compartments and takes out his pills. Instinctively, I give him a water bottle. He swallows the pill and takes a sip of water.

"Is it bad?" I ask in a soft voice. I can see the car rattled him. Maybe I shouldn't have said anything.

He's tense, the veins in his arms bulging as he grips the steering wheel tightly.

"I'll be fine," he bites out, but his demeanor tells me he's not fine.

"Maybe we should pull over," I suggest.

He shakes his head.

"I said I'm fine, Luce," he repeats, his breathing growing more labored.

God, I really shouldn't have said anything. Just the mention that someone might be following us triggered something in him —and given his past, I don't blame him.

"You can admit if you're not fine, Nikki. I don't care if we have to cut this short..."

"Luce." He takes a deep breath, turning toward me. His eyes are wholly black, his intense gaze swallowing me up. "I'm *fine*," he grits out. Sweat beads on his forehead, his hands trembling slightly.

He's *not* fine.

"I don't feel good. We should stop," I say weakly. Anything to get him to stop and get through the attack he's having. He thinks I don't recognize the signs? We've been together long enough for me to see when he's on the verge of breaking down.

"I said I'm fucking fine," he yells, banging his fist against the wheel.

My eyes widen at his outburst and I instinctively shrink back.

"No, Luce. I didn't mean it like that," he immediately says, raking a hand through his hair and giving me an apologetic look. "Please." He reaches out for me.

I blink a couple of times, breathing in and out.

"You scared me," I whisper.

"I'm sorry. I'm an idiot. I'm so sorry." He closes his eyes with a deep sigh. When he opens them again, there's so much pain in them, I feel it penetrating my heart.

I reach out and take his hand. "I—" My words get stuck in my throat as Nikki suddenly veers to the side. Turning, my eyes widen when I see a truck heading straight for us.

"Hold on!" he shouts at me.

But by that time, it's too late. Instead of letting us to the side, the truck veers at the same time as we do. No matter how much Nikki pulls on the wheel, the collision is imminent.

Seconds turn into an eternity as the front of the truck hits the middle of our RV, sending us spinning down the road. I try to hold on to something, but the force is so strong I'm thrust forward out of my seat.

My eyelids are heavy as I release a harsh breath. My chest feels constricted, and as I try to move around, I realize everything hurts.

A low moan of pain escapes past my lips as I finally open my eyes to see the blue sky. What...

My head is spinning, my sight becoming blurry. For a moment, I'm so disoriented, I don't know what happened or how I came to be like this. It's only when I hear another pained sound that the events finally come to me.

Accident. We were in an accident...

Nikki!

I release a pained whimper as I roll around, scanning my surroundings. The RV is a distance away, parts of it already obliterated from the impact, others catching fire. There's debris everywhere on the ground.

And Nikki... My eyes land on him, a short distance from me. He's bloody and still, but I can see his chest moving up and down—he's still breathing.

I crawl forward to the best of my ability, pushing against the pain.

"Nikki?" I wheeze out.

Another pained moan. I push myself harder.

"Nikki," I repeat as I finally reach his side.

He's on his belly, his shirt ripped to reveal a nasty wound on his back.

"Luce?" He says my name in a ragged voice. He can barely move as he turns his head toward me. There's a big cut running from his eyebrow to his hairline, blood pouring down his face and blinding him in one eye. "My Luce?"

I reach for his hand, threading my fingers through his in an attempt to draw strength from him and give him mine in return.

"I'm here," I whisper, tears pricking at my eyes—of pain and anguish, but most of all of worry. I don't know how badly I'm hurt, but most definitely not as bad as him. "Help will come. We need to hang on." I force the words out of my mouth even though I see the truth reflected in his gaze.

"I...love...you." He coughs, blood splattering onto the ground. "Will always...love—"

"Don't speak," I stop him. "Please don't speak. Help will come. Please..."

A sad smile clings to his lips as he continues to look at me, the love in his gaze hurting more than the physical pain I'm feeling—because it has a finality to it that shakes me to my core. He squeezes my hand once, twice, before he loses all strength.

Slowly, so, so slowly, the corners of his lips drop down and he stops blinking.

His eyes are wide open, and he's not blinking.

"Nikki?" I call his name, pushing myself closer to him. "Nikki, please answer me," I call out in a frantic voice.

He has a vacant look, and no matter how much I yell at him, he won't reply to me.

"Nikki, please," I wail. "Please..."

I hold his hand tightly in mine as I bring my face to his, nuzzling my cheek against his, his blood smearing on my skin.

"Nikki, say something. Please don't leave me..." I continue to whisper frantically.

The physical pain is but a distant sensation as I feel every fiber of my being disintegrate at the realization that he might be gone—that he *is* gone.

No. No. He can't be gone. My Nikki can't be gone.

"You're fine." I nod to myself, kissing him on the lips. "You're fine. Help will come and we'll both be fine."

I wrap my arms around him even as I feel my bones cracking, and I hold on to him for dear life.

He's fine. He's just taking a nap. He's preserving his strength.

I tell myself that until I convince myself.

But as I wrap my arms tighter around him, an explosion erupts from behind me.

"We're fine. We'll be fine." That's what I keep whispering to myself as a blunt piece of metal hits me from behind, and I black out.

THREE

Present day

Nikki's family stares at me with narrowed eyes. I shrug my shoulders—or as much as I can considering I'm still sporting a cast.

I can only imagine what I look like. I've never been prone to vanities, but maybe I should have taken a look in the mirror before coming here.

Lifting my hand to my face, I brush my hair aside, arranging it so it doesn't seem so messy. The doctors had done the craniotomy on the occipital bone, so even though they'd shaved the area, you can't tell since the rest of my hair covers it.

Oddly enough, my attending physician had told me that I'd recovered miraculously considering the many injuries I had—to my dismay. You'd think that a broken heart would slow down the process, not speed it. Although, watching my husband's killers in the eye now, I realize it had all been for this moment.

Just you wait.

You will *all* pay. I now have all the evidence that the accident was *not* an accident. It's all safely ensconced in a security box at a bank downtown. Soon, they will all pay!

My smile widens—to the discomfort of Nikki's family.

"Good. Everyone is here," Mr. Daniels chirps as he walks inside the conference room, taking a seat at the end of the big round table.

"You're looking quite good, Mrs. Archibald," he notes, his eyes surveying me from head to toe.

Someone snickers.

"I've been better," I shrug.

"Right. Why don't we begin?" He gives us all a saccharine smile as he removes some documents from an envelope.

Placing his glasses on his nose, he starts reading the will. It doesn't take me long to realize this is the same one Nikki told me about—the one that leaves most of his assets to me.

"I don't understand why *they* are here if I'm the beneficiary. They don't get anything." I point to the family when Mr. Daniels finishes.

"Actually," Mr. Daniels clears his throat. "They are here because Mr. Archibald"—he nods to Nikki's uncle Matthew —"wants to contest the will."

"Contest?" I burst out. "What for? I'm his wife, and his will states that I get the majority of his assets, including the company. What is there to contest?" I get to my feet, giving Mr. Daniels a belligerent look.

"Lucero, dear. You've been in the hospital for quite some time, so you may not be aware," Ophelia addresses me in a fake voice. "But once we discovered that Nicholas was using hard drugs, we did our duty and talked to his therapist and his physician." She feigns a sound of distress.

"What are you talking about?"

"His doctor told us that he hadn't been in his right mind since that accident years ago. The therapist confirmed it, too. Since the accident took a toll on his brain, it caused some issues with his frontal lobe. It's that part of the brain that deals with decision-making."

"I know what the front lobe is," I snap.

"Frontal," she corrects, her finger delicately raised.

"Your point?" I arch an eyebrow.

"We've talked to his other therapists, of course, and they all confirmed that he suffered personality disturbances after the accident. We've brought the medical records here. They've already been notarized."

"I don't see what that has to do with the will."

"Of course it does. He ratified the will after his accident."

"Nikki said his doctor cleared him for that." I narrow my eyes.

"And who knows what other lies he might have told you? All his therapists said the same thing. The boy was living in a delusional world." She flutters the documents in her hand. "Why, those houses of his alone were more secure than Alcatraz. To say he was paranoid would be an understatement."

"I still don't get what you're trying to do with this. Even if that were all true—and I know it's *not*—I'm still his wife and that means I stand to inherit his assets."

"Not if the marriage happened under duress, too. Not if he wasn't able to make a sound decision. He did marry you after his accident, after all. Didn't you move in with him only a few months after he woke up from his coma? Who's to say you didn't influence him in some way?" she says innocently, although the malice is evident.

"What?" I whisper, horrified.

"And of course, if he wasn't of sound mind to make these decisions, that means there are grounds for the annulment of your marriage, too."

"How can you believe a word she says?" I ask in a hurt voice as I turn to Mr. Daniels. "They planned this from the beginning. They've been trying to kill Nikki for years to get their hands on his money. Do you think that accident was a fluke? Or do you think *this* accident was just that, an accident?"

"Now, Lucero. I won't allow you to accuse us of something so heinous," Matthew interrupts.

"Heinous? You sent your thugs to burn down our home, just a few hours ago," I accuse, pure hatred bleeding from my voice. I'd gone back to check Nikki's computers for evidence of Nikki's innocence when a bunch of thugs had broken in and set fire to the house. Luckily I'd managed to get away, together with a USB filled with security footage that *proves* Nikki did not cause the accident and it was all a set up.

Thank God for secure Cloud storage.

"That is a vile accusation!" Ophelia intervenes.

"Is it? I have the evidence to prove it. Because that's what you were after, weren't you? You wanted to destroy the evidence that proved it wasn't an accident, just like you wanted to erase the fact that you had your people in *my* home—"

"Mrs. Archibald, they are correct in that these are serious accusations. If you have the proof you say you do, you should give it to the police and let them do their job," Mr. Daniels interrupts, his voice calm. "But in the meantime, the documents Mrs. Lockwood and Mr. Archibald have provided are sufficient to dismiss the will and your claim to any portion of Mr. Archibald's assets."

"What..." I blink furiously, unable to believe what is happening.

Ophelia smirks, and all the others smile furtively.

"And if that is all, I'll be in touch with the division of assets very soon," Mr. Daniels explains before he leaves the room.

"Lucero, dear. I'd tell you not to take anything from the house since it doesn't technically belong to you. But all your stuff is gone anyway." She laughs as she passes by me.

All of them leave—all but Matthew.

"You might want to be careful with that so-called evidence," he warns.

"Is that a threat?" I look Matthew straight in the eye.

"Of course not. Call it friendly advice. We were family, were we not?" He chuckles. "Although..." His eyes linger over my body. "Maybe I could help you out," he adds suggestively. "If your marriage gets annulled, you'll get deported."

His meaning sinks in, and before I know it, I curl my hand into a fist and aim it at his smug face. He doesn't expect it, which makes it even better when I nab him in the nose. He's

pretty sensitive, too, because blood pours down his face immediately.

"You fucking bitch," he bites out right before he strikes me
back, his palm making contact with my cheek.

The blow makes me lose my balance and I fall backward.

"You should be fucking thankful I offered you a way out.
Hell, you should be kissing my damn shoes for even entertaining
touching your pathetic little self, you fucking gold digger."

I tilt my chin up defiantly, my eyes shooting daggers at him.

"Even if you gave me all of Nikki's fortune, I would *never* let
you lay one finger on me."

He takes a handkerchief and wipes the blood off his
upper lip.

"You'll regret this." He shakes his head, his lip twitching in
displeasure.

"Bring it on," I mutter.

He takes a step closer to me, his hand raised. But right at
that moment, Mr. Daniels's assistant walks in, and Matthew
immediately puts himself together, pretending nothing is
wrong. And just like that, he's gone.

"Are you all right, miss?" the assistant asks me, coming to
help me to my feet.

"I'm fine, thank you." I give him a slight smile before I ask
him if there's any back exit I can use. He points me to the
service elevator, and without looking back, I'm out of there.

I walk for a couple of streets before I stop, realizing that I
have no home to return to. Of course, there is Noelle, and she is
likely waiting for me to contact her. I reach into my pocket for
my phone, but instead of dialing her number, I just stare at the
screen.

My stomach releases a low growl, and I swallow hard.

It's been hours since I last ate, and right now I'm not
pleasant company. Maybe I'll call her later.

After a few moments of going back and forth on what's the
best course of action, I decide to grab something to eat first and
talk to her later. Likely, she'll want to talk to me about Nikki,

about the accident, about...everything. And no matter how much of a strong front I put on, I'm not ready to delve into those subjects. Especially not now after I realize the dangerous lengths his family is willing to go to in order to get their hands on his money.

Slipping my phone back into my pocket, I keep moving.

I have some money left, and although not much, it should be enough for a hot meal. Not one to waste unconscionable amounts on food, I try to find a cheaper place to eat, even as my stomach keeps protesting the decision.

God, but just thinking about Matthew's smug expression and his indecent proposal makes my skin crawl. His blow hadn't been unexpected, but it had certainly done a number on my already frail body.

Absentmindedly, I bring my hand over my cast, rubbing my fingers over the rough material. Maybe I should buy some painkillers too...

"Damn!" I halt, my eyes widening in shock.

My medicine. I forgot it.

Squeezing my eyes shut, I fight back against a wave of hopelessness. I can't succumb to it, no matter how much I'd like to.

But how much bad luck can one person have in one lifetime? I can barely afford to think about Nikki because then I'd truly lose it, but every little failure seems to push me further in that direction anyway.

I have to keep my head clear to punish his murderers, but how can I do that when every second is a struggle? How can I *not* think about him when he's all I've been thinking of for the past eight years?

I've always looked at my life as before and after Nikki.

For the first sixteen years of my life, I was simply a *thing*, not a person. I served my purpose, but there was nothing more to me. Nikki was the first one to see me as a person and not an object. He was the first to tell me my thoughts mattered, or that I was smart despite my obvious lack of education. He was the first to truly see *me*.

Before, I'd never felt any of those things. I saw myself as cursed because everyone saw me as such. But he... He made me realize my worth.

Tears swim in my eyes, trickling down my cheeks as I move slowly, aimlessly.

A jolt in my left arm startles me and makes me lose my balance. I take a step backward, my eyes alert as I scan my surroundings. When I don't see anyone around, I frown. I could have sworn something bumped into me. My arm reels from the impact, the sensation growing in intensity as it spreads down my body. There's a silent hum just underneath my skin, almost as if portions of it caught on fire.

I breathe in and out, assuming it's just the start of a panic attack—Nikki always had those. But the pricking sensation persists—so much so that it makes me sway lightly on my feet, my vision swimming. Backing into a corner until my back hits a wall, I crouch down, dropping my forehead to my knees and rocking back and forth.

FOUR

I don't know how long I remain like that, barely in control of myself. I only know that once awareness starts to seep in, my eyes zone in on the empty street—more confirmation that there's no one around.

Once I'm able to get myself out of that dangerous zone, I shake my head in exasperation. The confrontation with Matthew must have shaken me more than I realized. After all, I've learned from Nikki that the mind works in mysterious ways, especially when it comes to traumatic episodes. And I'm barely starting to experience the full-blown effects of his death.

Squeezing my eyes shut, I wobble to my feet and go to the first convenience store I find to grab some ibuprofen for the pain. That should do the trick until I can get the rest of the medicine the doctor provided. But since I can't take the pills on an empty stomach, I resolve to go to the pizza place next door that seems to have some affordable items on the menu. Considering my current circumstances, I really need to budget properly.

If only things weren't so expensive in New York...

Grumbling to myself, I quickly scan the menu, choosing a basic pepperoni small pizza and asking for a glass of tap water—at least that's free.

I eat slowly to avoid indigestion. But as I sit in my secluded corner in the restaurant, I can't help but feel eyes on me. The hair on my arms stands to attention, goose bumps spreading all over my skin. Uneasiness settles deep in the pit of my stomach. Furtively, I glance back a couple of times, but there's no one of consequence. Everyone is minding their own business, eating.

"I'm just being paranoid," I whisper to myself, grabbing another bite.

Living with Nikki's paranoia for so long must have rubbed off on me. But is it *really* paranoia when he ended up killed by the very people he was afraid of?

I take a deep breath as I try to keep my calm. But how can I when I think about all the injustices my Nikki suffered? We might have been happy together, in our little world, but that happiness was always overshadowed by the perpetual danger his family posed to us.

The more I think about it, the more I realize Nikki likely never had a moment of peace in his life. Perhaps when he was a child and his parents were still alive, but after their deaths, he was thrust from one nightmare to another—tortured both physically and psychologically.

I scan my surroundings again for fear I may be the next on the Archibalds' list. Maybe I should have tried to understand Nikki better. Maybe if he hadn't noticed my longing for the outside world, we wouldn't have left the safety of our home, and he'd still be alive.

Maybe...

I sigh audibly as I stare at the leftover crusts.

If he were here, he'd eat those since they were his favorite part of the pizza—we'd always complemented each other in that regard.

But now...

I grab the first one, biting into it and forcing myself to chew. I do the same to the next until the plate is empty.

He's not here anymore, and I need to get used to it—*for now*. I can't afford to go through those five stages of grief I'd read about online. I only need *one*—vengeance. But to do that, I know I can't let myself succumb to my sadness. I just have to use it to fuel my thirst for revenge.

I nurse my tap water until it gets dark out.

Releasing a deep sigh, I venture out into the night, deciding to take a small walk before going to the apartment.

I don't trust the police who investigated Nikki's death any more than I trust the Archibalds, and that means I need to ensure the USB with the evidence doesn't fall into the wrong hands. It's the only way I can rehabilitate Nikki's name.

Lost in my thoughts, my feet take me to the Brooklyn Bridge, and I tentatively go to the pedestrian side, admiring the view of the Hudson River.

I can still remember the first time I'd seen it and how awestruck I'd been by the size and magnificence of New York City. After all, wasn't this what I'd always dreamed of? The type of freedom that you could find only in movies because real life would never be that fair. I'd first learned about it from Nikki, and he'd described the opulence and sheer size of the buildings in a way that shaped my dreams of the outside world. Yet I fear it's those dreams that have steered us on this path—that wretched desire of mine to experience...more.

I bring my fist to my chest, banging it against my heart in admonishment.

I'd dared to want too much, and now this is my reward.

The city stretches out before me, the buildings taller than ever, with their blinding lights and the raucous car noises.

But I'm alone.

I'm all...alone.

I fiddle with my wedding ring as I stare into the distance, Nikki's face as I'd last seen it appearing before my eyes—bloody, hopeless...unmoving. That vacant look that had descended upon his features as life left his body will haunt me forever, as will the knowledge that I'd been there—that I'd *seen* him give his last breath. And yet... I wouldn't change it. I'd rather keep this suffering deep in my heart as long as he was able to die peacefully, with me by his side—as long as he told me the words that were so dear to his heart.

His *last* words.

Will always love you.

I draw a deep breath into my battered lungs, tipping my head back and blinking back the tears that threaten to flood my eyes.

Those words. Those four words.

I'll let them caress my soul and imbue it with the necessary courage for the days to come—I'll keep them nestled in my breast for as long as I have left on this Earth. And when I finally draw my last breath too, I'll whisper them to him, so he can utter them back in the afterlife.

Slowly, I raise my hand to the sky, watching a few stars as they sneak between my fingers. I've never been a believer. Not since I saw all the evil in this world and wondered how a deity that was supposedly good could bring forth so much tragedy. Then I watched Sergio spin his god-like narrative, fool people and manipulate them for his own gain. And even then, I still wondered, how was it that a god would wish ill upon anyone? Shouldn't gods be above people?

I'd always had questions, but only when Nikki had come along had I gotten some answers. Yet now, I find myself wishing it were true—that there was some type of heaven where we could be reunited in the end.

Because if not...

My eyes snap shut, pain vibrating under my skin with increasing frequency. Like an earthquake waiting to be set loose, it echoes through my being, pushing me closer and closer to the brink.

It would be so easy to end it all...to take a step closer and stare the abyss in the face. But that would be the easy way out. How could I let Nikki's killers walk free?

With a deep sigh, I open my eyes. I should probably head back before I get some more foolish ideas.

When I step back, my phone vibrates in my pocket. A text

message from Noelle has the address of her downtown apartment she graciously allowed to let me use for the time being and the passcodes to the building. With a weary sigh, I plug in the address in the maps app and follow the directions.

But as I turn, I come face to face with a masked man standing less than one foot away from me.

What... When did he get so close?

Before I can say anything, he slaps my hand so hard, my phone flies over the bridge, plunging into the water with a thud.

My eyes widen in shock before fear settles in.

Adrenaline surges through my veins as I turn to run. But I barely take one step forward before his fingers are in my hair, dragging me back.

"Let go." I grit my teeth as I try to fight him—not that easy with my cast on and the other injuries that make it hard for me to move.

He doesn't say anything, simply tightening his hold over my scalp. All at once, he pushes me toward the railing, my entire body reeling from the impact.

"Help!" I scream. "Help me!" Yet what good does that do when there's no one around? My assailant knows this, for he doesn't even bother to muffle my screams.

He maneuvers me around until he has a good grasp on me.

I try to hold on to the metal with my good hand, but he's much bigger and stronger than me—so much so that he can effortlessly lift me up over the railing and...

One moment, I see the blinding city lights and the clear night sky full of stars. The next, I'm diving headfirst toward a turbulent abyss that is anxiously waiting to swallow me up.

I can't even react. I can't flail my arms. I can't move or do anything. I can only fall freely.

I fall at an odd angle. My shoulder is the first that makes contact with the water, then my head. Pain becomes my second skin as I dive toward the bottom. Even my good arm is useless, the pain from the impact spreading from my shoulder down my entire right side.

I sputter at being suddenly deprived of oxygen, but it's an instinctual reaction and one I'm paying dearly for as my mouth and nose fill with water. The more I try to keep it out, the more it seeks to rush inside.

I kick my legs, moving them in a fluttering motion in an attempt to stop myself from sinking even deeper. But no matter how much I try, it's useless. The current of the river spins and twirls me, the depths of the water reaching for me and pulling me closer.

Is it at that moment that I give up? Is it when I sink deeper and deeper? Is it when there's no oxygen left inside my lungs, or is it when my entire body becomes so filled with water it's almost *one* with the water?

My eyes are unblinking as I stare at the darkness—at the abyss that slowly calls my name. Slowly, I stop struggling.

This is my fate, it seems. But maybe it's a mercy. Maybe, just maybe...

More water gurgles down my throat.

My thoughts are in disarray.

I'm not sure if I can focus on anything specific as the seconds trickle down before my imminent death, but if I could, I'd always choose Nikki.

Nikki who saved me. Nikki who loved me. Nikki who...left me.

Nikki who is now waiting for me.

Everything slows down until I'm truly one with the darkness.

Water comes out of my mouth and nose as I cough and cough. My throat is on fire as I hold on to my stomach, spitting up every bit of liquid I swallowed.

I retch until there's nothing more to expel, at which point I collapse on my back.

It doesn't register that I'm alive yet. Not until blinding light washes over my face, the morning sun moving higher and higher in the sky. I squint my eyes, groaning as pain erupts from all places of my body at once.

My broken arm is completely numb, while my right one is bruised and battered. At this point, I doubt there's any spot on my body that hasn't been absolutely obliterated.

But against all odds, I'm alive—I guess.

"Lucky me," I mumble, my voice coming out thick and ragged.

Dragging myself into a sitting position, I look right and left, noting I'm on the shore of the Hudson but quite a distance away from the bridge. I guess the currents must have carried me here.

"Can someone have worse luck than me?" I mutter dryly as I wobble to my feet. My clothes are semi-dry at this point, but I feel dirty and gross and...

"Oh my God," I groan when I think of all the water I swallowed. Who knows what could have been in it. The unbidden thought of an article I'd read about sewage sometimes draining into the Hudson makes me retch again, but at this point I've thrown up everything in me.

My breathing is patchy, a wheezing sound coming from my throat that is *not* normal. Well, I guess neither is being attacked by a masked man and thrown into the river. The mere fact that I'm still alive is a miracle considering I was already half incapacitated *before* diving from a couple hundred feet.

Quickly, I scan my surroundings to confirm that I am indeed alive and this isn't some farcical afterlife. But going by the acute pain I'm feeling and the putrid smell that somehow's made its home in my nostrils, I think it's safe to say this is *not* the afterlife—who would be *that* cruel?

Yet as I take a few steps, something else catches my attention.

Next to the place I woke up, there's a white, sparkly note. Frowning, I stoop to pick it up, only to drop it back down when cursive writing appears on it out of *nowhere*. Like one of those fade-in animation effects, black letters stain the sparkly note.

"You've been invited," I read out loud the first line. Right underneath, my name appears in purple letters—*purple?*

Lucero Archibald.

"I've been invited to what?" I blink in confusion. Yet no sooner do I utter the words than a third line appears on the note.

101 W 54th St.

I barely get to blink before the writing fades out, the note becoming blank once again.

What is this? Is it some kind of sophisticated technology? I've never been too good at technology, barely able to operate my personal smartphone. But this... Now this is the stuff of the future.

Am *I* in the future?

I shift my gaze to the tall buildings on the other side of the Hudson. Surely, if I'd fallen through some wormhole and arrived in the future, it wouldn't still look this bad?

I blink slowly, satisfied with my train of thought. Maybe it's just some kind of tech I'm not familiar with. I can allow that considering I'm barely familiar with *anything*.

"I must be going crazy," I sigh. I don't even have the strength to panic about the odd note—or the possibility that I might have arrived in a futuristic but still as dirty NYC. Instead, I simply write it off as being a side effect of my almost drowning. Before I can turn and walk away, though, more letters appear on the surface of the note.

What do you wish for more than anything in this world?
Money? Fame? Revenge? Love?

I rub my eyes vigorously before I look at the note again.

We can make it all come true.

"What the..."
A date appears underneath—

Today at 8:00 p.m

Then there's one more line.

Dare to take the leap.

And just like before, the writing vanishes again, the sparkly note blank and unblemished.

I close my eyes, inhaling deeply. Right, I'm probably hallucinating. It wouldn't be the first time. Extreme conditions tend to do that to a person. Back when I'd worked in Sergio's temple, I'd had periods of utter exhaustion coupled with a lack of nourishment that made me see things that weren't there. But I'm also smart enough to realize that's all it is.

Shaking my head for even entertaining the possibility that the writing might be real, I turn my back to it, leaving it on the ground as I slowly make my way to the main road. There, I hail a taxi to take me to the address Noelle gave me.

FIVE

The loud sound of the ringtone wakes me up. I rub at my eyes as I swing my legs over the bed, walking like a zombie to get the phone.

"Yes?" I answer sleepily.

"Lulu? Where are you?" Noelle's panicked voice startles me.

"I'm at the apartment." I frown, looking at the time. Damn, I've slept almost seven hours. It's already dark outside.

"You need to get out of there right now. Use the back exit."

"What—"

"I don't have time to explain it, but the police issued a warrant for your arrest and they're on their way to the apartment as we speak."

"I don't understand. Why? How would you know? How would they know I'm here?"

My confusion mounts as my brain tries to awaken and make sense of the situation.

"Raf heard about it from one of his contacts in the force. They're claiming you withdrew money from Nicholas's account after the reversal of the will. Apparently, they got a tip from someone that they saw you get into this building."

"I didn't do that. I didn't touch his money."

"I know. But it seems someone did in your name, and now

they think you're trying to run away with the stolen money—potentially leave the country. They marked you as a flight risk."

"But I—" My mouth hangs open in shock. "What should I do?"

"Grab a cab and go to Brooklyn. Raf's friends live in a secure warehouse there. I'll try to get you a new identity as soon as possible. I'm so sorry."

"I don't understand," I whisper slowly, hopelessly.

"I know. But we don't have time, Lulu. If they arrest you, it's game over. You know that."

"I'll put on my shoes and leave."

After I hang up, I put on my shoes and hurry out. But just as I reach the door, the intercom rings, and I see Detective Reynolds on the screen.

Damn.

The front desk must have recognized me and told them which apartment I was in.

Wow, they were fast.

Following Noelle's instructions, I go out the back exit of the apartment block, but as I round the corner, I see more than a few police cars waiting around. And since that's the only route available, there's simply no way for me to walk right by them—not with my cast being such a recognizable feature.

Police cars swarm around the apartment building.

Noelle is right. If they arrest me, it's game over.

The Archibalds will concoct whatever accusations necessary to take me out of the equation so they can inherit all the money. Add in some xenophobia and disdain for immigrants, and it wouldn't take much for them to convince everyone that I was nothing but a gold digger looking to get rich and get a green card—all the while taking advantage of a poor man who suffered from mental illness. I can already see the story they'll spin.

And the worst thing? It's persuasive enough.

Pursing my lips, I take a few steps back to avoid being heard. And as I find a sturdy metal bar at the base of the building, I use all the strength I can muster and hit my left arm against it. The sound echoes, and the first hit doesn't do much except give me a jolt of pain. But it's a life and death situation, and that means I must push through the pain.

I hit again.

And again.

On the third hit, the plaster cracks. Hope soars in my chest. I take a deep breath and will myself to hit harder.

The cracks widen, small fissures spreading all over the cast. Another two attempts and parts of the plaster fall to the ground. I quickly peel all the pieces off my arm, noting the purple color of my skin.

There is pain, but there is also numbness.

I focus on the numbness.

Without the plaster, I should be a little less recognizable, but that doesn't mean I can be reckless. I walk to the corner of the building, waiting until more people flood the street before I lower my gaze to the ground and do my best to get lost among them.

As I put one foot in front of the other, getting farther and farther away from the police cars, my heart beats loudly in my chest as my optimism soars.

I can do this. I can...

"Right there! Stop right there," someone yells.

I turn my head only for a second to see a few policemen point at me, already running toward me. Without even thinking about it, I run.

It doesn't register that running from the police will only make it worse. The only thing I know is that if I get arrested, I'll never be able to get justice for Nikki.

The sea of people parts for me as I run, the police behind me. I may not be too familiar with New York City, but I know that Noelle's place is within walking distance from Times Square. And once I'm there, I'll be able to get lost in the crowd. My plan made, I turn to the right, going down onto 56th street. If I keep straight, I should come across Times Square—*I think*.

The police are hot on my trail, but it's not just officers running after me. The sound of sirens echoes from behind.

Oh, God. I'm screwed.

Not only do I have short legs, but I'm also still recovering from a car crash, in addition to having a broken arm that's now freshly out of its cast—*before* its time. I'm no match for some officers who undoubtedly run for a living or a bunch of police cars that have priority *everywhere*.

Just as I start to give up hope, I notice one of the billboards on a building shift to a new ad on a sparkly background.

You've been invited.

I frown at the familiar words.

Just two more blocks.

The words change again.

101 W 54th St.

The invite! It's the same address as the invite!

Dare to take the leap!

I maintain my stride, but one glance backward and I can see that the police are getting closer and closer to me.

As I round the corner to 54th street, in a moment of complete madness, I decide to go to that address, hoping it could at least help me elude the police for some time.

A neon flashing light with a flickering 101 W 54th street is above the entrance to a historical building. And that solidifies the decision for me.

I dash to the door and knock, waiting anxiously for someone to open and counting down the seconds until the police spot me.

The door creeps open, but there's only darkness inside. I

can't spot anything. Slowly, a figure appears in the doorway. His face is covered by a red mask, his eyes barely visible in the dim lighting.

"Invite," he demands.

"I lost it." I give him an apprehensive smile. "Can I come in?"

"No invite, no come in," he states in a resolute tone before he slams the door in my face.

What...

I don't even have time to ponder my rejection as the police sirens get louder and louder. Stepping into the street, my heart begins to race as I deliberate what else I can do. No matter which way I go, I'll be caught and...

As my right arm brushes against my side, I feel a pricking sensation. Frowning, I touch my hip, noting a pocket in the dress and something that pokes through the material. To my utter surprise, as I remove the item from my pocket, it's the invite.

The same invite I'd thrown away.

But it might be the invite that saves me in this moment.

Twirling, I knock once more on the door. Just like before, it opens and the same gruff voice demands an invite. I shove it into his face, my gaze on the end of the block as I spot one of the officers rounding the corner.

I only hear a grunt of approval before I find myself inside, the door closing with a thud behind me.

"Go to the end of the hallway and down the steps," the man tells me before turning his back to me.

My lashes flutter in confusion.

I'm still not entirely sure what I got myself into or what type of establishment this might be, but as long as it provides me with some cover to escape the police, I'm willing to keep an open mind.

I walk slowly to the end of the tunnel, and as I come across the stairs leading down to the basement, I stop, somehow waiting for the police to come barging in at any moment. My body is tense, my heart in my throat as I can already envision myself behind bars, wasting away before I'll have the chance to get justice for Nikki.

No... That's out of the question!

I take another step as my conviction strengthens.

A gust of wind brushes against my right side, blowing my hair in my face. I raise my hand to tuck the stray strands behind my ear, but I stop midair as I feel the slightest touch against my face and a gentle blow of warm air on my cheek. Goosebumps spread all over my skin and a light tremor goes down my back.

I shake my head, hurrying to pull my hair back. It's just a current of air. It's not the time to give in to my overactive imagination.

But as I march forward, stabs of pain erupt all over my left arm. Without the benefit of the cast to keep it immobile, every little movement causes me anguish. And now that my adrenaline has started to wear off, the pain becomes increasingly more nuanced.

If only I'd grabbed some pain medication on my way out.

With a sigh, I continue on, curious to see what I'd been invited to. It's not as if I have anything better to do with the police still outside looking for me.

As I descend, the sound of music becomes louder and louder, and when I get to the bottom of the stairs, I notice an odd array of colored lights.

It's only when I step inside that I realize this must be a club.

The room is packed with people, dancing and swaying to the music. The lights alternate between red, blue, and pink, giving everyone an ethereal look. They look lost to the sound, their eyes closed, their bodies moving to the beat as if they were chasing the high of carpe diem—or, in this case, carpe noctem.

A melancholic smile flickers on my lips. Nikki would be so proud of my Latin—he taught me the basics himself.

"Welcome, Mrs. Archibald," a man greets me as I step inside.

I frown, confused at how he'd know my name, but I assume the person at the entrance might have let him know.

"Please, have a complimentary drink." He takes a fancy glass from his tray and hands it to me.

My mouth opens to refuse, but an errant thought pushes me to take it.

"Thank you," I say as I accept the drink. It's a neon color, something I've never seen before. But as I bring it to my mouth for a sip, a strong mango flavor with only a hint of alcohol hits my tongue. The drink is so yummy that I end up drinking it in one go.

"You may dance or go to the sitting area by the stage. The main event should start soon," the server continues, handing me another drink with a knowing smile.

Despite knowing I shouldn't, I accept it. It's too delicious to pass, and I don't think it's too strong to affect me—not that I'm an expert in alcohol. Nikki had never been a big drinker since it triggered his anxiety, so we've mostly had a glass of wine here and there with dinner. But this? This is just fabulous.

I take another sip as I walk toward the sitting area. My body is already becoming more relaxed, my heart rate dropping as my fear slowly melts away. I find an empty seat in a more secluded corner and sigh deeply as I finally sit down.

God, I don't think I've ever run as much or as fast as I did today. Then again, I don't think I ever imagined the police would chase me either.

The club is divided into three sectors. There's a rectangular dance floor in the middle, facing a main stage that's big enough to host a live show. All around, there are seating areas—tables with chairs, sofas, bar stools. There are a variety of enclosed spaces that allow for more privacy for those who don't wish to exert themselves.

If at first glance I'd thought that everyone was dancing, now that I have a better look around, I realize that the people on the dance floor are in the minority. Most people are on the fringes, glancing around suspiciously, some curiously. They're holding tightly onto the sparkly invite, their bodies tense and anxious.

Although there are some dressed normally, the majority are

wearing odd costumes. I spot a few animal ones, some wolves, lions, and panthers. My eyes widen in appreciation as I study them. Their costumes are so realistic, it's as if they'd stepped out of a video game. There are also some more... eccentric ones. Some people are painted from head to toe in different colors. I spot a few pink ones, some green, and even some purple ones, all with some special features. The pink girl has translucent wings and the purple one has a fluffy tail.

"So pretty," I whisper to myself.

Compared to all these extravagant costumes, I'm only wearing a simple black dress. But the invite hadn't specified a theme, had it? My brows bunch up in confusion. I hadn't perused it enough for that, and now I wish I'd paid more attention.

But just as I think of the invite, I'm also reminded about its odd appearance and the fact that it kept following me around—or did it? There's no denying that there's something very odd about the entire situation. But I'm still not sure if this isn't a by-product of my accident.

Have I gone... mad? Is that what's happening? Maybe I'm seeing a distorted version of reality due to my head injury.

"Another drink?" A server stops in front of me, her tray full of the same neon drinks.

"I shouldn't." I lick my lips as my eyes zero in on the liquid.

Damn my sweet tooth! Why did it have to be so delicious?

"Are you sure?" she asks, pushing a glass toward me.

I'm ready to refuse, but somehow, I end up taking the drink and thanking her. Everyone is drinking the same thing, and I don't see one drunk person around. My initial assessment that it shouldn't be a strong cocktail was likely spot-on.

Sipping quietly on my drink, I realize that the pain from my arm is completely gone, my body so much more energized than before—and that's a feat considering how hard I ran.

"Is that seat taken?" A voice startles me from my reverie.

I slowly lift my gaze, blinking as I take in the owner of the voice.

She's around my age, but she has the most stunning pair of dark blue eyes I've ever seen, contrasted with the fiery red of her hair. She's wearing a pair of black high-waisted jeans and a yellow crop top that accentuate her hourglass figure—well, at least someone else is dressed in mundane clothing.

She gives me a beaming smile as she awaits my answer.

The girl is so pretty, it's hard not to be blinded by it. And I'm not the only one noticing, as everyone around is staring at her as if in a trance.

"Yes, of course. Sorry, I didn't mean to stare," I mention as I pat the seat next to me for her to join me. "You've got lovely eyes."

"Aren't you a sweetheart?" She smiles at me. "Thank you."

"I'm sure you're used to people telling you that."

"They rarely dare," she mutters under her breath.

I flutter my lashes in confusion.

"I have an overprotective brother." She waves her hand dismissively as if that's what all brothers do. "I'm Thea, by the way. What's your name?"

"Lucero." I smile warmly. "But you can call me Luce."

"Nice to meet you, Luce. Are you ready for the big adventure?" She squeals excitedly.

"Uhm... What big adventure?" I ask warily.

"What? The Game, of course! We're here for the Game!" She presses her hands together as she directs her gaze to the empty stage. "It's going to start soon."

"What Game?" I frown.

She suddenly sobers up as she turns to me.

"You don't know?"

I shake my head slowly.

"Then why are you here?"

"I couldn't get rid of the invitation." I strain a smile. I can't very well tell her I'm on the run from the police, can I? At least this is a half-truth.

"Odd. That's not how it usually happens."

"What happens?"

"Never mind." She shakes her head. "It's a game of wishes. You were specifically chosen to compete for the chance of getting your wish fulfilled."

"I don't understand."

"You will." She winks at me. "Soon enough, everything will make sense."

That sounds ominous. Is this some type of organ harvesting ring? Did they lure us out here because of our medical history? I've just gotten out of the hospital. It would have been so easy for them to get my medical records. It wouldn't be the first time I've heard of something like this, where they lure unsuspecting—usually desperate people—with the promise of wealth, only for them to never be heard from again.

Anxiety prickles under my skin as all my senses become high on alert.

Oh, good God, did I escape a murder attempt just to be dissected for my organs?

My palms become clammy as I keep a forced smile on my face, all the while planning for an exit. From what I can see from my angle, the only way out is through the door I came in. But there should be some type of emergency exit, no? Aren't there regulations for clubs to have multiple exits?

"So what's your wish?" Thea continues happily, not noticing my darkening mood or my slow descent into a full-blown panic attack.

"Uh, I," I stammer, my eyes wildly seeking a way out. "Do you know where the restroom is?"

"Sure. It's right behind the stage." She points out to the back. "But don't take long. The event's about to start."

I nod awkwardly, standing up and doing my best to wade through the throng of people without jostling my frail arm. Up close, I'm even more surprised by how real these costumes look. Why, the fur feels like genuine animal fur! I jostle my way through the crowd, but as I near the other end of the room, I stop, shocked at one girl's costume.

She has a beautiful white fluffy tail that sways in rhythm with the music.

"Is it mechanical?" I can't help but ask.

"Huh?" Her brows shoot up.

"Your tail." I point to it just as it moves in a slow circle. "Wow," I whisper.

"What are you on about?" She frowns, staring at me strangely.

"How do you move it? Do you have a remote control for it?" I ask as the fluffy end brushes against my right hand. It's so soft and cute! Oh my, I'd love a purple one...

"Shut the fuck up, *human*," she sneers at me, and I belatedly realize that she wasn't inviting me to pat her tail. She was swatting me away.

A yelp escapes me as I jump back, blinking furiously in an attempt to understand what I'd done wrong. But even as I open my mouth to apologize, the girl glares at me belligerently.

"Uhm, I'll just...go?" I put on a fake smile as I slither my way back, putting distance between us. A little hopping, dodging, and ducking, and I make it safely to the end of the stage.

Was I rude? Sometimes I may mess up the words in English, but I didn't offend her—or at least I don't think I did. I release a weary sigh as I step away from the rest of the crowd.

Maybe I just came across as a creep because we were both in a crammed space and she wasn't sure of my intentions? Although the situation rests heavily on my mind, I decide my focus should be on finding an escape. But still, I don't like that my intentions were misconstrued...

Shaking my head, I continue walking, ignoring all the other cute costumes around me—even the purple ones. There's a small corridor in the back, which is eerily empty. The restrooms are on one side, but the corridor extends farther. Assuming that the emergency exit should be located at the end of the hallway, I venture deeper.

I walk for a few meters before I realize that the lights have gone out.

A sliver of fear goes down my back.

Well, damn. If I go back, I'm going to get killed for my organs, but if I go farther, I may get killed for a different matter altogether.

For a moment, I falter, stranded in the darkness. I sway lightly on my feet, a little dizzy—not sure if from fear or from the alcohol. Damn it, I shouldn't have had three cocktails either. Who knows what they put in them...

Squeezing my eyes shut, I decide to take my chances with what I may find at the end of the corridor. Maybe I'll be lucky enough to find an exit.

As I walk farther, the music becomes only a soft ringing in my ear as silence slowly envelops the hallway. Everything is so dark, I can't even see where I'm walking.

"Luce?" An echo travels down the corridor and I stop, slowly turning back as all the hairs on my body stand up. The same voice calls my name again, and pure terror grips me as I make to run.

But I barely take another step before I bump into someone.

"Ah!" I scream, reeling backward and falling down. "Don't hurt me," I whimper, squeezing my eyes shut and defending my face with my right arm while my left one hangs limply to the ground.

SIX

<p style="text-indent: 2em;">A spark of light erupts in the darkness, slowly illuminating the entire hallway.

"This area is off-limits," a harsh voice says.

I squint my eyes as I try to make out the figure in front of me.

The color of his eyes is the first thing I notice—a deep swirling amber. I blink, unsure I'm seeing it right, and the next time I look at him, his eyes are just a regular warm brown. He straightens his back as he regards me skeptically, rising to his full height and towering over me. Good grief, how tall is this man? He must be well over two meters—that makes him over sixty centimeters taller than my slight frame.

"I-I'm sorry?" I whisper, forcing a smile. With that size, he could crush me with one hand. It's better to get on his good side.

"You need to leave. Now," he orders as he takes a step closer.

I instinctively back away. Right, so my options now are between being harvested for my organs and being murdered by this giant.

"I—" I wet my lips as my brain tries to find a proper explanation.

"Luce! There you are," Thea calls my name as she jogs toward us. Even in this low lighting, she looks absolutely stunning, her mane of red hair bouncing in the air. When she sees the newcomer, she comes to a halt, her eyes narrowing at him.

"What are *you* doing here?" She points a finger at him, her other hand balancing on her hip.

The stranger grinds his jaw as he shakes his head.

"I should be asking you the same. You know you're not supposed to be here."

"So that's it? You just came to ruin my fun?"

"Your fun? Do you hear yourself? You know what this is. You can't be here," he states resolutely, bypassing me and grabbing her hand.

"Don't you dare tell me what to do, Cer," she hisses, her eyes shooting daggers at him. "I'm sick of you ordering me around and following me wherever I go. You're so overbearing." She stomps her foot.

He shrugs.

"You're still coming back with me."

"No, I'm not."

"Yes, you are."

"No, I'm not, and you can't tell me what to do," she huffs, blowing a strand of hair out of her face. A twitch appears in his jaw as he attempts to stare her down in order to intimidate her, and that's enough for me to get red flags out of this interaction.

"Yes, you are. And don't make me repeat myself again, Thea. You know I hate that more than anything else," he speaks slowly, intently.

Thea swallows hard, her lips pressed together in worry.

Immediately, I think of the worst—that maybe he's her pimp and he's afraid she's going to tell people she's being exploited.

"Uhm, it doesn't seem like she wants to go anywhere," I interrupt, slowly getting to my feet and dusting my dress. My left arm is eerily numb despite the fact that I should be howling in pain given the fall I just took.

"Did anyone ask *you*?" The man—Cer—raises a condescending brow at me before turning to Thea once more. "You're hanging out with humans now too?"

"Humans? Geez, I guess I should probably be happy you didn't call me a peasant," I add dryly.

He looks me up and down, seemingly disapproving of my appearance.

"That would, indeed, be more appropriate."

"Cer! You're being rude to my friend. Apologize!" Thea stomps her foot again, this time punching him lightly in the shoulder.

"Why should I apologize to a human?" He rolls his eyes. "It's almost time for the Game to start. We can't be seen here."

He makes to turn, his fingers tightly wound around Thea's arm as he drags her after him.

"Let her go," I muster all my courage as I insert myself between the two of them. "She doesn't want to go with you, and you can't force her."

"I knew you were going to be a good friend, Luce," Thea says dreamily. "Great minds think alike." She smirks at Cer before sticking her tongue out at him.

"Tell your human pet to stand down or she'll get hurt."

"She's not my pet!" Thea bursts out at the same time as I say, "I'm not a pet."

"I'm not leaving, Cer. I'm honor-bound to be here, and you know that means you *can't* remove me from the premises," Thea adds smugly.

Cer stops, pivoting to stare at her.

"Honor-bound? To whom?" He closes his eyes for a moment before he groans out loud. "What did you do, Thea? What did you get yourself into now?"

"It's nothing bad, I promise. It's just that I'm doing a favor for someone who did *me* a favor some time back," she says nervously.

Cer takes a deep breath, stepping away from us.

"How long do you have to stay?"

"Until the end."

"And her?" He points toward me.

"She's my new friend. Be nice," Thea quips as she hooks her arm through my right one.

Cer's gaze meets Thea's and for a moment, it looks as if they're having an unspoken conversation. The tension in the air is as thick as a cloud of dynamite, and I'm still wondering just what their relationship is.

I sit by idly, quietly thinking of *my* next move if Thea is indeed in danger—and if *I* am in danger. Maybe we should both make a run for it while we can...

"Fine. Let us go back, then."

"Us?" Thea blinks in surprise.

Cer's lips flatten into a thin line as he exhales wearily.

"I'm not leaving you here alone. Let's go."

He doesn't wait for any of us to reply as he turns his back, walking toward the club.

"Ugh!" Thea grits out. "He had to show up here, too."

"Who is he?" I ask before I lower my voice to a whisper. "Are you in danger from him? You can tell me if you are and we can figure out a plan to escape together. I'm not in peak physical condition, of course, but I can get rather inventive if need be and—"

"You silly goose." Thea giggles. "We're not in danger from him. Hmm..." She pauses, stroking her chin thoughtfully. "Maybe it's even better that he's here."

My lashes flutter in confusion.

"I thought you didn't want him here..."

"I said that because I love ruffling his feathers. He's my brother." She waves her hand, dismissing my concerns. "We should follow him back. The game will start any moment."

She leads me back to the club, the corridor suddenly full of light.

"I don't understand... What game are you talking about? What is this place?"

"The Wishing Game is—"

"Please don't give me another cryptic answer." I sigh. "I only came here forced by circumstances, and without knowing what it is, I'd like to leave."

She takes a deep breath.

"I'm sorry to be the bearer of bad news, Luce, but you can't leave. Once you stepped foot into this building and the doorman validated your invite, you can't leave until the event is over."

"But... What... That can't be legal!" I squeak, although it's a little ironic of me to invoke legalities when I *am* on the run from the law—albeit for nothing of my own doing.

She gives me a sad smile.

"I guess someone really wanted to make sure you came here."

I'm about to ask her what she means by that, but the music becomes louder as we get back to the club. Thea doesn't let go of my hand as she leads me back to our seats—which are still, miraculously, unoccupied.

Her brother is already sitting there, his hand on his chin as he intently studies the people around. He's...odd. Besides the fact that he insulted me to my face and never even deigned to apologize, there's something *off* about him.

Thea plops herself on the seat next to him, seemingly deriving great amusement from her brother's grimace. She pulls me into the seat next to her.

"At least tell me we're not in any danger," I murmur as I fidget with my fingers.

"For now, no. But don't worry. Cer's always ready to save us. Isn't that right, big bro?" Thea giggles as she rubs her shoulder against Cer's.

He grumbles something under his breath, but he makes no attempt to extricate himself from her. In fact, I could almost swear I note a slight curl of his lips. Hm... Maybe I misjudged him and he's actually a good, caring brother who was just worried about his sister.

"Can't you at least give me a hint about this? I'm really wary about all the secrecy."

"I'm guessing you didn't read the invite properly, did you?"

My cheeks heat up as I slowly shake my head.

"I had more important things to do," I mumble.

"And yet you're here," she says, watching me intently.

"I just happened to be here at the right time." I sigh. "Someone was following me and I thought I was lucky to find this place. Now, I'm not so sure anymore..."

"Someone was following you?" Her eyes flash.

"It's a long story." I give her a tight smile. I'm not about to tell a person I just met that I'm wanted by the police.

"Maybe it's fate. Right place, right time? Don't you humans have a saying for that?"

"There you go again with 'humans.' Is this some slang I'm not aware of?" English is my second language and while I've learned a lot in the past few years, I'm still not the best when it comes to slang or online speech.

Thea shoots a quick look at Cer, but he just shrugs as if telling her *it's your mess.* Clearing her throat, she gives me a wide smile.

"Something like that," she says, the words forced.

My skepticism increases despite liking the girl. There's something off about her and her brother. They know more than they're letting on, and that only makes me feel more uneasy about what's to come.

I could try to make a run for it again, but somehow I doubt I'd even make it to the exit, let alone past the bouncer. One glance at Thea and Cer, and I realize they must have guessed what I was thinking about because they both shake their heads at me.

"Tell me what was on the invite." I change the topic as I feel the air around us grow thicker. No way out, got it—for *now.*

"It's exactly what the name implies—a wishing game. Everyone is here to compete to have their most ardent wishes come true."

What? Is this some sort of reality show? I look around, but I don't spot any cameras. Then again, they could very well be hidden to get our natural reactions.

"And how does that work?" I ask apprehensively.

"Do you think people care about the *how* as long as they get their wish?" She shrugs, and it's not lost on me that she evades answering. "You, too, must have a wish, or you wouldn't be here," she further prevaricates.

"I—"

Do I? Yes, of course I do. I want revenge for what happened to Nikki. I want his killers to pay for *everything* they put him through.

I nod slowly.

"Vengeance," I whisper. "I'd wish for something the law will not give me."

She smiles kindly at me.

"*Just* vengeance? If you could have anything in the world. *Anything* at all, would it be just vengeance?"

I stare at her, my mouth hanging open as a thought flashes through my mind.

My most ardent wish.

Nikki.

"I see that you do." She nods, her expression almost sad. "Whatever happens next, Luce, I want you to always ask yourself if what you wish for is worth the sacrifice."

Sacrifice? What sacrifice?

More alarm bells go off in my brain, and this time, not even the alcohol I consumed can keep me from freaking out.

"What do you mean by that?"

SEVEN

Thea opens her mouth to speak, but Cer places his hand on top of hers. She inhales sharply at the contact, her body tensing. Eventually, she just shakes her head at me, her lips tipped up in an apologetic smile.

And by God, that scares me even more.

I don't get to ask her further as the music suddenly stops and the lights dim.

Thea claps her hands, her eyes sparkling with joy.

"It's starting. Oh my, it's starting," she squeals.

"Why are you so excited?" I frown. Looking back, she's been this way from the beginning—ecstatic to just be here. Does she want to compete in this so badly? Is it for a wish? What is her wish?

More questions flood my mind as I realize I know nothing about these strangers, just like I know nothing about this supposed game I've been invited to.

"It's my first time here," Thea breathes out in awe, her eyes searching the room for something. "I wasn't allowed here before," she says, almost absentmindedly.

"It's him! That's Inu." She jumps to her feet as she points to the stage.

With my attention on Thea, I didn't see that someone

appeared on the stage. The lights surrounding the outer area have turned a deep red, while the floor lighting of the stage is a bright white. The audience is mostly invisible now as the focus is solely on the two newcomers.

The man—who I assume to be Inu—is dressed in a pair of black leather pants paired with a sparkly silver tank top. His bleached blond hair is spiky, reminiscent of the early 2000s. He has a pair of black sunglasses on, obscuring most of his face. He must be one of those people I've seen memes on the internet about who doesn't remove his sunglasses indoors.

Next to him is a woman, her hair just as blond as Inu's. She's wearing a silver pleated skirt that matches Inu's tank top, and she has a glittery bra as her top. Her breasts are...generous. That cleavage area alone has the men in the audience audibly panting at the sight of her, whistles and lewd jokes flittering through the club.

They both smile at the audience, waving to get more reaction out of the crowd.

"I can't believe he's here!" Thea jumps up and down.

"That's enough, Thea," Cer grumbles as he pulls her back down onto her seat. "You're going to make a spectacle of yourself."

"So what?" She shrugs, her eyes still glued to the stage. "When will I have the chance to see Inu again?" She gushes audibly.

"Who is he?" I ask, frowning.

"He's the most famous entertainer. His parties are legendary, or so I heard..." she trails off when her brother shoots her a look of annoyance.

Entertainer? So this is a reality show after all? But where are the cameras?

Oh my God! Is this live? Will I be on TV? Then the police will know exactly where to come look for me and...

"Is this being recorded?" I ask warily.

"Recorded?" Thea frowns. "No, of course not. This is an exclusive event that only a few people can take part in. It's very secretive," she tells me before redirecting her gaze to the stage and sighing dreamily as she stares at Inu.

Her brother doesn't seem too pleased about that. His facial expression is the definition of *if looks could kill*. I guess he doesn't share Thea's enthusiasm about tonight's hosts.

"Good evening, everyone, and welcome to the seventy-ninth edition of The Wishing Game. Are you all ready?"

The crowd follows the cue, erupting in a chorus of glee. "Yes!"

"Seventy-ninth edition?" I whisper to Thea.

She nods. "It happens once every one hundred years."

"We are your hosts for this evening. My name is Inu, and this bombshell next to me is my twin, Inara. We're going to explain all the rules and officially welcome you to the game."

More raucous cheers erupt from the crowd, together with chants of the hosts' names.

Inu smiles, putting a palm up. The crowd falls silent.

"Is he that famous?" I ask. Most of the people in the crowd seem to know them somehow.

"I told you. He's one of the biggest entertainers, but he's a very elusive figure. He DJs at clubs and hosts some of the most extravagant parties in this world."

"In this world?"

Cer clears his throat, giving Thea a warning look.

"Anyway, he's very famous in the party circles."

"I see..." But I *don't* see. I don't understand what everything has to do with me. Although I'm grateful to have a respite from being chased by the police, I'm starting to think I may have gotten myself into something worse.

"Your messengers should have already explained why you were chosen and what you stand to win if you prevail in the game. But I'm here to tell you that only the *best* can win. Are you the best?" He pauses for effect, glancing at the audience. "That remains to be seen."

"Messengers? What messengers?" I inquire, trying to subdue the panic in my voice.

Thea purses her lips.

"Doesn't matter." She shakes her head. "Just pay attention to what he's saying and you'll be fine."

I blink in confusion. Both Thea and Cer ignore me as they focus on the stage, and once more I get the feeling that they're hiding something.

"There are two hundred of you outcasts in this room today. And thousands more across the universe. You will all be competing at the same time for a chance to get your most ardent wish fulfilled. But this edition's game will be a little different," Inara says, a smile pulling at her lips. "Only five individuals out of one hundred thousand outcasts from all over the universe can win the game. That means this time you will not only be competing against the trials we've set for you, but also against each other."

The audience gasps, some voicing their complaints while others express their excitement about the more competitive nature of the game.

"Just like in our previous editions, we want the scales to be even for everyone at the start of the game. That means that all the participants will be gifted the chance to compete at peak condition. Of course, as per the rules, this gift is to be used *only* while you're competing in the game"—he gives Inara a look —"and at our discretion, of course."

"A gift?"

"What is it?"

"Inu is the best!"

Voices echo in the room, everyone showing their excitement.

Both Inu and Inara smile at the crowd.

"I trust you've all indulged in the special cocktails we've prepared for tonight?"

The audience responds with a resounding yes.

I find myself nodding as well, licking my lips as I remember the sweet taste of the beverage. Just a while ago, I'd chastised myself for drinking one too many glasses, but now I'm craving another one. It's quite the addictive flavor...

"What you all enjoyed was a punch mixed with a drop of ambrosia—just enough to give you *all* a fair chance in this competition."

I frown at the mention of ambrosia. What is that? I'm not familiar with the fruit. Others seem to be equally confused, but as the complaints resound in the room, they seem to be more concerned about the effects of the drink—or *lack* thereof.

"No, I'm afraid immortality is not on the menu tonight." Inu chuckles. "Although you can wish for it—and get it if you win."

"The drop of ambrosia was meant to get everyone in peak condition for the game. Shall we, Inu?" Inara shares a glance with her brother.

He stretches his arm toward her. As they join hands, a bright light engulfs the entire room. I squeeze my eyes shut, blinded by the blast.

A panicked breath catches in my throat as I bring my hands to my eyes, rubbing furiously. I dare to blink, moisture clinging to my lashes. Yet I can see—there's nothing wrong with my eyes.

My brows furrow as I glance around, trying to ascertain what just happened. But when I reach for Thea to ask her if she's all right, I'm shocked to discover the ease with which I can use my left arm. There's no...pain. No numbness. No discomfort at all.

I can move it perfectly fine—as if it had never been broken in the first place.

My eyes widen as I incredulously pat my torso, feeling for my bruised flesh and broken ribs. Where they used to hurt with just one touch, now there's absolutely no pain. Still in shock, I pull my hair to the side, searching for the place the doctors drilled a hole in my skull. If before I could feel the ridges of the sutures, now there's only smooth scalp.

"How is this possible?" I mumble in shock.

I'm not the only one in awe. As I look at the other side of the room, I spot someone who'd been in a wheelchair suddenly stand up and walk. Others who'd had various disabilities are healed as well. Even those costumed are rejoicing, although I can't see how the ambrosia worked for them.

The most striking, though, is a guy weeping on the floor. I vaguely remember noticing before that he had crutches and he was missing one leg.

But now...

How the hell could a person suddenly *grow* a leg?

Murmurs envelop the entire area, and while I can't make out what everyone is saying, I'm willing to guess they are all exhibiting some sort of life-changing healing.

Thea is watching raptly, a wide smile on her lips. Her brother, on the other hand, looks entirely bored. Resting his chin on the back of his hand, he releases an annoyed sigh.

"What is this, Thea? What is happening?"

Panic swells in my breast, yet at the same time, I'm physically perfectly fine. How is this possible? Am I dreaming? Am I in an alternate reality? Or, worse, am I still in a coma? That must be it because otherwise how can this be real? How can someone be healed with the snap of a finger? How can *ambrosia* grow a leg?

I'm either going crazy or something seriously messed up is afoot here.

"Sometimes it takes seeing with your own eyes to believe something, doesn't it?" Thea smiles at me. "Inu and Inara are minor deities of mischief and gossip, respectively. Together, they have a bit more power, hence the hand holding. But they're not *that* powerful. The ambrosia healed you. They merely activated its effects," she notes glibly.

"What? You... Deities? You're messing with me."

I stare at her, my mouth hanging open in shock.

"Please tell me you're joking," I whisper.

"I'm not and you know it. You can *feel* it," she says as she grabs my left hand. "How else would this be real, Luce?"

"I'm going crazy," I mutter to myself. A mixture of calm and restlessness fights for supremacy within me. One side of me wants to accept this as truth—the evidence is right in front of me. But the other side—the skeptical one—would rather believe I'm going crazy than admit that this *could* be real.

I lived most of my childhood believing that a *god* controlled our homeland, only to find out it was a charlatan who only wanted to take advantage of people's worship. Back then, too, I believed the so-called miracles and his divine intervention. So how can I believe this now when I've been burned before? Yet the evidence...

There's no pain. That's all I can think about. There's absolutely *no* pain.

"You're not going crazy, Luce." Thea pats my thigh. "Just open your mind to the impossible."

The impossible... That there are gods among us. Gods who have the power to stop pain, heal wounds, and grow limbs.

There are gods among us. And I have never in my life been more confused.

Because if there are gods among us; if there are beings with powers—*true powers*—then nothing is impossible.

Not even death.

"This is our welcoming gift to you," Inara says. "But as we mentioned before, this is only for the duration of the game."

"Shall we explain more about the game, Ina?"

She nods.

"The Wishing Game consists of five trials." As Inara speaks, the screen behind them lights up, showing five empty panels, each containing a question mark. "Each trial will be announced after the previous one is completed. The trials will become increasingly harder, and the last one will declare our winners. If more than five people pass the fifth trial—although that's unlikely—there will be another round to decide the winners. If not, you will get your wish upon the fulfillment of the fifth trial."

"And the rules are..." Inu pauses, a mischievous smile pulling at his lips. "That there are *no* rules."

Murmurs echo through the crowd.

"Yes, it's exactly as it sounds. You can use any means to win —even cheating."

"However," Inara intervenes, "you may *not* quit at any point during the game. Once you stepped foot into this venue, you officially entered the game. There is no way out except if you pass to the next round."

Inu nods.

"Once you've passed a trial, there will be a break before the next one starts. That is the only time anyone is allowed to withdraw. Of course, the gift we've offered tonight will be taken back, and your memory will be wiped of any knowledge of the game," Inu continues in a nonchalant manner—as if he didn't just say he'll erase the memory of anyone who wants to leave the game.

My mouth drops open in shock, but somehow I can't tear my gaze away from the stage.

"If you die at any point *during* the game, you forfeit your right to *any* future incarnations," Inara casually chimes in.

EIGHT

"What does that mean?" I turn to Thea since she seems to have more knowledge on this than me.

"Are you familiar with the concept of reincarnation?"

"Somewhat?"

"The short version is that the soul is immortal and goes through many cycles, incarnations if you will. Forfeiting your right to reincarnation means your soul will simply cease to exist."

"But that's—"

"A steep price to pay." She smiles sadly. "The risk must be equal to the reward. When you make that wish, you'll be gambling with your soul."

I stare at her, my mind a whirlpool of confusion.

There's only so much a person can take in, no?

Not an hour ago I was running from the police, and now I suddenly find out there *are* deities out there, with powers, who actually healed my broken body, and who expect me to wager my soul for the chance to fulfill a wish.

But...if there *are* deities, that means that nothing is impossible, doesn't it?

"Do deities have the power to bring back the dead?" I whisper, unable to believe I'm even willing to contemplate this. It could all still be just a nightmare—the rational side of me is inclined to believe that. But it could also be real and my one chance at saving my husband. My brain tells me it's the former. But my heart... My heart yearns for it to be real.

"Of course. There's nothing they can't do," Thea explains. "The messengers you were asking about earlier? They should have given you the invite in person and told you all of this."

"There was no one." I shake my head, recounting how I'd gotten the first invite and the subsequent ones.

"That is an anomaly," she notes thoughtfully.

"Now that we've gotten the boring talk out of the way, who's ready for the game?" Inu asks, eliciting cheers from the crowd.

Thea too claps enthusiastically until her brother gives her another one of his dry looks. The corners of her lips lower, her gaze dipping to her feet.

"Your brother is an asshole," I lean to whisper.

"Tell me about it," she grumbles. "I can never enjoy anything." She sighs dramatically. "But now I'm here. And I met you. And we're going to have such a fine time. Of course, you can't withdraw now, but you can do it after the first trial and—"

"Wait a moment," I stop her senseless rambling. "Who said anything about withdrawing after the first trial?"

"Well, you wanted out. That's your way out." She smiles blithely.

"Not if the prize is *any* wish," I oddly find myself saying.

Until a moment ago, I didn't even think I believed this whole god talk—I'm still not entirely sure I do. But if there is the slightest chance I can get Nikki back, I'm going to take it— regardless of how crazy it sounds. The flames of revenge, previously raging uncontrollably, slowly fan out, replaced by a much more potent fire.

The goal I thought I had is all but gone until only one objective remains.

Nikki.

My beloved Nikki.

To have him in my arms once more, I would pay *any* price. I would even gamble my immortal soul.

"But... Luce..." She blinks in surprise. "You can't... You're..."

"I am?" I raise a brow.

"Never mind." She strains a smile.

"You didn't tell me what your wish is," I shoot back. "Why are *you* here?"

"Yes, do tell, Thea. Why are you here?" her brother interjects, leaning in to watch her closely.

"My wish is"—she pauses, a look of uncertainty crossing her face—"to find love!" she suddenly declares. "Yes, that's it. I want to find love."

"You want to find love?" Cer repeats ominously.

"Uhm, yes..." she stammers, looking anywhere but at him. "Like at least a quarter of the people present here do. The others want money, power, immortality, or just like you," she addresses me, turning her back to her brother, "to get back someone they lost."

I nod thoughtfully. Everyone here must have their own circumstances, and knowing my own desire, I can't judge anyone for their choices.

Turning my attention to the crowd, I note that everyone is debating the merits of the competition and if their wish is worth their immortal soul. Out of the corner of my eye, I spot the girl I'd bumped into previously—the one with the fluffy white tail. My eyes slowly widen as I note that her entire body is now covered in white fur—*is that even her?*

"Thea?" I ask tentatively. "This isn't a costumed event, is it?"

"Costumed event?" She frowns. "Where did you get that idea?" She pauses as realization dawns on her. "Oh, Luce." She giggles.

"That's why everyone kept referring to me as *human*. It's because some are *not* human, is that right?"

Even as I utter the words, I find it hard to believe that any of this could be true. Yet if gods exist, if they have the power to heal extensive injuries, then it stands to reason that other creatures could exist, too. And considering the girl's control of her tail...that only leaves me with one conclusion. It wasn't a mechanical tail. It was a real one. Just like the other people I assumed were costumed as animals—they're not. They *are* the animals.

My God—or is it Gods now? This is too much information for my feeble *human* mind. And although I find that I am oddly okay with the existence of all these creatures, it doesn't make the experience any less eerie.

Thea gives me a tight smile.

"Yes, you would be correct." She takes a deep breath. "Most of the individuals here are *not* human. And those who *are* either have ties to the underworld, or their messengers explained the situation in detail when they were invited to the game. It's why I was so surprised you had no idea about...well, anything. It's certainly not done to not explain the situation, least of all to a human."

"You mean I'm the only one here who was clueless about it," I add dryly.

"I don't know why you got the invite and nothing else. It's not how it's done. It must have been a glitch or something," Thea adds. "But you're taking it very well considering this is your first exposure to this world," she praises.

"Thank you, I'm trying." I crack a smile.

At this point, I've come to terms that this is actually real, or I'm having a full mental breakdown. And even if the latter turns out to be true, at least in my delusion I can have a chance to get Nikki back.

"You're funny, Luce." Thea laughs. "We'll have such a good time together," she says as she pulls me into a tight hug.

"Wait a second," I suddenly say, drawing back. "You called me *human*, too. So if you're not human, what are you?"

Thea shares a look with her brother, who simply shrugs at her.

"We're..." she stammers. "We're..."

"She's a harpy," Cer intervenes.

Thea gasps, a horrified look on her face.

"What are harpies?" I ask.

"You've never heard of them?"

I shake my head. It's not the time to be embarrassed by my lack of knowledge.

"You should show her, *sis*." Cer raises a daring brow at Thea.

She rolls her eyes at him and, lifting her hand, I notice her fingers turning into claws.

"That's..." I blink. "Impressive?" I force a smile.

Maybe I actually died that day on the bridge and now I'm stuck in an afterlife limbo filled with all types of creatures. Yes, that might actually make more sense.

"You're so cute." Thea gives me a genuine smile before she turns to her brother, baring her teeth at him. "You'll pay. Later," she hisses at him.

He shrugs, leaning back in his seat, his lips curling at the corners.

Their relationship is...peculiar.

Before I can dwell more on the fact that my new friend is *not* human, Inu's voice echoes in the room.

"Now that we've covered the basics, it's time for the high-light of the night. The Wishing Well."

Claps resound from the audience while I'm even more confused.

Inu takes a step to the side, and Inara does the same. Within seconds, cracks form at the level of the stage in the shape of a perfect circle. As all the dots connect, the ground collapses, leaving behind a gaping hole.

What...

Instead of the panic that I expect to see from the crowd, more cheers erupt.

"It's starting. It's so exciting, Cer," Thea exclaims, grabbing her brother's arm. He grumbles something under his breath, clearly not sharing the sentiment.

Is he even allowed here without an invite?

I hadn't considered that before. But if he came here in

search of his sister, then he's not here in an official capacity, is he?

My train of thought is interrupted as Thea jumps to her feet, taking my hand and steering me down the stairs to where the main crowd is.

"Come on, we need to line up," she mentions, and I notice that everyone is forming a line in front of the newly appeared hole.

"We're not supposed to worship that hole or something weird like that, are we?" I ask in a hushed tone. My perception is a little screwed from everything I've witnessed at the hacienda, and worshipping a hole would not be the strangest thing.

Thea stares at me for a moment before she bursts out laughing.

"What? Of course not. The Wishing Well collects all the wishes. Think of it as locking in your wish before the game starts."

"Oh." I nod slowly. "So once you make your wish, you can't change it?"

"No. The wish you start the game with is the wish you end the game with."

We take our places in line. Thea is in front of me and her brother stealthily joins us, giving death stares to everyone around.

I crane my neck to see what's happening at the end of the line. The first person walks up to the stage, stopping right by the hole in the ground.

He exchanges a few words with Inu and Inara before he takes a step forward, plunging into the hole.

"What?" I gasp.

He resurfaces a second later. His clothes are wet—a sign that there is an actual well and not just a metaphor. He has a wide smile on his face as he walks to the side of the stage, getting down and taking a seat at a table. He seems fine, but that doesn't make me any less wary about this.

Think of Nikki, I urge myself. I'm already down the road of no return—I have no family, no home, and a warrant on my name. There's nothing waiting for me outside of this. No matter how crazy it gets, at least there's a chance that at the end of it all I'll have my husband back. For that sliver of hope, I'm willing to put aside all my disbelief and surrender to this madness.

Surprisingly, the line moves fast. Even with at least a couple hundred people in here, it takes only a few seconds for each person to jump in and be right back out. As we reach closer to the stage, I see that Inu and Inara greet every person in turn, exchanging platitudes.

"That's nice of them," I mention to Thea.

"Isn't it?" She sighs dreamily. "I can't believe I'll get to talk to him."

While Thea gushes about Inu and his celebrity status, I continue to look around, studying the other participants and wondering what their wish could possibly be. Now that I know most are *not* human, I see them with different eyes, and I can't help but wonder how their different advantages will play out during the game. Inu had mentioned that this will not only be us against the trials, but also against the other participants. Does that mean that suddenly everyone here is an enemy?

Despite the fact that my injuries have healed, I am aware that I'm neither the strongest nor the fastest person for a *human*. Compared to mythical creatures? I likely don't stand a chance. Regardless of that, though, I have something they don't—my love for Nikki. Conviction slowly fills me as I envision having him by my side once more. For that, I'm able to withstand anything— even the deepest circles of hell.

The line moves swiftly, and before I know it, it's Thea's turn.

She's giddy as she jumps on the stage. Stopping in front of Inu, she looks at him with stars in her eyes.

"Do I know you? You seem familiar." He frowns as he peruses her.

Her eyes widen.

"You remember me?" she asks in a small voice.

Inu smiles, taking a step closer to her.

"That little..." Cer mutters. I turn to him, but he's already gone. What...

He appears out of thin air onto the stage, grabbing Thea's hand and pulling her into the well with him.

"You're not supposed to go two at once," Inara cries out as she rushes toward them. But by the time both Inu and Inara get to the mouth of the well, they're already gone.

"You need to be more careful." Inara's eyes flash at her brother. "We can't afford any mistakes."

His brows furrow in confusion as he stares at the well.

"I could have sworn I've seen her before." He scratches the back of his head.

"You and your girlfriends." She rolls her eyes. "She could be any one of your flings and you wouldn't remember anyway."

"I'm not sure..."

The seconds pass, and Cer jumps out of the well, holding a wet and shivering Thea in his arms. Inu opens his mouth to address them, but one look from Cer and he takes a step back. Even Inara, who seemed on the verge of a fight, backs down, averting her gaze.

That is...odd.

Cer storms off the stage and deposits Thea on one of the seats—or rather, he drops her with a resounding thud. Fuming, she opens her mouth to rebuke him, but he's already turned his back to her, thereby ignoring her.

Yes, these siblings are very odd, indeed.

It's my turn to go onto the stage.

"Hello there," Inu greets me. "When you go in, think about your most ardent wish."

I nod, already picturing Nikki's face. Taking a deep breath, I jump.

Wha—

The fall is much steeper than I would have expected—at least a few hundred feet as I keep plunging down. Water breaks my fall and I sink to the bottom of the well. Still, I try not to be overwhelmed by fear as I focus on my wish.

Nikki. I want my Nikki to come back to me.

A pulsing light flashes from the ground up, charging at me and swallowing me whole. I open my mouth to cry out and water rushes in, yet my breathing isn't impacted. Somehow, I'm not drowning.

"Luce?" I hear an echo, accompanied by a soft caress.

My heart stops in my chest.

"Nikki?" I whisper, my eyes wide open as I search for him in the depths of the water.

"Luce," the voice is closer. Then closer.

NINE

Just as the sound of my name on his lips brushes against my ear, I cough water, inhaling deeply. Staring at my feet and the floor I'm currently sitting on, I realize I'm not in the well anymore.

"Luce! Come here!" Thea waves me from the side.

My thoughts are in disarray as I slowly move to the side.

"Are you okay? You look a little pale."

"How long was I there?"

"A few seconds. Just like everyone else," she replies. "Well, except for us because Mr. Grumpy over here had something to prove." She sticks her tongue out at her brother, who's currently still giving her the back treatment.

Groaning loudly, she shakes her head.

"After everyone is done, they'll finally announce the first trial. I'm so curious about what it's going to be. They change it from edition to edition, you know. You never know what to expect."

"You know quite a lot about this," I murmur.

"There are rumors, of course. You always hear about it and how much fun it is. But I've never been allowed to go to one before."

"Uhm, you said the last edition was a hundred years ago."

"Oops, I did say that, didn't I?" She giggles.

"That means you're over a hundred years old?" I blink.

"Around there," she says with a mischievous smile—which I take to mean she's much older than that.

"And your brother?"

"He's a few... decades older than me."

I nod, storing that bit of information. I'm a baby compared to them—hell, probably compared to anyone in here.

Soon, a whooshing sound envelops the room as the hole fills up, the ground appearing once more as it was before.

"The well has absorbed all of your wishes. Now you are officially part of the seventy-ninth edition of the Wishing Games!" Inara says excitedly.

"That means we can finally reveal what awaits you for the first game."

The screen behind them lights up again, showing five squares, each corresponding with a trial. With the wave of a hand, Inu brings the first square into focus, the question mark slowly disappearing to be replaced with the picture of a bridge.

My brows furrow in confusion, and I'm not the only one baffled by the ambiguous clue.

"For the first trial, you are allowed to work in teams of up to *five* individuals," Inara starts. "Of course, if you don't trust anyone, you can attempt it alone." Her lips tip up in a cunning smile.

"There are, of course, advantages and disadvantages to this. If any member of your team dies during the trial, you *all* die. You will be putting your fate in the hands of strangers—and potential enemies," Inu adds smugly. "You have five minutes to choose whether you will compete in the first trial as a team or by yourself."

Hushed whispers and suspicious glares abound in the crowd.

"We'll be a team, right? Me, you, and Cer." Thea immediately grabs my hand, her smile intoxicating.

I find myself nodding despite myself. As a human, I doubt

I'd do much by myself. I don't yet know how demanding the contest will be, so I'll benefit from having them by my side. But what's in it for *them*? Because if I die...

"Are you sure? I'd be the weakest link," I admit honestly.

"Nah," Thea dismisses my words. "We'll make it through this, trust me," she adds confidently, pointing to her brother with an amused grin. "Cer is practically unbeatable," she whispers in a low voice.

He scoffs, but he doesn't turn, nor acknowledge our conversation.

"If you've decided how you will compete, please form a queue in front of the stage to receive your task for the first trial."

"Wait... Is there a different task for every team?"

"It seems so." Thea nods as she gets to her feet. Her hair is magically dry while mine is still soaking wet—well, I guess being *human* has some downsides.

She takes my arm and hops over to her brother, looping her arm through his, too. She's probably the most excited and energetic person in this room. Everyone else is wary, suspicious, and greedy for the prize. Not Thea, though. She seems to be in it just for a good time—or maybe annoying her brother.

To my surprise, there are a lot of people who form teams, only a few choosing to compete in the game individually. But as I study the teams, I note that almost all have partnered up with their own species, or at least as close as possible.

As if reading my thoughts, Thea explains.

"There are a lot of enmities in the underworld. Half of the people in this room hate the other half. I'm surprised no one has started a fight yet. Especially with humans."

"Do you guys hate us so much?"

"Hate you? Of course not. I find you rather cute," Thea adds vehemently. "But not everyone shares my opinion. Most hate humans because they're different—and powerless. But mostly different."

"Awesome," I mumble, suddenly realizing why everyone was staring at me with distaste. In fact, the people I suspect are also humans have partnered up together. I'm probably the only one with non-human teammates.

"Don't mind it. The wolves over there *hate* the foxes." She points to two teams that are currently baring their teeth—fangs?—at each other. "The nymphs abhor the satyrs." She points to another cluster. "And it goes on and on. Very few get along." She shrugs as if this is simply the nature of things.

"Is there any wiki page for the underworld that I can use for reference?" I joke lightly.

"Wiki?" She frowns.

"You know, like an encyclopedia."

"Of course not!" she says, horrified. "To have all that information in one place would be extremely dangerous. Every kind viciously defends its secrets."

"Then how do you know stuff about them? How do you even know they hate each other?"

"Oh, you just observe who kills whom, how they do it and why they do it. That should give you a general idea," she explains matter-of-factly.

I open my mouth to say something, only to snap it shut when I realize I'm rather speechless.

The underworld sounds...awesome—*not*.

On the stage, Inu and Inara materialize an odd-looking board that is mirrored on the screen in the back too. One by one, the teams go up to the stage and, using a small needle, they prick their fingers and let a drop of their blood fall onto the canvas of the board. Each time, the blood flows around, filling some invisible crevices until they transform into numbers—that, if I'm not mistaken, are coordinates.

When it's our turn, I offer my blood, but Thea doesn't allow me, pushing me behind her as she takes the needle and stabs her pinky. The red liquid stains the canvas, traveling around until it settles into a combination of numbers and letters.

40°45'22"N 73°59'17"W

"Congratulations, this is your location," Inu says, transcribing the coordinates onto a piece of paper and handing it to us. Before Thea can grab it, her brother does, barely acknowledging Inu.

"You're so rude sometimes, Cer," Thea grumbles in annoyance. And just as I've come to expect from him, he doesn't answer back.

When all the teams have received their locations, Inu and Inara finally announce the theme of the first trial.

"At every one of the locations you've received, you'll encounter a spirit that refuses to cross over to the afterlife. Your job is to do whatever it takes to convince it to leave this world and continue its incarnation cycle. Each spirit will be different. They will have different motivations and different reasons for why they are still stuck in this world. You need to help them cut their ties so they can move on."

Of course ghosts would be real too. And our job is not only to find one and interact with it, but somehow convince it to stop being a ghost?

I'd laugh if the situation weren't so dire. This is exactly the scenario I would picture in a bad movie. Nikki and I used to have this oddly cute tradition on Fridays. We'd find the worst-rated movie and watch it. Most often, it was something involving the supernatural and they all featured very bad special effects.

My lips tip up in a melancholic smile as I remember cuddling with him on the couch and laying my head on his chest, the thud of his heart the sweetest melody. He'd hold me in his arms and soothe me with his gentle voice whenever a jump scare would pop up on the screen. We'd be initially taken aback, but then we'd laugh it off.

But my smile quickly falls as one of our conversations suddenly echoes in my mind.

"If I were a ghost, I'd never leave your side," he joked as we watched a movie. "I'd haunt you for an eternity."

I smiled lazily at him, taking his words as jest.

"But then you'd never have peace," I countered, thinking about the movie's idea of an afterlife where souls go to either Heaven or Hell.

"You are the only peace I seek," he whispered.

Back then, I never thought I'd be a moment without him, or that life would be so cruel to take him away from me so young. Back then, I thought it was the two of us against the world, in our little world, and no one could ever intrude on that.

But I was wrong.

I was wrong to take everything for granted.

Yet here I am, being given a second chance.

Every breath I take, the world I live in changes irrevocably, and with it my perception of what's real and what's not—of what's good or bad. Every second, I feel as if my sanity is under threat by all this new fantastical information foraging its way into my brain. But the truth is, my sanity's been slipping away from me from the moment I heard that last love confession on my Nikki's lips. When he died, I died too. That I was still alive was a cosmical farce—or so I thought.

I have another chance. Against all odds, I have another chance to see my love again. And it doesn't matter if this game is just another farcical collection of absurdities. It doesn't matter if I can make sense of it or not. As long as I get him back, I'm willing to do anything.

A gong sound echoes through the entire building, startling me from my musings.

"It's midnight. You have until midnight a week from now to resolve your cases. If not, you will fail. Those who succeed will receive an invitation to the next phase of the game."

"Wait, what happens if we fail?" I ask in a low voice. Had they even mentioned it? They'd only told us what happened if we died *in* the game.

"You die," Thea states in an empty voice. "If you don't complete the trial, you die."

"How will we find the location?" Thea asks as the three of us leave the club.

The chilly air of the night hits my face. I inhale deeply, glad for the absence of pain in my chest.

"We need a smartphone with GPS," I answer.

Both Thea and Cer stop in their tracks, their brows furrowed as they stare at me.

I raise my brows in question.

"What is a GPS?" Thea asks. "And what is a smartphone?"

"You don't know?"

Both shake their heads.

A smile tugs at my lips. Ah, but it seems that for the first time I am the one with the knowledge—and I'd be lying if I said this doesn't feel good.

"GPS is like an automated map. You plug in the coordinates and it shows you how to get there."

Thea's eyes widen.

"Oh my! That's so exciting! And where do we get this GPS from?"

"We need to buy a smartphone. Unfortunately, I forgot to bring mine with me." I sigh. With the police on my trail, the last thing on my mind was taking my phone with me—though in hindsight, maybe I should have been more careful.

"What is that?" Thea frowns.

As I explain what smartphones are, I notice that her brother is no longer by her side. Just as I'm about to inquire about his whereabouts, he appears from around the corner with a paper bag in his hand, which he thrusts toward me.

A little weirded out, I accept it, peeking inside to find over ten phones, stacked one on top of the other.

"Uhm, where did you get these?" I ask as I look at him.

He stares me down, his mouth closed shut.

"Did you take them from someone?" I rephrase my question.

The phones are all without their original packaging, and some exhibit signs of wear.

"Open that GPS," he barks in a low voice.

Shaking my head at him, I mutter a sorry to the people he must have robbed. If I weren't wanted by the police, maybe I would have dropped them off after we're done with them. Unfortunately, the situation at hand precludes me from acting like a Good Samaritan.

"Let me see," Thea interjects, grabbing a handful of phones from the bag and studying them with curiosity. While she's playing with those, I find a phone that is unlocked and access the GPS, plugging in the coordinates.

"It's in the city," I add, surprised. I would have thought it would be some remote destination just to make it harder for us to get there. Alas, maybe this trial won't be *too* difficult.

When no one speaks, I look up to find Thea taking apart the phones with her overgrown nails—or claws? Cer is behind her, looking over her shoulder and doing a great job of looking uninterested even though his eyes are glued to her hands.

I sigh as I clear my throat to get their attention.

It's only been hours since I found out that there are other species out there—*non*-human species—just as there are gods. Against all odds, I've ended up participating in some sort of supernatural deadly game that might very well kill me. Now, I'm teamed up with two very odd *non-humans* who are even more technologically illiterate than me. And somehow I'm very calm.

Maybe I'm still in shock.

"Oh." Thea smiles, dropping the phone parts to the ground. "Where to, then?"

"It's actually very close to here," I say as I show them the screen, pointing at the distance between us and the location we've been given.

New Amsterdam Theatre.

For a haunted place, I would have expected an abandoned building, or at least something out of use. This is, however, very much in use. There's a musical performed there almost every day, which might make our mission a little more difficult.

"I know that place!" Thea exclaims. "I've been there before."

"You have?" Cer echoes.

"I saw a musical there a while back. What was it..." She frowns. "Ah, Alice in Rabbitland."

"Wonderland?"

"Yes, that one! It was so cool."

"And when exactly were you there?" Cer crosses his arms over his chest.

"Oh, a while ago." Thea waves her hand.

"You know you're not allowed to—"

"If I can have your attention," I interrupt. "You can fight about that later. We need to focus on our assignment."

Thea sticks her tongue out at her brother before she gives me her full attention.

"Since I know where it is, I can lead you there," she offers. "We can tele—Ouch!" she exclaims, slapping her brother's hand aside. He glares at her.

I shake my head, releasing a weary sigh. It's not going to be easy with these two, is it?

"There's a subway station right around the corner. It's one stop away from the location," I tell them. "Once we get off, Thea can lead the way."

We could walk, of course, but I don't want to take any chances that the police might still be in the area. And with the hour growing late and the streets becoming emptier, it would be so easy to spot me...

I rummage through the pockets of the dress, sure I'd felt some money before. Since it had been on the left side, I hadn't noticed until my arm healed. My fingers brush against a few crumpled dollar bills—likely forgotten by Noelle inside the dress at some point. And as I peek to the side, I count a ten and a couple of fives—plenty for a subway ride and maybe for a snack later.

"S-subway?" Thea flutters her lashes, her smile a little forced.

"Don't tell me you've never been on one before."

Even I have, and I've rarely been out and about the city.

"Doesn't matter. It's a new experience." She shrugs. "Let's go."

She grabs both my arm and her brother's as she marches forward to the subway station. For someone who's never used the subway before, she sure is confident. Especially as we go down the stairs and come face to face with the turnstiles. Both Thea and Cer stare at them with a puzzled expression on their faces.

Leaving them alone for a moment, I head to one of the cash ticket machines to grab tickets for the three of us. The process is smooth as the machine feeds me the tickets.

A satisfied smile flickers on my lips—ah, but it feels good to be independent for once. Sadly, looking back, there have been very few instances in which I had any type of freedom. My childhood had been defined by the hacienda and my lowly status. After that, I married Nikki, and despite it being the happiest period of my life, we were both trapped by our circumstances—Nikki caged by his illness, and me, his faithful companion.

But as I walk back to Thea and Cer, I stop in my tracks, my mouth hanging open in shock. Cer is holding the detached turnstile in his hand, out of Thea's reach. She jumps up in an attempt to get it, but she's no match for Cer's height. He seems to derive pleasure from baiting her, chuckling as he moves the turnstile around while Thea chases after it.

"Guys," I call out. "You can't just..." I trail off when I realize that my words will fall on deaf ears. "Here." I stop by their side, handing them each a ticket. "Now put that down and let's go."

It seems that soon I won't be the only one wanted by the police.

TEN

They squabble for a few more seconds before they dutifully follow me to the platform. The train is set to arrive in a couple of minutes, time I decide to spend by laying down some ground rules.

"Here's how this is going to work. You may be non-human or whatever you are, but we're officially a team, which means that what you do reflects on me, and what I do reflects on you."

"I know that," Thea starts to protest, but I put a hand up, stopping her.

"I'm betting everything on this game, and I'm not going to lose. That means you two need to cut it out and behave. Don't draw unnecessary attention to ourselves. Don't steal from people and don't destroy public property. Is that clear?"

They both stare at me as if I've grown two heads.

"You're rather confident for someone who didn't even know what the game was about a few hours ago," Thea huffs aloud.

"Maybe." I shrug. "But I know what I want. It doesn't matter what I have to do to get it."

"So now you believe the underworld is real." She smiles.

"Is it, is it not? I don't really care. As long as there's a chance for me to get my husband back, I'm going to take it—be it real or imaginative."

Thea nods slowly as she regards me.

"Fine. But I'm not the only one who has to behave," she says as she narrows her eyes at her brother.

Cer grunts, but he doesn't give any verbal assurance.

"Good. And since you're not familiar with how things work around here, please ask before you do something."

The train arrives, and we step inside. At this hour, it's mostly empty, so Thea and I grab a seat while Cer positions himself in front of us, his feet spread apart, his arms crossed over his chest.

"Uh, Luce?" Thea leans in to whisper.

"Yes?"

"I think I sat on something wet." She wrinkles her nose. "It smells."

"Just ignore it. It's only one stop."

She blinks.

"But it's really wet and smelly, Luce," she whines.

I sigh.

"We can change seats," I offer.

She nods fervently, getting up for the exchange. As she turns, however, I note *why* she was so wet. There's a yellowy-brownish wet stain on her pants, and as soon as she turns to me, the putrid smell wafts to my nose, intoxicating me. I'm sure I can see some bits of food, too.

"Uhm." I clear my throat. "I think we should just stand."

Cer, however, takes one look at Thea and bursts into laughter. She frowns in confusion until she makes the mistake of brushing her hand against her ass, the foul substance sticking to her fingers.

It takes a whole of two seconds before it dawns on her what she sat on. Her mouth opens and a shrill scream resounds in the entire train. Luckily, just at that moment, the doors open, and she dashes out of the train, still screaming into the night.

Cer is still furtively chuckling, and I look at him suspiciously.

"You knew," I note quietly.

He pins me with his gaze, his lips quirking up just as he angles his shoulders in a lazy shrug.

"I don't know what it is with the two of you, but you need to stop taunting each other," I say in exasperation.

He doesn't answer, simply stepping out of the train. I trail behind, wondering where Thea could have gone.

We get out of the station and still there's no sign of her.

"Don't worry. She'll find us. *Eventually*." He smirks.

Taking out the phone, I choose our location as a starting point so the GPS can give us a route to the theater.

"Okay, this way." I point ahead.

Despite being well after midnight, the area is bustling with tourists. Lights flash from the huge advertisements placed on every building, and for a moment, I just take a deep breath, absorbing everything.

It's not a dream. This is actually real. I may have a chance to get Nikki back.

It might be jarring that I've suddenly been thrust into this foreign world, but from the moment I was born, I've done nothing else but make do with the information I was given.

At sixteen, I found out there were no ancient gods and that there was freedom in the world—of thought, of speech, of being whoever I wanted to be.

At nineteen, I experienced that world for myself, savoring every moment of happiness after being deprived of it for so long.

Now, at twenty-four, I find out that gods *do* exist, as do other creatures. I find out that the world is much vaster than I'd ever thought possible. But somehow, it's the knowledge of that infinity that helps me digest this new information. Just because I don't know something, that doesn't mean it doesn't exist. I've been proven that time and time again.

My lips tremble with optimism as hope blossoms within me.

Nothing is impossible. Just like nothing will stop me from achieving that impossible.

Wait for me, Nikki. We'll meet again.

Cer clears his throat and I give him a tentative smile.

"Sorry," I mumble. I turn the GPS compass right and left as I try to make sense of the orientation. When I finally get it right, I nod to the building a few feet from us.

"This is it," I say as I stop in front of a flashy building. "Doesn't seem very haunted, does it?"

"Things are rarely as they seem," Cer grunts, taking a step forward as he studies the facade of the building. A billboard runs over the top part of the entrance, the banner highlighting the current show being played at the theatre. The entrance leads right into the middle of the busy street, and that might pose a problem if we're to break in.

Break in?

My mouth parts in a silent O as it dawns on me that if I want to win this game, I need to get rid of my previous sensibilities.

"There you are, guys," Thea exclaims.

We both turn to see her running toward us in a zig-zag pattern to avoid the tourists meandering about. She's dressed in a knee-length pink dress that's covered in glittery feathers, and to complete her look, she also added a sparkly pink headband and equally sparkly pink heels. Paired with her rich red hair, she looks as if she stepped out of one of those billboards.

Yet as she comes closer, I note that she can barely walk in those heels, bouncing from side to side as she tries to maintain her equilibrium. All the while, the smile has never left her face —until she sees her brother's expression, that is.

"What are you wearing, Thea?" He pinches the bridge of his nose as he takes her in.

"I think the most important question is—where did you get this?" I ask as she reaches our side. "All the stores are closed."

"Oh, that." She licks her lips. But whatever answer she was about to concoct is useless as I pluck the tag from the dress—still attached to it.

"Did you break into a store to steal these?"

"What? Of course not. I, uhm, I—"

"Couldn't you have at least stolen something less...conspicuous?" I close my eyes with a sigh.

"But it's pretty," she whispers. "And pink. Your world has such fun colors and clothes."

That gives me pause.

"And yours doesn't?" I frown.

She shakes her head.

"It's all boring and conservative and agh." She stomps her foot—a little *too* hard, because her heel breaks.

That attracts the attention of the people around, who stop to stare at her, which is enough for Cer to intervene and put himself in front of her. But just as I think he's going to chastise her some more, he goes down on one knee, grabbing her other foot and breaking that heel as well so Thea can walk properly.

"Okay, now that we've found the location, we should make a plan of action."

"What plan? We just go in and spook that spirit into going to P'asala and be done with it. How long can it take, a few minutes?" Thea says casually.

"P'asala? What is that?" I frown.

Cer and Thea share a look. Thea releases a sigh.

"Remember the bridge on the screen? That is B'Isalat. It's the place all souls go after they depart this world."

My brows shoot up in curiosity.

"And where does it lead?"

"It all depends on the quality of deeds performed during their lifetime."

"That's enough, Thea," Cer intervenes, raising a brow at her. She rolls her eyes but complies.

"Right," I add drily. They are likely wary to share too much information with a *human*. "We should devise a plan."

"Why don't we just—" Thea starts again, but her brother stops her.

"The first trial ends in a week. That means it will likely not be as easy as *spooking the spirit* into crossing over." He gives his sister a look. "I think we should scout the location first and see what type of spirit we're dealing with. After we find out who the spirit was, we'll research the history and find its motivation for staying behind. As long as we're methodical about it, we should finish the task with ease."

"That's a good idea," I say, surprised at his insight—and the fact that he said more than a few words for the first time. "One thing to bear in mind, though," I note as I point to our surroundings. "This is too public to simply break inside. We'll have to scout the location during operating hours."

Cer nods pensively.

"Why?" Thea pouts.

"In this world, there are rules and the body that enforces those rules is the police. If we break in, *steal*, or destroy public property, we'll get in trouble."

"We have such a body in our world, too," Cer notes. "But that doesn't mean *some* obey it." The jibe is clearly meant at his sister, who shrugs.

"Not my fault that you're all so boring. Live a little, big bro."

He narrows his eyes at her.

"Okay, what did I say about behaving? Please stop baiting your brother." I point at Thea. "And you." I turn to Cer. "Stop glaring at your sister."

Silence descends as he glares at her some more and she sticks her tongue out at him.

Good Lord, maybe I should have chosen a different team...

"You're no fun, Luce." Thea sighs. "This is the adventure of a lifetime. Take a risk. Or two. Or maybe more." She giggles.

"There is such a thing as calculated risks," I grumble. "Given what is at stake, I prefer to be more judicious with my decisions."

"B-o-r-i-n-g," she mouths.

"As I was saying." I clear my throat. "We should come back tomorrow during open hours. We can meet here at noon."

"Meet here? Where are we going?"

"I don't know where you're going. But I'll be heading over to my friend's place." Hopefully, it's not too late for me to make my appearance at the warehouse.

"You can't," Thea bursts out.

Both Cer and I look at her curiously.

"That is to say, it's not safe. This is a competition and others will want to defeat us. That means we need to stick together."

I frown at her explanation.

"You have guesthouses, no? We can check into one and stay there for the duration of our mission," she adds, quite pleased with herself.

"You mean a hotel?" I ask, intuiting what she's referring to. It's clear both are not very familiar with how this world works, but they seem to have at least some equivalents in *their* world—wherever that is. As that thought arises, I decide to carefully probe more in the coming days to arm myself with more knowledge.

"Yes, that. I saw quite a few on my way back."

"There's only one issue. You have no money. I have maybe ten dollars left. We can't afford a hotel."

"Pfft, leave that up to me," Thea declares.

Not even ten minutes later and we find ourselves in the lobby of a very expensive-looking hotel. Thea says something in a low voice to the woman at the front desk, and in a matter of seconds, she's offered the key to an apartment—their most deluxe apartment.

"How did you do that?" I ask as we all cram into the elevator to head to the tenth floor.

"I can be *very* charming." She winks at me.

The apartment has two bedrooms, one for me and one for the siblings. Maybe I should have offered to room with Thea considering how much they squabble, but I'm too tired and Thea has too much energy. If I'm to rest tonight and regain my strength, I can't have her hop around and talk incessantly—regardless of how endearing she might be while doing so.

After we've divided the rooms, we say good night and agree to reconvene in the morning.

As I enter my room for the night, I'm surprised by how luxurious it is. Thea's charm must be quite potent for her to be able to get this apartment with no money. It makes me wonder about the extent of her powers. I'm not entirely sure what being a harpy entails besides those sharp nails she displayed on occasion, but maybe it includes some hypnotic abilities.

Everything is possible at this point. I don't think I would be surprised at anything anymore.

Releasing a weary sigh, I go to the bathroom, once more surprised by the luxurious amenities. There's a waterfall-style shower that could accommodate half a dozen people. I glance longingly at it. I'm so tired, but I also feel dirty considering how much I've been running around. The dip in the well notwithstanding, I truly need a shower.

Before my eyes can become more sluggish, I shrug off the straps of my dress, shimmying it down my body until it lands at my feet. Stepping out of it, I enter the shower stall, pursing my lips as I get acquainted with the controls.

Once I figure out the settings, I turn on steaming hot water, letting it drape over my body just as steam envelops the entire stall, the glass panels fogging. Warmth caresses my skin, a change from the coldness that's made its way into my bones. Maybe it's the hot water, or maybe it's my newfound optimism. All I know is that the beats of my heart align with the drops of water dripping onto my body before sliding to the floor. The anguish that had previously consumed me melts away as I envision a new future—one where my husband is beside me.

Turning to face the jet of water, I close my eyes as I shift reality in my mind. Stepping back, I feel a block of hard muscle meet my back, his body molding to mine.

Hands caress my rib cage, big palms splayed over my stomach as he draws me closer. The harsh pads of his fingers scrape against the softness of my skin, his nails digging into my flesh.

My breath hitches in my throat as I lean into him, throwing

my head back as his searching lips meet the side of my neck, sucking, nibbling, licking.

He cocoons my weary body, laying siege to my mind as he makes me lose myself to the euphoria of those sweet kisses.

The water turns scorching hot, leaving behind red angry trails on my skin, but the pain is but a pulsing sensation, eclipsed by the urgency of his touch.

I pant low in my throat, pushing myself into him, only to lose my balance as I belatedly realize there's no one there with me. It's just me and this aching emptiness in my heart.

The water sprays onto my face as I find myself immobile on the shower floor, my feet spread apart, my gaze fixed on a nonexistent spot.

From a welcoming heat, it becomes an unbearable inferno as panic strikes in my breast, causing my heart to erupt into an unsteady rhythm. Dragging myself on my knees, I reach the controls of the shower after what feels like an eternity, turning the water off and taking a deep, anxious breath into my lungs.

"Soon," I whisper to myself.

I take a moment to settle my nerves before I turn on the water again, this time washing my body thoroughly. As my hands move around the planes of my chest, my eyes widen in surprise when I can't feel any of the old scars or indentations.

For as long as I can remember, my body has been a mosaic of scars, some gotten through beatings and abuse, others through the backbreaking labor I was subjected to.

My fingers trail up my shoulder, feeling for the small pucker of skin that had formed after my gunshot wound had healed five years ago. The skin is smooth and blemish-free.

I search lower on my back for the lashings I'd gotten when I disobeyed the orders of the master of the house, but even those have disappeared—as if they'd never been there in the first place.

Had that ambrosia-infused drink healed all of this? Had it erased even my deepest scars?

Does that mean that my marks...?

Quickly rinsing myself, I turn off the shower and step out. I plant myself firmly in front of the mirror, almost afraid to gaze at my new self but excited to see those marks removed nonetheless.

I wipe the steam off the mirror and slowly regard myself, a crushing disappointment settling in my chest as I spot the black lines staining my skin.

All other scars are absent.

All but the worst of them—these marks that have been the bane of my existence since the day I'd gotten them when I was sixteen and about to become the mistress of El Señor of the hacienda. In a bout of madness, I'd fought back, preferring death over having my body violated in that manner. Against all odds, I'd survived. But for my rebellion, I'd been marked for life.

Outcast. Pariah. Cursed.

Although I'd been saved from that ignominy, I'd been sentenced to a life of servitude and perpetual labor.

"You should never be ashamed of these, Luce," Nikki would tell me whenever I became hung up on them. "They're not a punishment. They're a mark of bravery. You fought and you won."

I would smile at him and nod, the rational part of me understanding his reasoning, but the other side of me, the hurt and belittled one, saw it as a way for El Señor to control me for the entirety of my life. The marks weren't ephemeral like an action or a word. They were always there, etched into my skin, proof of my lack of agency.

I release a shaky breath, my lashes misted with tears.

I stare at my reflection in the mirror for what feels like an eternity, my mind going in circles as I try to decipher why all of my other scars and injuries went away but these marks remained.

Could it be that Sergio truly had connections to the divine? Is that why these won't go away? Because they're not seared in my flesh, but in my soul?

The thought makes my legs tremble, and I grasp onto the sink to keep myself from falling.

He's taken so much from me already...to take even more?

Pain stabs in my chest as I choke a sob.

"*Maldito perro*," I rasp, my voice thick and filled with pain. "*¡Espero que te pudras en el infierno!*"

Too bad he died before I could take all my frustrations out on him. If there's one regret I have, it's that I wasn't there to see him suffer as he drew his last breath. That will forever haunt me as my hatred for him grows instead of abating.

I trail a finger down my naked body, following the sinuous curves of the black markings etched on my flesh. A shiver goes down my back just as a gust of wind blows in my direction.

My head snaps to the side, but the bathroom door is closed. No window in sight.

I blink, my breathing becoming more erratic.

It's just my imagination.

Turning, I note the mirror is once more fogged up. My brows bunch together in a frown as I take a towel and wipe it again. Yet as the contour of my form becomes visible in the mirror, so does something else.

My mouth opens on a gasp.

It's barely perceptible, but it's there.

The hairs on my back stand up as a shadowy form sways lightly in the air just behind me, smoke-like fog surrounding me like an outline.

I swallow hard, my heart drumming in my chest.

Is there a rule that if you suddenly become aware of the supernatural it also becomes aware of you? I could swear I've seen something like that in a movie...

Is it a ghost? Or another entity? Is it a creature...my senses go into overload as my rational side meets my fanciful one who'd like nothing more than to believe that if the supernatural is real, then maybe Nikki's ghost could also be real. That he'd still be with me, haunting me, glued to my side for an eternity. Yet even as that hope pulses inside of me, becoming more and more ardent with each passing second, the logical side of me tells me to tread carefully.

The black mass of air floats around me, so, so close. It doesn't make to leave, nor does it seem inclined to move.

I wet my lips as I force myself to slowly turn.

It remains rooted to the spot, even as I tip my chin up to gaze at it.

Swirling black, there's a shimmery mist in it, like a myriad of eyes glistening in the dark. It watches me—or so I think. It stares me down just as time ceases to exist.

The breeze blows again, gently brushing my cheek in the lightest caress.

"It's you, isn't it?" I whisper before I can help myself.

My pulse jams against the surface of my skin, my heart about to burst out of my chest.

With a courage I never knew I possessed, I raise my hand, tracing the foggy outline with the tips of my fingers.

The shimmery particles flash, almost like a blink.

I freeze with my hand midair, waiting for some type of confirmation. The mist neither acknowledges me nor responds to my quiet inquiry. It simply exists, hovering, observing.

"You can understand me, can't you?" I ask gently, moving my hand until I almost reach the top of the outline. As my fingers connect with those particles, they sway lightly, blinking more and emitting a flash of light that tickles as it meets the surface of my skin.

A light giggle escapes me as the shimmery black mist touches my palm, tingles spreading down my back.

"You were there. That night," I continue, digging into the depths of my memory for the same sensation—for the same light brush of satin against my flesh.

The mist closes itself, the black becoming more pronounced before a million lights erupt within the darkness.

My lips tremble with hope and mirth and unending optimism.

"I know you." I smile. "I'll *always* know you."

He's been with me from the beginning, but I couldn't open my mind to it. I was blind to the world beyond, and that blindness caused me to miss him.

Raising myself on the tips of my toes, I press both palms against the cloud of smoke. Tingles of awareness spread down my body as well as an ineffable sense of déjà vu. But before I can come closer, the mist disintegrates and disappears.

I stumble back, blinking furiously as I look everywhere around me.

"Nikki?" I call out, my voice thick and painful. "Please come back."

Only my own echo greets me, his name reverberating in the room like the most crippling lash against my skin.

"Nikki? Please..."

Surely, I didn't imagine it, did I?

He was here, with me. Just like he promised.

"Oh, Nikki," I cry out, exhausted and alone.

ELEVEN

The elevator doors slide open on the ground floor and Thea's voice rings out from the lobby.

"Luce!" she calls my name as she dashes toward me. "I got us a table at the restaurant. They're just serving breakfast. Let's go," she says as she grabs my hand, steering me toward the entrance of the restaurant.

A waiter shows us to a table for two and takes our orders. I opt for hash browns, eggs, and avocado toast while Thea chooses eggs and bacon.

"What about your brother?"

"He'll come eventually." She waves her hand, her nose wrinkling in displeasure. "He won't be able to stay away for long," she grumbles under her breath.

"Right," I murmur. "You have a peculiar relationship."

"You could say so." She strains a smile. She doesn't offer more and I don't ask.

The food arrives relatively quickly, and we both start eating.

"This is marvelous," Thea sighs, her mouth full.

"I gather you don't have bacon in your world?"

"We have some equivalent. But I was never allowed to eat it."

"What? Why?"

"Let's just say it wasn't part of my diet," she answers evasively.

I nod. Silence descends as she munches with gusto while I can't help but dwell on what had happened last night. Was it possible? Could it be that the shadow I saw was Nikki? That he kept his promise after all?

There had been a deep sense of familiarity in that brief interaction—as if my soul had known what my other senses had been unable to decipher.

But I'm also aware that it could just be my wishful thinking. Now that I've found out there's an unseen world out there, I might be tempted to equate every unusual encounter with the supernatural when the answer would be much simpler. It could be an otherworldly spirit, or it could simply be my wretched longing.

Yet no matter how much I replay the events of last night in my mind, I get increasingly more convinced that I hadn't imagined it.

The shadow had been real.

"Thea," I start, biting my lip in apprehension.

"Huh?" She gives me her full attention, slowing down her chewing.

"Tell me more about these spirits that stay behind."

She swallows her food, reaches for her glass of water, and takes a big sip.

"It doesn't happen very often. If it did, this world would be teeming with ghosts." She chuckles. When she sees I'm not amused, she clears her throat. "It usually happens when a soul is particularly strong. When an individual is about to die, a messenger of death appears at the scene and calls the soul out of the body." She pauses as she pops another piece of bacon in her mouth. "That messenger is a neutral being whose sole purpose is to lead souls across P'asala for their judgment."

"Judgment? Is that like St. Peter and the gates of Heaven?"

"I don't know any Peter dude," she frowns. "Anyway, long

story short, after the souls are judged, they can go on to pay for their deeds during that lifetime and hope to qualify for reincarnation. After they drink from the well of oblivion and all their past memories are erased, of course."

"And?" I probe, but her attention is momentarily distracted as she calls for the waiter to bring her another portion of bacon.

"And what?"

"We were talking about the spirits that stay behind," I repeat.

"Oh, right. Sorry, this bacon is truly divine."

"No one's taking it from you. You don't have to eat so fast," I mention when she digs into her plate the moment the waiter places it on the table.

"Have to," she says, her mouth full, her eyes moving suspiciously from one corner of the restaurant to the other. "Have to finish this before my brother comes."

"Oh," I murmur. It's on the tip of my tongue to ask her about her conflict with her brother, but I don't want to distract her from the subject at hand.

"Back to those spirits," she continues. "When the soul exits the body, most are confused and easily malleable. It's very easy for the messenger to get them to follow him into P'asala. But there are a few more... strong-willed spirits whose emotions are so powerful at the time of death that they refuse to leave this plane of existence under any circumstance."

"Can't the messenger force them?"

"Nope." She pops the P just as she bites down on a crunchy piece of bacon. "They're neutral, remember? Their job is simply to lead the souls to P'asala. They can't otherwise intervene. They wouldn't want to either. Messengers have no feelings. They are like your machines—entities that fulfill a role."

My mouth opens in awe. That's fascinating—and so, so smart. If the messengers have no feelings, they cannot be swayed. I nod to myself, intrigued by the world Thea's describing. But there's something that doesn't quite make sense.

"So those souls are simply left to their devices?"

"Of course not. There's a special team in charge of collecting rogue souls—the Collectors. But it's not the most desirable job, so there are usually a lot of vacancies. My guess is that they decided on this trial because they wanted others to do the job for them."

I blink, slowly digesting all the new information. Not only are there ghosts and deities and other creatures, but also different types of grim reapers—who seem to be oddly unionized. Growing up, my experiences with the supernatural had been solely through the prism of El Señor. It had been chaotic, illogical, and at times inane. Although I had been forced to believe without questioning, it had been questionable even to my young, untutored mind.

Back then, even with all that alleged proof, I could see the man behind the godly mask, and I knew it to be a farce. Now, though... I'm the living proof of this truth.

Some people pretend to be gods. Others...*are* gods.

The world is suddenly a lot more complex and complicated than I ever realized—or gave it credit for.

"Being a collector is a job?"

"They're the equivalent of bounty hunters in your world," she explains further. "They get a list with all the rebellious souls, and they choose their assignments. Some souls can be a pain from what I've heard, so they just never get picked. I imagine that must be the case with the theatre."

My optimism plummets as I consider her words. If even a special team tasked to recover rebellious souls avoided the theatre, what will that mean for us? Have we been set up to fail from the beginning?

"I see." I nod slowly, taking a sip of water. "You mentioned powerful emotions at the time of death. What would that entail?"

"A violent death?" Thea shrugs. "A deep regret? A desire for revenge? Every case is different."

"And how do these ghosts look?" I ask tentatively, holding my breath for her answer.

"I haven't seen one myself, but from what I've heard, the more time a spirit spends in-between realms, the more powerful they become and the more they resemble their former selves. It's also why the Collectors avoid them, because their sense of self is so solidified—pun intended"—she chuckles to herself—"that it's sometimes impossible to get them to drink from the well of oblivion."

I'd love to question her more about this well of oblivion, but I need to take advantage of the discussion at hand and find out more things about these ghosts—or, in my case, a particular ghost. Who knows when is the next time she'll be this forthcoming with information? Certainly not when her brother joins us and their never-ending cycle of bickering resumes.

"What about newly deceased souls? How do those look?"

Thea puts a hand up, ordering yet another portion of bacon. People all around the restaurant stare at her. Even the waiter is giving her an odd look, probably wondering if he should call the ambulance after she's done. It's likely not every day that they see a girl eat her weight in fat, greasy bacon.

"Newly deceased souls are rather shapeless particles of energy. From what I've heard, they're harmless and barely have any powers."

Shapeless particles of energy? That sounds *very* similar to the dark shadow I saw last night. Hope blossoms in my chest and I swallow hard to curb down the excitement that flows freely through my veins.

"Can they communicate?" I probe further.

"I doubt it." She taps her finger against her chin. "But then again, I'm not an expert in ghosts."

"But you *do* know a lot." I raise a brow.

"I hear things here and there," she murmurs, a guilty smile playing on her lips.

Right. I'm starting to notice a pattern with her. She knows some things and is completely clueless about others—like phones and GPS. That, coupled with the way her brother keeps her under close surveillance, tells me she's been sheltered most of her life.

The waiter brings the third plate of bacon.

Her eyes sparkle in anticipation. She licks her lips as she reaches out to grab a strip of bacon, but before she can touch it, the plate is snatched away from her.

Her eyes widen, and we both gaze up at her scowling brother.

"You know you're not allowed to eat this." He grits his teeth. Barking an order at the waiter, he hands him the plate, throwing a couple of hundred-dollar bills toward him.

"We're done here." He levels his sister with his icy stare. Yet just as I think Thea is going to protest—as she usually does—she hangs her head in resignation as she gets up from the table.

"What's going on?" I ask as I follow after them.

Cer doesn't stop until we're out of the hotel. He suddenly comes to a halt, pivoting to face us.

"Here." He hands us each a ticket to a musical being performed at the New Amsterdam Theatre. "The show starts in a couple of hours."

"Thank you," I murmur, glancing down at my ticket.

The title of the musical is in bold letters on top of a colorful background—Penelope's Odyssey.

In small script, the description of the musical implies it's been adapted from Homer's Odyssey but it's focusing instead on Odysseus's wife, Penelope.

"There's only one show today and none until Friday," Cer continues. "If we remain in the theater after closing hours, we'll have at least a couple of days until the staff comes back to work."

"How do you know that?" Thea fires back.

"I asked around." He shrugs. "There's a national holiday the day after tomorrow too, so it's unlikely anyone will be present. That gives us plenty of time to deal with that rogue spirit."

I nod, impressed.

"Since we're going to be there for a few days, we should get some supplies," I suggest.

"Like what?" Thea frowns.

"Food, some spare clothes, flashlights, and maybe a few sleeping bags."

Cer stares at me intently before his gaze moves to his sister. He purses his lips, pensive for a moment. Thea sports a contrite expression as she meets his eyes, almost as if they're having a silent conversation.

Or maybe they are? I'm not sure what their abilities are—besides Thea's extreme charm—but I can't discount the fact that they could be capable of some crazy stuff. Just like I can't discount the fact that for all intents and purposes, they are strangers. We may be on the same team now, but I'm still unsure about their intentions or their plans. For that reason, I need to keep my guard up.

"Fine. We can do that," Cer says.

We go to the nearest convenience store and stock up on essentials—water, some non-perishable food, and a few snacks. Next, we stop by one of those touristy shops and get some hoodies and mini flashlights with NYC on them. Cer pays for everything in one-hundred-dollar bills, just like he did at the restaurant. I don't know where he got that money from, but I'm not about to ask. Given their cluelessness about how things work in this world, I wouldn't be surprised if he robbed a bank. And since I'd rather not become an accessory to yet *another* crime, I'll gladly embrace my ignorance.

With a little under one hour to spare until the show starts, we go to a coffee shop across the theatre and wait. As we order some refreshments, I notice that Cer is monitoring Thea's choice closely, grunting in approval when she asks for a lemonade. I get the same, while Cer orders plain water.

After we get our beverages, Cer slides a few pieces of paper on the table, nodding at us to have a look.

"A short history of New Amsterdam Theatre," I read aloud the title of what seems to be a newspaper clipping.

"There wasn't a lot of information available, but this should give us a starting point," he mentions as he leans back.

Thea comes closer to me as we sift through what her brother found.

"Here's a mention of a ghost! A man claims to have seen a lady in a green beaded dress holding a blue bottle and walking through walls a few months ago," I read off the page. "He recognized her as former silent film actress, Olive Thomas." There's a brief biography of Olive Thomas, once a Broadway superstar. "It seems she died of an accidental poisoning in 1920."

"That's odd." Thea narrows her eyes, shooting a subtle look at her brother. "What type of poisoning?"

"Apparently, she ingested a mercury bichloride mixture that had been prescribed for her husband's syphilis," I add as I peruse some of the details.

"Syphilis? What's that?" Thea inquires innocently.

"It's a sexually transmitted disease. Now it's treatable with penicillin, but in 1920 that hadn't been discovered. Mercury was the de facto treatment back in the day, but it was also highly toxic. Poor girl, I can't imagine the torment she must have suffered after ingesting the mercury..." Just thinking about it makes the hairs on my body stand up. Such a cruel way to die— and she didn't die immediately, either. She languished for days on a hospital bed before her final demise.

"You humans have such diseases?" Thea blinks in surprise.

"Welcome to being human," I mumble under my breath.

"An accidental death doesn't seem like prime material for a haunting," Thea continues, picking another newsletter slip from the table. "Look here. She didn't even die at the theatre. She died in Paris. That makes it even more unlikely for a haunting."

Her brows furrow as she peruses article after article, seemingly searching for something.

"Why?" I ask.

"Spirits usually remain tied to the place where they died."

"You forget one thing, Thea," Cer interrupts. "Spirits can also cling to objects they prized during their life."

"What about people?" I suddenly ask.

Cer shrugs. "Could be. Spirits are fickle. When a soul exits the body, it's usually very confused and cannot remember too well what happened during its life. A messenger intervenes at that point and leads them quietly to P'asala. But there are times when the spirit becomes obsessed with something. It could be a place, an object, a person...a feeling. That obsession is what usually prompts a spirit to go rogue."

I nod slowly. His explanation makes more sense than Thea's. But it also opens the door for more questions. Is Nikki trapped in between realms because he can't let go of me? Is he still by my side because I'm the object of his obsession? And if so, what would I do? Would I try to help him cross over, or would I feign ignorance and keep him by my side? A cynical smile twists my lips. The former question is moot because no matter how much I'd like to think of myself as ethical and virtuous, my husband is where I draw the line.

"Maybe there's something at the theatre that keeps Olive there. She was part of the Ziegfeld Follies, and one of their shows, Midnight Frolic, was staged at the New Amsterdam Theatre. It says here she was also having an affair with Ziegfeld, the show's impresario."

Thea and Cer share a long look, and once more I get the feeling that they're communicating without words.

"I tried to find out more about Miss Thomas, but given that this happened more than a century ago, there aren't a lot of details," Cer adds. "That means we've got to do this the old-fashioned way."

"Old-fashioned way?" I frown, while Thea releases a loud squeak.

"That should be a lot of fun!" she exclaims excitedly—but at this point, what is she *not* excited about?

"Wait a moment. What are we talking about?"

"We need to catch Miss Thomas and interrogate her. With her age, she should have cognitive abilities. Once we know what's keeping her here, we can resolve the issue and help her move on," Cer explains matter-of-factly.

"And how does one go about *catching* a ghost?" I ask drily. "Do we need some crucifixes and holy water?"

"What? No!" Thea's eyes widen. "You humans and your silly tales." She waves her hand around, shaking her head.

My lips flatten in a thin line as I barely stop myself from commenting on her use of *humans*. I know she doesn't mean it, but it comes across as a little condescending.

"The first step is to get her to appear before us. After that, Cer will trap her and we can chat. She's an actress. I'm sure she'll love to talk about herself."

"Uhm..." I look back and forth between the two of them, wondering how the hell we're going to pull this off. "And if she's *not* cooperative?"

"We'll cross that bridge when we get there." Thea shrugs. As she leans in, she whispers, "Pun intended." She waits a second before she starts giggling. Wherever she heard that line, she's definitely taken it upon herself to include it in her daily vocabulary.

With a plan in mind—or the *semblance* of one—we pay the bill and head to the theatre for the start of the musical.

The theatre's hallway is filled with framed pictures of influential people from the history of the theatre. Walking around, I catalog all the images, half in awe at stepping inside such a historically rich venue, but mostly attentive for any potential clue.

"That's her." I point to one of the frames. The picture is in black and white, and Olive is wearing a French-style fur ensemble.

"I don't think anyone has a problem with her ghost," Thea adds as she catches up with us. I turn slightly. I hadn't even realized she'd remained behind.

"What do you mean?"

"All the people at the entrance were talking about the ghost and were excited about potentially seeing her. Even the person at the ticket booth was joking about it, saying she's been around for decades. He was instructing men—apparently, she's partial to men—to greet her and blow her a kiss."

"Hmm," Cer grunts, his eyes narrowing as he looks around.

"You're thinking about the same thing I am, aren't you?" Thea pulls on her brother's sleeve, their eyes meeting.

TWELVE

"**W**hat? What are you two thinking about?" I ask, my gaze moving from one to the other.

Cer purses his lips.

"Most of the places that claim to be haunted are likely *not* haunted anymore. They may have been at one point, but the moment a spirit makes itself known to a living human, a Collector is specifically dispatched to bring it back since that type of interaction is forbidden."

I frown, slowly digesting the information. Does that mean that if Nikki has made himself known to me, a collector will come after him? I gulp at the thought. I've just gotten him back—granted, in a shadowy, barely human form—but I know deep in my gut that it's him. I'd recognize the warmth he instills in me anywhere because only *he* has the ability to make me feel like that.

He's my person. In life or in death.

"What he means is that if everyone knows this place is haunted, it should technically *not* be haunted anymore. Collectors may be capricious bastards, but they get the job done when they get a direct order. That's the only time they cannot choose their targets. But still, we were sent here to deal with *a* spirit."

"So what are you saying? That the spirit isn't her?"

Thea nods apprehensively.

"What if the collector just hasn't gotten around to getting her? That could happen, no?"

"Technically, it could, but... I don't like this. It's too out in the open for them to just ignore the issue." Pursing her lips, she turns, her screwed eyes taking in all the details of the foyer. "I've been here once before," she remarks. "And I never felt the presence of a spirit."

"And you didn't think to mention this earlier?" I ask drily.

Thea gives me a guilty smile.

"We didn't want to alarm you until we gathered more information. But if these people have been aware of the ghost for *decades*, that changes everything. It's not just a sighting a few months ago that could be explained away with the fact that a collector hasn't come to, well, *collect*."

"Hence the trial." Cer cracks a smile. "Of course it wouldn't have been *that* easy."

"You've both lost me," I mumble, confused.

"We'll see what we're dealing with soon," Thea says. "Don't you worry, Luce. We'll protect you." She winks at me.

I strain a smile. I'm not sure how much I trust them to protect me when I can't even trust them with the facts. Every time they give me one piece of information, it's incomplete. But at the same time, they also have something I don't—some type of superhuman abilities that will prove useful in this game. Despite the fact that I don't trust them, I have to admit that I *need* them.

Taking a deep breath, I suggest we head to our seats.

Yet as we get to the auditorium, I spot a mini-museum in the back. There are a few artifacts from the original Ziegfeld Follies, including shoes, bags, and ostentatious headdresses.

"Maybe one of these objects could be keeping the spirit in the theatre? If it *is* Olive Thomas, that is."

"Mayhap," Cer answers noncommittally, scanning the display in his usual bored manner.

Thea, on the other hand, is getting increasingly closer to one of the displays, and from the corner of my eye, I note the lengthening of her nail as she searches for the lock.

"Thea, no!" I say through gritted teeth. "Can't you see how many people are around?"

"But it's so cute." She pouts, gazing at one of the headdresses adoringly.

"And not yours. What did I say about stealing?"

"After everyone leaves?" She bats her lashes at me.

I look at her brother for help with her little sticky fingers—or in her case, *clawy* fingers—situation, but he pretends he doesn't know us.

I sigh.

"You can borrow it after the show as long as you put it back when we leave," I tell her, knowing that even if I say no, she'll still do whatever she wants.

Her eyes sparkle and she gives me an effusive nod.

When it's time to go to our seats, we barely get her away from the display. As we reach our designated area, I'm surprised to see Cer had gone all out and booked one of the private boxes on the side of the auditorium. The privacy is welcome, as is the opportunity to study the location from a vantage point.

We place the bags with our supplies on the floor just in time for the curtains to go up. Silence descends in the room, the orchestra starting with a lulling violin sound. Turning to the stage, I take a moment to soak in the beauty of the auditorium. There's a vaulted ceiling surrounded by paintings in an Art Nouveau style. Green, mauve, gold, and a muted red swirl around in a contrast that speaks of the Gilded Age of New York, with its lavish decorations and illusions of grandeur. Floral details are depicted in a bas-relief style—which I only know about because I took art history as one of my electives. There's an assortment of new and old pieces, preserving both the history while keeping up with modernity.

A pang of regret reverberates in my chest. I've been living in this city for over a year and I've barely visited *anything*. For the first time, I should have been here with Nikki, not with two odd non-humans, and certainly *not* ghost hunting.

The musical ends up being surprisingly enjoyable—so much so that I barely realize when it ends and people stand up to leave the premises.

I make to get up, too, but Cer raises a hand to stop me.

"We can wait here until everyone leaves."

"But the staff will come to clean and—"

He gives me a bored look that simply says *trust me*.

"He's right, Luce. Sit down and wait. It will be easier to evade detection here."

I don't know how, but apparently, they have some plan I know nothing about.

Just as I predicted, the staff comes to the auditorium to clean up after the spectators. Someone opens the door to our box as well, and just as I prepare to make up an excuse for still being there, I realize that they don't come in. They stare at us as if they aren't seeing us. A moment passes, after which they close the door and leave.

"What just happened?" I mutter, confused.

"Told you there was nothing to worry about." Thea winks.

Hours pass and the sun goes down. The lights go out in the theatre, and the last staff member leaves, which allows us to finally move around freely.

Turning on our flashlights, we make our way out of the box and back to the ground floor.

For a supposedly haunted place, I expected to be more afraid. Instead, there's only an odd sense of anticipation that blooms within me with each step I take. If this ghost is real, then so is the one from the previous night—or so I tell myself.

The night air is cool and moist. Despite the continuous use of the theatre since its inauguration, there's still an old, musky smell clinging to the walls. While the main auditorium has been entirely restored, the rest of the theatre not so much. The vintage wallpaper in the hallways is one peel away from falling down, the various decorations adorning the walls and the ceiling chipped and discolored. Once upon a time, this would have been a vibrant, ostentatious place. It's still ostentatious, but in a way that speaks of decadence and decay—perhaps fitting considering its history.

"We should check backstage," Thea suggests. "The article mentioned the sighting of the ghost was on the stage. Maybe we can sense something there."

While Thea and Cer go down the stairs that lead backstage, I remain rooted on the spot in the middle of the stage.

My mouth parts in awe at the grandiose view of the auditorium from the center of the stage. I imagine that every seat is filled, their eyes on me as they follow my every move. There's a sense of exhilaration—of fear laced with excitement.

Is this how stars feel when they perform?

Is this how Olive Thomas felt?

"Luce?" Thea's voice rings out and I shake myself from my reverie.

"Coming," I call out, turning to leave.

I back away slowly, somehow unable to tear my gaze away from the sprawling empty seats.

The wooden floor creaks as I place my weight on the heels of my feet. The sound vibrates in the silence of the auditorium, and I wait for fear to seep into my bones. I wait for many things —a sudden drop in the temperature of the air, the foul smell of sulfur, the flickering of lights and all the Hollywood signs that point to a ghost infestation. Most of all, I stare intently at a spot in the back of the auditorium, almost as if willing the ghost to show itself. Alas, I may have watched one too many movies.

My lips quirk up and I shake my head at my own foolishness. I pivot, rotating on the ball of my right foot.

A gust of wind hits my face, but I welcome the breeze. It's only when I blink, my eyes fluttering open, that I come face to face with a red, mottled mass of skin. There are no eyes, just scar tissue that had never mended properly. A mouth with rotten teeth slowly opens, the movements of the jaw emitting a low, clanking sound, almost as if it's popping out of place.

I gulp down, keeping myself absolutely still.

There are two canine-like teeth in the front, discolored and verging more on black than white. And as the creature releases a blood-curdling scream, a wave of pure force blasts me backward. I hit the side wall of the stage with a deafening thud. A gasp escapes me as the wind is knocked out of my lungs. Yet as I glance again at the spot, I find it empty.

What the...

"Luce?" Thea hurries to my side, worry etched on her features.

"I'm fine," I croak, slowly getting to my feet.

"What happened?" Cer materializes from behind Thea, his eyes narrowed as he surveys the area. His nostrils flare as he inhales deeply, his expression tense.

Thea looks back at him, her eyes widening as he gives her a brisk nod.

"It was...something. But it wasn't Olive," I say as I manage to catch my breath. I give them a quick description of what I saw, and the siblings fall silent.

Cer crouches to the ground, swiping the pads of his fingers against the floor and bringing them to his nose.

"What is it?" I frown.

"You and Thea should leave," he suddenly says.

"What? Why? What's going on?"

"This isn't a regular ghost." Cer gets up, his gaze swallowing up the entire auditorium. He doesn't explain further, and my patience runs out.

"Can you just tell me what's happening? Both of you," I say in exasperation.

Thea purses her lips as she takes a deep breath.

"I might have omitted some information." She flashes me a guilty look.

My brows rise in question as I tap my foot impatiently against the floor.

Thea gazes at her brother, nodding at him.

"Sometimes rogue spirits are...consumed by other beings."

"Other beings?"

"Demons."

I gawk at the two of them before I slowly shake my head, amusement bubbling inside of me. Of course there would be demons too. Just what I needed.

"Explain," I demand sharply.

Thea opens her mouth to speak, but Cer interrupts her.

"When the soul leaves the body, it's either led by a messenger to P'asala, or it refuses to move on and remains trapped on Earth. In this case, there are two outcomes. First, a collector comes and retrieves the soul. This usually happens within a short period of time after death. The more time passes, the stronger the soul becomes, and Collectors typically don't like to deal with them unless they interfere with humans directly. In the second scenario, the soul goes on to haunt whatever place or object they've become attached to until they become a demon themselves or they catch the attention of a demon. But it's rare for a soul to turn into a demon. That only happens when the soul is evil. Most often, souls become other demons' prey. Since unblemished souls are the purest source of energy, they are a delicacy for a number of beings."

I blink slowly, dread forming in the pit of my stomach. If what he's saying is true, then...

Nikki!

As a newly deceased soul, he's either going to be retrieved by a collector, or he risks becoming food for a demon. And if he's attached to me...

I might have led him straight into danger.

THIRTEEN

"What happens to the souls that are consumed?" I ask as my heart hammers in my chest.

"Generally speaking, that is the end of them. But there have been cases where the souls were retrieved after the demon was exterminated. But these are very rare cases and only when the soul has been recently consumed. As time passes, the essence of the soul merges with that of the demon and they are forever lost."

"So this entire trial is a hoax. Is that what you're telling me?"

Cer's lips flatten into a thin line.

"Well, isn't that so?" I turn to Thea. "If the soul merged with the demon, then we won't be able to help it cross over. That means we lose."

"No one said this game is easy," Cer says.

"More like impossible," I mumble.

"Which is why you two need to leave. I'll deal with the demon myself."

"What—"

"We should listen to him, Luce," Thea suddenly says as she hops over to me and grabs me by my arm. "He fights them for a living."

"He does what?" I blink.

She nods fervently.

"If anyone knows how to hunt and kill a demon, it's Cer. And once he kills it, the soul will be freed—if it hasn't been ingested, of course."

My mouth curls in disgust as I think about that process of...ingestion. Not the image I wanted in my head.

"And how might one kill a demon?"

Cer gives me a chilling look.

"You don't need to know," he grunts, his features tense as he scans the auditorium.

Oh, well. I can see why Thea has an issue with him. He's not very friendly, is he?

As much as I hate letting someone else do the work for me, in this case, I'll have to make an exception. This isn't just about me anymore—although God knows how dangerous these demons are to a mere human. No, this is about my Nikki and the fact that if I'm in danger, so is he—even more so. As long as he's by my side, my recklessness could cost him his soul.

That is the last thing I would ever want to happen.

"See, now let's go. He'll meet us at the hotel, right, Cer?"

He grunts again, barely paying her any mind.

"He's in hunting mode," Thea whispers. "Come on."

Pulling on my arm, she leads me toward the entrance of the theatre.

A part of me is guilty for abandoning this mission. Somehow, not being directly involved makes it feel unearned. But I can't expose Nikki to it.

The hallway is dark as we head to the main exit. As we reach the door, Thea uses her claw to unlock it. A click resounds through the stillness of the night and she pulls on the knob. The door easily opens, but as we're about to step into the night, we collide with an invisible barrier that thrusts us back.

"Wha—" I mumble, wincing as I hit the ground.

"No, no," Thea whispers, getting up and running toward the door at full speed. Yet it's in vain because she's once more thrown back.

"What is it?"

She wobbles toward me, her features tense.

"We're trapped."

"What do you mean we're trapped?" My eyes widen.

"The demon created a barrier," she mentions as she extends her claw toward the invisible shield put in place by the door. She uses her force to push her hand, but nothing happens. The more strength she exerts, the more the barrier acts *against* her, the tip of the claw slowly bending inward.

As if burned, she withdraws her hand, softly caressing her bent nail.

"But... Then how... How are we going to leave?" I stammer as pure dread envelops me.

"We can't. At least not until Cer neutralizes the demon. And on that note, we're better off by his side just in case it makes another appearance."

"It didn't hurt me when it had the chance." I frown.

Thea's lips tighten in a sad smile.

"Demons don't go straight for the kill. They like to take their time, terrify their victims so they can feed on that terror. Supposedly, the soul has different, ehm...properties if it's ruled by fear."

"Oh," is all I can say, internalizing that tidbit of information. So these demons not only like to ingest souls but also terrify them before that. Sounds like a proper way to die—or die twice? I'm confused.

"Do you also hunt demons?" I ask Thea on our way back to the auditorium.

"Oh, no." She rolls her eyes. "I'm not cut out for that. Actually..." She pauses, her lips trembling with mirth. "Between you and me, I'm not cut out for much of anything, which of course drives Cer crazy. He's one of the brightest of his generation and I'm, well...still training."

"To hunt demons?"

"No, of course not," she answers emphatically. "I'll likely

never be at that level. I'm still training to reach an average level."
She shrugs.

"Average for a harpy?"

She blinks twice before she shakes herself.

"Yes, of course." She forces a smile.

"The claw is part of it, no?" I continue to probe—my attempt at gathering at least some information about my new teammates on which my immortal soul depends.

"Yes. Unfortunately, it's the only part." She sighs. "Told you I'm still training. The rest will follow...at some point."

"What are you still doing here?" Cer barks when he sees us.

"We can't get out," Thea explains, describing the barrier surrounding the theatre.

Cer frowns. Pinching the bridge of his nose between two fingers, he lets out a loud sigh as he turns to face us.

"Then we have a problem. Only mid-range demons and higher have that type of ability," he mentions, pacing around. "Sure, it won't be as hard to exterminate it once I draw it out, but with you here... That changes things," he mutters to himself.

"You can do your thing, and Luce and I will stay out of your way. What do you think?" Thea offers with a wide smile. "You can add your own barrier to a room, no?"

He tilts his head to the side, considering her words.

"You know my abilities are constrained," he bites out in a low, rough tone. His eyes meet hers, flashing a thunderous gold.

"A small room?" She bats her lashes at him.

"What room, Thea?"

"The dressing room!" She almost jumps up out of excitement.

I slowly turn to her, my mouth open in shock—or is it outrage? We're in a life-and-death situation with a loose demon that hasn't only consumed the soul we need to liberate, but might also consume ours, and she wants to play with clothes?

"You can't possibly—"

"Fine," Cer interrupts me. "That is a small enough enclosure. But"—he pauses, looking both of us straight in the eye—"you stay put. You do not leave the room until I tell you it's safe to do so, understood?"

"Yes, sir." Thea cackles, while I mumble a low, "Fine."

Cer pivots, heading backstage, and we follow.

The women's dressing room is not very spacious, but it's filled with colorful gowns that immediately catch Thea's eyes—and if I'm honest with myself, mine too.

"Remember what I told you. Stay here," Cer warns once more before he closes his eyes, white-blue light shimmering in his palms as he directs it to the door and the walls around. "This will keep anything out of here, but the moment you step outside of the barrier, it will automatically dissolve."

Thea and I nod, while Cer seems rather conflicted about leaving us here by ourselves. Eventually, though, he shakes his head and exits the room.

"Oh my, Luce! Look at these gowns! I'm in love!"

"Shouldn't you be... I don't know, more worried about our lives?"

"Nah." She waves my concerns away. "I trust Cer with my life. Always. He's good at what he does, Luce. He would never let a demon harm us."

"If you say so..." I mumble, taking a seat on a chair at the vanity table.

With the barrier in place, I feel more at peace, but that doesn't mean I'm not still worried. Is Nikki here as well? Is he by my side and I don't know it? Or is he trapped outside the barrier, somewhere in the theatre where he could be the next meal for this damned demon?

"Thea," I suddenly speak. "How can you talk to a spirit?"

She's already taken off her clothes, standing completely naked in front of me—unabashedly so. She's holding two dresses in her hands, one blue, one purple, regarding them with her lips pursed.

"It's very hard to say," she adds absentmindedly. "You can bait them, but usually they are the first to make contact. It also depends on the level of awareness they have. An old spirit like

Olive would be easier to goad into showing herself to us—if she weren't demon food, of course."

"Not a newer one?"

"Those are the most unpredictable. I pity those teams who got assigned to a fresh soul." She shakes her head.

"Your brother mentioned mid-level demon. What's that?"

Thea turns slightly toward me.

"Demons have hierarchies too. A mid-level demon means that it's sentient and often cunning in how it lures its victims. It could be why people have been seeing Olive's ghost."

"You mean he might have been masquerading as her?"

She nods.

"At this level, however, they are still monsters. The higher up the ladder you go, though, the more humanoid they look. They also don't get their hands dirty like this. They have their army of minions to do their bidding."

"Do they also possess people?" I ask, thinking of those horror exorcist movies I would watch with Nikki.

"The low-level ones. They have no corporeal form, so to speak, so the only way they can consume a soul is from within," she explains.

"So how do exorcisms work then? Because there are a lot of stories about that... Also, how do Christianity and God and the Bible fit into all of this? How do any religions fit into this?"

Her lips curl up.

"It's the intention that matters. Your Christian priests are no different from Buddhist priests or any other priests—they all pray for the good of the soul. The legend goes that eons ago, the Primordial gods created mortals in their image as an experiment —or, if I'm honest, as toys. But after mortals were created, the gods saw that mortal souls, created from the purest source of energy, were actually *immortal*. And soon, these souls developed their own free will, thinking themselves omnipotent. Not wanting their toys to turn against them, the gods combined their forces and wove into each soul nine threads of fate—controlled by the Gods of Fate. This way, they regained control over that mortality, and the Gods of Fate were able to sever the threads whenever they wished. Naturally, the soul would survive to be reincarnated at a later date, but without memories or knowledge of the past, thus making it impossible for them to ever rebel."

Thea pauses, taking a big gulp of air.

"Cultures evolved, religions were created, gods appeared and perished. Yet when mortals invoke a higher power, it doesn't matter under which name they do it—the gods listen. So when you have your exorcisms, regardless of what tradition they are carried out in, they channel the same purifying energy."

I gawk at her in shock. Did she just tell me an abbreviated history of the human race? And all of it while naked? Her kind certainly doesn't have the same sensibilities as us mere mortals.

"Of course, by mortals I don't mean only humans," she adds, almost as if reading my mind. "Mortal is any species that is not eternal—that is not godly. Whether humanoid, non-humanoid, or shapeshifting, they are all considered mortals because their bodies age and decay. Some might have increased life spans, and others lower. But they all die in the end."

"So you mean prayer works? What about holy water? Is that effective against demons?"

"Lower-level demons, yes. Those prayers are purified by our priestesses, as is the water you call holy. It's a temporary weapon against demons, but the higher the level a demon is, the more you're just going to piss him off."

"I don't get it. Then what happens to higher-level demons?"

"You have people like my brother, who dedicate their lives to eradicating them. It's why he's much more comfortable with your world than I am because he's sometimes sent on missions to kill rogue demons."

"I see," I murmur. But I don't see it. At least not at this moment. It's too much for me to digest and wrap my head around.

And just like that, once more, everything I thought I knew about the world is moot. Damn! But now it makes sense why those other *species* were competing in The Wishing Game.

Although they look different, they share the same circumstances with us humans—wow, it's so weird to refer to myself as *human* now.

"Does the cross have the same effect then?"

Thea nods.

"It's a holy symbol, imbued with power by the priestesses."

Okay, so various religious paraphernalia work against *some* demons. Good to know.

Done with the lesson for today, Thea proceeds to ignore me as she looks pensively at the two dresses she picked, turning them around and assessing them in great detail. Before I know it, she throws the purple dress toward me.

"You try that on. I'll try this."

"They're not ours, Thea," I muster a feeble protest. The material is luxurious in my hands and the color happens to be my favorite. I know I shouldn't, but...

"No one will have to know." She winks at me, already halfway dressed. She quickly shrugs the sleeves on and buttons her top before adding the belt.

Gliding to the mirror, she twirls around, her features rapt as she watches the material float in the air.

"Come on, Luce." She turns, pouting at me.

Relenting, I stand up, sliding the straps of my dress down my body. Thea's watching me curiously, her eyes taking in the marks on my body.

For a moment, I'm frozen in place as I realize this is the first time someone other than Nikki sees my naked body and my marks. She comes closer to me, and just as I'm waiting for her to comment on my scars, she surprises me by pointing at my bra.

"What's this?" Her eyes are full of curiosity as she pokes a finger into the material. Her gaze dips lower to my underwear, and she blinks repeatedly, as if in shock. "And this?"

FOURTEEN

"You don't know what underwear is?" I frown.

She slowly raises her gaze to meet mine as she shakes her head.

"This is a bra." I point to my chest. "It helps support your, ehm, breasts." I clear my throat. "And these are panties and, well..." I pause. I'm not even sure what exactly they do.

"Fascinating," she whispers, sparing me the painful explanation of what panties are. "I need one of these *bras*," she says, her hands cupping her breasts and lifting them higher. Going back to the mirror, she checks her reflection, nodding to herself. "Yes, I need one as well."

As I button my purple dress, Thea rummages through the wardrobe in search of a bra, somehow finding a red glittery one to fit her. She's so happy about her find I don't have the heart to tell her that's a bra for an adult show, not one you'd normally wear under clothes. Discarding her blue dress, she soon finds a pair of red boy shorts that she puts on in an effort to emulate my lingerie.

"What do you think?" she asks as she admires the way her breasts sit higher and perkier than before.

"Uhm, you look good?" And she does. More than good. With her voluptuous figure, she looks like a model.

"I never knew of this contraption before, Luce. This is revolutionary," she marvels at the lingerie.

Shaking my head, I tie a belt around my midriff, going to the mirror to check how it looks. The dress is made out of silk, the color the lightest purple, complemented perfectly by the darker color of the belt. I turn right and left, a smile creeping on my face.

It's...pretty. Even better, the long sleeves and high neckline cover all my marks.

"You look so beautiful." She comes up from behind me. "This color suits you."

"Thank you." I smile faintly. Memories of Nikki and his little purple gifts intrude in my memory and make my heart clench with longing.

A lone tear falls down my cheek, but I wipe it away before Thea can notice it—although with how enraptured by her new finds she is, I doubt she would.

Oh, Nikki. If only you were here...

I may be thrilled to find out that there's a world beyond our knowledge, beyond the visible or even the fathomable. But without Nikki, it's all moot. I would love nothing more than to explore all this new and arcane knowledge, but it will never be the same without my best friend—without the only person in the world who completes me.

A sigh escapes my lips as I try to regulate my pulse.

It's okay. I'll have him again. I'll fight this until the end, and we'll be together again.

A strangled noise makes me turn around, my eyes widening as I see Thea on her knees, her eyes red, her claws extending.

"Thea?" I ask tentatively.

She opens her mouth to speak, but nothing comes out. She brings her clawed hand to her neck, the sharp tips penetrating the skin and drawing blood. Yet her blood...it's not red. It's a swirling silver that drips down her skin, shiny particles sparkling in the dimly lit room.

"What's happening, Thea? Is it the demon? Is it here?" I get to my knees in front of her, my features a mix of worry and help-lessness as I watch her without knowing what I can do to ease her suffering.

She shakes her head.

"C—" She opens her mouth. "Ce—"

"Your brother? You want me to call your brother?" I quickly ask.

She gives me a pained nod just as more of the silvery liquid pours down her neck, nestling into her cleavage.

Panicked, I get to my feet, dashing out the door as I call out for her brother. I feel the pressure of the barrier for a brief moment before it dissipates and I'm out of the dressing room.

"Cer?"

"What are you doing here?" he asks in a low, chilling voice as he appears in front of me—almost as if out of thin air.

"It's Thea. I don't know what's wrong with her..."

His eyes flash for a second before he dashes into the dressing room, finding his sister writhing on the floor.

"Damn you, Erithea," he rasps. "Didn't I warn you this would happen? You little fool."

She raises her head slightly, letting out a throaty groan as she reaches out with her clawed hand toward him.

Shaking his head, he bends to gather her in his arms, her claws automatically lodging deep into his skin.

"What's wrong with her?" I ask, biting my lip in worry as I take in the drastic change in her appearance. That silvery liquid continues to flow out of her wounds, her face losing color. Where she was so lively just a few moments ago, now she's barely alive.

"The meat. She knows she's not allowed to eat it, but she does it anyway. And this time..." He stops himself. "You foolish girl. This is what you deserve for stuffing yourself with that bacon."

Thea releases a choked sound, which some might take as agreement, but knowing she hates agreeing with her brother, I'll interpret it as a protest.

"What can we do? How long will this go on? Is she in any danger? Do we need to call an ambulance? But we can't get out and..." The questions pour out of my mouth as the most awful scenarios fill my mind.

"She'll be fine," Cer grits out. "Wait in here while I tend to her. And *don't* leave the room. Understood?"

I blink, slowly nodding. He doesn't acknowledge me as he storms out with his sister in his arms.

What does he mean that he needs to tend to her? Why not do it here? Where are they going? The questions fill my brain as I stare at the open door.

Taking a deep breath, I plop myself on the chair, folding my hands in my lap.

What just happened?

Why was there silver flowing out of her wounds?

Too many questions and no answers.

Around half an hour of pure worrying passes before I decide I can't stand still anymore. While Cer tends to Thea, I can at least take care of my little ghost problem. Thea said that it's harder to initiate contact with new spirits, but I don't have anything to lose. In fact, the mere thought that Nikki could be attached to me, wandering around the halls of the theatre, all ripe for plucking by that damned demon, makes me want to hyperventilate.

"Nikki? Please, if you can hear me, give me a sign," I say aloud as I pace around the dressing room.

I'm not even sure if a spirit can leave the object it has attached itself to, but at least I can warn him about the danger.

"Nikki? Are you there?"

Minutes on end pass as I utter plea after plea, but they all go unanswered.

I release a sigh as I fall back into the chair, watching the gossamer fabric of the dress swoosh into the air. Such a pretty dress. If only Nikki were here to see it, too.

My lips tremble lightly as I stare at my wedding ring and the commitment it signifies. I'd promised to be by his side, in life and in death. He'd promised it back, too.

So where is he now?

Why isn't he here when he promised me?

"You said you'd never leave me," I utter a broken sob. "You said you'd never leave me," I repeat, louder this time. "You *promised*, Nikki. You gave me your vow. So why did you? Why did you leave me?"

Breathing hard, I clench my hands, fisting the material of the dress. A light rip echoes in the air and I still, almost paralyzed. Slowly, I gaze down, noting the tear in the light fabric.

"Oh, Lord." I let out a cry of frustration.

Getting to my feet, I reach behind to undo the belt. I need to take this dress off before I do more damage.

As I struggle to untie the knot, a light, pulsating noise reverberates from the side of the dresser. I half turn, frowning. Maybe it was just my imagination. I focus again on undressing when a bang on the wall makes me jump up in surprise.

"Jesus," I whimper, half scared to death.

Not a couple of seconds later, and the same pulsating noise resounds in the room, almost as if someone is knocking on the outer wall in small, precise beats.

My hands fall to my side, the belt still intact. I take a few steps toward the dresser, parting the row of costumes to the side to reveal the wall. I stare at the blank patch, the darkness even more pronounced in this corner. When I don't notice anything else amiss, I make to step back.

Thud.

I stop, blinking.

Thud.

This time, the sound is louder and coming straight from the wall in front of me. Pushing more clothes to the side, I step deeper into the wardrobe, letting my palms be my guides when my eyes are not of much help. I feel around the wall in an attempt to decipher the odd sounds it's emitting—my foolish heart perhaps thinking it might be a sign that Nikki is near. At the same time, though, my rational side knows that I'm still within the barrier Cer had created and not only is there no way for the demon to breach it, but it stands to reason that Nikki wouldn't either.

I purse my lips, letting out a small sigh as I nestle against the wall, placing my ear next to its surface.

"Is it you, Nikki?" I ask wistfully.

My eyes flutter closed as I lean back, placing my entire weight against the wall. The rack of clothes is like a rich foliage that cocoons me inside, the light from the dressing room a faint flicker at the end of the tunnel.

I breathe in and out, calm settling over me as I rest my back against the wall, my palms hot against the cold wall. Still, I imagine a warm presence caressing my senses, wrapping me in its protective embrace and vowing to never let me go—to never leave me again.

Inhale. Exhale.

A light push and a deafening sound penetrate my eardrums. Then I fall. My mouth opens with a scream as the void swallows me up. But it's not for long as my bones crack in the eerie silence of the night. The pain is as sharp as it is sudden as I hit the ground.

I roll on my back, a low howl of pain wheezing past my lips. My eyes are wide open, yet I cannot see anything. There's only darkness—and a lingering flicker of light up above. Did I... Did I just fall from that height?

"Damn it," I mutter as I make an effort to get up. Pain erupts in my joints, and I grit my teeth against the sudden weakness in my knees.

Turning, I look right and left in an attempt to figure out where I am and what the hell happened. I don't let panic overtake me, doing my best to keep calm despite the fact that I'm in a dark room, outside of the protective barrier, where the demon could very well come for me.

"Damn your curiosity, Luce," I chastise myself, mumbling a few curses for good measure. Of course I had to investigate the sound of that noise, only to find myself trapped in a hidden room within the wall—and above ground!

Bringing my hand against my chest, I bang it over my heart.

"You foolish girl," I mumble, shaking my head at myself. So lost I was to the possibility that my Nikki would be around that I'd *lost sight* of all the other potential dangers—*and* the fact that someone could have made those noises on purpose.

A frisson of awareness goes down my back, and a sliver of fear spears through me.

Someone or *something* made that noise. It wanted to draw me here. And like the lovesick fool I am, I fell right into its trap.

Gulping down against the anxiety rising in my chest, I realize I need to act fast and find a way out of here. Given my dim vision, the only recourse I have is to feel my way around and hope for the best—clearly *not* a very optimistic course of action, yet the only one I have at the moment. I stretch my arms out as I walk a few steps forward, and my fingers graze a piece of metal. Frowning, I wrap my hands around the metal bars, realizing it's a staircase—an old, rusty, industrial-type of staircase.

Realization dawns on me. It's a secret room. God, but had I fallen just a little to the right, I would have hurt myself a great deal more than I already did.

"Thank God there's a staircase," I whisper, already raising one leg so I can climb up. Yet I don't make it more than one step up the ladder when a cold gust of wind blows against my neck, my hair flying forward.

My eyes widen just as my heart starts hammering in my chest. Without looking back, I keep climbing, hoping I'm fast enough to evade whatever's behind me.

Another gust of air hits me, yet this time it has a certain warmth to it. A light scent wafts forward, one that speaks of comfort, lightness, of...*home.*

I freeze.

My self-preservation be damned as my heart pounds in a mixture of anticipation and relief. And following the cues of my body, I slowly turn.

At first, I don't see anything—not with how the darkness seems to swallow everything up. Slowly, though, particles of dust light up, creating the vague outline of a body.

I blink once. Twice. I bring one hand to rub at my eyes, convinced I must be seeing things. But no. It's real.

The shimmery dust I've seen before is here again. And that means...

FIFTEEN

"**N**ikki?" A choked sob escapes me as I all but jump off the staircase in my attempt to get closer to him. "Is it you? Please tell me it's you," I plead.

This is what pure madness is. Prizing the potential of one more moment with my beloved above my own safety.

It could be anything. It could be anyone. But I throw caution to the wind and focus only on what he makes me feel—on what my heart tells me is true.

How could anyone but him awaken this raging storm of longing in my heart?

I reach with my hand for him, curling my fingers inward as I hesitate to touch him.

"Nikki?" I ask in a whisper.

He doesn't answer. Of course he doesn't answer. He's shimmery dust, not a person, and according to Thea, his spirit would barely have awareness.

Yet in spite of that, the shimmery mist that makes up his shape flickers, the light particles growing in intensity.

I stare at it with my mouth wide open, my brain working fast on a solution.

He can't mean me harm. I sense no malicious intent from him, only curiosity and protectiveness.

"You can't speak, can you?"

The mist shimmers again.

But against all odds, he *is* trying to communicate with me.

My pulse is in my ears as I stare at him, almost unable to believe this is real. But if gods, demons, ghosts, and who knows what other creatures exist, why can't this be? Why can't I have at least this after suffering so much in this lifetime?

"Can you light up once for no and twice for yes?" I ask tentatively.

The mist lights up once. Then another time.

Oh God. It's happening. Excitement courses through me as I take a step closer.

"You can understand me, right?"

He lights up twice. *Yes*.

"Are you attached to me?"

I wait for a moment for him to answer, but when he doesn't, I rephrase my question.

"Have you been following me?"

Two shimmers. *Yes*.

I nod to myself.

Okay. Good. That is good to know.

"Have you been following me since the game?"

One shimmer. *No*.

"Before?"

Two shimmers. *Yes*.

Oh my. I'm close to hyperventilating the closer I get to the most important question.

"Have you been with me since the accident?"

He doesn't answer. Of course he wouldn't really remember the accident, would he?

"Are you my... Nikki?" I wet my lips as I stare intently at the mass of black-silvery swirling dust.

One shimmer. My stomach drops. It's not him? There's a heartbeat pause before his body lights up again in a second shimmer.

I bring my hand to my mouth to cover a gasp. I knew it. Oh, I knew it.

"You're my husband, aren't you? My Nikki," I repeat, struggling to keep the emotion out of my voice.

Two shimmers. *Yes.*

Adrenaline rushes through my veins, and I lose sight of everything but him. Before I know it, I throw myself over him, my arms reaching out for him, to hold, to caress, to love.

Yet the most I feel is the cold air that brushes against my limbs—*his* cold air. That is the only evidence he exists in this space—the only way he can physically interact with me.

"Oh, Nikki," I cry out. "Thank you! Thank you for staying by my side," I say as I search for the gathering of dust that represents the essence of my beloved.

The mist lights up twice. A yes.

Even knowing I can't touch him, I move closer to him, lifting my hand and swirling my fingers through the mist. It's cold to the touch, but also warm—a warmth that goes beyond physical temperature.

Another step, and I move closer, so close I'm almost one with him. Every particle of his shadowy body brushes against my corporeal one. Every atom of his being caresses my own. Icy wind skims my right cheek, and as I close my eyes, a sigh escapes me as I imagine it's his lips that lay a trail of arctic kisses that melt into my skin.

Seconds turn to minutes that seek to turn into an eternity as we succumb to this unorthodox embrace. All the yearning I'd buried deep within erupts to the surface, and I can feel the yearning in him too. It's right there, in the erratic flicker of light, the shift in temperature, and the storm of dust that swirls everywhere around me.

"I missed you," I murmur. "I missed you so much, Nikki. But don't you worry. I'll bring you back. I'll do everything in my power to make sure you come back to me."

The mist swirls around me, almost like a pat before stepping back. I want to protest at the sudden feeling of bereavement, but before I can voice that out loud, I'm reminded of what I had wanted to tell him from the beginning—as well as my own precarious circumstances away from the other siblings.

"Can you leave this place, Nikki? There's a dangerous demon that feeds on souls roaming around the theatre. If you stay here, you'll only be in danger, and I can't have you in danger," I tell him breathlessly. The mere thought of him being away after I just found him again causes me visceral pain. But this is for his good—for his safety. And that is the one thing I can't risk.

He doesn't answer me, nor does he flicker or emit any light. He's just...there.

"Please, Nikki—" My words are interrupted by a piercing sound coming from behind me. I swivel, my eyes wide as I search through the unyielding darkness.

"You need to go, Nikki. *Now!*" I tell him, this time more pronounced.

I step backward, my arm thrust back to find the metal stair. But I don't reach it when I feel another presence with me in the tunnel. The same foul smell as before lingers in the air, becoming more potent by the second. Loud, thudding steps echo before an inhuman howl physically thrusts me back.

Fear clogs my throat, but my thoughts are all centered on Nikki. Scanning the area the best I can, I manage to make out Nikki's shadowy self and the outline of the other entity present. My mind is blank as I jump up from my spot, placing myself in front of Nikki in one last attempt to protect him.

"Go, Nikki. I'll hold him back. Please leave," I beg him.

He gives me a shimmery signal to mean yes before the mist dissipates, in its place remaining only faint rays of light coming from up above.

I release a sigh of relief. At least he's safe...

The sound of wet lips smacking together brings me back to the present. Now that Nikki's gone, I need to find a way to get back to the dressing room too.

The pungent smell becomes stronger, to the point that I

have to stop myself from bending over to retch. I swallow hard, taking one step back at a time so I don't set the demon off by any chance.

Another roar explodes in the tunnel, causing me to stumble and almost fall. Grabbing onto the wall, I quickly stabilize myself, only to feel a sticky hand grab me by the throat. In no time, my hands stop touching the ground as he lifts me in the air, his fingers tightening over my flesh.

He brings his snout to my face, sniffing me.

"*Lora re*," he hisses in a strange tongue. His voice holds two layers. A broken, sinister one that is the most clear, but also a second layer that sounds like a choir of a thousand people.

His breath wafts directly into my face now, the smell so putrid I can barely breathe. This is the smell of rot, of decaying flesh that's been forgotten in the sun. The fact that I've seen and tended to dead bodies before at the hacienda is the only thing that's keeping me from casting my accounts in that very moment. That and the fact that with Nikki out of the way, my self-preservation makes its belated appearance.

"Let me go," I barely get the words out.

Fear grips me as I rack my brain for a way out. Remembering some of Thea's words, I bring my hands together, using my two forefingers to make the sign of the cross and pressing it into his gross face.

He lets out a roaring screech as he shoves me backward, his sharp claws scraping the sides of my neck in the process.

I whimper as I hit the ground. Wetness pours from my neck, flowing down my chest, making my dress stick to my skin.

The demon howls in pain momentarily before he stomps toward me, his steps making the foundation of the building quake.

My body shakes as I drag myself backward, hoping I'll bump into the staircase so I can haul myself up. But it's not long before he's on me.

I barely see him, but I feel his foul stench as he extends his claws toward me, gripping me by my bodice and pulling me toward him. I push at his hand in an attempt to get loose, but it's in vain. His force is so immense, he easily lifts me up again, my feet dangling in the air.

"Damn you," I force the words out as I lash out, hitting him with my fists. Although I get some blows on him, they do little else but enrage him.

Opening his mouth, he lets out a deafening roar that not only physically hurts my eardrums but also pollutes the air all around.

I can't even die with dignity, can I?

Yet just as I think he's going to swallow me up with that stinky orifice some might call a mouth, I drop to the ground.

Whaaat?

I draw in a ragged breath, my pulse becoming more and more erratic as I dread to imagine these are my last moments on this earth.

But before I can blink, the entire corridor comes alive, light infiltrating every particle.

SIXTEEN

I blink slowly, taking a moment for my eyes to adjust to the
light. And then, I blink again, afraid I'm seeing wrong.

A giant of a man is with his back to me, dressed in an all-
black ensemble and wielding a marble-white sword as he faces
the demon. But that's just the first startling detail. The second is
that the demon is writhing in pain, muddy blood flowing from
his severed arm.

And that severed arm...well, that's currently still attached to
my bodice.

As my eyes dip to where his claws are tightly wrapped in
the purple material, I let out a shrill scream, pulling with both
hands on the grotesque arm in an attempt to dislodge it.

"Be quiet, human," the man in black states in a deadpan
voice, not even bothering to look at me. All at once, I realize yet
another thing. This isn't Cer—though his physique is similar.
His voice is nothing like Cer's.

The rebuke instantly quiets me, and I frown at my odd
acquiescence. My mouth opens and closes, but I can't find any
reply—not when he might be my only chance of survival.

The stranger maneuvers his sword to the side, the white
catching some of the light and reflecting it directly at the

demon. There is a flash of foreign symbols on the sword that seem to be pulsating with life. The demon gives another loud yelp of pain before he disappears.

Just like before in the auditorium, he simply vanishes.

I stare at the empty spot, shocked that the demon would leave like that. Yet my shock only mounts when a hissing sound directs my attention to the severed arm currently lying by my side. Bubbles erupt to the surface, and like a corrosive acid, the arm dissolves until there's nothing left behind.

What the hell...

"Why are you not getting up?" the same harsh voice demands.

I whip my head up, my gaze instantly becoming belligerent at his tone and word choice.

He has cropped dark hair, a strong jaw and cheek-bones, and the darkest irises I've ever seen. His eyes are big and round, framed by thick, black lashes that would make any woman envious. His expression is neutral as he stares down at me. With slow, deliberate movements, he stashes his sword away in the scabbard secured at his waist.

"And who are you?" I ask curiously.

He continues to stare at me. From this angle, there's some-thing familiar about him.

"Do you know Cer and Thea, by any chance?" I inquire. Once more, I'm struck by an odd familiarity. His features are reminiscent of Cer's. Although their coloring might be different, the bone structure, eye shape, and even the nose are almost identical.

He regales me with a grunt, his eyes scanning my bloody neck and bodice with assured disinterest.

"Get up," he orders, and something about his tone irks me.

"You should say please," I shoot back in annoyance.

His expression doesn't change.

He merely blinks in a bored manner.

Pushing my palms to the ground, I attempt to stand up, only

to fall back on my ass again, a low whimper of pain slipping past my lips.

I look up at him, expecting to see at least some compassion, maybe even offer a helping hand. Instead, he's sporting the same uninterested expression. No muscle in his body has moved. He's just staring at me.

"It's good manners to help a lady in need," I grumble when he makes no attempt to move.

I wonder if I sprained my ankle when I fell. It's a little tender to the touch and I can't put my weight on it. I might need to ice it up later...

"You're not a lady," he simply states, taking a step to move past me.

"W-what?" I sputter, my eyes widening in incredulity at his words.

He stops in his tracks right by my side, gazing down at me with that inscrutable expression of his.

"You do not hold a noble title. Therefore, you are not a lady."

I blink. Slowly. As slow as possible so I can properly digest his words.

"A noble title... You..." I take a deep breath. "I was speaking figuratively, not literally."

"I do not understand your words, human," he states blankly, still staring at me.

"It means you should be a gentleman and help a woman in need," I explain, exasperated.

"But I am not a gentle man," he replies evenly.

My lashes flutter at him, my brows creasing with confusion.

"Will you help me or not?" I huff out.

He surprisingly nods, leaning down toward me. I extend my arms, thinking he's going to help me get to my feet, but instead, he swoops me in his arms in one smooth movement.

"You should have said that was what you wanted from the beginning," he mentions as he carries me to the staircase.

What? Another frown mars my forehead. Just what the hell is wrong with this man? I didn't think there could be someone out there with worse manners than Cer and Thea, but it seems I've barely scratched the surface.

I'm about to question how he's going to climb with me like this, but it seems I don't have to worry when he all but floats up, using only his feet to keep himself stable on the narrow steps.

We emerge through the wardrobe and into the dressing room. There's still no sign of Thea or Cer.

The stranger carries me to the center of the room, where he stops. His eyes are scanning around the room, his expression focused. But he doesn't let go of me. I open my mouth to tell him to put me down but close it when I realize that he might be sensing danger. Considering my ankle is not in the best shape, I won't take my chances. And he seems quite a proficient fighter.

To my surprise, he's not on the lookout for demons. His brows crease lightly as he moves to the vanity, picking up a bottle of pink glitter, likely left behind by one of the actresses. Keeping me in his arms with one hand, he uses the other to check its contents, looking thoroughly intrigued by it. With a nimbleness you wouldn't expect of someone using only one hand, he unscrews the cap, shaking the bottle and scattering the glitter all over the table. His gaze is intent as he stares at the glitter, almost like a child in a candy shop. Some fine particles of powder end up in the air, tickling my nose until my eyes tear up. I attempt to draw a breath in, but I ultimately cannot stop myself from sneezing. The power of my sneeze scatters the glitter even more, some of it ending up on the mirror and some of it on us.

My eyes widen in shock as I gaze down to find glitter all over my gown, with some of it sticking to my bloodied gashes. And as I slowly turn to the stranger, it's to find him too completely draped in pink glitter, the shade complementing his black ensemble.

He blinks slowly.

"What is the meaning of this?" he asks in a low, outraged voice.

"Maybe you shouldn't have messed with the bottle." I wrinkle my nose in discomfort.

"What is this magic, human? Explain," he barks out, still fiddling with the glitter bottle with his free hand. "And why is it this...cheery color?"

I stare at him open-mouthed.

"It's glitter. It's not magic."

"It *sparkles*," he adds, the corners of his mouth curling in disgust.

"That's what it's made for." I roll my eyes. "To make things sparkle."

He frowns, and I think it's safe to say this might be his first experience with glitter. But he's not deterred as he continues to study the items on the table, picking up a perfume next. Instead of spraying it, however, he unscrews the entire cap until the liquid spills everywhere, the scent wafting in the air.

Well, I must say it is a nice change from the sulfurous smell of the demon—just a tad too pungent.

"I'm not sure what you're trying to do, but you should stop destroying the makeup," I add as he touches another container.

"Makeup?" he repeats, the word foreign in his tone.

"You know, the stuff you apply on your face and body."

"I know no such thing," he huffs. Ignoring me, he continues to check every item.

"Hey, you're ruining people's property," I rephrase my words, reaching out to grab his hand.

He turns his head toward me, giving me a deadly stare.

"Do not touch me without permission, human," he states, potentially forgetting that I was already touching him before since he *still* has not let go of me. If anything, considering I'm in his arms, I'd say *he* is touching *me*.

"Just stop whatever you're doing."

"I must check all these odd containers for any potential threat." The words flow out of his mouth. "I do not know what type of magic you humans dabble in."

Now it's my turn to simply stare at him.

I thought Thea was odd, but she certainly wasn't *this* level of crazy.

I attempt to get him to stop once more, but he ignores me and continues to check *every* single item on the vanity. Alas, after some time, he is done, and he moves away from that area. But I'm still in his arms!

"You can put me down, you know," I grumble.

He doesn't reply as he simply lets go of me.

Just. Like. That.

I yelp in pain as I fall down. Luckily, the carpet is fluffy enough to make it less painful, but the impact still jostles my bones.

"What the hell is wrong with you?" I burst out, looking up at him belligerently.

He stares me down, his eyes narrowing.

"You asked me to put you down. I did."

"You *dropped* me," I point out.

"I put you down," he counters.

"Ugh!" I let out an annoyed huff. "You're not from around here, are you?"

His eyes narrow further.

"You're not from *this* place," I reiterate.

"I am not," he replies proudly, pushing his chin up.

His tone tells me he doesn't have the highest consideration for us *humans*.

"Why are you here anyway? And how did you get past the barrier?" I decide to change the subject since it's a chore to have a normal conversation with someone who cannot understand normal language—and who already sees me as a primitive human.

"I can get through any barrier," he immediately answers, a hint of indignation in his voice—as if he's insulted I'd even suggest otherwise.

"Right. Well, thank you for saving me from that demon," I reluctantly offer. No matter how odd his behavior might be, he *did* save my life.

"As you should," he replies smoothly.

I stare at him unblinkingly. He stares back, his expression puzzled. He tilts his head to the side, his eyes dipping from my face to my neck.

"You're bleeding," he states blankly.

Bringing my hand to my neck, I feel the wetness coat my fingers, together with particles of glitter. Although it doesn't hurt too much, there's quite a bit of blood.

He crouches in front of me, his shrewd eyes inspecting my wound. He looks at it from every angle, pursing his lips. Before I realize what he means to do, he pulls on the hem of my gown, ripping out two strips of material. Using the first one, he dabs at my neck, cleaning the wound. But he soon realizes that some of the glitter is not coming off, remaining stuck to my skin. The microparticles are abrasive enough that every time he wipes the fabric over my neck, I wince in pain.

"You're in pain," he observes, his tone clinical.

I force a smile. "It's the glitter. It's scratching my skin when you dab at it."

He considers my words for a moment before he nods to himself. Removing the fabric from my neck, he brings it to his lips and spits on it.

He...

My eyes are the size of two saucers as I watch in shock as he spits a couple more times on the cloth before he dabs it over my wounds again. The moisture from his saliva helps with the glitter particles, but I'm still processing the fact that he *spat* on it.

He works nimbly, cleaning my wound as best as he can before using the other strip of material to tie it around my neck in two layers.

Pleased with the result, he gets up, proceeding to ignore me.

I'm still frozen to the spot, staring at a blank spot while he's already curiously inspecting the rest of the room, as if he didn't just...

"You spat on me," I say in a low voice when my shock starts to wear off.

He half turns, raising an eyebrow at me.

"You spat on me," I repeat. "On my wound. You..."

"Yes. I am still awaiting your gratitude," he says smoothly.

My mouth hangs open. I didn't think I could be more shocked, but there it goes.

"You what?" My voice goes up in outrage.

"I shared my precious healing saliva with you, human. You should be *more* than grateful that I would deign to do so," he continues, and with every word, he manages to render me even more speechless than before. "Others would prostrate themselves at my feet for such an honor."

"Prostrate at your feet?" I repeat numbly. Just who the hell does he think he is? Yet even as I ask myself that, the previously pulsing pain stops. I reach for my ankle, feeling for the tender spot from before, only to find that there's nothing there.

Yet before I can say anything else, or before he can insult me some more, the door to the dressing room opens. Thea and Cer stride in, both looking perfectly fine. Thea is once more wearing the blue dress from before. But as they see the new guest, they both stop in their tracks, unable to hide their surprise. At least Thea, who gasps audibly. Cer is more subtle in his reaction.

"Ze!" Thea bursts out, dashing toward him. He immediately extends his arm to stop her just as Cer grabs her arm and drags her back.

"What are you doing here?" Cer asks, and somehow he doesn't seem too pleased about Ze's presence.

"I was in the vicinity and I realized you might need help," Ze haughtily professes.

"You can't be here, Ze. You know that," Cer says through gritted teeth. "Not when there's a war brewing."

War? What war?

I look from one side to the other, confused about their exchange.

"Aethon took over for me," Ze shrugs. "He can handle it until I come back."

"Excuse me? What's going on? Who's he?" I point at Ze.

It's at that moment that Thea notices my torn and bloodied gown, quickly rushing to my side.

"What happened, Luce? Are you all right?"

"She is, but not thanks to you," Ze adds pointedly, probably fishing for some more praise.

"I'm fine. He saved me from the demon," I admit reluctantly. He smirks, and God, I could swear he's preening. Arrogant ass!

"What? Oh, I'm so sorry, Luce. This was all my fault for eating that bacon. But it was so good..."

"Yes, it was your fault," Ze comments. "You left a defenseless human alone, Erithea, when you knew you should not," he adds with a strange glint in his eyes.

"Can you guys just explain what's happening and who this"—I wave my hand at him, unable to find a good or even neutral word to describe him—"thing is?" My eyes widen at my slip, as do everyone else's.

"Thing?" Ze sputters. "Thing? You puny little human." He takes a step closer, his eyes flashing at me.

"Well, I don't know who you are, do I?" I quickly make the excuse.

"Don't mind Ze too much, Luce. He's Cer's friend," Thea hurries to say.

"I am his superior," Ze adds smugly.

Cer rolls his eyes at that, but a smile pulls at his lips—one of the very few times he's smiled since I've known him.

"Superior in what?"

"Oh that," Thea stammers. "Remember I told you my brother fights demons. Ze fights them too."

My brows shoot up in surprise.

"Why is he here then? Is he taking part in the game too?"

"That's right. Are you part of the game, too, Z?" Cer asks, narrowing his eyes at him.

"You could say I am a late arrival. But now I will be on your team. You may rejoice," he says, entirely serious.

My God, but I don't think I've ever met someone as arrogant.

"Who invited you?" I grumble under my breath. His head whips to me, his eyes boring a hole in me.

"Your opinion is of no consequence, human."

"Human this, human that. I have a name, damn it," I burst out, shocking myself.

"I have not heard it," he replies, staring intently at me.

SEVENTEEN

"It's Luce. You can call me Luce."

"Luce," he repeats my name, his voice rough. "Very well, human. From now on, I shall call you Luce."

I sigh deeply. On one hand, he might be a good addition to our demon hunt. On the other, he'll be a pain in the ass to deal with, so I guess I'll just have to limit my interactions with him.

"Is he always like this?" I whisper to Thea.

She fights a smile as she nods.

"This is Ze being nice. Most days he's much worse."

"Lord," I groan. "At least he can help us catch the demon."

"For sure. With Ze and Cer by our side, we'll definitely win in no time," Thea adds enthusiastically.

As Thea helps me to my feet, I'm happy to see that my ankle is fully healed. But since my gown was destroyed, I need to find something else to wear.

A little snooping through the wardrobe and I find a pair of pants and a loose blouse that should be comfortable for the remainder of our sojourn here.

The men agree to wait outside while we change, and Cer tries—rather pointlessly—to convince Ze to change into some non-glittery clothes too. Of course, he immediately refuses, going on a soliloquy about how worthless human clothes are, not worthy of touching his skin. I barely hold my laughter as they exit the dressing room, Ze's voice still booming from a distance.

"Ze is quite the character, isn't he?" I chuckle when we're alone in the room.

"I told you this is him at his best. Back home, no one likes him. Well, except Cer and Aethon, and sometimes Molokai."

"I can't imagine why." I crack a smile, which she returns.

"He's...different. Don't take his words to heart. He doesn't realize if he says something offensive or how his words might come across to someone else."

"Why's that?" I frown.

Thea's lips flatten into a thin line. She looks as if she wants to tell me more but cannot, perhaps from a sense of loyalty—they are friends, after all.

"He doesn't socialize much." She eventually shrugs. "I'd be willing to bet this is his first time in this world."

"Now that would make sense. He thought the makeup was dangerous." I point to the broken makeup containers on the vanity.

Thea laughs.

"Just don't judge him too harshly. He might be a bit of an asshole, but he's not that bad. My brother wouldn't be friends with someone he didn't like or respect, and against all odds, Cer looks up to Ze the most."

"He said he was his superior?"

She nods.

"They're part of the military—or the equivalent of a military in your world. Cer has been with Ze since he was little. He trained under him, and he not only sees him as his best friend but also his beloved mentor."

"He's that old?" My brows go up.

"I'm not sure how old he is, but yes. He's much older than Cer and me."

I nod slowly while I shrug the blouse over my head and button up my pants.

"I think I'm done," I tell her, and she wastes no time in calling the men back into the room.

Ze walks in first, his spine straight, his hands behind his back as he assesses me with narrowed eyes. Cer trails behind him, maintaining a protective stance.

"What is that monstrosity you're wearing?" he demands.

"What do you mean?" I frown, looking down at my outfit. It's comfortable and casual, but it's nothing to scoff at.

"Why are you wearing that?" He points at my pants.

"What do you mean?" I ask, confused.

"Females don't wear pants in our world." Thea leans in to whisper. "And no one wears pants this tight," she clarifies.

My lips tremble as I fight a smile.

"I'm sorry for offending your alien sensibilities. But you're in my world now. You don't get a say in how I dress in my world," I fire back.

"You impertinent little—"

"My name is Luce," I state in an even tone, meeting his icy gaze.

He stares at me, and I know fully well that the word human was about to leave his lips.

"Very well. I shall not comment on your lack of taste in garments," he says, pleased at his magnanimity.

I roll my eyes.

All the while, Thea and Cer are trying their hardest not to laugh at us.

"If we could focus on our task?" I interrupt.

"Yes, indeed. Why don't you tell us about the demon encounter," Cer suggests.

We draw a few chairs to sit, but Ze is the only one who refuses, claiming he's more comfortable standing.

I do my best to describe the events in the secret passage, omitting the fact that I saw Nikki. For some reason, I don't want them to know that his ghost is with me.

"And you fought the demon," Cer addresses Ze, his tone strange.

"I merely cut his arm," he shrugs. "As soon as he saw my sword, he ran away."

"You used just your sword?"

"I know the rules well enough, Cerenios," Ze states, and the air suddenly becomes chillier.

I frown at their exchange but think nothing of it as I focus on the matter at hand and how we're going to work as a team when we're constantly at each other's throats.

"Can you break the barrier for them to get out?" Cer continues.

"It is only I who can come and go. To break through the barrier would draw unwanted attention."

Cer nods, his gaze straying to Thea. I don't fault him for being worried about her after what happened.

"We don't need to leave. We'll just nab the demon and move on," Thea intervenes. "Why don't we draw him out in the auditorium and you guys can end him or whatever you've got to do to him?"

"That is a sound idea." Cer nods.

"I'll do it. He must already be mad at me from before," I offer. With Nikki out of the way, I don't have to worry about the demon being a danger to him. And despite the fact that my teammates seem to possess some special abilities, I want to pull my weight in this team. Maybe I can't do a lot, but I'll at least try.

"No," Ze immediately says.

"Why? I'm a lowly human after all." I narrow my eyes at him.

"It is precisely because you are a lowly human that it will not work. Erithea can do it," he says as he turns to Thea.

"No." Now it's Cer's turn to refuse. "She's not well. There's no telling if she'll have another fit."

"And who allowed her to eat meat in the first place?" Ze comments. "You should take better care of your sister, Cerenios," he adds in an odd tone.

Damn, why do I feel like they're speaking in some sort of code?

"Erithea will do it," Ze insists. "She is better suited for this."

"I said she will not," Cer reiterates, getting to his feet.

They're both giants, and although of similar heights, Ze is slightly taller, his features more fearsome due to his inherent coldness. Although Cer tends to be aloof and sometimes reserved, there's a warmth to him that is completely absent in Ze.

"Stand down, soldier." Ze gives Cer a deadly stare.

"I'll do it. There's no reason to fight over this," I interject, getting between the two of them.

"You're going to get yourself killed." He pins me down with his gaze. I hold it, not letting his impressive height intimidate me, even though I barely make it to his chest.

"I'll do it," I repeat, turning to Ze and ignoring Cer.

I can feel Ze's gaze boring into my back just as an arctic air descends upon the room. Damn, the man is the definition of *chilly*.

"She's our best bet, Ze. Twice the demon has shown up until now, and both times it was when she was alone," Cer says.

Ze doesn't reply, but he doesn't agree with the plan either. He's just intently watching us as we start plotting.

"You can wait on the stage," Cer continues. "Ze and I will be on either side of the auditorium. The moment he shows up, we'll corner him from both directions."

"Then what?" I ask.

"We need the demon alive to check whether the souls he swallowed are still alive within it. After we ascertain that, we perform an extraction and subsequently we exterminate the demon."

"It sounds so easy when you say it." I smile.

Ze grunts from behind.

"And me? What am I supposed to do?" Thea suddenly asks, getting to her feet and dusting her pretty dress. Her long red hair's waving back and forth as she moves, swaying in a hypnotic rhythm. For someone who was struggling to breathe just a few hours ago, she certainly looks the picture of health. I wonder how she managed to get well so quickly—not that I'd begrudge her that. But I'm curious about these odd teammates of mine, and if I'm honest, a little skeptical too. Especially with our new arrival. Ze makes it very hard not to be even more suspicious considering his even odder behavior.

"You can stay in the back, at the museum we saw earlier," Cer tells her.

Thea's eyes positively sparkle with joy.

"That is perfect," she gushes, probably already thinking which pieces she's going to steal. I sneak a look at Cer, noting the light curl of his lips. He did it on purpose! He remembered she liked the museum, and instead of making her feel useless on the mission, he gave her something else to think about so she wouldn't place herself in danger. Smart.

He notices my gaze and raises a brow. I smile.

Yet as I look away, it's to find Ze glaring at me. Of course, that seems to be his favorite pastime.

Once our roles have been decided, we head to the auditorium. As I take my place on the stage, Ze comes toward me, withdrawing a small pouch from his clothes. He doesn't say a word as he pours some black dust onto the floor in a circle around me.

"What's this?" I frown.

"A barrier. It will protect you. But don't step outside of it until the demon is caught."

"Oh. Okay. Thanks."

After he finishes, he places his pouch back in his clothes and turns to leave.

"I'm not as weak as you think I am," I call out after him. I don't know what makes me say that, but I hate that he sees me as a *lowly* human. "I can do this."

"See that you do," he replies, his back still toward me as he walks down the stage.

Thea is already in the back while Cer takes his position on the left flank of the auditorium.

Soon, everyone is out of sight, and I'm left alone in the middle of the stage, my movements restricted by the circle Ze has drawn around me.

Silence descends in the auditorium and time passes. After about half an hour of waiting, my legs are starting to cramp up, so I stretch a little, jogging on the spot.

My stomach emits a low growl of hunger, and I pat my pants for the protein bar I sneaked earlier. Considering it's been too many hours since I last ate, *and* the fact that I don't know how long I'll be stuck here, I had to make sure I won't starve.

I peel off the packaging and take a big bite out of the bar. It's chocolate flavor, and the sugar is already doing wonders for my mood. I close my eyes, letting out a soft sigh as I nibble at the chocolate crust.

Despite playing bait for a dangerous demon, I'm in quite high spirits. My husband's ghost is somewhere around, attached to me. I'm competing for a chance to bring him back to life, and I actually stand a chance to make that reality.

Maybe my luck hasn't completely run out.

I munch slowly on the protein bar, and though filling for the moment, my mind can't help but conjure up pictures of sumptuous dinners, a nice steak, maybe roast potatoes and some greens—but mostly steak. Oh, my. I take another bite and imagine the taste of juicy beef flooding my mouth.

Soon.

After we're done here, we must have a celebratory dinner. And if Thea can't eat the meat, then more for me. I smile cheekily to myself.

Maybe I should have packed more than one bar. I'm clearly *too* hungry if I'm already dreaming up these types of scenarios.

Just as I'm about to eat the last bite, the typical demon smell hits my nostrils. The food barely goes down my throat. I gag a couple of times as I try to swallow everything before our guest makes his appearance. God, but this smell is really something. For as long as I live, I don't think I'll be able to delete it from my olfactory memory. It's right there with the smell of death at the hacienda.

The air, too, becomes colder and thicker, so much so it's increasingly harder to breathe.

I stuff the packaging of the bar in my pocket as I get into position, knowing that the demon is not far behind.

A sudden noise erupts in the middle of the auditorium, and the demon appears in his full monstrous appearance.

This is the first time I see him fully as he walks toward me. Yet there's something different about him than before. His arm has healed, and his face now has eyes.

Where did that come from?

His teeth are still the same rotten yellow that gives off toxic fumes, but his face resembles more of a human face. His body is semi-naked, his skin a rusty, peeling color, almost as if he's about to shed a layer. As he walks closer, I note he *did* shed parts of his skin, the remaining tissue looking normal and healthy.

Thea had mentioned that there are levels to demons, and the more souls they ingest, the more humanoid-like they become, losing their monstrous appearance for a normal one. Is this what's happening? Did the demon consume more souls? When? From where?

As he steps toward me, I note that it's an ongoing process. He's continuously developing. Oh, God. Does this mean he's more powerful now? If so, what does that mean for us?

Panic grips me as the demon approaches. But when he's a few meters away from me, he suddenly stops, his eyes on the black circle around me. He snarls at me, the power of his breath almost knocking me over—and making me double over from the smell.

"Easy, buddy," I murmur as I hold on to my balance.

His nostrils flare as he glares at me, but suddenly, he tilts his head to the side, sniffing the air.

What...

One moment he's in front of me, the next he's gone. But he doesn't go into hiding.

"He's here!" Thea cries out from the back.

My eyes widen in shock, and without a thought for my own safety, I step out of the circle, dashing off the stage. Cer and Ze are already there when I reach the museum, the two of them circling the demon while Thea is nestled behind Cer.

"He's evolving. We don't have much longer before he reaches the next level."

"Then we'll have to end him quickly," Ze responds in that calm, unruffled tone of his. He takes a step toward the demon, but Cer's voice rings out in warning.

"We need to check the status of the souls first."

Ze doesn't give a verbal answer, but his features tense, his eyes on the demon just as his hand is on the top of the scabbard of his sword.

"He's ascending, Cerenios," he grits out.

"My guess is that he needs one more soul for the process to be complete," Cer adds.

When I step inside the small enclosure, the demon turns toward me, his eyes gleaming with greed as he licks his lips.

"*Lora Re*," he whispers again, a semblance of a smile appearing on his face.

The others are completely forgotten as he focuses his attention on me.

Before I can blink, though, Ze is in front of me, his broad back filling my field of vision. His sword is in his right hand, and he rotates it once in the air before he drives it straight into the demon, severing his head from his body.

Yet just as I think the demon's dead and the entire ordeal is over, the head that just fell to the ground dissolves into a caustic mist—like his arm did before. The demon sways lightly on his feet as the flesh at his neck starts melding together, muscles and skin knitting right as bone lengthens from his spine. In less than a minute, his head is back on his body. But this time, his features are even more humanoid-like than before.

"What the hell is happening?" I mutter in shock.

"He's ascended," Ze adds quietly. "We were too late."

"What do you mean too late?"

"He's consumed the energy of the souls and now he's on a different level. Stay behind me, human," he says tensely.

It's on the tip of my tongue to tell him that my name is Luce, not human, but maybe now's not the time. Not when his words create even more panic in my breast. If the demon has already consumed all the souls, then is this all in vain? Is the trial already lost?

Ze's right hand holds his sword, and with his left one, he reaches behind, holding on to me.

"When I move, you move. Understand? I'm your only cover," he instructs.

"All right," I whisper.

Fear travels down my back, small tremors overtaking me. No matter how much confidence I have in the guys, this doesn't seem like a development they were expecting.

"Be mindful of our limitations, Ze!" Cer calls out.

I frown. This is not the first time I hear them mention limitations. I wonder if this is related to them being in a foreign world. But if that is so, then what does that mean for us? Do we stand a chance?

"Don't worry. I know what I'm doing," Ze states, his voice even and calm.

Okay, maybe he knows what he's doing. He's supposed to be an expert in this, right?

He steps back, coordinating with me to move alongside him. His eyes are on the demon, his attention unshakable.

I gulp down as I reach for his hand, grasping tightly onto it. I'm not sure if this is for his sake or mine, but I find that I'm truly terrified the more I stare into the morphing face of evil. My hands are hot and clammy. His are cold and dry. Yet they provide the modicum of comfort I desperately need.

The demon now looks completely human—except his eyes. They are two black swirling orbs of shadows. His mouth is set in a grim line, and as he sets his sights on us, he lets out a loud howl that materializes into black clouds of pure energy—all aimed at us.

The white of the metal of Ze's sword gleams against the darkness of the demon's shadows. I blink as I take in the smooth appearance of the surface of the sword. I could swear I saw some indentations on it earlier.

With inhuman swiftness, Ze wields his sword around as he cuts through the shadows. He's only using one hand, the other still firmly grasping mine.

Every blow the demon throws our way, Ze deflects it with his sword, waltzing around and keeping the exchange purely defensive.

"Why aren't you striking back?" I ask in a whisper, almost afraid to ruin his concentration.

"If there's the smallest chance that the souls are still alive, I can't destroy him yet." His reply surprises me.

"But how can you know for sure?" I frown.

"I'll know."

Slipping his hand out of mine, he reaches into his inner pocket to withdraw the same pouch he used to create the magic circle before. He puts it in my hands.

"If he comes at you, blow this in his face."

"What do you—"

I don't get to finish my question as Ze grabs my wrist, twirling me around as we get farther from the demon. When he's satisfied with the distance, he pushes me to Cer's side before going back to face him alone.

My heart beats loudly in my chest as I join the others. Thea grabs my arm, squeezing it tightly.

"Are we going to let him face the demon alone?" I ask, my eyes wide with worry as I watch him parry all the blows the demon sends his way.

"Don't worry about him. He knows what he's doing," Cer comments, watching the fight intently.

"But—"

My words die on my tongue as a deafening noise explodes in the museum. The air crackles around the demon as the shadows envelop him further, becoming a third arm, a fourth, and so on. It's almost as if from mist they have become matter, uniting themselves with the humanoid-looking body of the demon.

"What's that?" I point to the appendages forming on the demon.

"The essence of the demon is coming to the surface," Cer explains. "It's the core of his power. Ze's been trying to draw it out in the open because that's when demons are the most vulnerable."

"When it solidifies like that?"

"Yes."

I turn my attention to the fight. Ze effortlessly wields his sword, parrying each blow from the demon while making him expend more energy in order to draw out the entire essence of the demon.

The building quakes as more black fumes exit the demon's body, spreading all around him. Yet this time, instead of attaching themselves to his body, they become new ones, slowly becoming smaller solid replicas of the demon.

"Where would he get the power to do *that*?" Thea asks with a frown. She's glued to Cer's back, watching the fight from the crook of his shoulder.

"I don't know," Cer mentions, his tone... worried? "I've never seen a demon ascend so fast before. Just how many souls did he consume?"

"There's a chance we won't win this trial, isn't there?" I ask in a low, hopeless voice. The possibility has been on my mind since they mentioned he had consumed the demons. And if there are no souls to save, doesn't that mean we're doomed too?

Cer's features are tense. Thea averts her eyes as she bites her bottom lip.

I guess that's my answer.

Regardless of whether Ze kills the demon or not, if the souls have been consumed, we've failed.

My God... All this effort for nothing.

I swallow hard as a wave of hopelessness overtakes me. But I won't let it swallow me up—not while the fight is still raging on. Yet seeing Ze battle the demon alone makes me feel more useless than ever. I wish I had some sort of power to help him. I wish I could do something more than just stand around and watch, fear my only companion. God, but how I wish I could have *done* something earlier, when the demon had not yet ascended.

Yet I must face the unequivocal truth.

I *am* useless. And if I want to stand a chance in this game— if I want to win so I can get my beloved back—then I must learn how *not* to be useless.

I must learn how to prevail.

Turning my attention to the fight, I see even more shadow minions arise from the essence of the demon—to the point that they are all surrounding Ze, with some of them turning their attention to us.

Cer removes his own sword and parries the attacks of the shadows—how have I not realized he was carrying one up until now? With his right hand, he maneuvers his sword to slay the shadows. At the same time, he extends his left hand to the side, telling us to stay behind him.

Thea, too, unleashes her claws, ripping at the shadows sneaking past Cer.

The enclosed space becomes overwhelmed with the essence of the demon that is seemingly infinite. As Cer and Thea tackle the incoming shadows, I'm jostled to the side, tripping and falling on the hard floor. I drag a deep breath in, trying to get to my feet, only to be knocked down again by a mist that's slithered its way past Cer.

I give a low yelp of pain as I feel a burn where the dark shadow touched my arm. Their touch... it's acidic. As the shadow comes once more toward me, I fiddle to open the pouch with the black dust. But I'm too slow, and before I can untie the end, the shadow is upon me, striking my hands.

"Agh!" I drop the pouch to the ground, red, gnarly burns forming on the back of my hand. The shadow moves to strike again, but it's cut down by a sword at the last moment. A familiar back is in front of me, wielding that marble-white sword and cutting through the shadows until they evaporate in the air.

"Thank—" I don't get to thank him because in the next second, he's gone, already on the other side of the room, fending off attacks from the main body of the demon—the one that now has doubled in height and width.

I quickly grab the pouch, though the burns look raw and angry. Slowly getting to my feet, I return to Thea's and Cer's side.

The two of them managed to drive most of the shadows away, but it seems that the main body is creating more. At this rate, he's just going to multiply ad infinitum and we're never going to get to the bottom of it. If we want to end him, we need to limit him somehow...

"I have an idea," I suddenly say, grabbing onto Cer's sleeve. "Are you as fast as him?" I nod to Ze.

"What are you thinking about?"

"What if we cage the demon in? I have the black dust from Ze. If we create a barrier around them, then maybe..."

"It will help Ze tackle them all in one place." Cer nods. "Could be worth a try."

I hand Cer the rest of the pouch, and before I can blink, he's gone.

"Wow," I mutter when a moment later he's back by our side, a circle of black dust in place surrounding the demon.

Ze gives Cer a smirk before he jumps into the circle with the demon.

"Does the barrier work against Ze, too?"

"No." Cer shakes his head. "He *made* that dust."

"Made?" I frown.

"From his blood."

EIGHTEEN

My mouth drops open in shock, and I turn my head to watch the makeshift cage we created. The space is crammed. There's only Ze and the countless shadows that are now screeching every time they come in contact with the barrier before disintegrating. The more shadows the demon creates, the more they perish as they try to cross over.

"They're not sentient," I note.

"No, they are not. At this point, I doubt the demon itself is too sentient. It's consumed too much energy to be able to think of anything else but the urge to attack—and the desire to feed. It needs to defend itself and find more sources of energy," Cer explains.

"That's why he was coming for me. The demon saw me as his next meal," I add drily.

"Could be."

"Will Ze run out of energy, too?"

"Unlikely," he answers tersely.

He's been fighting relentlessly and only on the defensive. I now see that it was all in an attempt to make the demon weaker because soon, the rate at which he's creating the shadows slows down.

"Are all demons like this?" I inquire, trying to imagine the effort it would take to defeat more of them.

"Ascended ones, yes. This is considered a level one, although he's a very developed level one."

"What's the highest level?"

Cer gives me a side glance—one I take to mean *do you want to know?*

"Twelve."

"What?" I blink repeatedly, thinking I haven't heard him right. If this is only one, then how powerful can a level twelve demon be?

"Level twelve are considered to be the most powerful. There aren't too many of those, and we've never encountered one in a fight so far," Cer explains.

"It's why we have an army dedicated to this problem," Thea interjects. "If these demons were let to roam freely around, there would be no more souls left in the universe."

"That's incredible. And no one knows you guys do that—that you're basically real-life superheroes."

"Well," Thea's expression sours. "They do have multiple fan clubs at home."

"His energy levels are going down," Cer interrupts us, nodding to the cage.

Ze's wielding his sword with both hands, rotating it in a circle. His speed is out of this world as only flashes of white remain as he moves it, taking out all the shadows in his vicinity. He takes one step at a time as he gets closer to the demon. And at some point, the demon stops producing those external shadows.

By the time Ze reaches his side, all the shadows are gone. The only thing remaining is the extended body that seems to be losing control.

When he's only one step away from the demon, Ze puts his sword away, his movements incredibly graceful as he slides it into the scabbard before resting his palm on top of the handle.

The demon releases a loud, roaring sound as he tries to

move forward. The added weight of his body makes the earth quake with each step, and it's quickly evident that he's slowed down by the additional limbs. He tries to land a blow on Ze, but he's too slow.

Ze looks entirely unbothered as he plants himself right in front of the demon. Bringing his hands forward, he clasps his palms together until a purple-like energy emanates from him. He looks up at the demon, his eyes full of focus as he presses his palms to his chest, pushing the purple energy into the demon.

The demon opens his mouth to release a deafening screech that slowly turns into a myriad of cries for help—all in different voices.

"What the..." Cer mutters, taking a step forward. His eyes are wide with shock.

"The souls," Thea whispers. "They're still in there."

I purse my lips. I don't dare to hope that might be true. But as I watch the energy emanating from Ze's hands and onto the demon, I start to make out different shapes emerging from that monstrous body.

"How is this possible?" Cer shakes his head. "I've never heard of a level one demon retaining the souls after ascension."

"Maybe we got in time?" I add.

"No. Without the energy of the souls, the demon would have been unable to ascend. So how the hell did he do it?"

Colorful particles of mist erupt from the demon, filling the room and creating a kaleidoscope of color. But I quickly note that they're trapped in the black circle, swirling around the air and hitting the barrier before floating away, only to attempt it all over again.

The demon's screeches intensify as he loses more and more souls, his additional limbs evaporating. From the giant hulking mass of flesh he was before, now he resembles a child in stature. His cries become sharper until suddenly they stop.

Ze takes a step back, the purple disappearing from around his hands. He regards his handiwork for a moment before he nods to himself. Before I can blink, he withdraws his sword once more and pushes the sharp tip into the demon's body. This time, it doesn't heal anymore. As Ze withdraws his sword, the demon's physical manifestation becomes fragmented, bubbles appearing on the surface. Slowly, the bubbles rip through its flesh as if it's being burned by a caustic substance. It gets eroded until nothing remains of it. Nothing but the empty floor with no stains, nor any trace of a past presence.

Ze sheaths his sword, turning his gaze to us. He steps carefully over the circle of black dust.

"The Collectors will be here any moment," Ze mentions.

"That demon... I've never seen anything like that," Cer says, his expression still one of awe. "How did you know it hadn't consumed the souls yet?"

"I didn't," Ze replies blankly.

Cer frowns.

"Why didn't you kill it directly then? You attacked it as if you *knew* the souls were still inside of it."

"Did I?" Ze muses, his gaze dipping to me. There's an odd gleam in his eyes that makes me question my previous impression of him. If he didn't know about the souls, then...

I give him a tentative smile. Maybe he's not such a bad guy after all. Sure, he might be a little gauche, socially inept, and overall rude, but he fought until the end without even knowing if it was worth it. And going by Cer's words, he could have killed the demon at any point.

But he didn't.

He seems puzzled by my smile, a frown pulling at his brows as he stares at me for a good moment.

My smile wavers under his intense perusal. What is it with him and staring—all without saying one word?

"You were really good in that fight," I add, just to fill the silence.

He's still watching me intently, a low sound erupting from his throat in what I think is meant to be a grunt of acknowledgment. But he doesn't open his mouth to say anything. He just...stares.

"Uhm," I stammer, looking at Cer and Thea for help. But they seem just as puzzled by Ze. Maybe he's just that odd. "Will I be able to see the Collectors when they come?" I decide to ask, once more to divert the attention from me.

"Probably not—" Thea starts speaking. But she doesn't get to finish as Ze interrupts her, taking a step forward and barking a low command.

"Give me your hand."

For a moment, I'm not sure what he means, but he doesn't await my answer as he grabs both of my hands in his big ones. My God, he really is a giant.

"What are you—" The words die on my tongue as he bends down, spitting on the back of my right hand before repeating the process on the other.

My mouth is hanging open in shock—for the thousandth time today? He spat on me not once, but twice now.

And on top of that, now he's smearing his spit on my arms.

Yet I can't find it in me to argue with him—not when the pain from the blistered skin is already receding. The red skin slowly heals, healthy tissue swallowing up the damaged one.

"Wow," I whisper.

I'd felt the healing effects before, but this is the first time I'm seeing his saliva in action.

"Thanks. I guess?"

He releases another grunt before stepping back. Yet his staring doesn't cease. Well, that must just be his manner. Who am I to judge after seeing him fight so well? He's officially won us the first trial, bringing me one step closer to getting Nikki back. For that alone, I'm willing to overlook any...eccentricities.

A white swirl of air appears within the circle, making the souls more erratic than before. It's almost like a portal, remaining open right in the middle while the souls move around it, almost as if being sucked inside.

"They're here," Cer says.

"I can only see a white mist." I frown.

"That's them. They're not visible to the naked eye," he explains further.

"Do we still need to convince them to go back?"

"I think at this point they're all pretty willing," Thea jokes, describing that the souls are overjoyed to have escaped the demon and that the Collectors are having an easy job getting them to cross over.

We wait for moments on end, and Thea relates to me what's happening that I cannot see. One soul after another, they say yes to the crossing. There must be over a hundred souls that the demon had accumulated over time.

"Is Olive there?" I ask, remembering the sighting.

Thea smiles.

"She is. I guess now we know how she came to be at this location when she died in another country. The demon must have eaten her soul there before coming here. And he used her projection to draw other victims."

I nod, happy with the outcome. At least now she'll be able to find peace in the afterlife.

"There are only a few left." She points out to the few particles of colored mist remaining.

When the last ones have left, the portal snaps shut and the entire room returns to its initial state.

It's rather shocking to realize that the first trial is done.

"We did it," I whisper, slowly turning toward the other three. "We did it, guys!" I squeak in excitement, jumping up and down. Thea joins me, grabbing my hands as we twirl and hop around. The guys, however, are merely looking at us with bored expressions on their faces. Cer shakes his head at Thea, already used to her shenanigans, while Ze simply stares at us. His hands are behind his back, his spine straight, his chin tipped up. He stands so still, no muscle moves on his face.

"We passed the trial," both Thea and I chant as we continue to jump up and down.

Yet our mirth quickly dissolves as I release a loud, startled scream, letting go of her hand and tripping on my feet. I fall back on my ass, staring wide-eyed at the translucent half-human, half-whatever-it-is thing in front of me. The torso resembles a young woman, but around the hips, the body is cut off, extending into a tail of sorts that doesn't touch the ground. She's floating, almost as if that tail was a cloud of smoke. She's a grayish color, wavering between a transparent white to a solid dark gray when her features are most pronounced.

"I think there's one more," I say as I point to the apparition, my voice trembling from the scare.

"That's not a soul," Ze steps forward, assessing the newcomer with curious eyes. "It's a wraith. They are used as messengers of the underworld," he explains before he sets his intense gaze on the wraith. "State your purpose," he commands her.

She floats in the air, her face serene and devoid of any emotion. It's just...blank.

"Congratulations. You have passed the first trial and are officially invited to join the second one. Is there anyone in your team who would like to withdraw?" she asks in a mechanical voice.

Ze turns to me, his eyes piercing.

"You." He points to me. "Now is the time for you to quit."

"W-what?" I burst out.

"You'll never survive in this, human. So quit while you can."

His words leave me flabbergasted. And here I was starting to warm up to him.

"No, thank you. I will not withdraw," I state firmly as I get to my feet.

"Noted," the wraith quips.

"Human," Ze addresses me in an exasperated tone, once more forgetting I actually have a name.

"Luce," I correct. "And I'm seeing this through. I wasn't useless in this round. I'm not going to bring the team down."

"Because I saved you," he fires back.

Well, I certainly can't argue with that.

"I helped," I repeat, pushing my chin up.

"The contestant has confirmed her position," the wraith continues. "What about you?" she asks the others.

Ze gives me a murderous look before he shifts his gaze to Thea.

"I'm in, too," she quickly adds.

And just like that, Cer and Ze confirm their participation, too.

"Congratulations," the wraith repeats in the same dry tone. "You can continue in the same formation or individually. How would you like to proceed?"

Before anyone can say anything, Ze responds.

"Same formation."

Thea and Cer raise their brows at him while I simply narrow my eyes, wanting to convey that I'm still mad at him.

"Noted. The second trial will take place in P'davi. You have until the end of the week to be present at the gates of P'davi for the convocation. You will be assigned your second trial upon arrival."

"P'davi?" I frown.

"It's another world," Thea whispers.

"But how will we get there?"

"You will need to find your way by following a list of clues."

Out of nowhere, she materializes an envelope that she hands to Ze.

"What happens if we don't find it?" I ask, confused.

"Since your ongoing participation has been noted, if you fail to make it to P'davi by the end of the week, you will be eliminated from the game."

I stare at her. How the hell is that fair? But I'm realizing very few things about this game are. I open my mouth to ask another question, but the wraith says a stilted goodbye before she disappears.

"What's in the envelope?" I ask as I go to Ze's side, getting up on the tips of my toes to get a better look.

He gives me a glare—shorter than his usual—before he slowly takes out a sheet of paper from the envelope. There's an illustration of five squares, one in the middle, one up, one down, one left and one right. In the middle of the first square, there's a drawing of a rising sun, together with two symbols.

I'm fairly sure the writing is Chinese. But the rest? How are we supposed to decipher that?

Cer and Thea come to get a look at the clues, but they don't seem overly concerned about the odd drawings. If anything, they look pretty indifferent, which is completely insane to me.

My blood is boiling just thinking about how unfair this is. It's almost as if getting to the second trial is a trial in itself. How else are we supposed to decipher those odd drawings?

"Why is no one freaking out about this?" I ask when no one says anything.

Ze turns his gaze to me. "Because it's not hard. Maybe for your little—"

"Human mind." I roll my eyes. "I got the general idea. So why don't you go ahead and tell me what this is all about, Mr. Know-it-all?"

He narrows his eyes at me, just watching me. For moments on end.

I clear my throat.

"You're probably just not as familiar with this as we are," Thea intervenes. "Here." She snatches the paper out of Ze's hands, earning herself a scowl. Drawing me to her side, she points to the squares. "The squares are equivalent to the five elements. Or, in Chinese mythology, it was a way to group the five sacred mountains. The second clue is the rising sun in the middle, which is associated with the east—and in Chinese mythology, that is Mount Tai. The last clue and the one that confirms the location is the Chinese symbols for *bi xi*, which is a mythological creature with the body of a tortoise and the head of a dragon. And some of the earliest and most famous representations of it are at a temple on Mount Tai."

As she finishes the small history lesson, I stare at her in awe. "How do you *know* that?" I whisper.

Wasn't she asking me what phones were just the other day?

How would she have no idea how the modern world works but know everything about Chinese mythology?

"Doesn't everyone know this?" she replies, looking genuinely confused.

"Um, no? I would have never in one million years thought of China or Mount Tai."

"But it's a holy place!" Thea bursts out.

I blink at her.

"Maybe to some people, but I've never heard of it before."

She turns to her brother and Ze.

"This is blasphemy, I tell you. *Blasphemy!*"

I'm shocked at how vehement she is about it. Thea's voice becomes increasingly distraught, to the point that her brother has to intervene, taking her in his arms and leading her to the next room over.

"What was that?" I turn to Ze, who's standing still as a stone and equally expressionless. "Why was she so hurt about that?"

His piercing stare meets mine.

"She's passionate about this subject," he answers casually.

"That was *more* than just being passionate."

"We need to leave for Mount Tai. How long will it take us to get there?" He changes the subject.

"I'm not sure. A day or so?"

He frowns.

"On foot?"

"Of course not. We'll need to take a plane to China, and then probably a car to reach Mount Tai."

He stares at me, unblinking.

"What is a plane?"

I take a deep breath. Right. These people are experts in Chinese mythology but have no idea what a plane is. But that's not the most pressing issue right now. To get on a plane, I'll need to go through passport control. It hasn't escaped me that I'm technically a fugitive—okay, maybe not that bad, but there's a warrant out on my name. The moment I check into a flight, the police will be notified.

My eyes snap shut as I ball my hands into fists in frustration. Of course nothing would be easy. How the hell am I supposed to bypass the police and get to China? Do I even need a visa to go to China? Do *they*?

need a visa to go to China? Do they even have passports?

"We'll talk more about that at dinner. I'm starving."

"Dinner," he repeats, an odd look on his face.

"Food? I don't know about you guys, but I need food to survive," I explain, my tone less than civil.

"Food. Fine. We will get food," he decrees with the same air of superiority as before.

NINETEEN

Maybe getting food wasn't such a good idea after all. I'd been so hungry after the events of the day that I ordered almost the entire menu. Knowing that Cer still had a wad of cash, I reasoned that he could afford this.

But now, noticing Thea's longing expression as she stares at my juicy steak while she's only having a mushroom risotto breaks my heart.

Her brother had been adamant she could not have meat—in any shape or form—going as far as taking the menu from her and ordering on her behalf. She clearly doesn't look too happy about that.

For himself, Cer ordered a hearty portion of vegan mac and cheese, while Ze refused to get anything. In his words, he would not deign to eat lowly human food. Well, his loss.

I stare down at the plate in front of me, my mouth already watering. Starving from all the ghost acrobatics, I'd decided to go for two portions of medium-rare ribeye steak with some mashed potatoes on the side. I've been thinking about this juicy meat for the last twenty-four hours. And now that it's in front of me...

The meat is crusted with pepper, the inner part a pink-reddish color as more juice pours out as I slice a small bite. Bringing it to my mouth, I chew slowly, enjoying the rich flavor and the soft texture.

"This is divine," I moan, unable to help myself. "Thank you for buying us dinner, Cer!"

He gives me a nod, though I doubt he heard me. He's too focused on his own food, wolfing down his mac and cheese. Going by the way he eats with so much gusto, I'd say he's pretty happy with his choice.

Even Thea, after a little pouting that she wasn't allowed meat, decides to give her food a chance. Her face lights up at the first taste of the risotto, almost as if she couldn't believe a non-meat dish could be just as yummy.

"This isn't that bad either," she notes, taking another bite.

Ze, on the other hand, is merely sitting with his spine straight, his arms crossed across his chest, and his chin tipped up —as if he's too good to even sit at the same table as us.

I notice from the corner of my eye that he's staring intently at me, probably judging me for my choice of food. But hey, I lived under the poverty line for eighteen years of my life. Back then, I could only dream of having a taste of steak. So of course the moment I could afford it, that became my favorite food. Maybe it was my way of proving to myself that I'd surpassed my circumstances—that I was now able to *afford* that type of food.

"Why can't you guys eat meat?"

"It's not that we can't eat meat. It's that we can only eat meat from a few select animals from our home," Cer explains. "We're not exactly compatible with your meat."

"Is that why Thea got sick?"

"Thea is a different story." His lips curl up as he glances at his sister. "She's still in training, so she isn't allowed *any* type of meat. Animal protein interferes with her energy flow and creates instability in her body."

I nod along, though half his words sound foreign to my ears.

"That's a poor explanation, Cerenios," Ze intervenes in a scholarly tone.

Cer raises his brows at him, tipping his chin in an amused fashion to prompt Ze to explain further.

"Do tell, then. What is a *proper* explanation?" I ask, refraining from rolling my eyes at him.

"There are only three animals in our world whose meat we can eat, but their meats are not equal," he says, raising a finger as he gets into his teaching mode. "After one has finished their training and passed their exams, they can consume the meat of the first animal, which is called a *luago*. After they have practiced for some time and have passed a few more levels, they are able to eat the meat of the second animal, which is called a *praga*. Only those who attain the highest level in their field are allowed to eat the meat of the third and most precious animal, the *doradora*."

"What do you mean by *allowed*?" I frown.

"Technically, after you've passed your first exams, your body can handle the intake of animal protein from all three," Cer fires at Ze.

Unbothered, Ze shakes his finger at him.

"Yes, one could theoretically consume meat from all three. But the *doradora* is a mythical beast that is very rare, and it's reserved only for those at the highest levels. It's actually codified in our law that no lower rank can hunt or eat its flesh. And after they made a law for the *doradora*, they made another one for the *praga*, since it's become endangered in the last few thousand years."

"I see." I nod. That sounds awfully tyrannical to me—limiting what people can eat based on their ranks. "Let me guess, you're one of those who can eat the *doradora*."

"Of course," Ze replies casually.

Thea stifles a laugh while Cer shakes his head at Ze.

"Oh, I see. So you cannot bring yourself to eat lowly human meat when you can eat your mythical beast."

"*Of course*," he replies again, this time in indignation. He narrows his eyes at me. Yet it doesn't escape me the way his gaze dips to my plate every now and then.

A mischievous smile clings to my lips as I cut another piece of steak, bringing it to my mouth. At first, his gaze is on the juice oozing from the steak, his Adam's apple bobbing up and down as he swallows. Slowly, he brings his eyes to my mouth, watching as I chew. And because I'm in an extra petty mood, I purposefully chew slowly, letting out sounds of enjoyment as I marvel at how tasty and delicious the steak is. I repeat the action, not surprised when he continues to stare at my food, his lips flattened into a thin line.

After I'm almost done with my first steak, he finally speaks.

"What meat is that?"

"Beef."

"What animal is it from?"

"A cow." I giggle. He's too clueless about this world.

Ze frowns.

Shaking my head at him, I pull out my phone—well, technically it's the phone Cer stole for me, but it's the only one I have for now—and I quickly google a picture of a cow to show him.

He nods to himself as he peruses the picture.

"It is very similar to our *praga*," he muses, bringing his hand to his chin.

"Nice," I say as I move to the next piece. What else can I reply to that? Cer and Thea are busy having a hushed conversation across the table, so that leaves me with grumpy Mr. I'm-too-good-for-you-humans—the same one who's still staring intently at my food.

"It is a good animal," he continues, almost as if he's trying to tell me *something*.

"Very good. It's the best in *our* world."

He nods again, seemingly pensive.

"And you say this is an illustrious establishment?"

"Didn't you see the prices on the menu?" I reply as I swallow my food. I reach for a glass of water to chase it down. "This is wagyu beef—the most expensive type. Those cows are more pampered than some humans."

"I see..."

I spare a glance at him, my lips trembling with mirth. He ruminates over that information, a deep frown on his face as he tries to steal peeks at my food.

"Do you want to try it?" I finally ask, knowing his dignified self would *never* ask for it.

He whips his gaze to mine, blinking slowly. He opens his mouth, and I already know he will utter some—clearly—fake outrage. So instead of waiting for his tongue-lashing, I cut half of my second steak and place it on a plate in front of him.

He stares at me, then at the steak, then back at me. He narrows his eyes at the meat for a few seconds.

"Fine. I will try this cow of yours," he says in the most serious tone ever.

I burst out laughing, and he shoots me an annoyed look. He straightens his spine and, picking up the utensils, he cuts gracefully into the steak. His movements are slow, precise. Grabbing a piece with his fork, he brings it to his mouth, his lips closing over the succulent meat.

My eyes are glued to him as I await his reaction. I'm not the only one as Thea and Cer have stopped their little tête-à-tête to gawk at Ze too.

He chews slowly, his expression pensive.

I watch his throat as he swallows, waiting for the verdict.

"So?" Thea is the first to inquire. "Tell us. How is it?"

"It is..." he trails off as he licks his lips.

We all lean forward, our ears perked. After all, what could be more important than what the mighty Ze has to say about the best cut of meat in this world?

"Passable," he eventually says.

I blink at him.

"Passable?" I repeat, my tone incredulous.

"It does not compare with a *praga*. And it is far below a *doradora*," he adds. Yet despite the meat being passable, he continues to eat. Bite after bite until the plate is cleared. Grabbing a napkin from the table, he presses it against his lips in slow, deliberate movements, wiping his mouth as if he were the King of England himself.

"Passable..." I mutter under my breath as I stab my fork into my steak, bringing the entire piece to my mouth and taking a huge bite out of it. I forgo cutting it into small bites altogether, simply eating the big chunk from the fork.

His eyes widen at me, his expression horrified.

I munch on it with gusto. He might think it's *just* passable for his *superior* palate, but it's perfectly fine for mine. And as I finish, I clean the plate with the remaining potatoes, not leaving a single drop of sauce on it.

"You humans have deplorable table manners." He tips his chin up, the corners of his mouth turning down.

That's it! I've had it with Mr. Superiority.

Taking the napkin off my lap, I dump it over my plate and get up.

"Luce?" Thea asks, her lashes fluttering in confusion.

"I'm going to the restroom to pick at my teeth since I don't want to offend His Majesty's sensibilities with my *deplorable table manners*," I grit out. Glancing at Ze before I leave, I give him a death glare that should convey my current feelings for him. For God's sake, it's always one step forward and a hundred back with this...*whatever he may be*.

And of course, since Ze cannot *not* have the last word, he raises his forefinger to make one last note.

"I am not a king—*yet*. You may call me *my liege*." His piercing gaze meets my incensed one. "But for you, *sir* will suffice." The corners of his mouth tip up.

My nostrils flare at him.

"Fine. Sir Sparkles, as you wish," I say, bending forward in a mock bow.

His mouth drops open in shock, his eyes wide. He peers down at his black outfit, which is still covered in glitter, and for the first time, he's speechless.

I stick my tongue out at him before I dash out to the restroom.

I splash water over my face, glancing into the mirror as I take in my bedraggled appearance. A shower would be nice. A change of clothes too.

Taking a deep breath, I turn off the faucet as I lean against the sink.

"Nikki?" I whisper out loud. "Are you here?"

I wait minutes on end for him to reply, but the only sound in the small restroom is that of my own breathing.

"Please, Nikki. Give me a sign if you're here," I speak louder.

For a moment, panic swells in my breast as the thought that he might have been taken by the Collectors crosses my mind. Would they do that? Take any soul in the vicinity? I must question Thea about it...

He can't be gone, right?

I know it's irrational to feel such fear strike me when I know I'll see him again at the end of this game. But just having him with me and knowing he is by my side is the support I highly need. Since we left the hacienda together, I don't think we've spent more than one day apart at a time. Certainly, never without speaking every hour or so. But now...

"Please let me know you're by my side," I whisper.

Yet it's in vain. I continue to wait, calling for him, pleading with him.

Maybe he can't show himself to me. Maybe his energy is depleted and he needs to recharge. Then he'll come back by my side.

God, even if I can't touch him, I just want to feel his presence around me. I just want to know that at a molecular or mystical level, his atoms hug mine. That is enough to keep me going.

Combing my fingers through my hair until I look halfway

decent, I prepare to go back to the dinner table. I close the door of the bathroom behind me, but as I whip my gaze up, I find Ze standing in the hallway, swaying slightly on his feet.

He frowns when he sees me, taking a step closer.

"Are you all right?" I ask, a little worried. Hadn't Cer said our food isn't compatible with their bodies?

"I... Where am I?" He looks disoriented as he rests his arm against the wall, bringing his fingers to his temples and massaging them lightly.

"You don't look too good, Ze. Maybe you should sit down?"

He doesn't answer me, merely letting out a soft grunt. His eyes are closed, his lips half-parted as if he's struggling to breathe.

"Ze?" I call his name again as I reach his side, tentatively reaching out to touch him. All previous animosities are quickly forgotten as I remember the way Thea had reacted to the bacon. It had been excruciating to watch. I can't imagine what it must be like to experience it. "Is it the meat? Is it making you sick?"

He mumbles something under his breath that I can't understand, but it's clear something's not quite right with him.

He's too much of a giant for me to carry him, but I manage to help him into one of the individual bathroom stalls. As soon as I close the door, he slips from my grip, falling to the floor with a thud. I catch myself just in time not to lose my balance and fall on top of him.

"Ze," I say as I crouch in front of him.

His eyes are droopy, his face flushed. Pursing my lips, I get to my feet and grab some paper towels, folding them together in a thick layer. I quickly wet them before I bring them to his forehead, gently tapping the makeshift cold compress across his skin.

"It's the meat, isn't it? Do you need to throw up?"

He lets out a mumbled, unintelligible sound.

"Is that a yes?" I ask, ready to help him move to the toilet.

He shakes his head lightly.

"I'll be fine," he finally says in a ragged tone.

"You don't look fine." I sigh, softly pressing the cold compress to his cheek. I slowly move it around his face. He's a little hot to the touch, but he doesn't seem like he's running a fever.

He's leaning against the wall, his head tipped back, his mouth slightly parted. His breathing is labored, and every inhale and exhale is rough and pained.

Worry mounts inside me as I don't know what I can do to help him. Should I call Cer? He seemed to know what to do with Thea. Maybe he can help Ze too.

"I should ask the others for help," I murmur.

"No," Ze rasps, catching my arm and stopping my movements. He wraps his fingers around my wrist, his hold soft but firm. "I told you I will be fine. It's just a slight inconvenience," he grits out.

His gaze pins me to the spot, lucid and unyielding.

"Cer helped Thea. I'm sure he could help you too—"

"No," he repeats. His eyes on mine, he studies me with a strange glint.

I raise my brows in question, rotating my hand in his grasp as I attempt to pull it back. He doesn't let go, however. Instead, he tightens his grip, pulling me closer.

"Why are you being nice to me?" he asks, his breath fanning my face. His voice is crisp and clear, a contrast to his previous mumblings.

"What do you mean?" I frown, trying to pull back.

"This... Why are you being nice to me?" he repeats. His expression is puzzled, his gaze searching for an ineffable something in my features.

"Why would I *not* be nice to you?" I counter. Sure, he might be a surly asshole who doesn't know how *not* to be rude, but he's not that bad. He might have attitude problems, but his actions so far have proven that he means well. And I'd rather judge someone by their actions than their words.

"No one else is," he states with a straight face. His voice doesn't falter. He truly means it.

"What about Thea and Cer? They're nice to you."

He snorts.

"They tolerate me. That is a different matter."

"How can you think that?" I blink in shock. Even to me, it's clear that Cer cares for Ze, and according to Thea, he respects and admires him.

He narrows his eyes at me.

"It is simply the way things are." He shrugs. "I know I am not...easy to be around," he admits reluctantly. He looks out of his element as he averts his gaze.

The corners of my lips tip up.

"Is that your way of apologizing for your abysmal behavior?"

"Of course not. I never apologize," he huffs out. "And you do have deplorable table manners," he points out matter-of-factly.

I shake my head at him, amused.

"You're a very odd person, Ze," I muse aloud.

"So I've been told," he replies, his shoulder blades angling up. There's that shrug again. It's the only sign that he's less than comfortable with the topic because it's the only time he's *not* his confident self.

He finally lets go of my hand, and I continue to tend to him. I swipe the compress over his forehead in slow, gentle movements, eliciting a small sound of approval from him—something akin to a kitten purring at being petted.

A hidden smile is on the edge of his lips as his lids flutter shut. His breathing is not as erratic as before, his body slowly relaxing. Even the tension in his muscles evaporates as he makes himself comfortable. His chest rises and falls in a steady rhythm, almost as if it were imitating the motion of my hand. When the compress becomes lukewarm, I lean back, about to get up to wet it again. But once more, he stops me, catching my wrist. The compress slips from my hand, but he simply flattens my palm, bringing it to his cheek and burrowing his face against it.

I'm at a loss for words as I simply stare at him.

His eyes are still closed, and his moves seem to be more

instinctual than intentional. He barely looks aware of what he's doing as he nuzzles his cheek against my palm.

"Ze?" I call out his name, but he doesn't answer. "Ze, are you all right?" I repeat, and with a deep exhale, he opens his eyes, dropping my hand.

He doesn't blink, simply staring at me intently. His eyes are almost like a swirling mass of silver, but there's a hint of color too. Curious, I lean forward to get a better look. Another flush stains his cheeks, spreading all the way to his hairline.

"Are you feeling ill again? Your cheeks are so red," I say as I swipe my thumb up his cheekbone.

His mouth opens and closes a few times, his piercing gaze still holding mine.

Before I know what's happening, he shrugs me off him, getting to his feet. Already unstable in my position, his sudden movement makes me lose my balance and fall back, landing on my ass.

"Ouch," I mumble. This is the second time I've fallen because of him.

"You've taken too many liberties, human," he states in his arrogant tone.

"A thank you would be enough." I roll my eyes at him.

He arranges his clothes, dusting himself off before turning to leave. I get up, too, still puzzled by his reaction—and, if I'm honest, his entire persona.

"Why did you eat the meat?" I inquire softly.

He half turns, and for a moment, I don't think he's going to answer me—not with the animosity I spot in his gaze. Spine straightened, eyes narrowed, he's back to the rude Ze from before.

"You liked it." He gives me a clipped reply, the tone almost... accusatory?

"But I *can* eat it," I point out with a raised brow. "You know you can't."

"I was curious." He shrugs, looking me straight in the eyes. *Another* shrug?

"And? Did you satisfy your curiosity?" I tilt my head to the side.

"Not yet."

My lashes flutter in surprise at his answer, but before I can recover and ask him what he means, he's already out the door.

I trail behind him, going back to the table.

Cer and Thea are wrapped in an argument about the dessert. Ze is back in his seat, leaning back and watching their exchange with disinterest.

As I resume my seat, Thea looks up at me, giving me a brilliant smile.

"Luce! You have to try this chocolate cake. It's absolutely delicious. And the server assured me it doesn't have any animal products in it," she says as she pushes a plate in front of me. It's then that I realize they ordered dessert for all of us.

Ze is staring at the untouched plate with reticence but also a smidgeon of longing.

I ignore him as I grab a spoon and take a bite of the cake, my eyes widening in surprise.

"Oh, wow. This is amazing."

"Isn't it? Cer is the only one who doesn't like it." She rolls her eyes at him. "But you know what that means? More cake for me," she declares enthusiastically before she swaps her empty plate for Cer's full one.

He shakes his head at her, but I can spot the slight curl of his lips as he watches her from the corner of his eye.

"You heard her. This is vegan. You won't get sick from it." I nod to Ze, avoiding looking at him.

He doesn't reply, but he pulls his plate closer, taking a bite of cake. Then another. And just like the steak, the cake is gone within minutes. Yet even then, he doesn't say a word.

Of course, it would go against his ego to admit that lowly human food would be so delicious that he would eat an entire portion.

"Right, Thea, I have a question," I say as I remember my

initial concerns. The whole Ze debacle made me lose track of my little ghost problem for a moment.

"Yes?"

"If there were any other souls around when the Collectors came, would they take them as well?"

She purses her lips as she thinks about it.

"Possibly. They'd see it as a bonus assignment."

Her answer deflates me.

"I see." I strain a smile.

TWENTY

od, but I hope that wasn't the case and Nikki is still around—he *has* to be around.

"Why are you asking?"

"Never mind." I shake my head. "We should probably plan our next steps since we have until the end of the week to get to P'davi." I change the topic. The most I can do for Nikki right now is to focus on the game and win. Regardless of whether he is with me or not, the end goal is the same.

"Here," I say as I pull out my phone and open the maps app. "This is the route we have to take to get to Mount Tai." I point at the screen. "First, we take the plane from JFK to Jinan Yaoqiang International Airport, and then we'll head to the mountain via train. Once there, we can figure out the best way to get to the temple."

"But that's...more than a day of travel," Thea bursts out, her expression shocked. "We can just tele—" She jumps out of her seat, yelping in pain. Turning to Cer, she gives him a wounded look.

"Sit down and shut up, Thea," Cer tells her, his voice holding an edge to it.

She opens her mouth to argue with him but eventually just sighs and plops back in her seat.

"We will do as you said." Cer nods at me.

"There is just one issue." I force a smile.

They all turn to stare at me, waiting for me to elaborate.

"Well, you can't travel abroad because you don't have a passport," I point out, my cheeks heating up as I think of the *other* reason we might not be able to leave the country.

"It will be fine," Ze comments nonchalantly. "No one will question us."

"But there is another *small* issue."

Once more, they wait for me to continue.

"You see, I'm wanted by the police, and the moment I step foot into an airport, they will come after me. They probably already have a notice out for me at all ports of exit."

Thea blinks at me.

"Why? Weren't you telling me just a few days ago not to commit any crimes because the police would come for me?" she asks, pointing her finger at me accusingly.

"Ah, well... I didn't do it. I'm innocent."

"Don't they all say that?" Ze snorts from the side.

"You're not helping, Sir Sparkles," I grit at him under my breath.

His eyes flash at me, his body tensing.

"Tell us what happened," Cer luckily interrupts.

"It's my husband's family. They're accusing me of stealing some money, but I didn't do it. If anything, they're the ones who stole from us." I sigh.

"Husband? You're married?" Thea's eyes widen, her eyes skirting from me to Ze.

Odd.

"Yes." I give her a sad smile. "But he died a couple of weeks ago."

"He's dead. That makes you *not* married," Ze grumbles.

I inhale sharply at his words. Of all the rude things he could have said...

"Not for much longer. Once I win the game, he'll come back to me," I say, my tone more biting than I intended. But Nikki is where I draw the line—always. I won't let anyone talk badly about him or our relationship.

Ze stares at me, his pupils narrowing to two slits.

"He is still dead. That means he is no longer your husband and you are not married," he continues, very much pleased with himself.

For God's sake, why is he focusing on the semantics?

"Regardless of whether he's dead or alive, he's still my husband and will always be my husband." I grind my teeth, clenching my fists as a wave of violence washes over me.

"I do not agree with you, human." He crosses his arms over his chest, pushing his chin up.

"I don't care if you agree with me or not. I don't care about your opinion at all," I huff out.

For some reason, that seems to strike a chord in him as he turns sharply, his hand suddenly on my wrist.

"Ze, what's wrong with you? Leave the poor girl alone!" Thea intervenes, reaching across the table to untangle his fingers from my wrist. "You're ruining the mood," she tells him, her words charged with hidden meaning.

Ze looks at her, then looks at me, then looks at her again. He takes a deep breath, letting go of my hand before proceeding to ignore us again.

"What the hell is wrong with him?" I mumble under my breath.

"Don't mind him, Luce. He's just...weird," she tries to assure me.

"Right," I say, giving him a death glare. "Well, they accused me of stealing his money," I start, telling them about the entire debacle with the inheritance and that they arranged everything, including Nikki's death.

"The bastards." Thea slams her fist on the table. "They need to pay, Luce!"

"Oh, they will. I haven't forgotten about them. I'm just prior-itizing my husband first."

A low growly sound erupts from my side, but this time I

don't even bother to look, knowing I'll likely just get angrier with him.

"You don't have to worry about the police," Cer speaks. "Thea can work her charm on anyone. That is a low-level skill that doesn't demand a lot of energy, so we should be able to get on the plane without any trouble."

"Low level?" Thea's eyes widen.

"You know what I mean, Thea." He sighs. I don't think he's in the mood for yet another fight.

"But still. *You* do it if it's so *low level*," she challenges, imitating his voice.

"You know I can't," he answers calmly.

Thea merely smirks.

"Okay, that's good. There's a flight that leaves tomorrow morning. That gives us just enough time to get some supplies before we leave for the airport."

"What supplies?" Thea asks.

"We need some new clothes, especially for you." I point to Ze. "You can't go around in your odd costume stained with glitter."

He glares at me.

"You too." I turn to Cer. "You need more casual clothes. Same goes for you, Thea. You can't walk around in a dress you stole from the theatre."

"You stole the clothes too," she quickly points out.

"And I can't walk around in stolen clothes either," I continue with a smile.

"Let's get that over with," Cer says as he stands up. Taking out a wad of cash from his pocket, he dumps it on the table. Thea and Ze stand up too, moving toward the exit.

I quickly run after them. "Uhm... That's not how you do it. You need to wait for the bill."

No one answers me.

"No." I shake my head vigorously. "That's not happening."

Cer and Thea are laughing behind us, giving me a hint into who the culprits behind this epic fashion fail might be.

"This has to go," I say as I jump up to grab the rainbow-colored hat off his head. "This has to go, too." I point to the washed-out overalls that are a few sizes too small. Even the shirt he's wearing is so tight on his torso the seams are about to burst.

"Are you having fun, guys?" I turn suddenly. Thea hides behind Cer, but she still can't stop herself from giggling. For themselves, they chose nice, proper clothes. Thea's dressed in a pair of thick tights, a white wool midi dress and a cashmere cardigan on top of it. Cer went for a pair of cargo pants and a sweater—all in appropriate sizes for him.

But for Ze... They really made a mockery of him, and I don't know how he accepted it.

"You look ridiculous," I mumble.

"He chose it himself," Thea chimes in.

I frown.

"You did?"

His lips are flattened in a thin line, his muscles straining against the flimsy clothing. Without saying a word, he raises his arm and points to something.

I blink repeatedly as I take in what he's showing me. It's the mannequin in the window, and it's wearing exactly the same clothes as him. Except, the mannequin is much smaller and skinnier.

"That's..." I take a deep breath. "That may be a good look for some people, but it's not for you. Come, we're going to find you some clothes that actually fit," I say as I grab the sleeve of his shirt, pulling him back to the clothing racks.

"But the shop seller said this is the latest trend," he finally speaks, his voice low. His eyes, too, are looking anywhere but at me.

"The latest trend doesn't mean it will work on you." I sigh.

"But—"

"No buts, Ze. We need to find you something else, and quick."

For some reason, he looks dejected as he follows me around the clothing racks. God, did he actually like those horrendous clothes? Not only were they not very nice, but they were not in the least flattering on him.

"But the shop seller said this is what popular people wear." He makes one last attempt at a weak protest, and I finally pause. Gazing up at him, I note a slight flush on his cheeks and none of his previous aggrandizing attitude.

"And you want to be popular?" I inquire softly.

"I... Forget about it." He shakes his head.

"I'm sure we could find something similar—"

"No. Just forget about it," he repeats, his voice thick. His blank, arrogant expression is back on, and I have to wonder if I imagined that small glimpse of vulnerability on his face.

"Okay." I nod, a little puzzled about his attitude. But as I watch him from the corner of my eye, I realize he's quite confused about himself, too.

Maybe it's the foreign world, and he's just trying to fit in. But at the same time, why would someone with Ze's ego *want* to fit in?

With not too much time to spare, I choose a similar sweater to the one Cer had gotten since that's likely to fit him properly. I get it in black and the largest size available. Next, it's pants. I manage to find a pair of loose black pants that might fit him. Since he's such a fan of black, this should work just fine.

With the clock ticking, I push him into the changing room to try on his clothes while I also quickly scramble to find clothes for myself.

Thea and Cer are having fun in the accessories section, and I fly past them as I quickly browse the available options. Since this is going to be a long journey, I need something warm and comfortable.

I grab a pair of leggings from the sports section, adding a pair of warm tights too—just in case. I also get a sports bra that won't be too much of a bother, then quickly survey the underwear aisle and pick up a few to have throughout the trip. For the top, I decide to go with a couple of warm layers topped by a big purple hoodie. I purposefully choose a large size so that it looks oversized on me, the hem reaching my knees.

Finally done, I get back to the changing rooms to check on Ze. This time, luckily, his clothes fit him. I give him a thumbs-up —which I realize he doesn't know the meaning of—after which we pay and we're finally ready to go to the airport.

As we get there, we successfully snag four tickets to Jinan, but the only available ones were in the economy class. With Thea's charm, we manage to get through airport security by only showing a blank agenda that they think is a passport. The staff doesn't even scan it, merely glancing at it and letting us move forward.

It's only when we're ushered into the airplane that the problems start to arise.

Thea is marveling at everything around while Cer and Ze look downright uncomfortable.

"Damn it," I mutter softly as I realize with their size, they won't have an easy time fitting in their seats. And this is such a long journey, too...

We're pointed to our seats by one of the air stewardesses, and though I'd planned to sit with Thea, I decide to ask her to switch places with one of the guys. It would be too torturous to have them both crammed in one place when they will barely be able to fit in a seat.

"But, Luce." She sighs, not too happy with the idea.

"You can sit with Ze if you don't want to argue with your brother," I offer, knowing how easy it is for them to squabble.

"No way! I'd rather fight with Cer a hundred times over than have"—she leans in to whisper—"that surly man next to me. No, thank you. You can endure his company for the flight."

"Fine." I chuckle. "I'll just ignore him and it will be fine."

Reaching our seats, I inform the guys of the changes. Cer

rolls his eyes while Ze merely stares at me unblinkingly—as is his habit.

While Thea and Cer make themselves comfortable in their seats behind us, I turn to Ze.

"You can have the window seat," I tell him. He should have a bit more freedom there than in the middle seat. And we don't know who's going to sit next to us either... Yes, the window seat is best for him.

He regards me for a moment before he gives me a brisk nod, folding his big frame in the seat. As I slide next to him, I lift up the armrest so that he can have a little more room.

"I'm sorry about this. You'll have to bear with it for a few hours." I give him a tight smile.

"Are all humans as small as you?"

"What?" I frown. "Not really. I'm on the smaller side for a woman. But the men are much larger. A lot have problems with these seats too."

He nods to himself.

"Was your dead husband small, too?"

My lashes flutter in surprise. He's staring forward, his back straight, his hands resting on his thighs.

"No, he was not a small man," I mention, a smile pulling at my lips as I remember how easily Nikki could carry me in his arms—even with his busted knee. Although he hated the outside world, he'd always had a fondness for physical exercise, and he installed a gym in every home we ever owned. We'd sometimes work out together, even though I was not the best at it. But I would just love to watch him, sometimes lying on a yoga mat with a book, spying on him as he was doing his sets.

When he was shot in the knee, he was devastated to find that he couldn't move as well as he used to, but he didn't let that keep him back. He was always a fighter. And even in his last days, all he was thinking was how to fight more, harder—how to go to war with himself and his own psyche. My eyes are moist as I bring the back of my hand to wipe the tears clinging to my lashes.

In the beginning, when the grief had been too strong—too blinding—I hadn't been able to see anything other than the pain in my soul. Now, though, I can look back and be proud of my husband and everything he did.

Four more trials, and I'll see him again.

And by God I will *not* give up. I'll see this through to the end and I'll get my wish. If only his soul were still around...

I sigh deeply at the thought.

Ze's fingers dig into his legs, his gaze still forward. He doesn't probe further about Nikki, and I don't say anything more, the silence offering a comforting embrace.

The plane slowly fills up, more people coming in. Ze is alert and curious as he watches everyone, probably taking note of how other people look since it doesn't seem that he's been around too many humans before.

"Is your species so much more different than humans?" I ask.

"Of course. We are much stronger," he replies smoothly—not that I expected him to say anything different.

"Then are all men similar in size to you and Cer? Thea isn't that much taller than me, so I'm assuming not all of you are giants."

"No."

"No? That's it?" I raise my brows at him.

He narrows his eyes at me.

"You harpies are quite odd," I muse, watching him closely.

"H-harpies?" He blinks, his eyes wide with shock.

"Well, that's what you are, no?" I smile sweetly.

"That is...correct." He swallows uncomfortably, probably finding it hard to keep up the lie when the mere notion of it offends his superior sensibilities. Yet this just confirmed my theory.

When I'd had a moment to myself, I quickly googled harpies in an attempt to learn more about them. The doubts had already been planted after what happened at the theatre, but I'm a complete newbie to this world, so what would I know? But Wikipedia does have an entry for *harpies* and it describes them as half maidens, half birds. More research into Greek mythology yielded the same results. Since neither Cer nor Ze are maidens, I fail to see how they could be harpies.

Now it remains to be seen what they really are. That little lie aside, I find it easy to trust them. My instincts tell me that I can count on them, and I've already seen the evidence of that during the first trial. But that doesn't mean I won't keep my guard up. I only have one purpose in this game—getting Nikki back. Anything else is moot.

The plane continues to fill up, and just when I'm about to rejoice that maybe the seat next to me will be empty, someone comes. A man in his thirties gives me a tentative smile as he places his luggage in the overhead compartment before he settles in his seat.

"Hi." He turns to me. "I'm Matthew. We'll be on this flight for quite some time, no?" he says with a nervous laugh.

I force my lips into a smile, not wanting to be rude. God, how I hate it when strangers are talkative for no reason.

Before I can answer, Ze suddenly stands up.

"Ze." I gasp, grabbing onto him for fear he might hit his head on the ceiling. "Careful, please," I whisper, and he barely avoids a direct hit as he bends forward.

"I do not like the window seat," he states in a tense voice. Turning ever so slightly, his gaze meets that of nervous Matthew and Ze regales him with one of his glares. Everyone is staring at us.

"You will change seats with me, human. Now," he commands me, his voice chilling.

"But, Ze, the middle seat is too small for you," I murmur a weak protest. "It's a fifteen-hour flight. You'll be miserable."

His eyes move from Matthew to me.

"You will move," he repeats.

Before I can say anything more, he grabs me by the waist, easily lifting me up and changing our seats. He carefully places me in the window seat while he wiggles his big frame into the middle one. Shaking my head at him, I scoot over to give him a little more space.

Ze nods to himself, a slight smile on his lips. But as he looks at Matthew, the smile turns into a scowl.

"You do not talk to her," he tells him in a stern tone. Matthew's eyes widen as he glances at me with concern. "You do not look at her," Ze continues, his voice tightening. "You do not acknowledge she exists."

"I-I-I'm sorry, man," Matthew stammers, quickly averting his glance and making himself small in his seat. "I didn't know she was with you."

"She is. With me." Ze nods, giving him one more harsh stare before turning away.

TWENTY-ONE

"What's wrong with you?" I pinch his arm, leaning in to whisper. "He was just making small talk."

"I hate small talk," he replies, baring his teeth.

"Well, it's something we humans do, so you'll have to get used to it."

He purses his lips as he gives me a strange look.

"I hate humans," he mutters under his breath.

"Wow, thank you." I roll my eyes. "You're just so full of compliments today, Ze." I shake my head at him as I lean back into my seat, crossing my arms over my chest and deciding to ignore him. Yet it seems that I'm not able to, especially as he continues to quietly seethe, his muscles tense and bulging even through his loose clothing. His chest vibrates with low, guttural sounds that once more attract attention to us.

"Excuse m-me?" Matthew raises his hand to signal a passing flight attendant. She stops by his side with a smile, and he beckons her closer so he can whisper something in her ear. It's soon clear what he must have said to her because she gives Ze a once-over before she nods to Matthew.

"There is another seat available in the back. Please follow me."

Matthew doesn't even look at Ze or me as he quickly gets his luggage out and scurries away to the back.

"What was *that* about?" Thea asks from behind.

"You should ask Ze," I reply dryly.

He doesn't say anything, but his lips curl around the corners.

The boarding is soon over, and we're instructed to put on our seat belts and prepare for takeoff. The plane taxis on the runway, gaining speed before it inclines for takeoff.

Ze's eyes widen, his hands fisting the material of his pants.

"Are you okay?" I ask softly.

"Fine," he gives me a curt reply, his gaze forward.

I watch him from the corner of my eye for a few moments, noting the tension in his body continues climbing instead of diminishing.

It's his first time flying. I can imagine how jarring the experience would be for him. I remember my first time on a plane. It had been after the fire at the hacienda, and Nikki and I had moved to Texas. I'd been petrified the entire flight, but having him there, holding my hand throughout the entire journey, had helped immensely.

Tentatively, I reach out, placing my hand on top of his.

I don't know what it is about him and his silent struggles with this world that tug at my heartstrings. Maybe it's that I relate to him because I was once a stranger in the world too. Yet the one difference is that I had someone to help me through the transition. He...well, he doesn't *want* anyone's help.

Somehow, I find that so pitiful and lonely.

"It takes only a few minutes," I assure him, squeezing his hand in comfort.

He turns toward me, his piercing eyes meeting mine. I brace myself for a few of his scathing words. But he doesn't speak. Slowly, he brings his gaze to his lap where our hands are. He stares at our hands so intently, he forgets all about the takeoff or the fact that the plane is already in the air.

"See, it wasn't so bad." I give him a tentative smile.

He doesn't return it—I don't think the man is capable of a genuine smile. He simply nods at me, softly taking my hand off his and depositing it in my lap. I guess it could have been worse. Something along the lines of—*how dare you touch me, human?* Yes, it could have definitely been worse. My lips tremble with mirth at the thought of those scenarios.

As the plane stabilizes in the air, I lower the armrest on my side and on Ze's side so he can have more space. Then I turn off his monitor and plug in the complimentary earbuds to show him what he can do to pass the time.

At first, he doesn't seem interested. But as I get to the list of shows he can watch, his interest is piqued. He leans forward, his eyes wide and curious.

"This magic of yours," he starts, his expression pensive. "It traps people inside the small box?"

"It's not magic. It's technology. Remember the billboards in Times Square? It's the same."

He blinks.

"So they were not actual people? I was under the impression they were putting on a live show from those boxes," he adds.

I try to hold my laughter in and fail.

"No, they're not." I giggle. He gives me a harsh look. Getting my mirth under control, I proceed to explain—to the best of my ability—how movies and TV shows work.

"I see." He nods. "So these are visual stories. But it's not magic."

"Yes, that's exactly right."

"And I can watch whatever story I want?"

I point to the screen, showing him how he can operate it with his fingers.

"It's like that smartphone of yours," he murmurs, a hint of excitement in his voice. He's entranced by it as he starts swiping in all directions, exploring every option. Eventually, he settles on a TV show called

Game of Thrones.

With Ze preoccupied with his show, I direct my attention to

my own device, wondering if I should watch something or try to sleep. I'm quite tired after all that ghost-hunting turned demon-hunting. While I debate my options, I browse the selection of TV shows. Suddenly, though, Ze pulls on my headphones to get my attention.

"What?" I frown.

"How dare you make me watch this, human?" he grits out in the most disgusted voice.

I flutter my lashes in confusion.

He points to the screen, his nostrils flaring with anger. Two fully naked people are going at it like rabbits. The woman's breasts are bouncing up and down. The volume is high enough that I can hear her moans from his earbuds.

"Oh," I murmur. "I'm guessing your world doesn't have R-rated stuff?" I try to make light of the situation, but Ze is not amused. If anything, he's incensed.

"This is blasphemous," he mutters as he presses all over the screen in an attempt to turn it off.

"Are you a prude, Z?" I raise my brow at him.

"It is against the law to have any licentious display in public," he hisses, "much less between an unmated couple."

"I don't understand," I frown. Reaching forward, I press the back button to take him out of the video since this is clearly offensive to him.

"Is Ze giving you any trouble, Luce?" Thea asks. Looking up, I see she's on her feet, resting her elbows on the top of my chair as she peeks down at us.

"He's offended about nudity in a TV show." I roll my eyes.

"Oh." She giggles.

Ze turns sharply to her, giving her his signature death glare.

"Is this really illegal in your world?" I ask, thinking I may have actually committed a faux pas.

Thea beckons me closer to whisper in my ear.

"It is *technically* illegal," she adds drily. "Of course, it's always the males that are the exception. As long as they're quiet and careful about their liaisons, people turn a blind eye. But if females are caught doing the same thing, they are ostracized, or worse."

"Then why is Ze so insulted by it?"

"Because he's...different? You've probably noticed that he doesn't understand nuances. For him, a law is a law." She sighs. "He's the only person I know who is beyond temptation in that regard."

"That is...odd."

Ze clears his throat, his eyes narrowed at us.

"He *is* odd," she says intentionally louder so he can hear.

He doesn't react to it, merely staring her down some more—which seems to be his only reaction in most situations.

"Then why is it illegal in the first place if there are exceptions?"

"It's an archaic law and when it was passed, it was supposed to reduce pregnancies between unmated couples. And when that didn't work as intended, they actually made it *illegal* for a female to have a child without being officially mated." Thea shakes her head in disgust. "We have a *lot* of archaic laws. It's all so they can control who reproduces and how they reproduce."

"That's...a lot of laws."

"Tell me about it." She rolls her eyes. "I can't eat what I want. I can't wear what I want. I can't do *anything* I want," she huffs out, annoyed.

"What happens if someone breaks those laws?"

She pauses, her features tense.

"It depends on the offense and who commits it. Some have more leeway than others, but if a female has a child outside her mated bond, then all bets are off. It's the one thing that no one will overlook. If it's with a different species, then... I don't even want to imagine." She shudders.

"Your world sounds even worse than mine." I give her a sympathetic smile.

"And that's just the tip of the iceberg."

"Why don't you leave? Come live here? Surely you could—"

"No," she states before I can even finish my sentence. "Just as there are Collectors for rogue souls, there are Trackers for us. Even if I tried to leave, they would *always* find me."

Ze snorts from the side.

"The Trackers are your last concern. Cerenios would never allow you to leave, Erithea."

Cer grunts an affirmative from behind.

"So you see, there's nowhere to go for me." She gives a fake laugh as she settles back in her chair, her features tense and weary.

"Why doesn't this all surprise me?" I mutter under my breath as I give Ze the side-eye. "Of course you'd come from a hyper-misogynistic society. Your rudeness should have clued me in."

"Watch your words, human," he warns in a biting tone before pausing. "What do you mean by misogynistic?"

"It means you hate women."

He frowns.

"That is false. I do not hate females. I do not care about them at all."

What? He's puzzled by the exchange, too.

"I meant your society, not you as an individual," I explain, realizing he took it quite literally.

"That is false as well. Females are revered in our society."

"Let me guess, for their wombs?" I raise a brow.

He opens his mouth then closes it.

"Yes and no," he says as he puts his forefinger up. Oh, here comes professor Ze again. "It is true that they are the mothers of our future leaders, but females can hold the same type of functions as men in our society, including warriors. In fact, despite the difference in size, females in our world can sometimes be stronger than their male counterparts. As such, your *misogynistic* comment is false."

He nods to himself as he finishes, clearly pleased with himself.

"Well, Thea has a different account," I shoot back.

"What Erithea failed to mention is that our laws apply to

everyone. If a male fathers a child outside the mating bounds, he is also punished. The same goes for food, clothes, and behavior. Depending on your level of skill, standing in society and responsibility, certain things are expected of you. Cerenios and I, for example, are held to much stricter standards because of our positions in the army."

"Oh... I'm sorry for assuming," I say. I'm embarrassed that I jumped so quickly to conclusions without hearing the entire story.

"You are forgiven," he smoothly replies.

"This is a bit of a trigger for me." I laugh nervously. "I grew up in a community that subjugated women and only treated them like objects," I continue. For some reason, I feel the need to justify myself.

"You were subjugated?" Ze frowns, his gaze on mine.

"Technically, I was a slave." I shrug.

"A slave? You humans still practice slavery?"

"There are people who still do. It doesn't mean it has to be legal."

"Who? Tell me who it was and I will annihilate them," he rasps, his nostrils flaring with anger.

On my behalf?

"They're already dead. But thank you." I give him a smile. He really isn't that bad once you get over the rough exterior.

He humphs.

"In *this* life..." he trails off, a smile pulling at his lips.

I don't quite get his meaning, but I choose not to dwell on it since the mere topic of the hacienda tends to make me deeply uncomfortable. Instead, I browse through the selection of shows and choose something PG-13 for Ze. And what other better option than anime? There are a few episodes of Naruto available, and I suggest he watch those. Of course, after the first episode plays, I expect him to have some more complaints. But to my surprise, he watches it with great interest.

I make sure that Cer and Thea are also comfortable before huddling closer to the window and closing my eyes to sleep.

TWENTY-TWO

"You need to evacuate the aircraft, sir."

I yawn as I nuzzle my cheek against the soft pillow cushioning my head.

"No." The tone is clipped, the voice familiar.

I slowly open my eyes, sleep still clinging to my lashes. Tipping my head up, my eyes meet Ze's steely ones. My hands are wrapped around his arm, my head resting on his shoulder. I quickly sober up as I realize I've been intruding on his personal space, using him as my pillow.

"Sorry," I mumble, pulling back with a guilty smile. He's going to tell me off any second now, I just know it. Yet to my surprise, he doesn't. He merely stares at me intently, his eyes roving over me curiously.

"You're awake," he notes.

I nod, rubbing my eyes and stretching my upper body.

"You need to leave, sir," the woman continues.

I blink a few times as I focus on my surroundings. The plane is... empty. There's only me, Ze, and the flight attendant glaring aggressively at Ze.

"Where's everyone else?" I ask, worried something might have happened while I was passed out from sheer exhaustion.

"Everyone else has left already. Half an hour ago," she

enunciates each word clearly. "Everyone but you two because your boyfriend refused to move and disrupt your sleep."

"What? He's not my boyfriend," I immediately reply. "Ze, what's happening? What did you do?"

"You were sleeping," he comments, folding his arms across his chest.

"I'm so sorry about the inconvenience," I hurry to say, getting to my feet and taking Ze along with me. Since the only luggage we have has been checked in—including his precious sword—it takes us only a few seconds to scramble out of our seats and leave. "So sorry," I repeat as I give a guilty smile to yet another flight attendant on our way out.

Just as we exit the aircraft, I spot a few security guards heading our way—intent on forcefully evacuating us, no doubt. We walk briskly before they can question us, though Ze looks more than ready to wage war.

"Where are Thea and Cer?" I ask as I pull Ze along by his hand.

"They left."

"And they just left us behind?" I frown.

"They did," he answers.

"Goodness, Ze, you can't just do whatever you want! The planes run on a schedule and people have to do their jobs."

"You were sleeping," he repeats.

"You should have woken me up when we landed."

"You were tired," he counters.

"It doesn't matter." I shake my head.

Stopping abruptly, I look up at him.

"Just as there are rules in your world, there are rules in mine too. You need to make an effort to respect that while you're here, okay?"

He studies me for a moment before he gives me a grunt—that I take as acknowledgment.

It doesn't take us long to find Cer and Thea.

Cer is grumpily trailing behind while Thea admires the

many clothes and handbags available at the duty-free. She already has a few bags in her hands.

"I see you've been busy," I note with a raised brow.

"Oh, Luce. There are so many stores! I got you something, too. Look," she says excitedly as she opens one of the bags to show me a purple dress. Immediately, my anger melts away at her thoughtful gesture.

"Thank you," I murmur. "Still, you should have woken me up. I was so embarrassed to hold the plane behind."

"You're awake now. That's all that matters," she replies nervously, her gaze flittering from Ze to me.

I roll my eyes. Ze and his peculiarities. It will take me some time to get used to all of his *quirks*.

Since nothing too bad occurred, I decide to let it slide. Thea continues to show me what she bought as we walk toward the food court to grab a snack before our next flight.

Luckily, our next flight is in a couple of hours, so that leaves us with plenty of time to dawdle.

After we eat, we manage to get to our transfer without any issues. The journey is a short one, and in no time, we arrive at Jinan Airport.

"I still can't believe how well your charm works," I tell Thea as we successfully pass through immigration. She only needed to tell security a few words, and we were let through, as if we had both official passports *and* a visa.

"It's a pretty useful *low-level* trick," she says, giving Cer a smug look.

As we head out of the airport, we grab a few snacks and Thea secures us train tickets to Mount Tai.

We embark on the train, oddly keeping the same seating arrangements from before. The only difference is that this time, the seats are facing each other. Ze is by my side on the aisle seat, and Thea is in front of me, next to Cer.

"Okay, guys," I say as I take out the map I bought at the station. "You said we need to reach Dan Miao Temple, which is here." I point to a spot on the map. "But what after? How are we going to find the entrance to P'davi? And how are we going to find that place, P'davi?"

"Don't worry about that." Thea waves her hand dismissively. "You'll see when we get there."

Somehow, that's not exactly reassuring. Especially as we'll need to hike up the mountain on foot since no car will take us up the narrow roads.

The journey to Mount Tai is unusually quiet. Cer is busy with a game he found in a magazine, Thea marvels at her new purchases, and Ze is polishing his sword. He's doing what...

I whip my head around, gawking at him.

"You can't do that in public," I hiss in a low voice.

People are already staring at him, some of them with fear in their eyes.

He doesn't reply, continuing to clean his sword with a disinterested expression. The conductor passes by to check our tickets, and although he clearly seems worried about Ze's sword, he doesn't dare voice his concern, merely giving him a reverent nod.

"I can't believe this," I mutter under my breath.

Ze's lips curl up at my annoyance.

We get off at our stop and head to the ticket booth at the base of the mountain. Not surprisingly, there are a *lot* of tourists around, which on one hand, makes me feel a little better about the length of journey we're about to embark on, while on the other, it makes me uneasy because that means more opportunities for the odd trio to get into trouble and attract unwanted attention.

The ascent up the mountain is strenuous. The online guide indicated it would take us around four or five hours to get to the top if we are in good physical condition. Of course *they* are in perfect shape. Me? Not so much. Which results in me being out of breath only one hour into our hike.

How the hell am I going to last for another four hours?

"Can we please take a short break? I need to catch my breath and drink a sip of water," I say as I huff out loud. Bent at a ninety-degree angle and with my hands on my knees, I do my best to breathe in and out to stabilize myself.

"Humans." Ze bristles.

Thea takes my hand, helping me to a boulder by the side of the road. She hands me the bottle of water and gently pats my back.

I look at the three of them looking entirely unbothered, not one hair out of place, not one drop of sweat on their foreheads.

"How are you guys not tired? My lungs are on *fire!*"

"They have military training," Thea points out.

"And you? What's *your* explanation?"

"I'm training now?" she answers sheepishly. I shake my head at her non-answer, gulping down some water as I rub circles on my chest. The shoes I'm wearing are not making this any easier. The soles are thin, causing my feet to chafe against the rough terrain. At this rate, I'll end up with blisters all over.

Despite that, however, it only takes looking at Ze's smug expression for me to launch myself to my feet and give them the signal that we can continue.

I need to push myself if I want to be rewarded at the end. I'm not that naïve to not realize that this game will likely sap me of all my strength, both physical and mental. But rewards like that are not given, they are earned. And I need to earn my place among the five who will make it to the end.

Gritting my teeth, I push my body forward, using my determination as fuel.

But every step hurts.

Maybe I should have taken Nikki up on his daily gym trips. Or, maybe, instead of reading while he was working out, I should have also put in some effort.

I trail behind, the distance between me and the others increasing with every step. In spite of my effort, I'm no match for them. Ze is the first, walking with unnatural ease. His spine is straight, his hands behind his back—his usual unbothered stance. Behind him, Cer always keeps a slight distance. I noticed this before, too, and I wonder if this has to do with their ranking in the army. Perhaps it's his way of showing respect to his superior.

Thea alternates between walking, hopping, and running, seemingly having an unlimited supply of energy. She's perpetually excited as she looks around at the scenery, calling my attention to this or that, or dragging Cer along to show him an insect or a plant. If I'm honest, the scenery *is* breathtaking—*and* breath-taking. If I didn't feel as though I'm dying, maybe I could enjoy it more.

We're nestled between the mountains as we follow a winding path to the top. I can see our destination on the horizon, but the distance is deceiving, as I'm learning every ten minutes or so when I check our progress. There are hundreds of other people around, maybe thousands. All taking pictures and stopping to admire the natural beauty around. They're not pressed for time as they go at a relaxed pace, valuing the experience itself more than the end goal of reaching the peak.

A sad smile tugs at my lips as I look to my right, at the green expanse of forest shadowed by the gray tips of the mountains. If only Nikki were here... We would take our time on the climb, walking hand in hand, joking, and playing around as we wondered at the beauty of nature. It would be one of our bucket list destinations, and we would revel in the feel of being outside, free and without any worry. He would no longer be weighed down by his anxiety, and there would be no more danger to our lives. We'd simply...be.

Did we ever even have that luxury? Ironic that we had so much money we couldn't have spent it in ten lifetimes, and yet, we never had the most important thing—peace of mind.

I suddenly stop, turning toward the edge of the road as I stare at the sprawling cliffs. Closing my eyes, I take a deep breath as I become one with the sounds of nature—tuning in to the very essence of life.

Are you here, Nikki? Are you with me?

Thea explained that young spirits are weak, and I wonder if that's the case with Nikki. Did he deplete his strength when he appeared in front of me at the theatre? Because the only other alternative would be that he got taken by the Collectors, and regardless of how insignificant that may be in the grand scheme of things, I would *hate* for it to be true. I need him by my side, always with me.

I just...need him.

A tear falls down my cheek, a cold breeze brushing against my skin and making me shiver. My eyes instantly snap open, my gaze greedily roaming around as I look for him. The breeze...that's his signature. Is he really here?

I run in circles, chasing the wind, all in hopes that he might give me another sign—that he might show himself before me.

Yet it's all in vain.

Maybe he's too weak.

Maybe.

My breath becomes ragged as I look for him in every crevice and nook, stopping short of checking under every rock for his presence. Either I'm too exhausted or I'm just going crazy—both plausible explanations.

There's just this chasm in my heart that's slowly expanding, leaving room for panic to settle in, for emptiness to grow and fester. Because without him... Who *am* I without him?

"You," Ze suddenly calls out, pointing his finger at me.

I blink as I shake myself from my silly reverie. For a moment, I truly forgot where I was and what I was doing, my mind simply honing in on the possibility that my husband might be around. God, but what wouldn't I give for one hug. Just one fleeting hug to keep me warm in this labyrinth of frost.

"What?" I frown.

"You're slowing everyone down, human."

My eyes widen at his words, yet I can't deny that he's right.

"I-I'm sorry," I whisper, lowering my chin. I realize my limitations and the fact that I'm likely dragging everyone down with me.

"You should be," he huffs, stalking toward me.

My heart lurches in my chest at his biting tone. Instinctively, I take a step back as he continues toward me. His features are knit in a tight scowl.

"I'm just smaller than you." I put my hands up in an effort to placate him. "And *human*. We humans aren't that strong, you know," I stammer, slowly backing away.

He has a murderous look on his face, and I fear I may have finally angered him. After all, I am the weakest link of this team... Oh, God! I hope they won't drop me because without them... I don't even know if I can get to P'davi without their help.

"Please," I whisper. "I'll try harder."

"Ze!" Thea calls out, rushing toward me. Cer, too, looks alarmed at Ze's behavior.

Ze reaches my side, and my eyes snap shut as I wait for whatever scathing remark he wants to dole out. Yet as I creep one eye open, I'm shocked to be at eye level with his chest. The tips of his shoes graze mine. The black in his eyes glints dangerously, almost like a prism reflecting a hidden rainbow. One moment he's staring me down with his intense glare, the next he turns with his back to me, dropping to one knee.

What?

"What are you waiting for, human?" he asks when moments pass and I don't say or do anything.

"W-what do you mean?"

"Climb on," he grits out, signaling to his back.

My lashes flutter in shock, then confusion, then finally settling on awe.

Tentatively, I reach forward, wrapping my arms around his neck and climbing on his back. Holding on to the back of my knees, he rises to his feet, moving forward with innate grace, as if he didn't have a whole human on his back weighing him down. But if what I've seen so far of him is any evidence, I'd say he's pretty strong.

"Thank you," I whisper, floored by his thoughtfulness. Or maybe self-preservation. If I lose, the entire team loses too. But right now, I can't focus on the self-serving aspect, choosing to be grateful for his thoughtful gesture.

He grunts.

"Ze's finally doing something nice for once in his life," Thea says as she joins our side.

"I'm not nice," he grumbles, and I feel the deep rumble of his voice through his body.

"I'd say you're pretty nice to me." I smile. "Although your conversation skills could use some improvement."

"Cer, if Ze's doing this, then you have to do it as well," Thea calls out.

Cer rolls his eyes, ignoring her. But Thea, being Thea, will not allow him to slight her like that. Running at full speed toward him, she jumps on his back, holding on to him. I expect him to throw her off, but instead, he secures her onto his back without a word, continuing to climb with her in tow.

"Are you and Cer related in any way?" I ask Ze as I settle more comfortably on his back.

"Of course not," Ze huffs. "He's my subordinate," he says, his tone almost offended. It also doesn't escape me that he doesn't call him his friend, whereas Thea and Cer consider him one. Our previous conversation comes to mind, and I have to wonder if he really thinks they only *tolerate* him.

"You're very alike. Though he's much nicer than you," I add playfully. They are so similar in temperament, saying one thing but acting completely differently. The only difference is that Cer is more circumspect and considerate. Ze is...well, Ze means well, but he doesn't know the first thing about communication and how *not* to be rude. But this could all be due to their training in the military, for all I know.

His body tenses.

"I can be nice," he barks out.

"You just said you're *not* nice," I counter.

"I can be *nicer*," he concedes, though his tone is so strained, it's almost as if someone was pulling the words out of his mouth with a pair of pliers.

"Oh, I'm definitely looking forward to seeing what *nicer* means to you." I laugh.

He emits a low, growly sound that I don't know how to interpret. Just like Ze doesn't know the first thing about being *nice*.

We continue walking, and I attempt to make some small talk to fill in the awkward silence. Yet by the time I comment on the scenery and the beauty of nature, Ze seemingly has had enough. "I hate small talk," he mutters anew before proceeding to ignore me. I guess that's the end of my attempt at small talk *and* the end of *his* attempt at being nice.

As we climb up the mountain, the incline increases, making it harder for everyone. The other tourists are tired out of their minds. The edges of the road are filled with people sitting on boulders or smaller rocks or whatever they can find to have a moment of rest. On our side, Thea is yapping happily about the clothes she bought and what she wants to buy next while Cer listens attentively—or at least pretends to. As for me and Ze... I think I'm slowly starting to enjoy the silence.

It's not long before we reach the peak of the mountain. As opposed to everyone else, Ze and Cer didn't have to take any breaks, and that helped us get to the top in record time.

Ze puts me down, and I take a sip of water as I survey our surroundings.

"So? What now?"

There are so many people around taking pictures that I doubt a gate to another world would simply be lying around.

"Follow me," Thea beckons, going to the side of the road and crossing a forbidden barrier. The security takes note, hurrying to her side to give her a warning, but she uses her charm to get out of the situation. When they get back to their jobs, we follow suit.

"How come you know where it is?" I ask, curious.

"Uhm..." She shoots a look at Cer and Ze. "It's included in our education?" She gives me a tight smile. "There are a few strategic places in your world, and everyone needs to know where they are."

"You too?" I ask Ze and Cer.

They both give a noncommittal grunt. I guess it makes sense they'd know about it. Otherwise, this would have been branded as another trial, no? Maybe they already counted on people knowing the locations.

As we wade a path through the forest, I notice we're getting farther and farther away from the beaten track. We seemingly go down the mountain on one side before resurfacing up on another. The entire journey is long-winded and confusing—so much so I'm surprised anyone would remember it. But I guess it makes sense that it would be so far away from curious eyes. It's not as if anyone is aware that there's a portal to another world right next to one of the most touristic destinations in China.

The foliage becomes increasingly thicker and lush. The grass reaches my knees, tree branches obscuring my sight. We walk for around ten minutes before we come to a rock formation that stretches into another, higher peak. There is less vegetation around, the stone gray and forlorn. Vines climb up the rock, twining together and forming something akin to a V-shaped vault. A few dots of color surface through the combination of dark brown and green, a stark contrast to the tepid gray of the rock.

As we get closer, I notice some carvings in the stone in the shape of the dragon-turtle, ensconced by grass and vines and making them barely visible.

A beaming smile stretches across Thea's face as she dashes forward.

"It's here!" she exclaims.

I trail behind, frowning as I don't realize what she's pointing to. Aside from the beautiful vines adorning the mountain, there's nothing else.

"Where?"

She doesn't acknowledge my question as she walks farther until she's in front of the rock. Reaching forward, her hand passes right through the stone, disappearing within it.

What...

Well, that certainly is unlike any portal I've seen in TV shows.

"Come on." She beckons to us. Without waiting, she walks straight into the rock, disappearing from sight.

If up until now I could have somehow logically explained away *some* events, this is beyond my capabilities.

She just passed through stone!

Cer is next, following closely after Thea.

That leaves only me and Ze. And while I have no doubt there's *something* at the other end, I'm still a little apprehensive about stepping into the literal unknown.

"What are you waiting for?" Ze barks out from behind me.

"Does it hurt?" I blurt the question out loud.

Thea and Cer left so quickly I haven't even gotten the opportunity to ask some questions, get a little more used to the thought of crossing into another world, or even the mere action of walking into a wall of stone. Some additional mental preparation would *not* have hurt.

"What? Of course not," he huffs out loud. "It's just a doorway."

"It doesn't look like one," I mutter under my breath as I walk a little closer. I study the rock and the vines, tentatively stretching my arm to touch them. But my courage seems to be in limited supply as I chicken out just as I'm about to make contact.

Mr. Impatience doesn't like that, and instead of helping me ease into it, he simply sweeps me into his arms and walks forward.

Straight into the rock.

My eyes snap shut as I grab onto him with all my might, holding my breath as I prepare for the worst. So far, I've been a good sport, but I don't know why the prospect of going into another world terrifies me so much.

"You can open your eyes." Ze's voice rings out not even a minute after.

I slowly creep them open, my lashes fluttering in shock when I see a mirror image of the place we've just left.

What...

I'm not sure what I was expecting. Maybe some sci-fi civilization, or maybe some type of ancient, intricate architecture. Instead, all I see is a stretch of green land and mountainous rock, with trees and rich vegetation scattered all over.

"Is this it?" I ask in awe. The words are barely out of my mouth when I find myself flat on the ground. *For the third time!*

Ze's goal to be nicer needs more work, and I make sure to point that out to him, but he doesn't seem that concerned with what I think. Instead, he completely ignores me as he narrows his eyes, walking in circles as if he's looking for something.

Dusting my clothes, I get up just in time to see the same wraith as before appear in front of us.

"Congratulations on reaching P'davi. The second trial will be announced in one day. If you continue down the mountain, you will reach a complex where the contestant quarters are located. You have opted to continue as a team, and as such, you will be placed in the same accommodation. Your suite number is 56."

Out of nowhere, the wraith materializes a key, which she gives to me—or rather, the key simply drops into my waiting hands.

"The announcement for the second trial will take place in the main courtyard of the complex. Until then, you are free to rest, move around, and get to know the other contestants. You are, however, prohibited from leaving the complex grounds. Whoever is found in breach of this rule will be disqualified from the game, together with their team."

By disqualified, I guess she means *dead*.

"Until we meet again." The wraith offers a salute before she vanishes from sight.

TWENTY-THREE

We arrive at the P'davi complex half an hour later. The journey down the mountain is smooth, and I'm amazed to see how similar the environment is to that of my world. There is a dense forest at the base of the mountain, and the complex is nestled right in the middle of it. It almost looks like a military center. There's a metal fence surrounding the entire area. Inside, there are rows of buildings painted in a nondescript gray. They are all the same height—some five or six floors.

The closer we get, the more I'm surprised at how well guarded the complex is. There's barbed wire around the metal fence, with armed guards stationed at every watch tower. We head for the gate of the complex, which, as we get closer, I realize must be quite a few meters in height.

I stare up at the intricate design engraved on the gate. It represents a circle cut in two. The bisecting line flares into a triangle at both ends of the circle, with vines entwining the line and flowers slowly blooming, one development phase at a time.

One of the guards comes up to us, requesting to see our key, which I hold up for him to see. Nodding at us, he gives his colleague the signal to open the gates.

There's a loud sound as the gate creeps open, the bottom

dragging onto the ground. When there's an opening wide enough for us to pass, it suddenly stops.

We go through and the first thing that greets us is a large courtyard—the area where the next trial will be announced. There are already people around, all of them with their own teams—none larger than five. In fact, there's no one around that's on their own, and as they turn their attention toward us, I can see the interest and curiosity radiating from them. We are competing for the same prize, after all. They're probably sizing us up for any potential weaknesses.

As we get to the accommodation, we see more and more people, and I realize that plenty of teams have made it past the first trial. But what worries me more than anything is the fact that they all look to have some ability of sorts. Especially as some make a point of displaying their powers as they glare at us.

"Don't mind them," Thea whispers by my side. "They're just trying to show off."

I give her a strained smile, nodding. I know they're just trying to intimidate us, but for me, it's working. I don't have any special abilities, and now I don't even have the advantage of being in my own world. My team is the only thing keeping me afloat, and as much as it pains me to admit it, it's the reality. Yet I'm not about to give up. I'll do whatever it takes to prove myself useful so they don't think I'm a burden.

A member of staff intercepts us and, seeing the number of our suite, he leads us to a building in the back, telling us that our accommodation is on the first floor at the end of the corridor.

The inside of the building is eerily similar to one in my world, except I don't think it's made out of concrete. Curious, I touch the walls, marveling at the spongy but firm material. They seem to have hard metals, but other than that, the rest of the materials seem different.

I don't get to dwell much on it as we arrive at our suite. Opening the door, we all step inside, surprised to see it's a small apartment with a rudimentary kitchen, a bathroom, and two bedrooms. It's sparsely furnished, but it should be enough for our stay here. If anything, it's quite extravagant considering we're not all crammed in one room.

"This is not bad," I comment as I look around. "Thea and I can take one room and Cer and Ze the other."

Thea nods, dropping her shopping bags to the floor—I'd almost forgotten she insisted on bringing everything with her.

"I know you guys didn't get much sleep on the plane. Maybe you can rest a little?" I offer with a smile.

Ze grunts, and he's gone before I can even blink, the door closing behind him.

"You two will be all right?" Cer inquires, his gaze drifting to his sister.

"I'm exhausted," Thea sighs. "I'll see you later, big bro." She winks at him as she heads into our room.

I give him an awkward wave before I follow after Thea.

There are two beds in the room, with two nightstands in between. There are clean, white sheets on each bed, a pillow, and a blanket. On the opposite wall, there's a double door wardrobe, the design incredibly similar to what one would find in my world. Most things so far have been very familiar, except they seem to be designed on a more basic level, without any advanced technology.

The moment the door to our room closes, Thea discards her clothes, changing into a light cotton dress she bought from the duty-free. As she gets in bed, she only lets out a loud yawn before her eyes close and she's deep asleep.

That was... fast?

Since the weather is pretty warm, I decide to change into the purple dress Thea got for me. It's a pretty sundress with a fitted bodice and a flared skirt. Too bad that I don't have any pretty shoes to pair it with since I only brought a pair of comfortable sneakers with me. Hopefully, that will be enough, or at least there will be some shops in this world to get some new stuff.

As soon as that thought arises, it dawns on me that I know nothing about this world. I have no idea what the geography is like, if there are countries and governments and what currencies and languages they use. What species are its inhabitants? I am absolutely clueless. But because my toxic trait is that I'm too curious for my own good, I can't let this slide.

While Thea and the guys are resting, I can go explore and maybe ask some questions around. I don't want to bother any of them with my mundane curiosity, given that they're all likely exhausted. Thea hasn't slept since we left New York. The same goes for Ze and Cer, but they put in additional effort as they carried us for *hours* up a mountain. I'd say they truly deserve a few hours of uninterrupted sleep.

There were staff scattered throughout the complex, including the guards. I'm sure that someone will be able to give me more information. Maybe I can even find a way to get us some food since I have no doubt they'll be starving when they wake up.

As I exit our bedroom, I wonder if I should tell the guys that I'm going to be out for a bit. I don't want them to worry about me if they don't find me. Stopping by their door, I raise my fist to knock, but I stop myself at the last minute. I place my ear against the doorframe, listening for any sounds.

It's completely silent inside, a sign that they've gone to sleep just as Thea had done.

With a sigh, I take a step back. There are a few bags scattered on the floor—the only luggage we'd brought with us. I do a quick inventory, noticing that not only do we not have any food, but we're also out of water.

A smile surfaces on my face as I imagine them waking up to hot food and fresh cold water. Maybe I'll even get a *thank you* from Z—though I'm not getting my hopes up.

Leaving the apartment, I take a moment to orient myself outside. All the buildings look the same, and I assume they're all used to house the contestants. I walk slowly, looking right and left as I absorb as much information as I can.

To my right, there's a team comprised of three people. None of them seem human. In fact, one of the men on the team is juggling small flames on his fingers. My eyes widen in shock. No matter how strong my team is, I haven't seen either Cer or Ze have any such abilities. Thea confessed herself that she's not very good at anything except her charm—and sharp claws. A tremor of fear runs down my back.

They've been my first introduction to people with powers, and I've been so in awe with what I've seen of them that I immediately thought them unstoppable. But that's only because I didn't know better. I haven't met anyone else with such powers. But now...

Despite my efforts to keep a low profile, they notice me staring at them. A smirk appears on the man's face, and with a flick of his fingers, he sends a few balls of flames toward me. I jump back just in time to see the fire go out on the ground in front of me.

I walk faster, keeping my gaze to the ground. Yet no matter how much I try to ignore my surroundings, I'm aware of others displaying their abilities. There's a girl wielding shards of ice, while another can morph water molecules. Some guys a distance away are having a sword duel, practically flying in the air.

As I pass by them, I feel their curious gazes on me, but I also hear hushed whispers.

Human.

Somehow, they know I'm the weakest link.

Spotting a staff member a distance away, I decide to inquire about food and water.

"There's a canteen on the other side of the complex. It's the only building with a red door. You will need your room card to get supplies," she mentions.

"Thank you," I murmur with a smile. Searching for the building with the red door, my mind replays our conversation as I wonder how we were able to understand each other. Although her language sounded foreign, it was also familiar at the same time and I could somehow understand it.

Maybe it's just a side effect of being in this world? I'll have to question Thea more about it.

After a few failed attempts and even more run-ins with other teams who glare at me snidely, I'm not any closer to finding the building. On the other hand, I'm starting to realize that *humans* aren't very popular with this crowd.

God, it's almost as if I had the word tattooed on my forehead. Otherwise, how else would everyone know that I'm human?

Shaking my head, I ignore all the sharp glares and snide remarks as I walk farther to the back. It's only after what feels like forever that I come across the red door. Smiling to myself, I go inside the building. There's a lady at the counter, looking bored out of her mind as she rests her head on the table.

"Excuse me." I clear my throat when she doesn't acknowledge my presence.

She lifts her head, raising her brows in question.

"I'm here for food and water?" I force a smile.

"Room number?"

I show her the key and the small tag that says fifty-six. She nods and points me to the left.

"You can grab food and water from there. There's a limit of four items per person per journey," she adds in a robotic tone.

I blink.

"So I'll have to come back if I need more?"

She nods, her attention half drifting away.

Well, there goes my idea of surprising everyone with a meal. But since I'm already here, I decide to go inside and grab at least *something*.

As I step inside, I'm surprised to see rows and rows of food and drinks. It's almost like a buffet, with a lot of options that you can fill your plate with. Whenever an item runs low, a staff member comes in to add more, making the entire experience very fast and efficient. There are a few other people around, but there's no designated space to eat inside. You can only come in, grab your food, and go.

Grabbing a plate and a fork, I peek around, curious to see what type of food they'd have in this world.

There's something that looks oddly like rice, and I put a spoonful of it on my plate. Next, there are some oddly shaped vegetables that are more colorful than any I've seen in my world. More options of grain-like foods that look familiar but strange at the same time. I get a spoonful of each on my plate so I can try all of them. When I get to the meat, there are five rows of different types. There's no name to suggest what animal the meat could be from, and though it looks thoroughly cooked and quite appetizing, I can't risk it—not after seeing what happened to Thea and Ze. Even the other foods are a risk, but I'm starving, so I'll have to pray I won't get sick from it.

After I fill my plate with food, I get to the dessert station and see some dark squares that look like chocolate, along with some weird-looking fruits. Since I won't be able to carry two plates with me, I scoot the food to the side and add a couple of those squares, my mouth already watering at the thought of eating something sweet.

Last in line is the drink station. There are five jugs placed one next to another and wooden cups next to them. I sniff each jug, deciding to go with the one without scent. I pour a little into the cup at first, take a sip, and nod to myself. Water. Okay, that's good, now I can get more.

When I'm finally done, I leave, intent on going to the back where I saw some empty tables.

It seems that although there are no seats to eat inside, everyone is having their meal outside. I take a seat at the farthest table, not wanting to draw even more attention to myself.

Once I'm comfortable, I hesitantly start tasting the food. To my surprise, everything tastes fantastic—not too different from the food in my world. As I get to the dessert, I'm surprised to see that the dark squares taste just like chocolate, but this is much sweeter and buttery.

"Oh my God." I release a soft moan as I close my eyes. This is just fabulous. I don't think I've ever eaten better chocolate in my life. Now I know for sure what I'm going to be stocking up on from the cafeteria—and hey, it's a good source of energy, and I'll likely be needing a lot of that in the future.

I'm soon finished and I can't resist the urge to go in again to get a few more pieces of chocolate. I take a fistful of chocolate and make my way out, going toward a pretty garden I noticed at the edge of the complex. Despite its restricted area, there seems to be everything one might need here.

Finding a small nook next to some yellow flowers, I take a seat on the grass. The many plants and flowers offer me an advantage as I'm not as easily noticeable. This way, I won't need to withstand all the odd glances coming my way from the other teams.

I bite into a chocolate square, and despite it being utterly delicious, a sigh escapes my lips as I wish my Nikki were here to enjoy this too.

"You'd like this," I whisper, taking another bite. "I bet I could make you the best cake with it. It would be so creamy and sweet..."

My voice trails off as I realize how silly I am, talking by myself to an imaginary version of my husband—and it's not even his ghost.

I release a weary breath as I bring my knees to my chest, hugging myself. For the last few weeks, I've managed to keep myself together and focus on one goal at a time. Yet there are brief moments when my confidence falters and grief swallows me whole.

"It's fine," I tell myself in a low, pained voice. Shivers erupt all over the surface of my skin, coldness penetrating my bones despite the warmth outside. "I'll be fine. I'll win..."

Yet the truth is that I'm not fine. I'm the furthest away from fine. I've just done a damn good job of burying everything so deep within myself that at some point I've managed to convince myself that maybe I *could* be fine.

All along, I've been living a lie.

And this one bite of chocolate was enough to remind me of

everything I lost. Of those stolen moments together where not even my deepest fears could get to me because I had him.

I press my lips together as tears stab at the back of my eyes.

"I need to be strong," I whisper as I swallow against the sudden wave of grief that strikes me in the breast. I allow myself a few moments to wallow in my pain before I put myself together. The only way I can win this is if I keep a level head.

I breathe in and out, closing my eyes and trying to get a modicum of control over myself. All my life, this is what I've been best at—compartmentalizing. When things got too hard, I focused on the bright side—on the future that was yet to come. Only that way could I withstand the pain and the suffering. Because I knew better times were ahead. I may have been hopeless at times, but I've always been an optimist by nature, so I harnessed that hopelessness and simply dropped the *less*.

If I could turn dearth into abundance, then I could prevail. So I focus on that.

Imagining all my grief, I focus on it until it turns into a tangible ball of energy. I wrap my hands around it and aim to change its meaning. Just like hope was born out of desperation, so is determination born out of grief.

My heart rate slows down as the last tendrils of heartache recede.

I slowly open my eyes, a gasp escaping me as I startle back.

A shimmery black shadow looms over me, the contour of a body clearer than it's ever been. And just as I'm about to fall on my back, a hand reaches out to stop me.

A hand that can... touch me.

"Nikki?" I croak as he pulls me back up. He's on his knees in front of me.

"Luce." His voice echoes, barely audible and distorted.

TWENTY-FOUR

"Oh my God, you can speak. You can touch me," I inhale sharply.

"Yes," he replies. His touch is cold and impersonal. It doesn't feel like skin, only like a hard surface that's being molded to my arm.

"How? What happened?" I ask, worry infusing my words.

"This world," he speaks slowly. "I have more...strength."

I stare at him, unable to believe this is actually happening. And just like that, all the hope I toiled to foster blossoms. His features are not discernible. There's still only a dark smoke that swirls with tinges of silver. But the contour of his body is unmistakable, as is his intoxicating presence.

Tentatively, I reach out, my palm fitting to the plane of his cheek. I caress him softly. I may not be able to see his face, but I can feel his features. It's him. My Nikki.

"Oh, Nikki," I burst out, throwing myself into his arms.

I wrap my arms around his neck, feeling the hard surface of his chest. Everything is familiar. Everything but one thing. There's no heartbeat. That soothing sound that has been my safe place for years is missing.

Of course it's missing. He's a ghost.

"You're following me, aren't you? You're attached to me?" I ask as I lean back.

He nods slowly.

"You have to...quit."

"What?" I frown.

"It's not safe. Please," he whispers. "Don't risk yourself for me."

"How can you ask me that? How can you even suggest it? You know I'd do anything for you."

He shakes his head.

"It's not safe," he repeats. "Please, Luce." He reaches with his hands, palming my cheeks as he strokes his thumb over my skin. "You have to withdraw after this trial."

"No. Absolutely *no*," I state.

"You can't see what I see from here. This is not something you can win. And if you die, your soul dies too. Do you know what that means? No more incarnations. We can *never* meet again. At least this way..."

"I can't do it, Nikki. I can't give you up. I *know* I can win this."

"You're human, Luce. They aren't. You can't win."

"My team will help me," I tell him. "They're stronger than me. With them by my side, I can win. I *will* win."

"Luce. Please... I can't bear if anything happens to you."

"And I can't bear to be without you," I whisper. "So you see, we're at an impasse."

He continues to caress me as he moves closer. The coldness of his cheek seeps into mine as he nuzzles his face against mine.

"Please. Do it for me. Leave this game and go home."

"Do you understand what you're asking me? You're telling me I should just go back home and live the rest of my life without you. How could I *ever* do that? How, Nikki? How?" I cry out.

"Because the alternative is much worse," he says calmly.

"I know the risks. I'm well aware of the danger and nothing you could say can change my mind. I know you're only thinking of me, while I'm only thinking of you. So we're bound to be perpetually at a crossroads."

His arms drop from my side as he takes a step back, rising to his feet. I scramble up too, stepping toward him, *needing* to be closer to him.

"You must drop out of the game," he reiterates, his voice sterner. "You must, Lucero," he says with an exasperated sigh.

I blink slowly.

He called me Lucero... He only calls me by my full name when he's angry at me.

"Nikki, please..."

He shakes his head, stepping farther away from me.

"If you love me, you will drop out of the game."

"What... No. It's *because* I love you so much that I can never do that. Please understand me."

He doesn't speak. He merely stands there, a large spot of black against the colorful background. The shadows within his body move wildly, like black flames fanned by his increased displeasure.

He takes a step back. The chasm between us widens. I step forward, raising my arm and reaching for him.

"Please, Nikki... Don't leave," I whisper, terrified that he'll disappear any moment.

He doesn't move, letting me come closer. Raising myself on the tips of my toes, I reach for him, gently touching his face.

"Can you feel me?" I ask in a whisper as I blow hot air to combat the iciness that pervades every atom of his being. "Can you feel my touch?"

He gives me a subdued nod.

Closing my eyes, I bring my lips to his cheek, breathing him in as I breathe life into him. I skim my mouth all over the hard surface of his face. There's nothing that denotes my Nikki, yet there's something that's so intrinsically him. Tears fall unbidden down my cheeks. Where he'd once been warm to the touch, now he's cold and unwelcoming. Where once his heartbeat had been the sweetest melody, now there's only a deafening silence —one that not even my erratic heart can fill.

I wrap myself around him, all in hopes I can lend him some of my warmth.

"Does my touch warm you?"

He takes my hand, threading our fingers together.

"It gives me life."

Moments pass, and I cannot move. I'm trapped in his spell as I stare at the faceless man I love.

The hard planes of his body are tightly pressed against my soft ones. Yet even as I rejoice at this closeness, there's no denying that while this is my Nikki, he also isn't.

"Why did you not leave when the messengers came for you?"

"Because then I would have forgotten you," he replies in a low, cracked voice.

Those words wrap themselves around my heart, squeezing it until only pain and longing remain. Nikki...my Nikki.

I hold on tighter to him, wishing with all my might that I could see him once more—feel his warm skin on top of mine. His handsome face is an echo in my mind that threatens to ebb with every passing day, and I can't allow that. I can't let my feeble memory erase him—not when he risked everything to remember *me*.

Pressing both of my palms to his face, I hold him close to me as I seek some light in the darkness of the shadows. His eyes were once the same color—a smoky obsidian that has haunted me from that first moment I saw him when I was sixteen. They were black against the darkness of the tunnels we were sentenced to labor in, and yet still, I found light in them.

Now...

"I love you, Nikki. I love you more than anything in the world—even my own life. So please don't ask me to give up the game. It's the one time I cannot fulfill your request. You may hate me for it. But know I'll love you more."

A cold current of air whooshes me in the face. Before I can

blink, Nikki's gone from my arms, already a few meters away. The shadows within him become more erratic and out of control to signal his anger. And though I can't stop the tears that pour down my face, I stand firm in my decision.

"I will win," I say as I straighten my back, bringing the back of my hand to my face to wipe the moisture away. "I will pass this trial and the next, and then the next until I get my wish. And I will have you back," I continue, leveling him with my gaze.

I can't see his expression. I can't tell what he's thinking or how he's reacting to my pronouncement. There's only the wild swirl of shadows that move around like tendrils of darkness. They sway in the air, destroying any semblance of a bodily contour. The wind picks up, the coldness of the air more biting than before.

Streaks of shimmery mist appear within the shadows.

"Nikki..." I whisper, my eyes wide.

I take a step forward. He walks farther away from me.

The swirling tendrils speed up until only small black particles remain. One moment he's there, the next he's gone.

Just like that.

A loud noise explodes in the background, the sound echoing the agony in my soul. My mouth falls open as pain slices me in half. He's mad at me. I swallow hard as I hug my arms to myself, hoping for a modicum of warmth.

He came with the cold, and now he stole my warmth, too.

And even though my determination doesn't falter, my spirits plummet until all I can feel is desolation.

Coldness and desolation.

TWENTY-FIVE

Still rooted to the spot, I'm so caught up in my own despair that I barely realize someone is next to me. A figure looms over me, and I slowly lift my gaze up, frowning at the familiar face. She's the girl from the club, isn't she?

"How did *you* get here?" she demands, a disgusted expression on her face. Black hair and equally dark eyes, she's wearing a cute costume that's cut in the back to make way for her beautiful white tail that even now sways from side to side.

"Huh?" I frown.

I stare at her, not comprehending what she's referring to. Is she mistaking me for someone else?

Behind her, I note three men with protective stances, glaring at me. She's not the only one who has a tail. The others do as well, only theirs are a combination of red, black, and white. I'm not sure what exactly they are, but maybe I should ask Thea to give me a lesson on all the species that I'm likely to encounter in this competition.

"It's her." She points at me, looking back at the other men. "She's the one who touched my tail," she accuses.

My eyes widen in shock.

Getting to my feet, I give them a shaky smile as I put my palms up.

"I didn't. It was just a misunderstanding..."

"A *human* touched your tail?" One of the men growls, taking a step forward.

What... How the hell did I get myself into this?

"I didn't. I really didn't. I only mentioned it was very pretty," I say, slowly backing away. But even if I had, why are they reacting like this for something as simple as touching a tail? There's a sense of danger that seeps into my bones. My fight or flight instinct is activated as I look right and left in an attempt to find an exit since I think it's high time I returned to the suite.

But just as I take a step back, I'm smacked across the face by a different tail—one that's not nearly as fluffy as the girl's. Losing my equilibrium, I fall to the grass. I bring my hand to my lips, wiping away blood from the blow.

"What the..." I mumble, half in shock. Looking back at them, I find the girl sporting a twisted smile while one of the men by her side is swaying his red tail in the air, a smug expression on his face.

"I don't know how you made it here, *human*, but you'll pay for your audacity," she sneers at me.

What audacity? I didn't do anything!

"You're insane," I mumble, wobbling to my feet.

She puts a hand up, calling one of the other men to her and giving him a signal. My eyes flare open with fear as I realize this won't stop at just one blow.

"Let's not get ahead of ourselves. You know I didn't touch your tail. I just complimented it." I try once more to reason with them.

But it's soon evident that not only does it not matter if I touched her tail or not, but that by taking me out, they're just eliminating competition. Since our first trial was isolated, I forgot that not only are we competing against outside obstacles, but also against each other.

The man's lips pull up in a smirk as he whispers something to her. She nods, giving him permission to act.

Oh, no, no, no. I'm not going to wait around for them to hit me again. Turning, I dash toward the apartment, running at full speed. Yet it's in vain as the man's tail extends and wraps itself around my ankle, pulling suddenly. I gasp aloud as I fall face down to the ground. Pain flares in my knees from the hard surface, and more red liquid trickles down my flesh.

I groan in pain as I raise myself on my arms. Footsteps resound behind me. Despite the biting pain, I push myself up, ready to make another go at an escape.

"Silly human," he mutters, his tone mocking. His tail moves, about to strike me again. Yet this time, the attack doesn't come.

I blink repeatedly, afraid I'm seeing things.

One flash of white and half of his tail drops to the ground, blood pouring from his open wound. He gives a harsh cry of pain as he drops to his knees.

"Why do you always attract danger?" Ze's voice echoes as he appears in front of me, blood trickling down his sword as droplets fall to the ground. The image is quite familiar as his broad back fills my entire field of vision. He's changed clothes, I notice. He's back in his black ensemble consisting of a loose tunic shirt and a pair of wide-legged linen pants. A belt holds the outfit together, which he uses to hang the scabbard of his sword.

Thea and Cer are here too, with Thea shooting murderous glances at the girl.

"I've got her," she motions to the girl, positioning herself in front of her just as her nails lengthen into claws.

"You..." the man sneers, his nostrils flaring as he stares at Ze. Releasing a sharp battle cry, he thrusts himself forward, ready to attack Ze.

My lips part in wonder just as my eyes widen in shock.

Ze doesn't move. He doesn't even dodge the incoming blow. He merely lifts his arm, his forefinger on the man's forehead as he keeps him at a distance. He stops the man's advancement with just one finger!

What the hell...

He flicks him across the forehead, and that small gesture

sends the man flying in the air until he crashes into the fence surrounding the complex.

The girl cries out when her partner releases a groan of pain as he hits the fence. She turns feral as she faces Thea, her entire body changing right under my eyes. More of the same fur starts covering her limbs until she changes from a humanoid form to something resembling an oversized fox. She jumps toward Thea, but she easily evades the attack, raking her claws on the underside of the belly. The fox yelps in pain, but she doesn't give up. Still, it seems that Thea can more than handle herself.

Ze sheaths his sword as he turns toward me. His lips are flattened into a thin line as he surveys the state of my injuries. My lip is busted. My knees are bruised and bleeding. He's no doubt thinking what a weak human I am.

Taking a step forward, he extends his hand toward me.

I blink at the unexpected gesture, but I'm not in a position to refuse his help, so I grab onto his hand, letting him pull me up to my feet.

His gaze is on my bloodied lip as a scowl permeates his features.

"Who did *that*?" His voice vibrates with tension.

"That guy." I point at the man with the red tail.

His cheek twitches dangerously. Pivoting on his heel, he pins the other two men with his icy glare.

"Cerenios, that one is mine," he says in a low, barely contained voice.

Cer smirks, shaking his head.

"As you wish." He inclines his head. "But remember our limitations," he mentions before he steps aside and focuses his attention on the other man.

Ze stares at the man and, raising his hand, he uses two fingers to beckon him. My lips tremble with mirth. Of course he would be awfully arrogant in combat, too.

The man bares his teeth at Ze, and with a loud howl, he shifts his form too. His fox is much bigger than the girl's, the color a deep auburn with streaks of black on the back. Its snout is protruding, its canines sharp. In this form, it's hard to believe that he was ever humanoid. There's nothing but the wildness of the beast inside of him as he charges toward Ze. Yet in contrast to the girl, whose only strategy seems to be close combat, the man can shoot power balls out of his mouth.

Wha—

"Get back, human," Ze commands. In one smooth movement, he removes the sword from his waist, deflecting the blast and sending it to the side. The fox continuously fires blasts at him, coming closer and closer.

Ze rotates his sword as he catches one blast. Tracing his fingers from the hilt of his sword to the tip, he absorbs most of the momentum of the blast before he returns it, using his sword to bounce the ball of energy back to the fox.

This catches Ze's opponent off guard and he barely has time to avoid the incoming blow. He veers to the side, but the blast is too powerful, catching him in his lower body and burning a good part of his fur. A strangled cry escapes him as he falls to the ground. There's a gaping wound in his right flank—so deep the bone is visible, the flesh around the wound raw and mangled. One would think that he'd give up at this point. But if anything, he's even more determined to strike at Ze as he gets up and inhales sharply, gathering all his energy for one last blast.

Ze is unbothered as he simply watches him with an emotionless expression. He smoothly rotates the hilt of the sword in his hand, the effortless display of strength intimidating even to my eyes—*and I'm on his team!*

But just as my focus is on the red fox and his incoming attack, I note movement from the corner of my eye.

I turn my head, following the motions.

To the side, Thea is still fighting the girl—or, better said, she's playing with her, baiting her here and there. Next to her, Cer is sporting a bored expression as he evades all the useless attempts of his opponent. He's clearly superior in strength and skill, but he doesn't seem to have the same thirst for blood that

Ze does. He's just toying with the other man, dodging every attack and wearing him out.

But as I move my gaze even farther right, my eyes flare open in shock as I recognize the other male, now fully shifted into his fox form too. He's running at full speed toward Ze, readying himself for attack just as the red fox opens his mouth to release his energy blast.

"Ze, watch out," I call out to him, running to his side. In the moment, all my coherent thoughts vanish. It never even crosses my mind that I'm powerless and I could never possibly help him. There's only this unnatural impetus to save him as I push my battered body forward. I only cover a short distance before it becomes clear that the fox isn't running toward Ze.

He's running *at me*.

Ze's head whips to me, something flaring in his gaze. He moves with frightening alacrity, his sword up in the air to absorb the blast of energy. One leg slips backward as the power of the blast strains his equilibrium. He holds on to his sword as the wave of energy washes through him, his body bent forward. His entire body shakes as currents of electricity travel from the sword through him, his expression pained. Still, his attention is fully on me. Yet the distance between us is a wide gulf that he can't possibly cross in time.

I come to a complete halt, my eyes wide, my heartbeat erratic. There's no time to retreat. Not with how unresponsive my body suddenly is and certainly not with how fast the fox is moving toward me.

Everything happens in slow motion as I squeeze my eyes shut, bracing myself for the impact.

But it never comes.

A loud bang erupts in the air, sowing panic in my chest. I crack my eyes open to find myself staring at Ze's back. He's breathing hard as he holds his ground, keeping the fox away from me. His fingers are wrapped around his opponent's throat, squeezing the life out of him. His hold tightens until a snap permeates the air, the neck of the fox bending at an awkward angle. His beady eyes are wide open, unblinking, his mouth parted—in regret or shock, who knows. Ze releases him and the unmoving body drops to the ground, morphing back into its humanoid form.

"Ze..." I whisper, reaching out to touch his sleeve.

It's the first time I see him *kill* someone. Before, when he'd dispatched that demon, I hadn't once had second thoughts about it because it was evil, no? He was saving the souls. But this... I'm not sure how I feel about it even though the fox was going to attack me. If it weren't for him, I'd be dead, or at the very least gravely injured. It's quite obvious that the foursome had started the conflict as a way to show off and take care of a weaker contestant. The flimsy pretext they had used to attack me had been a mere front.

Ze doesn't answer. He shrugs my hand off as he stalks toward the red fox, his steps heavy and measured. By now, the man must have realized that Ze is not someone to mess with because he tries to run away. But Ze will not allow him that mercy. He vanishes from his current spot, reappearing in front of the fox. With unnatural speed, he withdraws his sword, decapitating the red fox with one smooth slide of his blade.

The head falls to the ground, rolling on the grass until it's only a few steps away from me. I stare in shock at the blood gushing from the neck, the sight of the severed spine and tendons an anatomy lesson I did not particularly need.

But Ze doesn't stop there.

It's almost as if he's no longer in control of himself as he flashes out of sight once more, appearing between Cer and his opponent. Cer's eyes widen, but he doesn't seem overly surprised, taking a step back to give Ze more room. I detect a small bow of reverence coupled with a sharp gaze as he surveys the situation in case his superior might need help. Despite their apparent friendship or friendly countenance, there's no denying that Cer is always behaving in a subtle deferential manner toward Ze—one that isn't necessarily borne out of their positions, but because he truly respects the man. That tells me everything I need to know about Ze and what type of person he is. He might be rude and arrogant and sometimes downright tyrannical. But he's someone who inspires trust and loyalty—both traits I happen to admire.

Ze doesn't hesitate. He strikes again with his sword, the head of the man flying a few meters away, rolling on the grass. I barely blink before he disappears again, only to show up in front of the girl—the last one.

He has a chilling expression on his face. Splatters of blood are on his cheeks and forehead, some droplets dripping from his chin. He looks utterly terrifying, yet it's his eyes that trigger a deep fear within me.

They're empty. Soulless.

They're a pool of nothingness as he stares at his last victim, his sword raised high.

"Ze!" I call out. He doesn't hear me.

One second the female fox is watching him with trepidation, the next she's split in half by his sword, her lifeless body parts falling to the ground, her organs spilling onto the grass and staining it with blood and various other liquids. The urge to gag is overpowering, as is the shock that claims my body and renders it immobile.

All around us, there's only destruction and bloodshed. The lush garden in which I'd hugged my husband for the first time in weeks has turned into a hellish scenery. The grass is a muddy brown. The flowers have been stained by death.

I stand there, frozen to the spot as I stare around me. My emotions are high, my morality caught in a loop, churning until it ripens, then rots.

At one point in my life, I would have regretted this, but now I can't.

Four fewer people to compete against. Four fewer people contending for the prize. It's selfish, I know. But in the grand scheme of things, it's them or Nikki.

Slowly lifting my gaze, I meet Ze's absent one. We stare at

each other for moments on end, the buzz of adrenaline the only sound as everything fades away.

There's a glint in his eyes, the swirling darkness giving way to a hint of color. Yet as he blinks, it's gone, as is his murderous rage. He slowly puts his sword away, his features clearing up. He's covered from head to toe in fox blood, but as I take a step forward to go to his side, I catch sight of something on the ground.

Red blood. But next to it, there's black blood. I follow the trail around, watching a pattern unfold and remembering something Cer had said about the black magic dust.

It's made from his blood.

Without caring for the pain in my limbs or my pounding heart, I dash to him. Reaching his side, I note the small hole in his shirt as well as the slightly deeper black staining the edges.

God, he got hit. When he put himself in front of me, he must have absorbed the blow meant for me—that's the only possible explanation. Panic swells inside of me as I grab onto the material, ripping at it to check for the damage.

Smooth skin meets my eyes, and I have to blink several times to make sure I'm seeing correctly.

TWENTY-SIX

"Are you done ogling me, human?" he drawls, amused.

I slowly lift my gaze to his face.

"You got hit. The blood. That's your blood." I point to the black liquid on the grass.

He grabs my hands, stopping me from inspecting his skin further.

"I'm fine," he replies curtly.

"But... How... How can you be fine..." I stammer, belatedly realizing I'm likely still in a state of shock. Yet if his saliva can heal, is it any wonder that he can heal himself, too?

"We need to go." Cer's voice resounds from behind me. "We already have an audience."

Tens of other contestants have gathered around the garden, all watching the spectacle with curiosity. Whispers travel through the air, and though I can't quite make out what they're saying, I imagine they're all in awe of Ze.

Good.

Maybe this will deter them from coming after us again.

"Let them stare." Ze shrugs.

"Are you all right, Luce? You're bleeding," Thea says as she touches my arm.

I look down at myself, noting the crusted blood around my

knees and down my tibia. With everything going on, the pain was the least of my concerns. But now that I'm reminded of it, it suddenly flares up, causing me to wince in discomfort. My lip, too, is tender and stiff, more blood likely dried around my chin.

"I'm good." I force a smile—or what should look like one considering my lips hurt too much to move.

Without warning, I find myself being lifted up. I release a yelp of surprise, instinctively scrambling to get away.

"Stop moving, human," Ze growls low in my ear. "We're going back," he declares, already moving toward our accommodation. Cer and Thea share a look, but they don't say anything, simply following suit.

The crowd of onlookers parts to allow us to move, all the while staring at Ze with a mix of awe and fear. Their eyes follow him around as they wonder who or *what* he is. As we leave the crowd behind, it dawns on me that staff members were around as well, all watching but not intervening. I guess this really is a matter of survival of the fittest. If the game doesn't kill you...the other contestants will.

Ze kicks the door of our suite open, heading straight for Thea's and my room. He steps inside the room and stops, turning his head sharply to Thea and Cer, who are right behind him.

"Out," he commands.

They blink in surprise, but they don't contest Ze's edict. He shuts the door in their faces before he stalks over to my bed and places me down.

"Uhm... What are you doing?" I ask, my brows creasing as I regard his grave expression.

"You're hurt," he states, his gaze lingering on my lips. Clearing his throat, he looks around the room, nodding to himself as he grabs Thea's sheet and rips it in half.

"That's Thea's sheet. You can't just..." I hiss, my eyes wide.

He pins me with his icy eyes, his glare shutting me up immediately.

I mumble a few profanities under my breath that he decides to ignore—although I'm sure he can hear them well enough.

He rips the sheet into four strips of cloth. At first, I think he's just going to help me dress the wounds. But he surprises me when he goes back to the door and wrenches it open. He comes face to face with Thea, who's holding a jug of water in her arms. He grabs it from her hands, then closes the door in her face—*again*.

"You said you'd be nicer. That's being the opposite of nice," I point out.

He doesn't answer, his face expressionless as he wets the cloth.

"Did you hear me? You're being rude."

"I am nice to *you*," he replies, exasperated.

"Well, it's not enough. You can't be nice just to one person."

"Yes. I can." He shrugs, going back to ignoring me as he drops to his knees in front of me. He gently grabs my ankle, his fingers brushing against my tender skin. His touch is both light and firm, the tips of his fingers pressing against the softness of my calf. The sudden movement startles me.

"What are you doing?" I ask with a frown, trying to wrench my leg from his grasp.

"You're dirty," he comments in a matter-of-fact tone. He tightens his grip on my leg as he removes one shoe.

"I'm what..." I blink.

"I need to clean your legs," he speaks as he removes my other shoe too, discarding it to the side. Grabbing the cloth, he starts wiping the caked mud and blood off my legs. His movements are brisk and efficient, his attention wholly focused on the task. I guess this is nice of him, but it still doesn't excuse his treatment of Thea and Cer.

When he finishes my lower leg, he pushes my dress up my thighs, the gesture taking me by surprise.

"W-wait a moment," I burst out as I push against his shoulders. He stops, raising a brow in question. "You should ask for permission first," I mumble as my cheeks heat up. I grab the hem of my dress and fold it nicely across my lap so I'm decent.

He frowns at me, confused.

"Remember how you were offended by the nudity in that TV show? This is the same, but in my world, people are offended when others see them naked without permission."

"But those humans were naked in the TV show," he says, even more perplexed.

"Well, yes. But that is entertainment and they agreed to be naked on screen."

"I do not understand this entertainment of yours."

"You said that in your world it's forbidden for people to engage in intercourse without being married, no?"

"Mated," he corrects.

"Mated. Same thing." I smile. "How is nudity perceived then?"

He stares at me unblinking.

"Only your mate can see you fully nude," he answers.

"Well, there you go." I chuckle. "Since we are not mated, from now on, ask me before you do something like this, okay?" I say with a smile. Sometimes it's like explaining things to a child.

His nostrils flare, his mouth set in a grim line as his eyes shoot daggers at me. He doesn't acknowledge my words as he returns his attention to his task. Silence descends as he finishes tending to my right leg. He switches to a new cloth for the left one, cleaning all the dirt off my skin until the previously white scrap of sheet is now a combination of brown and red. Every time he brings the wet cloth to the injured area, I wince, a stinging pain erupting from the site of the wound. He stops each time, raising his gaze to check in with me. I give him a small nod to continue, doing my best to withstand the pain.

When he's done, my legs are clean save for the wounds that are still glistening red, fresh droplets of blood threatening to trickle down my tibia. I expect him to focus his attention on the knee injuries, but he surprises me once more when he takes the third cloth to wipe my left arm, cleaning my palm and the back of my hand. He does the same with the other and soon we're out of cloth.

Oh, God, he's going to tear up another sheet to bandage my knees.

I'm about to ask him to take it from my bed this time, not Thea's, but I don't get to utter a single word as my mouth drops open in shock.

Ze leans forward and places his mouth on my right knee. He flicks his tongue across the open wound, lathering it in his saliva. He trails his lips all over my knee, cleaning the last drops of blood with his mouth.

"Ze..." I trail off, unsure of what to say.

He takes his time, making sure he licks every part of my injured knee. The effect is immediate as the pain subsides. I can feel the skin knot around, mending together. He does the same to the other knee, wrapping his lips around my flesh and trailing his tongue all over the bloodied injury. When my knees are as good as new, he takes my hand, then licks the small scrapes and scratches I got when I fell. As the last wound starts healing, he gives it one last lick before he gets to his feet.

It's only when he tilts my chin up and he leans forward that I realize what he means to do. My eyes widen and I scramble back, pushing him away at the same time.

"Thank you. I think I'm fine." I give him a tight smile.

He frowns.

"But you're still hurt."

"This." I touch my split lip. "It's nothing." I wave my hand. I'm not sure what the stance is on kissing in his world, but in mine it means something. And regardless of whether this is just for healing purposes, a kiss is a kiss.

And I'm married.

He straightens his back, crossing his arms over his chest and regarding me with overt skepticism.

"But it hurts." He narrows his eyes at me.

"It's a manageable pain. I'm sure it will heal in a few days."

"You may get an infection. You don't know how your human body will interact with this world," he points out.

I blink rapidly. He's right. I don't know what germs are in this world and how they will react with my human DNA. A simple cold could prove deadly here for all I know.

I nibble at my lip as I debate on what I should do. I'm not going to let him kiss me, that's for sure. But maybe...

"Here," I say as I extend my hand, pointing the inside of my finger at him. "You can spit on my finger and I'll rub it on my lip."

He stares at my finger for a moment before his gaze meets mine.

"Why are you being so difficult, human?" He sighs in annoyance.

"Because in my world, kissing is reserved for mates only," I explain in his terms.

"Kissing?" he repeats, his brows knit together.

"You know, touching lips. Only mates do that. So you'll have to either do it on my finger or let me die of an infection because you're not going anywhere near my lips," I say with a huff.

He glares at me.

I glare back.

"Is that so..." he grumbles in a gruff voice. Taking my hand, he brings my finger to his mouth. But instead of spitting on it as I expect, he wraps his lips around the tip of my finger, all the while staring me in the eyes.

I swallow.

He lazily strokes his tongue against my finger before he sucks it into his mouth. The black of his irises shifts ever so slightly, a hint of color swirling in that darkness. A shiver goes down my back, my rib cage suddenly constricting my breathing.

"That's enough," I croak, pulling my hand from him.

He lets my finger fall from his mouth, his eyes still on me as I bring it to my lip, massaging his healing saliva into my flesh. In a matter of seconds, the wound heals.

"Thank you," I nod awkwardly.

He's still staring at me, his scrutiny making my skin erupt in goosebumps.

I fidget around, arranging my dress and pulling it down my legs, hoping he'd get a clue and leave before this becomes more awkward than it already is.

"'Tell me I am nice," he suddenly demands, startling me.

"What?"

"Say it," he prompts me.

"You're...*nice?*"

He waits a moment as he stares at me. Then he nods and turns on his heel, leaving the room.

What the hell was that?

TWENTY-SEVEN

"Luce, are you all right?" Thea asks as she comes into the room.

"Yes. Now I'm fine. My wounds are healed, see?" I point to my knees.

"Your lip, too," she notes, raising a brow. "Ze was quite busy, wasn't he?"

"Oh, it's nothing like that," I hurry to add, thinking she's going to imagine the worst. "I dabbed some of his, ehm, saliva on my lip." I strain a smile.

She doesn't look particularly convinced as she takes a seat on the bed next to me.

"You should be careful with him," she suddenly says as she takes my hands in hers. Her expression is serious—entirely unlike the Thea I've come to know.

"What do you mean? Isn't he your friend?"

"He is, though I'm sure he wouldn't call me that." She lets out a dry chuckle. "But he's also...unpredictable. Until a while ago, I thought I knew him well, but now I'm wondering just how much I truly knew him."

"I don't understand." I frown.

"I've known Ze since I was young. My brother went to train under him when he was very young, and Ze would come visit our family home every now and then. He's always been...cold. Emotionless. Some say that's why he's the best at what he does—because he relies on cold logic and unbendable rules. But more than anything, that's what makes him ruthless. He doesn't have a moral compass. For him, there's no such thing as right or wrong, there's only his position and the orders he receives."

I blink as I slowly take her words in.

"Why are you telling me this?"

"Because Ze has never broken a rule before. In all of his existence, he's *never* broken a rule."

"I kind of gathered that," I add dryly, thinking back to his outraged remarks.

"What he did today. He broke a rule. And it's not the first time."

"What rule?" I frown.

"He's not allowed to dispatch someone unless he's directly under attack."

"But he was," I add, confused.

She shakes her head, the corners of her mouth curling up.

"*You* were under attack."

"We're a team. What happens to me reflects on all of you," I point out.

She just smiles at me indulgently.

"I like you, Luce. I don't want anything to happen to you. Just...keep this in mind, okay?"

"Okay..." I answer, still not seeing the point of this conversation. Ze has been nothing but nice to me—granted, in his own, surly way. He might not be the best with words, but his actions prove that his heart is in the right place.

"Speaking of today. Why were those people so incensed about a tail?"

"Those damned foxes." She rolls her eyes. "They're very particular about their tails. To touch their tail without permission is the most offensive thing you can do. They're usually pests and no one can stand them. They probably picked on you because you're human and they thought they could eliminate a contestant easily."

"Is it going to be like this from now on? Are people going to keep attacking us?"

"I reckon they'll try. It's about to get more and more vicious, Luce. You need to keep your guard up."

I nod.

Thea gets up, stretching languidly and proclaiming she's exhausted. Her demeanor changes back to normal, mischievous Thea as she jumps on her bed, bouncing on the mattress.

Shaking my head, I get up, telling her I'm going to take a shower before bed. I gather a change of clothes and go to the bathroom. At first glance, the place is eerily similar to a bathroom in my world, except the bathtub is made of wood.

Interesting.

I carefully explore the plumbing until I manage to turn on the hot water, then get in the tub and wash myself thoroughly. Yet no matter how much I try to relax and forget today's events, I can't. Nikki's plea to quit echoes in my head.

But how could I willingly give up when it's my only chance to get him back in this lifetime?

I can't deny that I'm at a disadvantage given my frail human condition. Even if there are other humans in the competition, considering the abilities I've seen displayed today, I doubt *any* will make it out alive.

And that leaves only one recourse.

I need to become better—*stronger*. And the first step is information. I need to find out as much as I can about the other contestants—their strengths and weaknesses.

Taking a deep breath, I rinse myself before dressing up and heading back to the room. Thea is already in her bed, fast asleep. I get under the covers and close my eyes.

I sleep like the dead. I'm utterly content under the blanket, my body cocooned in warmth and comfort. Maybe it's the exhaustion of the day, or simply my mind being in dire need of a break, but I don't think I've ever had a better sleep.

And it's all being made even better by the fact that Nikki appears in my dreams, hugging me from behind and resting his chin in the crook of my shoulder. His breath is on my skin, the beat of his heart loud in my ears.

"Luce? You need to wake up," a voice calls out to me.

I groan, pulling the covers over my head.

"Five more minutes," I grumble. I'm not ready to give up this perfect dream yet. If only I could hang onto it just for a few more moments...

"Luce! Come on, the second trial announcement will start soon."

My eyes snap open at hearing that, and I jump into a sitting position.

"Come on, get ready. I'll be outside," Thea says, waving at me and getting out of the room.

I rub my eyes as a yawn escapes me. Damn, but that was a fine dream.

Scrambling off the bed to get dressed, I almost don't notice the imprint on my bed. I carefully pull the blanket off the bed as I study the sheet and pillow with a frown. There's the outline of my body, but there's another outline—particularly on the pillow, there's the impression of another head.

"Nikki?" I whisper, hope blossoming inside my chest.

After the way he disappeared yesterday, I was heartbroken at thinking he might be mad at me. But if he was here... If my dream wasn't just a dream...

"Thank you," I say with a smile, hugging my arms to my chest and imagining it's his embrace instead.

My mood vastly improves as I realize that Nikki likely spent the night with me, holding me in his arms. With a smile on my face, I quickly get dressed and go to meet the others.

"I'm ready," I call out excitedly. "Let's do this!"

"My, my, you're in a terrific mood today, Luce." Thea chuckles.

I nod vigorously.

"I'm very optimistic about this," I say, happily hopping

around until I reach their side. Ze's mood, on the other hand, is right about the opposite as he glares at me.

I ignore him as I squeeze between Thea and Cer.

He scowls at Cer, which prompts him to offer his spot to Ze.

"It seems someone didn't sleep very well last night," I quip playfully as I look up at Ze's sour expression.

He narrows his eyes at me.

"I did not," he replies in a strained voice.

"Well, I did, so keep your surliness to yourself, okay?" I smile, skipping about, unable to contain my energy. I'm not about to let him or anyone ruin my good mood.

"Why are you smiling like a fool, human?" Ze barks out.

"Maybe I am a fool." I shrug. "But I'm a happy fool," I say as I stick out my tongue at him.

"Stop smiling," he grits out.

"Nope." I shake my head.

"I forbid you to smile without my approval, human." He stops in his tracks, his eyes shooting daggers at me.

"Good thing I don't *need* your approval." I wink. Not even his arrogance can make me lose my temper today.

"Human," he growls low in his throat. Coming toward me, he stops just as his chest meets mine. With how tall he is, I need to crane my head back to the maximum to be able to look into his eyes.

"Yes, Sir Sparkles?" I ask innocently.

His cheek twitches dangerously.

I raise a brow at him, daring him to tell me more of what I can and can't do—just to prove him the opposite.

"Stop. Smiling," he repeats.

"Make. Me." I stretch my lips into a wider smile.

Out of nowhere, his hands shoot out, his fingers on the corners of my mouth as he pulls my lips down. His brows are knit together in concentration as he tries to stop me from smiling.

Damn, someone *really* didn't sleep well last night if he's so bothered by a simple smile.

He somehow manages to pull my lips into a flat line. His own lips twitch in response. He proudly nods to himself as he continues to stare at me with those intense eyes of his. There's something odd about the way he regards me, and in a weird twist of fate, I don't know whether to feel flustered or incensed at his behavior.

"I think we shouldn't start the day with a conflict," Thea intervenes, sneaking between us. His hands drop from my face, but his expression doesn't change. If anything, I catch a note of wistfulness, but I could be wrong. I don't think Ze has more than two basic emotions—annoyance and arrogance.

"We need to show a strong front. People are watching," she says as she inclines her head toward the audience gathered around us.

Ze mumbles something under his breath as he pushes his chin up in indignation, but not before he gives me one last scathing look.

Just what the hell is his deal today?

I roll my eyes, taking Thea's arm and continuing toward the courtyard. On our way, we have the opportunity to see more teams. Most of them are in pairs of four or a maximum of five, with very few in duos or trios. Some are humanoid-looking like the foxes from yesterday while some are less...normal-looking— at least *my* kind of normal. There's a wide variety of horns, tails, and other...appendages.

"In Christian lore, demons are the ones with horns general- ly," I mention quietly to Thea.

"Oh, those?" She points directly to one of the horned groups —who immediately take note of her interest. "They're some incubi species. Right, Cer?"

"Don't look at them, Thea. They'll take it as an invitation."

"Invitation?" I frown.

"They...feed on sex," Cer explains, doing his best to keep a straight face.

"Oh." My curiosity immediately plummets as I avert my gaze.

"Oh, indeed." Thea chuckles. "I guess they would be seen as demons in your world, but it's not what we'd technically call a demon. Humans tend to call any being with less than honorable intentions a demon."

Cer nods. "They're known to usually prey on humans since they are the easiest to control. They've been around for thousands of years in your world."

My lashes flutter in disbelief. First, there are demons that feed on human souls. Now there are other creatures that prey on humans? My God! A shudder goes down my back as I realize just how unsafe my world is. And here I thought that my past was the epitome of fucked up. But it seems it doesn't even begin to cover the reality.

"Does no one stop them from taking advantage of people?" I ask, horrified.

"No one has reason to." He shrugs. "A lot of the species you see here are parasitic in one way or another. They're all looking out for their best interests."

"What about you guys? You fight demons. Can't you fight them, too?"

Ze snorts from the back. I turn and notice he's walking right behind me. "It is not our duty," he intervenes in his scholarly tone. "Although some species may cause human death, they don't cause the total annihilation of the soul. We're merely charged with protecting the cycle of the soul. Human life means little to us."

"I wasn't talking to you," I tell him before turning my attention back to Cer. He's still not off the hook after his behavior.

"Your world has a trophic chain. In the grand scheme of things, these species also occupy a position in the universe's trophic chain," Cer notes.

"You mean to tell me humans are not at the pinnacle of evolution? What a controversial statement." I laugh.

"Cerenios," Ze calls his name, a warning echoing in his voice.

Cer gives him an odd look and, shaking his head, he steps to the side to allow Ze to get in line with us.

God, he's like a petulant child upset he's not the center of attention.

"Your reality is merely one of many," Ze continues as he resumes his spot by my side. Hands behind his back, he walks as if he owns the entire place. "There are many worlds out there, and even more realms. But most of them are in agreement on one thing—humans are at the bottom."

I roll my eyes at him. What did I even expect him to say?

"Might I remind you that you have a *human* on your team?"

"I am aware," he states blankly. "You should thank the fates for bringing me into your life."

Thea can barely contain her smile, while Cer isn't far behind. Only Ze isn't laughing—because he's actually *serious.* He believes what he's saying.

"Oh, I am *so* very lucky," I add sarcastically. "What would have become of me if it weren't for your magnanimity?"

"Good of you to recognize your good fortune." He nods, pleased. "I knew you were wise for a human," he continues.

My hands curl into fists by my side as I barely resist the urge to tell him just how lucky I feel.

"It's not worth it," Thea whispers in my ear.

I blow out an annoyed breath. Yes, it's not the time to get mad at him. The man can't even recognize sarcasm. If anything, I should pity him and his narrow worldview.

As we reach the courtyard, I note just how many people there are. There must be a few hundred—if not more. Since we came a little late, we're in the back.

We make our way a little farther into the crowd before Ze suddenly puts a stop to it, placing his arm in front of me.

"That is enough," he commands, his eyes monitoring the movement of everyone around us. Although he's been a grouchy asshole all morning, I value his insight when it comes to the competition.

He pulls me backward, placing himself behind me as he

rests his hands on my shoulders. I blink in confusion, but I don't question it when Cer does the same with Thea. A few moments roll by before a noise erupts from the front. The crowd grows wild as people start chanting an odd name.

"Milado, Milado!"

"What's happening?" I ask Ze. With everyone taller than me, the only things I can see are people's backs—*lots* of backs.

"Someone is on the stage," he answers laconically.

"I kind of gathered that." I sigh. "But who is it? Can you tell me what's happening? I can't see anything, in case you haven't noticed," I add drily.

"I have noticed," he replies glibly. "You are a very small human. Somewhat like a little pet."

"W-what? A pet?" I sputter, my eyes widening in shock. I turn to face him, ready to let him know that he's crossed the line. But in his nonchalant style, Ze doesn't stop there.

"Yes." He nods thoughtfully. "A cuddly little pet. If you strayed on my grounds, I would spare your life. Maybe feed you. Maybe I would even keep you," he says as he taps his finger against his chin.

"Wow, Ze. That's so generous of you. I would *love* to be your pet. Why, I can't believe you'd even feed me!" Of course, the full-on sarcasm is lost on him.

"You do need more meat on your bones," he points out as his eyes scan my frame.

"I think you should stop there," I warn, narrowing my eyes at him. "Jesus, you need to read a book on sarcasm," I mutter, shaking my head.

Suddenly, he frowns.

"Who is this Jesus and why are you suddenly bringing him up, human?" he demands, his eyes glinting dangerously.

"What? You don't know who Jesus is?"

"You are forbidden from saying that name again." He places his finger against my lips. "You cannot simply say another man's name in conversation with me."

I blink slowly as I stare at him. He doesn't even know who Jesus is...

Why do I even try?

Removing his finger from my person, I release a sigh as I turn my back to him. Ignoring him is the best course of action when he's so vexing. Otherwise, I may end up saying or doing something that's entirely unbecoming.

"And I still don't know what's happening on the stage," I mumble, squaring my shoulders.

"It's the host for this trial," Thea says, finally taking pity on me. "He's a minor Earth deity if I'm not mistaken."

"He is," Ze grunts, inserting himself in the conversation—*again*. I sneak a glance at him and note that he doesn't seem very pleased with Milado's appearance.

"You know him?"

"I know his kind."

"And?" I probe.

"I do not like them," he growls. He doesn't explain further. He merely directs his attention to the stage, no doubt imagining countless scenarios in which he could harm that Milado person.

"He hates Earth deities," Thea leans in to whisper. "He's been badgered for a long time by a slew of Earth nymphs—among others."

"Earth nymphs?"

"Minor deities, but they always think themselves so important." Thea rolls her eyes. "They think he's a catch, so there's a running bet on who's going to land him first."

I blink in surprise.

"Are we talking about the same Ze?"

He might be good-looking, but I doubt anyone would consider his *extraordinarily sociable* personality a prize.

"Yes, I don't know how *that* happened." She laughs.

"I will have you know that I am *very* sought-after," Ze intervenes with a huff. "I have been branded the most eligible mate at every court I have been to."

"I can't say I know why," I say, struggling not to laugh.

He narrows his eyes at me.

"Of course you would not. Your human mind is too narrow for that."

"I will accept that as my fault." I nod, amused.

He stares me down.

I shake my head and turn, ignoring him and his *too* inflated ego. *Most eligible mate,* my ass. I truly wonder how *that* happened.

Leaning closer to Thea, I whisper, "Is this the part where you finally admit to me that you're *not* a harpy?"

She blinks repeatedly as her eyes widen.

"Is it that obvious?"

"I was waiting for you to tell me on your own, but yes. It is very obvious."

"Drat it," she mumbles. "I thought I was good at it."

"You were quite mediocre." I pat her shoulder. "Except the claws. Those were a good addition."

She releases a dramatic sigh, though the corners of her mouth twitch in amusement. "We're from a realm called Arche," Thea mentions with a tight smile.

"Arche?" My brows go up. "Why the lie then?"

"Don't take it personally, Luce. I didn't want to lie, but we're technically not supposed to be here," she whispers. "So please, don't tell anyone or we'll be in big trouble."

"Of course. I wouldn't say anything that might harm you."

"Everything else I told you is true. Ze and Cer are part of an army that fights demons. I'm...well... I'm still taking my exams." She sighs.

"You are overly gregarious today, Erithea," Ze comments in his imperial tone.

She whips her gaze up, wariness entering her eyes. It's not the first time I've seen this. She's always careful around Ze, almost as if she fears him. And then there's also our conversation from last night in which she told me to be careful with him. I can't help but wonder what happened between them...

"She's not dumb, Ze. She was bound to figure out I lied," she shrugs.

"Because it was not a good lie in the first place," he shoots back. "Harpies," he snorts. "It is little wonder that you have failed your exams five times already."

Thea's eyes widen with hurt. She blinks slowly as she nibbles at her lip.

"Ze! That was uncalled for." Cer shoots him a look—the first time he's been anything but deferential with him.

"Stop bullying my friend, Ze," I intervene in a stern tone. "You are being mean for no reason."

"I am only speaking the truth," he points out matter-of-factly.

"Sometimes it's better to be silent than be so insensitive."

He looks down at me, his eyes narrowing dangerously.

"You think I am insensitive?" he asks in a low voice.

"That's an understatement." I roll my eyes. "You've been behaving abysmally the entire morning. What's gotten into you?" I ask, exasperated with his behavior. In the past, I might have seen his cluelessness about the world as cute. But this is straight-up mean.

He blinks slowly.

"I see. I shall attempt to be more sensitive, then." He nods, pursing his lips.

"I think you owe us an apology."

TWENTY-EIGHT

He looks at Thea, a soft warning in his gaze. Turning back to me, he simply stares at me for moments on end, his mouth opening and closing as if it's physically hurting him to say the words.

"I," he starts, swallowing in discomfort. I lean into him, ready to hear the magic words. "I—" He clears his throat, his Adam's apple bobbing up and down.

"Welcome to P'davi," a voice resounds from the stage, saving Ze from having to swallow his pride and, God forbid, apologize!

Shaking my head at him, I turn my attention to the stage. I should have known he wouldn't be capable of an apology—he who wastes no time in pointing out how inferior the rest of us are compared to him. I blow out an annoyed breath as I try to calm myself down. It's not worth it to get so incensed over him. Not when I have more pressing things to focus on—like getting ready for the second trial.

Ze puts his hands on my back, his big body a barrier between me and the rest of the crowd. In an unprecedented gesture, he leans down, placing his chin on my shoulder, his mouth angled toward my ear.

"I apologize," he whispers in a barely audible voice. The

crowd is so raucous that for a moment I think I'm imagining things. "Will you forgive me?"

I swallow, the heat of his body seeping into mine.

Never did I expect him to *actually* apologize.

"Do you promise to try to be nicer?" I murmur, looking straight ahead and ignoring his proximity.

There's a pause as he breathes deeply, blowing hot air into my ear.

"For you." He sighs, his voice low and gravelly.

Before I can question him about what he means by that, he resumes his position, his attention back on the stage. Meanwhile, all I can think is how odd Ze is. He keeps surprising me, and at times such as this, it's a rather pleasant surprise. Maybe not all is lost when it comes to him.

"I am so pleased to see so many of you here. I trust that the first trial hasn't been too hard?" Milado calls out.

A chorus of *no*s resounds from the crowd. They probably didn't encounter a soul-eating demon in their trial.

"As you know, each trial will become increasingly harder. I see a few hundred of you here. I wonder how many of you will make it to the next round." A chuckle. "Some of you might not be aware, but P'davi is an intermediary realm that connects all other worlds together. Every place outside of this complex might lead you to an unknown world, some of which could prove quite hostile. All of you come from different worlds, with different evolutionary mechanisms that enable your species to thrive in *one* particular environment. But to compete in this game, you'll need to be able to thrive in *all* environments.

"Regardless of your abilities, or *lack* of, you all have something in common. All of you have *mortal* bodies," he proclaims, eliciting displeased sounds from the crowd. "And if you die in this game, you forfeit the immortality of your soul."

I wish I could see him to associate a voice with a face, but with everyone so much taller than me, the only thing I can see is the back of some random person. It's in vain even if I raise myself on the tips of my toes.

"And that brings me to the second trial of The Wishing Game. Are you ready to know?"

"Yes," everyone shouts.

"Good. I like the enthusiasm." Milado laughs. "You see, the moment you stepped into P'davi and left your worlds behind, your clock started ticking."

I frown. What does he mean by that?

"There are only a few worlds whose atmospheres are similar enough for multiple species to live in, as you well know. But that will not be the case with the ones you will encounter in this game. In plainer terms, that means you are all currently *dying*."

Gasps erupt from the crowd.

"No need to panic. Yet." Milado chuckles. "The air is toxic for mortals in P'davi, as it is in a lot of the worlds P'davi connects to. Some are more toxic, some are less. Here, you have a fortnight until your body will fail you. Until then, you will get increasingly weaker and slower, until you won't be able to move at all. Of course, if you happen to stumble upon a worse world, that process will be accelerated."

What?

I blink slowly as I take in the new information. Sneaking a glance at Thea, I note she's avidly listening to Milado. But is she surprised? Did she know about this? I find it difficult to believe she wouldn't when she knows so much...

"In response to that comes the second trial. Those who survive at the end of the fortnight will automatically pass to the next trial."

"What is he talking about?" I ask as I turn to Ze.

"Listen." He nods, pointing to the stage.

"Since we want to be as fair as possible, I have a few clues for you. P'davi is the only realm that hosts a wide range of healing plants, among which there are three of them that can give you immunity not only within P'davi, but in every world in existence."

My eyes widen.

"For the next two weeks, your task will be to search the

wilderness of P'davi for these three plants. But the ticking clock isn't your only enemy. You must be careful not to stray into another world—it might prove fatal. And you must be wary of your competitors. Starting with this trial, inter-contestant fighting is officially encouraged. You can take out competition as you like, or only when you feel they are a threat to you."

"How is all that even possible?" I ask, appalled. It seems like a straight-up death sentence. Not only will we weaken progressively over the course of the two weeks, but now we also have to contend with traps that lead into other worlds and belligerent competitors who will have all the incentive to attack us.

"Now for the clues. The plants you will need to gather are as follows: *ridea*, *doyen*, and *saelica*. Every team will receive illustrations of the plants. But you will have to be *very* careful, as there are plenty of other similar-looking plants that have completely different effects."

Great! Add poisoning by the wrong plant to the list of obstacles of this trial. Everything is a double-edged sword here. I wouldn't have expected it to be simple, but not *this* difficult.

"There is a library in the complex, and you may avail yourself of its resources to track down the plants. But remember, the clock is ticking. If you survive your death day—exactly fourteen days from the moment you arrived in P'davi—you will be visited by the messenger wraith to secure your spot in the third trial. If you die..." he trails off.

"That will be all for today. The illustrations will be waiting for you at your accommodation. The second trial has officially commenced!"

The crowd erupts in claps and shouts and soon, everything turns to mayhem.

Ze grabs my hand, steering me away from the crowd. Cer and Thea fall into step with us, their expressions grave.

"We need to come up with a plan," I say. "And fast. We only have thirteen days left."

Ze's lips flatten into a thin line as he nods.

"You three will go to our accommodation to get the illustrations. I will meet you there."

"Where are you going?" I frown.

"Library. We will need maps of P'davi, perhaps a book on flora and fauna if there is one. Everyone will be crowding the libraries soon, so having a head start will be useful."

He doesn't wait for our acknowledgment before he disappears.

"Did you know about this?" I ask as we reach our suite.

Thea purses her lips.

"I was aware of the incompatibility issue, but I didn't think they would make a trial out of it. In past editions, the brew was provided to participants on arrival."

I take a deep breath, slumping into a chair. Just as Milado said, three illustrations await us on the table, each depicting a plant. One of them has blue, elongated flowers, another yellow ones, while the other is comprised solely of leaves—very *common*-looking leaves.

"Can *anyone* pass this trial?" I whisper, hopelessness lacing my voice.

There are just so many variables involved, which makes the entire ordeal even more dangerous.

"Of course," she promptly replies.

"There are some species that have an affinity for plants," Cer adds grimly.

"Great," I mumble.

In less than a minute, Ze makes his appearance in the room carrying a stack of books. He drops them onto the kitchen table with a thud.

"I took everything that might be of help to us. Maps, botany books, and some history tomes."

"There's just one issue," I point out as I pick up one of the books. "We don't speak this... language."

The letters look like hieroglyphs. The maps, too, are not designed in the way a map would be in my world. Everything is foreign and strange, and tears of frustration stab at the back of my eyes.

My hands tremble as I put the book down, and with a startling realization, I note that I may be close to my boiling point.

From the start of the game, everything has happened so fast, I've barely had time to grasp all the strange events leading up to this. But this goes beyond just the game. It all started with the accident, after which I became semi-numb to reality. Maybe if I weren't so desperate for any modicum of hope, I would have never entertained the thought that other worlds might exist— that there might be other species out there.

But because I was so devastated by Nikki's loss, I was able to push aside the rational part of my brain and give in to the *irrational*.

Yet now that it's slowly catching up with me, I can't help but wonder.

What the hell did I get myself into?

From demons, fox people, gods, and other strange beings to toxic worlds and other hellish dimensions, I've barely had a moment to catch my breath. And now? If we don't get these plants in time, I'm going to die.

I swallow hard, closing my eyes as I try to get a hold of myself.

Inhale. Exhale.

My heart is pounding in my chest, my anxiety poking its head at the most inopportune moment. Reality dims until all I can hear is my erratic pulse.

"You may not, but Cerenios and I do," Ze replies with a huff.

I take a deep breath, holding onto his voice as I attempt to hold onto my sanity.

"It's part of their military training," Thea whispers.

My eyes flare up with renewed hope just as I succeed in calming myself.

"You do?" I squeak, all but jumping out of my chair. "Then what should we do first? Where to?"

I don't say, however, what I'm really thinking—we have to *do* something before I become a slave to my emotions and dangerous thoughts again. I force a smile on my face so they don't see the turmoil inside of me. The less time I have to over-think, the better.

Cer spreads out a map on the table, pressing the palms of his hands onto the edges to hold it in place. The illustration is nothing like the high-resolution maps you can find in my world. The design is more antiquated, with mountains depicted by raised peaks, water by wavy lines, and other elements in a basic composition that reminds me of ancient parchment maps.

"We're here." Cer points to a spot on the far right of the map. There are drawings of trees all around, indicating a large forest.

"The host said P'davi is an intermediary realm. What exactly is that?"

"It is a buffer zone between worlds. These realms were specifically created to avoid conflicts," Ze replies. "It is why their atmosphere is poisonous for all who trespass, so that it would prevent the imperialistic ambitions of certain worlds."

"But how come there were other species in *my* world? Like the foxes? Or the other furred people?" And how the hell do humans not know about their existence? How are we coexisting with such different species without realizing it?

Ze's lips flatten in displeasure.

"There was a Great Migration some thousands of years ago when the intermediary realms were weakened. Worlds meshed together and people were separated from their families. Back then, the inhabitants of Alopea, the fox realm, originally could only maintain their humanoid form for a brief period of time. But after the Great Migration, they adapted to living longer in their humanoid skins in order to avoid detection by humans. It is the same for other species that made Anthropa—your world— their home as well. They can pass as human, but they are *not* human. You will notice that others prefer their non-humanoid form in this game, and that is because they are endemic to a different world," Ze explains.

"That's a lot to take in," I swallow.

"There is more to it that I will not get into at the moment, but the aim of intermediary realms is to keep individual worlds at peace and independent. The only beings who can traipse freely are deities."

"What about demons, then? They are able to move between worlds too, are they not?"

Ze straightens his spine, his hands behind his back as he paces back and forth while talking.

"They can only travel between worlds in their spiritual form. Once they become corporeal, they are stuck in that world. But you do not need to concern yourself with demons. They are unlikely to make their home in P'davi because there are no souls to consume."

"One less problem to think about. Yay?" I laugh nervously before I quickly sober up. "But how come *you* guys are able to cross worlds?" I raise a brow. Now that I know they are from a world called Aperion, that only raises more questions as to what they are. I don't doubt that Ze and Cer are part of the military, or that Thea failed some exams, as Ze is prone to point out, but I don't know more than that about them. What's their relationship with the game? Or with the deities hosting the game, for that matter, since they seemed to be familiar with them?

"We *hunt* demons," Ze replies curtly.

I nod thoughtfully. That makes sense, but why do I feel like there's more to it? It hasn't escaped me that they've been quite cagey with their identity aside from a few crumbs that they let drop here and there. It's odd that despite that, my gut is telling me that I can trust them. And so far, all evidence points to the same conclusion. Their origins might be mysterious, but they are on my side.

For now, that's enough for me.

If what Thea said was true and their presence here would endanger them, then I will not force them into revealing their identities. I trust that they will tell me themselves when the time is right.

"Does that mean you don't need the plants?"

Both Thea and Cer turn to look expectantly at Ze.

"That is correct." He clears his throat. "We are, however, a team. Your weakness, *our* weakness, isn't that so, Cerenios? Erithea?" he asks in a booming voice.

"Yes," they both answer, amusement brewing between the two of them.

"So it is settled. Rest assured, you will not die, human." Ze gives me a confident nod.

He might be annoying with his supercilious attitude, but he *is* good at what he does. That means I have to put my trust in him—well, not that I have much choice considering I'm the *only* one dying here.

"Back to the map?" Cer interjects.

"You may proceed, Cerenios." Ze gives him a nod.

"As I said earlier, we are here. There are two major forests in P'davi. There is one that is located right next to our complex, here." He points to the gathering of trees represented next to our complex. "But there is another one here."

Ze narrows his eyes. Picking up one of the history tomes, he rapidly sifts through the pages, his pupils moving at the speed of light. Before I can even blink, he closes the book, placing it back on the desk.

"One of the plants is endemic to the western forest while the other two are found in the eastern one."

Did he just read the entire book in a matter of seconds?

"That's...impressive," I mumble in awe.

His lips curl up as he soaks in the praise.

"The most efficient way is to split up. Two of us will go to the eastern forest and two will go to the western one. We would then meet again at a designated location to make the brew."

Ze nods.

"It should be a medial location to the two forests. The farther away from the complex the better. We don't want to risk an ambush when we return with the plants," I offer.

"Cerenios and Erithea will tackle the eastern forest. I will take the human to the western one," Ze declares.

"And we have no say in this?" I raise a brow.

"No. You do not." He pins me with his gaze. "This is the optimal division of labor." He doesn't wait for a reply as he turns his attention to the botany books, flipping through them and absorbing all the knowledge.

"I am ready," he proclaims, grabbing my hand and pulling me to my feet. "I will communicate a meeting place at a later date," he tells Cer.

"Just be careful, Ze. Don't overdo it. Now more than ever..."

Ze gives him a tight nod.

"What are you doing..." I hiss as he all but drags me toward the door.

"The western forest is a good distance away from here. We need to depart now if we want to make it in time."

"Fine," I exhale deeply. Wrenching my hand from his grasp, I follow behind as he leads the way.

Thirteen days.

In thirteen days, I will be dead if we don't find those plants.

A shiver goes down my spine as I realize just how precarious the situation I'm in is. And it's not even *just* about me anymore, or Nikki. It's about my teammates too. If anything happens to me, not only will I cease to exist. So will they.

Maybe Nikki was right. Maybe this *is* too dangerous. But what is the alternative? Living without him for the rest of my days? Taking my own life so I could see him faster? But even then, who's to say we'll even meet again in the next life?

I *cannot* continue on without him. The only reason I've managed to do it so far has been because I refused to give in to my grief. I chose to focus on my goal to bring him back instead. But until now, I haven't let myself think of the possibility of failure. I could *not* even entertain the thought that I might lose.

But what if...

No! I shake myself the moment that thought enters my mind.

I can't let myself get distracted.

Gazing up ahead at Ze's broad back that radiates with strength, I get a renewed burst of confidence.

"Ze?"

He half turns toward me.

"I'm glad we're on the same team." I smile tentatively.

His brows shoot up, his expression one of surprise. His cheeks heat up before he suddenly looks away.

"As you should," he grumbles—but his tone isn't as biting as before.

And that, ladies and gentlemen, is what I call progress.

TWENTY-NINE

It's night when Ze finally suggests we take a break. The soles of my feet ache, and my muscles are so tense, it takes Herculean strength for me to continue forward. Yet in all this time, I haven't complained—not when everything rests on this journey and successfully finding the third plant. Ze already considers me the weakest link of our team. I don't want to give him more reason to look down on me.

We've probably walked for close to ten hours now. The road was a mixture of desolate desert and steppe before we finally spotted a hint of tall, green trees.

"We shall rest here for the night," he declares as he stops in the middle of a patch of grass nestled among towering foliage and sprawling trees.

He doesn't need to say it twice as I plop myself on the ground, the soft grass cushioning my ungraceful fall. I take a deep breath, a whimper escaping me as I bring my fist against my thighs and calves, hoping to unknot some of the residual tension.

Ze takes one look at me and shakes his head. But he makes himself useful as he gathers some stones, twigs, and dry grass to make a fire. His movements are swift and confident, and a spark bursts to life from the first attempt.

I drag myself closer, letting the heat from the flame caress my skin. Although the temperature was warm during daytime, the moment it got dark, it started getting chillier. I made a good decision to wear my hoodie, but even with it, a shiver goes down my back.

He drops our small bag with supplies by my side before joining me next to the fire. Despite our sudden departure, I was surprised by his comprehensive planning. By the time he dragged me out of our apartment, he already had a bag packed with snacks and water to last us a couple of days. Even more surprising had been the fact that he'd packed *only* non-meat options.

He sits cross-legged, his palms on his knees, his expression blank. His clothes are in perfect order, not one drop of sweat on his forehead, whereas I'm almost drowning in mine. Even his features are as fresh as if he just woke up from a nap.

"I'm surprised you know how to make a fire," I mention.

"Huh?" He raises an arrogant brow.

"That right there." I point at him, my lips quirking up. "You're such a snob I didn't think you'd know basic skills like the rest of us."

"And how is it that you have come to that conclusion?" he inquires lazily.

"You probably live in a palace and are waited on hand and foot by an army of poor servants." I shrug.

He stares at me for a moment before he throws his head back and starts laughing.

I blink.

Is this... This is the first time I've seen him laugh, no?

As if he could read my mind, he suddenly stops, his features frozen in place like he surprised his own self with his reaction.

"Your assumption is erroneous." He clears his throat. "I do live in a palace," he continues.

"Aha, I knew it." I grin.

"But"—he puts a finger up—"I do not have any servants."

"You don't?"

"As for how I learned to make a fire," he continues, ignoring my cry of surprise. "I am a soldier. I have lived most of my life on the battlefield, where you sleep under the naked sky. On the rare occasion, I slept in a tent. The palace is a rather...new addition," he adds awkwardly.

"But Thea said you're the boss, general or commander or whatever."

"That, too, is a rather recent development."

"How recent?" I arch a brow. I don't think our conceptions of time are the same.

"A few thousand of your human years."

"What?" My mouth is agape as I stare at him. "That is recent for you? Just how old are you?"

His lips flatten.

"Old," he replies flippantly.

"Oh, come on." I smile as I scoot closer. "How old are we talking about?"

He gives me a side-eye.

"Too old for your human mind to comprehend."

"I assure you I can comprehend numbers just fine. Come on, Ze." I pout at him. "You don't have to be embarrassed. You look fine for your age. Why, you don't have any wrinkles," I joke as I pat his hand.

He looks down where I'm touching him before his gaze snaps up to mine, his eyes narrowing.

My smile freezes on my face, and for a moment, I'm afraid I might have offended him somehow. We've already established that nine times out of ten we don't speak the same language.

"I do not know," he utters in a low voice.

"What?" I blink, thinking I didn't hear him right.

"*I do not know*," he grits his teeth.

"What do you mean you don't know? When is your birthday?" I probe, ready to do the math for him. Maybe he's so old that he's lost track of time, or he simply stopped counting altogether.

"I do not know that either." He presses his lips together.

I frown. "Do you guys not celebrate birthdays in your world?"

"Others do," he replies curtly.

"But not you."

A single nod.

"Why?"

"*Human*," he growls, the sound vibrating in the stillness of the night.

Oh no... Did I hit a sore spot?

"I'm sorry if this is something you don't like to talk about," I murmur softly. God, but now *I* am the insensitive one.

He grunts, and just as I'm about to take my hand away, he grabs onto it, covering it with his own.

"I was a soldier for a few thousand years before I advanced to my current position," he starts, his voice the same steely baritone as before, yet there's a light tremor to it. "I have no living relatives who could comment on my age or birthday, but I would estimate I am over seven thousand years old in your human years."

"Oh..." Is there anything else I can say to that other than *oh?* The man is older than the Bible—*and* Earth according to the Bible.

"That is quite old," I nod.

His brows furrow as if deep in thought. He emulates my nod.

"So you've never celebrated your birthday?"

He stares at me. Another nod.

"Ze..." I trail off, my gaze softening.

"Don't you dare pity me, human," he warns, squeezing my hand.

"No, of course not," I hurry to say. Someone as proud as Ze would hate to be the object of pity. "I just feel sad for you. Birthdays are awesome." I smile tentatively.

He's still staring at me, his gaze intent.

Recognizing this is a rare moment in which he's sharing

something about himself, I decide to do the same to make him feel better.

"I didn't celebrate my birthday for a long time either," I confess.

His eyes flare.

"Why?" he asks quietly.

A melancholic smile plays across my lips.

"I was extremely poor growing up. My mother barely had enough to feed me on a day-to-day basis. I never got a gift or even a special meal. Then I was a slave for many years, so no one cared about me." I swallow.

His features harden.

"You said the people who enslaved you are already dead?"

I give him a tight nod.

"That's a pity," he sighs dramatically. "I would have enjoyed breaking their bones."

My lips spread in a genuine smile as I turn my hand palm up, lacing my fingers through his. He's startled by it but doesn't seem averse to it as his gaze drops to our fingers.

"Thank you for saying that. It means a lot to me." And that is the real Ze. He might be surly and rude and socially inept, but he's a real friend.

"Maybe not all is lost. I'm sure we can do something about it..." he trails off as he sinks deep in thought.

I shake my head at him, but I appreciate the initiative. And this time, it's not because we're a team and what happens to one reflects on the others—he's simply mad on my behalf.

"As I was saying," I clear my throat. "I was nineteen when I escaped the hacienda, and after that..." Warmth floods me at the vivid memories, my features lighting up.

"After that?" Ze asks curiously, leaning in. He has an avid expression on his face, waiting for me to continue.

"After that my husband made sure to celebrate my birthday every year. It became our tradition. He would prepare surprises for me and I would do the same for him. We made it a competition on who would come up with the best gift each year..." I add wistfully.

Ze's body tenses, and an indecipherable emotion enters his features. He tightens his hold over my hand, his thumb rubbing circles on my wrist. He squeezes his eyes shut as he takes a couple of deep breaths, almost as if he were in physical pain.

My brows furrow as I stare at him. Suddenly, his eyes snap open, jolting me closer as he pulls on my arm.

"When is *your* birthday?" he asks in a slow, deliberate voice.

His eyes bore into me, the dark of his irises glinting dangerously.

"September sixth."

"That would be sixth of Ananke in my world."

"Ananke?"

"There are fifteen months, each one dedicated to one of the ruling royal houses. Ananke is the ninth one."

"Sixth of Ananke," I repeat, tasting the words on my lips.

"Ananke is a good month," he mentions, nodding thoughtfully.

Silence descends as a look of concentration enters his features. Suddenly, he bursts out, "I have decided, human." His voice booms in that arrogant lilt of his. "I will allow you to give me a birthday. You may choose a month and a day."

I blink at him.

"You want me to choose a birthday for you?" I squeak.

"That is what I said, human. It is a great honor. You may rejoice." He nods, his lips twitching.

I refrain from rolling my eyes—such an honor!

"Fine. What month would you like?"

Although he still needs work on his delivery, I can sense that him *asking* for it would be revealing too much of a weakness— that he *wants* a birthday. Somehow it reminds me of his ridiculous encounter with *trendy* clothes and the way he'd desperately wanted to fit in but would have never admitted it aloud.

"It is up to you."

"Hmm. What about the third month?"

"I do not like the number three."

"Seven?" I throw out a random number.

"That is Flora." He wrinkles his nose. "I do not care for it."

"One?"

"I am banned from it," he mentions, shaking his head.

"Five," I say.

"They do not care for me," he echoes yet another objection.

I frown. Okay, fine. Ten more options.

"Eight?"

He immediately shakes his head.

"It is an unlucky number."

I give him another three suggestions, which he promptly rejects.

Throwing my hands up in the air, I blow out an annoyed breath. "I give up. Just tell me what month *is* okay with you."

He licks his lips, his eyes never once leaving mine.

"Ananke is a good month," he adds slowly, uncertainly.

"Okay. Ananke it is then. What about the day?" When he simply stares at me, I add, "What is a good day? Or a lucky day for you?"

He presses his lips together.

"Sa," he answers firmly.

"Sa? What is that?"

"It is a number in my language."

"What number?" I inquire curiously.

He pushes his chin up, for the first time averting his gaze.

"Six," he replies casually.

"Six of Ananke?" I repeat, a little taken aback.

"Yes. Do you have something against it?" he quickly asks, folding his arms across his chest and narrowing his eyes at me.

"No. But we share a birthday now," I point out with a smile.

"Indeed." He nods pensively. "I wager I can give you a better present than you can."

My brows shoot up, my lips trembling with amusement. Oh, Ze. He can never just say something outright, can he?

"Then I shall accept that wager," I chuckle.

He nods to himself. Seconds stretch into minutes as he starts fidgeting in his seat. Eventually, he picks up our bag with supplies. Grabbing a couple of nut bars, he pushes them into my lap.

"Eat," he commands.

I frown at his sudden change in demeanor. But when I don't obey his order, he takes the bar, tears the paper package, and pushes it against my mouth.

"Wha—" I don't even manage to voice my question as he pushes the bar past my lips. I reluctantly bite into it, munching slowly.

"You need your strength. We have walked a long distance today," he says awkwardly.

I nod, taking the bar and biting into it. I'm not *that* hungry, but I guess it wouldn't hurt to eat a little more.

"You should eat, too." I hand him the unopened bar.

"That is for you as well." He pushes the bar back to me. "You are human, and as such weaker. I have plenty of strength," he proudly explains.

Who said Ze doesn't have a way with words?

As I silently eat, he watches me from the corner of his eye. He opens his mouth and closes it a few times before he finally utters the most shocking words, "You did well today."

I stop eating, my eyes widening.

"Did you... Did you just compliment me?"

He shoots me a warning look.

"For a human," he adds.

"Nah." I shake my head in amusement. "You said I did well. Period. You can't just change it."

"Yes, I can. They are my words and I can do as I like with them."

"Which you clearly *always* do." I fight the urge to laugh.

"Precisely. You can take it or leave it."

"My, but if the mighty Ze said I did well today, then I shall count myself forever grateful that he has decided to bestow such a rare and marvelous compliment on this unworthy subject," I add sarcastically—knowing full well it's not a language he's fluent in.

"Indeed." He nods, pleased. "You are a fast study, human."

My facial muscles are betraying me as a snort escapes my lips. I slap my hand over my mouth, but I'm unable to stop the incoming fit of laughter.

"You are mocking me?" Ze leans back, his horrified eyes on me.

"Mocking? You? Of course not." I wave my hand. "I'm...p-praising you."

He stares at me for a few more moments before he nods, seemingly mollified by my words.

"You are an odd human." He tsks to himself.

"I shall attempt to do better." I incline my head in a half-bow.

He swings his sharp gaze to me. I swallow, unmoving. Slowly, his lips curl up. Mine do, too. We just stare at each other, amusement hanging between us.

"Finish your food," he grumbles, the hint of a smile still painted on his lips.

"Yes, sir," I add immediately.

He shakes his head, his lips spreading further into a full-on smile.

I take another bite from my bar, watching him curiously.

"You said you've never been to my world, but have you ever been to *other* worlds?"

"I have. It is the nature of my position to go where duty calls," he replies smoothly.

"What do you do when you're not fighting demons then?"

"What do you mean?" He frowns.

"Do you have any hobbies?"

"Hobbies? What is that?"

"You know, things you do in your spare time," I explain.

His brows are still furrowed, confusion echoing in his features. I purse my lips as I realize he truly has no concept of a *hobby*.

"For example, I love reading books," I say.

"I read books too." He nods.

"Really? What type? What books are there in your world?"

"On military treaties, of course," he scoffs.

I stare at him, my mouth agape.

"That's not fun reading."

"You read for fun?" His eyes widen.

"That is the definition of a hobby. Something you do for fun. Have you never read fiction?"

"That is a frivolous pursuit," he immediately replies. "Only people with no prospects engage in it." A pause. He blinks a couple of times before he leans in, serious. "What is fiction?"

I school my features so I don't laugh.

"Stories. Adventure. Romance. That type of thing."

"And you enjoy this fiction?" he probes, his eyes sparkling with interest.

"I *love* it. My favorite genre is romance. I used to devour one book a day." I sigh wistfully. "Nikki had been a fan as well, and we'd sometimes buddy read books after which he'd surprise me with the recreation of *some* scenes."

"Tell me more about this... romance. What is it exactly?"

"It's a story about two people falling in love and overcoming obstacles before they live happily ever after," I explain excitedly. "Usually, it's a handsome billionaire hero who falls for a sweet and innocent heroine. It's a bit of a cliché, I know." I chuckle. "But clichés are my comfort reads."

He nods slowly, seemingly deep in thought.

"Why billionaire?" He frowns.

I shrug. "I don't know. I guess it's the female desire to be protected and taken care of, and romance novels feed into that fantasy by having a rich, strong, and handsome man as the hero."

"And you say all women want that?"

"Not all, but a great deal do."

He nods again to himself.

"Why do *you* like that?" he suddenly asks.

My cheeks heat up at being put on the spot.

"I-I guess it's because I like the idea of being saved?" I murmur, averting my gaze. "It feels odd to think about it *that* way when I had been saved—Nikki had saved me. Yet I think that a part of me was forever lost at the hacienda—the same part that never got over what happened to me. But how could I say that aloud? Because admitting that would be akin to admitting that Nikki hadn't been enough for me, when he had—hell, he'd been *more* than enough. The failing is solely mine for being unable to move on and forget."

"Let me tell you about this book." I change the topic. Instead of talking about me, it's easier to talk about one of my favorite books. And so I recount a story in which the heroine is a poor seamstress and the hero is a handsome duke. Due to the difference in their stations, their relationship is forbidden, and the duke wants to make the heroine his mistress. The heroine, however, could never live with herself if she had to stay on the sidelines and watch her beloved marry someone of an appropriate station, so she decides to run away, but not before seeing the duke one last time.

Ze listens attentively, which makes me surprisingly happy. It's such a pity that he doesn't believe people should read for fun, but I aim to remedy that. Stories give us life. It's unfair that he's never experienced this before.

His eyes are on me, vivid emotions playing on his face as I reach a poignant scene in the story where the heroine gives the hero one last kiss before she's about to leave him.

"And?" he asks impatiently when I pause. "What happened?" He leans forward, his lips parted almost as if he held his breath for what's to come.

I smile at his enthusiasm.

"He realized she left him the next day and went after her."

I spare him the raunchy details of their reunion since I remember far too well his reaction to *The Game of Thrones* episode. Instead, I give him the PG-13 version of how they made up and the fact that the hero decided to defy society's expectations for her and make her his wife.

"That's it?" He blinks.

"After they married, they lived happily ever after," I finish, releasing a soft yawn.

"That can't be the end," he complains. "There must be more to the story!"

"Nope, that's it," I say, my voice sleepy. "You can use your imagination for what happens next."

"But I want *you* to tell me." He pouts.

My brows shoot up in surprise.

"I can tell you other stories. But not now. I'm too tired..." I trail off.

He stares at me.

"Tomorrow?" he asks in a low, hopeful voice.

"Yeah, sure," I answer automatically just as my eyes close.

I snuggle closer to the warmth of the fire and the soft material cushioning my face. And as I drift off to sleep, my thoughts stray to Nikki.

Is he around, I wonder...

THIRTY

Warm sunlight bathes my face. Slowly, I creep my eyes open, rubbing them gently with my hands to chase the sleep away. But as I turn on my back, I have to blink twice to make sure I'm seeing right. That's when I notice that I'm lying down on a soft material. Ze's sitting with his legs crossed, holding his hands by his side so he won't touch me. But that doesn't change the fact that I've been sleeping on his lap.

"Ze?" I get up, sleepy confusion still clinging to my lashes.

"You're awake?" He looks at me and nods, getting to his feet to stretch.

I gape at him.

"Did I... Did I sleep on your lap the whole night?" I clear my throat.

He nods.

"Oh my God, I'm so sorry! Did you get any sleep?" I burst out, ashamed of myself.

"No. I kept watch," he answers tersely.

"Are you tired? Do you want to take a quick nap while I keep watch? Damn it, you should have woken me up sooner to change places."

He stops, slowly turning toward me.

"Change places?" he asks in a low voice. "Would you allow me to use you as a pillow?"

I'm taken aback by his question, and for a moment, I consider saying no. But it's my fault he didn't get any sleep. It's also imperative that he is rested since I'm relying on his strength in case there's any danger as we continue our journey.

"All right," I eventually answer.

"I suppose a few minutes would not hurt," he mumbles, coming to my side. He plops himself on the floor and places his head on my lap. Everything happens so quickly that I can only stare at him as he makes himself comfortable in my lap, closing his eyes and releasing a deep breath.

I hold myself still even as he relaxes.

Damn it, why did I agree to this? It somehow feels too intimate, not only him sleeping on my lap, but also me sleeping on his.

He doesn't sleep long. In fact, he's up in a matter of minutes, dusting his clothes and looking entirely unbothered.

"Okay, so what's next now? Where are we going?" I ask as I get to my feet.

He scans the ground for a twig, which he uses to draw in the sand the map he memorized.

"We're here. We need to go north and then farther west to reach the forest," he explains. "You will need to be more vigilant as we get closer to the forest. We won't be the only ones searching for that plant."

"Do you think the others already got there?" I ask as I nibble my lip.

"Yesterday at the convocation, I studied some of the competition," he says as he uses his foot to wipe the map. "There are people who I am sure will not make it. But there are also plenty of dangerous species in the competition—even some that have powers to rival those of a god."

My eyes widen.

"What does that mean for us?"

"We will need to be more careful. I am not at my full potential in this realm," he adds as he clears his throat. "Otherwise, of course, I could take each and every one of them," he amends. He straightens his back, his hand going to the hilt of his sword as he caresses the dark handle.

"Of course." I nod, a smile pulling at my lips. His pride would never allow him to admit anything less.

"As I am limited, however, we shall have to avoid a direct confrontation," he continues. "We will also have to avoid drawing too much attention to ourselves, although I suppose killing the foxes did not help," he muses to himself.

"Why would someone so powerful join this competition then? If they are so strong, why would they need a wish from the game?"

"Not all desire a wish," he says, his lips flattening in displeasure.

"What?" I frown.

"There are some that make a sport out of this competition, training in between editions to get greater results."

Realization dawns on me. If they've trained in between editions, they must be hundreds of years old.

"You mean there are some who've participated in the game before? And won?"

"Participated, yes. Won? A few might have. The ones who did not were smart enough to quit at the right time."

"But why? Why would anyone do this?"

"Recognition. Ambition. Pride," he answers glibly. "There is one resolute rule in this competition that has been around for thousands of years. No god or demon can participate. This is all to make the game fair to participants, but that doesn't mean that distant relatives of gods are not competing. And if they are hybrids of another powerful species, that is all it takes for someone to have powers to equal those of a god."

"Oh. Wow. I didn't realize this was *more* than just a game of wishes." I force a wobbly smile.

"The gods are watching this game closely," he explains in a

tight voice. "Those who will make it to the last trial may even gain the favor of one. The opportunities are endless."

"Is that why you're here? To gain recognition? Or is it to gain the approval of a god?" I ask, tilting my head to study him. How is it that until now I haven't even questioned *his* reasons for participating in the game.

A sardonic smile takes possession of his lips, and he stares at me for a moment.

"I am here to gain...something."

"Something?"

"There is *something* of interest to me in this competition," he amends, but his vague reply suggests he doesn't want me to probe further.

I nod slowly.

"Well, I hope you'll get what you wish for. I promise I'll try not to die," I joke, since we're all aware I'm the weakest link of our team.

"You will not die," he grits out, his expression icy.

"Of course. We'll win this game. You'll get your *thing* and I'll get my husband back, and everything will be perfect." I beam at him. Except my words don't seem to warm him up. If anything, his features are taut, his hands clenched into fists by his side. He stares at me, his nostrils flaring. Before I know what's happening, he stalks toward me, his body rippling with unreleased tension.

My eyes widen, and I flinch just as he stops in front of me, instinctively closing my eyes and waiting for an imaginary blow.

Nothing happens.

He doesn't come closer.

I count to ten in my mind before I creep my eyes open. He's staring at me with an odd expression on his face, his arm hanging midair as if reaching for me but never quite making it.

"We're leaving," he states in a rough tone, his arm dropping to his side.

Grabbing the bag off the floor, he swings it over his shoulder. And with that, the conversation is over. He turns his back and marches forward. Silence descends as he continues to walk, with me trailing a few steps behind him.

His broad back fills my vision as I wonder if I said or did something wrong.

We walk for about an hour before I decide that I don't like this awkward silence. Hopping to his side, I grab onto his arm, looking up at him and playfully batting my lashes.

"Want me to tell you another story?"

He gives me a sharp look, but the subtle wiggle of his brows denotes his interest.

He releases a noncommittal grunt, but I don't know if that's a yes or a no.

"Yes? No?" I ask hopefully. When he doesn't reply, I continue. "If you don't want a story, we can talk about something else," I offer. I *hate* awkward silences, just as I hate feeling I said something wrong and upset him.

His gaze dips to me, his lips twitching.

"Why don't you tell me more about that new palace of yours? Did you decorate it? How many rooms does it have?" The questions are out of my mouth before I can help myself. But going by the slight smile I detect on his lips, he's not *too* bothered.

"Are you bored, human?" he suddenly asks, raising a brow at me.

"Are you mad at me for something, Sir Sparkles?" Although I meant for it to be a playful question, I fear that my insecurities must have bled through.

"I am not mad at you." He shakes his head.

"Promise?" I insist.

He purses his lips, giving me a long look.

"I am mad at myself," he reluctantly admits.

I frown.

"Why? You did nothing wrong."

"I scared you," he states in a low voice.

My brows shoot up in surprise.

"You thought I was going to hit you," he continues stiffly.

"I-I..."

Reaching down, he catches my hand in his, holding it tight.

"What happened to you?" His voice is soft, entirely belying his previous countenance.

I swallow hard, directing my gaze to the ground.

When I don't answer, he comes to a halt—and me with him. He moves in front of me, tipping my chin up with his thumb.

"I have witnessed this type of behavior before in the people we rescue from abusive situations. They recoil at sudden close contact in fear of being hurt. You thought I was going to hurt you."

I bite my lip as I look at him and the concern I spot in his gaze.

"What happened to you, Luce?" he murmurs in the softest, most comforting tone.

"What happens to most slaves, I guess," I say, forcing a smile.

"You were beaten," he states.

I nod.

"Were you...raped?" It's almost as if it hurts him physically to ask the question.

I slowly shake my head.

"I was lucky," I whisper. "It never got that far."

"But you were hurt."

Another nod.

He closes his eyes, releasing a deep breath.

"I apologize," he finally says.

My eyes widen in surprise.

"I shall attempt to be more careful around you. I do not wish to cause you any distress."

"Thank you..." I murmur, utterly shocked at his words.

He nods awkwardly, silence descending between us.

I'm staring straight at his face. He's looking anywhere *but* at me.

Clearing his throat, he tugs me along as he continues walking.

"So about that palace of yours." I smile as I switch the topic to something more pleasant.

He snorts.

"You seem very interested in my palace."

"Of course. Who doesn't like palaces?"

He regards me for a moment before he nods to himself.

"How many rooms does it have?" I ask.

"Some fifty rooms, I believe. I have never counted them."

"Wow. It must have been expensive to decorate fifty rooms," I breathe out.

He gives me a side glance, his lips twitching.

"Indeed." He straightens his back. "*Very* expensive. It is one of the most ostentatious palaces in the realm."

"And you live there alone?" I blink. "Don't you get... lonely?" Fifty rooms is a *lot* for a single person.

His brows furrow.

"Lonely? What is that?"

I stare at him. At first, I think he's joking, but his expression of confusion is genuine.

"You know... alone?"

"I am used to being alone." He frowns.

"But you shouldn't be. Don't Cer and Thea visit you?"

"I *prefer* to be alone," he replies smoothly. "Cerenios and Erithea know better than to show up unannounced. I have wards all around the premises, and if an intruder thought to enter, he would be turned to dust."

"No one prefers to be alone," I remark softly, my heart clenching at the certainty I hear in his voice. "Have you never invited *anyone* to your palace?"

"Why should I? It is my home. I do not like strangers in my home."

"You're telling me you're *completely* alone in a fifty-room palace?"

"A *very* expensive palace," he interjects.

"Right. You're the only person in a fifty-room *very* expensive palace?"

"Indeed." He nods, pride emanating from his voice.

I thought talking about a mundane subject like his palace would lift up our spirits, but instead, this is even more depressing. What's worse is that he doesn't even realize how strange this is.

"Okay, got it. You live alone in your *very* expensive fifty-room palace. But who cleans? Who cooks? Who keeps the palace in shape?" Something of that size is usually maintained by a crew of tens if not hundreds of people.

"Me, of course," he answers in indignation. "I would never trust a stranger with my belongings."

Well, at least he's self-sufficient. I guess that's something...?

Although Nikki had a similar outlook, at least he had me. We were never lonely because we were together.

"You don't have to live like that, you know?" I add softly. "You're not a bad guy. I'm sure you'd have more friends if you tried."

He slowly turns to me, his eyes pinning me to the spot.

"Does that mean you think I am nice?" he asks, his lips twitching.

"Yes. You are quite nice." I smile. "You're a good friend, Ze." I pat his arm.

He preens at my praise. "You can't take it back," he warns.

I chuckle. But my laughter is cut off as Ze moves with shocking swiftness. I don't even have time to react as he engulfs me in his arms, tackling me to the ground and rolling with us so that he cushions our fall with his body.

As we come to a stop, I'm flat on my back with Ze looming over me, his body draped over mine. His arms are around my waist, holding me tight but making sure he's not overwhelming me with his weight. His face is a razor's edge away from mine. Up close, I can see his features better—the almond shape of his eyes and the swirling darkness of his irises, his high cheekbones and his strong, masculine jaw. I rectify my assessment of him from earlier. He *is* a very handsome man. It's odd that I've never quite realized that before.

I study his features at leisure, my eyes dipping lower to his straight nose and full lips—he has very full lips for a man. If he weren't such a peculiar man, I'm sure he'd have women falling all over him—of course, I don't believe his claims that he's sought-after. The man can barely string together two sentences without offending someone—that someone being me in particular. I fail to see how any woman would find that attractive. Maybe it's cute in a maladroit way, but mostly rude.

Still deep in thought, I feel tendrils of hot air bathe my face. I lift my gaze back to his. I blink slowly. His eyes... Are they...purple?

My lips part in wonder. Bringing my hand to his face, I brush away a few rebel curls from his cheek before I mold my palm to his skin, tracing the area around his eyes. Wow... I've never seen eyes this color before. But...how?

As my thumb brushes against his skin, he inhales sharply, his muscles tightening. Thinking I must have offended him somehow, I pull my hand back. At the same time, his hand shoots out, holding mine in place.

His eyes close, his chest rumbling with a rough and wild sound.

My heart thumps in my chest, adrenaline pumping through my veins.

"Ze?" I whisper.

He doesn't answer, taking another deep breath as he presses my hand tighter against his skin, slowly moving it around until his lips brush against the inside of my wrist. A strangled noise erupts in the stillness of the forest—one that I'm not sure whether it's coming from him or from an unknown foe.

I try to wiggle under him.

"Don't," he barks the command, his eyes snapping open.

He stares at me with those swirling purple eyes, his black pupils fading into a mix of silver and purple, as if the starry sky met aurora borealis.

"Don't move," he grits out.

"What?" I whisper.

His lips compress into a thin line, his expression changing as he glares at me. One moment we're on the ground, the next he's up, helping me to my feet too.

"Why did you..." I start to ask but stop when I see him march toward a tree in the back. He removes an arrow stuck in the bark and studies it closely.

"Traps," he states. "Someone was here before us," he says as he directs his gaze to the path we were supposed to take. "We need to be more careful."

"But it's just an arrow, no?" I ask as I go to his side.

His mouth curls in a lopsided smile.

"Not just an arrow," he notes, swiping some yellow residue with his finger from the arrowhead. Bringing it to his nose, he sniffs it.

"Venom."

"What?"

"Naga venom. Deadly to almost any species. A painful death, too."

"We'll need to be more careful then. Can you spot the traps? You were pretty fast there."

He nods, but his expression is grave.

"You need to stick by my side at all times," he tells me in a strict voice as he throws the arrow to the ground and destroys it with his powers.

"All right," I say softly. "Thank you for saving me. You were awesome!" I exclaim enthusiastically as I give him two thumbs-up. Of course, he doesn't know what that symbolizes, so he merely shrugs.

Yet as he gazes at me, I note that his eyes are still the same swirling purple. It wasn't a play of lights or my erroneous perception.

"Ze... Why are your eyes a different color?"

He blinks, shock enveloping his features.

"They...are?" he asks in a low voice.

I nod, worried.

"What color?" he demands.

"Purple."

He frowns.

"My eyes? You are sure?" he adds, confused.

"Yes. They're *very* purple, Ze. Has this never happened before?"

"Never," he rasps. His brows crease in confusion, and for a moment, he looks so lost, I get an overwhelming urge to give him a hug and tell him we'll work it out—that regardless of what's happening to him, it's all going to be all right.

"Do your eyes hurt? Can you see fine?" Now *I* am getting worried. If it's never happened before... Oh my God! What if he got hit and this is a side effect? What if...

Before I know what I'm doing, I'm circling around him, my hands on his back and chest as I look for an entry point from the arrow. Panic bubbles in my chest. What if he's dying? What if he got hit by the venom and he's going to die?

Tears prick at my eyes, and oddly enough, my first thought is about him, not about the competition or my chances of getting Nikki back. I just...don't want him to die.

"Human, cease!" His voice echoes.

I'm a sniffling mess as he grabs my hands, stopping me.

"Why are you crying? Answer me!" he demands in a strict voice.

"You..." Tears roll down my face in rivulets. "You're dying," I sob aloud.

"What nonsense are you spouting?" He frowns.

"You got hit," I sniffle, using the back of my hand to wipe the moisture from my cheeks. "That's why your eyes are purple. You got hit and...now you're dying. I don't want you to die!" My throat closes up as fear engulfs me.

He simply stares at me. He removes my hands from my face, placing them by my side. Without a word, he uses his own sleeve to dab at my face. His touch is much gentler than I would have expected as he brushes my tears away.

"I am not dying, human," he finally says with a sigh. "I do not know why my eyes have changed color, but it might be a side effect of this realm."

"Oh," I whisper, feeling extremely silly for my outburst. "Sorry," I murmur.

"Were you worried about me?" He clears his throat, pushing his chin up.

I nod as I swallow painfully.

He gazes down at me, pensive.

"No one has worried about me before," he muses quietly.

"No one?" I ask in a low, wobbly voice.

"You are the first." He nods, his lips twitching.

I mirror his smile, and we're gazing at each other like two fools.

My runny nose, however, breaks the spell.

"Do you mind if I use that..." I tug at his already wet sleeve.

He takes one look at my runny nose, then another at his sleeve before he pulls his hand from my grasp, wrinkling his nose.

"Do not push your luck, human," he mutters under his breath.

THIRTY-ONE

"How are you feeling? Are you all right?" I ask as we walk farther into the forest.

His features are tense as he sweeps his gaze across the lush foliage, his mind attuned to danger.

"Fine," he answers in a clipped tone.

"Are you sure? Your muscles are a bit tight," I murmur as I pat his straining biceps.

"This is the twenty-fourth time you have asked me in the last twenty minutes. That is more than once per minute, human," he adds drily, easily waltzing us around more of the incoming arrows.

We've been shot at countless times so far. Whenever we advance a little, more traps are triggered, shooting those venomous arrows at us.

Ze is in control, however, as he senses the motion and is able to dodge each one. Although I feel safe with him, I'm still a little worried.

"But your eyes are still purple," I mention in a small voice.

He gives me a side glance, his eyes glinting a deep purple. It's almost as if they have a life of their own, the color swirling from light to dark and back to light.

"I am *fine*," he grunts, pulling me by the hand into his arms and twirling us around as a flurry of incoming arrows pass by us.

"If you say so..." I grumble.

He rolls his eyes.

We walk another hour or so before Ze suddenly stops, placing his finger against his lips and motioning for me to be quiet.

I give him a nod, watching as he orients himself around, his narrowed eyes taking in his surroundings. His ears perk up as he turns sharply to the right. Before I can ask what's going on, he grabs me in his arms, jumping up just as more arrows are dispatched toward our direction.

Yet this is different.

Whereas before the arrows had come from booby traps, now they're being handled by people. Three men come out from the rich foliage, all dressed in green camouflage suits and fitted with weapons from head to toe.

"Finally, they reveal themselves," Ze mutters, tightening his hold on me. "You will do what I tell you," he commands.

Since it's not the time to argue with him, I nod.

Jumping around the trees with me in his arms, he evades every incoming arrow while managing to confuse the men with his swift movements. When he's satisfied that they've lost track of him, he quietly lands a few meters away from the clearing, depositing me in a hidden spot in the bushes. The forest is teeming with rich trees and mid-sized bushes, making it the perfect spot to hide—but also to ambush someone.

"Do not come out until I tell you to," he whispers.

His gaze lingers a moment over my features before he disappears from my sight.

A sudden noise erupts from the clearing, and I move forward on my knees, pushing some of the foliage away to make a small hole through which I can see what's happening.

Ze is in the middle as the three men circle him, their bows and arrows raised to strike. My heart is in my throat as I watch helplessly, cursing myself for my weakness.

Until now, I'd made peace with my human condition, counting myself blessed for the fact that my teammates could help me advance in the competition. Somehow, I'd thought that the strength of my conviction was enough to get me ahead. But I never counted on the uselessness I'm feeling now.

I could be helping him. Instead, I'm just hiding in the bushes, only able to look on as Ze risks his life for a plant only I need. Cer and Thea, too, are taking unnecessary risks for me.

I bite my lip in frustration. If only I could be of more use to them...

Ze removes his sword from his scabbard, the stark white a contrast to the black of his clothes and the green of the forest. Holding it with one hand, he waves it around as he focuses his attention on one of the men. And when they least expect it, he strikes.

His movements are sharp and brisk. It's almost as if he's one with his sword as he reaches his opponent in two steps. Dodging an arrow from behind, he increases the momentum of the shot by using his sword to hit the arrow back to the sender. The pointy end hits one of the men in the leg. His knees buckle as he falls to the ground, his previously light countenance becoming a deep blue. In just a matter of seconds, he stops breathing.

A gasp escapes me just as I slap my hand over my mouth.

When Ze had said the venom was potent... This is on a level I've never seen before. It acts so fast that you're dead within seconds of being hit.

"Please be careful," I whisper, my heart in my throat.

One hit.

That's all it takes for him to die.

Just one hit.

Ze slowly lifts his head up, the wind blowing his hair to the side as his purple eyes connect with mine. As if he heard my words, his lips curl up in a self-assured smirk.

"Watch out," I yell before I can stop myself.

One of the other men is aiming at him, his fingers pulling on the string of the bow, ready to send the arrow flying.

Ze's lip twitches before he disappears, only to reappear like a flash of light in front of the man. He wields his sword confidently, and in one smooth movement, both man and bow are cut in half.

Red blood spills onto the ground, together with other bodily liquids that mix in the middle, pooling around the leftover bone and flesh.

I take a deep breath. *He's got this.* I nod to myself.

As he finally turns his attention to the last one standing, another two men appear from behind.

My eyes widen.

But if that wasn't enough, something else is coming.

It all starts with the noise.

The sound of branches cracking and leaves whooshing. Then there's the echo of the birds flying out in the distance, their habitats destroyed by something enormous. The ground, too, trembles with its approach. I barely balance myself on my hands as I'm thrust forward by the quaking of the forest.

The men don't seem surprised.

Ze's features are hard to read, but he must be expecting the worst as he assumes a rigid stance.

After a few moments, the beast that disturbed the forest finally appears, leaving behind a deep trail in its wake.

It slithers closer to the clearing, its big body breaking through the green fence before it finally makes its appearance.

It's blue.

That's the first thing I notice. A combination of dark and light blue, the former on its back while the latter is on its front. Sixty to seventy percent of its body is that of a serpent, the inside of its skin marred by reptilian rings that spread from its belly to its sprawling tail that stretches for meters in the back—so much so I cannot even see where it ends. The upper part of its body is humanoid, or as close as possible to the appearance of a humanoid bar the blue skin.

Its abdomen ripples with strength as it flexes its muscular

arms. Its mouth opens on a loud screech, two sharp teeth glinting dangerously.

That is...that must be the naga with the deadly venom.

Oh God!

Ze could handle the arrows, but can he handle the raw source of the venom?

My body trembles as anxiety builds inside of me. Fear engulfs me as my fight or flight response is activated. The logical move would be to run—save myself. But how could I ever do that to Ze? How could I abandon him when he's fighting for *me*?

The men align themselves to one side, forming a three-man formation, while the naga positions itself on the other side, trapping Ze between them.

"Ze..." I whisper, worried for him. He might be strong, but that venom... I don't even want to imagine what would happen to him if he got hit.

The naga releases a loud howl before it uses its tail to strike at Ze. He easily evades the blow, but I belatedly realize he wasn't the target in the first place.

A strangled cry is wrenched from me as the end of the tail wraps tightly around my midriff. The hold is bordering on painful as it restricts my breathing. Without warning, it yanks me out of the bushes and into the clearing, throwing me into the trunk of a tree. I yelp aloud as I fly through the air.

I squeeze my eyes shut as I expect the pain to ripple into my insides. An impact like that would surely break my bones...

But instead of excruciating pain, I'm met with softness, familiar hands gripping me firmly.

Slowly, I open my eyes and notice the trail Ze's feet left on the ground as he got dragged by the sheer momentum of the throw when he caught me. He used his body as a shield to ensure I didn't get hurt. But what about him?

"Are you okay?" I ask in an alarmed voice.

His cheek twitches, the purple in his eyes becoming a deeper, more pronounced shade.

"I am fine. They? They are *not* fine," he spits out.

Placing me carefully by his side, he scans me from head to toe to ensure I am not hurt before turning his attention back to his opponents. The change in his expression is immediate—just as it is frightening. His gaze on me is soft, concerned. But as he stares down the enemies, he transforms into the epitome of a deadly warrior.

His hand is on his sword, and just as I've seen him before, he trails two fingers from the top of the sword to the tip. The touch awakens some type of magic as the sword starts glowing a strange light—one that is similar to the new shade of his eyes.

"Stay back," he orders.

I don't get to reply as he vanishes from my side. No one gets to blink, and he's suddenly in front of the three men, their heads dropping to the ground before they can even think to engage their bows and arrows. Blood splashes onto the ground, the green leaves, and Ze's tense features. It splatters across his cheeks and forehead, dripping lower down his neck and onto his clothes.

His eyes flare, the color glowing.

"W-w-what a-a-re y-y-you?" the naga asks in a booming hiss.

Ze smirks.

"What do you think?"

Then he's gone again, appearing midair in front of the naga and wielding his sword, ready for attack. My lips quiver with optimism. If he so easily dispatched the others, this naga shouldn't be a problem, right?

But my smile quickly falls apart as the naga opens its mouth, the hiss becoming a shrilling cry that makes the entire forest tremble. It sweeps the grass and everything in its path away, advancing like a hurricane. Ze's thrust backward before he disappears again, unable to withstand the marauding wind.

I grasp onto the tree trunk with my arms, holding on to it so I'm not hurled away by the sheer force of the naga's roar.

"I have you," Ze murmurs in my ear as he appears behind me. He wraps his arm around my waist, keeping me in place.

Despite the power of the wind coming from the naga's mouth, Ze stands strong, his feet firmly planted on the ground.

My hair flies to the side, my ears ringing from the velocity of the air.

"Hold on to me," he whispers, his voice lulling me to safety.

I swallow hard, fisting my hands into the material of his shirt and holding on to him tightly.

"Can we win this?" I ask in a small voice.

"Do you doubt me?" he fires back, his voice amused.

"No, but—"

"No buts. Do you see the rings on its stomach?" he inquires as he moves us out of the destructive path of the wind.

I nod.

"A naga's weakness is the eleventh ring."

"Oh," I murmur weakly.

"Do not worry about me, human. I will be fine. But you..." he trails off.

My lashes flutter in question as I lean back to study his features.

"Me?"

"You need to stay put. I can only focus if I know you are safe," he states firmly.

"Oh. Okay." I wet my lips. "I can do that."

The corners of his lips curl up.

"Good." He smirks as he flashes us again, this time depositing me behind a couple of trees out of the naga's sight.

"I shall be back soon." He winks. And with that, he's gone from my side, only to appear in front of the naga once more. The serpent is still blowing wind from its mouth, doing its best to aim for Ze. But it's in vain because nothing seems to rattle him.

Ze skillfully cuts through the wind with his sword, steadily gaining distance. The naga's mouth closes briefly—presumably to rest—and Ze takes advantage of it to appear right in front of its belly, slashing a long line through the light blue tissue.

I quickly count the rings, hoping he got the eleventh one.

But just as blue blood pours out of the wound, the naga opens its mouth again, this time the sound becoming a screeching noise of pain mixed with anger. Ze is about to strike again when the naga coils its tail, lashing out. Ze flashes out, appearing at another side, only for the naga to aim for him again. It goes on for minutes on end, and I wonder why Ze won't just go for the kill.

It's only when I catch a small glimpse of his features as he's baiting the naga that I realize why he's taking his time.

He's enjoying this.

Just like the previous fight with the foxes or the demon confrontation, he's utterly in his element when he's fighting. He's drawing the fight out on purpose.

The next moment, he gets closer again, cutting through the snake's hide and drawing more of that eerie blue blood.

A smile plays at my lips as I watch him fight like that. He moves as if he were born on the battlefield. Now I realize why he's such a poor conversationalist. He only knows how to speak with his sword.

The naga becomes increasingly more enraged the more Ze evades all its attacks. It swipes its tail back and forth at Ze with increased strength. He jumps over it, under it, to the side, to the other side. His smile widens with each failed blow, a carefree expression painting his features—one I've never seen before. It's almost as if he's using the naga's tail as his personal jumping rope.

I can't believe I was ever worried for him when it seems he's not afraid of anything—not even deadly venom.

Dashing forward, the naga tries to use its wind power at the same time as its tail, but Ze's ability to move in the blink of an eye makes it impossible for the naga to catch him. One second he's in front of it, the next he's in the back, his sword raised high as he cuts half of the naga's tail.

A sharp shrill erupts in the air, and for a moment, I feel bad cheering at someone else's misery. But as Ze gives me a glance, red and blue blood soaking his face, his lips widen in a dashing smile. I find myself returning the smile, excitement building inside of me.

The naga crashes to the ground, rolling around in pain. Ze casually walks to its side, counting the rings with the tip of his sword before cutting another line straight through the naga's body. In just a few seconds, it stops moving, slumping to the ground.

I dash to Ze's side and throw myself in his arms.

"You did it," I exclaim, giggling.

"It was nothing," he mumbles grumpily, but he tightens his arms around me.

"You don't have to be modest," I say as I lean back to look at him.

He's a mess, his face stained with the combined blood of all his opponents.

Pursing my lips, I lift my hoodie, taking my undershirt out of my leggings and tearing a small strip of cloth from the hem. Lifting it up, I dab it around his face, doing my best to clean the residual blood.

Ze stares at me in wonder, utterly still, his purple eyes swirling like a beautiful galaxy.

"Are you always this messy when you fight?" I ask jokingly.

He blinks. Slowly, he shrugs.

"I believe so," he answers gruffly, averting his gaze.

Underneath all that blood and grime, his cheeks are still red, and no matter how much I try to scrub them, the redness won't come off.

"You are not disgusted by me?" he asks in a quiet voice, his eyes on me, unblinking.

"Why should I be?" I raise a brow. "You're a wonderful fighter, and you saved me." I smile, shrugging.

He stares at me.

One second. Two. I lose count of the seconds that pass as he stares at me, never once blinking. My hand stills on his cheek, and I return his regard, curious as to what got his interest.

Slowly—painfully slow—his lips tug up into a hesitant

smile. One that is as precious as it is beautiful because it shows a vulnerability in his gaze that I haven't encountered before.

"You are a very odd human," he remarks in the same low, gravelly voice.

"Haven't we already established that?" I chuckle. "Just as you are a very odd...whatever you are," I shoot back, waiting for him to correct me.

"Warrior. I am just a warrior, Luce." He smiles sadly.

It strikes me that this is the first time he hasn't used his title to signal our societal differences—just as he hasn't once been rude or condescending. Who *is* this Ze?

"We are an odd pair, are we not?" He muses quietly as he places his hand on top of mine, keeping it in place on his cheek.

I blink in surprise, not sure I understand his meaning.

"Ze..."

The rustling of leaves has him on high alert, his eyes regaining the focus from before just in time to pull me to his chest, rotating with me to avert an incoming attack. My heart beats loudly in my chest. I hear *his* heart beating loudly, the beat in tandem with mine.

Grabbing his sword, he hurls it at the barely moving man on the ground, severing his head.

"I do not want you to panic," he starts in a tight voice.

I frown.

"What do you mean?"

"I... I might have gotten hit."

"You might?" I gasp, immediately jumping out of his arms. I circle around him and sure enough, there's an arrow sticking out of his back.

But...how? How could he have missed the fact that one of the men wasn't dead yet? Unless... It's my fault. I distracted him. Not only did I disturb his focus by rushing to his side, but he also got hurt protecting me.

"Ze... No... Tell me you're immune or something," I plead in a thick voice. He's not yet blue, so maybe that's a sign? The other man had turned blue within seconds.

"I am not immune, but it is not deadly for me, either. I will be fine shortly," he says as he coughs. "My body needs some time to fight off the venom." Reaching back, he pulls the arrow out of his back and throws it to the ground. A little unsteady on his feet, he walks to the dead man, recovers his sword, and places it in his scabbard.

"What do you need me to do?" I offer immediately.

"We need to find shelter for the night. I cannot protect you in this state and I do not know how much longer I have before..." He pauses as he sees my aghast expression.

"Before?" I probe, already frightened by what he's about to say.

"Before I become incapacitated."

"But... But you said you will be fine," I cry out, tears already coating my lashes.

He smiles a sad, weary smile.

"I hope so."

He wheezes and coughs, and my worry mounts. Knowing time is of the essence, I hurry to his side, wrapping my arm around his waist and trying to give him some support as we move forward.

"That way." He points to an unbeaten track. "I remember from the map," he rasps.

I nod. There's no point in arguing with him now.

The vegetation becomes increasingly harder to traverse, the foliage thicker than before. We walk for another thirty minutes before he motions me to the right, down a windy path that gets us out of the thick vegetation and into a rockier environment.

Ze seems to get weaker by the moment, his breathing harsh and pronounced. But every time I ask if he's all right, he tells me he's fine and we should push forward.

It's some ten minutes later that we come to the location he had in mind—a big rock with a hidden opening in the back. How the map would have had this small detail is beyond me, but I don't question it as I help Ze inside the cave-like structure.

It's hidden enough from sight that we should be fine for a

while. But the size of it is a little concerning. The mouth of the opening is small—so much so that we both need to get down on our knees to crawl inside.

"Wow," I whisper as we both make it on the other side.

Although the entrance was tiny, the interior is certainly not. The ceiling is high, with a few small holes on each side to let light in.

Ze slumps to the floor, dropping our bag next to him, and gets a sip of water. Leaving him there, I walk around a little, noticing some odd constructions that are certainly *not* natural. This makes me suspect that the entire rock is some sort of shelter, especially as I find a small pond at the end of the cave that leads into a subterranean river. Getting to my haunches, I put my palms together and take a bit of water to taste.

It's sweet. If we boil it, we might be able to drink it. If Ze's body will be weakened from the venom, then he'll need a lot of hydration.

Spending a bit more time looking around, I find some dusty cloth, some animal bones, and a few containers—signs that someone lived here before.

"We need to make a fire," Ze croaks. He gets to his feet, wobbling toward the center of the cave. We find some materials for the fire, after which Ze teaches me how to light one—in case he will not be able to in the future.

The more he talks, the more anxious I get that this is more serious than he's been making it out to be. Is he dying and he doesn't want to tell me because I might freak out?

As the sparks from the fire flare to life, the cave is inundated with light and warmth. That's when I notice some strange illustrations on the wall of the cave.

"Is that..."

"Language," Ze states. "The language of those who make P'davi their home."

"But you said it's an intermediary realm." I frown.

His lips twitch.

"Precisely. If you are not welcome in your world and if you cannot go to another one, what do you do?"

"You're stuck in limbo."

"Indeed." He coughs.

I hurry to his side, offering him a little more water. Seeing his wan complexion, I place my hand to his forehead, checking his temperature.

My eyes flare open in shock. He's...burning.

"Ze..." I whisper, my voice cracking with pain.

He did this for me—to save *me*.

He grabs onto my hand, slowly looking up at me, his eyes now a light purple.

"I will be fine," he assures me.

"You better," I sniffle. "You can't die, you hear me?"

A sad smile plays at his lips.

"You know... You are the first person to tell me *not* to die."

Before I can ask him to clarify what he means by that, his eyes flutter shut, his body slumping against the wall.

"Ze!" I cry out, shaking him.

He doesn't answer.

THIRTY-TWO

Panic courses through me as I lie frozen by his side, uncertain of what to do next. I'm just staring at his unmoving body, my heart thumping mercilessly inside my chest. It takes me a few seconds to get myself under control enough to go closer to him and feel for his pulse.

He's still covered in blood and bodily fluids, but feeling my way around his neck, I manage to find a heartbeat.

I sigh in relief.

He's not dead.

Yet.

No, no. I won't let him die. No one else is dying under my watch ever again.

Nibbling at my lip, I stand up, cataloging my surroundings to gauge what I can and cannot do. Well, first, I need to get him into a comfortable position. I should also clean the rest of the naga grime off his body since who knows if that's venomous too, and it might only make him sicker.

Nodding to myself, I grab some of the abandoned containers off the ground and hurry to the pond in the back. I clean them the best I can, but I'm aware that they are still not sanitary enough to be used for consumption. But they might work to clean him and make some lye for starters.

Filling the containers with water, I go back to the fire, using a bone shard to pull some ashes from the bottom of the fire. I add them to the water and place it over the fire. While that's boiling, I grab the other container with water and bring it closer to Ze's body.

There are a few rags around, but I don't want to use them until I can properly wash them with some lye. That leaves me with only one option.

Shrugging my hoodie off, I carefully place it to the side while I take off my undershirt. A shiver of cold goes down my body, and I quickly put my hoodie back on.

I rip my undershirt into smaller pieces of material and fold them neatly on top of the bag. With that ready, I shuffle closer to Ze, reaching for his shirt. I undo it with shaky fingers. I'm aware he might not approve of this when he wakes up, but now it's imperative I clean all that blue blood off him.

Since his clothes are wholly black, I didn't realize just how much blood had soaked through, staining his skin.

I undo his shirt from the string that holds it together at his midriff, parting it to reveal his stained chest. There are large blots of blue mixed with red blood.

My lips flatten as I shake my head.

Releasing a deep breath, I slowly try to remove the shirt from his body. He's completely unmoving, and his size makes it a little hard to maneuver him around. Raising his arm, I pull one sleeve, then the other, and lay the shirt aside so I can wash it later.

Instinctively, I avert my gaze, my cheeks turning red. It would take a blind person not to notice how well-defined his chest and muscles are. Hell, the man probably has a twelve-pack, if that's even a thing. I don't think I've seen someone as ripped as him before—not even bodybuilders on TV. Curiosity gets the best of me as I allow myself a small glance—for purely aesthetic reasons, of course.

Despite the splotches of red and blue covering his chest, his bronzed complexion peeks through. His shoulders are broad, his arms even bigger than I imagined.

No wonder he can carry me in one hand alone.

His waist tapers down to narrow hips, his muscles even more defined as I spot a trail of black hair starting from his navel and leading into his black trousers.

I startle back, shaking my head at my foolishness. He's not some specimen to be ogled, and he would no doubt take offense to this as well. After all, it's not as if it's entirely surprising that he has such a beautiful physique. He said it himself—he's a warrior. He probably spends his entire time training to kill demons.

It's also not as though this is my first time seeing a half-naked muscular man. Why, my Nikki was quite muscular himself, with all those hours he spent in the gym. Maybe not demon-hunter level, but he was perfect for me.

As usual, when my thoughts revert to Nikki, I find the chasm in my heart widening, my loneliness creeping out once more.

"Ugh," I let out a cry of frustration. This is not good. Ze needs my full attention at this moment. Nodding to myself, I turn him on his side to examine the site of the wound.

"Damn it," I mutter when I realize it's gone—healed. I should have expected that given his natural ability to heal. But that also means that the venom went straight to his bloodstream. Who knows how well he can deal with something attacking him from the inside. I'm not an expert in healing, but I assume the body won't have such an easy time fighting off the venom if it spreads through the blood.

Not very pleased with my findings, I decide to do what I can —namely clean the rest of the blue residue off his skin. I softly lay him on his back again before I set to work.

Reaching for the pieces of cloth I laid aside, I grab one, soaking it in the water.

I start with his face. Though I wiped his cheeks before, they are still stained. Tracing his forehead, I move the cloth softly over his skin. The planes of his face are a surprising combination of sharp and soft. Where his cheekbones and his jaw are sharp, his lips are full and soft. As I peruse his face, I wonder if his species is similar to ours, with more than one race. His features are reminiscent of East Asian ancestry, yet there's still something foreign to them. Something that's both alluring and frightening.

As I finish with his face, I move lower to his neck. His pulse is strong, which gives me hope that this isn't too serious and that he'll awaken soon. His neck and collarbone have the most direct splatters, the rest of his torso only stained by the fluids that have seeped through his clothes.

I exchange the dirty cloth for a clean one and continue wiping down his torso. His chest rises and falls, his breathing steady yet punctuated.

Trailing down his abdominals, I make sure there's nothing left in the grooves of his muscles. But as I trail lower and lower, I get a little apprehensive. Taking a deep breath, I quickly clean the skin peeking through the band of his pants before I discard the cloth as well.

When I'm done, I go back to the fire to check on the boiling water. Seeing that it's done, I carefully move it to the side, letting it settle for a few moments before adding his shirt and the dirty cloths in the container and stirring them together. It might not work as well as soap, but it should at least remove *some* of the dirt.

"Ah," a sound echoes in the cave.

Turning sharply, I see Ze turning around in his sleep, his features tense, his brows bunched together.

"Ze? Are you all right?" I ask, my voice full of worry.

He doesn't answer me, but as I note the goosebumps on his skin, I realize he must be cold.

Damn!

I look around, but there's nothing to cover him with. His clothes will take a while to dry too, and I can't let him freeze to death.

Without any other option, I take off my hoodie, remaining only in a thin white sports bra. It's a little chilly, but I'll be fine. He, however, will not.

I cover him with it to the best of my ability, but he's too big even for my oversized hoodie.

"What next?" I mumble to myself. "Oh, right. Water!"

I empty the dirty water from the cloth in a corner and scoop some lye to scrub it as clean as I can before rinsing it off, careful not to contaminate the pond with the lye. When it's relatively clean, I fill it with water and place it over the fire to boil.

In the meantime, I rummage through our bag, happy there are at least a few sips of water left in our jug that I can give him.

"Ze," I whisper. "Drink some water," I say as I cradle his head in my lap, trying to angle his head so he won't choke on the liquid. Yet as I bring the jug to his lips, I realize he can't drink it. Placing my fingers on his jaw, I slowly part his lips as I incline the jug, letting a few drops fall into his mouth.

I stare intently until I see the small movement of his throat.

He's swallowing!

I repeat the motion, feeding him a few drops at a time, giving him time to swallow them. I do this until the jug is empty.

"You did great," I praise him, gently brushing my fingers through his hair.

The water is boiled and I pick it off the fire, then place it on the floor to cool off. Then I turn my attention to the clothes, doing my best to clean them before placing them to dry on the floor near the fire.

I glance back at Ze every now and then. He's still cold, trying to wrap himself in my hoodie but with no real success. He covers one part of his body, only for another to become uncovered.

"Ze? Can you hear me?" I ask in a low voice as I come by his side.

I swipe my hand over his forehead, checking for his temperature.

"You're not running a fever," I breathe in relief.

"Mmm..." He releases a guttural sound as he scrunches his nose, a visible shiver racking his body.

"You're still cold, aren't you?" I murmur, getting closer to him.

He mumbles something in his sleep, moaning lightly as if in pain.

"Shh, it's okay," I whisper, softly caressing his hair. "It's going to be okay."

The words are barely out of my mouth when his arms shoot out, pulling me next to him. The hoodie falls to the side as he brings me close to his giant body. I momentarily tense as he wraps his arms around my waist, holding me close to him. Light vibrations emanate from his chest, a sound that's oddly calming and familiar.

"Ze... Maybe you should..." I stammer in an attempt to extricate myself from his hold. This is not very proper considering he's naked from the waist up.

His hold is firm, and as I wiggle against him, it only serves to make him hug me tighter. Releasing a weary sigh, I stop moving. I suppose a life and death situation might void propriety in this case.

Despite his abrupt embrace, I don't feel threatened by his presence or the closeness of his body. A shiver runs down his spine, the clatter of his teeth a small echo that reverberates in my ears.

He's cold. Of course he's cold.

"I've got you," I murmur softly as I relax in his arms. Grabbing the hoodie off the floor, I place it on top of us. But even like this, he's still cold. A little reluctant, I wrap my arms around his neck and I bring him closer to me, hoping to lend him some of my body heat. He lays his head on my chest, nuzzling his cheek on top of my bare skin.

Slowly, his breathing evens out as he hugs me tightly. His trembling, too, subsides as his cold naked flesh meets my warm one.

"That's it." I smile. "You'll get well soon," I whisper as I press my chin on top of his head, trailing my hand down his back in a soothing gesture.

I yawn softly, my eyes becoming heavy with fatigue as we both slowly warm up. My body is lethargic, but after today's events, it's not surprising. The stress alone must have taken quite a toll on me.

I try to keep my eyes open in case Ze might need me, but the inviting heat lulls me into sleep.

Maybe I can rest my eyes for a few minutes or so...

I startle awake as I feel the small sunrays filtering through the holes in the ceiling. My short nap turned into an all-night sleep!

The hoodie is hugging my body, but there's a marked absence. My eyes widen with worry as I turn over and don't find Ze next to me.

"Ze?" I call out as I fumble to my feet. The hoodie covering me drops to the ground, and a sliver of cold washes down my back. Yet my mounting worry for him supersedes my physical discomfort. My lips tremble with alarm as I look right and left, rubbing my eyes to chase the sleepy confusion away. The sound of splashing water attracts my attention, and I hurry toward the pond, fearing the worst. What if he's still out of it and he falls into the water? I didn't check how deep it was, but he could drown or further hurt himself.

"Ze," I call his name again, rushing forward. Yet just as I reach the edge of the pond, I stop in my tracks, my eyes widening.

He's in the pond with his back to me, his hair wet, droplets of water dripping down his skin. The water reaches his waist, ripples of movement making it clash against his skin. Hearing me, he slowly turns. Water clings to his face and chest, his vivid purple eyes a contrast to his bronzed skin and black hair. He raises his brows at me, a frown marring his features as he scans my body. He takes a step toward me, but he somehow loses his footing and slips, plunging below the surface of the water.

Seconds pass, and he doesn't resurface.

"Ze!" I shout, fear reverberating in my chest.

Without thinking, I quickly remove my shoes and dash forward, jumping into the pond and wading against the water while frantically searching for him. Yet it quickly becomes clear that the pond is much deeper than I thought. The first few steps, my feet meet smooth, slippery stone, but in my hurry, I don't pay too much attention to my surroundings. I don't even realize that the farther I go from the shore, the deeper the water gets.

"Ze," I call out, wildly moving my arms around as I attempt to find him.

One more step, though, and I lose my footing. The bottom stone suddenly becomes steep, and I find myself freely falling to the depths of the pond.

I move my arms and legs as I try to prevent my quick descent, but there's a hidden current that seems to pull me down. I struggle against the invisible force, but the more I try, the more forcefully it seems to drag me down.

Panic swells in my chest, but I quickly realize that it's not going to help me—if anything, it's only going to make matters worse.

So I stop struggling.

I simply let my body fall down—after all, how deep could this be?

At the same time, I force my eyes open, looking around for any signs of Ze. The water is an unnatural blue color, and the more I descend, my vision gets clearer.

There are odd constructions around, almost like a subterranean city. There are buildings carved in stone and swallowed by water, the darkness of the rock a contrast to the crystalline blue water. The windows of the buildings are wide open, as if something had shattered the glass until only the frames remain. Intricate ornaments embellish the facades of the buildings, making them seem aristocratic, even regal in appearance.

There are vines climbing all over the rocky edifices, curling around the open orifices and hugging them in an elegant embrace. This must have been someone's residence at some point in time.

The buildings continue down a narrow, darkened lane, and I catch sight of statues depicting all sorts of foreign creatures. Some are still standing, somehow still rooted to the spot, but some have fallen, faces and bodies broken and battered by the currents.

I'm struck by the beauty and the tragedy of it. Unfortunately, I'm not able to enjoy it seeing as my oxygen supply is nearly depleted. My lungs are nearing their capacity, and it takes everything in me to stop myself from gasping for air.

Still, there's no sight of Ze.

Although I do my best to keep calm, my impending doom as well as Ze's uncertain fate have my heart racing to the maximum. My eyes become sluggish the more I'm deprived of oxygen, so much so that I think I start seeing things. Otherwise, how would I explain the jelly-like translucent being that Ze is currently wrestling in the narrow tunnel?

I blink once.

Twice.

Bubbles erupt from my mouth as I slap my hand over it to keep myself from accidentally ingesting water.

Ze's head turns to the side, noticing me. His features are tightly drawn together as he turns sharply toward the jelly-being. It's almost as if the water is not affecting him in any way, able to both breathe and move freely as if he were on land.

His hands grasp onto two tentacles, purple energy emanating from his palms and spreading to the jelly-being. From the point of contact, the energy permeates the entirety of his opponent, like an eternal flame that can survive anywhere— even in the depths of the ocean.

A blink of an eye. That's how long it takes for the jelly-being to disintegrate, leaving behind only some purple sparks that now float into the water.

Ze turns his attention to me, swimming toward me. It takes him a few strokes to reach my side. I do my best to motion to him that I can't swim upward—that the water is somehow caging me and dragging me down.

He frowns.

Frustration gnaws at me as precious seconds trickle by. Pointing to my mouth, I attempt to tell him that I'm moments away from running out of breath and that we need to go back up.

I'm not sure if he understands my urgency or if he misconstrues my meaning. But as he plants himself in front of me, he cups my cheeks firmly in his hands, leaning forward.

My eyes widen as it dawns on me what he means to do, and I turn my head just in time to avoid the brush of his lips against mine. His mouth grazes my cheek, and I bang my fists against his shoulders, pushing him backward.

He seems equally frustrated at my refusal.

I shake my head at him, pointing again upward to the surface. Although I appreciate his offer, I'm still not quite at death's door. Since I've seen him wade through the water, I know he can have us back to the surface before my lungs give out.

He leans back, his eyes narrowed as he watches me. I motion up again, this time with increased urgency. His features are still full of tension as he wraps his arms around my midriff, pulling me close to him until our bodies are flush together. Using only his legs, he propels himself upward.

His movements are brisk and sharp, cutting through water at an alarming speed. In no time, we both break through the surface of the water, back in the cave.

I draw a sharp breath in. Then another. I cough and splutter as my lungs get used to getting a steady supply of oxygen again.

God, but it feels good to breathe normally again!

My heart is beating in my chest like crazy, my adrenaline levels probably through the roof. I don't know what happened down there, or what that creature was, but I don't want to experience that again. Although I've never particularly had a fear of water, I now realize I'm not overly fond of it either.

Ze doesn't let go of me, carrying me along until we reach the stony shore. Only then does he hoist me up on the rock before hauling himself up too.

We're both soaking wet. I'm breathing hard, barely able to get up on shaky legs.

"What the hell was tha—" My words die on my tongue as my mouth hangs open in shock.

He's... He's... Was he before, too? How did I not notice? Well, I might have been too focused on staying alive, but still...

Ze is naked. Entirely naked. Head to toe naked. As in, there's not a stitch of clothing covering his body. He's with his back to me, droplets of water falling from his hair down his broad shoulder blades and his...

Oh my god, I don't need to see that!

"Huh?" He raises a brow as he half turns.

My eyes bulge in my head as my jaw drops to the floor.

He's naked. He's *utterly* naked.

"Cover yourself!" I squeak, jumping up and swiftly turning around as I cover my face with my hands. But my slightly delayed reaction meant I saw more than I needed to see. I couldn't help it. I mean, it's not my fault, right? He's the one walking around naked with...that outrageous *thing*. It's bound to get people's attention.

"You can turn," he adds a few moments later.

"Are you sure?"

"Yes. I am sure," he says, and I detect a hint of amusement in his voice.

Slowly, I turn around, but I don't remove my hands from my face. I part my fingers to peek through them. Okay, he's wearing his pants and shirt now. That's an improvement.

Clearing my throat, I drop my arms by my side, walking away from the pond and deeper into the cave.

"Don't do that again, all right? I thought we established that it's not okay to be naked in front of people who are *not* your mate." I feel the need to mention. Who knows, maybe in his solitary *very expensive* palace he walks around naked all the time. But I'd rather he do that only when I'm *not* around.

"We did," he agrees, his eyes boring a hole in me.

I avert my gaze, suddenly flustered. Heat climbs my cheeks as I find myself stammering.

"W-well, since you know, don't do it again."

He doesn't reply, merely staring more at me.

Damn, this is awkward.

Without warning, he comes to my side, grabs my hand, and leads me to the spot where we'd slept. "Sit," he commands, pushing me to the ground by my shoulders.

I go along with it, especially when I notice he's gathering some more twigs to make a fire. That would be heavenly now, since I don't want to put on my hoodie while my sports bra is wet. It might be a little uncomfortable to show so much bare skin in front of Ze, but the last thing I need is to catch a cold.

Once the fire is ablaze, he takes a seat right next to me.

"What was that down there?" I finally ask.

"It was once a town. But these lands are not meant to be occupied like that. The gods flooded all settlements in the intermediary realms when they found out about it."

"Oh," I whisper. "And that creature?"

He shrugs.

"It must have slipped through a portal. You do not have to worry about it. It is gone now," he assures me.

"Okay." I nod. "Thanks for saving me. Again." I let out an awkward laugh.

"Of course," he replies with a huff. "You are my person. I will not let anything happen to you."

"You mean I'm your teammate," I correct him lightly.

"You are my person," he reiterates, his voice firm.

Glancing at him, I'm startled by his intense expression. Wet locks of hair frame his face, droplets of water clinging to his dark lashes and emphasizing the otherworldly color of his eyes. Every time I meet his gaze, I can't help but be utterly captivated by that ever-changing shade of purple. It's unlike anything I've ever seen, and I don't think there are words that could do it justice, just as there's no matching Pantone to describe it.

"What is this?" He reaches out to trail his finger up my arm and toward my collarbone.

My eyes flare open as I realize what he's pointing to, and instinctively, I jump back, pushing his hand away.

"Are you all right, human?" he demands in a low tone.

"Yes, sorry about that," I murmur as I hug my arms around myself. "I don't like talking about it."

He frowns.

"It seems to be embedded in your skin," he muses, his eyes still arrested on the marks on my body.

"Ze..."

"But why did it not heal when the game started? Or when I healed you?" He continues, ignoring my silent pleas to drop the subject.

"I don't know." I sigh. "I've had them for over ten years. They are...brandings."

"Brandings?" he repeats, his brows furrowing together.

"From when I was a slave," I whisper.

Realization dawns on him and he freezes.

"I see." His lips flatten into a thin line, and his eyes are back on my chest.

Goosebumps erupt all over my skin and I find myself suddenly colder than before. A shiver runs down my back, his intense regard making me squirm.

"Would you allow me to attempt to heal them?" he asks after a moment.

"What?" I blink.

"I can focus solely on your brandings. If it is something that has been done to your skin, my healing should work."

"You mean..." I trail off as I point to his mouth.

He gives me a nod.

I ponder his suggestion, ashamed to find myself actually considering it. Somehow, it feels a little too intimate to allow him to put his mouth on my skin after... I swallow uncomfortably.

I shouldn't think too hard on the fact that I saw him naked. He's hardly the first naked man I've seen. Yet there's this continuous feeling in my chest that tells me it *is* wrong. I am married. And I am certain Nikki would *not* like any of this. My heart clenches in my chest at the thought. I would *never* want Nikki to think I would betray him in any way—alive *or* dead.

At the same time, if there's a chance I could finally get rid of these markings forever... I'm ashamed to admit that I would take it.

I'll just have to pray Nikki will understand this, too. He knows how much it means to me to finally be free from my past, so I'm certain he'd never begrudge me this. It's not as if I see Ze as anything but a good friend. And he certainly only sees me as a pesky human he's charged with protecting.

"Fine. You can...try," I say as I take a deep breath.

He shuffles closer to me, his hand circling my wrist as he pulls my arm toward him. Leaning forward, I feel his breath brush against my skin as he hovers his mouth over my upper arm. He trails his lips over my skin and a tremor travels down my back.

I squeeze my eyes shut as I await for him to do...whatever he needs to do.

Moving from my shoulder to my collarbone, he finally presses his open mouth over my skin, his tongue trailing along the contour of my marks.

A scorching heat envelops my entire upper body, almost as if the marks themselves were on fire. My pulse speeds up, my heart racing unlike ever before. More heat coils in my stomach as my breathing grows labored until I'm panting. My body tingles all over, from the tips of my toes to the top of my head, there's an insane pulsation that grows in intensity with every lick of his tongue.

"Agh," I cry out, pushing him and falling on my back in an attempt to get away from him.

His eyes widen in shock, but it's not because of my outburst. Following his gaze, I look down to find the previously dark markings on my body lighting up like a Christmas tree.

"What's happening?" I ask in a wobbly voice. "What's happening to me, Ze?"

The burning sensation continues, although it's not entirely unpleasant. It's just...foreign.

"I am not certain," he answers, his expression puzzled.

I rub my hands down my arms and chest, and slowly, the light goes out until my marks become the same dull dark spot of ink as before.

"But I can tell you one thing," he continues, looking conflicted. "Those are not brandings made by a human."

THIRTY-THREE

"**A**rms up," he commands, holding the hoodie up for me.

"You're being awfully bossy," I mumble under my breath, but I do as he says. I raise my arms, allowing him to slide the hoodie down on my body.

My clothes are now dry, and I'm no longer cold. But more questions than ever are clamoring inside my head.

"I told you before, human. You are my person. That means I protect you," he mentions smoothly before he throws a few more twigs over the fire. He tugs me closer to the flame, his hand moving up and down my back as he emulates the comforting gesture I used on him.

"What did you mean by that? If the markings were not made by a human, then who..."

He compresses his mouth in a flat line as he tightens his hold over me, pulling me closer and sliding his arm over my shoulder.

"A god," he answers grimly.

"W-what? But how? Why?" I burst out. "I don't understand..." I add weakly.

"I do not understand it either. But I aim to find out." He grinds his teeth, his body tensing.

"You'll help me figure it out?" I ask in a small voice.

He breathes harshly.

"I will not spare anyone who laid a hand on you, human. You have my word," he assures me. "For now, you need to eat. We have a long day ahead of us."

I nod weakly.

He grabs our supply bag, taking out a couple of nut bars and handing them to me. I blink in confusion when I note he's not eating any. Then it dawns on me that I never inquired about the most important thing.

"How are *you* feeling? I'm so sorry. I should have asked that first." I sigh dejectedly.

His lips twitch, though he forces himself not to smile.

"I am perfectly fine. The venom is out of my system and I am back to my optimal functioning capacity."

"That's good to hear. You scared me last night."

"You were that worried about me?" he asks hesitantly.

"Of course. You're my friend, Ze. I don't want anything bad to happen to you." I smile.

He doesn't return the smile. Instead, he just stares at me, mumbling something inaudible under his breath.

"Let us depart," he suddenly declares, getting to his feet and sheathing his sword at his waist.

"What's wrong with you?" I mumble the question, quickly chewing on the remainder of my nut bar. "I haven't even finished eating."

Wasn't he the one who told me to eat earlier? Now he won't even let me do it at leisure.

He glowers at me, his lips tight and unmoving.

I pop the last piece of the bar in my mouth before placing my hands on my hips and returning his intimidating glare—all the while chewing *very* loudly. To my surprise, that doesn't seem to bother him. Annoyance gives way to amusement as his lips curl at the corners, his features softening. Grabbing the bag off the floor, he searches for something inside of it.

I frown at his contradictory actions.

"Here," he says, throwing something at me.

I catch it instinctively. But as I open my fist and peel the thin tissue away, I notice a few squares of chocolate.

What...

"What's this?" I whisper.

"Chocolate. You like it."

"Yes, but why do you have it? We didn't pack any."

"I packed some for you," he immediately replies, folding his arms across his chest and proudly pushing his chin up.

My lashes flutter in confusion as I look back and forth from Ze to the chocolate squares.

"But *why?*" I ask again.

Now it's his turn to frown, staring at me as if he doesn't understand why I'm questioning his goodwill when that's exactly why—Ze is *not* known for his goodwill.

"You like it," he reasserts. "The journey is long and harrowing. It is good to have something you like along the way."

He states it as if it's self-explanatory.

"How did you know? That I like it?" My voice is softer, a smile trembling on my lips.

"It is all you eat, human," he huffs. "When you are not eating that cow of yours, of course."

"Of course," I repeat, amused.

"It would not have been ideal to bring a cow with us on this journey," he continues. "I could have carried it, of course. That would have been no hardship. But I am not sure whether the vegetation in this realm would have agreed with it," he muses quietly.

"You would have carried a cow on your back?" I blink numbly.

"Do you doubt my strength, human?" He thunders.

"No, no, of course not. I would *never* doubt your strength. But cows are not small..." I trail off, not sure how I should react to his statements. Should I laugh? Should I thank him? Should I tell him that no one carries cows around like he described?

"They cannot be bigger than you," he says with unnatural certainty—despite never having *actually* seen a cow in person.

"Did you... Did you just say I am the size of a cow?" My eyes widen, and I barely keep myself from bursting out into laughter. This man...

Ze shakes his head, coming closer.

"You do not have enough meat on your bones," he says as he circles around me, his eyes studying my body intently. "It is quite strange," he continues as he pokes a finger at my chest, right above my breast. "This part of you is disproportionately larger than the rest."

"Ze," I squeak, jumping back. "You can't just touch my breasts as you like."

His brows shoot up as he gazes at me, and he looks the picture of innocence.

"I am just stating a fact," he adds nonchalantly. "But do not fret, human. I like you as you are," he states confidently, nodding to himself. "After much deliberation, I have handpicked you as my person, and I happen to have very sound judgment."

"Right... Because you are so glorious and awe-inspiring and I bow in front of your magnificence," I reply drily, shaking my head at his antics.

"You forgot the most important thing," he suddenly interjects, placing one finger up.

"Huh?"

"Nice. I am nice to you." He smiles to himself.

I blink in confusion.

"Yes. That is true." I nod. "I'll even give you extra points for the chocolate." I chuckle as I bite into a square.

He stares at me for a moment.

"Extra points?" he inquires, almost unsure. "You mean"—he straightens his back and clears his throat—"I can earn extra points? Then I can be *more* than nice?"

I nod, my lips spreading into a genuine smile. Who said even Ze wasn't teachable? After I'm through with him, he'll be the *nicest* man ever.

"Yep. Every time you do something nice, you'll get extra points."

Excitement shines in his eyes, his mouth slowly curving into a smile.

"I do enjoy a challenge," he adds slowly.

I take another bite of chocolate as I gaze around to make sure we haven't forgotten anything. Then, both Ze and I resume our journey into the forest.

"Is it good?" he asks a few moments later. "That chocolate." He points to my hand.

"You've never had it?"

"I did once try that chocolate cake you have in your world," he recalls thoughtfully.

That's it? The only time he tried chocolate was back then? And not even by itself, but only as a cake? Somehow I find that hard to believe. He's over seven thousand years old, for God's sake. And clearly, chocolate exists in other worlds too. Why has he never tried it? It's just odd.

But then again, when is Ze *not* odd...

"Ze, what the hell do you usually eat?" I ask him.

A look of panic crosses his face.

"I eat," he quickly adds in a defensive tone. "I have a strict regimen... because I am a soldier."

I watch him from the corner of my eye. No doubt his menu is just as dry as his empty *very expensive* palace.

"Well, allow me to awaken your taste buds," I declare, handing him the last square. "Come on. Try it. Cake has nothing on pure chocolate."

He's skeptical as he stares at the chocolate square. Using his other hand, he breaks the square in two, popping the first half in his mouth.

I surreptitiously watch for the play of emotions on his face. At first, he frowns, his jaw working as he munches on the chocolate. His tongue darts out to lick his teeth, his expression one of contemplation. Still, there are the small signs. The way his eyes flicker in surprise or how his lips smack together as he searches for more of the flavor. Finally, his Adam's apple bobs up and down as he swallows, a low, guttural sound escaping him.

"So?" I ask, eagerly awaiting the verdict.

"You may have the other half," he says, dropping the last bit of chocolate in my hand.

"That bad?" I sigh. Although I'm happy to have the other half, I'd still secretly hoped he'd like it—at least to have some sweetness in his life since it seems so utterly bare. Alas, if he doesn't like it, then maybe I should think of something else he'd like. He *needs* that—to unwind and enjoy life.

I still can't believe he's thousands of years old and he's more sheltered than me—and even more alone.

"There are better things out there," he muses, his gaze lingering on me.

I give him an awkward smile as I redirect my attention ahead of me. But since I can't stop myself from talking, I end up recounting to him another one of my favorite romance novels as we walk farther into the forest.

We fall into a comfortable routine. Walking for a few hours before taking a short break and resuming our journey. All the while, Ze continues to ask me to tell him more and more stories, listening attentively to every detail. Who would have thought that Mr. Warrior would be so invested in romance novels? There isn't a quiet moment, and as it gets dark once more, my throat becomes sore from talking too much.

"How much longer do we have?" I ask a while later, tired and out of breath. My muscles have started to ache again. God, what I wouldn't give for a hot, steamy bath to soak in right now. But it's a luxury I don't know when I'll be able to afford again.

I let out a weary sigh as I prop myself against a tree trunk.

"By my calculations, we should be close to the area where that plant grows," he replies as he studies our surroundings.

"What does it look like again?"

"We will not miss it. It has a flower with white petals and a black pistil. The stem is a light green, but if broken, it oozes a black liquid and the inner tissue is a dark blue."

"That is...very specific."

"Finding the plant itself was never the hard part."

"How do you think Thea and Cer are doing? They need to find two plants."

"That are just as easy to find. Do not worry about them, human. Cerenios is my most skilled warrior. He will not let anything happen to Erithea."

Now *that* is high praise coming from someone like Ze.

"But who will protect her from him?" I joke. "I've never seen two siblings fight the way those two do."

Ze's lips flatten.

"They are indeed...unusual."

"Thea mentioned you've known each other for a long time?" I probe, curious about their acquaintance—especially after her warning.

He frowns.

"She said you used to go to her house when she was younger," I add.

"Rubbish," he huffs aloud. "I have only ever been to her home on official visits. I do not simply go to people's houses."

"But you're friends?" I ask tentatively.

"I am her brother's superior. Nothing more, nothing less."

Why is this so complicated? Thea tells me they're friends but that I should be careful with him. Now he's saying they are not friends. Just what the hell is going on?

"What about Cer?"

"He is"—he pauses—"agreeable."

Well, I guess that's as much of a praise as I'll ever get from him.

"Cerenios exhibited abilities similar to mine from a young age. His parents wanted him to have the best training, and they beseeched me to take him under my wing," he continues to explain. "Of course, I initially refused since I do not like people around, nor am I good with children." At my confused expression, he clarifies, "He was only a few hundred years old at the time. Around seven years of age in your human biology."

Oh, wow. I didn't expect him to be that young.

"I gave him a series of tests in order to accept him, and he surprised me by passing them all. Although it wasn't the most ideal situation, I could see potential in him, so I decided to take him as my apprentice and protégé."

"How long was that?"

"Our kind matures differently than yours," he notes. "He was a juvenile for hundreds of years. He reached his majority when he was three thousand years old, after which he was allowed to return home."

"You mean you spent three thousand years with him? You basically raised him!" I exclaim.

"Indeed. Which is why he is such a good warrior," he adds proudly, a smile playing at his lips. "He has displayed the highest degree of skill. Soon after he was finished with his training, he was voted to represent his family in my army, and he's been my subordinate ever since."

"I see..."

"As for those visits"—his lips curl—"they were merely official meetings with Cerenios when he was on his break at his home. My acquaintance with Erithea is merely a by-product of my association with her brother. But whereas Cerenios is cool and disciplined, Erithea is the opposite. She has quite the reputation, and it is unlikely she will secure a good mate—or any at all," Ze comments, his biting tone suggesting he disapproves of Thea. Even without telling me that, I could see that there's some undercurrent between the two of them. I wonder what exactly happened that made him dislike her so much.

Sure, she's bubbly and energetic, but she's also nice, kind, and thoughtful. I don't see why she would not be able to find a mate.

"You don't seem to like her very much."

He narrows his eyes.

"I do not like her effect on Cerenios. She rattles his focus and has become his weakness. In our line of work, one cannot have any weakness."

"Well, if there is any consolation, it seems she considers you her friend," I say with a smile, hoping I can put in a good word about her.

He rolls his eyes.

"Perhaps because she has none."

There he goes, being mean again.

"I could say the same about you," I quickly fire, raising my brow.

"I do not require friends, nor do I want them. That is the difference between us," he states unequivocally.

"What about me then? I'm not your friend?" The question was supposed to be jocular, but the moment the words are out of my mouth, I feel a sharp pain in my heart. It's quite strange, but despite not knowing Ze for long, I've come to understand him and consider him a good friend. It saddens me that he might not feel the same.

"You are different," he replies smoothly.

My brows shoot up.

"Different how?"

"You are my person. That is a category reserved only for you."

My lashes flutter in confusion.

"I don't understand what you mean, Ze."

"It means I am responsible for you," he adds gruffly.

"So I'm your new protégée?" I giggle. "Will you teach me how to fight too?" I ask enthusiastically.

Now, that wouldn't be such a bad idea. If I've learned anything so far in this game, it's that I'm far from properly equipped to deal with the competition. Almost everyone has some sort of power, or at least combat knowledge. And then there's me... The only reason I'm able to move forward, despite my ardent but useless desire to win, is due to my team—and more importantly, due to Ze. If it weren't for him, I'd be dead.

I have no trouble admitting that, and in a way, maybe it is foolish of me to continue on while knowing I don't have the ability to win even one battle. Maybe it's even more foolish to put my trust in others. But it's that foolishness that fosters my hope and the fact that I'd do *anything* in order to win and get Nikki back. There is no place for pride or shame.

There is only persevering and enduring. Although I may benefit from having strong teammates, I cannot always count on them. That means I must learn to fend for myself, too—one way or another.

After all, this is kill or be killed. And I have no intention of being on the losing side.

Ze gazes at me intently.

"You want to learn how to fight?"

"Oh, I'd love to!" I nod fervently.

He ponders it for a moment, his eyes narrowed as he gazes at me.

"Fighting requires close contact...*physical* contact," he muses quietly.

"I know. I promise I'll do my best and I won't complain if it gets too hard," I'm quick to assure him. Yes, it might be physically grueling, but I'm ready to put in the work. I'm not afraid of pain—not anymore.

"I shall teach you," he eventually nods. "I am, after all, the best suited for this job."

"Yay!" I jump up to my feet in excitement, clasping my hands together in front of me. Unfortunately, my feet are too tired to withstand the sudden movement, and just as I find myself upright, I totter to the side, my knees buckling just as my ankles bend sideways.

Ze's eyes widen, and with his characteristic swiftness, he catches me before I hit the ground.

"What happened?" he barks out, scooping me up in his arms.

"I'm fine." I muster a smile. "My legs hurt a little. I'm not accustomed to walking this much," I admit, although I don't say the entire truth—the fact that I've been pushing myself far above my limits. That I've made it this far is a wonder, but *because* of that I'm not going to give up when we're so close to our goal.

"Your legs hurt?" He frowns, a panicked expression appearing on his face. "Do you need me to heal you?"

"No, no," I hurry to say. "I'm only tired from walking. I *am* human after all," I try to joke lightly.

He doesn't seem to see the humor in my statement. Placing me on the tree trunk, he gets to his knees in front of me, extending my legs to have a look at them. He examines them on one side, then the other, not finding anything wrong with them. Still, he isn't satisfied.

"We are not far from the location. It should take us a few more hours to get there. I shall carry you so we can reach it before nightfall," he simply states.

Turning with his back to me, he motions for me to climb on him.

I may be a little reluctant to keep taking advantage of him and his kindness, but he *is* right. We do need to get the plant as fast as we can.

"Thank you," I murmur, wrapping my arms around his neck and hopping on his back. "You're *very* nice to me today," I praise him gently, knowing he loves being called that.

He tightens his hold under my knees as he starts walking. I'll never fail to be amazed at the easiness with which he's able to carry me. Somehow, I have no doubt he'd carry a cow just as easily. My lips crack in a smile as I get the mental picture of Ze giving a cow a piggyback. That would certainly be something to behold.

"Remember to add another extra point," he suddenly mentions.

"What?"

"You said you would give me extra points. Remember to add this, too." His voice is brighter than usual; his countenance, too.

I frown.

Oh, God! Of course he wouldn't realize I was speaking metaphorically. I open my mouth to explain what I meant but end up closing it and swallowing my words. He seems so excited about the potential of earning more extra points that I can't ruin it for him.

"Yes, it's added," I end up saying.

"Will you give me a boon if I accrue a certain number of points?" he asks sheepishly after a moment's thought.

"How many points are we talking about?"

"What about... one hundred? Will I get a boon if I get one hundred points?" he inquires in a rather hopeful and innocent tone—almost like a kid asking for something off his wishlist.

"I don't see why not," I agree, leaning in and placing my chin on his shoulder.

If the points matter so much to him, then I'm sure he'll put in the effort and be nicer, not just to me but to everyone else too. A smile plays at my lips. Ze is competitive—and proud. By turning this into a competition, I can give him the incentive to stop being rude to people.

"Good," he purrs, satisfied. "Make sure you do not forget to add up my points."

"I won't, I won't." I chuckle.

"I shall hold you to that." He smiles.

Pleased about our deal, he hums lightly to himself as he continues walking. I can feel the deep vibrations reverberate from his warm body, melting into my own and lulling me into a sense of peace and comfort. I nuzzle my cheek against the material of his shirt, releasing a soft yawn as I feel my eyes slowly closing, my body demanding some rest.

"Sleep, little human," I think I hear Ze whisper.

THIRTY-FOUR

I don't know how long I sleep for, but as I open my eyes, I'm happy to see that it's not dark out yet. I'm still on Ze's back as he walks through the dense forest.

The sound of birds chirping from the branches of the trees startles me back to reality, and I blink the sleep away as I take in our surroundings.

Though there is still rich foliage all around, the environment is slightly different.

Leaves and twigs crackle under Ze's weight as the ground is a mix of dirt, moss, and stone. The trees are larger than before—so much so that I can barely see traces of the blue sky. For the first time, it dawns on me that despite being a foreign world, with a toxic atmosphere for outsiders, it's so very similar to my own world. The vivid green of the leaves, the earthly brown of the tree branches and the muddy ground, the clear blue of the water and its refreshing taste, the textures of the plants and rocks; they are all so similar. I may not be too knowledgeable in science, but I wonder if perhaps this is not a universal requisite to produce and maintain forms of life. Maybe they are similar yet different enough to ensure a parallel evolution—from cells to complex systems.

Where my world is mostly devoid of supernatural dangers

that could promote the evolution of certain abilities, other worlds are not. Maybe it's just my simplistic and ignorant way of thinking of things, but I still can't help but marvel at the things around me—at everything I'm experiencing that I would have never thought real before. There's so much more out there than I could have ever imagined. Yes, there's danger, terror, and evil. But there's also beauty. It's in the nature that seems ubiquitously serene and peaceful. But it's also in the attempts to build civilization, to create a language, a culture—something to live on. There's so much commonality that for the first time I don't feel as foreign. Not to this world, and not to my new friends.

"You are awake?" Ze inquires as he half turns his head to me.

"Yes. Thank you for letting me sleep."

"You have been holding out well, human," he acknowledges in a soft voice. "I sometimes forget how small and frail you are."

"Hey." I pinch him. "I'm not *that* frail."

"Compared to me, you are," he continues. "You forget that I could crush you with one hand."

"Don't worry, Sir Sparkles, I haven't forgotten about your *strength*," I mutter drily.

"I am not saying this to antagonize you."

My eyes widen in surprise at his words.

"I am merely reminding myself that we are different, and I should not expect you to keep up with me, or with Cerenios or Erithea for that matter."

"Wow, Ze..." I whisper. "You just scored yourself another point," I joke. Did I wake up in yet another world where Ze is not arrogant, rude, and overbearing? Maybe I should pinch myself to make sure I'm not dreaming.

"I have been reflecting," he states, his tone serious—almost as if he was about to tell me he had the most important epiphany.

"Oh, and what did you reflect on?" I ask curiously.

"You are weak. I am strong. It is a perfect match."

"I don't—"

"Because you are so weak," he continues, cutting me off, "you can never be alone with another male." He pauses. "Or female."

"What are you talking about?" I ask, thoroughly confused by his so-called reflection.

"I, of course, shall always be by your side to ensure your safety and I will vanquish anyone who means you harm."

I blink.

"I appreciate that, but—"

"I acknowledge it is not your fault you are so weak," he interrupts me again. "You were simply unfortunate to be born as a human. Do not worry, I will not hold it against you. In fact, it might be for the better."

"Ze, I have no idea what you're talking about," I mutter, confused.

"Alas, that is another one of your shortcomings. But I will not hold that against you either. You have plenty of good qualities, too," he speaks, his voice booming with self-assuredness.

"Oh, really? And what are those?" I ask ironically. I'm curious what he'll come up with after insulting me not once, not twice, but three times! I guess I should start taking off points, too.

"You are small."

"You just said I was weak." I raise a brow.

"I like small." He nods to himself with a smile.

That's not exactly a quality, though.

"What else?" I ask, even though I know I'll probably regret wanting to know.

"You are nice," he says, his voice dropping an octave. "To me."

I blink.

"I am not...good with people. And I admit I may have, at times, offended you."

I resist the urge to roll my eyes since I doubt even he knows when he's offensive and when he isn't.

"But you have not held my idiosyncrasies against me. You are a good person, Luce." He smiles, turning his face toward me.

My lashes flutter as I find myself suddenly *too* close to him, his warm breath fanning my face, his purple eyes fixed on mine.

"Uhm, thank you?" I whisper, heat traveling up my cheeks.

"You are very welcome," he replies in that dignified tone of his. "From now on, I would rather you were not as nice to others, though. I suppose I could make an exception for Erithea, and maybe even Cerenios since he knows his place. But any other individual is out of the question."

Now I'm confused... Is he telling me not to be nice to other contestants?

"Is this because it might be dangerous?"

I experienced firsthand what happened with the fox when I only tried to be nice and compliment her tail. Maybe he has a point with this. Despite my instinct to be cordial and kind to people, it's not the place to do so. We're all enemies here.

"Yes. It is"—he nods before adding under his breath—"*for them.*"

"You're right," I eventually agree. "Sometimes I just can't help it." I sigh. "But I realize it might not be in my best interest."

"Do not worry. I will ensure I am the only object of your attentions," he declares.

"Well, I guess that gets you an extra point." I laugh. "Thank you for always having my back." I pat him lightly on the shoulder.

He preens quietly at hearing about the extra point.

Ze might be downright offensive sometimes, but he's lucky that another one of my *good qualities* is that I don't take his poorly phrased words to heart, nor am I quick to anger.

We walk for a while longer before I anxiously tap his chest.

"Do you see that?" I point at the spot between the trees. "Those colors..."

White petals with a black dot inside are attached to a light green stem that's a contrast to the deep green of the grass.

"It seems we have arrived at our destination," he nods.

I ask him to put me down and the moment my feet touch the ground, I run forward. Once I pass the last of the trees, my eyes widen in wonder as I take in the beauty of the landscape.

"It's an entire field, Ze! Oh my," I exclaim in excitement as I hurry forward.

The flowers are quite tall, reaching my waist. And as I run around, the silky texture of the petals brushes against my hands.

Turning to Ze, I continue to walk backward as I beckon him forward.

"Come on!"

Ze smiles as he watches me.

"Should we take it out with the root?" I ask as I gaze at one particular plant.

"Yes," he replies, handing me our bag before getting to his knees and digging his hands in the ground. He pushes his fingers in the damp soil, moving around until he has a good grasp on the root. Carefully, he starts taking it out. To help him, I get down next to him, brushing away the dirt so he can perform a smooth removal.

"There. One," he says, giving it to me. But instead of stopping, he moves to the next.

"Isn't one enough?" I frown.

"You should always aim for a backup plan," he mutters as he repeats the process with the other plant.

"I see." I nod.

We get a total of three plants, carefully placing them inside our bags.

A foolish smile pulls at my lips, my insides trembling with mirth and happiness and optimism.

"We made it, Ze! We found it. I'm so happy." I jump up and down as I twirl around.

He just stands there, an inscrutable expression on his face as he stares at me.

"That we did," he speaks slowly.

I raise a brow at him, but he simply shakes his head.

"Happiness looks good on you, Luce," he murmurs, walking toward me in that dignified manner of his, spine straight, hands behind his back.

"I bet it would look good on you, too. Come!" I grab his hand

and pull him along with me, running around in the field until we reach a portion where the plants are not as tall. Without saying a word, I throw myself on my back, cushioned by the softness of the grass.

I wave my arms and legs back and forth, creating the shape of an angel and feeling the light caress of the grass against my skin. The ground is damp and cool, but I barely register the discomfort. At the moment, the only thing that matters is that we did it. We found the plant!

Ze tilts his head, a frown marring his features.

"What are you doing?"

"Having fun, Ze. You should try it!"

He looks at me, then at the grass, then back at me, the frown on his face deepening.

"Just come," I urge him.

He ponders it for a few moments before he stiffly lies down on the grass next to me. He's on his back, his hands glued to his sides as he stares up at the sky.

I glance at him, noticing he doesn't move a muscle as he lies there as if he were made of stone.

"How do you feel?" I ask as I turn onto my side, propping my head on my arm to look at him.

"It is wet," he replies drily. "And cold."

I roll my eyes.

"I didn't ask how the ground feels. I am very much aware that it's not comfortable. But how do *you* feel?" I inquire anxiously, hoping to spark at least some joy in his barren heart. The more I learn about him and his life, the more I feel sorry for him and the prison he's locked himself in—all in order to excel at his job. I admire him for wanting to do his duty and protect people from demons, but that doesn't mean he cannot take time to himself, relax, and simply enjoy life.

He's over seven thousand years old, for God's sake, and he's never read a book for enjoyment.

If that's not a crime, then I don't know what is.

He seems confused by my question.

"I... I do not know," he blinks.

"What do you mean you don't know?"

He's silent for what seems like forever, his body tensing until the high definition of his muscles becomes visible through his loose clothing. Still gazing at the sky, he swallows hard, his Adam's apple bobbing up and down as he releases a deep, agonizing breath.

A sliver of anxiety courses through me as I shuffle closer to him, my hand midair as I reach for him. But just before I can touch him, he speaks.

"I do not have a frame of reference for feelings. I may rationally understand them, but I do not know what feelings *feel* like."

My lids flutter rapidly.

"Are you serious? You're joking, right?" My voice ebbs as uncertainty grips me. It seems like a joke, but his countenance indicates it's not one.

He turns his head toward me, the purple of his eyes intensifying.

"Why would I joke?" he asks with a straight face.

"But... I don't understand. How can you not know what feelings feel like? You just have to *feel*..." Maybe he has a hard time putting his emotions into words. We've already established he's not the greatest communicator.

"I cannot. Or at least..." he trails off, his lips flattening as a scowl mars his features. "I thought I could not. I am not sure." He blinks, emotions warring on his face. They're out there in the open, fighting for supremacy despite his proclamation that he cannot feel.

"Can you explain what you mean?" I ask softly. I can see he's struggling with this, and I hate the uncertainty mirrored in his expression.

His features tighten, his brows knit together as he muses quietly.

"I have been this way for as long as I remember. I can logically understand joy, sorrow, love, hate, envy and so on. I *under-*

stand them, but I do not experience them. Or, at least, I could not experience them before."

"Before?"

He sighs.

"I was gravely injured in a battle and after I recovered, everything was...strange."

"Strange?" I probe further. He has a lost expression on his face, which tells me he doesn't understand what's happening to him.

"My compulsions have become...unnatural."

I frown. "Unnatural how?"

"They are...illogical. Irrational. *Instinctual*," he rasps in a rough voice. "As if there is another *me* inside of me that dictates my actions. An *absurd* me."

"And you think your injury caused this?"

He nods.

"I am who I am because of my immutability. I do what I do because I do not waver. But now... I fear I am not unshakable anymore."

My heart clenches at his admission. It's rare to see Ze being so open and vulnerable, admitting to his own weaknesses. But as this information sinks in, more things start making sense—his lack of awareness, his rudeness, his outbursts. Just like I had initially intuited, he doesn't do it with malice. He does it because he doesn't know any better.

I place my hand on top of his, patting him lightly.

"I'm sorry," I whisper.

"You are forbidden from telling this to anyone, human," he suddenly declares in a booming voice, turning his hand palm up and threading his fingers through mine, the action belying the severity of his words. "You are the only one who knows about it."

"Thank you. I'm flattered you'd trust me." I smile.

He stares at me awkwardly, seemingly at a loss for words.

What is it about him that hurts my heart so? It's almost as if his pain and confusion echo in the air, sending an arrow straight to my chest and making me *feel* his struggle. From the beginning, I could sense there was more behind his seemingly haughty facade, but I would have never guessed it would be something so monumental—or that he'd be so lonely and scared in the face of the unknown.

"I could help you navigate it," I offer with a smile. "If you want to talk to someone about it, that is."

"You would do that for me?" His voice is tinged with surprise.

"Of course," I assure him. "We can start with what you experienced *after* you awoke. What was different than before?"

He's pensive for a moment.

"Before, I would not react to anything. I would do my duty on the battlefield. I would sleep and feed because my body demanded it. I would interact with others only when duty required it," he starts. "I did not care about anything or anyone. People... They do not like me, and they are not afraid to make their dislike known, even to my face. I would be insulted, but I did not mind it, nor did I punish them unless it was a sanctioned action."

Oh, God. The more he speaks, the bleaker a picture he paints. How is that a life? How can *anyone* live like that?

"After I recovered, everything changed. I became annoyed at every little thing. I am prone to anger unlike ever before. I can feel...*hurt*, even when there is no discernible wound on my body. It is entirely too strange," he marvels in a low voice.

"Oh, Ze," I whisper. "You must be so confused at everything. I can't imagine what you're going through," I say as I squeeze his hand. In hindsight, his past behavior makes sense. He wasn't rude—that was his default mode. If anything, his newfound feelings must have made him question everything he thought he knew about himself and the world.

I can't possibly imagine what it would be like to go through something like that—to have everything you thought you knew stripped away from you. Yet, still, he's handled everything much better than I think I would. For someone who's practically experiencing the world for the first time, he's shown an impressive amount of self-control—especially considering his destructive abilities.

"I do not want your pity, human," he rasps, his eyes flashing at me.

"I'm not pitying you." I shake my head. "It's called compassion. It means my heart hurts for your pain."

His frown deepens.

"I do not understand. How can you hurt for someone else's pain?" he asks, entirely confused.

"When you care about someone, their pain becomes your own. You want to see them happy all the time, and when they're not, their lack of happiness influences your own, too."

He nods to himself as he mulls over my words.

"You care for me?" he speaks slowly, hesitantly.

"Of course." I smile. "You're a good man, Ze. I don't care what others say or think of you. So what if people don't like you? They just don't know you because they never tried to know you. And that's their loss," I state with all the conviction I can muster.

He stills, staring at me with an odd glint in his eyes. The color of his irises, too, becomes a deeper purple that swirls into an infinity pool, specks of silver flashing brightly.

Shifting onto his side, he comes closer to me, his gaze a mix of confusion and curiosity. But there's something more, too. Something strange and exciting. I can barely blink because I cannot tear my eyes from his, afraid that the spell would be broken any moment.

A low tremor goes down my spine as he takes my hand and lays it against his chest.

"I," he starts, licking his lips as he searches for the right words. "I think mine hurts for you too."

A wide smile stretches across my face, just as a hopeful look crosses his.

"This is called friendship, Ze," I tell him gently. "We care about each other because we're friends."

His expression falls, a scowl pulling at his features as he tightens his grip over my hand. Taken aback by the sudden change in his countenance, I pull my hand from his. It takes me a few tries to dislodge it from his iron grasp.

"Right, uhm... What else happened after you recovered?" I ask in an attempt to redirect his attention to the previous topic. I'm not sure what I said that triggered him, but judging by the tension in his muscles, he's not very happy with where our conversation was going.

He narrows his eyes at me.

"I am overwhelmed by these new...urges," he states, watching me intently. "And I do not know how to quench them."

Seconds trickle by as he awaits my response, but I find myself at a loss for words.

"What...urges?" I ask hesitantly.

He stares at me, the answer clear without him having to verbalize it.

Right. Awkward. Why did I have to offer to help him navigate his newfound feelings?

"Uhm..." Is this really the time to give him the sex ed talk? Given his disinterest in females and his prudishness, I am sure he's never done anything of that nature.

Damn... Why does it have to be me?

I may be married, but I've always been shy about these things. Nikki used to laugh about it all the time when my cheeks would turn red at the mere mention of the word sex. But then, he'd tease me about my blushes and one thing would lead to another and we'd end up in bed, where somehow I'd forget all about my shyness.

But that was Nikki, my husband and only lover. Even with him, it took me a long time to come to terms with the abuse I witnessed at the hacienda. Our courtship lasted over a year, and in that time, we only kissed a handful of times. It was only on our wedding night that we became intimate, and although I'll always cherish that memory, I must admit that it was a disaster. We fumbled awkwardly together, and the entire thing was a painful ordeal. It took us months of practice to become comfortable with it and enjoy each other.

I can already feel heat travel up my neck as I imagine stumbling my way through an uncomfortable explanation. I should just give him a romance novel and let him figure things out on his own.

"I'm sure you'll find a way to...erm...quench them," I say nervously. No matter how much I want to help him, this isn't something I feel comfortable talking about, nor do I think it would be a proper topic to discuss with a male friend. It's better if we just focus on the emotional aspect.

His mouth curls around the corners.

"I am sure I will," he drawls, his eyes boring into mine.

I swallow uncomfortably.

"We should make our way back," I suggest, getting up and dusting my clothes.

He rises, his posture straight and imposing.

"Let us depart," he states in an icy tone, barely sparing me a glance.

He walks ahead, not bothering to wait for me.

What the hell is his deal?

I hurry after him, gazing up at his lofty profile. His expression gives nothing away, a neutrality resembling the one from when I first met him encasing his features. Almost like a switch, he went from the vulnerable man he let me glimpse just a few seconds ago back to the ice block that thinks himself better than everyone else.

Perhaps he's regretting opening up to me? Ze strikes me as a man accustomed to showing no weakness, and he just admitted a huge one to me. At the same time, I'm also torn because the thought of being his only confidante warms me. But his current attitude makes me wonder why he said anything in the first place. His words implied that he cares for me, his previous actions too. His current ones, however? Not so much.

I sigh and hunch my shoulders. Since he's new to this feelings business, I'll cut him some slack. But that doesn't erase the fact that *my* feelings are slightly bruised.

We walk in silence for roughly two hours.

Every time I try to initiate a conversation, he mumbles a few brief words and then ignores me. Sometimes, he just stares intently at me, almost as if he's trying to decipher something.

When my stomach growls with hunger, we take a short break at the edge of a forest, right by a rocky cliff that feeds into a canyon. From a green and rich environment, we're now in the middle of a dry and arid one—a polar opposite. It's quite hard to imagine that these two landscapes would coexist in such proximity, but at this point, I don't think I should question the logic of the universe anymore. Anything is possible.

I take a seat on a boulder at the peak of the cliff, unpacking some of our remaining snacks in front of me. Ze's a few meters away, standing tall and mighty and doing his best not to glance my way as I munch on a nut bar. His attention is focused on the forest, and I assume he's trying to be alert in case of an attack.

Clearing my throat, I call out to him.

"Ze? You should come and eat something."

He turns sharply to me, his lips compressed into a thin line.

Does this man *ever* get hungry? I can count on one hand the times I've seen him eat, and we've been by each other's side for days in a row.

"I am not hungry," he replies in a dry tone before turning his back to me.

"You've barely eaten anything. You must be hungry."

"I am not hungry, human," he grits out.

"Come eat something." I put on a hesitant smile as I beckon him closer, waving the bar in my hand at him.

He half turns, his brow raised as he looks from me to the nut bar.

"Pretty please? I'll give you an extra point."

He blinks, his ears suddenly perking up.

"An extra point?" he repeats, already walking toward me.

Without saying another word, he takes the bar from my hand, peels the wrapper, and bites into it.

"Tell me you're not mad at me," I say as I lean into him, rubbing my shoulder against him playfully.

He frowns.

"What are you on about with this nonsense again, human? Why would I be mad at you?"

"I don't know." I shrug. "You've been ignoring me for the last few hours. If I did something wrong, please tell me so I can fix it," I add hesitantly.

"I was not ignoring you," he states, and I detect no falsehood. "I was just ruminating."

"Oh." I gulp. "About what?"

"About our conversation. About our *friendship*." His face screws up in disgust as he utters the word.

"And?" I ask anxiously. I can't help but think that I did or said something wrong.

He's about to answer when something else grabs his attention. Eyes flashing with determination, he grabs my hand, pulling me into his arms right as a static noise permeates the air.

"Quiet," he whispers in my hair, keeping me close as he glances at the bottom of the canyon. I follow his gaze to a bluish swirling mass of air in the shape of a sphere. The color becomes increasingly more pronounced, and as a loud thud echoes through the valley, a mangled foot steps out of it. Soon after, the owner of that foot makes its appearance—a monstrous demon like the one we encountered at the theatre. And he's not alone.

He steps out of the portal, leaving way for another demon to come after him. And another.

Four demons enter the realm, and just when I think that's it, someone else comes out. Yet this person doesn't have the typical demonic appearance. Dressed in a dark blue suit tinged with red, he appears to be humanoid.

The moment his feet touch the ground, the portal behind him closes.

I sneak a glance at Ze and note the tightening of his jaw.

"What's going on?" I whisper. "Who's that?"

"A son of Tenebreis—an archdemon."

"But what are they doing here? Didn't you say they can't move around in corporeal form?"

"They should not be able to," he answers tersely.

The archdemon is talking to the four demons, seemingly giving them some orders before they flash themselves out of sight. Alone, the archdemon removes something from his pocket. From this distance, I can't see what it is, but as he holds it in his hand, a red light emanates from his palm, surrounding the object. His lips move, too, and I assume he's chanting something just as the light intensifies.

Ze's arms tighten around me, his breathing harsh against my flesh.

When the archdemon has finished chanting, he throws the object onto the ground, the light infiltrating through every crack and crevice, melting onto the very fabric of the earth.

Then he disappears as well.

"What the hell was that, Ze?" I whisper, still staring at the canyon.

"Something that should not have happened," he says with a twitch of his cheek.

"I don't understand..."

"This is bad," he mutters to himself. "This is bad," he repeats, almost like a robot. He takes a step back, his shrewd eyes taking in his surroundings, his body taut and primed for war. "I need to send a message to my generals. Stay here," he orders, but his attention is not on me.

"But... What if they come back?" I blink.

"They are no longer around," he replies absentmindedly, moving away from me without sparing me a glance.

"I'll come with you," I quickly say, hurrying after him.

He doesn't acknowledge my words, and before I can blink, he's gone from my sight.

"Ze?" I call out, my eyes widening with fear. I run toward the spot he disappeared from, anxiously calling out his name.

"Don't leave me alone..." My lips tremble as a sliver of fear washes through me. Maybe it's because we've been inseparable until now, but the thought of being alone in this world terrifies me.

Foolish thoughts and scenarios inundate my mind as I dash after him, still calling his name. It's as if between me and doom there's only him—only Ze. He's my buffer... my rock.

So focused am I on finding him that I no longer mind my surroundings or watch my steps.

A sharp pain erupts in my knees and palms as I trip and fall to the ground. But in my desperation, I barely register the fall. I get up, ready to continue my search for him.

But as I turn around, I note the sudden shift of the landscape as well as the dimming colors—as if darkness has suddenly consumed the entire sky.

"Ze..." I call out once more, my chest aflame with a spark of terror. Yet just as the word is out of my mouth, I frown, slowly forgetting my initial purpose. A cracking noise reverberates from my side, and as I turn to search for its source, my eyes are blinded by a sudden light. White tendrils slither forward and grip my body, pulling me into that light.

THIRTY-FIVE

I blink my eyes open, a whooshing noise erupting in my ears as I find myself in the middle of a hallway. The walls are a familiar cream color, decorated with Mesoamerican motifs. The illustrated deities watch me from their lofty place near the ceiling, ready to mete out judgment on those who step out of line. A flurry of movement startles me, and I watch a few servant girls hurry up and down the corridor.

I take a step forward, but an insidious pain makes me gasp loudly. Slowly, I bring my hand to my shoulder. My fingers become coated in blood, the pain getting worse by the second.

W-what happened?

One moment I was in a forest... I was in a forest, wasn't I? My brows furrow together in confusion as I strain to remember. There's something inside of me that tells me I was doing something else—something important. It's on the tip of my tongue as I strain to remember.

There was another person with me too.

"Who was he?" I whisper. I can almost make out a tall, broad-shouldered figure in front of me. But as the seconds trail by, a thick fog descends upon my mind, the mist concealing all that important information until I no longer remember why it was important in the first place.

My wound pulsates, the pain assaulting my senses until I hunch over, breathing erratically. Taking one more look around, I realize I'm close to the staff kitchen—my initial destination.

Why did I stop in the middle of the hallway? I, better than anyone, know what will happen if Sergio catches me. Then it's not just going to be a bullet in my shoulder. It's going to be a lot more than that.

Pushing against the onslaught of pain, I hurry to the back kitchen, getting inside and closing the door behind me. Since this is a secondary kitchen, it's not often used, which allowed me to smuggle some sanitary items in case I ever needed them.

Going to the back, I open the pantry, looking for the hidden compartment on the bottom shelf. As my hand brushes against the handle of the secret door, I pull it open and take out the small first aid kit I stashed away. It's nothing fancy, since it's mainly comprised of items I've managed to steal from the drug testing facility. But it should be enough for now to ensure I won't get an infection. With Noelle so close to going into labor, I can't afford to become incapacitated. That would jeopardize her health and that of the baby, and I could never forgive myself for it.

I spread out the sanitary items over the kitchen counter, quickly surveying them and forming a mental plan. A quick glance at the clock on the wall tells me I have an hour to spare.

I purse my lips. Since time is limited, I need to work fast. Taking off my shirt, I undo my makeshift bandage and hold up a small mirror to see the extent of the damage. I wince at the red, angry wound and the red liquid oozing out of it. Every little movement hurts, the bullet wiggling inside my flesh and causing me more pain.

Goddamn it. Why did this happen today of all days? Why are we so unlucky? Since Sergio caught us attempting to escape a few months ago, it's been getting perpetually worse. He wants to make Noelle suffer for what she did to him, and he knows that he can do it through her baby and...through me.

I stifle a broken sob as I try not to think of the future. It's bleak anyway. As long as I can help Noelle and her baby survive this nightmare, I won't care what happens to me.

She has her whole life ahead of her.

Me... What is there left for me?

I have no family. No friends aside from her and...*him*. God, I have nothing but some broken and delusional dreams about a boy I once made the mistake of falling for; someone who for all intents and purposes might be married now, living his best life while I...

A tear rolls down my cheek.

There's no one waiting for me... At one time, I may have made the mistake of imagining what life would be like outside of the constricting walls of the hacienda—what I could do if I were free. But that's only brought me more misery for something that's never going to happen.

I've lived my worst moments on this land. But I've also had the most happiness. Maybe it was brief, but I'll always cherish the memory of the man who gave me a purpose...an identity. Because it's that identity that I'll take to my grave.

Somehow, that gives me an extra dose of courage as I pick up a pair of tweezers and douse it in disinfectant. I close my eyes for a moment, breathing in and out. The pain is unavoidable. I know that. I've had so much pain my entire life, I should be used to it by now.

"I can do this," I whisper to myself.

But just as I lift the tweezers to my shoulder, the door behind me opens. My eyes flare open with panic, just as the tweezers slip out of my hand, dropping to the ground. Before I can scream or run, a hand covers my mouth, the other circling my waist and bringing me against his chest. A male chest.

Terror suffuses me.

I'm naked from the waist up, with a gaping wound in my shoulder. I'm at my most vulnerable and now at the mercy of a stranger. I know far too well how this will end. After all, I might be shunned by everyone at the hacienda—the cursed one as they call me for my blasphemous marks—but what no one sees, no one knows. Sergio may have decreed that I'm worse than a leper, but that hasn't stopped his men from trying to assault me when no one's watching.

"Don't scream," a voice speaks in my ear. It's an oddly familiar one, and I frown as I try to recall where I heard it before.

"I'm not going to hurt you, I swear. If I take my hand off, promise not to scream? No one knows I'm here and I'd rather keep it that way."

His words are even more confusing, but I slowly nod my assent.

He drops his hand from my mouth, but his arm is still around my waist. Instinctively, I draw back, turning to face him.

"You..." I whisper in awe.

He gives me a lopsided smile.

"I'm a little late, aren't I?"

I blink, wondering if this is a dream—*is it?* How many times had I conjured him before me just like this? Yet every time, it had only been a mirage that shattered the moment reality intruded on the fantasy.

"What are you doing here?"

"I promised you I'd come," he replies effortlessly.

God, he's even more handsome than I remember. His hair is shorter, his body leaner. But there's no way I would never not recognize those dark eyes—the eyes that still haunt my dreams. For years, his face has been the only thing I could fall asleep to, his presence the most comforting thing I've ever known in my life.

And now, to see him here, in the flesh? How is this possible?

"Are you real?" I ask in disbelief. "Is it really you, Nikki?"

"I'm here. I'm just so fucking sorry it took me so long, Luce. But I promise you, there's a good reason for it."

I nod numbly. How can I care about anything when he's *here?* In front of me. So close...

A smile trembles on my lips as I reach out with my non-injured arm to touch him, trailing one finger over the back of his hand. My eyes close and a shiver goes down my back at the contact. Not even the pain in my shoulder could detract from the utter delight of the moment.

"You're really here," I mumble incoherently, touching him some more—just to make sure he's real. Maybe on any other occasion, I wouldn't have been as bold. But as it happens, I've lost too much in the last years not to grasp onto this chance.

He catches my hand in his, giving it a tight squeeze. He slowly brings it to his lips, laying a chaste kiss on the inside of my wrist that has me blushing to the roots of my hair. Yet what's most striking is the look on his face. He's staring at me intently, his eyes caressing my face. There's a dangerous hunger radiating from him. One I don't remember seeing before—or, maybe I hadn't noticed? His body tenses, his nostrils flaring as he continues to drink me in.

My eyes flutter in confusion.

"Nikki?" I ask tentatively.

He snaps out of his trance and gives me a wide smile—as if he hasn't been looking at me like a starved man. I'm about to return the smile with a timid one of my own when I note the dip of his gaze, his eyes zeroing in on my chest. That's when I recall my state of undress. And it's not just my naked body that I don't want him seeing but also the marks that cover most of my torso.

I quickly wrap my arms around my body to cover myself, but the movement is so brusque that I end up bending over in pain.

"Who the hell did this to you, Luce?" He's next to me in two steps, his big hands splayed over my shoulder as he peruses my wound.

"Sergio." I give him a tight smile. One word that encompasses both of our experiences in this goddamn forsaken place.

His features darken, cold anger emanating from him.

"He needs to *suffer* for hurting you," he grits out, and my heart speeds up in my chest at the fact that he'd so readily avenge me.

"Thank you for saying that," I murmur. "But right now, I

need to take care of my arm. Will you..." I wet my lips, surprised at myself for putting my trust in him so readily. "Will you help me?"

"I'm here for *you*, Luce," he punctuates each word. "I'll help you with anything you want. But we need to get you to a doctor. It's not safe to do this here."

I shake my head.

"I can't." I tell him about the precarious situation Noelle is in. "So you see, I don't have time for a doctor. I need to get the bullet out and sew the wound."

He's about to disagree with me, but I slowly lift my hand to his face, fitting my palm to his cheek. At the same time, we both inhale deeply, our eyes connecting. Something flickers in my chest, almost as if my entire being sparks alive at the merest contact with his flesh.

"Luce," he rasps out.

"Please," I plead.

He doesn't speak, seemingly at war with himself. Eventually, he gives me a tight nod. Without a word, he bends down to pick up the pair of tweezers and goes to the sink to wash it before disinfecting it.

"Come here." He motions me to him. I take a seat on a chair while he positions himself in front of me. Placing a hand on my back, he eyes the wound with concern as he takes a deep breath. "This will hurt."

"I know."

"I wish I could take your pain onto myself, Luce," he murmurs huskily.

"Do it," I urge him.

He pushes the tweezers into my wound, doing his best to avoid hurting me more than necessary as he digs for the bullet. I close my eyes as I suffer in silence, not making even one sound. Somehow, I know that would distress him, his pain perhaps more profound than mine. How I know this, I'm not sure. There's only this certainty deep within, borne perhaps out of my own foolish romantic notions but also out of the friendship we shared in the past—a bond so deep, I've been living as a shell of myself since he's been gone.

To my surprise, he finds it fairly fast, pulls it out, and drops it on the table.

At the same time, though, more blood gushes out of the wound, and he hurries to press gauze to it.

"Can you sew it, too?"

He nods. His lips are pressed into a thin line, his breathing growing labored—more so than mine, and I'm the one with a hole in my shoulder.

He disinfects some needle and thread, and with a precision I wouldn't have expected of him, he sews the wound in just a few strokes. His features are tense as he focuses on his task. When he's done, he presses more gauze, wiping the last bit from my wound and cleaning it up with some disinfectant before he adds a bandage on top of it.

"How are you feeling?"

"Good," I wheeze. "It didn't hurt *that* badly." I attempt a smile.

He grunts.

"You did really good, Nikki. Thank you."

He doesn't answer as he takes the shirt I previously discarded, offering to help me put it on. I accept his help, and I try to ignore the way my nipples tighten, my skin covered in goosebumps. He tries to ignore it, too—I can tell. It's almost as if he forces his gaze *not* to stray to that area, realizing that it's making me uncomfortable.

After I'm dressed, silence descends between us.

"It's the first time you've seen my marks," I note softly. I told him about them since they were the reason I was the most hated person at the hacienda—the one even the other slaves snickered at. These ugly marks branded me as cursed, and that made people both fear and abhor me.

"You're beautiful, Luce," he says, his voice trembling with sincerity. "You're the most beautiful thing I've *ever* seen. Never doubt that."

I blink in surprise.

"You... mean that?"

He smiles.

"You're the only thing that's been keeping me alive until now. The thought of seeing you again carried me through my darkest moments."

"I—" I bite my lip as I study him. "I don't know what to say, Nikki."

"You don't have to say anything now," he murmurs, stepping closer and touching his forehead to mine. He inhales deeply, and I can feel his breath on my lips. "I'll help you with your plan. But after that, you're coming with me," he states.

"I am?" My voice wobbles, warmth spreading through my limbs.

"You are. Now that I've found you again, I'm never letting you go. *Never*," he emphasizes, his words sounding both like a promise and a threat. In fact, there's a slight edge to his tone, but it's not something I pick up easily on. In my euphoria, I can only see him, here, with me. In my naiveté, I don't ask any questions, simply satisfied with what he decides.

"We should go now," I stammer, still caught in his intense gaze.

"There are ten more minutes until we need to leave," he notes glibly, barely sparing a glance at the watch.

"But—"

"I've missed you, Luce. Tell me you've missed me, too," he says in a low, anguished voice.

"Of course I missed you. You were my best friend, Nikki."

His features darken.

"Your best friend? *Just* your best friend?"

"I... Well..." I moisten my lips as I gaze up into his eyes. He's so close... "Maybe a little more."

"How much more?" he rasps, his deep voice sending a shiver down my back.

Suddenly, there's no more physical pain. There's only a light pulsation that starts from the center of my chest, traveling up and imbuing all my senses with a euphoria I've never experienced before—one that makes me even more lightheaded than blood loss.

"You must know I had a crush on you, Nikki," I answer bashfully, my cheeks reddening.

"*Just* a crush?" He raises a brow.

"Maybe a little more."

"How much more? Tell me, Luce. Spare me from this torment I've been drowning in for the past two years. Tell me," he murmurs, the cadence of his voice changed. It's more suave, more... God, my face must be burning, and despite my injury, I don't think I have a fever. No, it's him—only him. It's his nearness when I've only dreamed about it before. It's his voice that makes me melt with every syllable he utters. And it's his intense gaze that has me pinned to the spot, so hungry and so desperate. It's almost as if he *is* drowning and I'm the only one who can save him.

"I was in love with you," I confess.

"Was?" he asks darkly.

"Am," I whisper.

A slow smile runs across his mouth, one that is as blinding as it is terrifying, and before I know it, his lips are on mine. His kiss is fierce and unrelenting, just like this side of Nikki I haven't known before. And though in the beginning I'm startled by this foreign sensation, I can't help but give in.

He's Nikki. He's *my* Nikki. The only man I'd ever allow such liberties because he owns my body just as he owns my heart.

His lips part over mine, his tongue skimming the seam of my mouth. At first, I'm confused about what he means to do, but as he brushes his tongue against mine, my entire body hums, a terrifying sensation enveloping me. One that threatens to overwhelm me with *feeling*.

Yet just as the kiss starts, it's over. He tears himself from me, his breathing accelerated, his features contorted in pain.

"Nikki?" I ask softly, bringing my hand to my lips.

"I'm sorry."

"I—What happened? Was it...bad?" I barely utter the last word as hopelessness forms inside me.

"Bad? What? No. It was *too* good, Luce. But I've been living for the past two years on your memory alone and that kiss... If we don't stop, we might *never* stop, and it's not the time for that. Not only do we have something to do, but..." He scrubs his face with his hand. "You're *you*, and that means you deserve more than just a quick tumble in the hay. You're also hurt." He shakes his head. "God, I'm a fucking idiot," he curses out.

I watch him in confusion, not understanding half of what he's saying.

"So you didn't dislike it?" I ask, needing direct confirmation.

"I loved it. Like I love *you*," he says, his piercing gaze meeting mine just as his hand comes up to caress my cheek. "Was it your first kiss?" he inquires before I can recover from his confession. His voice is tense, almost as if he's already hating my answer.

I give him a slow nod.

He lets out a relieved breath.

"Good. Good," he repeats, more to himself. "You saved those lips for me, didn't you, Luce?"

I'm so embarrassed, I try to avert my eyes, but he won't let me, tipping my chin up so all I see is him.

"Tell me you saved your lips for me," he rasps, his hungry eyes on my lips.

"Yes," I whisper.

He smirks.

"You're telling me everything I need to hear, Luce." Leaning further in, his mouth stops next to my ear. "Me too."

I don't get to question him on what he means as he points to the time.

"We need to leave," he says, taking my hand in his. "Lead the way, Luce."

I give him a smile, once more marveling at the fact that he's really here, with me. It was something I would have never dared hope for, yet something I wished for ardently.

As we take Nikki's car to go to the nearby village for an errand, he tells me about his cover story and how he'd managed to get an invite to Sergio's banquet by pretending to be a high-level investor interested in the inauguration of his new drug.

"What happened to you, Nikki? What happened after you left?" I muster the courage to ask. His features darken instantly, and he averts his gaze.

"I would have come earlier for you. Believe me that I wouldn't have taken so long if it hadn't been out of my hands."

"What do you mean?" I whisper, almost afraid to know.

"I made it home all right." A dry smile tugs at his lips. "But within a day, I was in an accident that might not have been much of an *accident*."

"Nikki." I turn to him, my eyes widening with worry.

"I was in a coma until a couple of months ago," he admits.

"What? Are you okay now? My God, Nikki..."

My heart is hammering in my chest at the thought of him in the hospital, fighting between life and death. Even before, when I'd never thought I would see him again, at least I was fine thinking he was happily living his life somewhere in the world. But to hear that it hadn't been the case? That he...

"There was something wrong with my head, but I'm fine now." He keeps one hand on the wheel, grabbing my hand with the other. "I'm not entirely sure what happened while I was in the coma, but you were there, with me."

"I was?" I blink.

He nods wistfully.

"I don't remember everything, but I know you were with me every day. We were by a waterfall, and I would lay my head on your lap while you'd tell me stories."

"That's... I don't know what to say, Nikki. I'm flattered," I murmur, a blush staining my cheeks. "I didn't realize you thought about me that way back then."

"You've been everything to me from the first moment I met

you in those cursed tunnels, Luce. I survived *only* because you were with me, and later, because I knew I needed to keep my promise to you."

I stare at him, mouth agape.

"I thought about you, too," I confess shyly. "Every day, I'd wonder what you were doing. If you were happy. If you...were with someone," I whisper as I avert my gaze.

How many times have I hurt myself over the thought of him with someone else? With a girlfriend, or maybe a wife. I never regretted helping him escape and leaving me behind. But just imagining him with another woman has chipped at my heart time and time again.

"There's only ever been you, Luce," he states emphatically.

His eyes hold mine for a moment before he returns his attention to the road. But it's enough to convey everything with that one glance.

He loves me. He *really* loves me.

I'm still in a state of disbelief over the events of the last few hours, but this piece of information is not only the most precious one, but the most unexpected, too.

"I'll come with you, Nikki. After everything is done. After Noelle is back with her family, too. I'll come with you," I tell him.

"You'll never want for anything in this life. That I can promise you, Luce." He smiles as he brings my hand to his lips for a kiss. "I'll cherish you always."

"I know you will." I return his smile.

Happiness brims inside of me, but just as I lose myself in the moment, I find myself physically wrenched out of that scenario and thrust into another.

I blink repeatedly as panic suffuses my chest, my heart beating wildly as confusion simmers in my mind. The image of the car falls away, walls slowly rising up around me to construct a different environment. For one brief moment, I remember a name. Someone I was looking for. Someone I care about.

Ze...

Yet as soon as the sound of a door closing reverberates in my ear, my previous thoughts disappear from my mind. I don't question anything but the present and the fact that Nikki is in front of me.

"We can talk here. But quietly," I whisper to him. Noelle is sleeping in the other room, and I'm almost certain she'll give birth today.

"Of course." He nods, walking farther into the bathroom. I follow after him, surprised to see him pull a small case out of his pocket. As he opens it, it's to reveal pills nestled inside. He takes a couple, popping them into his mouth.

"What are those?" I point at the pills. "You said you were fine," I add, a hint of worry in my voice.

"It's for something else." He strains a smile.

I wait for him to explain, but he seems reluctant to do so.

"It's okay if you don't want to tell me," I assure him.

"It's not that." He sighs. "It's just that... It's something I had from before the accident."

I frown. "What do you mean?"

"It's not...physical. It's psychological. The pills help me function more or less normally."

"Nikki..." I take a tentative step toward him. "I would never judge you for anything. I hope you know that."

He gives me a tight nod.

"You remember the panic attacks I used to get?"

"Yes."

"After my accident, I was formally diagnosed for the first time." He smiles ruefully. "PTSD, severe anxiety and agoraphobia, among others. The pills work to lessen the anxiety and agoraphobia—in as much as they helped me get out of my house and come here."

"And you're here..."

"I'm here." He nods.

I can't imagine the kind of strength it must have taken him to come, especially since I remember the panic attacks he'd get— I used to help him deal with them in the tunnels.

"Is it because of your childhood?" I ask in a hesitant voice.

He strains a smile. "My childhood and my entire life." He shrugs. "But I'm getting help, Luce. It's not just the pills. I started seeing a proper therapist, and I'm taking everything seriously. I'd never subject you to someone unstable—someone who can barely function by himself. I promise you that I'm getting better," he hurries to say.

"Oh, Nikki. Don't you dare go there! Don't you dare think I'd ever see you as less because of that. How can you even think that?"

"Because I don't want to save you from a prison only to lock you up in another," he says on a ragged breath.

"You won't." I shake my head. "Just the fact that you're here, with me, despite all your impediments, means the world to me. *You* mean the world to me, Nikki. You always have."

"Sweetheart," he rasps, coming closer to me. His hand curves over my jaw, his thumb caressing my lips. His hand moves lower down my throat, stopping atop my breasts, just under my clavicle. "Does your shoulder hurt?"

"A little," I whisper. *A little more.* But I don't want him to needlessly worry about me—not when there's so much left to be done.

"Just a little?" He raises a brow at me. "Don't think I didn't notice you wince in the car."

"Okay, maybe a little more. But I'm fine. I'll be fine."

"So brave," he murmurs, and his hand trails lower, reaching the valley of my breasts. Instinctively, I grab his hand, stopping him.

"I—" I swallow hard, my eyes meeting his.

"I'm not going to hurt you, Luce."

"I know that. It's just that..."

How do I explain to him that I've seen too much violence against women in my life? That I may trust him above everyone else, but that my body still trembles with fear in his presence for the mere fact that he's a man? I've been leered at and groped since I was only a child. Because of that, I've never felt truly comfortable in another person's proximity. The only one who's managed to break those barriers has been Noelle, but she's different. She's a woman, and she's my best friend.

But this... I'm not sure *how* to react to this since I've never been touched with such gentleness, such kindness by a man. Yet at the same time, I can also sense the desire beneath his civil mask, a type of lust that both scares and intrigues me.

"Did anyone hurt you?" His gaze darkens.

"Not like that. I was one of the lucky ones." I force a smile. "But it's never been for the lack of trying."

A million emotions cross his face, from disbelief to sadness to pure anger.

"Who?" he demands in a harsh voice. He takes a step closer. "Who touched you, Luce?"

"They're all dead," I say. "Noelle made sure they're all dead."

"I am in your friend's debt then," he murmurs, bringing my hand to his lips, skimming them over my knuckles.

"Debt?" I frown.

"She saved you when I could not. For that she has my gratitude."

"It's fine, Nikki. Nothing happened. They just copped a feel here and there," I try to explain, but my words seem to make him madder.

His nostrils flare, his eyes narrowing at me.

"Where?"

"What?"

"Where did they touch you?"

"Nikki..."

"Show me, Luce. Show me and let me erase the bad memories," he says huskily.

I lick my lips, a shiver going down my back at the intensity I see in his gaze.

Do I dare to do this? *Can* I do it?

Taking his hand, I bring it to my breasts, then I press it to my back, right above the swell of my ass before lowering it slowly.

"They touched you here?" His voice vibrates, an unnatural growl coming from him.

I nod.

"Fuck! Fuck, Luce. And I wasn't here for you," he rasps, his features anguished.

"You're here now. That's all that matters."

"I'm sorry." He bends his head down. "I'm so fucking sorry it took me so long to come."

"How can you say that?" My eyes widen. "You were in a coma, Nikki."

"I should have been more careful. If only I hadn't gotten in that accident. If only I hadn't left my house that day..." he trails off, and I notice the regret mirrored in his eyes.

"Don't," I whisper. "You're alive. To me, that's all that matters."

"I should have killed them," he continues as if he didn't hear anything I just said. "But I'm going to kill that bastard Sergio. He won't get away after what he's done to you. God, it's not even just your shoulder." He shakes his head as he looks me up and down. "The calluses on your hands, the marks on your body..." he drifts off when he sees the change in my expression.

I avert my eyes.

If there's one sore subject I'm uncomfortable discussing, it's the marks on my body.

"I didn't mean it like that," he quickly amends. "You're beautiful to me, Luce. No matter what marks you have on your body. There's nothing more beautiful in this world than you."

"You're sweet to say that. But you haven't seen the rest of them. They're not just on my chest, Nikki. They're on my belly, on my hips, and on my thighs. They're *everywhere*."

"So? Do you think I care?"

"I-I don't know," I stammer.

"Ah, sweetheart. I guess I'll have to prove to you just how much I don't care. But not now. Not here. And certainly not until your shoulder is healed and you're not in pain anymore."

I blush lightly, averting my gaze.

Is this too fast? Maybe. But it's been years in the making, too. I just never dared hope that my dream would become a reality. I always held him in my mind as my one ideal—my one connection to the outside world. I might be foolish to agree so readily to everything he's offering, but it's a risk I'm willing to take. So what if I'm still not very comfortable in my own skin, or that I'm a little wary about the intimacy that takes place between a man and a woman? I trust that with his help, I'll slowly break out of my shell—no, I *know* I will.

"Okay," I answer, my lips tipping up. "I just have one request."

"Hm?" he asks, returning my smile as he pushes a strand of hair behind my ear. "Anything for you."

"Can we..." I clear my throat, a little embarrassed by my request. "Can we take it slow? Physically, I mean. I'm a little scared," I admit. I know Noelle assured me that sleeping with the man you love is not the same as the violent rapes I've witnessed, yet the images will not leave my head—nor the times I've come close to being a victim too.

"Oh, Luce," he exhales pointedly. "You don't even have to ask. I'll always go at your pace," he vows. "It's going to be something new for both of us, and I want it to be equally special and comfortable for you."

I smile, pleased with his answer.

Taking a step forward, I raise myself on the tips of my toes and plant a quick kiss at the corner of his lips. Yet just as I lean back, his image starts distorting, the memory shaky.

"Nikki?" I frown, reaching out for him. Before I can touch him, I'm thrust back by an unknown force, almost as if I'm being swept in a vacuum.

Before I can blink, I find myself between four familiar walls.

THIRTY-SIX

Tears course down my cheeks as I stare at the broken mirror and the shards of glass scattered across the floor. My white dress is stained with red, blood dripping from my hands onto the lace I'd so carefully chosen for this special occasion. There is pain. But it's not just physical. There's a fire burning inside my chest that no medication could cure.

I heave loudly as sobs rack my body, my legs shaking uncontrollably until I buckle to the ground, my knees hitting the hard floor. Pieces of glass break through the surface of my skin, and a muffled cry escapes my lips as I bottle up even more pain.

There's one last intact piece of the mirror in front of me, my pathetic reflection staring back and taunting me with all my shortcomings. I should have never left the hacienda. How did I survive when everyone else died? Why the hell am I still here?

Images of my last day at the hacienda flash before my eyes. Instead of saving Noelle, I doomed her to a worse fate. And it was all because I left when I shouldn't have; it was all because I let Nikki convince me to leave.

It should have been me who died in that fire, not Noelle.

From the start, it should have been me...

My hands wander around the floor, picking up a piece of glass and tracing my fingers around the sharp edge. The pain helps, the familiar sting jolting me back to the past—to an era I can't possibly forget.

The door to my room bursts open, Nikki charging inside with a wild expression on his face. He's wearing a three-piece suit, looking dashing for what was supposed to be a happy occasion.

His eyes widen as he sees me hunched over in my bloodied dress, holding tightly onto the sharp glass in my hand.

"Luce, sweetheart..." he whispers in a ragged, pained voice.

He falls to his knees beside me, unclasps my fingers from around the glass, and throws it aside. My blood transfers onto his hands, seeping into his skin, forging yet another connection between us.

"What's wrong? What's happening?" he asks, breathing harshly.

"I can't do this, Nikki..." I sob. "I can't do this..."

"What? What is it? Tell me and we'll fix it," he tells me in a pleading tone, his eyes glistening with tears as he takes in my disheveled appearance.

"I can't marry you," I whisper, slowly raising my gaze to his. My throat is dry and painful as I force the words out. Yet the devastation that strikes his features pains me even more.

"W-what? What do you mean?" he speaks slowly, his lips trembling.

"I can't do it, Nikki. I can't..." I break down even more, the tears flowing down my face. "How can you marry me? How can you stand to look at me?"

"Luce, I don't understand. What's wrong? What prompted this? We were fine this morning. We..."

"It should have been me, Nikki. I should have died. Not Noelle..." I cry out.

"How can you *say* that?" he rasps, pulling back and looking as if I'd physically struck him. "How can you even think that?"

"Because it's the truth. She should have lived to be with her baby. She should have lived, not me." I take a deep breath. "She had a family. People who loved her. And I..."

"You what, Luce? You what?" he demands in a rough voice.

"I..." I blink slowly.

"Finish your sentence."

"I have no one," I utter in a low, barely audible voice. Shame eats at me as I avert my eyes, not wanting to see the disappointment in his.

"You have no one?" he asks bitterly, letting go of my arms and stepping away from me. "Is that what you think? That you have no one?"

"No, Nikki... I didn't mean it like that." I shake my head.

He squeezes his eyes shut, the pain in his expression ripping a hole in my heart.

"I've done all you asked of me. You wanted time. I gave it to you. You wanted to grieve, I let you grieve. But how much longer will you punish yourself for this? How much longer will you punish *me*?"

"Nikki... I'm sorry," I say, bringing my hands to my face to wipe the tears away, but in the process, I'm only smearing more blood on my skin. "I didn't mean it like that..."

"What did you mean then?" His features darken. "One year, five months, two days, and ten hours. That's how long it's been since the fire. That's how long it's been since..." He takes a deep breath, scrubbing his hand over his face. "That's how long it's been since you let me touch you."

My lashes flutter in distress as I register the pain and frustration in his voice.

"Sometimes... I wonder if you truly love me, or if I was just an escape for you."

"What?" My eyes flare open in shock.

"Maybe I fooled myself because I was so goddamn in love with you." His lips flatten in disappointment. "I thought that as long as I gave you space, you'd come back to me. When you finally accepted my proposal, I was over the moon thinking *finally, she's ready to move on*. But you're not, are you?" He pauses. "Are you *ever* going to be ready?"

"Nikki... That's not true. You know that's not true. I love

you," I tell him from the bottom of my heart, dragging myself closer to him even as my skin bleeds and peels off.

He shakes his head.

"Then how come you've never shown it to me before?"

My mouth hangs open as I simply stare at him.

"I—" I drift off, not knowing how to answer. He *is* right. I've been so wrapped up in my grief I've never once stopped to consider how *he* might be feeling.

"I'm sorry," I whisper, lowering my head in shame. "You're right. I've been horrible to you. I *am* horrible to you right now when you don't deserve this—you don't deserve any of this. I know it's not what you signed up for and—"

"Stop right there," he interrupts me.

I slowly look up to see him come closer to me, kneeling next to me.

"*You* are what I signed up for. *All* of you, Luce. I just wish you wouldn't shut me out. Let me share your pain. Let me help you through it," he whispers, his features softening.

My lips tremble as I cup his face in my palms.

"It's not just that, Nikki," I tell him sincerely. "I think I'm...damaged," I confess. It takes everything in me to admit this since I've barely had the courage to admit it to myself. But as much as I can put the fault on my grief, I know there's more. There's the deepest issue and the fact that I don't think I deserve him.

"What?" he barks, his eyes flashing at me.

"Look at me," I say with a quivering smile.

"I am. You'll always be the most beautiful woman I've ever seen, Luce."

I shake my head at him.

Bringing my hands to my bodice, I pull on the lace until it gives way, shattering to reveal the marked skin beneath. But I don't stop at that. Picking up a sharp piece of glass, I continue to rip and cut into the dress until it falls from my body. Until I'm naked in front of him—bare for the first time ever.

He may have seen some of my marks. But he hasn't seen the

rest. He hasn't seen the scars that mar my skin, the rough bumps and the gnarly, red tissue that never healed properly.

"I can't look at myself and not see the past," I whisper. "I can't stand to look at my own self, so how could you?"

His features tighten as he wipes my tears away with his thumbs. But he doesn't look at my body. He only looks at me.

"Let me help you build a new past, present, and future. Let me love you until you love yourself, too, Luce. Just... Let me love you."

"But what if... What if I'm not enough?" I swallow a sob as I stare into his eyes, struck speechless by the unconditional love I see there.

"You'll always be *everything*, Luce." He smiles at me. "I just hope I can be everything for you, too."

Tears trickle down my cheeks as I nod fervently.

He brings the rough pads of his fingers to my calves, trailing soft touches all over my skin until he reaches the bleeding wounds caused by the broken glass. He carefully plucks all the residual glass from my flesh before swooping me up in his arms. I don't question what he's doing or where he's taking me. I simply wrap my arms around his neck, burying my face in the crook of his shoulder and breathing in his familiar scent. My breathing evens out as my sobs subside. But as the fog over my mind starts to clear, embarrassment and regret fill me to the brim.

I tighten my grip on Nikki, wondering how I'm going to face him after my outburst. God... I've put him through hell, haven't I? I've made him suffer without even realizing it, and still, he's stayed by my side.

Nikki takes me to the adjacent bathroom and lays me in the bathtub. He turns the water on, making sure the temperature is perfect before he redirects his attention to me.

"Don't." He stops my hand when I try to cover myself. "You wanted me to see. So let me see," he murmurs, bringing the shower head to my skin and washing the blood away.

His hand follows the jet of water as he touches me softly.

First my shoulders, then going lower, tracing the contour of my ribcage before reaching my belly.

"It's okay." I give him permission as he proceeds lower.

"You're so beautiful, Luce," he speaks huskily, his eyes hooded as he regards me with love and...lust. There's no disgust. No aversion. There's only a reverent love that warms my insides.

"I'm sorry," I say as I reach to touch him. "I love you, Nikki. I truly didn't mean it like that. I was just... I let my weakness get the best of me. I never meant to hurt you."

He covers my hand with his, closing his eyes and inhaling deeply.

"I know you didn't, Luce. I know." He gives me a sad smile.

I blink away tears as I look at him. I hurt him. I hurt him, but he won't admit it.

"Come in." I pull lightly on his hand, urging him to join me.

His eyes scan my features, perhaps to ensure that I mean it, or that I'm ready for it.

"Please, come in," I repeat.

He swallows hard, his gaze dipping lower to my body.

"Luce... I'm not made of stone," he admits in a thick voice.

"Please."

He stares at me for a moment before he places the showerhead next to me in the tub and stands up. Slowly, as if giving me time to change my mind, he starts taking off his clothes. He undoes the bowtie at his neck, throwing it to the ground before unbuttoning his shirt.

I lick my lips as he shrugs the shirt off, letting it drop to the floor. He's always been beautiful to me, but I never imagined he'd have such a powerful physique. Isn't it pathetic? We've been living together for more than a year and I've never seen him without his shirt off.

As he reaches for his belt, he raises his brows at me.

I nod, pushing my anxiety aside.

He quickly discards his pants too and stands entirely naked before me.

I gulp, doing my best not to avert my gaze as heat climbs up my cheeks.

Getting in the tub, he sits behind me, pulling me to him and laying his cheek against my back. Slowly, he nuzzles his face against my skin, his palms splayed across my stomach. One hand moves higher, the tips of his fingers grazing my breast.

I inhale sharply.

"I'm not going to do anything, Luce. Not now. Not today."

"But—"

"We're not married yet. And I'm not marrying you today."

"What?" I burst out, turning to face him.

He gives me a sad smile as he tugs a strand of wet hair behind my ear.

"Today we talk. We grieve. We cry for the past," he tells me, taking my hands and bringing them between us. With gentle movements, he washes my scratches before bringing my knuckles to his lips to kiss the pain away. "Today we face everything we didn't dare face before."

I bite my lip as I stare at him. Renewed sobs bubble in my throat just as tears stab at my eyes.

"And tomorrow?" I ask in a whisper.

"Tomorrow is another day." His lips pull up.

"Please don't be mad at me. I couldn't bear it if you were mad at me," I mumble as I drag myself closer to him, wrapping my arms around his neck. My chest brushes against his, and we both suck in a breath at the sensation. Goosebumps cover my body, a tingle of awareness spreading to my core. Raising my gaze to meet his, I note the darkening of his eyes. His pupils are dilated, his lips half-parted as his breathing intensifies.

"I'm not mad at you, sweetheart. I'm mad at myself because I didn't realize what you were going through. I thought you were healing. I thought time could cure it, but it didn't, did it? It only made it worse."

I stifle a sob at his words and give him a slow nod.

"We'll get through this together. Because you have me, Luce. You'll *always* have me."

"I know. I was foolish to say that. You're the most important person to me, Nikki."

He pulls me flush against him, his arms resting against my lower back as he urges me to wrap my legs around him. We're so close, I feel that hard part of him resting against my core.

"Nikki..." I moan softly.

His breath fans my face as he skims his lips across my cheek.

"Are you in pain, sweetheart? Tell me where it hurts and I'll kiss it better," he murmurs lovingly. I turn my face, catching his lips with mine, brushing my mouth against his in slow, gentle movements.

"Nikki," I call his name, wiggling my hips to feel him better against me.

I brush my tongue against his mouth to deepen the kiss, but instead of tasting his lips, I taste the empty air. A whooshing sound makes me jump back just in time to avoid the cut of a sword. Wide with shock, my eyes take in the sharp blade and the person handling it. He's wearing a black tunic over a pair of loose pants, his dark hair curling over his forehead. His eyes are a deep purple that glints with dangerous intentions. A twitch appears in his cheek, his muscles tense as he pulls his sword back, sheathing it in the scabbard at his waist. Still, he doesn't take his eyes off me, staring me down with a mix of loathing and anger that's apparent in the clench of his jaw.

"Who are you?" I shout, scrambling back. At the same time, I notice that the spot previously occupied by Nikki is empty.

What? Where did he go? What...

It also dawns on me that I'm fully naked in the presence of a murderous stranger. Is he here for Nikki? Did his family send him to kill us before we got married for fear they might lose access to his money?

I struggle to cover myself with my arms, my eyes dipping quickly to the floor where Nikki had discarded his clothes. But there's nothing there.

"What—"

My words are cut off as the stranger advances toward me.

Without thinking, I get out of the tub and make a run for the door. But I only manage to take one step before he grips my arm, pulling me toward him.

"Stop moving," he barks in my ear, his voice barely contained.

"Please don't hurt me," I whisper, squeezing my eyes shut.

"I will not hurt you, human," he grits out. "Though I have never in my life experienced such an all-encompassing rage," he states and I feel a current of anger course through his body as he struggles to keep himself from smothering me to his chest.

"What are you talking about?" I ask weakly, daring to open my eyes to look at him.

Those eyes. Those purple eyes. Why are they so familiar?

A sharp pain echoes in my brain and I sway from side to side. He's there to hold me, lowering his arm to my waist.

"Ze?" I whisper, blinking hard against an onslaught of images that inundate my brain. "What's happening?"

His features are tight, his lips compressed in a scowl.

"I told you to wait for me," he speaks in a slow, thick voice. "You fell through a portal."

"What do you mean?"

"This..." He nods to the area around us. I turn to look, and that's when I notice that we're no longer in the bathroom, nor am I naked anymore.

I'm wearing the same hoodie and tights I was wearing before —when we were in P'davi. And just like that, I remember everything.

Nikki is...dead. And I'm in a foreign world, competing in a game to get him back.

Our surroundings are bleak. A barren earth enveloped by a blood-red sky.

"It's a parasitic world," Ze explains. "Once you are inside, it starts consuming your life force."

"But... I saw..."

"What you saw were all memories. Parasitic realms lure

their victims and trap them in their memories so they do not realize as their life force is being consumed."

"Am I dying?" I ask in a whisper.

"You are not dying," he answers dryly. "You have not been trapped in here for long. But we need to return to P'davi."

"So let's do it," I add quickly.

"I cannot do it. It will have to be you," he says tightly.

"What? How?"

"You have to *want* to leave. The memories shown to you are not random. They are chosen specifically to make you want to lose yourself in them."

I look around me. "But I *want* to leave," I mutter.

The corner of his mouth pulls up in a wry smile.

"If you did, we would already be back."

"Then how?" I frown.

"What is your happiest memory?" he suddenly asks.

I purse my lips as I try to think of it. But before I can even identify it, our surroundings change. Shock envelops me as I recognize the dark tunnels of the temple I was sentenced to work on at the hacienda.

My breath hitches just as a shiver of fear runs down my back.

What... Why... Why would this be my happiest memory?

Sensing my discomfort, Ze comes closer to me, threading his fingers through mine.

"This can't be..." I whisper. Yet just as the words are out of my mouth, I recognize what this memory is.

I'm right there, digging into a wall with some shabby tools. But instead of crying in pain from the blisters on my hands, I'm smiling. My eyes are on the person next to me, the affection I bear him evident.

"*Vamos, trata de nuevo.*" He chuckles.

I clear my throat. "My name is Lucero," I say in a thick accent. "You are Nicholas." I point at him. "I am sixteen. You are nineteen."

"Perfecto." He claps at me. "Seguro que no has aprendido ingles antes?"

"No." I smile. "Es la primera vez."

"Eres muy inteligente, Luce," he praises me softly. "Vas a aprender hablar ingles rápidamente."

"Solo gracias a ti," I tell him, sliding a little bit closer. "Cuéntame mas de tu país."

Still working, he watches me indulgently as he tells me yet another story about his home, about those big cities I can hardly imagine and all the possibilities available to the people living there. He tells me about a land of freedom.

And for the first time, I have hope.

For the first time, I also...love.

Tears fall down my cheeks as I realize that was the beginning of who I am today. Before that, I never dreamed about the outside world. I never dared dream that I could be free. Before that, I never heard anyone praise me before.

Nikki was the first to see me as a person.

"Why are you crying?" Ze's booming voice snaps me out of my thoughts. Somehow, he's in front of me, tipping my chin up and wiping my tears away. "I command you to stop crying."

"It doesn't work like that, Ze," I tell him with a tremulous smile. "I cannot just stop crying."

"It is because of that *man*?" he grits out, his voice holding a violent edge to it.

"That man is my husband. He's also the only man to ever acknowledge me as a person and see my potential. Without him... I wouldn't be standing here today."

"I do not understand you," he frowns.

A sad smile tips at my lips, just as the background of that memory fades away.

"Before I met Nikki, I was depressed. I was not going to last long there. People hated me. The work was hard. Food was barely enough. I was living from day to day, thinking—no, wishing that the next day would be my last. Back then, death was the only way out. But then Nikki showed up and he opened my eyes to a world full of possibilities. He taught me English and spoke to me of the wonders of the outside world. He appreciated me as a person and not just a means of production. And just like that, he gave me hope that life could be...more."

Ze's brows are bunched together. He's staring at me as if he doesn't understand a word of what I'm saying. But he doesn't need to. Because *I* finally understand.

It would be so easy to give in to this parasitic realm just so I could reside forever in my memories of Nikki. But that wouldn't solve anything, just as my death at the hacienda wouldn't have solved everything. Because Nikki taught me something else too.

Perseverance.

You can't just hope and wait for things to fall into your lap. You have to work hard to make those things a reality.

I *could* choose dream Nikki—an easy way out. But it wouldn't be real. Nikki wouldn't be real, and in the end, as my life's essence dissipates, I would cease to be real as well.

The only way to win this game is to not give up. No matter what happens, I cannot give up. I may not have encountered these supernatural trials in the past, but I've encountered plenty of hardships along the way. If I've survived so far, I can survive until the end.

"Let's go, Ze. I'm ready," I say as I give him a decisive nod.

He stares at me intently as he takes my hand and leads me down a foggy path. It's only a matter of seconds before we're back to our starting point in P'davi. But the difference is the sky is dark, where before it was light.

Just how many hours was I trapped in there?

"We need to camp for the night," Ze declares in a rough tone.

He doesn't let go of my hand as he leads me back into the forest—to a place he scouted before. It's a rather remote area at the base of a mountain. There's even a small aperture inside the rock that we can use as shelter for the night.

After placing our bag on the floor, he sets about making a fire, all the while not exchanging one word with me. In fact, there's something entirely off about him as I catch him staring at me every now and then, his expression inscrutable. There's anger and irritation as if he'd like nothing but to strangle me on the spot. But there's also something akin to longing, as if he wants to tell me something but stops himself just short of uttering the words.

"I'm sorry." I take a deep breath, deciding to offer him an olive branch. "I should have stayed put. But you shouldn't have left me alone either," I point out.

He's sitting by the fire, polishing his sword. Slowly, he raises his gaze to me.

"I should not have left you alone." He gives me a nod before turning his attention back to his sword and ignoring me.

"Am I forgiven then? I'm sorry I jeopardized the team." I force a smile. My stunt not only would have cost *me* my life but also theirs. I belatedly realize how deep my foolishness ran.

He doesn't reply, merely releasing a guttural grunt, his eyes glued to his sword.

"Uhm... Did you see anything?" I muster the courage to ask.

He lifts one brow at me.

"You know... In the bathtub?" I swallow against the wave of embarrassment that grips me.

He watches me intently, the purple of his eyes darkening as he pins me with his stare.

"If you did, can you please forget that happened?"

He suddenly stabs his sword into the ground, his upper lip lifting to reveal sharp teeth bared at me.

"No," he rasps out, and a wave of purple energy blasts from his sword toward me, making me lose my balance and fall on my back. I blink slowly, confused about what's happening. Yet before I can say anything, he's by my side, lifting me up.

His lips are compressed in a hard line, his muscles bulging in his forearms.

He grips my shoulders tightly as he stares at me with a hardened expression the likes of which I have never seen before.

"Why him?" he demands in a barely subdued tone.

"What?" My lashes flutter in confusion.

His fingers dig into my skin. He clenches his jaw as veins protrude up his neck.

A rush of adrenaline goes down my back, my limbs suddenly weak in the face of danger.

"I don't understand you, Ze," I mumble weakly, pushing at his hands.

"Why him, human? Why does it have to be him?"

THIRTY-SEVEN

"You're scaring me, Ze," I whisper, blinking back tears. Fear courses through me as I take in his crazed expression. His nostrils flare as his eyes zero in on me.

A lone tear falls down my cheek, and it seems to snap him out of it. Muttering a string of foreign curses, he lets go of me and takes a few steps back.

I sway in the wind, my legs made of jelly.

After a few deep breaths, my heart is still beating like crazy in my chest, my whole body trembling. I wrap my arms around myself, stealing a glance at him.

He's pacing around like a madman, stomping his feet into the ground with a force that makes the entire earth quake.

"Ze?" I probe gently, both afraid of him and for him. Just what prompted this display?

"Why would you risk yourself for that male?" he asks on a ragged breath, a hint of purple staring my way.

"I don't understand. He's my husband. Of course I'd risk everything for him," I answer weakly.

"But why?" he repeats. "What is so special about him?"

I bite my lip as I look at his savage manner, and it suddenly strikes me that he may be confused about emotions—about what prompts someone to sacrifice themselves for another.

"Because I love him," I say, my tone more confident than before. "He might not be special to anyone else, but he's special to me."

He narrows his eyes at me.

"You wouldn't understand." I give him a small smile. "All my life I've been told how insignificant I was, how little I mattered as a person. But Nikki... He treated me like I was *everything* to him."

"Is that so?" He raises a brow, coming toward me. Instinctively, I take a step back. He stops right in front of me, his expression twisted. "Then are you doing this out of a sense of duty to him?"

My lashes flutter in shock.

"What—"

"Is that not so? Was he not an escape for you out of your living situation?"

I stare at him, unable to recognize this Ze in front of me. There's a vicious edge to his tone, a sharpness in his features that wasn't there before. The corner of his mouth twitches up in a cruel smirk, and for the first time, I find myself at a loss for words.

"How much did you see?" I whisper.

He lets out a dry laugh.

"Too much." He shakes his head.

"Why would you intrude on such an intimate moment of my life?" I ask, disappointment filling me to the brim. "Why would you violate my trust like this?"

"You should be happy I *only* saw that, human. Otherwise..." he trails off, a twisted smile pulling at his lips.

"Otherwise what?"

"I am not a good male, human. And I find that I am not a patient one, either. You do not want to see me at my worst," he adds, the words a subtle threat.

"Ze... What is the meaning of this? Why are you behaving like this? I don't understand," I add weakly. I'm so thoroughly confused by his words and actions, and I can't possibly pinpoint what I did wrong or why he's so angry.

"You do not know?" He lets out a dry laugh. "You are *my* person, human," he grits out, charging at me. Before I know what he means to do, his hand grips my throat, his fingers digging softly into my skin. It's not painful, but it's not comfortable either. He stares down at me in such an odd manner as if he cannot understand himself why he's so mad about this.

"You will not sacrifice yourself for a trifle. You will *not* forfeit your soul for that. Do you understand me?" he asks in a punctuated tone.

"It's not a trifle," I murmur, swallowing a sob.

He laughs.

"Then what is it? Of course I can excuse your simple human nature. You merely clung onto the first male to give you attention. You are not the first to fall for such a trick." He nods to himself. "But your human foolishness ends now. I will not allow you to continue down this path. I *forbid* it," he states.

I squeeze my eyes to stop the tears from falling.

"Is that what you think of me?" I ask softly, hurt emanating from my voice.

He frowns at me, his hand falling from my throat.

"It is what you have displayed so far, human." He nods to himself, continuing his tirade without realizing how much his words are hurting me. "You are far too senseless and foolhardy. Your judgment leaves much to be desired. From now on, you are not allowed to do anything without my express permission," he decrees. And just like that, he's back to his usual overbearing self. Spine straight, hands behind his back, he preens around, satisfied with his tongue-lashing and the fact that he just made me feel like the scum of the earth. It's very clear what he thinks of me—that I'm stupid and reckless and I lack any judgment. I'm not worthy to be on the same team as him, let alone breathe the same air as him.

"Why are you here with me then? Why are we on the same team at all?" I ask, raising my eyes to look at him. I bring the back of my hand to my cheeks, wiping the moisture away. "If you think so little of me, why are we even doing this?"

"Because I am magnanimous enough to take care of you," he replies with a huff.

"Oh, wow. Lucky me," I say dryly.

"Indeed. You should consider yourself fortunate for having me by your side, human," he continues.

"No, thank you." I push my chin up. "You are *not* nice, Ze," I say, doing my best not to burst into tears. "You are a callous and mean man, and I don't want to listen to your vile words anymore."

He turns to me, his intense gaze finding mine as he crosses his arms over his chest, leaning back and daring me to speak further.

"You have no right to question my motives for participating in the game when you've never even told me yours," I continue, pointing a finger at him. "But most of all, how *dare* you question my love for my husband when you're not even capable of feeling it?"

Maybe I'm stooping a little too low with this jab, but it's *his* fault for bringing me to this point.

His eyes flare with a shadow of hurt at my words, but I don't stop.

"You are right about one thing. I *am* foolish but not for trying to save my husband. I'm foolish because I thought there might be something good in you. Silly me." I screw my face in disgust. "I thought you were misunderstood and that in spite of your unkind words, your intentions weren't bad. But I see I was wrong. You are just another bully and I will not stand for this treatment." I swallow, struggling to keep my bravado up. "I'll be civil to you until we get back to the complex, but after that I'm done."

His lips pull up.

"You will finally give up on the competition?" he asks, his tone oddly cheerful as if he didn't just hear me tell him how much I dislike him.

"No. I'll give up on this team. I'll continue with the competition, but I don't want to be anywhere near you." I shake my head at him.

He blinks in surprise.

"Asshole," I mutter under my breath, turning my back and heading to the aperture in the rock. I lie down on my side, pulling my knees to my chest and forcing myself to sleep. Tears burn behind my lids, but I won't give him the satisfaction of hearing me cry. Not when it would only make him see me as weaker.

"Do not turn your back to me, human," he calls out.

I don't answer, tuning out his words.

"You are not allowed to ignore me," he continues, coming closer.

I feel him lie down next to me, heat radiating from his body.

Squeezing my eyes shut, I will myself to sleep.

"Human! Luce," he drones on, calling my name and trying in vain to get my attention. It's too late, however. Words have been spoken, and my heart is still raw from his behavior.

God, but I am dumb, aren't I?

I really thought he was my friend, but how could he be when he has such a low opinion of me? Not only am I still a little shaken by the visions of Nikki I got in that realm, but now I have to deal with a mean Ze, too.

I'm still confused about what his deal is. If he's so concerned that I'm bringing the team down, then he shouldn't have offered to be paired with me in the first place.

Swallowing my sobs and sorrows, I force myself to go to sleep. There's little I can do by dwelling on this, especially when every time I replay our conversation, I hurt myself even more.

It's not worth it.

But as I drift off to sleep, I find that my heart hurts more at being on bad terms with him than at him... I am foolish, indeed.

I get up at the first sign of sunlight. Ze is already awake and ready to go and, giving him a silent nod, I march ahead. He tries to speak to me a few times, but when all he receives is the silent treatment, he mutters a few words and decides to give up.

We walk continuously until nightfall, and we manage to cover a great distance. Despite the pain in my legs or the fatigue that soon overtakes my body, I refuse to give him another reason to call me weak. We take a small break until dawn, and then we're back on the road.

All this time, I don't speak to him. No matter how much he's trying to get my attention, I pretend he's not there. Even when he offers me food, I refuse it if it comes from his hand. Instead, I wait until he puts it down before picking it up. Of course, that elicits more words from him about how foolish I am, but it's safe to say I'm long used to that word by now.

It's on the second day that we finally see the complex in sight. My body is already on the verge of giving up, keenly feeling the effects of the long journey and the lack of assistance from Ze. But as the image of him carrying me on his back from before appears in my mind, I scowl.

Not worth it, remember?

As we arrive at the complex, I note the presence of other teams on the sidelines, all staring at us as we head to our apartment building. I keep my head high, ignoring the jibes I hear, the word *human* being spat around as if it were the worst condition in existence.

I guess Ze is not the only one who has a certain distaste for *humans*.

Ze trails at my back, always a few paces behind me.

Luckily, just as my legs are about to give up on me, we reach our suite. Opening the door and stepping inside the apartment, my eyebrows go up in question as we spot Thea and Cer in the living room, looking mighty cozy together on the couch.

"You're finally back!" Thea exclaims when she spots us, jumping up and hurrying to me.

"We are," I strain a smile. "How was your quest? Did you get the plants?"

"Of course. We killed some competition on the way too."

She flashes me a smile. "Well, Cer did. I just told him who to kill." She chuckles.

"We got our plant too. I don't think we have much longer, so we should get the brew ready," I mention, but Thea doesn't hear me as she stops in front of Ze, her eyes going wide with shock.

"What happened to *you*?" she asks, pointing at his eyes. "Why are they purple?"

Cer moves stealthily, his expression worried as he stops by Ze's side.

They share a look, almost as if they're communicating without words. I wonder if it has anything to do with the demons we spotted in the forest.

"It is how they are now," Ze slowly replies.

"You mean it's permanent? But how? That's impossible. I've never heard of something like that," Thea continues.

Cer is still staring at Ze, reaching out to touch him on the shoulder. It doesn't surprise me that he'd be so worried about him considering the man basically raised him. At the same time, it's jarring to realize there's someone out there who genuinely cares about the guy—regardless of his rude personality. After experiencing his exquisite diatribes myself, as his teammate, I can't imagine how bad he'd be as a superior, or on the battlefield. His poor soldiers... They must be more scared of him than of the demons they're supposed to slay.

Since they're so busy fussing over Ze, I head to the kitchen, remove our plant, and place it on a table. As I look around, I spot the other two plants Thea and Cer got, and I grab them too, then rinse all three. Removing a pot from a cupboard, I fill it with water and place it over the stove. Unfortunately, I can't seem to find how to turn the stove on.

As I'm struggling to figure it out, a hand reaches out from behind me, pressing a few buttons until a small flame flares to life. I sneak a glance behind, not surprised to see Ze, who's looking at me with a puppy-like expression as if he's waiting for me to pet him and tell him what a good boy he is. Alas, that's exactly what he is *not*.

It's on the tip of my lips to thank him, but since I'm not speaking to him, I simply roll my eyes and redirect my attention to the pot.

When the water boils, I place the whole plants inside. Since there are no instructions on how to make the brew, I will not take any chances with it. Better to be safe than sorry, so I'll cook both the root and the stem with the flower. After everything is brewed, I drain the water into a cup and bring it with me to the table.

Ze silently trails behind, taking a seat next to me and giving me an odd look. He purposefully moves his chair closer to mine, his body brushing against mine.

I bring the cup to my lips for a sip, but before I can drink, Ze's hand shoots out and he wedges it between my mouth and the cup, stopping me.

"It is hot," he mumbles, wrenching the cup from my hands. I stare at him dumbfounded as he blows some cool air at the steamy liquid before drinking from it. He screws his face in disapproval, blowing some more cold air and tasting it again.

"What the hell are you doing?" I grit my teeth, incensed at his behavior.

He repeats the action a few more times, eluding all of my attempts to get the brew back.

"You can drink now." He nods, finally handing it back to me. He has a very pleased look on his face as he waits for me to praise him.

I blink, looking at the half-empty cup and getting the sudden urge to spill the rest of it over his head. But I can't waste more of the brew. My lips twitch in annoyance as I drink the remaining liquid. While it's only slightly warm now, the taste is bitter and unpleasant.

He clears his throat. "That is an extra point," he has the gall to say.

I gawk at him. He's impossible. I've never been prone to violence, but Ze has an unusual effect on me.

"I'm revoking your extra point privileges," I snap at him,

unable to keep my tone civil. His face immediately falls. He blinks a few times, taking a few breaths and pushing his chin down.

"I'm sensing some bad energy here," Thea notes as she stares between the two of us. "What happened?"

"Nothing," Ze says.

"He's an asshole," I add at the same time, turning to give him a murderous look.

I slam the cup onto the table and get up. Ze gets up too, his eyes on me.

"I'm going out. I need some time alone," I declare. "You can ask him what he did wrong." I point at Ze.

"I knew it," Thea grumbles under her breath. Cer just stares at the two of us, shaking his head. "I told you." She turns to her brother. "He's awful and cannot be trusted to be alone with anyone."

My lids flutter in surprise at the vehemence of her tone. I didn't expect her to defend me. Alas, I don't want to stick around to listen to them argue.

"Why did you even come here? You said you'd stay away, Ze," Thea tells him as I stealthily head out. But just as I open the door, I feel a looming presence behind. Stopping, I suddenly turn to find Ze right behind me, following me like a shadow.

"Do *not* follow me," I tell him pointedly.

He doesn't acknowledge my words, so I simply shut the door in his face, walking away from the apartment. But it's not before I hear Thea yell, "He's *your* friend, Cer. I've been patient enough with him for your sake, but I can't do it anymore."

Well, it seems I'm not the only one who has a bone to pick with Ze. Poor Cer, he might be the only one who *doesn't* dislike him.

Shaking my head, I walk to the canteen to get some fresh food and chocolate, after which I find a remote spot to rest and eat. I'm so tired, I would have liked nothing more than to go to my room and sleep. But after being forced to share a space with Ze for the last week, I find that I need some time alone. And for all I like her, not even Thea's company is welcome at this point. She'd undoubtedly ask me what happened, and I don't know if I can relate everything without breaking down into tears—and that's the last thing I need.

I take a deep breath.

Ze's behavior affected me more than I expected. We might only know each other for a short time, but I felt an affinity to him and I thought he did as well. Yet what I saw as friendship was anything but that for him. I'll always be a puny human not worthy of his attention—too dumb to make my own choices. How could we be friends if he'll always see me as someone inferior?

I slowly munch on some chocolate as I lie on my back on the grass. I found a small patch away from prying eyes, and as I stare at the clear sky, I wonder if I can get away with a small nap. The meal I ate was mostly comprised of carbs, so that should put me right to sleep.

A yawn escapes me.

Ah, if only Nikki were here. It's been too long since he last appeared before me. Although I wish I could spend every waking moment with him by my side, I also understand the dangers. Thea made it clear that rogue souls are hunted, never mind the fact that young souls have little to no energy.

I sigh.

The past memories I saw renewed my longing for him.

After escaping the hacienda, I thought for the longest time that my friend Noelle had perished there, and I'd blamed myself for it. Day and night, I'd lost myself to my grief, hating myself for being the only survivor. And in a way, I'd hated Nikki a little too for being the one to take me away. He knew it, too.

A wry smile pulls at my lips.

Even when I blamed him; even when I cursed him for taking me away, he was still there. Faithfully by my side, ready to pick up the pieces of my shattered self. And when I found out that Noelle was still alive, he was there to share that happiness with me.

My eyes become moist with unshed tears.

I miss that. I miss having my best friend by my side—through thick and thin. I miss having someone to share all my thoughts with—someone who loved and respected me.

Our relationship was never perfect. God knows, we've had plenty of ups and downs, some of which we never recovered from. In a way, both Nikki and I were—*are*—still slaves to our past. The only difference is that his got him killed while mine is *slowly* killing me. But our differences made us challenge each other.

Lying on my back, I stare at the clear sky, somehow unable to believe this is my life.

Out of nowhere, a dark shadow appears in front of my eyes.

I startle up into a sitting position, blinking repeatedly just as the dark mist starts taking shape, materializing into the form of a man.

"Nikki?" I whisper, my eyes widening.

THIRTY-EIGHT

He doesn't answer, merely coming closer to me. He reaches with his hand, the ghost of a touch brushing against my face. My eyes snap shut as I inhale sharply, the warmth left behind by his caress making my pulse spike up.

"It's you, isn't it?" I murmur, nuzzling my face against the ghostly palm.

"Luce." His voice reverberates through my being. "My Luce," he whispers as he dips his head, his diaphanous cheek brushing against my own.

Tears of pure joy cling to my lashes as I let myself feel him, my soul rejoicing at being near his again.

"You stayed away for so long." I stifle a sob.

"I couldn't come. I'm not that... strong."

"It's okay." I shake my head, realizing I'm being unreasonable. "You don't have to excuse yourself. The fact that you're here means everything to me. Especially after we parted on such bad terms."

"I only want what's good for you," he continues, his voice raspy and pained. "I don't want you to get hurt. Not on my account."

"I'll be fine, Nikki. I've already finished the second trial." I smile.

He leans back, the mist swaying in the wind, waves of shimmery dust sparkling inside him.

"You will not quit, will you?" he asks with a sigh.

I shake my head.

"I know I can do it," I tell him confidently.

"At least you have your team... I feel better that you have people by your side who can help you."

My smile falls, my features tense.

"I'll be on my own for the next trial," I tell him reluctantly.

"What?" His voice booms, echoing in the stillness of nature. "Luce! You've seen the competition! How can you defeat those people?"

"I know. But I can't in good conscience continue with my team. Not after..." I take a deep breath.

"What happened?" he barks, my ever so protective knight.

I give him a tight smile.

"Maybe I'm foolish." I sigh. "But all my life I've been disrespected by everyone around me—treated as less than human. Now... well, the mere fact that I'm human makes me less."

"I don't understand."

"Please don't be mad at me. I don't want to argue with you again. Not when I'm already barely hanging by a thread. Just... I know you're worrying about me, but please respect my choice. Please trust that I'll do the right thing."

He's silent as he mulls over my words. Plopping himself by my side, he takes my hand in his—light against the darkness of his shadow.

"I always worry about you," he finally says. "You can't stop me from doing it."

"I know." I nod.

"What prompted this?" he asks slowly. "Last time you were very happy with your team."

"There's... someone." I swallow. "His name is Ze. I thought we were friends, but almost from the beginning, he's been insulting and belittling me. I ignored it, even thought he didn't mean it." I shake my head at my foolishness. "He was so nice to me at times that I actually thought he might appreciate me."

There's a slight pressure on my hand, and I turn to look at him.

"How close did you get to this man, Luce?" he asks tightly.

"No, no," I hurry to say. "It's nothing like that, I promise. We were only friends."

"Is that so... You sound as if you care about him."

"I do—or did." I sigh. "But I realize that my affection was misplaced."

"You're telling me you care about another man, Luce?" He enunciates each word carefully, but I can sense the tension.

"I care for him as a friend, Nikki." I purse my lips. "He was good to me, he protected me, so I thought he cared about me, too. But he doesn't see me as anything but a worthless human."

Nikki doesn't reply. His hold over my hand tightens, a prickly sensation permeating my skin.

"Men and women cannot be friends, Luce," he grits out.

"Nikki!" I blink in surprise.

"Maybe you don't know it because you've barely been out into the world, but there is no such thing as friendship between a man and a woman," he continues. "He either wants to fuck you, or he's already fucked you. Which one is it?"

"W-what..." I stammer, at a loss for words.

The dark mist intensifies, the form barely contained.

"Which one is it, Luce?" he repeats in a harsh voice.

"Neither! Good God, who do you think I am?" I ask, scandalized. "Ze doesn't see me like that, and I certainly would never do that. How could you even think that? You know me."

"I know that you're a beautiful woman, Luce. I know that you're the most goddamn amazing woman I've ever met. And I doubt I'm the only one who thinks this," he bites out. "Everywhere you go people stare at you, and I know what they're thinking. I can *see* what they're thinking. Don't be so naive."

"What do you mean?" I ask in a small voice.

I forgot about this side of him, and I instantly regret bringing up Ze. I should have known better than to mention another man to him, but I felt the need to share my pain with someone. Nikki's always been insanely jealous. It was a blessing that we rarely went out because he'd snap whenever another man even glanced at me. The few times we went on vacation, we'd inevitably end up spending most of the time at the hotel because he had a tendency to start fights with whoever looked at me for more than five seconds.

"What do you think goes through a man's mind when he sees you smile?"

I open my mouth to answer, but he brings his ghostly finger against my lips, shushing me.

"They think exactly what *I* think," he states emphatically, angling his shadowy body toward me. Warmth radiates from him, seeping into my body as he traces the seam of my lips, dipping the tip of his finger inside.

My breath hitches.

"And all I can think of is how hard and fast I'd fuck your mouth. How sweet you'd smile with your lips stained with—"

"Stop," I whisper, heat traveling up my cheeks. My heart beats fast in my chest, goose bumps spreading all over my skin.

"You're adorable." He chuckles, caressing my cheek. "But you're so woefully naive, Luce. Men aren't nice to you in exchange for nothing."

"Ze's not like that," I protest weakly.

"He's a man, Luce, is he not?"

I swallow, averting my gaze.

"We should talk about something else. We have such little time together, I don't want to waste it talking about someone else," I propose, not liking where this conversation is going.

Silence stretches between us for a few moments before he nods.

I slide closer to him, tentatively wrapping my arms around him and laying my head on his chest.

"You have to be careful, Luce. I might not like it, but I'd

rather you stayed with your team. It's too dangerous on your own."

"Oh, Nikki..." I sigh. "I don't know."

"Think on it, okay? For my peace of mind."

"Okay," I agree.

We both lie down on the grass, our bodies wrapped around one another as we simply hold each other. It might have been odd in the beginning that I'm talking and touching a dark shadow. But now it's second nature. It just feels like home.

Time passes awfully fast as I tell him everything that's happened since we last spoke, and he assures me he'll do his best to come to me whenever he feels at his best.

"This state... It's unpredictable. I can never tell when I'll have enough strength to show myself to you, let alone touch you like this," he murmurs, his voice full of wonder. "And depending on where the next trial will be, I might not be able to see you at all."

I tighten my hold around him, blinking back tears.

"I will win this," I tell him vehemently.

He doesn't comment about the dangers or my abilities anymore. He simply hugs me, whispering how much he loves me. Yet all too soon, his strength fades.

It starts with the flicker of his shadow, and soon, he becomes transparent.

"I'll be back," he whispers right before he disappears.

After he's gone, I lie there for minutes on end, thinking about our discussion and my next steps. As it gets dark out, I finally get up and head back to the suite.

When I open the door, I find the three of them still where I left them, the tension palpable in the room. Their stances are also telling. Ze is by the window, his hands at his back and a bored expression on his face. Cer and Thea are in the middle of the room, arguing. Or rather, Thea is chastising Cer while he pretends to listen to what she's saying.

They turn to look at me.

"Please don't tell me you've been arguing since I left," I say.

Thea's gaze snaps to Cer and then to Ze, suggesting she's not pleased with either of them.

"I have not been arguing with anyone. I've just been making my opinion known," she says as she gives her brother a harsh look. "And the fact that I do *not* like certain people."

The implication that she's referring to Ze is clear, but he doesn't bat an eye at it.

"I do not care about your opinion, Erithea," Ze comments with a shrug.

"No one asked you," she snaps at him. "Just because you're stronger than anyone doesn't mean you get to treat us like shit. I've put up with you for far too long, Ze."

"On the contrary," he notes, raising one finger up. His voice is serene but cold. Calculating. "I am not the one people have to put up with. Shall I remind you what your last stunt caused? You are here for a reason," he says, narrowing his eyes at her.

I blink in confusion.

"What is he talking about?" I ask her.

"It doesn't matter," she quickly answers, but she doesn't meet my eyes.

"You may think I am harsh with Erithea, but has she told you about her reputation back home?" Ze asks, casually taking a seat on the couch.

Thea's eyes widen, her lips compressed in a thin line.

"Ze..." she warns, her voice grave.

"It is not the moment for this, Ze," Cer finally intervenes.

"Why? Are you ashamed of your past, Erithea?" Ze raises a brow.

"You damn asshole," she grits her teeth.

"Cut it out, Ze. Leave her alone."

"And of course, Cerenios is always there to fight her battles for her." He rolls his eyes. "Are you not tired of cleaning up after your sister?"

"Ze, I said stop," Cer enunciates clearly, his entire countenance changing. "You are taking this too far."

"I have barely started." He smirks. "Although, Erithea, I

wonder what your family would say if they knew your little secret. Do you think they would disown you at last?"

The temperature in the room suddenly drops. Thea's eyes darken, her nostrils flaring with aggression. She reaches for the cup I left on the table, and with a single touch, the material changes shape, becoming slim and elongated, the edge sharp like a spear. She doesn't waste a moment as she throws it at Ze.

He doesn't even blink as he tilts his head to the side, letting the spear embed itself in the couch.

"Don't you dare say anything, Ze, or I'll—"

In a flash, Ze is gone from the couch, appearing in front of Thea. His hand is wrapped around her throat as he pushes her against the wall, his eyes swirling an explosive purple.

"You forget yourself, Erithea. I can end you with one snap of my wrist." His voice is cold, unyielding. All of a sudden, I see the same Ze from the night before—the cruel, violent one—and fear courses through me.

Thea struggles to breathe, but she doesn't back down, her eyes shining with anger.

"Stop!" I call out, rushing forward.

But before I can reach them, Cer is by Thea's side, putting himself between her and Ze. He presses his hand on Ze's chest, propelling him back until he hits the wall, leaving a big dent in it.

Thea's hand goes to her neck, massaging it as she inhales deeply.

"Are you all right?" Cer whispers.

She gives a brisk nod, but her eyes are still on Ze, beams of hatred directed at him.

"You do not put your hands on my sister," Cer decrees in a harsh voice. "You do not touch her. You do not *breathe* near her," he states, addressing Ze.

Ze merely smirks, dusting his clothes and coming forward, his walk as nonchalant as his expression.

"I hit a nerve, did I not, Cerenios?" Ze chuckles. "So this is what it takes for you to turn on me," he muses silently, the ghost of a smile touching his lips.

"Just stop it, Ze. You're only making things worse," I call out. The last thing I expected is to see *them* at each other's throats. And with the way things are going, I'm pretty sure they'll end up hurting each other.

"Of course. All I ever do is make things worse, is that not right?" He finally turns to me, his purple eyes swirling in a myriad of shades, dark and light blending together in a hypnotizing manner.

"Why do you do it if you know it? Why do you have to be so mean to Thea? And now Cer, too? Isn't he your friend?"

He doesn't answer, the corner of his mouth curling up in disgust.

"Oh right, I forgot. You don't have friends, do you?" I let out a dry laugh.

His features tighten and he steps closer, his hard steps thundering against the wooden floor.

"That is correct. I do not have any friends. I do not want to have any friends," he declares, his words clipped.

I shake my head at him in disappointment.

"Then why are you still here?"

"Why, indeed." He stares at me. He takes another step until the tips of his feet meet mine, and I instinctively back away, the memory of his previous outburst still fresh in my memory—as is the way he manhandled me.

"You fear me, human?" he asks in a low voice.

I swallow.

"Have you given me reason not to?" I whisper.

His intent gaze pins me to the spot, the hairs on my body all standing up to attention. The proximity reminds me of our size differences—the fact that he's a giant next to me. That intimidates me even more as I find myself taking another step back.

"So this is how it is now, human. You turn on me, too?"

"Turn on you?" I repeat numbly, shocked at his accusation. "It was *you* who hurt me, Ze. But what's new? All you know is how to hurt people, how to insult them and make them feel insignificant. Because no one can possibly be as great as you."

His jaw hardens, his fists clenching by his side.

"Luce, it's not worth it," Thea quips from the back, but I'm done with his behavior.

"You're a hateful, *hateful* man, Ze," I tell him.

He straightens his back as he pushes his chin up.

"You hate me that much, human?" he asks in a low, raspy voice, his body shaking with unreleased tension.

"I just don't want you anywhere near me," I tell him honestly.

He stares at me for a moment before he nods, moving past me toward the door.

"You never even apologized for last night," I add quietly. I don't know if that would help, but it would be a starting point.

He half turns, his profile shrouded in darkness.

"I am not sorry," he states.

And before I can blink, he's gone.

I sway on my feet, finding a chair and sitting down. Thea comes to my side, her features stricken.

"Are you okay?" I ask her, carefully scanning her body. "Did he hurt you?"

"Nothing I can't handle." She shrugs.

"Why is he like this? Why is he so..."

"You're finally getting a glimpse of the real Ze." Thea sighs as she takes a seat next to me. "He's not a good person."

Cer grunts, although he doesn't offer any insight. I guess he's still his subordinate, technically.

"Why did you sing his praises when he first arrived then? Why would you lie that you're friends when it's clear you hate each other?"

She purses her lips, her eyes straying to her brother.

"Because he made me." She takes a deep breath.

My eyes widen in shock.

"He...made you?"

"I can't give you more details, Luce. I wish I could, but it's not something I can talk about. He knows things about me that would get me killed if they got out," she whispers. "He is the last person you would ever wish to know your deepest, darkest secrets. Because I have no doubt he would make good on his threat to tell my family."

"What does he have on you, Thea?" Cer demands sharply.

She shakes her head.

"Something that would make you hate me, too, Cer." She meets his gaze as she gives him a sad smile. "And I can't risk that."

"And he used that to what? Blackmail you?"

She nods grimly.

I inhale sharply.

"That is so low of him. I can't believe I ever felt sorry for him."

"You don't know him as we do, Luce. Cer would never speak ill of him, of course, even though I have no doubt he has plenty of such opinions as well."

Cer has a grave expression, but he neither agrees with it nor denies it.

"But that's only because he feels some misplaced loyalty to him," she continues. "But back home..." She shakes her head. "There's no one more hated. And it's not just because of his rude manner. I doubt there's any House that hasn't lost someone to his sword."

"What do you mean?" I frown.

"His duties don't only involve demons, but also—"

"Thea, that is enough," Cer interrupts her.

She gives him a harsh look.

"She has a right to know, Cer," she says before she turns to me. "Ze is the executioner of the law. If anyone missteps, he is the one who comes to deliver the punishment. And he never blinks an eye. In our family alone, he's executed at least five people that I know of in the last few hundred years. With him, you don't get second chances."

"Why is he here then? Why would he participate in the game?"

She shares a hidden look with Cer.

"I'm not sure. He didn't tell me, and with him, you never know. I'm sorry I lied." She sighs. "I didn't want him getting so close to you, but I didn't know how to tell you without risking his wrath."

"I understand." I smile as I reach to pat her on the back.

"What a touching scene," a familiar voice says from the back.

We all turn and watch Ze lean against the wall, his shrewd eyes taking in everything.

"How long have you been there?" I ask.

He doesn't reply. The corners of his mouth lift up in an eerie smile. Thea's face drains of color, and Cer reaches for her hand, squeezing it in comfort. She's already trembling, on the verge of a breakdown, and Cer is doing his best to calm her down.

Ze's eyes zero in on their interaction, his displeasure clear. Before he can say or do anything that might hurt Thea, I take a step toward him.

"Don't, Ze. Please don't do anything to hurt her. I'm begging you."

He slowly turns his gaze to me.

"You would beg?" He raises an eyebrow. "For a stranger."

"She's not a stranger. She's my friend."

He scoffs.

"Like *I* was your friend?" he asks, staring at me intently.

I don't answer, biting my lip to stop myself from blurting a caustic reply.

"Beg, then."

"W-what?" I blink.

"Beg me not to reveal her secret. *Beg* me."

"Ze. We should take this privately," Cer mentions. "We should leave them out of it."

"Why should we when they are at the core of this issue?" He

laughs. "Although if you knew what Erithea is hiding from you..."

"Please don't," Thea whispers as she drops to her knees. "Please don't tell him. Don't tell anyone," she pleads, tears rushing down her cheeks. "I'll do anything. Just please..."

"If you truly meant that, you would have done what I asked from the beginning. But no, you had to let your flawed emotions get the best of you."

"If you tell them... You know what will happen to me," she sobs. "You know I'll be dead."

"Of course." He smiles, although it never reaches his eyes. "And I will be the one to deliver you to your death."

My mouth hangs open in shock as I stare at the casual way in which he just told Thea he would kill her—regardless of the fact that she is his friend's sister, or that he's known her for years. To get what he wants, he'd kill her.

I have grossly misjudged him, haven't I?

Who is this Ze and where is the slightly awkward but well-intended protector? Where is the man who made me feel safe and made sure no danger touched me?

But the truth is staring me right in the face.

That man never existed. And considering what Thea told me, I'm sure he's had a secondary purpose for joining the game and our team from the beginning.

He was using us for something, wasn't he?

Disappointment settles deep in my stomach, and something more. A tingle spreads through my entire body, almost as if his actions are physically making me ill. The revulsion is so strong, I barely keep myself from being sick.

"That's enough, Ze." Cer's voice booms as he gets to his feet, his body radiating pure energy.

Fearing a fight between them would hurt everyone, I swallow my pride and meet Ze's eyes. I've seen enough of his abilities to know that no one would survive. Cer might be his disciple, but I doubt he's as strong.

"What do you want me to do? I'll do it," I slowly say.

He turns his attention to me, coming closer. His steps are measured, his expression icy. Whatever vulnerability I might have seen in him in the past is gone. There's just ruthless indifference. One that cuts me to the core.

As he reaches in front of me, he tips my chin up with his hand, his thumb brushing against my lips. I gulp down as a sliver of fear courses down my back.

With how unpredictable he is, I'm truly not sure what he would ask of me.

The caress is soft, gentle—belying his arctic countenance. He touches me almost reverently, and a small alarm bell goes off in my head.

What if...

"Give up," he says in a deadpan tone.

"What?" I whisper.

A smirk pulls at his lips as his hand dips lower. Slowly, he wraps his fingers around the circumference of my neck, bringing me closer to him.

"Renounce the competition and return to your world." He lowers his head to whisper in my ear. "If you do that, I will give you my vow that Erithea's secret will be safe."

THIRTY-NINE

My breathing accelerates as I blink repeatedly, thinking I haven't heard him right.

"Why? Why would you care if I give up or not?"

"Because I do not want to see you win, human," he states smoothly.

His words are like an arrow to my heart, the sharp tip penetrating deep and embedding itself in my flesh. Of all the things he could have said... I shield my face so he doesn't see the hurt reflected in my features.

God, how silly I am. How could I have seen anything good in him?

Moments pass as silence molds to the room. We all stare at one another as Ze waits for me to agree to his outrageous terms. To my greatest shame, I cannot bring myself to do it.

I sneak a glance at Thea on the floor, her face red from crying, and I still can't open my mouth to say the words. Yes, she's my friend. But Nikki... He's my everything.

Does that make me a bad person? I'm not sure. I only know that I have one limit only—my husband.

"As I suspected." Ze leans back, laughing. "You are not such a nice person now, are you, human?" he asks sarcastically. "You could not even save your friend."

"Ze, please..."

I don't get to plead my case with him because a cloud of smoke appears in the room, the messenger wraith materializing in front of us.

"Congratulations. You have passed the second trial and are officially invited to join the third one. Is there anyone who would like to withdraw?" The rehearsed speech flows out of the wraith's mouth.

Ze stares at me, his purple eyes glowing.

Does he think that tactic of intimidation will work?

"You know what you have to do," he adds in a low voice.

My hands clench into fists by my side, my anger growing by the second.

Why?

From the beginning, he's tried to make me quit, yet he's also tried to shield me from danger. Why would it matter so much to him whether I continue or not—whether I win or not? There are so many contradictory things about him that I no longer know what to believe. Was any of what he told me in the forest true? Or was it just a tactic to make me feel sorry for him? Capitalize on my empathy to get me to trust him unconditionally.

The more I find out about him, the more I think I must have been the perfect idiot for Ze to work his lies on because as it stands, I believed *everything*.

He was at least right about something. I *am* a fool. But I am a fool who learns from her mistakes.

"No," I answer, pushing my chin up. I avoid looking at Ze or at Thea, for fear my guilt might shake up my conviction. "I will continue."

"Noted." She turns to the others.

"I will continue as well," Thea answers.

It's Ze's turn to answer.

Time stops as he levels me with his intense glare. It's almost as if he's trying to communicate something but does not have the words to do so. But at this point, it's useless. He's already revealed his true colors and as far as I'm concerned, I don't care whether he continues or not as long as it's not going to be anywhere near me.

"I forfeit," he declares a second before he vanishes, this time for good.

"Noted," she quips. "And you?" She turns to Cer.

He's staring at the place that Ze vacated, indecision written all over his face. Thea grabs his hand, shaking her head at him.

"Thea..." He blinks.

"You have already risked too much, Cer. You can't afford to get caught," she whispers with a sad smile. "I can take care of myself."

"No. I will not let you do that."

"He will forfeit," Thea addresses the wraith before lowering her voice to say to Cer, "You owe me one, remember? I am claiming my boon."

His lips are compressed in a thin line as he stares at her for minutes on end.

"I will forfeit," he reluctantly utters the words, his eyes still on her.

"Noted," the wraith quips. "Congratulations," she tells the two of us. "Will you continue as a team or individually?"

"Together," Thea speaks first.

I glance at her, surprised she'd offer me this grace after failing her.

"Noted. The two of you are officially enrolled in the third trial. The destination is Aperion, House of Gaia. A portal will be opened tomorrow at midday, and you will be able to travel to your destination. The third trial will commence in a month from tomorrow, and you will receive your assignment seven days before the event. I wish you luck."

And just like that, the wraith is gone.

I slowly walk back to Thea's side.

"I'm sorry," I whisper. "I..." I swallow. How do I explain to her that I cannot give this up for anything in the world? That getting my husband back is the only thing that drives me forward. Without him... Without hope... I'm nothing.

"No. You don't have anything to be sorry for, Luce. It's not your mess. It's mine." She takes a deep breath. "I made my bed, now I need to sleep in it."

"I don't think he'll reveal your secret. If that was his intention, he would already have."

She forces a smile. "For now. He's too unpredictable. He has his interests, and if it's in his interest to reveal everything... I have no doubt he will."

"What can I do?" Cer asks, his voice tinged with worry. "Tell me what I can do to help, Thea. I can k—"

"Do not say it," she blurts out in a panic. "You know it is treason. And that is far worse than any death."

"I do not know how to help you if you will not tell me what he has on you." He sighs.

"It is my cross to bear, Cer. But I appreciate your offer," she says with a smile. "Maybe at some point in time..." She shakes her head.

"I'll always be there for you," he murmurs, and suddenly I feel as if I'm intruding on an intimate moment between the two. "Regardless of whether I am in the game or not."

Thea sighs as she lays her back against the kitchen counter. "Now that we know the trial will be held in Aperion, I'm even happier you forfeited. You cannot get caught, Cer," she murmurs.

"I would have been careful." He purses his lips. "We have not been caught so far. It is not hard to blend in as long as we do not use our abilities."

"I won't risk it." She shakes her head, reaching out to take his hand.

"You are that worried about me?" he inquires softly. "So much so that you would use your precious boon?"

A light smile appears on her face as she squeezes his hand.

"You protect me, I protect you. That's how it will always be."

They stare at each other in silence for a moment before Thea clears her throat.

"At least Ze had the decency to leave, too. I didn't think he'd ever do that of his own volition," she mentions drily.

"I was surprised about that, too." I sigh. In a way, I'm happy he won't be around since I already decided that I didn't want to be around him. At the same time, I'm still a little disappointed. "Do you think we'll manage by ourselves?" I ask, a little scared by the upcoming game. And to top that off, we don't even know what it will entail.

"Don't worry about it, Luce. We'll manage just fine." She gives me a smile. But as she turns to her brother, a frown mars her features. "I'm confused about something, though. Wasn't Aperion off-limits for the game?"

"It used to be. After the disaster of the first Wishing Game, it was decreed that Aperion was off-limits for any future competition." He nods.

"What do you mean?" I ask.

"The first Wishing Game was held entirely in Aperion, but each trial was in a different House," he explains. "One man made it to the end, but it was revealed he was a deity who had just come into his powers but did not know how to use them. He almost destroyed Aperion."

Thea frowns. "Is that where they say seven out of fifteen Supremes were killed in one day? But how is it that a young deity would have that type of power? To kill one Supreme is unheard of, but seven? That's impossible."

"It's a legend, Thea. I doubt he killed seven Supremes by himself," Cer adds drily. "You know those things can get blown out of proportion."

"Um, what is a Supreme?"

Thea and Cer both look at me as if they just realized I'm still around.

"Oh, right. I forget you're not used to this." She chuckles. "But now that we're heading to Aperion, you should probably know it," she says as she gets a confirmation glance from Cer. "There are fifteen royal houses in Aperion. Each House is a realm, with its own monarchs, military, and people. But from each realm, the most powerful individual is chosen to become a Supreme. Well, almost." She pauses. "There are two Houses that are the exception to the rule." She doesn't expand further. "But the most important thing is that the fifteen Supremes are the ultimate force on Aperion, and they rule over *everyone*."

"That sounds interesting." I nod thoughtfully. It's almost as if all the mythology I'd read in books is one step away from becoming a reality. Despite my precarious situation in the game, I can't deny that I'm giddy about what's to come and exploring the unknown.

"It might be, but not for us," Thea adds dramatically.

"Why?" I frown.

Her lips compress in a tight line as she sighs. Cer has a similar expression.

"Aperion is our home."

"But... Didn't you say you were from a place called Arche?" I frown.

"That is the House of Arche, within Aperion," she adds sheepishly.

"Oh," I whisper.

"And since the third trial starts in a month, I think we're due a visit home, Cer."

He grunts, seemingly not too pleased with the prospect.

"Of course you're invited to join us, Luce. My parents are wonderful, and you'll also get to meet our sister," Thea exclaims.

"You have another sister?"

"She's the youngest." She smiles fondly. "It's actually the first time I'm away from her for so long, so I can't wait to see her."

"I'd love to. Thank you," I tell her sincerely.

We don't get to talk for much longer as I announce that I'm going to sleep. The fatigue is starting to get to me, and I'll need all my strength for what's to come.

I bid them good night and plan to regroup in the morning. Thea surprises me by saying that I can have the room all to myself for tonight and she'll just sleep in the same room as Cer.

I don't refuse since I've been craving some alone time from the beginning.

As I go to my room, I change and take a quick shower before getting between the sheets. Yet despite being so tired, sleep doesn't come so easily. Not after everything that happened today.

Ze and Cer are out of the competition, leaving Thea and me in a team of two to fend for ourselves. If before I was contemplating going into the third trial by myself, now I'm wondering if we'll manage just the two of us. It's a little jarring to realize just how much I was depending on the others to win. And if that's the case, what does that say about me?

That you're human, a voice inside my head whispers.

I might be human, but I need to rise above my condition if I am to pass the third trial. Who knows what they'll ask of us, and for that reason, I need to amass as much information as possible and to get myself in better physical shape.

There are only two weeks left until it starts—*not* enough time. But I must make do.

I nod to myself as my conviction grows stronger. I might not have any fancy abilities, but I shall win based on my sheer will alone. Besides, now I have one more reason to fight until the end. I trace the marks on my chest, thinking back to what Ze said—that these are marks made by a god. The only way to find out what they mean and why I have them is to get to the final trial and meet these *gods.*

Curiosity brims inside of me as I wonder if, maybe, these marks I've so dreadfully abhorred my entire life might have another meaning. If they have a purpose that I may not be aware of.

A smile pulls at my lips as my mind strays into fanciful territory, imagining that the marks might make me special in some way.

I've never been special before.

But at the same time, I don't want to get my hopes up. This isn't a movie or a romance book where the heroine gets her happily ever after. This is the real world, with real challenges and dangers. If I let myself dream in vain, only I will be hurt in the end.

As I think about the way my marks lit up when Ze touched them, I can't stop my thoughts from straying to him and consequently remembering the deep disappointment I felt at his betrayal.

I *trusted* him, and he took advantage of that. And if what Thea's saying is true, he's been doing this from the beginning.

Just what was his goal with this competition?

Why was he so nice to me, only to turn around and be...not so nice?

I just cannot understand any of it. His behavior is contradictory, his words even more so.

"Why did you make me care for you, Ze?" I sigh to myself as I turn to the side, hugging the pillow to my chest.

My chest is heavy with hurt, my heart aching when I think of all the vile things he said to me.

I do not want to see you win.

Why? Why would he say something like that when he knows how important this game is to me? Why would he help me during this trial, saving me repeatedly if he didn't want me to win? I just cannot make sense of any of it.

"Ugh!" I cry out, banging my fist against my chest.

It's not worth it. Stop thinking about it, Luce. Just focus on Nikki.

Unfortunately, it's easier said than done. As I close my eyes and drift off to sleep, it's not Nikki that I dream about. It's Ze and those precious moments we shared on our trip.

FORTY

"I'm so excited to show you my home, Luce." Thea clasps her hands together as she gushes about her sister and their home, describing all the things we can do together and all the places we should visit. The way she's talking about it makes it seem like we're going on a vacation, not embarking on a potentially deadly trial.

I nod as I put on my shoes, signaling I'm ready to head to the courtyard. We head out of the apartment, walking alongside the other teams who qualified for the third trial. To my great surprise, there are quite a few people—at least half of those who were present at the inauguration. And that tells me one thing— these people are *strong*.

A shiver goes down my back as I wonder how we'll fare in this trial without Ze and Cer. We don't even know what the trial will entail, but if it's something to do with strength, then I'm already at a disadvantage.

"There's this place in the city that I think you'll love," Thea continues in a sing-song voice, barely minding the glances she's getting from the other contestants.

"This is as far as I can accompany you," Cer interjects. "I will see you in Aperion." He turns to his sister. "Until then, you should come up with an excuse for our parents. They will want to know where their precious daughter has been," he says with the hint of a smile.

Thea's eyes widen in realization and she stops speaking, her lips trembling.

"What will I tell them?" she whispers. "They'll be so angry if they find out I sneaked into the game."

"What's going on?" I frown. She mentioned before that if they were found out to be participating in the game, they'd get in trouble, but she never specified why.

"I think it's time to come clean, Thea. She'll find out sooner or later anyway," Cer tells her. Thea licks her lips as she glances at her brother, fidgeting on the spot.

"Well... There might have been one tiny, *very* little detail I omitted."

I wait for her to continue, but she stalls as she keeps looking at Cer.

"There is a clause in the game that gods cannot participate." She starts in a hesitant tone, fiddling with her fingers. "And well... technically, I haven't passed my exams yet, so I haven't qualified as a deity, but..." She gives her brother a worried look. "You won't tell them, will you?" she whispers to him, pulling on his sleeve as she nestles closer to his side. She bats her lashes at him adoringly, and he doesn't seem immune to her charm.

"So you two are deities?" I raise a brow. At this point, I don't think anything can shock me anymore. In fact, all of Thea's vague answers so far and the fact that she has so much knowledge of everything should have given it away.

"He is." She points at Cer. "I am going to be too, at some point," she grumbles.

"How does this work? You *become* a deity? You're not born one?" I ask, a little confused. In all the mythological stories I'd read, gods were born to other gods, and in rare cases, mortals were granted divine powers from other gods. But I haven't seen anywhere anything about exams.

"You must be born one, but you only qualify as a deity when your powers mature and you exhibit extraordinary abilities.

That doesn't happen to everyone. There are those like Cer who are naturals, or there are those like me who need some time to get better," she explains. "It's not a very clear-cut system. In many ways, it is a meritocracy. Only the best get appointed positions, and only the most exceptional ones get nominated for the position of a Supreme."

"I'm sure you are familiar with human myths," Cer interrupts. "Many of the ancient ones have a pantheon of gods, and each god is assigned to different phenomena."

I nod.

"The Supremes *are* those gods. But unlike your mortal stories, each main god is a position rather than a person. Take for example the God of Fire. There is no one being who is the God of Fire. Across time, multiple people have borne that name. Gods may be immortal, but they are not impervious. If one dies, another is elected to take its place to maintain the balance of the universe."

I blink slowly as I take in the new information.

"That is fascinating," I whisper. "But I'm not clear why you would participate in the game if you're not allowed to. Aren't you immortal? What more could you want?" Shouldn't that already give them the ability to have whatever they wish for?

"Well..." Thea stammers, a panicked look on her face. "I vowed to do it." She gives me a guilty smile. "And in our world, a vow is an unbreakable promise. Cer just followed me to make sure I'm safe. And Ze... He does what he wants." She shrugs, bitterness reflected in her tone.

"And of course, Ze is a deity too, isn't he?"

Why doesn't that surprise me? He's so powerful, I should have gotten an inkling about it. But we've already settled that I am far too foolish and too trusting.

"Not just *a* deity." She takes a deep breath. "He is one of the most powerful gods. And with the elections coming up, he might end up being the new Supreme."

FORTY-ONE

Cer disappears, leaving us alone in the middle of the courtyard as we await our turn to use the designated portal. Thea is still happily chatting away, but I'm too busy churning the new information in my mind.

They are all deities. Forbidden to take part in the game.

Then what the hell are they doing here, and more importantly, why with me?

Why would they get involved with a powerless human?

Now it makes sense why Ze was so condescending or why he never stopped using the term *human* in such a derogatory manner. For him, I'm an ant—if that. But though this sheds some more light on his personality, it doesn't excuse what he's done or how he's behaved with me, or Thea.

He crossed a line, and for that, I can't bring myself to forgive him.

The line moves at an insane pace, and soon, we are almost in front of the portal. I shake myself from my Ze-ridden thoughts and try to put it all behind me—though it's easier said than done. Even when I should be watching for the competition and cataloging those who are left in the game, my thoughts always go back to my disappointment toward Ze.

"Do you think there are other deities participating?" I ask Thea.

"Hmm, who knows. The only way they can sense if a deity participates in the game is by their power signature. You see, to qualify as a deity, your abilities need to be at a certain level. It's why you undertake a series of exams that track your power signature until it's within the acceptable parameters for a deity. The game tracks god power signatures. It's why Cer and Ze were so careful with their abilities so they wouldn't trigger the game security mechanisms."

I mull over her words.

"But what if someone is as strong as a god but is not actually a god?"

I remember Ze telling me that although gods are forbidden from entering, others descended from deities or hybrids are not.

"That is reflected in the power signature. There is a level, but there is also a *type* of power that denotes whether someone is a god or not. The first thing that triggers the game is the level. If it's high, they look into the type of power used to determine if it belongs to a deity or not."

"And what happens if a deity is caught participating?"

She purses her lips.

"They're sent before the Supremes, who decide on a fitting punishment. The few times it's happened before, those deities barely got away with their lives."

I nod thoughtfully.

"I didn't realize it was this dangerous for you."

"I could get away through the loophole—technically." She forces a smile.

"It was Ze, wasn't it?" I ask softly. "The one who made you vow."

She purses her lips, yet her lack of answer is answer enough.

"I'm sorry. I cannot speak of it. I've already said more than I should have."

"It's fine," I assure her. "I do have one question, though."

She nods, urging me to speak.

"Do you know any god who would mark a human?" I say as I tug on my neckline so some of my marks are visible. She's seen them before, though, so she knows what I mean.

"No." She shakes her head. "Gods don't concern themselves with humans. They rarely leave Aperion. Why do you think a god had something to do with that?"

"Ze tried to heal them for me, but he couldn't."

She frowns, touching her chin with her forefinger as she thinks.

"You can ask my parents. They should know more. I am a youngling compared to them—*and everyone else.*" She chuckles.

Our conversation is cut short as someone purposefully bumps into Thea, making her stumble forward and almost fall to the floor. I grab onto her, helping her balance on her feet.

"Oh, I'm sorry. Did I hurt you?" a fake voice calls from behind, followed by a crowd of laughter.

I look back and see a group of guys leering at us.

Thea's lips twitch with annoyance as she releases a loud huff.

"Don't mind them," she whispers. "It's not the time to get into a fight."

I nod, although I'm not so sure. She seems fine with it, but the more I hear them chuckle behind our backs and purposefully belittle us, the more I wish I could just tell them to shut it. No matter my impulses, though, I'm aware that Thea is right. This is not the place, nor the time.

We continue quietly toward the portal as our turn finally arrives.

Thea grabs my hand and gives me a smile as she urges me to follow her.

One moment we're in P'davi, surrounded by the complex and the other participants, the next we're in a foreign location.

If before we'd been in the middle of nowhere, with a scant few buildings buried in the middle of the woods, now we're in the midst of a bustling street, people walking right and left all around us. What's more startling, though, is the fact that I don't see any of the other contestants around us.

The street is lined with shops on both sides, as well as street vendors supplying different kinds of merchandise. I spot some selling fabrics, toys, jewelry, and food. People are marching from one stall to another to look at the goods, and to my surprise, I can understand everything they're saying as they barter with the sellers to get a better price.

"Five asim," a woman says as she touches a luxurious beige silk.

"Seven," the seller counters.

"How is it that I can understand what they're saying?" I murmur to Thea.

She gives me a sly smile.

"The brew you drank doesn't only give you the ability to survive in any realm, but it also endows you with the ability to understand all spoken languages in the known worlds."

I nod numbly as I continue to stare around.

The pedestrians walk around unbothered, going about their day as if we haven't fallen right out of the sky. But perhaps this is a usual occurrence for them. The men are wearing tunics and pairs of loose pants, with belts fitted around their waists, which hold weapons and small pouches. The women are all wearing long dresses, their bodies fully covered. There's a corset molded to their waists that flows into a long skirt. Some have additional layers underneath, peeking out of the hem with laces and pretty frills. The gowns remind me of Renaissance dresses. Similar to my world, there's an immediate class distinction based on the material out of which the dresses are fashioned. The wealthier ones are wearing silky, bright colors while the others are wearing what seems to be cotton or linen.

"Where are the other contestants?"

"They probably ended up in different areas of the Kingdom. These portals aren't known to be extremely reliable," Thea says as she scrunches her nose.

Turning around, she studies her surroundings.

"We need to go that way." She points east. I can make out some tall buildings in the distance. "I'm not sure where we are now. I haven't been to Gaia all that often, but I know my way around the capital. I'll send a message to Cer to meet us there."

"Send a message?" I blink.

"Uhm, telepathically." She gives me a sheepish smile.

"Right. Because you're deities."

"*Almost* deity," she corrects, winking at me.

"Fine, lead the way." I nod at her, and we start walking.

All the while, I continue to study this new world, surprised to see many similarities to mine. But as I gaze up at the sky, I find one glaring difference.

There are two suns.

They half-overlap each other, creating an eerie effect of two semi-circles bound together. Yet the added heat doesn't blister my body, nor does it make me feel odd considering the different environment. So this is why that brew is required. Without it, I wonder what would have happened to my body under this double sun.

"How far is the capital?" I ask after we've been walking for almost an hour. No matter how much distance we cover, the tall buildings we spotted before seem to be just as far away, their shapes marring the horizon.

She purses her lips.

"I'm not sure. We just have to reach there. This is likely just a peripheral town."

"It's very busy for a peripheral town," I note. "Are these people deities too?"

"Oh no." She shakes her head. "Ninety percent of the living inhabitants of Aperion do not possess any powers. They're called s'Aperiotes. I should have warned you." She sighs.

"Why?" I frown.

"There is a hierarchy in Aperion, like in any other world. S'Aperiotes are at the bottom, and because of that, they're often treated as such. Aperion is a meritocracy, but that merit is based on power. The hierarchy is based solely on who has the most power. The Supremes are at the top, followed by the monarchs of each Royal House, then the nobility, the military, and the minor deities. These are the classes that have abilities. S'Aperiotes are last, even though they make up the majority of the population. No one really knows why they lack abilities. Some say it's because of migration patterns eons ago. Others say it's because they've been bred out to be powerless since the other classes mate strictly with each other. The law specifies that it is illegal for someone with abilities to mate with someone without. For that reason, the five classes have to get approval from the House of Moirai if they want to mate with someone. S'Aperiotes do not need this."

"I didn't realize your society was *that* strict," I note.

"You haven't heard half of it." She rolls her eyes. "To a degree, I understand *why*, but it doesn't make it any less constricting. Deities might be immortal, but most are not impervious. That means if one dies, another has to be ready to take that place so that the universe is in balance. Because of that, the fates check all potential futures and decide on which mate would be most suitable to produce offspring that could benefit the society—and the entire universe."

"If you don't like it that much, why don't you go somewhere else? You clearly have no trouble traveling between worlds, and compared to Ze and Cer, you're much more social."

A sad smile pulls at her lips.

"Alas, that is yet another law. Some classes are forbidden from ever leaving Aperion. You must always notify the military legal office of your departure and return plans. Otherwise, the Trackers would come for you." She sighs. "Because how could Aperion waste its precious resources?" She rolls her eyes at that.

"I see," I mumble. It seems utterly insane that deities would have so many rules. But I guess it's the whole *with great power comes great responsibility* spiel.

"Anyway, what I meant to say is that since s'Aperiotes are at the bottom, they're often mistreated. You have to be careful and only go out with me or Cer. You don't want to be mistaken for a s'Aperiote by a minor deity or one of those military pricks. They always like to pick on people," she explains.

"Got it." I nod, though the more I hear, the more I wonder how this could be a godly realm when it's rather ungodly.

Aperion really doesn't seem like a great place so far, despite the lively and bustling ambiance or the beautiful blue skies and the dual suns. If anything, the outside might be pretty, but the inside seems rather rotten. For one, Thea has made her dislike of it quite clear, and it's so sad to see the change in her demeanor now that we're here. Somehow she's more subdued, a sadness underlying even her usual smiles.

"I'm sorry you're stuck here," I whisper as I pat her lightly on her back.

"It's fine." She shrugs. "At least I have my family. I don't know what I'd do without them."

"You're lucky." I smile fondly. "I've seen the way you and Cer care for each other, and I am quite jealous. I'm all alone. I've never had siblings, and I can barely remember my own mother. My husband is all I have."

She takes my hand, giving it a light squeeze as she turns to look at me.

"It's why I want to help you win this. You deserve to know happiness. No matter what Ze says or does, you deserve to win. At least one of us should get a happily ever after," she adds sadly.

"Thank you," I murmur, tears of gratitude stabbing at my eyes. "I really appreciate this, Thea. You're a good friend."

She has a wistful expression on her face as she tips her gaze up to look at the horizon line.

"If only." She sighs, pressing her lips in a tight, sad line. She doesn't say more, but it's enough for me to realize this has something to do with the secret Ze was threatening her with. Considering how many rules there are in their society, her transgression could be very minor and still get her a dire sentence.

The mood changes, and Thea seems lost in thought as we

continue walking. Every now and then, I notice her lifting her hand to her face and rubbing moisture out of her eyes.

There's a marked difference between the carefree Thea I knew outside of Aperion and the one now, and her words only serve to reinforce the fact that she's entirely unhappy about being back home. She's also remarkably quiet for someone who's always chatting about this and that.

I don't speak either, not wanting to intrude. But that doesn't mean I'm not sad about it, and I wonder if there's something I can do to help her.

Releasing a deep sigh, I turn my attention to the road, taking in our surroundings.

Now that we're out of the popular area, there are fewer and fewer people walking around. Every now and then, I see carriages being drawn around by something akin to a horse, but with the body of a human.

The suns climb up the sky, hitting their highest point and suggesting we've been walking for a while. Yet the capital is still nowhere near. The tall towers remain a dot on the horizon, and the more we venture out of the previous town, the more derelict the buildings by the side of the road look.

There are houses, but they're in poor shape. They are made of thin brown wood, and they all seem to be a similar size—a one-bedroom. The design is the same for the entire row, and that makes me wonder if these were not built by the state—otherwise, who would go for the exact model?

People go about their day, working on their gardens or drying their clothes in their yards. The families aren't small, certainly too big for a one-bedroom, but it quickly becomes clear this intermediary area isn't particularly well-off.

Isn't it hypocritical that a godly realm would have such poverty? When one thinks of deities, there's a rather romanticized version of perfection—not only are they powerful, but they are also wise and well-intended.

The evidence in front of me speaks of the opposite. The

treatment of s'Aperiotes as the scourge of society makes it even more clear that nothing is perfect here.

Despite Thea's assurances that this is a meritocracy, I don't see it. How could it be when s'Aperiotes are never even given a chance? The upper echelons intermarry and preserve their wealth, powers, and status, creating new gods and new Supremes, while the others are stuck in a continuous cycle of suffering.

It's. Not. Fair.

Maybe as a human, I'd gotten used to life being unfair from the moment I was born. Everyone knows there's no such thing as a utopia of fairness. Yet humans still hope for one—they still cling to the belief that one day, that could be achievable. But how could that be when gods themselves ascribe to discrimination and unfairness?

I may have only been here for a few short hours, but already, I am...disappointed. Which in itself is such an odd thing considering I've never been overly religious after my brush with cult fanaticism. But I guess I still had the hope that there was something better out there—that there were higher beings looking out for us.

Instead, what do I get?

More entitled assholes who make rules to only serve themselves.

I guess some things never change, whether you are human or deity. But Thea did say that gods created mortals in their image. That must be where we got our selfishness and delusions of grandeur.

I'm so lost in my thoughts that I barely register the voice calling out to us. Startled out of my reverie, I turn to see an older man in shabby clothes by the side of the road. His hair is long and unkempt, his beard reaching his chest. He rests his weight on a twig as he limps toward us.

"Don't mind him," Thea says with a wave of her hand.

I frown.

"Spare a coin, miss," he wheezes in a groggy, rough voice.

"Do you have a coin?" I whisper to Thea.

"I don't have any money." She shrugs. "But even if I had, I wouldn't give it to someone like him." She scrunches her nose.

"What do you mean?" My eyes flare in shock.

"Can you see the blue stains on his shirt?" She nods to the old man who's getting closer to us by the moment.

I nod.

"They're from *zantrax*, a highly addictive substance that is *extremely* illegal. He's just going to use the coins for that."

"What does it do?"

Thea purses her lips.

"It momentarily gives the user god-like abilities. It's very brief, and it does irreparable damage to the body. It's also very expensive, which means people will do whatever they can to get more money to buy *zantrax*."

I stare numbly at her. I guess not even godly realms are immune to drug problems.

"Let's go." Thea grabs my hand, urging me forward.

I let her lead me away from the man, still processing the information.

"Spare a coin, miss," he continues, his voice getting closer.

Fingers coil around my arm in a tight grip as I'm pulled backward.

"Spare a coin." He snarls, his face scrunched up in distaste.

"I'm sorry. I don't have any." I give him a polite smile as I try to take his hand off my arm.

"I. Don't. Believe. You," he enunciates each word as he lodges his fingers deeper into my skin.

I release a small whimper of pain just as Thea intervenes, placing herself between us as she tries to get him off me.

"We don't have any money. Go beg somewhere else," she tells him harshly.

"Give. Me. Coins," he continues, almost like a robot.

"Let her go or I'll hurt you," Thea warns, her claws growing in size. She uses them to prick at his hand, but he doesn't react to the pain.

His eyes are crazed as he looks at me, wide in terror, his pupils engulfing the whites of his eyes. His grip becomes even stronger as he bares his teeth at me, aggression rolling off him. He doesn't seem in control of his actions, merely responding to his instinctual need to get more of the drug.

"I'm really sorry," I try to placate him again. "We really have no money."

Thea digs her claws into his hand, drawing blood. At last, that seems to get a reaction out of him as he turns to her, his lips slowly pulling up in a sly smirk.

"You," he hisses. "You're one of them."

Thea blinks, her hand suddenly falling away as she takes a step back.

"We need to run, Luce," she whispers, and before I know it, she brings her clawed hand over his arm like a sword, detaching it at the wrist. His fingers dangle off my arm, but he doesn't even notice.

His expression turns covetous as he glances from Thea to me.

"You both are," he continues, taking a step forward.

His arm is bleeding onto the ground, but he ignores it. There's no flicker of pain on his face, nothing to denote he felt the blow. There's only his tunnel vision as he looks at us as if we're his next meal.

"Run," Thea says, taking my hand and pulling me into a sprint. And just like that, he follows, his feet moving with unnatural swiftness for someone his age.

"What's happening?" I ask, willing my legs to keep up with her speed.

"He doesn't need the money anymore. He knows how to get the zantrax from the source," she says, her breath coming in short spurts.

"The source? Us? But—"

"Zantrax is made from the essence of a god. Blood. Body parts. Hair. You name it. It's why it's illegal. And it seems our friend over there is still on his last dose, which means his strength might be even greater than mine," she adds in a scared voice.

I chance a glance back at the running old man. He has a crazed look on his face as he's maybe a few meters behind us. In a matter of seconds, he's going to catch us. There's no doubt about it.

"Faster," Thea urges.

There are other people on the sidelines. But they mind their own business, pretending we're not in danger—that nothing of consequence is happening right on the road in front of their house.

"I'm trying," I breathe out. My lungs are burning from the effort, and I don't know how long I can keep this up.

"He's almost—" She doesn't get to finish her sentence as we both fall to the ground. The man tackles us down, using his good arm to grasp at Thea while waving his amputated one in front of me, splattering blood in my face.

He's spouting some gibberish as he digs his fingers into Thea's arms, all the while hitting me with the protruding bones from his wrist.

I kick my feet at him, hitting him in the stomach, but he doesn't notice or budge. He's single-minded in his focus of getting to us.

Thea's panicking as she kicks him too, and she manages to get him to lose his balance enough for us to slip from under him. I drag myself to my knees, ready to sprint. Thea pulls me up, helping me. But we barely get to make a few steps as he throws himself forward, grabbing us by the legs and making us stumble again.

I fall flat on my belly, the pebbles in the hard asphalt molding to my skin. I groan in pain, my body momentarily shocked as adrenaline and fright fight for supremacy within me.

The man howls, a sharp, gut-turning cry as he blankets us with his body. Not a second after, though, and another sound pierces the air—one that sounds like an explosion.

Hot liquid sprays on top of us, together with other bits of debris as the weight on top of us is suddenly gone.

I blink in shock, slowly turning to look at Thea, who is equally stunned.

We both roll over and find ourselves in a bath of blood and guts. The man is gone. Liquefied. There's only the stain of red and putrid smell that's left behind.

We stare at each other for what seems like an eternity. We're both covered in blood...and other substances from head to toe.

FORTY-TWO

"W-what was that?" I mumble numbly.

She shakes her head, confused.

More people have appeared by the side of the road, coming out of their houses after hearing the commotion. But no one tries to help. No one asks us if we're okay, just as no one tried to stop the man assaulting us.

They're just watching the show, their expressions completely blank, as if this is just another everyday occurrence.

"Where the hell are you, Cer?" Thea screams out as she wobbles to her feet, shaking the remains of the man off her. I try to do the same, but my entire body is trembling, the fear I experienced locked inside of me and running in a loop.

"Are you all right, Luce?" she finally asks, breathing hard.

Her red hair is caked with a mix of blood and some of that blue substance, her clothes ruined. I glance down at my body, finding myself equally dirty.

Raising a hand up, I feel bits and pieces of organic matter stuck in my hair and on my hoodie, and I barely stop myself from heaving.

Slowly, I shake my head.

"What the hell was that?" I whisper.

"*That* is why I'm not allowed to go out on my own." She

sighs. "Gahh, where is Cer when I need him?" She stomps her foot on the ground.

But not a second after she utters his name, Cer appears in front of us. He looks us up and down, his nose wrinkling in disgust.

"I cannot leave you alone for one moment, can I?" He shakes his head.

"You could have come to get us! We just ran into an addict."

"You did that?" He raises a brow as he points to what's left of the man on the ground.

"No." She frowns. "He just exploded."

"Hm." He narrows his eyes. He scans the surroundings and notices the amassing crowd, as well as the glares he's receiving from the other people. "We need to leave."

Without waiting for us to reply, he grabs our hands and tele-ports us out.

Just like going through the portal, one second we're in the middle of the road, the next we're in a lush foyer the likes of which I've seen only in museums.

Marble columns are on each side of us, flowers in all shades of yellow and red curling from the ground up to the ceiling.

"Mother and Father don't know you're here yet. Make your-self presentable before you meet them," Cer says, turning to leave.

"Wha—" Thea blinks, grabbing his sleeve. "Where are you going?"

"I am needed. Aethon has gone missing."

"What do you mean?" She frowns.

Cer purses his lips.

"I don't know. It's not like him not to respond to summons."

"But he's *Aethon*. How could *he* have gone missing?" Thea pales.

"I aim to figure it out. Ze sent him to look into the demon incursions into the intermediary realms you witnessed." He nods at me. "Something is going on, and I don't like it."

"You don't think he's... dead?" Thea whispers.

He doesn't reply, his features taut. Removing her hand from his sleeve, he takes a step forward before he disappears.

Thea is left staring at the spot he's just vacated, her expression one of sorrow.

"Who's Aethon?" I ask, curious why she reacted like that to the mention of his name.

She takes a deep breath.

"He's Cer's best friend." She gives me a sad smile.

"I'm sorry," I try to comfort her.

"I'm sure he's fine. He's one of the most powerful deities I know. There's no way some demons could hurt him." She closes her eyes, her lips trembling. "Anyway." She blinks as she smiles forcefully. "Cer is right. My parents can't see me like this. Let's go inside and wash up."

I follow her as she opens a back door and leads me inside her home. We follow a narrow hallway, going up some stairs before we reach the ground floor. Yet what I failed to realize while being in the small yet beautiful foyer was that the main house would be so striking and so grand.

It must be the size of a football field. Or maybe two. Hell, the ceiling alone must be over fifty meters tall.

Everything is white and clean. While we are decidedly *not*.

The floors are polished to perfection, so much so I can see my grimy reflection in them—not to mention the fact that we're both dripping blood onto the ground. With everything so spotless, I have this unnatural urge to get down and scrub the stains away.

"Thea..." I whisper as I stop to simply stare at my surroundings.

Raising my gaze, I note a dome made out of diaphanous glass. The center is clear, allowing the unadulterated light from the sun to come down into the hallway, but surrounding it are stained glass windows of different colors containing artistic depictions. In fact, I'm shocked that they aren't too different from the church stained glass from my world.

I slowly take in the other features of the hallway—how is

this *just* the hallway? The most similar comparison I can think of is the Greco-Roman exhibit at the Met, but even that pales in comparison to the beauty of this place. There's a level of detail that's as close to perfection as I've ever seen.

Surrounding us are five marble busts, while in the center of the room, there's a statue that's about three times as tall as me.

There are more white marble columns to the right and left, all situated in a circle around the hallway. At the back, there's a double staircase leading up to the second floor. The stairs are wide and long, the balustrade containing battle scenes etched in marble. From the bottom up, the scenes feed into each other almost like a movie that tells the story of a historic event.

"That's Alithea, the first Supreme from our family. The busts are the subsequent ones." She points to the statues.

"I think this would be the best time to tell me if you're a princess or something," I mumble, utterly in awe of the beauty before me.

I might have been to some luxurious places on Earth, but this? Nothing I've seen compares.

"Not a princess." She laughs. "My father is just a duke."

I swivel to stare at her.

"*Just* a duke?"

"Well, there are also archdukes and princes, and then there's the king. So we're not anywhere in the top three." She chuckles.

"If this is not even top three, I can't imagine what that would look like," I mutter.

An army of servants descends upon the hallway, all getting into a well-rehearsed formation as they surround us.

"Welcome home, my lady," they all say in chorus, not even daring to look at Thea.

"Are my parents home?"

"Their graces are away," one servant answers.

"What about Arwyn?"

"Her ladyship is with them as well. They are scheduled to return late afternoon."

Thea clicks her tongue against her teeth.

"When they arrive, tell them I'll meet them at dinnertime. Also let them know I brought a friend with me who's going to be our guest of honor."

"Yes, my lady."

"Thank you." She nods with a smile before she scans the servants, zeroing in on a woman. "You." She points at her. "Please see my friend to one of the guest rooms. The best one."

The servant immediately nods.

"And you." She points to another. "Please go to my seamstress and see what readymade gowns she has. Get everything she has available and deliver them to my friend's room."

"Yes, my lady," the servant bows.

This is all so foreign to me, I can only stare in wonder.

"Go with her, Luce. She'll show you to a room and you can clean up and rest. I'll have some food sent up as well, and I'll come get you when it's dinnertime to meet my parents."

I nod slowly.

"Do you think"—I swallow—"that they're going to have a problem with me being human?"

Considering what I've experienced so far, I need to ask.

"Don't worry about it." She waves her hand. "They'll love you."

I give her a faint smile, somehow not convinced.

She doesn't go into detail, though, telling me to follow the servant while she goes to her room.

The servant stops in front of me, her head bowed down. She's a woman in her forties or fifties, but I can't make out her features because her eyes are rooted to the floor.

"This way, please," she says.

"Thank you," I murmur as I follow her up the luscious staircase. We make a right turn, and that's where the real beauty of this place is.

Painting after painting adorns the walls. They're all so damn beautiful, I wish I had the time to stop and admire them. But with the brisk way the older lady is walking, I find it hard to keep up, let alone linger.

We move swiftly through another gallery, and I vow to take my time later on to study it—if I'm allowed, of course. As we walk down a long corridor, there are doors on my right and left—I assume these are all rooms.

She leads me all the way to the end of the corridor, where an ornate alcove separates the area from the rest. Upon stepping foot inside, I note two more doors, one on each side.

"This will be your room," she motions to the door on the right. "It is ready and equipped with everything you should need. The washroom has fresh towels and toiletries, but should you require something more, please ring for me."

"Ring?" I blink.

She opens the door, pointing to a button in the door's frame.

"One touch of a button and I shall be right with you."

"Oh. Thank you."

"If you'll excuse me," she says, still not looking at me as she scurries away.

I step inside the room, closing the door behind me.

I'm not sure what I expected. Certainly, after seeing the *hallways*, I don't think I had any expectation, since I was sure nothing could live up to any prior knowledge I had of luxury.

But this...

The entire room is rose gold, the walls adorned with marble panels in the same shade, containing more artworks.

In the middle, there's a double king-sized bed—that's the only way I could describe it since I've never seen something so utterly immense. The bedding is a darker shade of rose gold, all matching the environment.

But the most stunning feature of this room is the back of it.

There are floor-to-ceiling windows across the entire wall. I walk deeper into the room, and the view simply takes my breath away.

There's a sprawling garden in front, with intricate shapes molded from trees. Intermingled in the green space are marble gazebos and other beautiful statues, while in the middle, there's an enormous fountain, water pouring out from a jug held by an equally imposing figure of a woman. Immediately, I recognize it to be the representation of the statue from the hallway—the first Supreme. The basin is surrounded by a mix of marble and flowers, highlighting the contrast between nature and man-made.

Only in the distance do I see other equally ostentatious palaces, though they're so far I can barely make out their shapes.

Thea had said her father is merely a duke. But this is far more extravagant than any ducal estate I've seen in history books or period dramas.

Though I'd like nothing more than to admire the view some more, the smell wafting from my body is becoming increasingly harder to ignore. While I wait for the dresses Thea asked for me, I should at least wash myself and remove this stench.

Throwing another glance around the room, I release a satisfied sigh as I imagine rolling around in those luxurious sheets after I've bathed. It feels like forever ago that I enjoyed a modicum of comfort, and my body yearns for it.

As I tentatively open the door to the bathroom, I'm once more taken aback by the extravagant design.

The walls follow the same rose-gold theme, with the furniture made entirely out of marble. There's a vanity right by the entrance, and I note a variety of products spread out on the counter.

In the middle of the room is the bathtub—if I can call it that. The sheer size alone makes it more like a pool than a tub. I get giddy just looking at it since I'm in dire need of a good soak. At the very back, I make out a waterfall shower.

Stepping farther into the room, I pass by the toilet and the accompanying washing facilities. Everything is spotless, and I'm at once scared to stain it with my clothes. I look around in search of an area to deposit my soiled garments, but I eventually decide to just place them over the sink.

Slowly, as to not drip more grime onto the clean surface of the bathroom, I remove my clothes. My hoodie is entirely ruined, and I don't think I can salvage it. But the leggings are still in good condition and would be wearable after a good wash.

Unfortunately, my white sports bra is completely stained, so I'll have to discard it. My socks are too dirty to keep, and even my shoes look as if they've been bombarded with a cocktail of blood and guts—not salvageable either.

I release a sigh as I place them by the sink, silently hoping Thea would give me a new pair of shoes, too.

Once I'm naked, I head to the tub, fiddling with the faucet until I get the right temperature for the water. While the tub is filling, I decide to use the waterfall shower to clean most of the grime off me. I may be dying to soak in warm, clean water, but if I step inside the tub as I am, that water will be decidedly *not* clean.

It takes me a good ten minutes of scrubbing to get everything out of my hair. But after I feel I've cleaned most of the blood off me, I turn off the water and move to the tub. I dip my toes into the warm water before slowly submerging myself.

"Oh my," I whimper as all that warmth envelops my body, cocooning me in sublime comfort. This is dangerous. I need to make sure I don't fall asleep since my eyes are already drooping.

Smiling, I let myself relax and forget everything that has happened in the last few days. Unfortunately, no matter how much I try to expunge the disappointment from my heart, I cannot seem to do so.

My thoughts stray to the *what-ifs*—if Ze had been with us, we wouldn't have been attacked. If he'd been with us, we would have never been targeted or singled out in the first place.

If he...

"I'm so damn silly," I groan, submerging myself entirely underwater.

I hold my breath as I squeeze my eyes shut, hoping that by cleansing my body I could cleanse my heart and soul too.

"Damn it," I breathe out as I come up for air.

My limbs are trembling, my heart beating loudly in my chest.

Instead of the relaxing bath I was hoping for, I just made myself more anxious with thoughts of Ze.

"He doesn't deserve it," I mutter to myself as I get out of the tub. "He's a bad man. A bad, bad man. So what if he was nice to me once?"

Grabbing a towel, I wipe my body and dry my hair as best as I can.

"Okay, maybe he was nice to me more than once. But that doesn't change his behavior or his insults," I tell myself with a nod.

Stopping by the vanity, I look around the various containers until I find some moisturizer. I leave my towel on the chair as I apply generous amounts of the cream all over my face and body. And because I haven't experienced such luxury in so long, I also dab some perfume behind my ears and on my inner wrists.

There's a wide selection available, but I go for a tuberose one, needing some flowery sweetness to banish the melancholy of my soul—but also because this happens to be Nikki's favorite.

When I'm done, I twirl around a few times to let the moisture sink in before I go back to the bedroom, ready to jump on the bed and close my eyes.

Yet as soon as I open the door, I spot a shimmering mist hovering right at the edge of the bed. The shadow takes the form of a man when I come closer, but particles of sparkling dust still hover in the air.

"Nikki?" I whisper in shock. I wouldn't have expected him to show up here, or now. "How did you get here?"

The shimmer intensifies.

"Where you go, I go. I thought you knew that by now," he says, his voice low and gravelly, echoing into the large enclosure. I don't think I'll get used to this disembodied voice of his anytime soon, yet I'll always be grateful to have at least this.

"You were able to follow?"

He nods.

I walk closer to him, ignoring the fact that I'm not wearing any clothes—it's not as if he hasn't seen me like this before. At least now I smell good—although I'm not sure if his ghost has any olfactory capabilities.

"Can you smell me?" I blurt out.

"What?"

"Never mind, that was a silly question," I mutter under my breath.

"Now I'm curious what you meant. Tell me," he murmurs, bringing his hand to my face, his cold fingers caressing my heated cheek.

I avert my gaze, blushing furiously.

"I felt good for the first time in forever. Clean. Pretty..." I trail off. "And I know you love this scent on me, so I thought maybe... I'm so silly, aren't I?" I shake my head, a sad smile painted on my lips. "You're just a ghost and here I am wondering if you can smell me, or if you're still attracted to me," I add in a low whisper.

"Luce, look at me."

He tips my chin up to look into his shadowy face. I try with all my might to imagine the features of the man I love in its place. He might not look like the man I'm used to, but he feels like it—mine, just like I am his. And to my shame, I crave him all the same. Black shadows or human form, I desire him just as much—maybe more due to this prolonged absence.

"I'm a mass of atoms. And they all vibrate in concert with yours. I may not be fully corporeal, but I can still feel you."

His tendril-like fingers caress my face, going lower.

"I'll *always* feel you," he whispers.

His touch is cool, yet it burns my skin all the same. Moving down my neck, to my chest, he pauses when he reaches my breasts.

I hold my breath as he makes contact with my sensitive nipples. A shiver goes down my back as desire pools low in my belly.

Is it unnatural to want him like this? Is it so abnormal to desire him in any shape or form?

"I missed this," I whimper breathlessly.

"You did?" he asks, his voice rough.

I nod fervently, keeping myself still for fear this moment will be over and I'll be left bereft once more.

"Tell me more, sweetheart. What else did you miss?"

He teases my breasts just enough to get my heart rate up and fill my head with countless scenarios. But as he continues his journey down my body, a new type of want blossoms inside of me. One that cannot possibly be normal, but it feels right nonetheless.

"You. Inside me," I whisper, my cheeks reddening. "Filling this aching emptiness."

I never saw myself as a sexual being before him. He awoke my desire, lighting a flame inside of me that's been fighting to stay alive after his death.

"

Sweetheart," he groans.

He trails his fingers lower, hovering over my belly.

I'm so gone that not even the presence of my scars bothers me anymore. They are a part of me, and *every* part of me is his.

"You're so beautiful," he rasps in a ragged voice. "Most beautiful thing I've ever seen."

He reaches between my legs, and before I can anticipate what he means to do, he plunges two thick fingers inside me.

I gasp at the sharp intrusion and struggle to keep my balance as I hold on to his shoulders. Shadowy tendrils wrap themselves around my arms as he keeps me in place, bringing me closer to him.

"So warm," he speaks, his tone one of awe. "So tight."

He thrusts his fingers all the way inside me, and I struggle to keep a straight face as he pumps them in and out.

"A bit slower," I tell him with a wobbly smile. "It's been a while."

My inner muscles struggle to accommodate the girth of his fingers, a stinging sensation echoing around my entrance.

"How long?" he barks as he rests his head on top of my shoulder, the shadows enveloping his body becoming wilder, more out of control. Shimmery particles circle around us like a cocoon.

"You know," I answer.

"Tell me," he demands, his fingers curling inside of me and making me tense. I dig my nails into his shoulders, but they easily slip through the undulating shadows that become increasingly more chaotic.

"Since the day of the accident," I whisper. "Please tell me you're not still jealous."

He doesn't reply.

"You're not jealous, are you?" I repeat, a little apprehensive.

"With you, jealousy is a constant state of being," he says tensely.

I blink in confusion.

"But you know I'd never..."

"Luce," he calls my name in a strangled voice. "You are mine. Do you understand that?"

He thrusts into me again, more forcefully.

"Say it," he urges, flattening the back of his palm against my mound and cupping my sex, his fingers buried deep inside of me.

The shadows cling to him like smoke clings to a flame, growing bigger and bigger as his emotions heighten.

Inside me, his touch is cold yet hot, a paradox I cannot explain. A pleasure marred by pain I should not enjoy—yet I do anyway.

"I'm yours." I swallow. "I'll always be yours."

More dark tendrils slither from him, enveloping me entirely. The speed of his pumps increases too, and tears stab at my eyes from the mix of pain and pleasure.

A sharp cry resounds in the air, one I barely recognize as my own voice.

"Please." I tug at him.

I'm unused to this side of him, but more than anything, I'm surprised by my reaction to it—by the fact that a part of me craves this harsh claiming.

Our lovemaking has always been gentle, mostly due to my past and the fact that he never wanted to do anything that might make me uncomfortable. But I've always known there was more to him—a raging storm masked by an undisturbed calm. There were moments I witnessed this untamed side of his, just as there were moments I wished he'd give in and simply take me.

Just like this. A wild, intense, almost primitive mating that has nothing to do with reason, only feeling.

Only unfettered desire.

Before I can draw in my next breath, I find myself on the bed with him looming over me, his fingers still inside me as he adds a third digit.

I thrash against the cool sheets, the sting of his possession searing itself on my flesh.

I'm full. So full.

"Nikki," I whisper, cupping his face and staring at those maddening shadows. "I'm yours. Never doubt that," I say as I tilt my hips, urging him on. A tingle goes down my spine, my muscles clenching as I tighten my grip on him.

I throw my head back as my breathing intensifies, the pain giving way to the sweetest pleasure. A little more. Just a little...

A knock at the door puts a stop to everything.

"Miss, I have brought your dresses," a feminine voice says from the other side.

Before I can blink, I'm all alone in the room, the shadows dissipating until the soreness between my legs is the only thing attesting he was here at all.

I quickly get out of bed and run to the bathroom to put on a bathrobe before opening the door and instructing the maid to leave everything on the table in the back.

She does as told, and as she leaves, I lock the door after her.

My heart is thumping loudly in my chest, my mind barely able to make sense of what just happened. A trickle of wetness slides down my inner thigh, and I get some tissue to wipe myself. As I part my robe to look between my legs, I'm not surprised to see a pinkish liquid cling to my skin—a combination of blood and arousal.

He wasn't gentle with me. He was rough and demanding. And despite the lingering sting of pain, I find myself wishing the maid hadn't knocked on the door.

Maybe I shouldn't even entertain thoughts of doing this with him as he is now, but the only regret I have is that we didn't finish what we started.

I didn't finish, despite being so close.

"Oh, Nikki. Ghost or not, you always like to torture me." I tsk to myself.

A smile plays on my lips as I wipe off the residual blood.

Yet now that this has happened, the idea of intimacy is sown into my mind, and I can't help but wonder.

Could we go further?

Could we...

The thought alone makes me blush to the roots of my hair. I don't care how taboo or wrong this may be.

He's my husband.

And shadows or not, I'll always welcome him in my body.

Even when his touch holds a bite of pain.

Maybe even more then.

FORTY-THREE

Incessant knocking at the door wakes me up from my nap. I yawn, rubbing my eyes as I fling the sheets off me and get out of bed.

"Luce! It's me!" Thea calls out from the other side.

As I unlock the door, she barely gives me time to react before she barges in, her arms full of boxes.

"My parents are home. We need to get ready for dinner," she casually says as she drops the boxes to the ground.

I blink at her, confused.

"Uhm, what?" I ask groggily.

"I brought you some shoes to choose from. I think I got your size right," she says as she eyes my feet pensively. "You have tiny feet, so I got the smallest size. I'll also do your hair and makeup," she drones on, and it's then that I realize that her hair is already styled in a prim bun at the back of her head, her makeup simple yet elegant, with lip gloss, peachy blush, and winged eyeliner. She's wearing a beige dress made out of a combination of silk and lace, the silhouette fitting her perfectly and accentuating the contours of her body but without seeming too risqué.

"Is it that formal?"

"Unfortunately." She rolls her eyes. "My father is a stickler for propriety. My mother is a bit more lax, but she still follows his decrees. If you are out of your room, then you must be presentable. It's all about image." She clicks her tongue.

"Oh. Let me quickly wash my face."

I go to the bathroom and splash some water on my face in an attempt to chase the sleepiness away. The cold water is refreshing, and I soon feel slightly more alert.

"Come." Thea waves me over to the vanity. "We'll do hair and makeup first and then dress and shoes. Okay?"

"Sounds good." I nod. "Are you sure it's all right for me to be here, though? You know, with me being human and all that..." I trail off. Her attempts to beautify me and make me presentable for her parents make me doubt I'll get a good reception, particularly since her kind seems to look down on humans.

"What? Of course not. I told you, they won't mind it. They'll be so happy I brought a friend, they won't even care you're human." She chuckles. "Besides, this is to my advantage as well since it will take the focus off me."

She takes a jar of cream and starts applying it to my face.

"What do you mean?" I frown.

"The same old." She shakes her head. "My parents, well, my father mostly, want to see me mated and married off as soon as possible, so he's been adamant about arranging meetings for me with single males. It's one of his greatest shames that his oldest daughter is still unmated at this age." She sighs dramatically.

"But you're not old," I protest.

She smiles.

"I might not seem old, but I'm six thousand eight hundred years. In our world, that's three thousand years over the marriageable age. I'm considered an old maid." She chuckles.

"But your brother isn't mated, and he's older than you. So is Ze."

"For them it's different. They are considered an asset for Aperion due to their role in the military, so no one is forcing them. For me, however..."

Opening a drawer, she studies the assortment of cosmetics, chooses a few, and places them on the vanity. She unscrews a jar with what looks to be foundation, and she starts applying it all over my face.

"I should have been mated a long time ago, but I managed to put it off because I was still working on my qualifying exams. But lately my father has become obsessed with finding me someone. In our world, especially for the upper class, it's frowned upon if a female is not married by a certain age," she explains.

"And you don't want that?" I ask. "You don't wish to have a family someday?"

A sad smile pulls at her lips.

"It is not that I do not wish to have a family. Rather, it's that I do not want any of the males my father thinks would be suitable for me. And..." she trails off, nibbling at her lip.

She's quiet for a moment as she finishes applying the foundation, after which she dusts some creamy pink blush on my cheeks.

"I trust you, Luce," she finally takes a deep breath. "This isn't something...that I normally advertise, because, well, Ze was right. It could get me shunned, or worse, killed."

I blink in surprise, but I don't probe, letting her tell me at her own pace.

"Our world is very strict. Unions within the upper class have to be approved by the Supremes. And despite Ze's protestations, this world is much harsher on females than it is on males."

"Is it because you haven't passed your exams then?"

"If only it were just that." She gives a dry laugh. "Females of my class are expected to be...pure." She swallows. "There have been cases in which a female did not come to her mate untouched, and the male reported her to the authorities. Not only was she and her family shamed, but she was also imprisoned for her offense."

"What?" I ask, my eyes widening. "Imprisoned?"

"Our class is in power due to our abilities. Without them, we wouldn't be here. The gods wouldn't be here. The universe as we know it wouldn't be here. So the rules are made to ensure those abilities are passed on. But more than anything, a female's first child is *always* the most powerful. And power is the goal of every union. The male that reported his mate? He did it because he considered himself cheated out of a powerful offspring."

"But what does her not being a virgin have anything to do with children?"

"Because if she came to him touched by another, he could not be sure she did not bear a child in the past, thereby depriving him of his powerful firstborn. That entitles him to compensation from the female's family and a harsh punishment for her."

"Wow... I have no words, Thea. I gathered that your world wasn't very nice to women, but I didn't realize it was this bad."

"Individuals don't matter. It's all about power and prestige. Every family measures their worth by the number of Supremes they produced."

I nod, my heart hurting for her.

"Were you...in love with him?" I ask tentatively.

She releases a bitter laugh.

"Maybe it would have been better if it had been some great love story. It was one time only, and I was so intoxicated I barely remember a single thing. Just...the morning after. The shame." She pauses, squeezing her eyes shut.

"Thea." I reach for her hand. "Did he take advantage of you?"

She shakes her head.

"We were both inebriated. Not that it makes it any better. But it was my fault... I..." She swallows a sob as she brings the back of her hand to wipe off the moisture clinging to her lashes. "If my father forces me to marry someone, it will be all over. I can't bring that type of shame to my family. I couldn't bear to see them disappointed in me."

"Why don't you tell him then? Surely, if he knows how this would affect you, he would stop pressuring you."

"That's the thing, Luce. I don't know which one is worse. My father finding out, or the world finding out."

I stare at her and it finally dawns on me that behind her

easygoing appearance hides a mountain of turmoil—oh, and how well it hides. She has everybody fooled that she's some type of carefree rebel, but she's only a woman trying to survive in a world that has her cornered.

"Is this what Ze threatened you with?"

She nods as she dries her tears, patting her face with a napkin to fix her ruined makeup.

"He saw me. The morning after, he saw me leave the male's room. And since then, he's been holding it over my head. One wrong move, and he threatened to expose me."

I shake my head in disappointment. How could he do that to her? Knowing the type of secret he's been blackmailing her with makes me realize just how badly I misjudged him.

"I have a question, and I don't want you to take it the wrong way." When she nods for me to continue, I ask, "Why would you tell me something so sensitive? If it's so dangerous for you, why would you risk it?"

A faraway look appears on her face.

"Ze was right about one thing. I... I don't have the best reputation in Arche. I have no girlfriends. No one to talk to, really. There is my sister, but she's too young to understand. I guess..." She sighs deeply. "I needed to tell someone and I thought you wouldn't judge me."

Getting up from my chair, I take a tentative step toward her. I open my arms for her and she comes easily, hugging me tightly as more tears fall down her cheek.

"Never," I whisper. "I swear to you I'll *never* say a word of what you just told me. Your secret is safe with me, Thea," I whisper.

She cries harder, sobs racking her entire body.

"I'm sorry to burden you with this," she says brokenly. "I think being home just got to me and I..."

"No. Don't even mention it. We're friends, are we not?"

"Thank you." She swallows hard. "Thank you."

"I'll do what I can to help you avoid any talk of marriage," I tell her, slowly patting her back.

She nods, leaning back to grab more tissues, blows her nose, and wipes the smudged eyeliner from under her eyes. It takes her a few moments to get herself under control as her sobs subside, but the same helplessness is still echoed in her features.

"Is this why you're still in the game? Why you didn't quit when Ze and Cer did?"

Her lips flatten into a thin line.

"If I can take advantage of that loophole, I want to do it. It might be my only way out of this."

"Then all the more reason to win." I smile.

"You're right. We need to win." She pushes her chin up, newfound confidence slowly suffusing her features. "Now let's get ready for this dinner."

She quickly does my makeup before fixing hers. For my hair, she does a single braid that she wraps into a bun at the back of my head.

When we're done with that, she helps me pick a dress and shoes suitable for the occasion. And to make me feel more confident since the dress has a lower neckline, Thea covers the marks on my chest with foundation.

"This is such a pretty gown," I whisper, feeling both pretty *and* like myself for the first time in forever. I glance at my reflection in the mirror, and the lack of dark spots on my skin shows me the *what-ifs*—who I would be without the stain of my past to always remind me I'm still a prisoner despite being free.

The dress is long, a light pink color, with an empire waist and square neckline. The sleeves are made of diaphanous lace that flows down my arms. Although simple in design, the luxurious fabric elevates the entire look.

For the shoes, she gives me a pair of white slippers with a little bit of heel and a single jewel on the tip.

"You look so beautiful." She nods, pleased with her work.

As she regards me, her head tilts to the side, a look of concentration on her face. Slowly, her lips spread in a smile.

"My sister is on her way here. I hope you don't mind," she mentions.

Not a moment later, someone knocks on the door.

Thea opens it to receive her, immediately wrapping her arms around her and hugging her tight.

"Thea, you were gone for so long," the girl cries out, her voice young and lively.

"I know. I'm so sorry I wasn't here," Thea comforts her.

They stay like that for moments on end before Thea draws back, a look of happiness unlike any I've seen before settling on her face.

"Come meet my friend," she says, pulling her inside the room and closing the door.

"Luce, this is Wyn," Thea introduces her, and I give her a bright smile.

"Pleased to meet you."

She returns the smile, bending down in a curtsy. She's so damn cute that I can't help but warm up to her right away.

She looks to be about seventeen or eighteen, her hair black as midnight while her eyes are a startling green. She's dressed in a pale green gown adorned by golden ribbons. The style is similar to the one Thea and I are wearing, with an empire waist and long, wide sleeves.

Her hair is tied down her back with a dark green silk fabric.

Yet the most startling thing is how much she looks like Thea. Aside from their different colorings, their features are the same, so much so they could pass as twins. The only difference is that Thea is much taller while Wyn is closer to me in height.

"You brought a friend?" Wyn squeaks as she looks me up and down. "It's so nice to meet you, Luce. Welcome to our home. I'm so happy Thea finally brought over a friend," she says excitedly, coming closer and grabbing my arms. "You're going to stay with us for a while, right? My debut is in a few weeks, and I would love for you to join us."

"Debut?" I blink, sneaking a glance at Thea.

"It's her official debut into adulthood," she explains in a soft voice. "Our kind reaches majority at three thousand years old. She's also going to start her qualifying exams soon."

Wyn turns to her sister and mouths, "Our kind?"

"Luce is human."

Wyn's eyes widen.

"You're human? I've never met a human before," she declares, her eyes sparkling with excitement—not at all the reaction I was expecting. She circles around me, studying me full of curiosity. "I didn't expect this," she adds pensively as she stops in front of me.

"That bad?" I chuckle.

"Oh no. You're so pretty. The humans I've seen in picture books were...not." She flashes me a guilty smile.

"I'm glad I surpassed your expectations."

"You have no idea how happy I am you're here," she continues. "When Thea told me she brought a friend, I couldn't believe it! She's never had anyone over."

"Luce is special," Thea adds. "You know I have high standards for people," she huffs in good humor.

"Maybe *too* high." Wyn coughs, and Thea raises a brow at her.

"You little..." Thea shakes her head. "Just because you're the queen of popularity doesn't mean I have to be too."

"No, but you could use more fun. When I heard you were away, I was so happy thinking you might meet someone and—"

The mood instantly changes as Thea's face drops. Wyn notices this too as she quickly amends with a blush. "Well, you met Luce. Our parents will be happy too. Mother's been worried sick when you were gone for so long."

"Were they too angry?" Thea asks tentatively.

"They were when they first noticed you were missing. But Cer assured them you were fine and that he was with you. You know how much Father trusts him."

"Right." Thea forces a smile. "He's the favorite."

"Oh, don't say that. Even with his assurances, Mother was constantly thinking of you. She tried to reach you countless times and she couldn't, so you'll have some explaining to do for that."

"I'm prepared for their lengthy speeches, trust me." She sighs.

"Don't worry too much." Wyn winks at Thea. "With my ball coming up, there's so much to plan and discuss, I'm sure they won't mind your disappearance too much."

"But that's just the thing, Wyn. Your ball is just another opportunity for them to make me meet eligible males. And you know how much I hate that."

Wyn sighs.

"I know, but I'll make them promise not to try anything. I'll tell them I don't want you to steal my shine." She giggles.

"You're a gem, Wyn." Thea smiles.

"In return, you must do something for me," her sister adds conspiratorially.

"What do you want?"

"You must ensure that Aethon will be present at my ball," Wyn says bashfully, her cheeks tinted with pink.

Aethon? The Aethon that is missing?

"Wyn, we've talked about this before." Thea purses her lips. "He's too old for you."

"He's *not*!" Wyn exclaims. "Why, Father is several thousand years older than Mother and their union was perfectly acceptable."

"We're talking about more than several thousand years," Thea adds in an exasperated voice. "He's close to fifteen thousand years old."

"So?"

"It's just a crush, Wyn. You'll get over it when you meet other males—more suitable ones."

"No." She shakes her head. "It's not *just* a crush."

"Wyn." Thea sighs. "He hasn't taken a mate in all this time. What does that tell you?"

"That he's been waiting for the right female to come along." Wyn bats her lashes. "As in, *me*," she says as she does a little twirl. "He just needs to come to my ball and see me all dolled up, and I'm sure he'll propose," she adds dreamily.

"I'm sure there's nothing wrong with her crush," I interject, unable to keep silent as I witness Wyn's enthusiasm.

Thea shoots me a warning look.

"There's plenty wrong with her crush. I don't want her to get her hopes up and get heartbroken."

"I won't!" Wyn protests. "He's the right male for me. I *know* it."

"He's not right for you, Wyn." Thea sighs.

Wyn takes a step back, her shoulders slumping.

"What you mean to say is that *I* am not right for him, no?" she asks in a low, hurt voice.

"That's not..."

"You don't think I'm worthy enough to be considered by him, isn't that right? After all, I'm only the thirdborn and I haven't exhibited any special abilities while he's the firstborn of the House of Pyros."

"I didn't say that."

"You didn't have to. I know very well what my place in society is. I know that he's far above me in, well, everything. But that doesn't mean anything. He *likes* me. I know he does. He always brings me gifts when he comes to visit. Just a few weeks ago he came and brought me this," she says as she rolls up her sleeve to reveal a pretty diamond bracelet with two Ws intertwined.

Thea's eyes widen as she grabs her hand, closely studying the bracelet.

"You saw him? When?"

Wyn blinks.

"When you and Cer were gone," she answers weakly.

"Tell me you were not alone with him, Wyn. Tell me," she demands sharply, her fingers tightening around the girl's wrist.

"Thea... What..."

"Were you alone with him, Wyn?"

"Y-yes, but I've been alone with him before..." she stammers, a look of confusion crossing her face.

"When you were a child!" Thea exclaims. "This is different," she murmurs, breathing harshly. "Did he touch you? Did he do anything untoward?"

"Thea, you're hurting me," Wyn whimpers.

"Answer me, Arwyn. Did he touch you?"

"He k-kissed me."

Thea's features darken, her nostrils flaring.

God, I've never seen her like this before.

"On my forehead," Wyn hurries to add.

"Thea, calm down," I whisper as I come to her side, trying to get her to release Wyn, who is already frightened by her outburst.

"He kissed you. And he's been giving you gifts," Thea repeats numbly. "Cer is going to kill him," she mutters under her breath.

"No, please, no. Don't tell him. Please," Wyn pleads with her. "It was just a friendly kiss. He wouldn't take advantage of me..."

"This isn't *friendly*, Wyn." Thea points to her bracelet. "Don't tell me you don't know what these stones are or how much they are worth."

Wyn swallows.

"He was just being nice."

Thea lets out a dry laugh.

"I'm going to have a serious talk with him about this. You're not even out in society and he's giving you gifts? Kissing your forehead? Goodness, Wyn, if anyone found out, you would be ruined. *Ruined*."

"But—"

"No buts. You are not to *ever* be alone with him. If he likes you so much, he'll go to Father and declare his intentions, though I doubt that will happen." She shakes her head. "And this?" She takes the bracelet off. "You can't tell anyone about this. Do you understand me?"

"You can't just take it. It's mine..." Wyn adds weakly as she tries to get back her bracelet.

"Do you understand me?" Thea repeats, raising her arm and keeping the bracelet out of reach.

Wyn blinks back tears as her eyes flit from her sister to the bracelet.

She gives her a reluctant nod before she flies out of the room, sobs echoing in her wake.

As the door closes behind her, Thea releases a deep breath as she sinks to the floor.

"Are you all right?" I whisper as I sit next to her, reaching out to pat her shoulder.

She shakes her head, her features tense as she tries to hold back her tears.

"She can't end up like me. I won't allow it. I won't," she mumbles as she draws her knees to her chest. "I thought her crush on Aethon was just a silly thing she'd grow out of. I didn't realize... I should have paid more attention to her."

"Is he so bad? He's Cer's friend, isn't he?"

"He's not bad. But he will *never* mate her. Of that I am sure."

"But why? She's such a beautiful and lively girl..."

"She is, isn't she?" Thea smiles. "But it's not enough. The Supremes will never allow him to mate with any random female. He's one of the last of his bloodline, and that means he has a duty to perpetuate his line. The only way he can success-fully do so is by mating with a compatible female."

"Does Wyn know this?"

Thea shakes her head. "No. She's so innocent. We've all done our best to keep her away from politics. But she will need to know soon."

"She'll understand you want the best for her."

"I hope so."

The time comes for us to head to dinner, and we head down to the dining room. I'm a little nervous about being introduced to Thea's parents, but I hope everything will be fine.

As we reach the dining room, there are servants lined up on each side.

In the middle of the room there's a giant table that must seat over twenty or thirty people—then again, I wouldn't expect any less considering what I've seen of the house so far.

Wyn is already sitting down and staring dejectedly into her plate.

She raises her gaze when we enter the room, but she doesn't say anything. Thea nibbles on her lower lip worriedly, and she takes a seat right next to her sister, motioning for me to sit next to her.

"Wyn, I'm sorry," she whispers as she places her hand over her sister's. "You know I just want the best for you, don't you?"

Wyn slowly nods, her lips trembling.

"It was my bracelet," she speaks in a low voice, not glancing at Thea. "I promise not to do anything improper, but may I have it back?"

Thea's features are tense as she debates what to do.

"Do you give me your vow that you will not allow any intimacy from a male who is not your mate?"

Wyn's eyes flare open as she stares at Thea.

"I vow it," she quickly says.

Thea sighs and, reaching inside her small reticule, she takes out the bracelet and fastens it around Wyn's wrist.

"Thank you," she says thickly. "I promise I'll be careful, Thea. I don't want you to be upset with me."

"I'm not." Thea smiles, patting her on her head. "I love you, Wyn."

"I love you too." She nods, a smile finally probing at her lips.

Watching their interaction warms my heart and makes me yearn for it too. Thea has no idea how lucky she is to have such a loving family, despite the unfortunate circumstances of her position.

Neither Nikki nor I had that, and to an extent, it made us closer since we were all the other had. It was perhaps the reason why we decided to wait to have a child, too. It had always been a goal, but we wanted to spend as much time with each other as possible first.

I gulp down against the deluge of feelings that clogs my throat.

We put it off so much and now we might not be in a position to have it.

I plaster a pleasant smile on my face as I try to immerse myself in the conversation and not dwell on those gloomy thoughts.

Animated once more, Wyn tells us about all the gowns she commissioned for her ball, as well as her vision for the event.

"According to the latest count, there will be at least five hundred people—" She pauses as both she and Thea stand up. She motions for me to do the same.

I blink in confusion as I look around, but not a moment later, a man and a woman enter the room—her parents.

They look to be in their thirties, barely older than Cer and Thea. The man has dark hair and tawny skin while the woman has Thea's red hair and a creamy complexion. They're both dressed in formal clothes, with Thea's father wearing a white suit adorned with gold while her mother is wearing a deep red gown with matching gold jewelry.

"Erithea, you are back," her mother exclaims when she sees her.

"Yes, Mother." Thea nods, a shy smile on her face.

They come around to greet us, stopping right in front of us.

Thea's mother moves to give her a hug while her father is standing behind. They don't seem to notice me just yet, their attention wholly focused on their daughter.

"You and I need to have a talk later. It is not at all like you to disappear for so long without a word."

"I thought Cer told you—"

"Your brother has a soft spot for you, Erithea. He will always take your side, even when you are in the wrong."

Thea blushes as she averts her gaze.

"But enough of that for now. I heard you have brought a guest?" she asks as she turns to me. Her eyes widen and she goes pale for a moment.

"You..." She opens and closes her mouth as she sways from side to side.

Her husband places a hand at her back, steadying her.

"This is my friend, Luce," Thea quickly introduces me. "These are my parents, Maros and Rhea, the Duke and Duchess of Sigmore."

"Pleased to meet you, Your Graces," I murmur, attempting a curtsy.

"Luce..." Rhea swallows. "For a moment, I thought you were someone else. She looks identical, does she not, Maros?"

"The resemblance is, indeed, uncanny," he grunts.

I frown, not understanding what they're talking about, but Rhea quickly recovers and gives me a smile.

"Do not mind me. You just reminded me of an old friend who has passed on. It has been many years since I last thought of her," she adds fondly.

"She's human, Mother," Thea whispers.

"She is?" Rhea's eyes widen. "Well, that is a surprise. We have never had a human over. Please be seated. It is our pleasure to host Erithea's friends."

"You mean her *first* friend," Wyn adds mischievously.

"Young lady." Rhea does a good job of appearing scandalized even as her lips curl around the corners.

Thea straightens her back as she threads her arm through mine, pulling me closer. "She is a dear friend, and she will stay with us for a time. I trust that is all right with you, Mother, Father?"

"Of course, of course." Rhea smiles, though Maros is still staring at me skeptically. "Why don't we start eating, and your friend can tell us more about herself."

We all sit down, and the servants bring the first course in. But just as they settle the plates in front of us, a sudden noise erupts from the back of the house, followed by a flurry of movement.

A man in a blue uniform enters the dining hall, and we all turn to stare at him.

"All rise. Commander Azerius has arrived," he declares in a formal tone.

Rhea and Maros promptly get to their feet, and I note that Thea and Wyn do the same, so I follow along.

"Who is that?" I lean in to whisper to Thea when I note the sudden change in her demeanor. Her lip is twitching in displeasure, her hands curled into fists by her side. Based on this grand entrance and the way her parents are reacting, it must be someone very important—at least someone with a higher rank.

Heavy steps echo in the hallway before the man in question, Commander Azerius, comes into view.

"You have got to be fucking kidding me," I mutter under my breath, my eyes widening with shock.

FORTY-FOUR

Commander Azerius. *Ze.* Just another thing he lied about. He looks different.

That's my first thought as I'm coming down from the shock of seeing him here.

His hair is longer, running past his shoulders. His clothes, too, are more polished. He's wearing a black linen shirt underneath brass armor that's molded to his broad shoulders and muscled chest. At his waist, he has a thick belt that houses the scabbard of his sword—a dusty gold metal embedded with red rubies. His pants are tight around his leg muscles, framed by leather straps that hold a collection of daggers around his outer thighs.

Like this, he looks even more dangerous than before.

Yet there's one more striking feature.

On the right side of his face, rune-like tattoos run from his hairline down his neck, disappearing into the collar of his shirt. Half of his face is marred by those swirling black designs, so stark against the deep purple of his eyes.

Everyone is on their feet for his entrance, bowing slightly as they don't dare to make direct eye contact with him.

But while Rhea and Maros are behaving reverently in his

presence, Thea is white as a sheet, her body trembling lightly as fear makes its home in her features.

Oh, God. She's scared he might be here to reveal her secret.

I stealthily grab her hand under the table, squeezing tight as I give her a comforting look.

She smiles sadly at me, her entire countenance dejected.

Damn you, Ze.

"Commander Azerius, what brings you here? We were not expecting you," Maros notes.

Ze doesn't acknowledge him as he surveys the dining room until his gaze lands on me. His jaw hardens, his eyes gleaming dangerously.

"Balthazar," he calls out, his voice thundering. All the while, he doesn't take his eyes off me as he lifts his hand, awaiting something.

A small man appears from behind, a leash in his hand, which he passes over to Ze.

He grunts, pulling on the leash to reveal the cutest brown cow I've ever seen. Striding into the room, he rounds the dining table, coming right toward me.

Everyone is staring at him dumbfounded, especially as he stops in front of me, extending the leash toward me.

"For you," he nods.

My lashes flutter in confusion.

"What?"

When I don't take the leash from him, he grabs my hand and places it in my open palm.

"It is for you."

"I don't understand." I frown.

"It is a cow," he mentions, his lips compressing.

"I can see it's a cow, but why would you give me a cow?" I ask, still confused.

"It is a cow from your world. For you. To eat."

I stare at him in disbelief.

"You... You brought me a cow?"

"A good cow." He nods. "It was the most expensive cow in your world."

A chuckle echoes in the room, and I look over to see Wyn holding her hand to her mouth to stop herself from laughing. There's a mix of amusement and bewilderment in the reactions around the room, but I can only share the latter as I have no idea what might have prompted this display.

I sneak a glance at the cow at the same time as she opens her mouth to release a loud *moo* before coming forward to lick my hand.

A smile pulls at my lips at how cute it is, and I bring my hand to the top of her head to pat her.

"You like it?" Ze asks as he pushes his chin up, his lips curling around the corners.

I don't reply. I have nothing to say to him. But since he brought me this cutie, I can't say no to her.

"You." He points to a staff member on the sidelines. "Take this to the kitchens and have them prepare it for her," he commands.

My eyes widen, and before I know it, I pull the cute cow into my arms, hugging it as I give him a death stare.

"You heartless heathen," I mutter.

The cow releases another *moo*, nuzzling her snout against my belly.

"Shh, it's okay, baby. I won't let the bad man hurt you."

A look of shock crosses his face.

"W-what? Bad man? I brought you a cow!" He thunders.

"And now you want to kill it."

"Because you cannot eat it raw!"

"I will not eat it at all," I huff.

How could he think I would eat this cute cow now that she's adopted me as her human?

His brows go up in indignation.

"But I brought it for you to eat," he repeats. "It needs to be slaughtered and cooked, or your weak human body will get sick." Of course he would find another way to insult me and my *weak human body*. Why the hell is he even here?

The mention of slaughter makes the cow burrow deeper into my embrace, and I give him another scathing look for scaring the cow.

"You're scaring her!"

"It is a cow!" He grits his teeth. "To *eat*. You have eaten cows before."

"But not a cute one like this. How could I eat it after seeing her?" I ask as I direct my attention to the cutie in my arms. "You're a cute girl, aren't you? We're going to be good friends."

"You are *not* keeping the cow," he suddenly states.

"You gave it to me."

"To *eat*! Not to keep as a pet," he groans.

"Well, it's your mistake for assuming I'd eat it," I retort. "But you've given it to me, so now it's mine and you no longer have a say in it."

"Human!" His nostrils flare as he stares me down.

I continue to pet the cow, all the while returning his glare with a mutinous one of my own. I've already established a connection with her—one that heartless Ze would have *no* idea about.

He continues to look at me for moments on end before he releases a deep sigh.

"You like it that much?"

I nod decisively.

"I shall make arrangements for her accommodation," he eventually relents, though it takes everything in him to accept this defeat.

"Balthazar," he calls out again, and his man scurries over to get the cow.

"I don't trust you," I hiss at Ze, holding on tightly to the leash.

"I give you my vow the cow will come to no harm, human." He rolls his eyes.

"Your vows are of no consequence to me. You are a liar and I don't trust you."

He narrows his eyes at me, his body tense.

"My vow is binding," he adds through gritted teeth. "You can ask anyone in this room and they will tell you that."

I sneak a glance at Thea's parents, and Maros gives me a brisk nod. Still, I'm somewhat apprehensive to part with her now that she's mine.

Looking down, I pet her a while longer.

"I shall call you Belinda." I smile. "Now be a good girl and follow the man out. He will not hurt you."

She gives me another *moo* as if understanding my words, and I reluctantly relinquish my hold on the leash.

Balthazar takes Belinda out, and I wait for Ze to follow, too, but he's still rooted to the spot. And to my everlasting surprise, instead of leaving, he takes a seat at the table next to me.

"You may sit now." He inclines his head at his hosts.

The insufferable oaf!

"It is a surprise to see you here, Commander," Rhea notes as everyone finally sits down.

"I have pending business in Arche. We are in Code Red."

Both Rhea and Maros appear stricken by the news.

"And Cerenios?" Maros asks.

"He is on a mission. I cannot divulge much else about it, but I have a meeting with His Majesty tomorrow and I will advise you what I shall advise him as well. You need to have your army on standby, with a division that is proficient in handling demon attacks."

"Demon attacks? In Aperion? You must be mistaken..." Rhea murmurs.

"There has been a new development." Ze's lips flatten in displeasure. "Demons have been sighted in the intermediary realms and I have reason to believe they have found a way to travel between worlds in their physical form."

Gasps erupt around the table.

"Impossible," Maros mutters at the same time as Rhea takes a sip of her wine, her eyes filled with worry.

"Do you think there is a chance of them entering Aperion?"

"We are not taking any chances," Ze explains. "It is clear the demons are planning something, but none of our sources have been able to find out what it is."

"That is terrible," Rhea whispers. "I have to ask... Is Cerenios in danger?"

Ze's lips flatten into a thin line.

"His mission is dangerous, but Cerenios is more than capable of handling it. I have trust in him and his abilities."

Although Ze's words are assuring, that doesn't stop Rhea from worrying, and she's not the only one. Glancing at Thea, I note the pallor of her skin and the light tremor in her limbs. Catching my gaze on her trembling hands, she removes them from the table, folding them in her lap as she straightens her back and attempts to act unbothered.

"The demons have never tried anything like this before. Why now?" Maria asks as she shakes her head in disbelief.

"I am not certain. It is possible they did not have the resources before. But after Elias's defection..." he trails off, and my brows go up in question. No one explains what that means, though, and a heavy silence descends upon us.

"That damn Elias." Maros strikes his fist against the table. "I cannot believe I trusted him."

"You were not the only one," Ze comments drily.

"We should have taken your counsel. If we had, none of this would have happened. The chalice wouldn't be missing either."

"It is what it is." Ze shrugs, though I note the ghost of a smirk touching his lips. "For the time being, I will reside in Arche to oversee the security detail for Arwyn's majority."

"What?" Wyn's eyes widen.

"Why would that be a problem?" Rhea asks.

"It is merely a precautionary measure. Arwyn's majority will be attended by some of the most important people in Aperion. It will be the perfect opportunity for an attack, if that is their plan."

I stare at Ze unblinking, a little taken aback by this new manner of his. He's surprisingly eloquent and persuasive, his words and tone demanding immediate attention and respect.

"You are right," Maros sighs. "You are welcome to stay in our home for any amount of time you require. Having you here for Arwyn's majority will, indeed, put my mind at ease."

"Why don't you go stay with the king?" Thea suddenly quips, not even bothering to hide her disdain. "Our home may be a little too lacking for a figure as lofty as yourself," she adds sarcastically.

Ze's lips curl around the corners.

"I have decided to lower my standards. You are welcome."

"Ze." I give him a harsh look as I kick him under the table.

He turns to look at me, the picture of innocence.

"I will have the guest room at the end of the hall," he says, not taking his eyes off me. It slowly dawns on me that the room in question is right across from my own.

"Of course. I will send the staff to prepare it for you." Maros nods, firing off instructions to some of the staff on standby.

With that settled, the staff brings an extra plate for Ze, and the duke and duchess nod at us to start eating.

I swallow as I gaze down at my plate, my mouth watering the more I stare at the assortment of appetizers. It's been a while since I've last eaten, yet I don't want to make a fool of myself considering the environment I'm in.

I pick up my fork and knife and carefully cut into the steamed vegetables, bringing a bite to my lips. The taste is divine, not that I expected anything less considering the fancy presentation.

Everyone eats in silence. Everyone but Ze, who's staring at his food with an inscrutable expression.

FORTY-FIVE

"Don't tell me you're not hungry? *Again*," I whisper at him. It's poor manners of him not to eat after barging into the dining hall and insinuating himself at our table.

He doesn't reply, appearing rather pensive as he picks up his fork and moves it across his plate.

Oh well, it's not as if this is the first time he's been rude, so I shouldn't bother too much—it's clear our hosts know it too since they don't pay him much attention.

Wyn starts talking about her ball, and soon the entire ensemble is too busy debating the latest fashions to notice Ze's fussiness about food.

I turn my attention to my plate, listening with one ear to the lively conversation at the table while I try each delicacy, setting aside those that are not to my liking.

"I still need to get fitted one last time for my midnight gown." Wyn sighs. "You will come with me, Thea, right?" she asks her sister enthusiastically. "You, too, Luce. Please." She flutters her lashes.

I nod. We have plenty of time before the third trial is announced.

"I would love to. I've already missed the other fittings." Thea smiles. "I can't wait to see you in that dress. It's going to be so special, Wyn." Her voice breaks.

"Don't get too emotional on me, sis. It's just a dress." Wyn chuckles, swatting Thea.

"It's *not* just a dress. It's *the* dress, Wyn. You've grown so much, darling." She sighs. "I cannot believe you're going to be an adult soon."

My lips stretch into a pleasant smile as I watch their sweet interaction. But a sudden flurry of movement from the side grabs my attention. Slowly turning, I catch Ze red-handed as he's swapping food from my plate to his.

I blink.

He blinks.

"What do you think you're doing?" I hiss at him in a low voice so as not to attract attention to us.

"Nothing," he quickly adds, straightening his back and placing his utensils next to his plate.

I narrow my eyes at him, then slowly glance down at my plate to see that the food I pushed aside has been swapped for the food I *did* like. At the same time, his plate is now filled with all the food I did *not* like.

My eyes connect with his, and he's still sporting the same innocent expression as he pretends to mind his own business. I glare at him so as to convey that these little tricks will not work on me—not after everything that's been said and done.

"You will *not* get extra points," I mutter under my breath.

Alas, it's at that moment that I get the first reaction out of him. His face falls, his shoulders slumping ever so slightly.

God, what is it with him and those extra points?

Shaking my head, I turn to my food, cutting into a slice of cheese when he once more intervenes.

"Let me do it for you," he murmurs, his hand already on mine as he attempts to wrench the knife away from me.

Annoyance spears through me as I elbow him away.

"For God's sake, just let me eat in peace," I groan, grabbing onto the knife. His grip is stronger, though, and in our tug of war, the knife slips, the sharp edge cutting through my palm.

"Agh." I jump back at the sudden sting.

Blood pours down onto the table, and Ze's eyes become affixed to it. Slowly, he raises his gaze to meet mine, a stricken look crossing his face.

"Oh no, are you all right, Luce?" Thea gasps.

Everyone is staring at us.

"Yes, it's just a small cut." I force a smile as I get a napkin to press to my cut. It's shallow, but it's bleeding quite a bit. "If you'll excuse me, I think I'll retire for the evening."

"Yes, of course," Rhea adds with a hint of worry. "Please let us know if there is anything you need."

I give her a tight nod as I get to my feet. I don't even look at Ze as I stomp out of the room, all the while muttering expletives under my breath.

That damn man! Couldn't he keep his hands to himself?

I barely reach the landing on the second floor when I hear the echo of steps following behind me. Slowly turning my head, I only need to glimpse the shadow of a giant to know who's following me. At once, I sprint to my room.

The steps, too, become more punctuated, more loud.

He's gaining ground.

Damn it! Why can't he leave me alone?

I dash to my room, get inside, and lock the door behind me. My breathing is out of control as I rest my back against the wooden frame of the door, pressing the napkin tighter against my injured palm. Despite being a shallow cut, it stings like hell.

The steps finally stop as he reaches my door.

"Human," Ze thunders. "Open up."

"Go away, Ze," I call out.

"You are injured. Open the door."

"I can take care of myself, Ze. Just leave me alone. You've done enough," I grit my teeth.

Silence greets me, but he's far from gone as I hear a deep intake of air.

"You did not finish eating," he says, his voice softer.

"So? Whose fault is that?" I grumble.

"I have chocolate."

My ears perk up.

"Ch-chocolate?" I clear my throat.

I did not eat enough considering I've been famished since we arrived in Arche. And chocolate does sound nice. But it's also coming from my number one archnemesis, the insufferable Ze, whose name isn't even Ze.

"Yes. I have chocolate. The most expensive kind," he adds proudly.

Once more, my stomach betrays me, my mouth watering just thinking about the chocolate.

Why does this have to be my weakness? Well, chocolate and cute things. I couldn't say no to Belinda either.

I release a weary sigh, the battle ninety-nine percent lost.

And the last one percent is not strong enough to hold out against *chocolate*.

Before I can think with the more developed part of my brain —the one that's not chasing the high of serotonin—I find myself opening the door and coming face to face with Ze.

Azerius, not Ze, I mentally correct myself.

I still can't wrap my mind around how different he looks. Those symbols on his face change his entire countenance, and up close, they are even more terrifying.

There's a deadlier edge to him that wasn't there before— even when I thought him dangerous enough. This new perception of him might have something to do with the fact that he appears even bigger than before—so much so I barely reach the middle of his chest, and I'm wearing heels.

There's an icy current surrounding him, the air crackling and vibrating around him with a heavy energy.

I don't let myself get rattled, though, and, pushing my chin up, I stare him in the eye.

"So?" I raise a brow. "Where's my chocolate?"

"I shall give it to you if you let me treat your wound," he replies smoothly.

I narrow my eyes, scanning him up and down. There's no chocolate! I should have known he was lying.

With an annoyed huff, I push the door in his face—locking it for good measure. As I turn, however, I come face to face with him.

"No door can hold me, human. You should have realized this by now," he murmurs, his tone oddly soft.

I regard him with suspicion. He's planning something.

"You're being rude, *Azerius*." I clear my throat.

His lips thin, his nostrils flaring.

"I am *not* being rude," he grits out. "I am being *nice*. I will heal you now."

He reaches for my injured palm, but I slap his hand aside.

"No one asked you. Please leave," I say as I move to the side and gesture toward the door. Or even better, he can use those disappearing skills of his to get the hell out of my room.

"It was my fault," he adds in a low voice, his eyes affixed to the red stain on the napkin I'm holding to my cut.

"I won't hold it against you." I roll my eyes. "You're absolved. Now you can go." I wave him to the door—again.

He doesn't move.

He's rooted to the spot as he stares at my hand.

"It will not take long," he murmurs, taking a step closer to me. "Just a moment."

"Ze, I said no. What do you not understand?"

"You are *bleeding*, human," he hisses.

"So? It's my business if I'm bleeding or not," I say, exasperated. "Why do you think I would let you *anywhere* near me after everything you've done?"

"Human," he grits out, coming closer.

"Stay away!" I move out of his reach, retreating deeper into the room. "You're rude and a liar, and I don't want anything to do with you," I tell him resolutely.

"When did I lie?" He swivels to stare me down.

"Really, Azerius?" I shake my head in disgust. "Are we going to pretend you didn't lie about that?"

"I..." He blinks. "I did not lie. I merely omitted the truth."

"And those tattoos?" I ask as I look him up and down. "You deceived me."

"You do not understand," he groans, still moving toward me.

"What is there to understand? That you're an awful person? Trust me, I already got that." I let out a bitter laugh.

He compresses his lips, his body taut.

"Everyone knows Azerius. No one knows Ze," he says as if that explains everything. "No one knows...*that* Ze."

"Well, it seems I don't know either, so please get out." I point toward the door.

"Human, stop being so stubborn and let me explain."

"What is there to explain? Thea told me what you've been threatening her with. I can't believe anyone would stoop that low." I sneer at him. "You are an awful man, Ze or Azerius or whoever you are. I thought there might be some good in you, but oh, I was sorely mistaken." I shake my head.

He frowns, tilting his head to the side.

"She told you?"

"That you would threaten her with something that would get her killed? Blackmail her, even? How could you?" I demand sharply.

"Erithea did it with her own hand and it is up to her to bear the consequences of her actions," he replies matter-of-factly.

My eyes widen at his nonchalance, anger spiking inside of me anew.

"You are *vile*. How could you shame her for something like that? And why? Because she's a woman? Because you have your fucked-up laws that look down on women?"

"I do not care whether she is a female or not. She broke the law. She—"

"Do not say another word about my friend." I grind my teeth, poking my finger into his chest.

I don't know when he got this close, but we're now millimeters apart, both breathing hard as we stare at each other. My heart rate continues to go up at his proximity as I envision all the ways in which I'd make him pay—despite the fact that I know I don't stand a chance. Still, a girl's gotta dream. And right now, I'd like nothing better than to have some cool powers so I could zap his ass out of my room and out of my life if possible.

A twitch appears in his cheek as he stares at me, the purple of his eyes glinting dangerously. His muscles tense, his sheer force rippling through the air. There's a heaviness all around us —one that's making me lightheaded. But I will not back down. I will not let him see how much he unnerves me, not when he thrives on intimidation.

He takes a deep breath, his irises swirling a deeper purple.

"I will vow not to speak of her secret again. Would that do?"

I blink in surprise.

"You...would? Just like that?"

"If you will forgive me," he murmurs in a soft tone.

I gawk at him for a moment before I burst into laughter.

He frowns.

"Of course you'd want something in return." I shake my head. "Not everything in life is an exchange. If you want to do something, you do it because it is the right thing to do, not because you expect something in return. As far as forgiveness goes, you don't barter for it, you *earn* it."

And with that, I turn my back to him, going to the window and waiting for him to leave. Surely, if I ignore him long enough, he'll get tired of this and do his hocus-pocus thing out of my room.

Steps echo in the room, and in a matter of seconds, I feel him behind me.

Of course he wouldn't leave.

It's dark out, and the windows are semi-reflective. I raise my gaze to see his shadowy figure behind me, his hands in the air as he tentatively lowers them down on my shoulders.

"I vow to never speak of Erithea's secret again," he speaks in a low voice.

"Is that so?" I raise an unbelieving brow at him.

"A vow once spoken cannot be broken. I will not ask for anything in exchange."

I don't reply. It's the least he can do.

"Now will you allow me to heal you?"

I half turn to glare at him.

"You're impossible."

"And you are still bleeding," he says as he takes my injured hand in his, peeling away the napkin to reveal the messy cut. He trails his fingers over my palm, and I wince at the sensation.

He stops.

"I apologize," he murmurs, bringing my hand to his mouth. He closes his eyes, inhaling deeply before his tongue peeks out to lick the entire length of the wound. A shiver goes down my back and I swallow hard as I keep myself still. He parts his lips over my palm, sucking on the residual blood. But even as the wound closes, he continues to slowly lap at it.

"That's enough," I say as I pull my hand away. "Thanks," I mutter awkwardly.

"I do not like you bleeding," he adds quietly. "You will not bleed again under my watch."

"Sorry to break it to you, but I bleed once a month whether you like it or not," I mumble dryly.

His eyes flash at me.

"What?" he thunders. "How?"

Amusement plays at my lips as I watch outrage flood his features.

"It's called menstruation," I chuckle.

He's staring at me, unblinking.

"An adult female bleeds once a month. I doubt it's any different in your world." After all, it's not only a human trait. Other mammals menstruate, too.

"I am not entirely familiar, but goddesses have different constitutions," he adds pensively. "This does not harm you?"

"I get cranky and tired, but it doesn't harm me."

He nods, though he still appears troubled by the concept.

"How could you not know this, Ze? It's biology."

"*Female* biology. I do not care for females," he grumbles.

"So you've said." I stifle a smile. "But you do realize this is part of a female's reproductive cycle, no?"

He blinks slowly. His cheeks redden and he looks away.

"Of course I am aware," he mumbles, avoiding my eyes.

Awkward silence descends between us.

"Well, you've healed me. Now where's my chocolate?"

His eyes widen, and he disappears. Not a second passes before he reappears, carrying a plate on which there's a chocolate figurine.

A figurine of *him*. A chocolate Ze.

"Here," he declares proudly as he thrusts the plate toward me.

"You... This is you." I point to the chocolate shape then at him.

He nods, a satisfied smile on his face.

"I found the best chef in all Aperion and I instructed him to make me the best chocolate."

"You asked him to shape it like you, too?"

"Of course." He nods. "So you know I am in earnest."

"Azerius," I sigh.

"Ze," he corrects. "For you, I only want to be Ze."

My lashes flutter at him.

"Ze." I clear my throat. "I don't understand you."

"It is chocolate. You like chocolate," he adds uneasily.

"I do, and this is nice and all, but why? You already told me how little you think of me. Why would you care to bring me chocolate, or a cow, or do all this"—I wave my healed palm —"when it's clear you believe me to be beneath you?"

"What?" His eyes flare with shock. "I would never—"

"You insulted me. Belittled me. Threatened me and my friends. Why are you trying to be nice now after you were so awful to me?"

"W-what?" he sputters. "I did not insult you. I insulted your actions."

"It's the same thing." I roll my eyes.

"No. It is not. I have told you. You are my person and I am responsible for you. That means I will ensure you make the best decisions. I cannot just sit by and watch you put yourself in danger for inane reasons."

"Ze... Is it so hard to apologize and admit you were wrong?"

"But I was not wrong," he argues, tipping his chin up.

"Please leave." I take a deep breath.

He's rooted to the spot, staring at me.

"I'm tired and I want to sleep. Please leave."

He doesn't move. He doesn't blink. He just stares at me.

God, this man is impossible! I don't understand him and I don't think I want to at this point.

"I..." He inhales a few times, placing his hands behind his back and straightening his spine. "I apologize if I offended you. It was not my intention to do so. I will weigh my words more carefully in the future."

"Good. Now you can go." I nod as I bypass him.

"Does that mean you will forgive me?" he asks eagerly as he trails behind me.

I close my eyes and count to ten in an attempt to calm myself and not rage at him.

"You have apologized, but that doesn't mean I'm required to accept your apology," I explain, and his face falls.

"But... I apologized," he whispers.

"You also need to show me you mean it, Ze. Words are easy. It is actions that are hard."

"But—"

"I really want to go to bed. Can you please go?"

He takes a deep breath, his shoulders slumping. Finally, he heads to the door. But just as I think he's going to leave quietly, he stops, his hand on the knob.

"Have a good sleep, Luce," he whispers in a barely audible voice.

Then he's gone.

I exhale deeply, my gaze finding the odd chocolate figurine.

Well, at least he brought me chocolate.

I plop myself on the bed and study the Ze-shaped figurine. It truly looks like him, down to the arrogance etched in his features. This version doesn't have the tattoos, though, and his hair is shorter—as I've gotten to know him. His clothes are simple, a shirt and a pair of pants, and his sword is sheathed at his hip.

A mischievous smile plays at my lips. Grabbing the figurine, I bite the head off, munching on the delicious chocolate and silently laughing at the now headless Ze.

Take that, you impossible man!

FORTY-SIX

"Are you sure it's okay for me to come along?" I ask Thea as we make our way down the stairs to meet with Wyn and accompany her to her gown fitting. It's early in the morning, and after a full night of sleep, I finally feel more like myself. Of course, I can't deny the slight disappointment I felt last night when Nikki didn't show up, but I trust that he'll make himself known to me when he can.

"Of course it is. Wyn likes you, and she's thrilled we're going to spend a girls' day out. She already planned the itinerary for today, and after the fitting, we're going to grab sweet ices from our favorite shop."

"That sounds heavenly. Thank you," I murmur with a smile.

"She's so excited about the ball. It's going to be a success, I already know it—much better than mine was, anyway," she adds, rolling her eyes.

"That bad?"

"Worse." She sighs. "Barely any people showed up. It was just my parents' friends, but no one my age. Later, I found out they had organized another secret party at the same time to spite me."

"What?" My eyes widen. "Why would they do that?"

"Because why would they not?" She shrugs. "I guess they

didn't see me as an equal. I wasn't exactly the best in my elementary training." She lets out a strained laugh.

"I'm sorry," I murmur as I reach for her, squeezing her hand.

"It's fine. I've had over three thousand years to forget about it."

"I don't think I'll ever get used to the way you guys casually speak about *thousands* of years. I'm barely an embryo compared to you," I joke, hoping to lighten the atmosphere.

"It's mutual, trust me." She laughs. "It's hard to wrap my mind around how little humans live..." she trails off as she suddenly stops, her brows bunched together in a frown.

She puts a hand up before placing a finger on her lips to tell me to be silent.

Tilting her head to the side, she looks deep in thought before a smile tugs at her lips, the tension from her shoulders dissipating.

"I'll have to make a small detour. Do you mind if you wait for me for a while? Wyn just got her first *ryoku* and she's freaking out."

"She got what?" I blink, but she's already walking away from me.

"It's her first ability," she says with a bright smile. "Feel free to roam around. There's a library at the end of that hall. You can have a look while I take care of Wyn."

"Sure." I nod.

"Great!" She exclaims, almost hopping with joy. "We'll join you in the library in a bit," she calls out, already at the bottom of the stairs.

I shake my head at her with an amused smile on my face. I'm still a little confused by what she meant by *ryoku*, but it must be something important if Thea is so happy about it. Truthfully, their relationship warms my heart, and for a moment, I just stare at her departing figure with a wistful expression on my face.

Family.

The most important thing in the world. And humans are not

the only ones to prioritize it. In a way, it makes the concept of deities less daunting to realize they have the same fears and desires as us mortals.

They might have powers beyond belief, but deep down, they also love and want to be loved.

Well, except Ze. He operates entirely outside that sphere.

The mere notion of a library gets me giddy, though, and turning toward the hall, I wander from door to door until I find the library Thea mentioned—although library is a bit of an understatement. The room is the size of a football field!

The door opens and I step inside, my heart beating wildly in my chest, a hum of excitement building in my stomach.

Wow.

I should have guessed that a palace such as this would house a grand library too.

The shelves are ceiling high—and considering the ceiling is over four meters in height, that says everything. The walls are entirely filled with bookshelves, with a few rows on either side, too. In the middle of the room, there's a spiraling staircase made out of marble that leads to a second floor. All around, there are tables with book weights on them, almost as if this were a study hall.

As I close the door behind me, I walk inside, brushing my palm against a massive oak table. I swallow hard in an attempt to temper my excitement and not run around like a kid in a candy shop.

This is fabulous.

Better than chocolate—okay, maybe *not* better, but equal...*almost*

equal.

I look right and left, not knowing where to start my exploration. But there's only one thought that permeates my mind.

Do deities have romance novels?

If I were to make an educated guess, if they do have them, they are going to be mostly censored. After all, with everything

I've heard about their world, even talking about sex is taboo. Of course, that would reflect in the literature.

A giggle escapes me.

Who would have thought that gods would have banned books? Yet it just goes to show that even when one has limitless resources, boundaries must still exist to allow for society to function and avoid mayhem. Maybe *because* they have limitless powers, they have to ensure that everything is carefully organized and curated.

If there's something that I've noticed so far about Aperion, it's the fact that it's not that different from my own world—they still rely on power structures. Maybe they're not as concerned with colorism or social class based on the people I've met so far, but they're definitely judging others by their abilities—or lack thereof. Even Thea, who is from a noble family, has encountered this issue, with people constantly putting her down because of her limited powers. In fact, social standing seems to be correlated with the abilities one has.

"Welcome, what can I help you with today?"

I jump back, startled by the sudden voice. Looking left and right, I don't see anyone around.

My brows furrow.

"Who's there?" I ask tentatively.

"I am Nigel, the librarian," the voice replies at the same time as a see-through figure materializes on top of the table.

I scramble back, my eyes wide.

"What?" I squeak in surprise.

A floating torso appears in front of me. His face is somewhat humanoid, but it lacks expressivity. The entire body is a shimmery white, and the only dot of color is his dark eyes.

"What are you?" I whisper.

"I am Nigel. The librarian. I am a wraith in charge of the Duke of Sigmore's library collection."

"Oh," I murmur, blinking rapidly as I take in the information.

Okay, this makes sense. They don't have computers to catalogue everything, so they would need someone—or something—to do it. And from what I remember from the wraiths in the game, they are similar to a programmed algorithm with no mind of their own. Just like Siri.

"What can I help you with today?" Nigel repeats.

"Hm." I take a moment to think. "Do you have any romance novels?" I ask sheepishly.

"I am not familiar with that term. Can you rephrase it?"

"Stories about love?"

"I am not familiar with that term. Can you rephrase it?"

What? Seriously? I can understand them not having romance as a genre, but stories about love?

"Stories where two people fall in love?"

"I am not familiar with that term. Can you rephrase it?"

Not one to give up, I try every combination I can think of. Yet the result is the same. Nigel does not know what I mean, which suggests that likely he wasn't trained with this terminology in the first place.

It's not too surprising that this world wouldn't have romance, but somehow I still hoped there might be something. Damn it, but the more I find out about this place, the more hopeless I become.

If gods have no notion of romance, then how do humans have it? We were modeled after deities. It stands to reason our capacity to love would come from them, too. But maybe these gods have been around for so long they've completely forgotten the meaning of love—after all, their marriages are all about power, nothing more.

"Do you have any books on The Wishing Game?" I ask instead. If I won't be able to find something to pass the time, I might as well do some research on the game.

"Yes, of course," Nigel answers. With a flick of his hand, a yellow shimmer envelops a bookcase on the second floor. "That is the selection of books we have on The Wishing Game. If you need further assistance, call my name and I shall be happy to guide you."

"Thank you." I nod.

His figure dissipates and I'm left alone in the library.

The bookshelf on the second floor still emits a low light, and I climb up the stairs before the beacon fades. Reaching the landing on the second floor, I stop in front of the section Nigel had pointed to and I browse the titles.

I'm surprised to be able to read the language perfectly, but then I'm reminded that the brew likely infused me with that ability.

Some of the books are about the rules of the game, while others are records of previous games and winners. I take a few of them out and lay them on the floor as I sift through them, thinking I can find some information that might help me in the third trial.

As I read, however, it becomes clear that each edition of the game has different trials. Not one trial appears to have been used twice.

I release a heavy sigh as I turn to the rules of the competition. One thing I've been exceedingly curious about so far has been what happens to the souls of the people who die during the game. It stated that the souls of the losers would forfeit their chances at future incarnations. But what happens to them? Do they just disappear? Where do they go?

I flip through the book, reading each line carefully, but as I reach that rule, the only additional mention I can find is that the energy from the deceased souls is used as fuel, but it doesn't specify for what.

I nibble on my bottom lip as I go back to the bookshelf, scanning more of the titles until I find a book on the first edition of The Wishing Game.

Cracking it open, I read the introduction.

After a series of debilitating daimon attacks, the Ananke Supreme Lyonas sacrificed his energy to enforce the weakening boundaries between the worlds. But as this scribe has witnessed in his eight thousand years of life, not even a Supreme's energy can hold up indefinitely.

The other Supremes became aware that they would either need to sacrifice one of their own every few thousand years, or they could find another source of energy that could continuously feed the boundaries.

Each Supreme brought forth a proposition, but none proved to be sustainable in the long run. That was until Lyonas's granddaughter and the favored candidate for the new Ananke Supreme, Lispera, came up with an idea.

Souls are the purest energy in the universe. It stands to reason that they could power the boundaries and keep them from collapsing. But a soul's cycle belongs to Psyche. It is not something that can be influenced, not even by a god. Yet Lispera found a loophole that not even Psyche could dispute. As long as the soul gave its consent and sacrificed itself, then its energy could be used to enforce the boundaries.

The Supremes were intrigued by the idea, but they did not know how they would find a soul to sacrifice itself, for that sacrifice meant utter oblivion. More than that, one soul's energy, though powerful, could not possibly feed the boundary indefinitely.

But Lispera came through again with another proposition. Souls may choose to sacrifice themselves in exchange for an opportunity to have their deepest desire fulfilled. If the Supremes joined their powers to bestow a boon upon a lucky winner, creatures from all corners of the universe would clamor for a chance to participate in such a competition.

The Supremes debated this topic for many years before they reached a consensus. They would hold a game for all the mortal creatures of the universe, and the winners would get the chance to have one wish fulfilled. But to participate, each creature had to consent to the fact that by losing, they would be forfeiting their souls.

As the boundaries between the worlds started to weaken again, it was time to organize The Wishing Game.

This is the account of the first Wishing Game that this scribe has witnessed with his own eyes. All the events that follow are true, and they bear the seal of approval from the Supremes.

I swallow hard as I put two and two together. Demons were recently sighted in the intermediary realms. Does that mean the boundaries are weakening again? Despite the ongoing Wishing Game?

I flip the pages of the book in search of more information, but the rest is merely an account of each trial and the favorite contestants. It's only at the end that I read about the winner and his wish. He asked for the hand in marriage of one of the Supremes, something clearly not done because the wish had been denied and the winner had been convicted and jailed for his offense—for it seems to have been an offense to even aspire to be with a Supreme.

There isn't much else in the book, so I turn my attention to others. Yet they all follow the same format. There is the exact same introduction after which the game is described in detail, almost as if the scribe was a sports commentator giving his opinions on his favorite teams.

"Nigel?" I call out, and the wraith materializes in front of me. "Is there anything more about The Wishing Game in here?"

"This is the only section that houses books on The Wishing Game," he replies in that monotone voice of his. The bookshelf is illuminated again as he points toward it.

"I see. Thank you."

"Are you finished with those books?" He points to the mess I made on the floor.

"Yes." I nod tentatively.

Before I can blink, all the open books close with a thud before levitating in the air and taking back their spot on the shelf—in the perfect order.

Okay, Nigel is far better than any computer.

"Do you require further assistance?"

"Do you have anything on Ze—Azerius?" I ask before I can help myself.

"Are you inquiring about Commander Azerius?"

"Uhm, yes."

A couple of bookshelves over, a few books light up.

"That is the selection of books we have on Commander Azerius. If you need further assistance, call my name and I shall be happy to guide you."

"Thank you," I murmur, getting up and heading to the designated shelf.

The wraith disappears. I pull out the books and spread them on the floor, making myself comfortable.

A low hum erupts in my stomach—a certain excitement at learning more about the mysterious figure that is Ze, because honestly, I do not understand him. He can be vile and mean, but he can also be nice and...considerate. I don't even know which one is the real Ze anymore because despite everything I've heard, he's been *mostly* nice to me. Last night is a main example. He surprised me with his apology, but even more so with his vow. And if it's true that a vow once spoken cannot be broken, then Thea no longer has to worry about his threat hanging over her head. I shall have to impart that with her later on when we are alone. Maybe it will ease some of her worries.

The first book is titled *Military History*. As I flip through it, I realize it's a history of battles in which Azerius has fought over the past four thousand years. It mostly describes military tactics, something I'm not well versed in, so I put it aside.

It's the second book, though, that catches my attention. It's titled *Prosecuted Offenses* and from what I can tell, it spans a hundred years. There is an index at the end, and my eyes widen when I see how many times the name Azerius has been mentioned in the book—five thousand times.

I quickly flip to the first mention, which details the case of a minor male deity having an affair with a number of s'Aperiotes and getting them all pregnant. The punishment had been death, and Azerius had been the one to dole it out. The details are gruesome as the book goes into depth on everything Ze had done to the male for his offense. He'd been strapped to a pole in the public square for thirty days. Each day, Azerius would be present to make a cut on his body. At first, it was shallow cuts, but with each passing day, they became deeper and deeper until his entire torso was cut open, his organs spilling out. He was left in the blistering sun, his blood draining from his body, until he drew his last breath.

Although the description is incredibly gory in the book, it's how Azerius is described that surprises me. The writer notes that he was so cold, so emotionless, that the people passing by couldn't help but be more shocked by his nonchalant demeanor than the guts hanging out of the male's body.

I gulp down. This is oddly reminiscent, isn't it? I've seen that side of Azerius when he kills. He does it so easily, so efficiently, it's almost as if there's nothing inside of him but the thirst for death.

Flipping some more through the book, I stop at a random page, my entire body freezing as I read the offense. A young female deity had been denounced by her husband for not being pure upon their marriage. After investigations, it was found out that the female had birthed a child in the past that she had abandoned. A s'Aperiote family had found the baby and they had raised him as their own. The female was convicted of several crimes, and because she belonged to an influential noble family, Azerius was the one to dole out the punishment.

I briefly close my eyes, reluctant to read on about what he must have done to her. I have never been able to stomach violence against women, and though this female did break the law, I cannot see how death is a fair punishment. Sure, she abandoned her child, but she was driven to do so by the same stringent laws that sought to sentence her to death. It's a vicious cycle whose only fault lies with the restrictions placed on people.

My breathing grows labored as I force myself to read on. No

matter how uncomfortable this is, I *need* to know who the true Azerius is.

Yet there's no avoiding the illustration of Ze aiming his sword at the woman's head, a swirl of energy and smoke surrounding his blade.

Decapitation.

That is the method he used on her. That is the method he would have used on Thea.

Good grief.

He was the executor of every high-profile case, thousands in total over a hundred-year period—a bleep in their existence. I don't even want to think of how many people he's executed in his seven thousand years of life. He probably doesn't have a number either, since all this killing is routine for him.

My eyes are glued to the pages as I skim over the many gruesome ways in which Ze delivered death to those people and I can't help but wonder if he has a conscience. Does he regret this? Do these deaths weigh on his conscience?

How can he sleep at night?

Yet the questions are moot since he already confessed he doesn't feel. He merely receives his orders and follows them—the perfect soldier.

The perfect *killer*.

Because that's what he is, isn't it?

A killing machine, and not just a regular one. He's a God Killer—a moniker given to him not only by the author of the book but by the entirety of Aperion.

The sudden noise of a door opening startles me, as well as the voices that grow louder. I close the book and slide to the floor, creeping closer to the balustrade to see who it is—the last thing I want is to be caught researching the God Killer.

An unknown man takes a seat at the table just as Nigel materializes in front of him.

"You are dismissed, Nigel," Maros tells the wraith as he follows behind. Ze is next, closing the door behind him. His hands are behind his back as he scans the room with disinterest.

Maros takes a seat across from the other man while Ze continues to pace around.

"I am sorry to call on you at this hour, Your Majesty, but Commander Azerius stated it was urgent," Maros informs him.

Majesty? So that is the king?

Even more reason why I should *not* be found here.

FORTY-SEVEN

"Go on then, Commander. What was it so urgent that you had me come here personally?" the king asks with affected impatience, tapping his foot on the floor.

Ze gives him a bored look, but he doesn't reply immediately, walking around the library.

"Commander!" the king barks out.

"Since Elias absconded with the chalice, the Supremes have been on high alert. They fear that other artifacts might be in danger, too," Ze speaks slowly, leveling the king with his gaze. "You have been made aware recently of the weakening of the boundaries between the worlds. Demons in their physical form have managed to sneak into the intermediary realms, and it will not be long before they will be able to cross between worlds."

"I thought that was under control," the king grunts.

"For now. But the situation is not looking good. One of my generals is missing."

"Who?"

"Aethon," Ze replies quietly.

"Pyros?" The king frowns. "How could he go missing? I wasn't aware there was anyone who could take him out."

"There should not be." Ze nods.

"But... You don't mean to imply he deserted, too? Blasphemy."

"Indeed," Ze drawls, rounding the table and taking a seat. He leans back, his posture relaxed. "Aethon is loyal. I do not suspect him of desertion. In fact, it was his last communication that gave me reason to be alarmed."

"What is it? Get on with it!" the king demands impatiently.

Ze raises a lazy brow at him, seemingly not impressed with the king's edicts.

"He was investigating the Sons of Tenebreis. It was a son of Tenebreis who was leading the demons into the intermediary realms."

"Tenebreis? Impossible. They cannot leave Tartareia."

"So we have presumed." Ze sighs. "I believe the situation to be more dire than we previously thought. Aethon relayed to me that he uncovered a demon plot not only to destabilize the boundaries between realms but also to awaken the Seven from Tartarstasis."

Silence descends in the room as both Maros and the king stare at Ze, their expressions full of disbelief.

"That's...impossible."

"Unfortunately, with Elias's desertion, it is highly possible. When the Primordials imprisoned the Seven in Tartarstasis, they each used a piece of themselves to perform the spell. As such, the only way the spell can be broken is by using the same type of energy to unlock the prison."

"The Primordials are long gone," Maros intervenes. "No one knows where they are, so I cannot see how the demons could get their hands on their energy signature."

"They might be gone, but you forget one thing. They left something behind."

"The artifacts," the king mutters a curse.

"Indeed. Each Primordial left behind an artifact to one of the Houses. And considering Elias took the chalice with him, the demons are already in possession of one. Now they need fourteen more."

"But—"

Ze places his hand up, stopping the king from speaking.

"Together, all artifacts could unlock Tartarstasis and free the Seven. But that is a concern for another day. By themselves, the artifacts are also far too dangerous to fall into the demons' hands. The chalice alone likely allowed them to leave Tartareia in their physical form. But according to Aethon's report, it is a temporary measure. The chalice allows their body to withstand travel between realms only for a limited period of time, which is likely how a son of Tenebreis was able to cross over. But there is one other artifact that coupled with the chalice could give them a more permanent solution," Ze explains.

"The vial of Arche." The king closes his eyes, pinching the bridge of his nose between two fingers.

"Yes. So you see why I am here and why it was urgent to meet with you. I will need the exact location of the vial so I can protect it."

The king shakes his head.

"I cannot tell you. I vowed to never disclose its location."

"You do not seem to understand the gravity of the issue," Ze speaks slowly, his voice chilly.

"If I tell you, I will perish. It is the same for everyone else who vowed to keep their artifacts safe."

"Damnation," Ze mutters, suddenly standing up. "Elias's desertion is a prime example of how to get around it. He did not have to break his vow to give the chalice to the demons. And his high priestess aided him. We *need* another safety mechanism in place."

"You..." The king's eyes bulge in his head. "You dare imply we would betray Aperion?"

"I am not implying anything. I am saying you could."

The king sputters as he stares at Ze, clearly offended by his remarks.

"Does anyone else know where the artifact is located besides you and your high priestess?" Ze repeats.

The king shakes his head, his cheeks reddening with frustration. "We both made a vow, Commander..."

"Perhaps. But two people knowing the location is two too many, and I do not like to take any chances."

"W-what are you going to do?"

"What I must, Your Majesty. We will all do what we must. This meeting is adjourned. Please relay to the temple that I will be visiting soon."

"You cannot!" The king rises to his feet, coming closer to Ze. He's at least a head shorter than him, a fact that makes him even angrier as he stares up at Ze. "Males are prohibited from entering the temple."

"And the high priestess is forbidden from leaving the temple," Ze adds drily. "I do not see any other recourse. She will not come to me, so I shall need to go to her."

"You... You are a *bastard*, Azerius. I should have you executed for merely implying what you just did."

In less than a second, Ze's entire countenance changes. His hand shoots up, his fingers curling around the king's neck as he lifts him up in the air.

"And you seem to be forgetting who you are speaking to," Ze drawls in a low voice. "I do not care about your lofty title, *Your Majesty*. Kings come and go. The only reason I am going after your high priestess is because you might still be useful to me in the future. But do not stand in my way, or I will get that location out of you, vow or not."

The king's body trembles, his expression a mix of fear and defiance. But as Ze's words sink in, he releases a deep sigh as he lowers his head in a sign of submission.

Ze releases him and takes a step back.

The king mutters something beneath his breath before he storms out of the library without looking back.

"You struck a chord, Commander," Maros adds with a shake of his head. "You should expect resistance at the temple. I doubt His Majesty will let this slide."

"I always expected it, Sigmore," Ze replies smoothly as he

exits. Maros follows suit, and the door to the library locks with a click.

I release a deep sigh of relief as I stretch my body, a little tense from keeping myself frozen to the spot.

The conversation I overheard was as confusing as it was revealing—at least when it comes to Ze's behavior with others. And therein lies my conundrum. He *can* be nice. But ninety-nine percent of the time he chooses not to be.

"Interesting choice of reading material," an amused voice rings out.

I scramble back, my eyes wide as I watch Ze grab my book, his brows going up in surprise as he reads his name. "If you are curious about me, human, you need just ask. These... accounts can be embellished."

"So you didn't execute all those people?" I fire back, still trying to get my bearings together from his sudden appearance.

"This is merely a fraction of the people I have executed," he mentions casually.

I purse my lips, narrowing my eyes at him.

He places the books back in their place on the bookshelf before redirecting his attention to me.

"Since when did you know I was here?"

"The moment I entered the room." He shrugs.

"Did... Did the others know, too?"

"No. Do you think they would have spoken freely with a human within earshot? I shrouded your presence from them."

"Why? Do you not care about what I overheard?"

"No. Not particularly," he says, and he surprises me by taking a seat on the floor next to me, sliding his legs through the empty spaces between the balusters.

I blink at him in confusion.

He's dressed in a black shirt and a pair of black loose pants, his sword faithfully at his waist. His dark hair is tied at his back, emphasizing the presence of his face tattoos.

"You will need to understand the politics of this world at one time or another."

"Maybe I don't want to," I grumble under my breath.

That somehow elicits a half-smile from him as he watches me from the corner of his eyes.

"The situation is as dire as you heard, Luce. And it does not only affect Aperion. In fact, I would wager that Aperion would bear the least brunt of it." His voice is serious, his features tight.

"What do you mean? I know there's a demon problem, but I thought there's always been one?"

"Yes and no. The universe relies on balance. There is no way to truly eradicate evil. But this goes beyond a mere demon problem. You heard me mention the Seven. They are Primordial beings born of pure evil who were barely vanquished eons ago. They cannot be killed, but they can be contained. Currently, they are imprisoned in the most secure prison ever designed—Tartarstasis. Just like the name implies, they are contained in a stasis-like state, perpetually frozen in time. But it seems the demons are trying to find a way to free them."

"What would happen then?" I ask as I mimic his position, sliding my legs between the balusters and letting them dangle in the air.

Ze's lips flatten.

"The universe would not stand a chance. The only ones who could fight against them are the other Primordials. But they have not been sighted in hundreds of thousands of years. No one knows where they are."

"So the best bet is to *not* allow the Seven to escape their prison. Got it."

"It has been so long since anyone thought of them that they have become something of a myth. Certainly, no one would have believed the demons would attempt something like this since their attacks have been rather uniform over time."

"I know I should have asked this before, but how does one become a demon?"

"There are those who are born—the Sons of Tenebreis. They are the descendants of the Seven just like the Supremes are the descendants of the Primordials. But after the Seven were imprisoned in Tartarstasis, the Sons of Tenebreis took it as a personal affront, and they declared war on Aperion. If I am completely honest, the war never ended. But seven thousand years ago, a Supreme sacrificed herself to lock Tartareia so they could not go out anymore. Unfortunately, it was not a permanent solution, and the seal has been weakening. I suspect that the artifact they now have in their possession hastened that process and it might be how they are able to walk freely out of Tartareia." He takes a deep breath, sneaking a glance at me.

I watch him raptly, utterly entranced by his words.

He swallows hard, his Adam's apple bobbing up and down as he clears his throat.

"But there are also those demons that are made. They are souls that have become corrupted. When the Sons of Tenebreis realized they could not escape Tartareia, they needed someone else to do their dirty work. That is how the first *demons* appeared. The Sons of Tenebreis found that a corrupt soul can grow in strength if it consumes other pure souls. The more souls a demon consumes, the more powerful it becomes. You have already seen an ascended demon. It was monstrous. That is only a middle state. If it consumes more souls, it becomes humanoid in shape. These demons will never be as powerful as a Son of Tenebreis, but they are a handful to deal with when they blend into a world and terrorize people from the shadows."

I nod slowly, taking all of it in.

"Why just *sons* of Tenebreis? Are there no daughters?" I blurt out.

He turns to stare at me.

"I just told you about demon hierarchies and your only question is why they are called *sons*?" he asks in disbelief.

"Well, yes." I bite my lip. "I want to know if they are *just* evil or also misogynistic."

"You..." he trails off, looking at me strangely. Then he suddenly bursts into laughter.

I gawk at him. When did I see him laugh before—*did I ever*?

His eyes crinkle around the corners, his face transforming

under my gaze. Gone are the edge of severity and the touch of arrogance etched on his features, replaced with a levity that makes him appear younger, more...handsome.

A low hum vibrates in my lower belly, and I avert my gaze.

"So?" I ask awkwardly.

"They do have daughters, of course. But you are correct in one aspect. Within their ranks, only males are warriors. Females are tasked with the rearing of children."

I nod pensively.

"Why are you telling me all of this? I'm an outsider and a human, after all." I crack a smile.

"Because I will need your assistance."

"What?" I squeak. "What do you mean?"

"You heard the king. He will not tell me where the vial of Arche is, and the only other person who knows its location is the high priestess. I have no doubt that he will warn her to put up her wards against me in the temple so I cannot enter, which is why I require the assistance of a female who can go inside undetected."

My lashes flutter in confusion.

"But why would he do that if the situation is so dire? Shouldn't he want to help you?"

"Theoretically. But because it is *me* who made the request, he will not budge. There is also the matter of his pride, and he believes he can protect the artifact on his own when I know for certain he cannot."

"What is so important about that artifact? What about the other thirteen? Aren't they as important?"

"They are, but in this case, it is the combination of the vial and the chalice that is dangerous. The vial contains the blood of a Primordial. If drunk from the chalice, it will give immense powers to its user. I do not want to imagine what the Sons of Tenebreis will do with that type of power."

I mull over his words, conflicted.

"I heard your conversation, Ze. If the priestess breaks her vow and tells you where the artifact is, she will die, won't she?"

"It is what it is." He shrugs.

"What exactly do you need me to do?"

Why am I even entertaining this thought? I should have told him no from the start. Yet I heard how dangerous these demons are, and I do not want to imagine what would happen to my world if they were to walk freely between worlds.

"I will not ask anything dangerous of you, rest assured. I will merely need you to infiltrate the temple and defuse the wards meant to keep me out. Then I shall find the high priestess and extract the location of the artifact from her."

"I don't know." I nibble at my lower lip. "I'm not sure I'm comfortable with aiding you in killing someone."

"It is for the greater good," he replies, his eyes boring into mine. "I will protect you, Luce," he continues. "*Please?*"

My brows shoot up in surprise. Who is he and what has he done with Ze? Last night he apologized and vowed he'd never threaten Thea again, and now he's saying *please?*

Fascinating.

"I guess I could do that."

His lips pull into a beaming smile.

"You are the only one I would trust with this," he murmurs in a low voice as he takes my hand in his. His thumb lazily strokes my flesh, his purple eyes glowing as he looks at me.

"Thanks... I think?"

"We make a good team, Luce." He nods proudly to himself.

My lips twitch, and I find myself smiling indulgently at him. I don't know if it's the way he said *team* or the fact that he used my name, but there's a strange warmth developing inside of me.

"You and me?" I challenge playfully.

He threads our fingers together, fitting his palm on top of mine. The size difference is unmistakable, his hand more than double in size. As the surface of his palm envelops mine, I feel a light pulsation at the top of my skin, one that grows in intensity just as it becomes louder and echoes in my ears.

"*Only* you and me," he speaks in a low, gruff voice.

His eyes find mine, gripping them in a tight vise that

squeezes the air out of my lungs. A tingle erupts at the center of my palm, traveling up my arm and making its home in my chest.

The door to the library suddenly opens, and Thea's voice rings out.

"Luce? Are you here?"

"Here!" I wave at her. Yet just as I look to my side, I note that Ze's already gone.

For a moment, I have to wonder if I did the right thing by agreeing to help him. Yet despite the high stakes, Ze is right in one regard—this is for the greater good. I'm not going to get Nikki back just to lose him again in a demon apocalypse. No, that's out of the question. Once I get him back, we're going to fully live our lives and grow old together. I'll accept nothing less.

I might, however, need to hide this from Nikki. He's already jealous as it is of Ze. I don't want to give him more reason to get mad.

I put on a bright smile as I join Thea and Wyn downstairs, ready to go into town.

This is the right thing to do...*right?*

The journey in the city is short. A luxurious carriage with the Duke of Sigmore's crest takes us to the seamstress's shop. As we step inside the shop, a bell rings, announcing our arrival.

"Lady Sigmore, I was expecting you." A middle-aged woman comes forward to greet us. She has a sweet smile on her face as she regards Wyn with eyes crinkling with warmth. Wyn takes her hands in hers, returning the smile, and a few other women in the back glare at her daring gesture.

"Wyn," Thea whispers, pinching her sister. "People are watching."

Wyn's smile becomes strained as she lets go of the woman's hands.

"This is my sister, Thea, and her friend, Luce," Wyn introduces us in a polite tone.

"Welcome. Please come in. The dress is in the back," she says, motioning us to follow her.

As we head to the back of the shop, I let my gaze roam around. The walls are draped in various colored fabrics, with a few gowns displayed on mannequins on each side of the shop. The materials appear luxurious, the gowns on display absolutely breathtaking. In particular, my eyes stray to a purple one with black flowers embroidered all over the bodice.

The other seamstresses stare at us, their countenances stiff and unfriendly. They barely nod at us as we pass by them, turning to whisper amongst themselves.

"Let's try the dress on, shall we? I've finished adding the details you asked me for last time," the seamstress adds as she ushers Wyn into the changing room.

Thea and I remain behind, wanting to give her and the seamstress enough space to get dressed and adjust the gown.

The seamstress gives us a pleasant smile before she closes the door to the changing room, assuring us Wyn will be back shortly to show us her gown.

"I'm so excited, Luce," Thea murmurs, her eyes glossy with unshed tears. "I can't believe my Wyn is already an adult."

"What happened this morning? If it's okay for you to tell me."

"Wyn's ryoku? I forgot you're not familiar with our ways. It means her body has reached full maturity and her main abilities are manifesting," she explains with a sigh. "She will soon start her qualifying exams and in no time, she will have offers from all eligible bachelors..."

"She doesn't seem very keen on that considering her infatuation with Aethon." I smile, remembering how I was at her age— just as infatuated with Nikki.

Thea's expression falls.

"Please do not mention him again in her presence. I don't want her to entertain the possibility that..." She takes a deep breath. "He is not for her. She will understand that eventually."

I don't reply, though I very much doubt it. I saw the way Wyn's expression changed the moment she mentioned Aethon's name. The girl is in love with him.

The door to the changing room opens and Wyn steps out in a majestic light blue gown. The bodice is the shape of a heart, a corset hugging her torso. Two dark blue straps mold to her shoulders, the sleeves a shimmery but sheer material that falls down her arms, leading to the floor. A pretty dark blue bow is wrapped around her waist, after which the skirt flares in a bell shape. The top layer is made of the same light blue as the bodice, but underneath there are three other layers of tulle, all a darker blue.

The pièce de résistance, however, is the embroidery. There's a dark blue dragon that starts from the base of the skirt, coiling up her body until it reaches her chest, its head resting lovingly on top of her breasts.

"Wyn...you..." Thea's eyes widen as she takes in her sister.

Wyn has a guilty expression on her face as she averts her gaze, looking down at her dress and biting her lip.

"This is absolutely gorgeous," I say, still in awe.

"It is not." Thea grits her teeth. "Do you realize that everyone will know the reference, Wyn?"

"I... I like it," Wyn whispers softly.

"Take it off," Thea suddenly demands. "Take it off and burn it. If anyone sees this... Goodness, Wyn, you will be disgraced before you even make your debut."

Wyn blinks back tears as she glances at her sister, her hands fidgeting uncomfortably in front of her.

"Did my mother approve this?" she asks the seamstress.

"Y-yes," she answers meekly.

"Oh, I don't think so. She didn't see the embroidery, did she?" Thea asks in a cutting voice.

"What's going on?" I whisper.

"Aethon is not just one of the most celebrated generals of Aperion," she starts in a scathing tone. "He is also the only blue dragon in existence. That, right there"—she points to the embroidery—"is the boldest statement I've ever seen. And I won't be the only one to think so. You promised me, Wyn," Thea adds in exasperation. "This will ruin your reputation. Take it off."

Wyn shakes her head.

"It's my ball, Thea," she protests. "I thought at least you would support me."

"Wyn, I would support you in anything but this. Not when it's your reputation at stake."

The bell to the shop rings. Glancing at the door, I note three women coming inside, all dressed in expensive dresses, their features stained by arrogance as they barely spare a glance at the staff.

The middle one, a dark-haired woman around my age, scans the shop until her gaze lands on Thea and Wyn, her dark blue eyes gleaming insidiously.

Her lips twitch as she gives a signal to the other two girls to follow her.

"Mrs. Bali, I specifically requested this time for my appointment," she starts in a haughty tone, her eyes narrowed at the seamstress currently helping Wyn with her dress.

"Your Highness, I am sorry. I already told you I was booked for this hour. Lady Sigmore will not take much longer. Why don't you come back in an hour? I will be able to attend you then."

"No," she replies resolutely. "I want to have my fitting now."

"Your Highness, as you can see, I am busy with a client..."

"Her?" The woman cuts her off as she assesses Wyn's gown, the corners of her mouth curling in disgust. "You might as well cut your appointment short. There's nothing anyone can do that is going to spare her the embarrassment with that gown."

"Elora..." Wyn seethes, her hands balled into fists. "You're going too far."

"Am I?" Elora smirks. "I'm not the one commissioning a gown with a blue dragon for my debut." She laughs. "As if General Aethon would ever look at someone like you."

"What's that supposed to mean?" Thea intervenes, taking a step forward.

"Stay out of this, Thea." Wyn shakes her head at Thea. "This is between me and Elora."

"And the entire Aperion that will laugh at you." Elora rolls her eyes.

"You're just jealous my brother happens to be Aethon's best

friend, and he's going to come to my ball. I doubt he'll come to yours," Wyn says as she pushes her chin up.

"You—"

"What was it in that letter that you sent him? *Dear General Aethon, it would please me immensely to invite you to my debut ball. It is going to be the grandest ball Arche has ever seen...*"

Elora's eyes widen. "How did you—"

"This?" Wyn raises an eyebrow as she opens her palm, materializing a stack of letters. "Sorry to say they got lost in the mail." She smiles.

"Damnation! Wyn's going to be in so much trouble," Thea mutters under her breath.

"I think she rather reminds me of someone I know," I add jokingly.

Elora moves to grab the letters, but Wyn takes a step back, holding her hand higher as the letters turn to dust.

"Oops. I do not think General Aethon is going to be able to come to your ball, Elora. Such a pity. But rest assured, I'll put in a *good* word for you when he claims the first dance. I'll tell him *all* about you."

Elora's chest rises and falls in frustration, anger evident in her features.

"Don't tell me they're fighting for a man," I whisper to Thea.

"It would appear so. It seems I have not been watching Wyn as closely as I should have." She grits her teeth, her body tense.

"You are going to regret this, Arwyn. My father will hear of this." Elora points her finger at Wyn, her nostrils flaring.

Wyn rolls her eyes. "Promises, promises. You might outrank me, Elora, but that doesn't mean I don't smell the jealousy off you from a mile away. You knew I was going to have my fitting today, at this hour. So you decided to bring your sour self here to ruin my day. Well, guess what? You've merely given me a boost of confidence because I just remembered that I have *no* competition for Aethon."

"You fucking bitch!" Elora rages before she throws herself at Wyn, removing a pin from her hair and slashing at her dress.

Pieces of tulle fall to the ground, the body of the majestic blue dragon ripped apart.

Wyn's surprised gasp echoes through the shop as she stares at the torn embroidery. Her lips quiver, her lashes misted with tears.

"Let go of me." She pushes at Elora, doing her best to avoid getting nicked by the dagger-like pin.

"Oh, no, no. You're not doing that," Thea curses before she intervenes to pull them apart.

Elora swivels, her eyes connecting with Thea's as she waves her sharp pin around.

"Ladies, please!" the seamstress calls out in distress from behind.

"What are you going to do, Erithea? Everyone knows you're the useless one," Elora spits out.

Thea's features become tense as she morphs her hand into claws, blocking the pin from cutting her face.

With Elora distracted by Thea, Wyn grabs a handful of Elora's hair, her fingers lodging into her scalp.

"Ah!" Elora yelps, her eyes watering. But that only prompts her to become more aggressive, slashing blindly at Thea with one hand while punching Wyn with the other to free herself. Their positions are awkward, and neither can land a good blow on the other.

Seeing that there are two against one in the fight, the other girls accompanying Elora rush forward to help. One of them tries to get Wyn's hand out of Elora's hair while the other attempts to push Thea off.

There's a cacophony of gasps, whines, and moans as they all get tangled within each other. One of the girls gets her hand in Wyn's hair, pulling on it. Wyn winces and she pulls even harder on Elora's hair, her fingers turning white from the deadly grip she has on it.

"Bitch," Wyn yells. "You're going to pay for ruining my dress," she vows, twisting her neck to push the other girl off her. She suddenly releases her grip on Elora's hair, but she doesn't let go. A black smoke erupts from the center of her palm, enveloping Elora's hair and turning it into ash, tip to root. Just like the letters, her hair disintegrates until there's nothing left.

Elora shrieks loudly, the other two girls joining in as they hit right and left, trying to land *any* blow on Wyn and Thea.

I bite my lip as I debate what I can do, being the only human in here. A glint of metal makes my decision for me as I notice one of the other girls grab a pair of scissors and aim it straight at Wyn's face.

"Watch out," I shout, pushing Wyn out of the way and inserting myself between her and the attacker.

My eyes widen as I watch the descent of her arm in slow motion, the sharp tip of the scissors gleaming menacingly as it nears my face. My breathing intensifies and I flinch back as the girl aims for my cheek.

Yet the blow doesn't come.

I blink repeatedly as I stare at the black drops of blood dripping to the ground. The scissors have perforated a hand, going through one side and coming out through the other. Slowly, I gaze up to see Ze next to us, his arm extended, his hand protecting my face from the attack.

The fight immediately ceases. Silence descends in the shop as they all gawk at him.

Grabbing the pair of scissors from the girl, he wrenches it out of his hand and drops it to the ground. His flesh starts mending, his skin knitting together until there's no blemish left.

"Ze..." I whisper.

His jaw is clenched tightly as he stares down at the three girls.

"Is that..."

"Commander Azerius," Elora whimpers.

"The God Killer," the other girl mutters in a low voice, her face going white.

Elora turns to him, tears falling down her cheeks as she rubs her bald head.

"Good thing you are here, Commander. She... She destroyed

my hair. Punish her!" she demands in an authoritative tone as she points at Wyn. "I command you to—"

Ze grabs two of the girls by their napes and flings them across the room. They hit the wall with a thud, sliding down to the floor, unmoving.

There's only Elora left standing, and she's slowly realizing that Ze is not there to help her.

He raises a brow at her, and without exerting any strength, he reaches with his arm and pokes her forehead, the strength of the blow sending her flying to the back where she joins her friends on the floor.

Ze takes a step forward, clearly not done with them.

"You... You can't do this. You're not allowed to hurt us," Elora whimpers, clutching onto her arm that appears to be dislocated.

The girls huddle together as they cower from Ze. His expression is tight and unyielding, a murderous aura surrounding him. Purple tendrils of energy swirl around him.

"You'll pay for this. My father will have your head," Elora continues, using her good hand to summon a blast that she sends toward Ze. He merely opens his palm, absorbing the brunt of it before the energy dissipates around him.

His nostrils flare dangerously as he takes a step forward.

"That's enough, Ze," I whisper as I grab his sleeve.

He slowly turns his head to look at me, his eyes narrowed.

"I'm fine. We're fine," I say as I point to Thea and Wyn.

Thea snickers as she dusts her clothes, glaring angrily at Elora.

"For once, I'm happy to see you, Ze," she mumbles before she turns her attention to her sister. Wyn is wiping her tears as she glances down at her ruined dress. I doubt there's much that can be done with the amount of damage Elora did to it. The embroidery is mostly destroyed, the layers torn. The bodice is relatively unharmed, but the sleeves have also been slashed.

"It's okay, Wyn. We'll get you another dress," Thea tries to comfort her.

She sniffles as she shakes her head.

"You have no idea how long we've been working on this dress." She swallows, a sob lodged in her throat. "It was supposed to be special. Aethon was supposed to see me in it and..." She squeezes her eyes shut.

"Aethon?" Ze swivels, raising a brow at her. "Why are you bringing up my general?"

"Don't worry about it, Ze. It's nothing."

He doesn't listen to Thea, striding to Wyn and looming over her.

"If she has information about Aethon, I must know it."

"She doesn't. She—"

"I'm going to be his mate," Wyn declares, bringing the back of her hand to wipe her tears. "Aethon will be mine. Just you wait and see. *All* of you," she states confidently as she glances at Elora.

"You are going to be Aethon's mate?" He raises a brow at her before he gives a dry laugh. "You are not very bright, are you? Just like your"—his gaze strays to Thea—"sister."

"Ze, please don't." I pull on his sleeve, whispering in a low voice. "You promised you'd be nice."

He pauses for a moment, deep in thought.

"I do not recall such a promise. My vow did not include that." He clicks his tongue, his gaze boring into Wyn.

Elora and her friends take advantage of this moment to slither past us and run out of the shop, but not before promising retribution for her hair—I assume also the humiliation. "My father will hear of this," Elora yells as the bell rings again to announce their departure.

Ze doesn't bat an eye at the threat. In fact, I'm surprised he let them leave so easily.

Maybe there's still hope for him...

"Tell me what you know of Aethon!" he demands sharply. "When did you last see him?"

"I..." Wyn bites her lip, blinking slowly.

"Leave her alone, Ze. She's just infatuated with him. He barely knows she exists," Thea intervenes.

"Is that so... I suppose that makes sense since the Supremes have already found a mate for him. If he is not already dead, that is."

Thea appears to be surprised by his words while Wyn looks stricken.

I retract my words. There is absolutely no hope for him.

"W-what?" Wyn's eyes widen, her lips trembling with fear.

"Don't listen to him." Thea pats her on her shoulder before turning to glare at him. "Stop this, Ze. Aethon can't be dead. He's as strong as you are."

He smirks. "Debatable."

"Ze," I groan.

He pulls me closer to him, keeping me glued to his side as his arm slides over my shoulders.

"What are you talking about? Why would Aethon be dead?" Wyn asks in a shaky voice. Tears cling to her lashes and she's on the verge of breaking down. If the fight with Elora didn't rattle her as much, this most certainly will.

"Ze, can't you just let this go? For bonus points?" I suggest, hoping he'd take the bait and leave the poor girl alone. Her dress is already destroyed. She doesn't need to find out that her crush is missing in action, or worse, that he already has a mate waiting for him when he gets home.

Ze's lashes flutter and he finally gives me his full attention.

"Extra points? Will you give me extra points again?"

I nod.

He stares at me.

"Good. For ninety-one extra points, I shall stop."

"Ninety-one?" I blink.

"I must recover my losses." He shrugs.

"Fine, you got it. Now let's go," I mutter as I try to steer him out of the shop. "Sorry about this." I give Thea a strained smile. "I'll find my way back to the house with Ze. I think you two need some time alone."

Thea nods, her expression worried.

In a lower voice, I whisper, "I think you should tell her that he's missing. She'll be even more disappointed when he doesn't show up for her ball."

She purses her lips, expelling a deep breath.

"You're right. Thank you, Luce. I'll see you later."

I incline my head and, leaving the two of them behind, I drag Ze with me out of the shop.

God, but the man doesn't know when to keep his mouth shut. And ninety-one points? That was stretching it and he *knows* it, especially with the smug smile he has plastered on his face.

FORTY-NINE

The two suns are blazing in the sky, a burning red against clear blue. As the door of the shop closes behind us, we step into the bustling street.

A few gasps erupt around us, and people stop to stare. Men and women of all ages come to a halt, their eyes widening as they take us in.

My brows scrunch up as I look up at Ze questioningly. His lips are pressed in a thin line as he glares at the pedestrians—his way of telling them to move along and mind their own business. But it's clear why they're gawking at him with a mix of awe and trepidation. He's easily the largest man around, with a good head taller than the rest. His shoulder breadth alone is the size of two normal males put together. He'd be a frightening sight to everyone, especially since his sword is dangling by his waist, the white of the scabbard a stark contrast to his black clothes.

A few kids here and there continue to stare at him on the verge of tears, while their parents are cooing to them in a comforting voice, dragging them away.

"So," I start, plastering a smile on my face. Thea had mentioned that s'Aperiotes don't particularly like deities, no matter their rank. They must have recognized Ze as one and they no doubt have plenty of opinions against him for that alone. Some people who haven't scurried away still glare at us, their nostrils flaring as they mutter something amongst themselves.

"Thea mentioned there's a shop around that serves sweet ices. Let's go there?"

Ze turns to me, his brows going up in surprise.

"You want to go get sweet ices? With me?"

"Why not? Thea and Wyn will likely be at the seamstress's shop for a while, and I don't have anything planned for today. Wait, do you?" My face falls as I ask.

"No. I do not," he hurries to add as he straightens his back, a smile tipping at his lips. "I will accompany you to get sweet ices."

"Great. If chocolate is so good in your world, I'm curious how this will compare."

"I would not know," he adds pensively.

"Of course. You do not engage in frivolities, and I bet sweet ices are the height of such frivolities," I say as I crack a smile.

He nods, his expression serious.

"You are correct, human. But for you, I shall make an exception."

"Happy to hear that, Ze." I chuckle, grabbing his arm and threading mine through the crook of his elbow. He blinks in surprise at my gesture, but his lips settle in a pleasant smile and he draws me closer to him.

As we walk to the ice shop, the whispers around us abound. The sea of people splits to make way for us as if we were a pair of diseased individuals no one wanted to be near. It's quite odd. I glance left and right, noticing men who hunch their shoulders in fear, averting their gazes as Ze and I pass, while others glare at us belligerently, cursing under their breaths.

I do my best to ignore it, but the heavy weight of their malevolent gazes makes the hairs on my body rise up. Ze does not comment on it, however, and I don't bring it up either. Instead, I make some small talk on the way, keeping his attention on me so he doesn't register the extent of people's dislike.

Knowing him, he would take umbrage at people failing to recognize his greatness and that could lead to a conflict no one wants.

Luckily, though, we reach the shop rather fast. The building is made out of red brick, with a white sign over the door saying: Jojo's sweet ice. As we enter the shop, a few waitresses run around the place, scribbling down orders with a pleasant smile on their faces. The place is almost full. Lively chatter fills the room, with customers engaged in animated discussions while they're enjoying their desserts.

The door closes behind us and everyone stops what they're doing to stare at us.

Silence envelops the room. One of the waitresses blinks, her smile falling. All the color leaves the customers' faces, the previously relaxed atmosphere becoming heavy and intense.

I clear my throat as I look at Ze.

"What about that table?" I point to a faraway corner.

He grunts, taking my hand and leading me there. And for the first time, I'm surprised to see a gentlemanly side to him as he pulls a chair for me to sit. He takes a seat across from me, though the chair is too small for him. Still, he doesn't complain, merely letting his calculated gaze roam around the room. Although he's not saying anything, his stiff manner alone is threatening enough, and people feel the shift in the air. The shop turns eerily calm, and although people are not openly staring at us, they're still furtively stealing glances, their voices now barely above a whisper.

The waitresses are gathered in a corner, talking amongst themselves and gesturing toward our table. Eventually, one of them hunches her shoulders and comes our way, bringing two menus with her.

She lays them on the table for us and scurries out of the way before we can even thank her.

Odd.

Grabbing one of the menus, I quietly study it, thankful it comes with pictures.

"This looks so good." I smile. The ice is served in a round cup the size of my fist, and it appears there are a multitude of flavors, all served with a syrup on top.

"What will you have?" I ask Ze.

His brows are knit together as he peruses the options, but he seems conflicted about his choice.

"What will you have?" he fires back.

"Chocolate, of course." I chuckle, pointing to the chocolate chip one.

A hint of a smile tugs at his lips.

"Of course, your favorite." He nods. "What is your second favorite?"

"Hmm." I bite my lip as I glance down at the menu. They have an assortment of fruits that I'm not familiar with, but there are also a few flavors that I know well. "This." I point to the mint caramel one.

"Then that is what I shall have," he declares, pushing his menu aside.

"Are you sure?" I raise my brows. "You don't have to get it just because I like it."

"If you like it, I will like it," he states, ending the conversation as he raises his hand and beckons the waitress to our table, barking out the order succinctly.

The waitress keeps her distance, swallowing hard as she scribbles down our order. She doesn't linger as she turns her back to us, disappearing toward the kitchen.

"Why are people so rude around here?" I ask him in a low voice.

His features tighten.

"I suppose it is my presence that makes them that way."

"What do you mean?"

He purses his lips.

"Do not concern yourself with that. You are here to enjoy yourself and you will enjoy yourself," he comments, leaning back and crossing his arms over his chest.

I blink repeatedly, taken aback by the vehemence in his voice.

"All right," I murmur, settling more comfortably in my chair. "Are you worried about Elora's threat? She's the king's daughter, isn't she?"

Ze grunts.

"She is his youngest daughter. I believe she is around Arwyn's age. It is my understanding she will have her debut at the end of the year."

"She seemed...difficult."

He shrugs.

"I do not like the king or his family. I have no doubt she will complain about me and in turn the king will have a reason to make it more difficult for me to gain access to the temple. Which is why I shall require your assistance."

"You anticipate that it will be that difficult?"

"It is a calculated guess. There is not one king among the fourteen Houses that bears me any affection. They see me as a threat."

"But surely that's more reason to try to be nicer to you?" I ask.

The corner of his mouth curls up.

"The politics of this world are...different. There are factions within the Houses, just as there are factions within the Supremes. Although...they all have one thing in common," he pauses, amusement playing at his lips.

I raise my brows in question.

"They all hate me." He releases a dry laugh—one that doesn't quite reach his eyes.

"W-what? Even the Supremes?"

"I am a necessary evil. Or so I am told." He shrugs.

"But why would you follow the rules of someone who hates you? Someone who only tolerates you for your abilities?" I frown.

He tilts his head to the side, thoughtfully considering my question.

"Because I do not know otherwise," he answers quietly.

My eyes slowly widen as the meaning of his words sinks in.

Seven thousand years. He's spent seven thousand years just...being tolerated? Because these people need him as much as they fear him? It hasn't escaped me that even the king was terrified of Ze despite putting on a strong front.

My lips quiver as it dawns on me what a lonely existence he must have led.

No frivolities. No relationships. Nothing. Just...existing.

No wonder he's never felt joy, or anything really. Was he ever allowed to?

He notices my reaction, and his features harden.

"Do not pity me, human," he grits out in a low voice.

I shake my head. Grabbing my chair, I scoot closer to him until we're next to one another. Forcing my lips into a smile, I tentatively reach out, curving my palm along his cheek.

He blinks, his eyes narrowed at me. His chest rises and falls as his pupils become larger in size. His countenance is tentative, as if he doesn't know what to expect—half leaning into me, half thinking to run away from me.

The corners of my mouth curl up.

Running—not something I would ever associate with him.

"How could I pity you when it's all you've ever known?" I murmur as I caress him gently.

A stricken look appears on his face, one that wounds me deep inside because I can see the fear reflected in his gaze, just as I can feel the loneliness emanating from him.

"But I want you to know you don't have to let yourself be tolerated. You don't have to live your life at other people's whims and take whatever scraps they throw your way. You deserve better, Ze."

His lips part, his breathing becoming labored.

"I know you don't need friends. But don't you wish to at least surround yourself with people who...don't hate you?"

Tension fills his jaw.

"I do not need to be liked," he grinds out. "It is the nature of my position to be hated. I do the job no one else dares to."

"But do you have to?"

He stares at me, his mouth opening and closing as if he cannot find the words to answer me.

"Why do you care?" he eventually asks as he averts his gaze, a flush going up his neck. "A few days ago, you were telling me how much you hate me—just like everyone else."

A hopeless sigh escapes his lips as he stares at the faraway wall. My heart clenches in my chest at that lone sound, and something akin to a punch in the gut makes me gasp for air.

I did say those things. I did tell him how much I hated him. Yet despite all he's done and said before... I understand. He was never given a chance to be better, and to my great shame, I behaved just like the others.

"I don't condone your actions, Ze. Hell, I don't like most of them. Yet even when I don't like you, there's something about you that calls to me." I give him a sad smile. "I may not agree with you, but I care about you. And I want you to be better. If you want that, too, that is."

He doesn't move, his eyes fixed on me.

"I would like"—he clears his throat as he rolls his shoulders and straightens his back—"to be nice. To you."

"Prove it then. Make an effort and be nice."

He gives me a brisk nod, his cheeks heated. My hand falls from his face and I tuck it by my side, not wanting him to misconstrue my actions.

"Does that also yield me extra points?" he asks eagerly.

My brows shoot up in surprise before I burst into laughter.

"Fine. I'll reward your good deeds with extra points."

A satisfied smile blooms on his face, and he once more leans back in his seat, resuming his relaxed stance.

Our conversation continues on a lighter tone, and I even manage to elicit a few smiles from him that are as foreign to me as they are to him.

Yet despite our easygoing interaction, the atmosphere is still tense. The hairs on my back stand to attention as I feel people's eyes boring into me. I glance around from the corner of my eye, not surprised to see people staring at us. Some do so directly, their distaste written all over their features, while others are more discreet. The staff of the establishment appears to have a problem with us as well. Since we've taken our seats, a few other people have come in, all ordering and receiving their orders within a short period of time. Meanwhile, we've been waiting for ages. I may not be sure how things are done around here, but I can feel when I'm unwanted.

I wonder if they haven't brought out our orders because they thought if we waited long enough, we'd cut our losses and leave. Alas, we will not.

Ze seems oblivious to the hostile atmosphere, and in order to avoid more trouble, I keep things to myself. The last thing we need is for him to say or do something that will just confirm people's opinion of him. So to distract him, I put on a pleasant smile and inquire about his general.

"Why did the Supremes choose a mate for Aethon? Is he not allowed to choose for himself?"

His lips press together in a tight line.

"Aethon is a special case. He is the only blue dragon in existence and the Supremes are afraid his line will die out. For thousands of years, they have been trying to find someone who is a biological match to him and who would be able to bear him blue dragon younglings."

"So he has no choice at all in who he takes as a mate?"

"If the Supremes decree it, he will have to obey it."

I nod slowly. Poor Wyn. She's going to be heartbroken.

"And who is this mate they've found for him?" I probe further.

"She is a silver dragon, but she has not yet reached maturity. Still, if the Supremes enforce a betrothal, it will be binding until she becomes an adult, at which point they will be mated."

"Isn't Aethon ancient? He has to wait even more?"

Ze shrugs.

"It is what it is. I have known Aethon for almost six thousand years. He has always been dedicated to his position. There was never any suggestion that he might wish for a mate, or younglings. But if the Supremes command it..."

"You obey. Got it. I just feel sorry for Wyn. She has a major crush on him," I sigh.

"Aethon is a desirable male, both due to his achievements and his unattainability. It is normal for young females to be infatuated with him. Most debutantes are. But compared to Arwyn, they realize their dreams are just that—dreams. I cannot fathom how Erithea has allowed her to nurture these fantasies."

"Thea thought it was an innocent crush. But Wyn went too far to embroider his dragon form on her gown."

Ze scoffs.

"That is how you know she is related to Erithea. Foolish females, both of them." He shakes his head.

"Ze." I side-eye him. "I thought you were going to try to be nice."

"Being nice and frank are two different things." He puts his finger up. "I do not lie, human." He glares at me intently.

"Right, sometimes I forget you have no filter." I sigh. "You don't have to lie, you know. Just... be more tactful."

His eyes narrow, his mouth tightening.

"Senseless females," he amends after a moment's thought.

I blink. Slowly, I release a deep breath. He is hopeless.

Our discussion is interrupted by the waitress, who places the cups of sweet ice on the table, the chocolate one in front of me and the mint caramel one in front of Ze.

"Thank you," I murmur, dragging my chair closer and licking my lips as I pick up a spoon to taste it. I dip it in the ice and grab a small spoonful, which I then bring to my mouth.

"Ah, this is so good," I exclaim as I smack my lips together to get more of the flavor.

Ze looks intently at me, nodding to himself. Seeing my reaction, he turns his attention to his own cup of ice, studying it.

"Here," I say as I push a full spoon of chocolate ice to him. "Taste. This is so amazing, Ze." I sigh. "You have to try it."

His eyes sparkle as he leans forward, wrapping his lips around the spoon.

"You like it?"

He nods, a look of surprise crossing his face.

"Oh, by the way," I whisper conspiratorially. "I hope you have money to pay for this since I don't have any."

His lips curve up in a lopsided smile.

"I have money, human. I told you, I am *very* rich."

"Right." I nod. "I forgot you also have a *very* expensive palace."

"Precisely." He pushes his chin up. "I can afford to feed you sweet ices for the rest of your life," he adds proudly.

"So nice of you, Ze. See, you're already doing better," I tease.

Heat climbs up his cheeks, and he struggles not to preen at the praise.

While I continue to eat with gusto, he dips his own spoon into the sweet ice and gets his first taste.

I pause, looking at him expectantly.

"How is yours?"

He gulps down, slowly licking his lips.

"It is... good," he finally says, though something about the way he scrunches his nose makes me doubt that.

"Let me try." I reach out with my spoon, but he swats it out of the way.

"Yours is better," he grumbles, pulling his bowl closer and out of reach.

"Ze." I pout. "You said you'd be nice. Let me try it."

He shakes his head.

I pull my chair closer to him, and with a mischievous smile, I try to get a spoonful again. This time, he takes the bowl in his arms, digging in with his spoon and eating half of the ice cream in just a couple of bites.

My lashes flutter as I stare at him.

If this is how he wants to play the game, he'll have a little surprise.

"Oh my!" My eyes widen in feigned shock as I point behind him. "What is *that*, Ze?" I call out in a frightened voice.

His features tense, and he turns to look behind him.

I take advantage of his momentary lack of attention to stick my spoon in what's left of his bowl of ice, take a little, and bring it to my mouth.

He's too fast, however. He grabs my hand, stopping it midair just as I'm about to finally taste it. Before I can blink, he leans forward, wrapping his lips around the spoon and eating all the ice. His eyes never leave mine, his tongue swirling around the spoon in slow motion.

"Ze..."

"It is poisoned," he whispers so only I can hear him. "You cannot have it or you will be gravely ill."

"W-what?"

"Yours is fine," he continues as if he didn't just drop a bomb on me.

"Are you all right? Will you get ill?" The words tumble out of my mouth as I drop my arm, staring at him in shock.

"I shall be fine. They were probably unaware that I am immune to most known poisons."

"They... You mean they did this on purpose? They wanted to..."

"Kill me?" He raises a brow, his lips curling at the corners. "It would not be the first time."

"What are you talking about?" I hiss as I lean forward until we're a mere breath apart. "How can you be so apathetic about this?"

"It is not a novelty." He shrugs. "Although it does not harm me, it does taste foul." He sighs. "I would not recommend it."

"Damn it, Ze. This is not the moment to joke around," I say pointedly as I jab my finger into his chest. "You can't just let this go. They tried to kill you!" I catch myself just in time so I don't yell the words. "Regardless of whether they succeeded or not, the intention was there."

The stares. The whispers. The blatant disrespect. Now it all makes sense. But it also makes me more enraged than I've ever been before—especially as Ze doesn't seem bothered in the least. His expression is relaxed, almost blasé.

"If I were to punish everyone who ever wished me dead, I am afraid Aperion would be sorely lacking in population," he says with a careless shrug.

"But... Aren't you mad?" I blink.

"I was, the first few times it happened. After so long, I got used to it and now I just ignore it."

"Well, *I* cannot in good conscience ignore it," I declare, fuming on his behalf.

His brows knit together as he tilts his head, his expression puzzled.

I shoot to my feet, sparks of anger humming under my skin.

"You." I point to the waitress. "Come here."

Everyone is suddenly staring at me, but I don't care. Someone needs to explain this, and I will not let it go until Ze gets an apology.

Ze gets up as well, hovering behind me like a shadow, quiet like one too.

The waitress looks right and left as she slowly makes her way to our table. Just as she reaches us, I grab the poisoned ice and shove it in her face.

"Eat." I nod at her.

"W-what?" she whispers.

"I said eat."

"I cannot," she stammers, looking at her colleagues for help. "It would not be right for me to do so." She feigns a smile.

"Is that so?" I plaster an equally fake smile on my face. And before she realizes what I'm about to do, I push my hand into the bowl, scoop the rest of the ice in my fist, and bring it to her mouth, forcefully feeding it to her.

She gasps and chokes. Most of the ice melts around the

corners of her mouth, but I have no doubt she must have ingested at least a little.

When she realizes what happened, she takes a step back, her eyes wild as she releases a sharp screech.

"Dora! Dora! I need the antidote," she screams, scrambling back and tripping. She falls to the ground, her mouth open as her voice becomes little more than background noise.

A few other women hurry from the kitchens, one of them carrying a small glass that she forces onto the waitress's throat. But while they're desperately trying to save that witch, I turn my angry gaze to the rest of the customers.

"It's the God Killer," the whispers abound.

"He ate so much of it and he's still alive," one man marvels.

"We should do something. I heard he can't strike back unless he gets permission from the Supremes."

"I heard that too. He's only allowed to kill demons and execute traitors."

"He shouldn't be called the God Killer." One laughs. "He should be called the Lap Dog instead."

The more I hear their vile insults, the more I feel incensed on Ze's behalf. One glance at him, though, and he doesn't seem in the least bothered. That tells me everything I need to know.

Seven thousand years of being treated like this. He's...used to it. He finds it normal.

"How the hell can you stand by and watch these people try to kill him?"

A gaggle of laughter erupts in the crowd.

"Good riddance," one scoffs from the back.

"You..."

"Do not get angry on my behalf. It is not worth it, Luce. We should leave," Ze whispers as he places his hands on my shoulders.

I clench my hands into fists. The laughter intensifies, as do the mocking words.

How can he not be affected by this? How...

"They should have poisoned her too," someone whispers,

indignation bleeding from her voice. "Any female willing to share a table with the God Killer is just as bad."

I purse my lips, my breathing intensifying as the urge to do something—anything—overwhelms me.

"I wouldn't be surprised if she's his whore." A woman steps forward, pointing her finger at me.

"She's too ugly to be anything but his whore," a man echoes.

My eyes widen.

"What did you just say?" Ze bellows, pulling me back and placing himself in front of me.

The crowd takes a step back.

Yet despite the overwhelming fear I sense from them, there's also the hate—so much hate.

Ze's expression changes, the air around him crackling as shimmery purple particles surround us. The ground quakes, the tables rattling furiously with each step he takes. His muscles are coiled, the purple of his aura becoming a deeper shade—the physical manifestation of his anger.

"Run! Run!" one man yells, but not before he takes his bowl of ice and throws it at Ze.

The others follow his example, flinging their ices at Ze before dashing out of the shop.

Ze could do more. I am sure of that. He could kill them with one finger if he wished. But he doesn't. Instead, he turns his back to them, letting them hit him with the bowls of sweet ice as he places his massive body in front of me, shielding me.

"Ze..." I whisper.

His mouth is a tight line as his nostrils flare, and I'm not sure whether he's in pain or not.

"They will be dead," he states in a rough voice. "They will be *utterly* dead."

I fit my hand to his cheek, brushing my thumb across his jaw and attempting a smile—more for his sake than mine.

"Let's leave. Please."

He breathes in and out, struggling to regain control of himself. His arms are around me, a protective cage as more bowls hit him, the flavored ice melting over his clothes, hair, and skin. He's thoroughly soaked and soiled, but he doesn't bat an eye at it. He might be out of his mind with anger, but his first thought is to protect me, not punish those who mocked him.

My heart squeezes in my chest, slow and steady, until my insides ignite with warmth.

"Take me back, Ze," I whisper.

He squeezes his eyes shut, and the purple mist around us starts dissipating.

FIFTY

Before I blink, we're back in my room at Thea's house.

A little dizzy, I take a step back.

"Oh, Ze..." I struggle not to laugh as I take a good look at him.

His black clothes are thoroughly stained by the melted ice, drops of it dripping down his body and onto the floor. His hair is utterly drenched in sweet ice, his black locks covered in a myriad of shades ranging from white to pink to brown—vanilla, strawberry, chocolate, and all the flavors in between. Smudges of chocolate sauce are on his face too, streaked across his forehead and his cheeks.

There's even a messy dot on his nose—though I have no idea how that got there.

I circle around him, quickly assessing the damage.

Though the front of his clothes is soiled, it's nothing compared to the back, where he took the brunt of the blows.

Those damn people!

Merely remembering that incident makes my blood boil again.

I reach out, brushing my hand over the back of his shirt and noticing the small cuts and tears in the material—he'd been hit.

The bowls likely broke against his back and cut into his shirt...and his skin.

Of course, he's likely already healed from it. But that doesn't change the fact that it happened—that he couldn't even enjoy a simple dessert in public because people tried to kill him.

He might be the most hated man in Aperion but... There's just something utterly lonely and heartbreaking about him that makes me want to protect him—show him that he can live his life differently. Because no matter what he's said and done in the past, the undeniable truth is that...he doesn't know better.

He's lived his life as he was conditioned to, only existing, never truly living. For that alone, I'm willing to give him the benefit of the doubt—give him a chance that no one else seemingly has.

After I'm done with my perusal, I plant myself in front of him, meeting his gaze directly.

He blinks.

"Are you all right?" he inquires slowly.

"I'm fine. But you..." I shake my head. "Let's get you cleaned up," I say as I grab his hand—and get some sticky ice onto my skin—and pull him toward the bathroom. He follows dutifully.

I invite him to sit down on a chair next to the sink while I wet a cloth.

I gently dab the cloth across his face, first wiping the dirt off his forehead before moving to his cheeks and jaw. Lastly, I wipe the little cute dot off his nose.

All the while, he doesn't say a word as he watches me intently, his chest rising and falling with each breath. The purple of his eyes is even more magical this up close, and heat rises up my cheeks when I find myself staring at him, our gazes locked in an intimate embrace.

Clearing my throat, I rinse the wet cloth and leave it in the sink as I turn my attention to the mess on his neck and torso.

"May I?" I murmur in a low voice as I point to his shirt.

He gives me a pointed nod.

Reaching for the buttons of his shirt, I slowly undo them.

He helps me by shrugging the shirt off his body and throwing it in the sink.

I swallow.

I've seen him without his shirt before. But that was when he was Ze. Now he is Azerius, and the changes are marked. The same tattoos that are on one side of his face run down his neck and torso, disappearing into the band of his pants.

Almost instinctively, I brush one finger against his collarbone, following the pattern of the tattoos downward. They're all symbols of some kind, ancient runes that remind me of mystical tales from mythology, of arcane knowledge. Some lines are harsh while others curl beautifully around his golden skin, contouring every ridge and emphasizing the pronounced muscles beneath.

"What do these mean?" I ask softly, slowly raising my gaze to meet his unflinching one.

His jaw hardens, a twitch appearing in his cheek.

I continue to trace the beautiful inked lines, allowing myself to touch him as never before. Yet as I reach lower, he suddenly stops me.

"My curse," he states in a rough voice.

"What?" I blink in surprise.

His hand engulfs mine, keeping it immobile. His expression changes, too, the lines of his face becoming harsher, more tense.

He stares at me, a million battles being fought behind his troubled gaze.

"It is how I am bound to the Supremes. You asked me why I let them use me, why I am the sword that delivers their sentences. Whether I want it or not, I am programmed to do their bidding."

"I don't..." I frown.

Bringing my hand to his face, he places my open palm against his tattooed cheek.

"To go against their mandates is to suffer dire consequences," he continues, his breath fanning the inside of my wrist. "But they did not think I would ever be capable of going against them."

"Why?" I whisper.

"Because they did not just program me to be their killing machine. They also stripped me of any emotion that might make me inclined to do otherwise—to think or want something else for myself."

"Then... The condition you were talking about?"

He nods.

"It is my curse."

My eyes widen.

"Then..." I swallow hard, dropping my hand from his face. "When you said my marks were caused by a god, did you mean..."

His expression tenses as he gives me a brisk nod.

"This is a curse?" I repeat feebly, my voice breaking.

"I do not know." He sighs. "It is the mark of a god," he continues, pulling me closer to him. His eyes dip to my neckline as he pulls on my bodice to reveal my dark marks. I gasp at the sound of the material tearing, but he doesn't give me the chance to pull back. He splays his palm over my chest, just above my breasts. Purple particles of energy envelop his hand, seeping into my skin.

"Ah," I yelp as the marks burn against my skin, humming as if alive.

Dropping his hand, he nods to me to look at myself. That is when I notice that the black of the marks is now a bright white.

"It is the energy of a god, though I cannot tell you what the purpose was. But I vow to you I shall find out."

Still staring at the changing color of my marks, now slowly going back to black, I nod numbly.

"Thank you." I smile as I bring my gaze to his. "We're quite similar, aren't we?" I chuckle in an attempt to make the situation less morose than it already is.

For years I've been thinking that these marks were merely

Sergio's punishment, and so I'd hated them as I hated him. But they're not. Instead, they might be a curse from a god...

"I will not let anything happen to you, Luce," he says quietly. "I will find whoever marked you and I will get to the bottom of it. I may not be able to save myself, but I will save you."

My lips part as I stare at him, his pronouncement ringing in my ears.

Tearing my gaze from him, I wet the cloth again and bring it to his chest to wipe the remainder of the sticky substance.

"Maybe we can both be saved," I murmur.

He takes a deep breath.

"If only that were so..."

"Don't be so negative, Ze. Aren't you the most powerful guy around? I doubt there's anything that can stop you." I laugh nervously.

But one glance at him tells me he doesn't share my optimism.

"There is only a matter of time before the Supremes find out that their curse is weakening. When that happens... I do not want to risk your safety."

"Ze," I call his name in a playful tone. "Are you being nice?"

He blinks slowly before he realizes I'm making fun of him. The corners of his mouth curl up, amusement entering his previously stern features.

"I am...nice," he says tentatively. "I am nice," he repeats, this time more confidently.

Suddenly, it strikes me why he's so adamant about being *nice*. He's never been seen in a positive light by anyone in his life, has he? I struggle to keep the smile on my face as moisture clouds my sight. Maybe it's better that he didn't have emotions before so he couldn't realize just how godawful his life was, but what about now?

A tremor courses through me as images of him, depressed and alone, flash into my mind. He might appear strong and unbothered to everyone else, but I know better.

He can feel pain.

And it fucking breaks my heart.

Stifling a sob, I swipe the wet cloth over his abdominals, and a hiss escapes him.

"Ze?" I ask, worried.

He grinds his teeth.

"Continue." He nods at me.

I wipe the rest of the smudged ice from his skin until I reach close to the band of his pants, at which point I waver. His stomach is taut and riddled with muscled ridges. That coupled with the black ink and the bronzed, healthy glow of his skin and he looks like the cover model of Men's Health magazine. I might be taken, but I'm not blind. He is a handsome man—maybe a bit too handsome for his own good.

I bite my lip as my cheeks redden. This is inappropriate. I doubt he would appreciate being ogled like this.

"I think we're done here," I announce in a chirpy voice, taking a step back.

Ze raises a brow at me, watching me as he lazily leans backward, his muscles rippling with every movement. And to my everlasting shame, my eyes follow those hard lines.

"You can look your fill," he drawls.

I blink rapidly, my face flaming hot as I realize I've been caught gawking at him.

"S-sorry," I mumble, turning to the sink and rinsing the cloth again—and again. God, can the earth open up and swallow me? This is mortifying!

"Do not be sorry. I gather that you find my form pleasing?" he asks with a twinkle in his eyes.

"Erm..." I stammer. "You must be aware you are a handsome man," I add quietly, avoiding looking at him again.

"But do *you* find me pleasing, human?" he asks, his breath suddenly fanning my ear.

"Oh," I jump up, turning and bumping into him.

He braces his arms on the sink on either side of me, leaning down to look at me.

"I... I guess so." I attempt a smile.

He stares at me.

"That is good." He slowly nods, his expression pensive.

"I doubt I'm the only one. Didn't you say you have a legion of admirers?" I laugh awkwardly as I try to make light of the situation, though his nearness makes all the hairs on my body stand up. I gulp nervously, a little unsettled by the way he's watching me—like a hawk with his prey in sight.

"I may have... exaggerated," he grumbles.

My eyes widen as I raise my brows at him.

"Those who do chase after me do not do it for *me*. Rather, they want to tame the God Killer." He sighs, squaring his shoulders.

"Surely you've been told you're a good-looking man before?" I say before I can help myself.

His lips flatten.

"Right...?"

"Not in those terms, no."

"What, then?"

A deep, growly sound erupts from his throat.

"It does not matter," he suddenly says, stepping away from me.

Whatever I said must have hit a nerve, for he turns with his back to me, pacing around the bathroom.

"Uhm, Ze?"

"What?" He pivots, his expression half-feral.

I wet my lips, surprised by this sudden change in him.

"I think you need to get in the shower to remove the sweet ice from your hair."

He glares at me for a moment before his expression softens, his muscles relaxing, not that I'm looking at them—*I'm not, really!*

"You do it for me," he says before he grabs my hand and leads me to the shower.

"W-what?"

He doesn't waste any time as he steps inside the shower,

taking a seat on the floor and waiting for me to wash him. He has half a smile on his face, his eyes sparkling as he looks up at me, and I find myself melting a little toward him.

Damn it, why does he have to be cute?

"Okay, I guess I can do that..." I trail off as I glance down at my dress. "Let me quickly change into casual clothes," I say and dash out of the shower. I quickly go back to the room and change into a pair of leggings and a plain shirt. When I get back, I find him fiddling with the settings on the mobile shower head, water spraying all around the shower stall. He's sporting an expression that's a mix of confusion and exasperation as he cannot get the shower to function properly. He's already wet, but not much cleaner than before.

"Let me take care of that," I mutter, taking the shower head and moving behind him.

Leaning back, he rests his weight on his elbows as he tips his head back. As I thread my hand through his locks, he closes his eyes, releasing a deep breath as he pushes himself further into my touch.

"Couldn't you have used those powers of yours to avoid getting hit?" I grumble as I set the water to warm before I place the stream over his hair, getting it thoroughly wet.

"I could have," he answers matter-of-factly.

"Then why didn't you?"

"I did not think of it."

"Why?" I frown.

"I did not want you to get hit." He shrugs, his eyes still closed.

I stare at him, replaying his words in my head until the meaning finally dawns on me.

"You foolish man." I shake my head, applying more force on his scalp and massaging it gently.

He releases a deep sound of satisfaction, something akin to a purr as a shudder travels down his body. He's like a cat. A water-loving, pampered cat, but one with the secret personality of a dog.

Grabbing the shampoo container, I pour a generous amount in his hair, working it up until his entire head is enveloped in foam.

"Smells good... like you," he murmurs, almost sleepily.

"Lily and tuberose are my favorite scents," I tell him.

"Is that what they are called..." he muses. "I shall have to acquire some for myself too."

"What do you usually use?" I ask as I bring the shower head over his forehead, gently rinsing the foam away. He preens, a gentle smile on his face as he sways his head from side to side, chasing the touch of my fingers.

"Plain soap," he murmurs absentmindedly. "I have never cared about scents before."

"No conditioner?"

"I do not know what that is."

"What you apply to your hair after you wash it. It makes it soft."

He suddenly opens his eyes, tipping his head farther back to look at me.

"Is that why your hair is so soft?"

I nod.

"Then you must use it on me too. Whatever you use to wash yourself, I shall have the same," he declares in his usual authoritative voice before he closes his eyes again, urging me to massage his scalp some more.

Since his hair was utterly soiled from the sweet ice, I apply another round of shampoo, working it into a foam before rinsing it again and applying some conditioner to make his hair softer. By the time I'm done, it's not just his hair that's soaking wet. We are, too. His pants are drenched, as are my shirt and leggings.

"Done," I declare, turning the water off and placing the shower head back in its place.

Ze releases a heavy sigh as he gets into a sitting position. Slowly, he turns his gaze to me.

"Thank you," he nods. "Now it is my turn."

I raise a brow at him, not understanding his meaning.

He gets to his feet, maneuvering me around in the shower stall until our positions are reversed. Hands on my shoulders, he pushes me down until my ass hits the ground.

W-what?

"You should take your shirt off," he suggests, already reaching for the hem.

"What are you doing?" I blink in confusion.

"You washed me. I will now wash you."

"But why? I'm not dirty, and these clothes are clean," I point out the obvious.

"I want to," he answers casually.

"But you don't have to," I say as I attempt to get up. He pushes me back down, starting the shower and placing it over my hair, getting it thoroughly wet.

I let out a surprised gasp.

"Your hair is so soft and long," he murmurs as he threads his fingers through my locks. "And it is such an odd color. Sometimes it reminds me of sunburnt sand, while other times it gives off a brownish hue, almost like the ancient rocks that have been eroded by time and the elements."

"Did you just say my hair is the color of a rock?" I ask as I stifle a laugh. I know he meant it as a compliment, but I think we've ascertained that Ze is not the best at giving compliments.

He suddenly stops the shower.

"Is that all you have understood from my words?" He tsks at me. "You are an odd human." He shakes his head at me.

"I rather think I am the *only* human you know."

"That does not mean you are not odd," he continues in his authoritative voice. "But do not mistake my meaning. I happen to like your brand of oddness. You are welcome." He nods to himself, satisfied.

My lips tremble with amusement, but I fear I may offend him if I burst into laughter. Despite his supercilious demeanor, Ze is quite the sensitive soul, isn't he? I know his words are all well-intended, which is why I'm going to give him a wide berth when it comes to his...unusual proclamations. If there's anyone here who is odd, it's most definitely him!

Done with his explanation, he shampoos my hair just as I'd done for him, carefully massaging my scalp.

My eyes flutter closed as a sigh escapes me. That does feel so heavenly.

He washes my hair thoroughly, rinsing it before adding a thick layer of conditioner.

He's so good at this that I can't help the way my body relaxes, sleep courting my lashes. I'm lulled into such a deep sense of comfort that I barely realize as I lean back against his legs, slowly falling asleep.

But it was too good to be true.

The jet of water hits me in the face, making me scramble in surprise. The shower head is right above my face as he sprays me.

"What are you doing?" I sputter, bringing my hands to wipe the moisture from my eyes.

"You cannot fall asleep yet," he tells me in a stern tone. "I am not done."

I blink at him, not understanding.

"Does it matter if I'm awake or not? You can continue what you were doing." I wave my hand at the shower.

"It matters." He gives me a decisive nod. "You need to be awake to judge my skills."

"What?"

"It is my first time washing someone's hair. I am sure I did a good job, of course, but you need to be awake to be able to assess my skills."

I stare at him as I rub my eyes.

"You did well, Ze," I add weakly, but no sooner are the words out of my mouth than a brilliant smile appears on his face. Oh, dear. He just wanted to be praised.

"Worthy of a bonus point?" he asks sheepishly.

I shake my head at him, once more stupefied. Even when I think I have him all figured out, he surprises me again.

"Fine. You've got your bonus point," I say.

Just as he rejoices at his meager bonus point, I take advantage of his lack of awareness to grab the shower head from him, spraying him in the face just as he did to me.

Take that! See how it feels to be sprayed unawares.

He jolts back, a look of surprise crossing his face. But it's soon replaced by a huge grin as he charges at me, wrestling me to the ground in an attempt to get the shower head from me.

Water sprays everywhere. On the walls, the ceiling. On his body, on my body. Even outside the shower stall.

Water is everywhere. So is the laughter echoing in the room as I try to keep him from gaining control of the shower head, spraying him with it whenever I get the chance. When he finally wrestles it from me, I take advantage of the shampoo container within my grasp and squirt a few drops in my hand, rubbing my palms together until it foams. Holding my hands near my face, I blow the foam into his face, rendering him immobile for a moment as I slip from under him and run out of the stall.

"You will pay for this, human," he thunders, his lashes covered in foam.

Yet how can I take him seriously with bubbles clinging to his hair?

My stomach hurts from too much laughter, and though I try to get away, I'm always looking over my shoulder, even more amused by the sight he poses. Black pants and white foam, he is the epitome of scary cute.

He realizes it, too, and to my greatest surprise, he doesn't take himself seriously as he strikes a pose, his stance that of a foam warrior ready for war.

I double over from laughter, giving him enough time to catch up with me. One last attempt to get away, and I enter the bedroom, my feet slippery as they meet the wooden floor.

"Oops," I squeal as I teeter back and forth. But then he's suddenly there, at my back, holding on to me.

Of course he's not being helpful out of the kindness of his

heart as his foam-filled hands cover my neck and arms, roaming around until I'm just as bubbly as he is.

"Stop it, Ze." I giggle, moving my head from side to side to avoid getting foam on my face.

"You started this," he rasps, a playfulness in his voice unlike any I've heard before. "Do you surrender?"

"Never," I call out.

"Oh, you will." He chuckles, leaning down to rub his cheek against mine, transferring some of the bubbles from him to me.

I squeak aloud, a sharp noise that is half scream, half giggle.

He wraps his arms around my midriff as he continues to assault me with his foam-filled cheek until we're both two bubble warriors engaged in a spumy battle for supremacy.

His laughter echoes in my ear, a warm, fuzzy sound that I've started to crave more and more.

But as the sounds we make become louder and more intense, the door to my room suddenly bursts open, Thea, her mother, and father standing in the doorway and staring at us in shock.

Both Ze and I freeze, his body still wrapped around mine, our faces glued together—or, rather, bubbled up together.

"I... I thought something happened to you. There was a loud noise and..." Thea stammers.

"We should have knocked," Maros adds awkwardly.

They don't move, though, quietly staring at us.

"Maybe we should leave," Rhea murmurs quietly.

"I do agree, love." Maros nods.

"That would be for the best," Thea agrees robotically.

But no one makes an effort to move.

It's only when Ze gets his bearings together that he shuts the door in their faces with a flippant wave of his hand.

"I hate people," he mutters under his breath. But as his gaze meets mine, his eyes widen slightly. "Not you," he quickly amends. "You are not people."

"Really?" I ask, amused. "What am I then?"

"Mine," he answers simply, unflinchingly.

FIFTY-ONE

"You don't know either, Belinda?" I ask the cute cow as I brush her hide.

She nuzzles her snout in the crook of my neck, tickling me.

"Moo." She releases a low sound as she nestles closer to me.

"I'll take that as a no." I sigh.

After the foam incident, Ze simply disappeared, saying that he had something to take care of and he would reach out soon with the details about his plan for the temple.

But that was almost a week ago, and since then, there's been no sign of him. And to my dismay, I've realized that I've become rather used to him. Certainly enough to miss him when he's gone. The fact that Nikki has failed to appear in so long has only made my days bleaker.

"You miss your friends, don't you? I've read somewhere that cows form deep friendships and they get depressed when they're alone. Are you depressed, too, Belinda?"

Another *moo* resounds in my ear, though I'm not entirely sure how to interpret it.

Since getting Belinda, I've tried to visit her at least once a day, but despite my good intentions, I have to admit to myself that this is not a suitable environment for a cow—for an *earthly* cow. Not only is she the only one of her species here, but even the food might have a different effect on her metabolism. I don't want anything bad to happen to her, and it would be selfish to keep her just because she's cute.

Taking another good look at her, I decide to ask Ze to take her back to Earth and find a milking farm for her so she will not be slaughtered.

"I'll ask him to get your friends, too, if you have any," I tell her as I relate my plan. I'm not sure if she understands me, but she's instantly happier when she hears that she'll go back to her friends.

Alas, my decision is made.

I lay a kiss on the top of her head before I step out of the room, ready to head back to my own.

Luckily, I managed to explain to Thea and her parents that nothing untoward was going on between me and Ze. Knowing Aperion customs, the last thing I wanted was for my hosts to think I was engaging in illicit activities under their roof. I merely explained to them that we'd been cornered by angry s'Aperiotes who'd tried to kill Ze, and upon realizing they were unsuccessful, they decided to throw sweet ice at us. To my relief, they all understood our predicament and assured me they wouldn't hold it against me.

However, that was a few days ago, and I've yet to see any of them since. Even Thea was rather scarce, though that's because she's been helping her sister find another dress for her debut. With a little under a week until the ball, both Thea and Wyn are, understandably, a little highly strung.

People are coming in and out of the place daily, working on decorations and preparing the ballroom for the event.

Since everyone is so busy, I've tried to stay out of their way and keep to myself. Although, with Ze's absence, things have been rather...lonely. Belinda has been the only one to keep me company, and technically...she's not even a person.

I release a weary sigh as I unlock the door to my room and step inside.

Right there in front of me, sprawled on my bed, is Ze. He's

wearing the same black ensemble, a long-sleeved black shirt paired with a pair of loose pants held by a thick belt that houses his sword. Sometimes I wonder if his closet consists of *only* the same clothes.

When he sees me, he tilts his head to the side, his mouth quirking up.

"I have been thinking," he starts nonchalantly as if he hasn't broken into my room.

"Do tell," I add dryly as I close the door behind me and walk to the bed.

"I have accrued one hundred points. I am entitled to a boon."

My jaw falls open as I stare at him dumbfounded. Of all the things... He's gone for an entire week and then he swoops in to tell me he wants his boon? The gall of him. My ire rises as I note his relaxed manner. His arms are behind his head, his legs propped up on the bed frame—of course he'd be too big for my bed. He's sitting there as if he owns the place.

"Is this what you came for? Where have you been in the last week?" I ask him before I can help myself. The moment the words are out of my mouth, heat engulfs my cheeks. That sounded rather...needy. But just as he is entitled to his boon, I'm entitled to know when he's going to suddenly pop up—*more like break in*—into my room. As that thought arises, I make a mental note for myself to remind him that it's not okay for him to simply barge into my room—or teleport himself or whatever. If a door is locked, it's for a reason. I value my privacy—not that Ze seems to have any notion of what the word means.

His gaze meets mine, an intense look crossing his face.

"You were expecting me?" he asks slowly, his voice gravelly.

"Right, it's my mistake for thinking you'd at least send word that you'd be gone for so long." I roll my eyes.

He blinks slowly as if it just dawned on him that he should have sent word. But then again, I don't think Ze is used to accounting for his whereabouts to anyone.

His entire body tenses, his lips fighting to stay still as the corners of his mouth curl up.

Time freezes as he stares at me, his Adam's apple bobbing up, a mix of awe, satisfaction and fear echoed in his features. Eventually, he swings his legs off the bed and silently walks toward me, stopping when the tips of his feet meet mine. I glance up at him to find him watching me pensively, his brows bunched together.

Reaching into the pocket of his trousers, he takes something out and thrusts it toward me.

"For you," he says as he unfurls his fist to reveal a gold bracelet crowned with a small purple pearl in the middle.

My lips part as a shaky breath escapes me, my eyes instantly arrested by the simple yet beautiful piece of jewelry. At the same time, my brain tries to make sense of the reason behind such an extravagant gift.

When I take too long to speak or react, he clears his throat, grabbing my hand and dropping the bracelet in my palm.

"What is this?" I ask as I brush my finger along the curved surface of the purple pearl. The gold chain is thin and elegant, consisting of small loops tied together by the slightly bigger pearl.

"It is a special pearl. As long as you carry this with you, I will be able to find you anywhere," he explains as he fastens the golden string around my wrist. "I apologize for not informing you I would be away for so long. My mission turned out to be more time-consuming than I previously thought. The situation is getting more dire with the new demon appearances. With Aethon missing, I need to take on more duties than before."

"You're forgiven," I say absentmindedly as I stare at the bracelet. "This is so beautiful, Ze. Thank you," I murmur. "Where did you get it from?"

"I forged it myself, of course," he declares proudly.

My brows shoot up in surprise. I was not expecting *that*.

"You did? That's impressive."

"Of course." He nods. "The pearl is an exceedingly rare one. I acquired it from the nereid queen herself. There are only two in existence," he proclaims proudly.

"I don't know what to say," I mumble in awe, unable to take my eyes off the bracelet. "Who has the other pearl?"

Silence greets me at that question.

I slowly look up to find him staring at the ceiling, his cheeks flushed.

"I do," he admits awkwardly, pulling his sleeve up to reveal a similar bracelet with a white pearl.

"Oh, we match." I smile, placing my wrist against his. The two pearls emit a sharp gleam when they're placed side by side, indicating they're a pair. As I stare at the two of them together, the purple and white swirl together, almost as if the essences of the pearls are getting combined. Moving my hand away, I note that my pearl becomes a deep purple again, while Ze's returns to its white state. "But how did you convince her to give you both of them if they're so rare?"

"I did not need to convince her. The pearls are the solidified tears of a mermaid, and they become the property of whoever makes one cry. Mermaids almost never cry, which is why they are so rare."

I stare at him in shock.

"You made a mermaid cry to get the pearls?" I ask numbly. Speechless, I do not know whether to be incensed or touched—both emotions are at war inside of me. This is Ze we're talking about, though. Am I really that surprised he'd do this?

The answer is rather obvious...*no*.

"Not...directly," he answers sheepishly. "I merely relayed to her that her mate was dead." He shrugs. "But she only shed one tear, and I needed two so we could match, so I told her *how* he died." He nods to himself, no doubt proud of his strategy.

I shake my head at him.

"That's cruel, Ze," I lightly admonish him.

"It is not. It is just the way of our world. Nereids, too, know that death is everywhere. Not even a god is spared from the ravages of injury or disease. We may be immortal in a timeless sense, but we are not impervious. Save for the Primordials, no one is invincible."

"That doesn't make it better," I protest. Humans may be mortal, and death may be a part of daily life, but we spend our entire lives *avoiding* the reality of death.

Ze shrugs again.

If it were any other person, I would have been more disturbed by this blasé display. But I've gotten used to him and his particular way of seeing the world—through a rather amoral lens. Does it make it better? No. But at least there's a logic to explain his actions—though I may not agree with them.

"I made the golden chain, though," he suddenly adds, his voice echoing with pride.

"Do I want to ask where you got the gold for it?" I raise a brow.

He swallows hard and panic flares in his eyes.

"I do not think you want to know."

"Good, let's leave it at that." I sigh, glancing once more at my bracelet. It's so pretty, though. I'll overlook its unusual provenance this time—and this time only.

I make to move, but he moves with me, blocking my way.

"Now let us talk about my boon," he says eagerly. He places his hands behind his back—his usual stance—as he glances down at me expectantly. He's almost like a kid waiting for his reward, though in this case Ze didn't do much for it since I got swindled out of ninety-one points for him merely *not* harming other people.

I sigh as I shake my head.

"Fine. What do you want?"

I'm almost afraid to find out what he wants. Although I've gotten to know him better recently, there's still that part of him that's unreachable, that *human* part that he's only discovering too. If he barely knows his wants and desires, then who am I to guess them? But that makes him unpredictable, too—dangerous even—because he could want the most outrageous thing.

I could refuse, of course. But I gave him my word, and that matters to *me*.

I'll just have to hold my fingers crossed that he won't come up with something *too* outlandish.

"It is rather simple. I would like you to give me permission to speak to you inside your mind."

"What?" My eyes widen.

"It will make things easier in the future, especially when you shall enter the temple. Otherwise, I will have no way to communicate with you."

"And you need my permission for that?"

"I could do it without, but it usually involves exerting force on a person's mind. The effects are not...pleasant." He winces. "Permission is the preferred method if you are not an enemy I need to extract information from," he explains, and for the first time I find myself truly without words.

Ze asking for permission? That is something novel. One would think he'd just do it without caring for the consequences. But the fact that he is asking for my consent beforehand makes me gain a new respect for him.

Perhaps not all hope is lost for him.

"Does that mean you will be able to read my thoughts?"

That is nonnegotiable. I would hate to think that someone could prey on my thoughts and hear all my intimate musings.

"I can only hear what you choose to share with me."

I bite my lip as I think this through. I did promise him a boon, and I'm not one to break my word.

"All right. Permission granted."

He cups the sides of my face as he leans forward. My lashes flutter in confusion as he brings his lips to my forehead, brushing them lightly against my skin. He then presses a firm kiss right at the top of my head.

I freeze, completely taken aback by this sudden gesture.

He doesn't move either.

His soft lips are tightly pressed against my skin, and a deep flush envelops me. The place of contact vibrates and a low hum travels down my body.

I swallow hard, my arms placid by my side.

An eternity passes in the span of a few seconds, yet this proximity messes with my mind. My thoughts are blank save for this unnatural awareness that echoes through my brain.

He leans back, his eyes a deep purple.

"Hello, little human," he purrs into my mind.

The sound of his voice inside my head startles me, the echo sending shivers down my back. It's different than I would have imagined—more intimate, more...

"Uhm." I clear my throat. "Is a kiss always required to gain permission?"

"You are the only one I have asked for permission from," he replies casually.

"Oh." I blink, once more surprised. "Thank you... I guess?"

"Consider yourself lucky, human," he starts in his supercilious voice. "You are also the only one who has had the privilege to be touched by these lips. You are welcome." He nods to me, satisfaction blooming in his features.

To say I'm flabbergasted would be an understatement. Yet to my greatest surprise, I find that I'm not mad. Perhaps I have finally gotten used to this odd manner of his.

"I'm deeply honored, Sir Sparkles," I murmur, leaning forward in a half-bow. At any other time, he would have asked me if I was mocking him. Now, his lips quirk up as he watches me indulgently, almost...tenderly.

A flush climbs up my cheeks.

"Now that we've gotten that out of the way, I'd like to have lunch. You can stay and eat with me or leave. Up to you," I quickly add, wrenching my gaze away from him.

He doesn't leave. He trails closely behind me and takes a seat opposite me at the table. I ring the bell and ask for lunch to be brought up, after which a servant arrives with the dishes not even ten minutes later. I lay everything out on the table, my stomach growling with hunger. Ze, on the other hand, is the picture of decorum as he watches me wolf down the food without eating one bite.

"Would you like some?" I ask as I push forward a tray of pastries toward him.

He shakes his head.

"When do you even eat, Ze? You're a big guy. You must need a lot of fuel."

"I have my feeding times," he grumbles, looking away.

"Your loss." I shrug. "This is marvelous."

"I like watching you eat. You humans get happy at the smallest things," he mentions casually.

My brow goes up as I side-eye him.

"Maybe you should learn a thing or two from *us humans*." I roll my eyes, grabbing a sweet pastry and shoving it in his mouth —half to shut him up and half to make him see why this human would be happy about it.

His eyes widen in surprise and he slowly munches on it, nodding.

"It is good," he agrees as he swallows. And now that he's had a taste of it, he doesn't stop at just one, going for another, then another.

Odd man. He claims I am the odd one when he can't even eat by himself, needing someone else to urge him to eat. I shake my head at him, though a slight smile plays at my lips. We eat in silence until all the food is gone, at which point Ze reclines in his chair, gracefully dabbing at his mouth with a napkin.

"Two days from now, the temple will open its doors to outsiders," he states, his tone suddenly serious. "It is an annual event in which they recruit a new apprentice. It is open only to females who exhibit spiritual abilities. They are required to go through a round of tests, after which the high priestess elects one female to join the temple. It is a highly sought-after position due to the training priestesses receive, and many Supremes have at one point been priestesses." He pauses, giving me a pointed look. "You have said our society is unfair to females, yet the temple is an institution that caters *only* to females. There is no equivalent for males."

I cross my arms over my chest, regarding him through narrowed eyes.

"What do you want me to do?"

"You will masquerade as a recruit to gain access to the temple," he answers simply.

"But how will I be able to enter the recruitment process if they only accept females with spiritual abilities? I fear I must remind you I am a mere human," I add sarcastically.

Now it's his turn to roll his eyes. He nods to my bracelet.

"That is where the pearl comes into the equation. The first test will measure your spiritual abilities. I have filled the pearl with my energy, so it should allow you to pass that test."

"Of course you wouldn't give me a gift out of the kindness of your heart," I mumble under my breath as I rotate my wrist, watching the purple of the pearl change hues depending on the light.

He doesn't acknowledge my words as he continues. "Passing the first test will gain you an invite inside the temple to participate in the second test. You will not, however, undertake it. You will sneak into the altar room and temporarily disable the runes keeping males out of the temple. I will then come inside, interrogate the high priestess, and get the location of the vial from her. If we are lucky, the artifact will be within the temple's premises."

I stare at him.

"It is all very simple." He nods, satisfied.

"Uhm, human here?" I say as I put my hand up. "I don't know how to recognize those runes you speak of, let alone disable them."

"You will have my voice guiding you." He smiles.

"You planned this all, didn't you?"

Everything makes sense now. He's been staging this from the very beginning, hasn't he? I don't know why, but an aching hole forms in my gut as I realize that he's been orchestrating all of our interactions to reach this point.

"Of course," he readily admits. "I have accounted for every probability. You are the best option. The king has undoubtedly told the temple to increase their security. They are expecting me, but they do not know how I will be able to get inside. And since I am not known to have any female friends—least of all one who would possess spiritual powers worthy of the temple—they will not suspect that a female will infiltrate the temple on my behalf."

"What if I get caught?"

"You will not," he assures me.

"But what if I *do* get caught? You said it yourself. They will expect you, so they will likely increase security. What will happen to me if they realize I'm human?"

"You will *not* get caught. If anything happens, I will get you out."

"But how? If you can't come inside, doesn't that mean I'm screwed?"

"You don't need to worry about that." He waves his hand. "There are two approaches to everything, Luce—with force and without." He pins me with his gaze. "I will raze the temple to the ground if need be," he adds casually.

My lashes flutter in surprise.

"What would you have done if I didn't agree to help you?" I ask hesitantly.

"I would have razed it to the ground." He shrugs. "So consider this charity work. You are saving lives." He smiles.

"You..." I trail off. For a moment, I'd forgotten this part of him. Perhaps it's because since arriving in Aperion, he's only shown me the gentle, rather playful side of him. But I shouldn't forget that's not who he is.

He's not nice...at least not to most people.

He is the God Killer, and his reputation isn't just false rumors. That is who he is—a killer.

"I will protect you, Luce. Nothing will happen to you. You have my vow."

I bite on the inside of my cheek.

He's never let me down until now, always coming to my rescue. If the past is any indication, then I don't see why the future would not follow the same pattern.

"Fine. I'll trust you."

FIFTY-TWO

The white dress is simple, flowing down to my ankles and hiding the nondescript shoes I'm wearing. When I woke up, I found a big square box by my bed that housed my outfit for the day. Ze left me a small note instructing me how to dress and do my hair, saying it's important to convey a prim and proper look—nothing flashy or ostentatious. Everyone would be wearing the same type of outfit to hide social status. In this test, the only thing that matters is spiritual ability, not a person's rank or family. Ze implied that because the process is so fair, even those rare s'Aperiotes who exhibit spiritual powers can participate in the selection—the only event of its kind that allows them to make something of themselves in spite of their humble beginnings. But there's a strong no-cheating policy, and that includes the zantrax drug. Although he has assured me that no one should be able to detect the pearl, I'm still a little apprehensive. The temple seems to take its rules very seriously, and I can appreciate that they want to give a fair chance to everyone.

After I'm finished dressing, I tie my hair in a tight bun at my nape and pull up the dark hood attached to the dress over my head. Done with the preparation, I take a deep breath, giving myself a quick pep talk before I leave my room.

Ze relayed that a carriage would await me at noon, and it

would take me straight to the temple, where the recruitment process would begin.

I exit the house, and a simple gray carriage greets me at the entrance. The door swings open, inviting me inside.

There's a driver and a horse, but he doesn't exchange one word with me as he waits until I'm fully boarded to begin our journey.

I make myself comfortable in my seat, though my anxiety runs high. I'm about to head into a foreign environment I barely have any information on. Sure, Ze described the temple and the priestesses to the best of his abilities, but he's only done so from the lens of a male outsider. The truth of what I'll encounter inside is yet to be revealed.

Each House has its own temple and the priestesses have been tasked with defending the Primordial artifacts. Their creation was a direct opposition to the Sons of Tenebreis—hence why only females can join the temple. But times have changed, and with the rise of demon attacks, Ze fears that the artifacts could fall into the wrong hands. It has already happened once when Elias, the King of the House of Bronte, and his high priestess defected to Tartareia with the artifact in their care. According to Ze, though, if the demons get their hands on the vial, it's the beginning of the end, and he's not one to speak in superlatives. For that alone, I'm willing to push against my discomfort and help him.

The silence of the journey is unbearable. Fidgeting in my seat, I pull on the thin cotton curtain, peering outside. The road is busy as we head into the main city. Merchant carriages are on both sides of the streets, people selling different items along the sidewalk. Most are s'Aperiotes, and I've learned to tell them apart based on their clothes. The materials are coarser, the colors washed out from too much wear. The wealthy individuals are garbed in silks and satins, the colors bright and vivid, immediately pinpointing their social status in a crowd. That in itself is reflected in the way they are treated. Shop keepers grumble when a lower-class citizen shows an interest in their merchandise, but when an upper-class person looks at the same item, they go above and beyond, their attitude sickeningly servile.

I suppose our appearance was not the only thing that was modeled after gods—our morals were too. Does every realm have a classist worldview? Is it a universal trait? Somehow, I refuse to believe it. Perhaps this is my past speaking, but I've seen the worst of mankind, yet at the same time I've also seen the best. So I choose to believe people *can* be better.

Nikki was one of the richest men alive. Yet he never once looked down on me, not for my lack of wealth, nor for my ignorance. Where I didn't know, he taught me. He never once made me feel bad for not knowing something. He's a prime example of someone born at the top, who lived his entire life at the top, yet never let that affect him and the way he interacted with those who had less than him.

My lips tug up as I tightly wrap my arms around myself, imagining it's his embrace.

I miss him. So damn much. But every day brings me closer to him. I just have to be patient.

The carriage breezes through the city, and soon we leave that boisterous atmosphere behind. Fields stretch around on either side of the road, and every now and then, there's a farm in the distance, with workers toiling under the bright suns. It's too far for me to see, but I think they're tending to crops and some domestic animals.

The journey continues for what feels like an eternity. I don't have a watch with me, but I think it must have been a few hours since I left Thea's house.

"Couldn't Ze just teleport me there?" I grumble to myself. Maybe I've gotten too used to that mode of transportation because this feels like torture. Thinking back on it, either he or Cer could have teleported us to China and it would have been so much easier—especially on them since they'd never flown before. The more I think on it, the more disgruntled I become at all the wasted opportunities. Now I understand that they were trying to conceal their real identities, but did they have to do it at the expense of their own comfort?

Another hour passes as we leave the plains behind, mountains appearing in the distance. The contrast is stark. The earth rises out of nowhere, lush, green pastures turning into a rocky, hostile environment. And before I know it, the carriage draws to a halt.

I blink, startled. The door opens, inviting me out. I gulp as I tentatively step out, but the moment my feet meet the ground, the door closes behind me, the carriage already doing a U-turn and disappearing from sight.

"What..." I mutter in shock.

Yet I don't have time to dwell on that as I note that I've likely reached the location of the temple. In front of me, there are two huge doors, on each side of them a thick steely fence going in either direction for what seems like kilometers. They are seemingly wrapped around the mountains, hugging them closely. Two women dressed in black clothes are at the gates, and as they notice me, they incline their heads, and with a wave of a hand, the doors open for me to step inside. I place one foot in front of the other, straightening my back as I attempt to keep my cool. I mustn't look out of place despite feeling absolutely out of my element.

A massive courtyard stretches in front of me. The area is so large I can only make out the base of the mountain on the horizon, the entrance of a steel building etched into the stone. The dark blue of the metal contrasts with the brownish hue of the rock that's peppered with hints of green.

I walk forward, marveling at my surroundings. There's a beautiful fountain in the middle, water flowing from a giant statue of a woman dressed in a dark cloak and holding a book tightly to her chest.

On either side of the courtyard, there are open pavilions, and priestesses walk around in pairs of two. I recognize them as priestesses because their outfits are different. All the recruits are gathered in the courtyard, the girls wearing the same white dress as me, the hoods drawn over their heads. The priestesses, however, are wearing black dresses, their hoods drawn back, their faces painted. There's a straight black line that runs from one temple to the other, shrouding their eyes like a visor.

The priestesses walk around the perimeter, keeping the recruits in one place and watching over them. When someone tries to go toward the pavilions, they intervene, stopping them and signaling them to move toward the fountain.

I move around slowly, studying my surroundings without drawing too much attention to myself.

There are tens of girls in white, maybe as many as a hundred.

From what Ze has told me, being a priestess is a sought-after position, not only due to its elevated status in society but also due to their rigorous training in the spiritual arts. Over time, they have perfected a secret technique taught only to its disciples, and it's said to help one develop great spiritual power—so much so that a few former priestesses became Supremes after spending time at the temple.

The competition is also fierce. Each year, the temple chooses only one girl. Once chosen, a priestess must complete at least one term, which is five hundred years. They cannot leave before the end of the term, but they can extend their position by an unlimited number of terms.

The bracelet rests heavily against my wrist, the purple pearl cold against my warm flesh. A flash of guilt slithers through me as I think of what I'm about to do. It might be cheating for a noble reason, but it's still cheating, and I've always despised that.

"Do not worry your pretty head, human. You are not taking anyone's spot," Ze speaks in my mind.

"Thank you for the reminder, Ze," I mutter drily.

"That is why I am here—to be your voice of reason," he teases.

I roll my eyes at him—though I try to do it in the least obvious way possible.

"Aren't you supposed to be busy somewhere fighting off demons?" I ask.

"*Who says I cannot do both? I will have you know that I am the best swordsman in all Aperion. I could slay demons with my eyes closed and my ears shut. It is second nature to me,*" he boasts as if I expected a different answer from him.

"*Ze,*" I groan. "*Just focus on your demon-slaying and leave me alone. I'll contact you if I need your help, but for now, you're just distracting me.*"

A pause. I can feel his presence in my mind even when he's not speaking. It's like a feather brushing against my skin, a light caress that leaves a trail of warmth behind.

"*But I am bored.*" He sighs. "*These demons are not fun. They are all mid-level, which means they are not only weak but also aesthetically challenged and my eyes are suffering greatly from it.*"

Only Ze would be able to use the phrase *aesthetically challenged* in an actual sentence.

"*It is your job,*" I point out.

"*You are not fun, either, Luce,*" he complains, and I can almost imagine him pouting. "*You are supposed to feel sorry for me and then promise me you will make it better.*"

"*What?*" I frown.

"*An extra point would help me get through this most harrowing time of my life,*" he adds in a dramatic voice.

"*Ze. What's gotten into you? Do I need to remind you that I'm on a very important mission—one that I'm doing as a favor to you?*"

He releases a deep sigh.

"*When one is surrounded by such ugliness, one tends to reminisce about the beauty in life,*" he suddenly says in a philosophical tone, not making much sense.

"*Please reminisce about it silently, or I'll have to kick you out of my head,*" I tell him as I move through the throng of people.

Another pause, and I imagine he's debating whether to push his luck or not.

"*Alas, I shall go back to battling my demons. If you require anything, I am but one thought away,*" he murmurs softly.

"Got it. Thanks," I reply absentmindedly, making my way deeper into the courtyard.

My attention is firmly placed on the priestesses on the sidelines, eyeing them surreptitiously. Despite my seemingly confident front, I still expect them to single me out any moment and tell me what an impostor I am.

I'm so busy making sure they don't find out about my charade that I unwittingly bump into another girl. We both lose our balance, and I teeter forward, grabbing onto her robe as I fall to the ground.

Damnation!

There goes my quiet and unassuming presence.

"I'm so sorry," I murmur as I wobble to my feet, dusting my dress and trying to do the same for the other girl. But as my gaze meets her startling green one, my eyes widen in shock.

"Wyn?" I whisper.

Her eyes flare in alarm as she brings her finger to her mouth, telling me to be quiet. Hooking her arm through mine, she takes me to a more secluded spot where no one can hear our conversation. We take a seat on one of the benches by the side.

"What are you doing here, Luce?" she asks as she pulls her hood lower to obstruct her features.

"I..." I stammer. "I can't tell you. I'm so sorry. But I'm not doing anything bad. On the contrary, I'm just doing a favor for someone," I quickly say.

She watches me intently for a moment before she nods.

"You are aware the first test will measure your spiritual power," she speaks slowly.

I nod.

"You are also aware you are human."

I nod again.

"What did you get yourself into, Luce?" She shakes her head at me. "Does Thea know?"

I shake my head.

Wyn sighs.

"I hope you know what you're doing. The temple isn't a playground, and the priestesses can be...harsh."

"Don't worry about me. I'll be fine, truly."

She stares at me for a moment before she nods as she releases a sigh.

"But what are *you* doing here? Isn't the priestess position for a minimum of five hundred years? You're just making your debut into society... If you join the temple, wouldn't that be for nothing? You've been waiting for your ball for so long..."

A sad smile pulls at her lips.

"Precisely why the position *must* be mine." She purses her lips. "I reckon Thea told you how hard our father has been trying to get her married. She's considered an old lady already." She lets out a dry laugh. "Not that it matters as long as he can find someone for her. But I know my sister. She's never going to go along with his plans. I also know that..." she trails off, shaking her head. "If Thea will not marry, I will have to. Otherwise, our family will be greatly shamed for having two unmarried daughters. My father knows this, which is why the moment I am out in society, he will start introducing me to eligible males. In a few months, or if I'm lucky, a few years, he will find someone for me and I will be unable to say no since it is expected of me."

"Wyn... I'm so sorry."

She half turns away, her lips trembling as she takes a deep breath.

"If Aethon is gone..." Her voice breaks. "If he is truly gone, I cannot marry anyone else. I will *not* have anyone else."

"So you're going to give up five hundred years of your life to the temple?"

"That is merely the beginning. If I have it my way, it will be until the end of my life."

"What?" I blurt out. "I understand that you have a crush on him, but surely... Why would you give up your entire life for someone you've never even been together with?" I ask, dreading the way my words sound—as harsh as her sister's.

Her eyes widen and she flushes a pretty pink.

I stare at her, my intuition telling me there's something more at play.

"Wyn... Did something more happen with Aethon? Something you didn't tell Thea?" I ask tentatively.

"I... It isn't like that," she murmurs, averting her gaze.

"I won't tell your sister if that's what you're worried about. Whatever you share with me will remain in confidence," I assure her.

Her lips tremble as she swallows audibly.

"It was just my foolishness." She shakes her head. "I do not think I can ever utter the words aloud."

"Did he..." I trail off, not knowing how to frame the question so that she does not take it the wrong way. It's just that he is so much older than her—far too old according to Thea. "Did you and Aethon..."

"No, no," she hurries to say. "Although it was not for my lack of trying. I..." She takes a deep breath. "While Thea and Cer were away, Aethon came to visit. It was then that he brought me the bracelet."

I nod, so far familiar with the events.

"He did kiss me on my forehead that day as I told Thea, but..." She briefly closes her eyes. "I am so embarrassed, Luce. Please vow to me you will not tell my sister."

"I vow I will not break your confidence," I assure her.

She still appears uncertain, her cheeks reddening as she tips her head up to gaze at the sky.

"He stayed the night at our house," she says in a small voice.

Already, alarm bells go off in my head, and I immediately think of the worst.

"Go on," I murmur.

"I snuck into his room at night. I know it was bad of me. I know it," she hurries to add. "But I thought if I gave him a little nudge...maybe he would finally see me as a woman and not a child. I..."

Her face is flaming hot at this point as she stutters through her explanation.

"I snuck into his bed," she quickly says, squeezing her eyes shut. "Naked."

"Oh, no... Wyn..."

"I kissed him. On the lips. But he woke up and he more or less threw me out." She sighs. "He told me to forget about the entire incident and gave me this sermon about how he would not tell my brother because he did not want to ruin my reputation but..."

At least Aethon had more sense than she did, all things considered. That earns the man my respect. But I don't let my thoughts show on my face—not when it is so painful for Wyn to recount those events. Poor girl, she didn't have anyone she could talk to, and considering how adamant Thea is about her having a stellar reputation and making a good match... I can see how alienating that could be regardless of how close the sisters are.

"He threw you out of his bedroom and you still think there's a chance for you?"

"Oh, Luce." She turns to me, her green eyes sparkling. "He kissed me back. Before he realized who I was, he kissed me back. And it was the most marvelous feeling in existence. And because of that one moment, I know I am ruined for anyone else who is *not* him. I'd rather live my entire life alone, reminiscing about that special moment than be forced to mate someone else against my will."

Her words are effusive, her features filled with the purest love.

"But you heard Ze—Azerius," I correct myself. "The Supremes already found a mate for him."

She shakes her head, a dry laugh escaping her.

"They're going to try to force the mating, but that doesn't mean he will agree. He will not," she says vehemently.

I sigh. I don't think there's any way to convince her that her dreams of being with Aethon are more or less unattainable.

Whether he's dead or alive, mated or unmated, for her it's him or no one else. And I'm ashamed to admit that I understand her and where she's coming from.

I try to remember the time before my marriage, when I was crushing on Nikki with no hope of ever being with him. Even as my future opened up with opportunities I never dreamed of, I never once thought of being with another man. To my young mind, he was the only person I could ever belong to. And even now, years later, the truth remains that he is the only one for me.

"Please don't tell Thea about any of this," Wyn repeats anxiously. "She will freak out and will never let me leave the house ever again. She's worse than my mother."

"Of course not. I gave you my word, Wyn."

"And please don't tell anyone you saw me here. The recruitment process ends a few days after my ball. By then I should know for sure if I made it—no, I *must* make it," she adds determinedly. "My family cannot know, or they will do everything they can to stop me."

"Even though the position is so prestigious?"

"Regardless." She smiles ruefully. "My purpose is to make a good match. There is already Cer in the family, and he has enough prestige."

"I see." I nod, pursing my lips. "Then I will cheer you on. You do not have to worry about competing against me since I will be gone after the first test."

Her brows go up in surprise.

"Hmm... It has something to do with Commander Azerius, doesn't it?"

I blink.

A knowing look crosses her face.

"Do not worry. I won't pry, nor will I tell anyone. Tit for tat." She winks at me.

I nod numbly. God, am I so transparent? I make the worst of spies. I should have never agreed to this.

"Be careful with Azerius, though," she mentions a moment

later. "I may not know him as well as my siblings do, but he is the most hated person in Aperion, and for good reason."

"I've gathered that," I mumble dryly.

"He's also the most powerful person I know. Rumors say he's more powerful than the Supremes."

My eyes widen at that.

"Really?"

She nods thoughtfully.

"So that begs the question... What could he want with a human?" She muses quietly, though the glint in her eyes tells me she's skeptical about my acquaintance with Ze.

A loud noise erupts in the air, distracting us and saving me from having to reply—thank God, for even *I* do not know what Ze would want with a human.

Wyn nods to me to get up and head toward the center where all the other recruits are congregating. The priestesses from the pavilion are also closing ranks and surrounding us from all sides. A loud voice calls to attention from the base of the mountain, but there are too many people for me to make out who's speaking.

"Count to ten, and then each number line up in a queue in front of the fountain," the voice intones.

We do as told, and when our turn comes, Wyn is five and I am six, after which we're separated into different queues. She gives me a smile, whispering a quiet, "Good luck," as I move away from her to stand in my own line.

I take a deep breath, willing myself to calm down. Although seeing that I've already been recognized by someone, it's pretty clear I'm not cut out for this James Bond stuff.

All the girls take their spots, and ten lines queue up in front of the fountain. It's only when we're more ordered that I finally see who was speaking.

She's the only woman wearing a wine-colored dress, her face painted white and red.

"Gazes to the floor. The high priestess will assess you,"

another priestess calls out from behind, and all the women tip their heads down.

I focus on the floor as my ears tune in to the click of heels as they tread closer and closer. Out of the corner of my eye, I make out the high priestess as she walks toward us, heading to the far left side where line one begins. She stops for a second in front of each woman, her gaze quickly flickering over them. A few girls are told to move to the side, though it's not explained why. The high priestess does the same to lines two through five, stalling when she stops in front of Wyn. She tilts her chin with her finger, looking her straight in the eye. With a satisfied smile, she nods before she goes to the next girl. She chooses another girl to look up at her before she switches to line six.

My nerves are killing me as I wait for whatever assessment she has in store. The seconds trickle by as her heels dig into the ground, the sound echoing ominously in my ear.

I cannot see behind me. But I can hear the hushed voice of the high priestess as she tells more girls to move to the side and leave the line.

Eventually, though, it's my turn.

The shoes are the first that come into sight, red pumps with a block heel. The hem of the dress reaches her ankles, but compared to my outfit, hers leaves perfect visibility of her shoes.

"You," she whispers in a low, eerie voice.

Her finger makes contact with my jaw and she tips my head up to look at her.

Her eyes are an almost translucent gray, rimmed with red paint that spans from one temple to the other. Her cheeks are angular and hollow, her mouth thin and pursed as she regards me. I cannot make out the color of her hair due to her hood, but based on her coloring, I'd assume it would be blonde.

"I sense male energy on you," she murmurs, her eyes narrowing as they traverse my entire body before settling on my right hand. "Move to the side, please."

She doesn't wait for me to reply as she moves to the next

woman. Meanwhile, her fellow priestesses come to escort me to the side where quite a few women have gathered up already.

A tremor goes down my spine, traveling down my legs until they become as soft as jelly. How I manage to put one foot in front of the other and continue moving, I do not know. There's only a foreboding sense of doom.

I got caught, didn't I?

FIFTY-THREE

The girls selected by the high priestess are led by the other priestesses toward the pavilion on the left, traversing one of the gazebos and heading into a small room at the end of the corridor. White, bare walls surround us, caging us in.

"The high priestess will be with you shortly for an in-depth assessment. Until then, please remove your clothes."

I blink at the pronouncement.

"What?" I blurt out.

The sharp gaze of the priestess pierces through me, making me freeze.

"The high priestess detected an unusual energy around you. To continue in the selection, we must ensure there's no foul play involved," she explains in a chilling tone.

The other girls all nod, already fumbling with the fastenings of their garments, and I'm forced to go with the flow.

"*Ze, what am I going to do?*" I reach out to him, my hands trembling as I pull the dress over my head and lay it on the floor next to me. We're all left in our undergarments, waiting in a line.

The priestess doesn't look over our naked forms, but that doesn't make it any less uncomfortable—not that I've ever been comfortable without my clothes on.

"*Ze?*" I keep calling his name, yet as seconds go by and he doesn't answer, it strikes me that something might be wrong.

My eyes take in the room, and I look around wildly for any clues. I almost miss it at first. But as I glance at the ceiling, the light from one of the windows reflects against a yellowish, almost transparent symbol, highlighting it. The symbol is only visible when directly hit by light. Otherwise, it blends into the white of the ceiling, remaining undetectable.

My breath catches in my throat.

If the temple has runes that prohibit males from entering, could they also have some to prevent *any* males from communicating with the priestesses? Going by those odd symbols and the way my brain is too quiet, that might be a possibility. This world does not have the advanced technology that Earth does simply because it relies on magic to get everything done. Those symbols could very well act like a Faraday cage to stop *all* types of communications—we were singled out as suspicious, after all.

But what does that mean for me?

My thoughts are interrupted as the door opens and closes with a whoosh, the high priestess suddenly appearing before us.

The red painted around her eyes makes her irises appear otherworldly. She lowers her hood, her hair a white blond pulled back in a bun at her nape.

She walks slowly, gracefully, her gaze swallowing the entire room in the span of a second.

One by one, she stops in front of each of the girls, staring intently for minutes on end before she gives a nod of assent—her way of deeming someone fit to continue in the recruitment process. Some girls pass, others fail. I don't know what her criteria are—not when all she does is stare blankly at us before the verdict is announced. The girls who don't pass are taken away by the other priestess and thrown out of the room.

Four have failed so far and have been removed from the premises.

I'm in the middle. A few girls separate me and the high priestess.

My legs won't stop trembling from the anxiety, especially since I don't have Ze's voice to guide me in my head. I'm on my own. Yet I find that I'm not as worried for myself as I am about what Ze will do if he cannot reach me should he try to because he *will* raze this place to the ground.

I don't doubt him just as I don't doubt the fact that he has the capacity to do so.

The high priestess approaches.

Drops of sweat form on my forehead, slowly dripping down my face. I swallow, trying to regulate my breathing. My heart is racing like crazy.

Will she find out about the pearl? Should I have taken it off? The questions continue to plague my mind, and I lose track of time and space, my hearing dimming until suddenly, the high priestess is in front of me, speaking *to* me.

I blink.

"What is your name?" she asks, her voice rough and husky.

"Luce," I murmur. Even my vocal cords are trembling, for God's sake.

I might be wearing a camisole and a pair of underwear, but that doesn't mean the rest of my skin isn't out there in the open —including my marks.

"This..." She brings her hand to my collarbone. "May I?" she inquires.

I nod, my tongue tied.

She lays one finger on the dark marks on my skin, tracing the flat designs.

"Why do you have this?" she asks, her gaze glued to my chest.

"I-I don't know," I stammer.

"Hmm..."

Her light eyes flash at me.

"Do y-you know what they are?" I find the courage to ask.

Her face screws up.

"It does not matter if you do not know," she says, half turning to move to the next girl. But something catches her attention as she suddenly stops.

She grabs my hand, her eyes narrowing as she peruses my bracelet.

Oh God! I'm freaking out on the inside and I'm doing my best not to show it, begging my muscles not to spasm uncontrollably—though that's exactly what happens.

I make a bad liar. I make an even worse criminal. And to think I was wanted by the police for fraud and whatnot. I almost snort at the thought.

The high priestess pulls the bracelet off my wrist, bringing the pearl closer to her face to study it.

"This." She purses her lips. "I will hold onto this."

She nods to herself, pocketing the pearl bracelet as she continues to the next girl.

I blink in confusion. That makes no sense. Half sentences that hold no real meaning to anyone other than her. She must have sensed that something was off with the bracelet, but I doubt she knows exactly *what*. Otherwise, she would have disqualified me. If she sensed Ze's energy, she wouldn't have been so calm.

I try to look at the bright side as the high priestess checks the rest of the girls. We slowly get dressed as she finishes, and to my surprise, all of us are good to go back. Yet as we exit the room, I can't help but feel the high priestess's heavy gaze on my back.

When we reach the courtyard, the priestess in charge divides us among the other lines, and somehow I end up in the same queue as Wyn. When she sees me walking toward her, her lips pull up in a wide smile.

"Everything all right?" she whispers as I squeeze between her and another girl—anything to have someone familiar by my side. My limbs are still trembling from the residual anxiety, adrenaline pumping in my veins and urging me to run away and never come back. Yet I can't do that. Not yet...

I nod, straining a smile.

"*Luce?*" Ze's voice resounds in my mind.

"Ze! The high priestess took my bracelet," I hurry to say.

"Do not fret. I presumed she might take it."

"But what will I do now?" I mutter, agitated.

"You will do nothing. Continue on, and should you fail the first test, you will come back to me."

"But... I let you down. I'm sorry." I sigh.

"You did no such thing," he immediately replies. *"Everything is going according to plan, Luce."*

"But she took my bracelet..." I grumble, realizing how disappointed I am that she took it from me. Will I be able to get it back? It was a gift after all, regardless of *why* Ze gave it to me, and I happened to like it very much.

"I will recover the bracelet for you," he intones confidently. *"I shall see you soon, Luce,"* he adds before he severs the connection.

I didn't even get to ask him how his demon slaying is going.

Huffing out a breath, I look around, noting that the high priestess has not made another appearance yet.

"Do you know what's going to happen next?" I whisper to Wyn.

She shakes her head.

"I am not entirely certain. From what I've heard, the first test measures spiritual power, after which, those deemed worthy advance to the next stage. But I don't know what the test entails," she whispers back.

My lips flatten into a tight line. Okay, so I'll wait to fail this spiritual power test and then I can be on my way. Still, I can't help but feel a slight disappointment at not being able to help Ze further. I promised him I'd disable the runes, yet not even five minutes into the mission and I'm singled out, my only advantage taken away from me.

A sigh escapes me, my fists clenched by my side.

Why can't I be just a little more useful? If only I had some cool abilities to help me navigate these circumstances... Then I wouldn't have to depend on anyone to help me in The Wishing Game either, and I could simply move from one trial to another until I'd get my crowning wish and Nikki would come back to me.

Yet things are not as simple as that, are they?

I'm just a lowly human to everyone around here, and no matter how much I wish otherwise, the truth of the matter is that I *am* rather useless.

Wyn's question echoes in my mind.

Why would Ze want to associate himself with a human? He told me countless times how weak and breakable I am due to my *human condition*, yet he still continues to hang around me, being *nice* to me.

What would a powerful god like Ze—one who is feared by most of his world—want with me?

My musings are interrupted by the sound of a horn reverberating through the air. My gaze snaps forward, my eyes focusing on the fountain where a flash of red announces the appearance of the high priestess. She's sitting on the ledge of the fountain, walking along the thin border in her high heels.

"Welcome, my darlings," she calls out as she spreads her arms. Her voice booms in the entire courtyard, snapping everyone to attention.

"Thank you for joining me on this marvelous day. I cannot wait to get to know some of you over the course of the next week. After the tests are over, one of you will join us at the temple for a permanent position."

Low cheers erupt among the participants, but a severe glance from the high priestess and the entire courtyard falls silent.

"The duty of the temple is to preserve tradition, and from its inception, priestesses have been tasked with protecting the ancient artifacts left behind by the Primordials. This is a duty that no one should take lightly. The temple needs its priestesses to be strong both in mind and spirit. Loyalty, honesty, and perseverance are the three qualities we look for in our recruits. As you have noticed, some participants have been excluded, and that is because they were caught using underhanded ways to secure a spot at the temple. I understand that this is a prestigious position, but trickery will *not* be allowed." Her eyes meet mine, holding my gaze for a second before moving on.

I swallow hard, somehow feeling that was directed at me. But if she thinks I was trying to use the bracelet to get ahead, why didn't she expose me? Why let me continue?

"Aside from a strong character, we also look for strong spiritual ability, which is why the first test is designed to measure your spiritual ability."

Holding out her hand, she materializes a white sphere the size of her palm. The sphere rotates in her hand, slowly floating in the air until it's above our heads.

I tilt my head back, watching it slither through the lines of participants until it reaches the first line, hovering over the first girl.

"This is the Elegian Sphere. It's empty inside save for particles of chaos that bind onto spiritual power. Depending on the level of spiritual energy, the particles will change color," the high priestess continues. "To establish your level, each one of you shall touch the sphere," she says as she gracefully steps off the ledge. She drifts to the ground, seemingly walking on clouds as she comes closer to us.

The white of our dresses in the inside quadrant is surrounded by the black of the priestesses' garb as they converge around us. The high priestess is a dot of color as she steps forward, infiltrating the tightly formed group, becoming the nucleus.

"There are five broad levels," she speaks as she walks farther into the middle of the crowd. "The first one is the bottom one, wherein the sphere will remain white. That means you have little to no spiritual power, and you will be asked to leave the premises immediately. If the sphere turns blue, then you are a first level—not bad, but not great either. You will also be asked to leave, cultivate more, and return in future years." She pauses. "Contrary to popular belief, spiritual power *can* be enhanced by up to fifty percent the amount you were born with. If you have blue at this time, you can cultivate and level up in time." She smiles—the first time I've seen her do so—as she meets the gazes of some hopeful participants. She nods at them, giving them a little boost of confidence.

"For the third level, the sphere will turn yellow. That means you have a good amount of spiritual ability—but still not enough. Just like blue, you will be asked to leave the premises and cultivate more. And that brings me to the last two levels—black and red. If the sphere turns black, you have a very good spiritual ability. You have likely trained for many years before you have come here, or you may have even failed before and tried harder. We do not judge those who've been turned away before. In fact, we value the perseverance, and if you did improve, that will be noted. The black level is allowed to remain and will pass to the next round.

"There is one last level—the best one. If the sphere turns red, then you have the best level of spiritual ability. You will, of course, advance to the next round."

Whispers ripple among the participants.

She pauses.

"You are probably wondering if black will be at a disadvantage compared to red in the subsequent rounds. The answer is no, for the simple reason that red is exceedingly rare. I have not encountered a red candidate in..." she trails off, pensive. "My, I don't believe I've *ever* encountered one." She chuckles. "In fact, working toward the red level will be part of your priestess training."

The girls bubble with excitement when they hear that—after all, it's one of the reasons they want to become priestesses. Red should be the equivalent of a Supreme in spiritual power if it's so rare, and as such, put them onto the path of becoming a Supreme in the future. That makes me wonder what color Ze would be. With his power, I have no doubt he would be an instant red. Hadn't Thea mentioned he is being considered for a Supreme position?

"What if there *is* "A red?" Wyn stuns everyone by taking a

step out of the line, directly questioning the high priestess. "Will she automatically become a priestess?"

The high priestess raises a brow at her.

"What is your name, child?" the high priestess asks as she comes closer.

"Arwyn," she replies confidently, looking straight into the high priestess's eyes.

"How old are you, Arwyn?"

"Three thousand years old." She pushes her chin up.

"A young adult, I see." She smiles. "Hopeful. Maybe *too* hopeful." She laughs. Turning with her back to Wyn, she addresses the others. "Arrogance is not something we welcome at the temple. And *youth* is no excuse for it," she adds, her voice cutting just as her features morph into a scowl. "Arrogance breeds recklessness, and recklessness breeds disaster. The temple is here *because* we have been steady in our devotion."

Silence envelops the courtyard.

"The sphere will now decide who leaves and who goes on to the next round." Glancing back at Wyn, she adds in a low voice, "And it might also give some a lesson in humility."

Wyn's lips flatten as she moves back into the line, her body tense. I reach out and pat her on the back, a small comforting gesture. She looks startled by it, but she musters a small smile as she inclines her head.

The sphere descends to the waiting hands of the first girl in line number one. Her palms are wide open, curving to the sides of the sphere. Her fingers press to the surface of the object as she stares at it intently, waiting for the color to change.

Seconds pass and nothing happens.

"That is enough," the high priestess intervenes. "Unfortunately, your level is white. Please pass it to the next person."

The sphere floats out of the girl's hands and into the next person's. Dejected, the girl takes a step back as one of the other priestesses comes to escort her to the exit.

As the next girl touches the sphere, it turns blue, eliminating her from this round too. The sphere continues to travel through the rest of the line, with most getting yellow, a few blue and white, and only a handful of blacks. The second line goes more or less the same, and it looks like there will not be too many people participating in the second test. Around two to three people per line get the black level. The most common level is yellow, which means they have a good level, but they aren't quite there. Still, with enough training, they will be able to return as blacks in the future.

The sphere passes from hand to hand until our row is next.

Wyn is still tense from her interaction with the high priestess, her expression a mix of confidence and rebellion. And when the sphere floats into her hands, she grips it tightly, her eyes fixed on it. Mine are too, my heart beating loudly in my chest as I hope she'll get black to pass to the next round.

Seconds trickle by.

The white matter inside the sphere vibrates, and we all wait with bated breath to see what color it will change into. Light shines from deep within, and at first, the color changes to a deep yellow. But the yellow quickly loses its intensity until a powerful beam of light erupts from the nucleus of the sphere, the color becoming the purest, brightest red.

Silence blankets the courtyard.

I sneak a glance at the high priestess, who for one moment has a naked expression of disbelief on her face, which she quickly masks with one of indifference. Pushing her chin in the air, she clicks her tongue against the roof of her mouth as she assesses Wyn with narrowed eyes.

"Very well, Arwyn," she murmurs. "You have proven yourself."

Wyn's lips fight to stay in a neutral position, twitching at the corners.

"Congratulations," I whisper to her.

"But you will understand why I find it hard to believe that a mere three-thousand-year-old child would get the red level on her first attempt. I will need to ensure that no rules have been broken," she intones, making her skepticism known.

"Of course." Wyn inclines her head out of respect, but she is not pleased with the high priestess's words. Yet it was to be expected, wasn't it? After ridiculing Wyn for her confidence and stating how rare it was to get a white level, she must find a way to save face.

"You can pass the sphere to the person next to you," the high priestess mentions, her tone biting.

I inhale deeply as I open my palms to receive the sphere.

"*Are you there, Ze?*" I ask in my mind. Yet only silence greets me. He must be busy. Damn it. I could have used his *boredom* now when my nerves are threatening to get the best of me. I know that the worst thing that can happen is that I'll get a white and be escorted off the premises of the temple. But at the same time, that means I will not be of any use to Ze, and for some absurd reason, I really wanted to help him. Maybe it's because I haven't felt needed in a long time—or perhaps it's because I could have finally done something he *couldn't*... Regardless, my time in the temple has come to an end.

The sphere slowly descends into my waiting palms. The crystal surrounding the white matter is cool to the touch despite having been in Wyn's hands just moments ago. My fingers grip onto the surface of the sphere as I gaze into the chaos within. The particles inside dance around each other, moving in a rehearsed tango, going back and forth and waiting to respond to my absent spiritual power.

Yet as I focus on those tiny meandering dots, my surroundings fall away, the whispers behind me muted until there's only the stark white of the atoms. The more I stare at them, the more it feels as though they are growing in size until I'm standing face to face with giant white balls that roll back and forth around me.

A bitter taste assails me, and I smack my lips together in an effort to isolate that odd flavor. The air around me thickens, the temperature dropping suddenly.

The sound of a waterdrop falling into a pond echoes in the background, along with a whispered voice.

Remember.

I blink.

The spherical particles flatten and change their shape, becoming mirror-like reflective surfaces. I'm slowly engulfed in a palace of mirrors with no way out. My heart squeezes painfully in my chest, the feeling of being trapped intensifying.

Remember.

The same voice yells from far away.

I blink again. This time, the mirrors reflect back my image, only it's not me.

It's me, yet it's not me.

A shrilling noise erupts in the air, and as my eyes flutter open, I note the crowd that's formed around me, caging me in. The sphere in my hands is no longer a sphere, only shards of broken glass lying on the ground. Muddy, mercury-like particles stain my hands, seeping into my skin and dripping to the ground. The moment they touch the pavement, a cloud of smoke erupts as they erode into the solid surface.

Startled gasps resound around me as the girls step away to avoid getting touched by the toxic substance that seems to destroy everything in its path—everything but me.

Slowly, I raise my gaze to meet that of the horrified high priestess, who in a loud voice proclaims, "The test is now postponed. Everyone leave." With one hand, she summons a cloud of smoke that envelops my hands, slowly traveling down my body and cleaning the corrosive substance out of the way.

I tentatively step back, my legs made out of jelly. Wyn is at my back, grabbing my arm and holding on to me.

"Not you two. You will come with me," the high priestess singles me and Wyn out.

FIFTY-FOUR

The crowd of participants dissipates after the high priestess's announcement. The other priestesses lead the girls out, until only Wyn and I are left behind. Two priestesses dressed in black appear at our backs, urging us to follow the Head Priestess as she heads for the entrance of the temple at the base of the mountain.

Wyn and I cling to each other, both worried and confused about what's happening.

"No one knows I'm here, Luce. What if she does something to us?" She bites her lip apprehensively.

"Azerius knows. He will not let anything happen to us," I assure her, though I don't know where that confidence comes from, especially as Ze is not answering any of my attempts at communication. Why did he even want access to my mind if he's not going to use it?

"Ze? I am in a little pickle here and I would appreciate it if you answered me," I call out to him again. Nothing but silence greets me. Damn it!

"I wish I had your confidence, Luce, but I don't think the high priestess likes me."

"I'm not sure she likes me either," I murmur, remembering the way she regarded me in the locker room.

"What if she kills us? What if she hides our bodies and we're never found again? I'm not ready to die!" she adds, getting increasingly anxious.

"You got red. I got nothing. At least you should be able to fight her off."

"It doesn't work like that," she whispers, her expression stricken. "I don't know how to use my powers. I haven't trained yet. It's only been a few days since my first ability manifested. I am just as useless as you are." She sighs.

"But...you're red..." I blink.

"I might have the spiritual power, but it's moot if I have no idea how to use it."

"Good Lord, what did we get ourselves into?" I close my eyes, the severity of the situation slowly dawning on me.

"It's the first time I've heard of a recruitment day being canceled," she adds warily. "I'm really not sure what's going to happen to us once we enter the temple."

"We can't go back either," I say as I glance behind us where more priestesses form a line, preventing us from leaving.

A few more steps and we reach the base of the mountain where two massive oak doors open before us. The Head Priestess steps inside, but as we reach the threshold, both Wyn and I hesitate.

"Move," the priestesses command us from behind, more or less pushing us over the edge.

We both stumble inside, our eyes widening as we take in the high ceiling of the hallway. The temple is built *within* the mountain, and the walls reflect that, rocks with specks of gold surrounding us. The streaks of metal in the stone glint as light from a window roof hits them, giving the sensation that the air shimmers with particles of gold too.

The priestesses stop at the entrance, not coming inside. As we look back, the doors close shut with a bang, leaving us alone with the high priestess, who is currently nowhere to be seen.

"We are *so* dead," Wyn mutters. "If she doesn't kill us, my parents will finish the job since there's no way they won't hear of this."

"Calm down. Maybe she just wants to talk to us... I mean, she did say she's never seen a red candidate before, and I technically broke the sphere, although that was just an accident."

"I bet you *she* doesn't think it was just an accident," she adds dryly.

We walk with our arms linked together, huddled against each other as we try to keep our calm.

Toward the back of the room, there's a ceiling-high golden statue of the same woman from the fountain, but this one is more exquisitely crafted, her hair and clothing made up of sparkling diamonds and rubies. There's a striking mix of rustic and ostentatious, the stones providing an almost medieval feel while the precious stones speak to the affluence of the temple.

We're both staring at the beautiful statue when a loud noise shifts our attention to the side of the room where a giant boulder slides to the right to reveal a hidden entrance.

"Come in." The high priestess's voice resounds, though she's not physically present.

Wyn and I share a look. I know we're both thinking about the same thing. We *could* take our chances and try to escape, but it would likely engender a struggle that would only end up with us getting hurt. The only option is to move forward. Nodding at each other, we hold hands as we slowly make our way to the hidden entrance.

It's dark and cold. That's the first impression as we step into the cramped tunnel. The moment we are out of the main hallway, though, the stone slides back into place, a loud thud denoting there's no way back. We can only go forward.

There's a flickering light at the end of the tunnel, and we take careful, tentative steps as we head toward it. Once we reach the room, we both shield our eyes at the sudden burst of light.

"Wow," Wyn whispers.

There are rows upon rows of books on either side of the room. Every nook and cranny of the mountainous rock has been fashioned into a shelf, while in the back, built on a bed of stones, is a bed. The more I look around, the more I realize that this is an inhabited space. Most likely...

"Welcome to my humble abode," the high priestess speaks, appearing out of nowhere to the right. She rests her palms against a wooden table, regarding us intently with those unusual eyes of hers.

"Uhm." I clear my throat. "Why are we here?"

"Why indeed." She smiles, turning her gaze to Wyn. "Who are your parents?"

"The Duke and Duchess of Sigmore," Wyn murmurs in a low voice, tightening her grip on my arm.

Her brows go up in surprise.

"I have not heard anything about Sigmore having a prodigy on his hands," she comments. "In fact, rumors have been swirling for years about his mediocre daughter, diametrically opposed to his son, a celebrated General of Aperion."

"My sister is not mediocre," Wyn bursts out.

The high priestess tilts her head to the side.

"It is rather unusual, is it not? Neither the duke nor his duchess has ever been particularly accomplished, yet two of their children are decidedly...*too* accomplished. Cerenios I could understand, he is the firstborn. But you? You are the youngest, are you not, and the thirdborn?"

Wyn doesn't reply, her lips trembling as she glares mutinously at the priestess.

"I have not encountered a red-level recruit before, never mind one so young, so you will have to excuse my skepticism," she murmurs as she manifests another sphere. "Please touch it again." She inclines her head toward Wyn as the sphere floats to her.

Gulping down her apprehension, Wyn drops her arm from my side, opening her palms to receive the white sphere. Like before, when the particles bind to her spiritual power, the color becomes deeper and deeper until there's only a bright red emanating from the sphere.

"Sensational," the priestess declares in awe, her eyes glued to the deep red of the sphere. "You are, indeed, a prodigy. Have you manifested any abilities yet?"

Wyn tentatively nods. "One," she answers.

"What is it?" the priestess asks eagerly, taking a step forward.

"I can manipulate matter, like my family, but I am not very good at it..."

"Show me," the priestess demands, her eyes sparkling with curiosity.

Wyn glances at me as she nibbles on her lower lip.

She presses her fingers against the sphere, and the light intensifies, the shape changing to an elongated lasso that bounces to the ground. Yet the moment it's out of her grasp, the red becomes white again, though still maintaining its new shape.

The high priestess nods. "Is that all?"

"Erm... Yes. I have not trained yet."

"I see. It is a good thing you are here then, for I shall train you."

"What do you mean?" Wyn blinks in surprise.

"I am accepting you as my new apprentice. Congratulations. The position starts in two weeks from now with an orientation led by my adjunct. You will have until then to say goodbye to your old life before you take your vow."

"Just like...that?" Wyn asks. "But you said everyone would have a fair chance and—"

The priestess's gaze snaps to her.

"Ultimately, *I* decide who will join the temple, and my followers trust that decision. There is raw power in you, young girl. So much you probably have no idea what to do with it, and I doubt the teachers at the academy would know either, since you likely outpower them all. You need a teacher worthy of your abilities. You need *me*."

"I..." Wyn stammers. "I would love to accept your offer, but I would not feel right depriving everyone else of a chance..."

"Nonsense," the high priestess scoffs. "You will join me two weeks from now at the temple. This is nonnegotiable. Is that clear?"

Wyn blinks, sneaking a glance at me as she fidgets with her fingers. I give her a comforting smile.

"Yes." She nods, though she doesn't seem very sure of her answer despite having been so determined to become a priestess just a few hours ago.

"Good. You are excused now," the high priestess intones as the boulder slides out of place to reveal the exit. We both turn to leave. "Not you." She points to me. "You are staying."

"But—"

"Arwyn, you are dismissed," she repeats, giving a harsh look at Wyn.

"It's okay," I whisper to her. "I'll be fine."

"Will you..." She bites her lip.

I'm not sure, but for her sake, I muster a smile.

"Of course. I'll see you later."

Wyn hovers around the exit for a few moments, reluctant to leave me alone. But one more warning from the high priestess and she eventually departs. When she's out of sight, the boulder slides back into place, camouflaging with the environment and sealing shut the room.

The entire room falls silent as the priestess stares at me in puzzlement.

"Who are you?" she asks as she slowly comes closer to me.

"Uhm, no one?"

She narrows her eyes at me.

"Your tattoos," she mentions as she circles me. "Who sent you?"

"W-what? I don't know what you're talking about."

"I have ways to make you talk. Do not test me."

"I really have no idea what you want from me. If it's about that sphere, I'm sorry. It was just an accident. I didn't mean to break it. I would offer to pay, but I see you have more of the same, so..." I mumble awkwardly.

"An accident?" She laughs. "That sphere is unbreakable. Not even *I* can break it."

My lashes flutter as I take a step back.

"Maybe that was a poor quality one?" I supply. "Oh, maybe it was a fake one!"

"Nonsense," she bellows. Stopping in front of me, her hand suddenly shoots out as she tears the top of my dress, revealing the marks scattered across my collarbone. "You mean to tell me you do not know what these are?"

"No, I swear I—" I put my arms up to defend myself as I take a step back.

"You don't know what this is either?" She screws up her face in disbelief, manifesting my pearl bracelet in her hand.

"Fashion jewelry?" I force a smile.

"Stop lying!"

"I am not," I protest.

"Maybe I could have overlooked those writings on your skin or this odd talisman that simmers with energy, but you broke an Elegian Sphere. You not only destroyed it, but you did something to the particles inside of it..." She grits her teeth, the red paint surrounding her eyes infiltrating her irises.

"I..." My pulse roars in my ears at the terrifying picture she strikes. Seconds go by and she looks increasingly less humanoid and more like a blood-thirsty monster—who is coincidentally out for *my* blood.

"What the hell, Ze? How could you send me to this crazy lady?"

"I will ask again. Who are you? Or better yet, *what* are you?" she demands, the ground shaking with each syllable she utters.

"You have the wrong person, lady. I really don't know about the marks on my skin. I've had them for years. And I have no idea why the bracelet would reek of demon. I have it from a mermaid," I explain, omitting *some* information, but still telling her the truth. "As for the Elegian Sphere or whatever, how could I break it when I'm just a human?" I end up confessing. This should be the easiest way to get rid of her. If she realizes I'm just a human—although I don't know how she didn't sense it before —maybe she will finally leave me alone.

She stares at me for a moment before she doubles over in laughter, the sound of her voice hitting the stones and causing the echo to reverberate in the entire cave-like structure.

"Human? Did you say human?" She cackles, a dry, sharp laughter that lacks any trace of amusement. "No human could bear to touch the sphere, let alone destroy it."

Her expression sobers.

"Stop. Lying. To. Me," she shrieks. Her hair breaks loose of that tight bun it was confined to, tendrils of it slithering in the air like Medusa's serpents.

"I'm not lying," I whisper meekly.

My eyes widen with shock, and my heart pounds in fear as I watch those tendrils coil around and move as if they have a life of their own. She takes a step forward. I take a step back.

I am cognizant I have nowhere to run. She has control of the exit, and at present she does not seem in the least inclined to let me go. Good Lord!

"Where the hell are you, Ze? Why did you need access to my mind if you can't be bothered to answer when I call?"

My legs tremble and I can barely keep myself upright. Far from the severe but distinguished priestess from before, she now looks like a raging witch ready to commit murder. Are priestesses even allowed to kill people? Or humans? I'm not sure I want to find out, though.

"Did a son of Tenebreis send you? You are not a demon from what I can tell," she says as she comes closer to sniff me. "But only someone related to the Sons of Tenebreis would have the ancient writings of Tartareia etched onto the skin."

"What?" I whisper. "Ancient writings of Tartareia? What do you mean by that?"

She leans back, studying me with her shrewd gaze.

"You really don't know?"

I slowly shake my head, my lips trembling with fear.

"This," she says as she brings her nail against the dark etchings on my skin. "It's the ancient script of Tartareia. I may not be able to read it, but I've seen it before in old scriptures." She pauses. "No one outside of Tartareia would be able to decipher it, which begs the question... Why would *you* have it on your skin?"

"I don't know," I whisper. "I truly don't. I was told someone in Aperion might be able to give me more information..." I attempt to explain, but she has none of it.

"If that is true, why would you have this talisman, too?" she asks as she holds the pearl between two fingers. "I can sense the vile energy coming off it. It is so strong it's making me ill." She scrunches her nose in disgust.

"It was a gift, nothing more..."

She cuts me off as she presses her fingers tighter against the pearl. A loud cracking sound permeates the air as the pearl snaps under the weight of her force.

My mouth hangs open in shock as I watch bits and pieces of the pearl fall to the ground before the priestess flings the chain of the bracelet away from her. She glances down at the debris, scowling as she further steps on the bigger pieces with the tip of her shoe, effectively turning everything into dust.

"Hm." She frowns. "Maybe I was wrong," she muses to herself as she creates a cloud with her hands, lifting the dust off the ground and analyzing it in front of her. She must find no fault with it because as she snaps her fingers, the cloud dissipates, together with what was left of the pearl.

"Odd." She frowns. "Nevertheless, it does not erase the fact that *you* are suspicious. To break the Elegian Sphere... I must consult with the Psyche Supreme..." She speaks to herself, deep in thought. "You are coming with me to see her," she suddenly decrees.

If before I might have been afraid of her, seeing her destroy *my* property just like that snaps me out of my anxiety-ridden state. A hot, velvety rage envelops me as I stare at the broken chain of the bracelet, lying forlorn somewhere in the back. Tears stab at the back of my eyes as I move past her, getting to my knees to pick up the gold band. Ze might have given this to me with an ulterior motive, but he did forge it personally for me.

"You had no right," I mutter, a tear falling down my cheek. "That was *mine*."

She raises a lazy brow at me, her lips trembling with amusement.

"I had no right? Who do you think you are?" She laughs at me.

My sight grows heavy as tears of anger stream down my cheeks. Without thinking it through, I run toward her, ready to tackle her. If I hadn't been so blinded by my rage, I would have realized I'd never be able to lay a blow against her considering the discrepancy in our powers. Before I can reach her, she smirks, throwing me in the air with the wave of a hand.

FIFTY-FIVE

I squeeze my eyes shut, bracing myself for the impact with the hard stone wall. Yet instead of pain, I only feel a warm embrace as arms hug me from behind.

"You did well, little human," Ze whispers in my ear.

"Ze!"

He holds me tightly in his arms as he slowly descends to the ground.

"How could you do this to me?" I ask through gritted teeth. The rage is still there, but now it's being directed to a different target—one equally deserving of it.

"I apologize for my slight delay, but I wished to see what she knew about your marks," he confesses.

I frown.

"When the high priestess singled you out, it dawned on me that she must know more about your marks from the way she reacted to seeing them," he adds, his voice pensive.

I nod slowly. That makes sense. And thanks to that, we do have more information about them—that they're written in some ancient Tartareian script.

"But the sphere... Did you do that?"

"No. I have never seen anything of the kind. But have no worry, Luce. We will get to the bottom of this."

I purse my lips. His tone sounds apologetic, but I'm still a little peeved by his marked absence when he said he'd be with me at every step.

"You could have answered when I called. Do you know how scared I was..." I grumble.

"I am sorry." He sighs. "I did not mean to do that, but the runes in this temple must be more powerful than I thought. I could hear you, but none of my attempts to reach you back were successful. There was a static noise that greeted me whenever I attempted to do so."

"Oh," I whisper, surprised. "At least you're here now. How did you manage that?"

"The pearl." He smiles as he speaks aloud. "It carried my essence within it, and when the priestess broke it, it automatically allowed me to enter this hallowed space."

"Did you know she'd break it?" I ask, regarding him with suspicion.

A sheepish smile crosses his face.

"It was a possibility I planned for," he admits.

"Ze! But it was my bracelet! How could you give me a gift knowing it would get destroyed?" I give him a deadly stare as I break free of his embrace. One look around, though, and I note that the priestess has been frozen in place, her eyes wide with shock, her arm stretched and ready for attack. There's not even the twitch of a muscle or the evidence of breathing. It's almost as if she's a statue made of stone. Even those serpent-like locks are frozen still in an awkward position.

Did he...stop time? Of course he did. He's Ze after all. I doubt there's anything he *can't* do.

He blinks, his smile slowly fading when he realizes he messed up.

"Oh," he murmurs, averting his gaze and scratching the back of his head.

Before I can blink, he disappears and appears again in front of me, taking my arm and slipping another bracelet on it with a similar purple pearl, yet this time it's a deeper color with streaks of black.

"I apologize." He sighs wearily. "I am afraid I am not used to caring about your human sensibilities."

I stare at him dumbfounded. *Human sensibilities?* The gall on this man.

"Tell me you did not make another mermaid cry." I shake my head at him, though I must admit, this new bracelet is prettier than the other. The chain is a rose-gold color that complements the purple of the pearl.

He gulps guiltily.

"I cannot tell you that, for it would be a lie."

I close my eyes, taking a deep breath.

"Fine. Let's just get this over with and leave. I think I've been traumatized enough for one day."

Snapping his fingers, he allows time to flow again, and the priestess moves anew.

"How *dare* a male come into the temple of her ladyship?" she grits out, her chest expanding with each labored breath. She doesn't wait for a reply as she summons her strength, sending blast after blast at Ze.

He dodges each blow easily, moving through the blasts as he stops in front of her, staring her down. Despite her high heels, he's much larger than her, and a sliver of fear enters her gaze.

"You know who I am," he notes, his voice suddenly changed. There's a coldness there that was not present before.

"You're the God Killer," she spits out at him, doing her best to keep her calm. "The king warned me you would attempt to come inside, but I did not think you would succeed."

A smirk pulls at his lips.

"Nothing can stop me if I want something," he drawls, walking in a circle around her. His hands are at his back, his sword still sheathed at his hip. He makes no effort to arm himself or even muster a defensive stance. "Your king must have also told you the reason for my visit."

"You will not get anything out of me," she straightens her

spine in an attempt to hide the tremor of fear racking her body. And I do not blame her. As Commander Azerius, Ze appears frightening even to me.

"That remains to be seen." He shrugs. "I am doing what is best for Aperion. If I entered the temple, a demon could do so as well. You were suspecting her to be related to a son of Tenebreis, were you not?"

She wets her lip, her body taut as she's undoubtedly gathering all her strength to attack him when an opportune moment arises.

"You are a rather half-witted female, high priestess," he drawls in a mocking tone. "You suspected her to be the enemy, yet you opened the doors of your temple to her. If she were an actual threat, she would have annihilated you and your precious temple just as she did that sphere."

"What are you—"

"You know I speak the truth. You have no one to blame but yourself. *You* invited danger. Well, do not be surprised when the danger strikes."

"What is she? Are you working with them?" the priestess asks, her tone as venomous as the hatred in her eyes.

"She is my person. That is all you need to know." He smiles, a sinister smile that does not reach his eyes. "And I do not appreciate it if *anyone* makes her anxious."

She narrows her eyes at him.

In the span of a second, he's in front of her, his fingers wrapped around her right wrist. "Was it this hand you used to attack her? Or this?" He grabs the left one as well.

She draws back, seeking to escape his grasp.

To my surprise, he lets her go easily. But it's only for a moment before he withdraws his sword and cuts her right hand in one smooth slice. Blood pours out of the wound, the bone visible where he cut it. She releases a sharp cry as she presses her other hand to stop the bleeding.

Ze doesn't even blink as he wipes the residual blood off his sword before sheathing it.

My eyes widen at the pure ruthlessness rolling off him.

"That is merely the beginning, Priestess," he adds casually.

"You will not get me to say *anything*. I made a vow."

"I am aware. And breaking that vow will mean death, but you will die regardless. The question is whether it will be peacefully or...violently."

"I cannot. You don't understand." She gasps, her features strained with pain. "No priestess would willingly betray her duty."

"Really?" He raises a brow. "What about Helen? Her duty to Elias was far more important than her duty to the temple."

"She is an anomaly. Priestesses have a duty..."

"Spare me the rehearsed speech. I am here because I have a duty as well, the only difference being that mine extends to the entire universe. Shall I remind you what will happen if the demons get their hands on the vial? We are already at a crossroad. If I could so easily break into your sanctified temple, it is only a matter of time before the demons will as well."

She shakes her head, her breath harsh and punctured. Her blood courses freely and her features become paler by the second.

"I will ask this just one time before I will be forced to get the answers myself. You either tell me of your own accord and embrace your death or you will die a slow and painful death as I examine every thought you have ever had."

Her lips flatten in determination, and with a loud battle cry, she hurls herself against him, using her other hand to conjure her blasts.

Ze releases a heavy sigh as he opens his palm and absorbs her energy.

The veins on her forehead are about to burst as she strains herself to send blast after blast. Ze indulges her, looking bored all the while. When he finally has let her play enough, he lifts her in the air with the snap of a finger, his eyes narrowed as he takes in her struggling features.

"You have chosen the hard way. So be it," he declares before his eyes flash a deep purple, his irises swirling with specks of silver.

A sharp, horrifying cry escapes her, her features contorting in pain as Ze tries to assault her mind to get the information out of her. Despite the fact that she wasn't the nicest to me, I cannot bear to watch her in such agonizing pain that mounts by the second.

Ze does not mind it, the corners of his mouth curling up in a twisted smile. He enjoys this. I've known for a while how blood-thirsty he is, but I don't think I'll ever get used to seeing him derive such pleasure from harming others. Especially since it's so at odds with the Ze *I* know.

How can two diametrically opposed people reside in the same body? Azerius, the God Killer and Ze, the thoughtful friend.

"Agh," the priestess cries out, and rivulets of blood flow out of her eyes, dripping down her cheeks as blood vessels burst from the effort it takes to block Ze's attacks.

The entire scene is horrifying and far too violent for my feeble human sensibilities.

"Wait," I call out, unable to watch this any longer.

Ze reacts to my voice, half turning to regard me from the corner of his eye.

"What if we got the location out of her without her breaking her vow?" I suggest.

His brows draw together.

"Continue." He nods at me.

"If she visits the hiding place of the vial, and we follow behind, wouldn't that work as keeping her vow? She's not directly revealing the location to us. She's not speaking of it."

"That would be a good idea if she were amenable to it," Ze notes as he returns his attention to the priestess. "It is how Helen and Elias worked around their own vow."

"But it could work, no? She does not have to die."

"You would have her live after she behaved so appallingly to you?" His eyes flash.

"She was only doing her job, Ze." I sigh. "Yeah, she's not the most likable person I've ever met, but she was only trying to do her duty. I think we should give her a fair chance."

"You have too soft a heart, human."

"And you have no heart, Ze." I shake my head at him. "The least you could do is let me balance you out with my soft heart," I fire at him, fighting a smile. "It would certainly make you more...nice," I add, knowing those magic words would get a reaction out of him.

"Nice?" He repeats the word with slow, deliberate strokes of his tongue. His eyes sparkle, the murderous aura surrounding him all but gone.

"Yes, that would make you *very* nice. You want to be nice, don't you?" I ask, fluttering my lashes.

He fully turns toward me, letting the priestess drop to the floor with a thud.

"If you say that would make me nice..." he starts, a little unsure but eager nonetheless.

"It would." I nod as I walk to the priestess, dropping to my haunches to be on eye level with her. She strikes a pitiful picture. If a few moments ago I'd been terrified of her, now I only feel bad for how the fates have turned. Her paint is smeared over her face, mixed with the blood she spilled. Her features are tighter, more strained, as if she's aged a hundred years in the span of a second.

"You have one chance to avoid a painful death, and trust me, if you refuse this, there will be nothing I can do to help you anymore," I whisper. "You know him. You've heard of him. You are well aware he is more than capable of delivering his threats."

She seethes quietly as she glares at me.

"What *are* you?" She hisses between her teeth. "You are no more human than I am."

"But the truth is that I am." I sigh. "Whether you believe it or not."

"You do not know what an Elegian Sphere is, do you? It is made out of pure chaos and while it can react to spiritual power, it *cannot* be destroyed. Chaos is a primordial force that simply...is," she says as she sputters more blood. "These writings..." she says, suddenly grabbing my torn dress and pulling me closer. She splays her bloody hand over my skin, tracing the marks. Ze immediately flashes himself next to me, ready to act. I put a hand up to stop him, curious about what she has to say.

"They can only mean one thing...doom," she utters in a low voice.

Turning her gaze to Ze, she addresses him, "You are concerned about demons, but *you* have brought danger within Aperion. The enemy might be closer than you think, God Killer."

"I advise you to choose your words carefully. Any insult to her is an insult to me, and I will not let it slide," Ze adds in a harsh tone as he fiddles with the handle of his sword.

I put a finger up.

"I am not the enemy, and regardless of what you may think of me, I only want to help. These demons...they've already infiltrated the intermediary realms, and from what I'm told, it's not long before they'll be able to jump freely between worlds. That means *my* world is in danger," I tell her. To Ze, I turn to ask, "How do I go about making a vow like hers?"

"You will do no such thing!" he immediately thunders.

"How, Ze? Tell me."

"You vow three times to our Vestal Ladyship and give a drop of your blood as offering."

"You will do no such thing," he growls.

I ignore him as I grab a pin from my hair, pricking my finger as I say the words.

"I vow to the Vestal Ladyship that I do not have any nefarious purposes planned for the vial." I repeat it three times just as a drop of blood falls to the ground, evaporating into the hard stone.

Ze continues to grumble in the background while the priestess merely stares at me.

"You foolish human," he says as he crouches next to me,

grabbing my finger and bringing it to his lips to lick the wound. His words speak of his disapproval, but his eyes express the opposite, a fiery warmth enveloping me as he caresses me with his gaze.

I gulp down hard, barely wrenching my eyes from his.

"It is done. You can see that I am in earnest now. Will you help us?" I put on a smile as I address the priestess. Her lips tremble as her gaze moves from me to Ze, who's greedily sucking on my finger. I pull my hand away, my flesh healed. He grumbles a small protest under his breath.

The priestess is quiet for a moment before she nods, her shoulders slumping down in defeat.

Getting to her feet, she waves the stone wall aside as she wobbles toward the main hall.

Ze and I follow closely. Skepticism is written all over Ze's features, and I can tell he's ready for attack at any point. The only reason he's going along with this is to please me and earn his designation as *nice*. As odd as that might seem, it appears to be the only thing he truly cares about. He doesn't mind when he's called names, not even when he is referred to as the God Killer. But being called *nice* seems to work wonders for his ego.

The priestess stops in front of the giant statue in the hallway. Going closer to it, she climbs the podium, placing herself at its feet. She reaches out with her good hand, touching the precious stones in some kind of secret combination. Her movements are fast—so much so I can barely follow. But as she uses her power to make herself levitate, she places herself in front of the statue and touches the lips of the goddess—her Ladyship as she'd called her.

A loud noise permeates the air as a fissure appears in the middle of the statue, the two halves separating to reveal the vial in the center. It is a small container—no bigger than my palm. The outside material is made of gold and encrusted with the same type of precious stones as the statue. Only at the top there's a translucent material that reveals the red of the blood within.

Ze uses his powers to bring the vial to him, the object infinitely smaller in his big hand. He closes his fist over it, and when he opens it next, the vial is gone.

"Your help is appreciated, Priestess. Rest assured that the vial will be safe in my keep." Ze inclines his head. "For your cooperation, I will give you back your hand."

The severed hand makes an appearance, floating toward us and fitting itself at the priestess's wrist. Her eyes widen for a moment, but as the hand is locked in place, her flesh begins to mend until it's as good as new.

"How did you do that?" I whisper in awe since he didn't use his healing saliva.

"I merely nullified the spell keeping her from healing." He shrugs. "It is not by chance that I am called the God Killer. My sword is the only weapon from which a god cannot heal."

"Oh." I blink.

I guess that explains why everyone's so scared of him.

"But I should mention one other thing, Priestess." He turns his attention to her, his voice cold and unyielding. "You will utter no word of what you have seen of my female. Not about her markings, nor about the sphere. If anyone asks, you shall say it was just a mishap. Understood?"

The priestess nods slowly, barely daring to meet his gaze.

"Good. That concludes our business here," he tells me.

Without waiting for my reply, he grabs my hand and flashes us out of the temple. As I blink, our surroundings change, and I'm back in my room at Thea's house.

I break away from him, a little shaken by everything that happened.

"No one in Aperion speaks ancient Tartareian. It is a forbidden language," he adds quietly.

"But you said a god must have left the marks on my skin. Who could it be...?"

He purses his lips.

"I am not certain. But I am concerned. If this has anything to do with the Sons of Tenebreis, I will find out. Until then, you must ensure that no one else sees your markings. We do not know who might also recognize the script and jump to conclusions," he advises.

"Do you..." I pause, searching his gaze. "Do you think I'm dangerous like the priestess said?" I ask tentatively. "I don't know what happened to that sphere, I swear. I just touched it and—"

"Do not worry," he declares swiftly. "You are my responsibility. I will protect you."

"But you didn't answer my question..."

"There is no answer, for it does not matter."

"But what if..." I swallow. "What if I *am* in any way related to those demons or to the Sons of Tenebreis? Aren't they your enemies?"

I can't believe I'm even contemplating this. This morning, I was just a human. A simple human. Now, the markings I bear might have demonic origin, not divine. The thought makes my stomach plummet. But nothing surprises me anymore, and instead of hiding behind a wall of ignorance, I'd rather face everything head-on. After all, knowledge is power. And only knowing the truth about myself will allow me to come to terms with my past...and my future.

"It does not matter," Ze states unequivocally, his gaze dipping lower. "You are not my enemy, Luce. I do not care *what* you are. *You* are not the enemy. Understand?"

I nod slowly, although I'm not entirely convinced by his words. His duty is to Aperion first and foremost. He is a weapon designed by the Supremes to battle demons. It might not be up to him whether I am the enemy or not...

I force a smile on my face as I awkwardly pat him on the shoulder. Moving about my room, I accidentally catch my reflection in the mirror, and a gasp escapes me as I notice how disheveled I am. My hair is all messy, some strands waving in the air, others sticking to my skin. Blood spatters are across my face and cleavage, my torn dress barely covering the top of my breasts. Dear Lord, have I been carrying on an entire conversation with him almost topless?

My cheeks burn with mortification.

Muttering a hurried goodbye, I dash into the bathroom to clean myself and change into something more comfortable. I take my time showering and removing all the traces of the day from my body, and when I'm done, I moisturize my skin and dab some perfume behind my ear. I settle on a dark blue silk dress—perfect to wear to bed for a nap.

But as I come back to the room, I note Ze has not left. He's sitting on my bed, his legs apart, his palms resting on his knees. I frown, concerned. It's been an hour since I left him there, maybe two.

His intense gaze is on me, his lips pursed as he just stares at me.

"Ze? What are you doing? Don't you have some demons to slay?" I ask, thinking he'd get the hint and leave. I did my duty and helped him. Now I deserve some me time, which is code for I'm tired and I want to nap the day away. After everything that happened today, I think I'm entitled to as much.

"I have been thinking," he starts slowly.

I raise a brow at him.

"You have been thinking for over an hour?"

"I have been thinking," he repeats, clearing his throat. "Today was a success."

"It was." I nod.

"Because of you," he surprises me by adding.

Now that's...unexpected. He looks mighty uncomfortable as he says that, though.

"You did well," he adds quietly.

"Thank you... I guess?"

He nods, his expression serious.

"You are, indeed, a worthy female."

"Okay..."

"We make a good team," he continues awkwardly.

"Right. Thanks. Now you can go."

He doesn't move.

"We shall celebrate," he declares, straightening his back.

"Celebrate?" I repeat numbly, still confused.

"I have decided to give you the honor of being the first female to go on a date with me."

"A...date?"

He nods proudly.

"You may rejoice."

FIFTY-SIX

I stare at him for a moment before I burst into laughter.

He doesn't share my mirth, however.

"What is so amusing, human?" He narrows his eyes at me.

"Do you even know what a date is?" I ask, my lips quivering as I try to curb my laughter.

"Of course," he answers in indignation. "I have performed thorough research." He opens his palm, manifesting a stack of about five or six books, all with the same mix of red and white cover and spine.

"What is that?" I frown, moving closer to examine the titles.

"The books you like to read. I procured them from your world to familiarize myself with those *hobbies* of yours."

Somehow, that statement warms my heart. He, who has never had a hobby in his life, wanted to learn more about mine.

"But... How did you think *those* are the books I like to read?"

The titles are not very inspired: *The Billionaire's Secret*; *The Billionaire and his Cinderella*; *The Italian Duke's Darling*; *The Tycoon's Nine-Month Secret*; *The Boss and the Maid* and *The Billionaire's Affair*. I cannot imagine Ze reading that, particularly the spicy scenes. My cheeks heat up as I picture him in my mind, book in hand, eyes narrowed as he reads the more risqué scenes, since there's no way those are clean romances.

"You like rich men. They are rich," he adds with a noncommittal shrug. "Not as rich as I am, of course," he makes sure to add. "You will not find someone richer."

"And what did you learn about dates from them?" I ask as I pick the top book from the stack and flip through it.

Big mistake!

My blush intensifies as I spot passages highlighted with notes in the corner. I only need to read a few words involving wetness, fingers, and moans to realize the type of passages he highlighted. I can't make out the scribbled notes on the margins, but I quickly close the book, *not* wanting to know more.

"It is an event during which a male and a female go out for a meal or an otherwise engaging activity whereby they have fun together," he quotes a definition as if he's spent eons researching it.

"You omitted one thing, Ze. Dates are for people who have a romantic interest in each other. We are *friends*," I emphasize. Although I don't think he sees me that way, I want to make sure he knows where we stand. Since he's been reading romance novels and has shown an interest in physical intimacy, it's a good way to remind him that our relationship is pure friendship—nothing more.

His eyes flash at me.

"You are my person," he speaks slowly. "You will go on a date with me. We will have...*fun*." He gulps down, the word *fun* burning on his lips as he barely keeps himself from cringing as he utters it.

"I thought the word fun wasn't in your vocabulary." I raise a brow.

"It is not," he quickly answers. His eyes widen before he amends. "It *was* not. I am willing to make a concession. For you."

"Ze. I am tired. It's late. I want to go to sleep," I explain gently. "I'm human after all, and today was a lot."

He stares at me for a moment before he slowly nods, though disappointment pulls at his features.

"Tomorrow. We will go on a date tomorrow."

"I promised Thea and Wyn I'd spend time with them since Wyn's ball is quickly approaching," I quickly make the excuse. Nikki would *not* appreciate me going on a date with another man. A low sound erupts from Ze's chest. His pupils become larger, the purple of his eyes intensifying as streaks of black and silver fight for supremacy.

"The day after tomorrow," he adds after a moment of deliberation.

"I need to get fitted for my dress for the ball."

He narrows his eyes at me.

"The day after the day after tomorrow."

"I don't know. It's the day before the ball..."

He can't take a hint, can he?

"Human," he growls. "You will accept," he decrees, his eyes flashing dangerously at me.

It strikes me that he's too insistent about this. Maybe he has something planned that he's looking forward to. The man's never had fun in his life, and that thought always makes my heart clench painfully in my chest. I cannot even imagine the type of life he must have led, or the loneliness he experienced. The more I note the determination in his features, the more I question whether I should just grant him this one small wish. He's already done so much for me; it wouldn't be that hard to show him how to have fun and unwind. This would be a first for him, too. And he wants to do it with me. Because we're a team, right?

"You really want to do this?" I ask slowly. I can't believe I'm entertaining this idea. But as long as he realizes that it's a *friendly* date, not a romantic one, it should be all right.

His jaw is locked tight as he nods.

"Do you have a plan? Something in mind?"

"Yes. I have given it much thought," he states, though he doesn't elaborate further. "The day after the day after tomorrow is mine. I will come for you in the morning. Be ready."

"Okay... Sounds good." I smile.

He doesn't reciprocate the smile, merely gazing at me intently. Moments pass, and he's still rooted to the spot.

"Now you can go," I say when he doesn't make to move. Pushing at his shoulders, I gently guide him to the door. "Good night, Ze. Go put the vial somewhere secure."

"I have already taken care of it," he scoffs. His eyes pin me to the spot, the colors swirling in a tempestuous whirlpool. "I will see you soon, human, for it seems you cannot wait to be rid of me."

His words give me pause, especially the tone of his voice.

"No, Ze, I..." I open my mouth to explain.

"It is fine," he cuts me off, a harshness underlying his words. "I am well accustomed to the sentiment."

With that, he vanishes from my sight.

My chest rises and falls as I stare at the spot he just vacated. I run our conversation through my mind time and time again. I offended him. I could tell in the way his demeanor suddenly changed, a veil of sadness underlying his otherwise biting words.

I hurt him.

Without intending, I hurt him.

I take a deep breath, squeezing my eyes shut. It appears that even the big block of ice that is Ze can get hurt. And for some reason, that makes it even worse.

"Ze?" I call out in my mind, hoping he might hear me, perhaps even reply. *It was not my intention to hurt you. I will see you in three days.*

Silence greets me. I release a heavy sigh. But just as I'm about to give up hope that he's going to acknowledge my words, his supercilious voice rings out in my mind.

"Nothing can hurt me, human. I do not share your feeble sensibilities," he huffs.

A sad smile pulls at my lips.

"Of course," I readily reply. *"I apologize for merely implying that."*

"Good," he says. *"Have a good sleep."* And with that, he's gone from my mind.

Feeling a little better—though not by much—I head to my bed, drawing the covers aside and nestling between them. No matter what he says, I know he *feels*, and perhaps he does not realize how much, but he *can* hurt.

Turning on my side, I hug the pillow to my chest, closing my eyes as I seek the oblivion of sleep. Briefly, I wonder how Nikki is doing. Is he fine? Is he losing strength? It's been quite some time since I've last heard from him, and I cannot help but worry. Thus far, I've done my best not to dwell too much on his absences, but that doesn't mean I don't fear for him, or that my thoughts are not constantly *with* him. We might be in Aperion, but even this world is not safe from demon attacks. If he should happen to come across one and be absorbed...

My heart swells with pain in my chest, but I cannot let my thoughts wander there.

Warmth greets my back as strong arms hug me from behind. A familiar presence that quenches all doubts. I let out a deep sigh, letting myself go, knowing I'm safe in his arms.

The following day, I wake up to an invitation to tea from Wyn. After I dress up, I make my way to the conservatory where Wyn is waiting for me with a steaming pot of tea and two cups. The room is made entirely out of glass, with flowers of all colors hanging on the walls. There are also beds of flowers on each side of the room, while in the middle there's only a table with a couple of chairs and a comfortable-looking sofa. The table is a pastel blue while the chairs and the sofa are a light pink, the colors complementing each other. Everything is muted, letting the bold colors of the flowers stand out.

"Where's Thea?" I walk inside and take a seat next to her.

"She's meeting with Father." She sighs. "He's probably lecturing her again for missing all the balls this season. She usually goes to a few at least, to placate him. But I can't remember the last time she went to one."

"Is it truly so bad if neither of you marry?"

She gives me a sad smile, averting her gaze as she pours tea into the cups.

"After my parents hear that I will be joining the temple, they might be harsher to Thea. And I still have not told her about my plans..." She shakes her head. "It will be a mess. But once I take my vows, they will not be able to do anything for five hundred years. That should be enough for their anger to abate."

"What about your sister? Do you think she'll be fine with this?"

She purses her lips.

"I do not know. She always supports me in my endeavors, but... I'll just have to hope she will forgive me. It's very cowardly of me, isn't it? Running away like this and leaving my sister to fend for herself with our parents." She laughs nervously. "I've been thinking about it too, and I *know* it might not be the best choice. But as of now, it is the best choice for me."

"I can't make any judgments since I barely know your family. But what I do know is that your sister loves you. She would never want you to be unhappy. Which is why I have to ask... Do you *really* want to join the temple?" I ask.

Wyn brings her teacup to her lips, taking a small sip.

"I have to, don't I?"

"You don't have to do anything you don't want to, Wyn."

She smiles.

"What happened after I left? Was the high priestess mad that you broke the sphere?"

I raise a brow at her, recognizing her tactic.

"No. It turned out to be a mistake. She let me go easily," I lie.

Wyn tilts her head to the side, her expression telling me she doesn't buy my explanation.

"I know you cannot tell me the truth. But I have something for you," she says as she fishes a small letter from her reticule. It's smaller than the size of a mobile phone, and going by the worn edges and yellowed paper, it's an old one too.

"What is it?" I frown.

"I cannot control my abilities, and it's been getting worse and worse recently. Sometimes... I know things. Things I should *not* know," she says pointedly.

I stare at her.

She places the letter on the table, silently pushing it toward me.

I glance down at the yellow, almost brownish hue of the paper, my eyes widening in shock when I see my name printed on top of it in cursive letters. The writing is elegant and feminine, the ink almost faded from the passage of time. But the meaning is unmistakable as is the timeline.

Luce. After the Elegian Sphere breaks.

"Where did you get this from?" I swallow uneasily.

"Ironically, I have had it for hundreds of years. My family and I were on a diplomatic trip to Aperionia, the official capital, and I was drawn to an uninhabited area of the palace. It was as if it was calling to me. I found the letter within the palace walls, nestled between bricks. Someone must have hidden it there. I did not intend to take it, but the servants came upon me and thinking I'd done something wrong, I hid it in the pocket of my dress and took it home with me. I haven't spared it a thought since. But after meeting you, I began to wonder, especially after what happened at the temple."

"But...how..." I stammer.

"I do not know how or why. I only know that it belongs to you."

"I don't understand," I whisper.

"Trust me, I don't either." She chuckles. "But it is yours and you shall have it. Now, if you will excuse me. I have to go for one last fitting, but you are welcome to use the conservatory as you'd like. I'll let the staff know not to bother you."

I can only nod, my eyes still glued to the letter.

Wyn gets up, the sound of the chair sliding against the

ground echoing in my ears. She steps away, slowly, until a click denotes the closure of the door to the conservatory.

Then I'm all alone.

Just me and this unusual letter.

I gulp, my hands trembling as I pick it up, slowly opening the envelope to reveal the folded sheet inside. Carefully, I pull it out, afraid any sudden movement might damage the paper and consequently the contents inside. I unfold the sheet of paper and start to read the message.

Dear Luce,

You do not know me, but I know you—intimately. In the future, we shall be best friends. In the future, everything will make sense, I promise. But for now, I need you to trust me that I have your best interests at heart—that everything I am about to impart is only meant to help and protect you.

By the time you read this, you should have already broken the Elegian Sphere at the Arche Temple. You may wonder how I know this. I am not quite ready to reveal that, but trust that you will find out eventually. After all, it is your fate. And the fates spare no one.

If you are not yet convinced of my words, there is one more thing that will hopefully change your mind. The ancient writings on your skin.

Do I have your attention now?

I pause, shocked. Writing. Whoever wrote this letter *knew* that the marks on my skin are an ancient script. That alone piques my interest. I continue reading.

You must quit The Wishing Game. You must do so

before the third trial. By now, you should have already given your consent to continue in the game, but before the third trial starts, you can, at any point, withdraw that consent. It is a small loophole that not too many are aware of, but no one will deny you should you summon a wraith and withdraw.

What the hell? Anger bubbles inside of me. Why is everyone telling me to quit the game? Yet the next sentence catches my attention before I can crumple the piece of paper and throw it aside.

You are probably ready to put the letter down, thinking you could never give up on your husband—that the only way to get him back is to win the game. Unfortunately, that is false. Winning the game will not get Nicholas back. On the contrary, your continuation in the game will jeopardize everything. Nicholas's soul is not with the House of Psyche. That means no god, and no Supreme can return him to you because to them, he does not exist.

But there is one way you can get him back.

He is with you, at every moment, whether you know it or not. But to get back the man you love, you will need to be free of the Game and free of any vow that might lay claim on your soul. I have laid out further instructions for you, which shall find you when the time is right. I cannot emphasize enough that this requires the utmost secrecy. It is why I cannot divulge too much in this letter for fear someone else might intercept it.

If anyone else should find out about this, it is not just your fate or that of your husband that hangs in balance, but that of the entire universe. I am being cryptic, I realize. But this is much more important than you realize—than even I realized. But for our loved ones, we must do whatever it takes to keep them safe.

I am aware this is a lot to take in, but as a sign of good faith and to show I can be trusted, I will leave you with this information. The writing on your skin—it is a promise. There is nothing evil about it, nor is it something to be afraid of. It is a vow written in blood, and in a matter of days, that vow will be fulfilled. When that happens, the mark of a new beginning will arise.

This is not the last you shall hear from me, but by the next time, I hope I will have earned your trust.

Yours,

A.S.L.

I stare at the letter for minutes on end. Who is A.S.L.? How does he or she know about me? The questions swarm inside my mind, making me more confused than ever before. A letter written hundreds of years ago knows so much about me, from the writings on my skin to Nikki and my participation in the Game. How could this happen when I was not even born when this A.S.L. must have written it?

Immediately, my gaze swings around the room as I search for an intruder—someone who could watch me closely enough to know how I'll react to the contents of the letter.

There's no one. I'm all alone. And even if there had been someone around, could they travel back in time to write about it in this letter? Is time travel possible? Who has that power?

The questions are endless. The answers... not so much.

I carefully fold the letter and place it back in the envelope before I stow it safely in my little bag.

If I cannot speak with anyone about this—that is, if I am to take this person's warnings seriously—then the library will be my best friend. Skeptical but curious, I drink the last of my tea before I make my way out of the conservatory. Although I'm weirded out by the letter, I cannot dismiss its contents—not when my actions could negatively impact Nikki.

At the very least, the next few days should tell me if there's any truth to what this letter is saying.

FIFTY-SEVEN

I set the letter down with a sigh after reading it for the hundredth time. Two days later, and I don't know more than I started with. The library didn't yield any new information, being even more cryptic on the subject of time travel. The most I could gather was that it's the job of the Supremes to ensure that the time and space continuum are not meddled with, and from that perspective, time travel is not only frowned upon but also forbidden—just like creatures hopping between realms. Deities might be allowed to do so, but even they are limited by scope and duration.

Just who could this A.S.L. be, and how would they even know about me, someone who would not be born for hundreds, if not thousands of years, since who knows how long the letter had been hidden in that wall before Wyn came across it?

The matter is entirely too strange, made even more so by the fact that it was as if A.S.L. knew all my worries regarding the new discovery that my marks might be demonic in nature and decided to ease my mind with this letter.

Yet if the writings on my body are neither a curse nor a demonic mark, what are they? What type of vow would be seared on my skin like this? What could have possibly triggered it? And if it doesn't spell doom, then what is it?

I cannot fathom how these marks could be a good thing, yet A.S.L. says exactly that. I tuck the letter in a secure place and occupy myself with getting ready for my meeting with Ze. As I browse my now fully stocked closet for a suitable gown, I take a small trip down memory lane to when the marks first appeared on my body.

I must have been roughly thirteen. My mother, burdened by poverty, could not afford to feed two mouths, so she decided to sell me—in her mind, it was the only chance I could have at life.

Ten thousand pesos.

That had been the price she'd fetched for me—a fortune by the standards of those days.

A vague sound whispers in my ear—her voice as she'd told me I was going to live with El Señor, and that I was to be obedient to him as a wife would be to her husband.

I don't blame her for selling me, though I was still a child with no understanding of the outside world. I was so naive, I had no idea what went on between a wife and a husband. Yet as I was wrenched away from the only home I'd ever known, I had to grow up fast.

And my first lesson was that El Señor was already married.

I was not to be his wife. I was to be his whore.

My eyes squeeze shut as I'm transported back to the moment I was taken to the hacienda. I was given a large room—larger than the small hut my mother and I had lived in. A pair of maids dressed me in the finest clothes I'd ever worn and told me to wait patiently for El Señor to come to me.

Had I known what was going to happen? No.

The only saving grace at that time had been my unquenchable curiosity. For all my stilted education growing up, I was starving for knowledge just as I was starving for any information about this new home I was supposed to live in.

Despite the warning that I should stay still, I did not. I opened the door and stepped out, wandering about the long-winded corridors and marveling at the impressive art that decorated the walls.

Some of the illustrations I was familiar with as they represented the gods of our tradition. Others, not so much. I walked and walked until I heard the sound of foreign voices that uttered my name. Slowly, information filled my brain—why I'd been brought there, and how I was to serve El Señor. Even in my innocent mind, I realized that his purpose for me was sick and perverted, and I quickly resolved to escape. Maybe I would not have a home to return to, but I at least would have my virtue intact.

Yet that was the second lesson I learned. No one left the hacienda. Not alive, anyway.

El Señor came to my room and didn't find me there. He had all his guards search the premises until they dragged me from my hiding place and brought me in front of him. Those fine clothes had already been torn and soiled in my attempt to fight the guards off. One look at my rebellious gaze, and El Señor decided to teach me a lesson. He ordered his guards to strip me naked, deriving sick pleasure from seeing me fight to keep what was left of my modesty. When I put up *too* much of a fight, he intervened personally.

That was the third lesson I learned. El Señor had a heavy hand.

I lift my hand to trace the contour of my cheek, the past sting reverberating into the present.

He smiled as he struck me. Again and again until my skin broke, until I was bruised and battered, and my blood stained the ground.

I remember doing my best to hold on, yelling at him that I wouldn't allow him to touch me.

But despite all my protestations, the pain soon proved too much even for my strong will. At some point, I must have passed out, for when I awoke, it was to find my entire upper body marked with strange writings, like a tattoo imprinted on my skin to remind me of the day my fate had changed, forever. After my rebellion, El Señor didn't want to be bothered with me, so I was sentenced to labor away in his temples, doing work that no woman, let alone a child of thirteen, should have done. Yet that was preferable to being his toy.

El Señor might not have raped me that night, but the marks on my skin were proof that he had done *something*—that he had stolen a part of me I could never get back.

Now, knowing that these strange tattoos are not his doing, I don't know how to feel about them anymore. For almost half my life, I've forced myself to hate them because they reminded me of him.

Big, manly hands cover my eyes. I inhale sharply at the sudden warmth that surrounds me. The scent of leather and spice fills my nostrils, pulling me back from that painful past and anchoring me into the present.

"I do not like that look on your face, human," Ze whispers in my ear.

I exhale, letting calm settle over me as his presence lulls me back into a safe space.

"What look was it?" I ask after a beat of silence.

"You were...sad. I do not like it when you are sad," he grumbles.

Taking hold of his hands, I lift them off my eyes as I turn to face him.

"And what do you know about sadness, Ze?" I lift a brow. "I thought emotions were not your strong suit."

His brows scrunched together, he tilts his head to the side as he considers my words.

"When you are sad, there is a hole inside your chest that nothing can fill," he muses aloud. "It hungers for *something* that is out of reach, creating a vacuum of emptiness that blackens every waking moment. But it is when you are slumbering that it is far worse, for it creates the mirage of getting that *something*, only to awaken and realize it was all a dream."

I stare at him, my lips parting in surprise.

"That is..." I clear my throat. "That is a very apt representation of sadness. Where did you read it? It's almost as if you've felt it yourself."

"It is all your fault, human," he huffs, pushing his chin up. "Because of your scathing words, I have lost far too many nights of precious rest. Instead of exterminating demons, I was researching those romance books of yours and scouring your world for the most expensive and worthy cow."

My eyes widen as my lashes flutter in confusion.

"You have caused me great distress and you need to take responsibility," he continues.

"W-what?" I stammer.

"I do not like it when you are sad. I forbid you to be sad from now on," he keeps going, ignoring my scandalized expression.

"It doesn't work like that, Ze. You can't just command feelings..." I attempt to explain.

"It shall be my new boon." He nods to himself, pleased.

"But you haven't amassed another one hundred points," I add drily.

"It does not matter. I will have my boon early." He crosses his arms, staring me down intently. "You may continue to add up the points, but this shall be my boon."

I gawk at him for a few seconds before amusement breaks across my face.

"You're impossible." I chuckle, shaking my head.

Slowly, his lips curl up in a smile just as he brings his fingers to my mouth, keeping my lips in place to mirror his.

"And you are not sad anymore," he hums to himself. "Mission accomplished."

I raise a brow at him.

"You shall wear this gown," Ze says as he steps forward and grabs a purple dress from my closet. "It suits you the most."

"Has anyone told you that you're awfully bossy?" I grumble, though I accept the gown and head for the bathroom.

"It is the nature of my position. I command, and others follow," he continues as *he* follows me, about to enter the bathroom, too. But I'm faster as I close the door in his face before he can step inside.

"Privacy, Ze. That's why doors exist," I call out as I take off my clothes to put on the purple gown.

"I hate doors," he adds grumpily from the other side.

I smile to myself, surprised to realize that his odd brand of bossiness did, in fact, accomplish the mission. Without even realizing, my sadness turned into good humor, the past promptly forgotten in favor of the much more entertaining present. If he keeps this up, Ze might very well get his new boon.

I shake my head at that absurd line of thought, but a small part of me may not think it's *that* absurd.

It takes me a couple of minutes to get ready. As I exit the bathroom, I find Ze pacing around my room with a deep look of concentration.

"So, where are we going?" I ask as I plop myself in front of him.

He suddenly stops his maddening pace, swiveling to meet my gaze.

"I have changed my mind," he declares.

"What do you mean?"

"I have, of course, planned an entire itinerary for today. I do not want you to think I would have come unprepared. But I find that there is one more pressing matter to take care of."

I blink in confusion.

"Are you canceling on me?" I ask, bewildered.

"Of course not." He pins me with his gaze. "But there will be a change of plans. Come." He takes a step forward and grabs my hand, pulling me into his arms. In the blink of an eye, our surroundings change.

A bleak landscape stretches out in front of us, the land barren and desolate as far as the eye can see. There's one narrow road in the middle of the rusty desert-like terrain, accommodating thousands of people as they slowly walk in a death march procession toward an unnamed destination. The sky is perpetually dark and unwelcoming, red clouds gathering here and there to obstruct the little light that exists.

"What's this?"

Ze places himself at my back, his hands on my shoulders.

"This is P'asala. The intermediary realm through which all souls pass before they head into the afterlife, and that is the Road of all Woes."

"But... It's so...so..."

"Simple?" he offers.

"I would rather go with sinister," I mumble drily. "Even good souls have to walk through here?"

"Yes. There is no differentiation until they reach the Apex." He points toward a vague dark spot on the horizon. "Each soul relives their past life during the Road of all Woes, the good and the bad. It is the last time they are able to remember their previous selves. The virtuous have nothing to fear, for they have led a noble life and they will be rewarded as such in the afterlife. The sinful become wracked by guilt and fear as they remember every bad deed they have committed," he explains.

A shiver goes down my back the more I stare at that bleak and somber road. I suppose the name of the road is an apt representation for the visual—it's truly woeful.

"Come." Ze takes my hand, pulling me into his arms as he levitates above the ground. We move speedily across the flat desert, and in just a few seconds, we reach the Apex he was talking about. The landscape changes from a flat surface to an uneven, hilly one. As we reach a tall dune, Ze descends to the ground. He releases me, placing me by his side.

"This is where everything changes," he notes.

There's a black patch of land where a masked figure garbed in a combination of red and dark yellow awaits each soul. As they step from the road and onto the black strip, the soul begins to glow. But not all souls are the same. Some are a light color, others a dark, muted one. But as they step off the black strip of land to continue forward, the glow doesn't change.

"That is the Apex where the souls are judged," Ze says. "That is Omorion. He is a Death deity from the House of Psyche. His task is to weigh each soul to determine where they are to go. The souls that have a light shimmer are virtuous. The darker the glow, the more sinful they are. Let us go to the next phase."

Taking my hand once more, he flashes us to the next stop. There's a huge well with intricate designs along the edges. It's so large, it covers the visible horizon, making it so there's nothing left north of it. A woman in a hood that obscures her face sits on the ledge of the well, holding a cup in her delicate hands that she fills from the well and gives to each soul to consume.

"This is Letharion—the well of oblivion. And that is Lethe, the Goddess of Oblivion. After a soul drinks from the well, all memories of their past life are erased until they become a blank canvas. But the souls never lose their glow, which indicates which part of the afterlife they will head to."

As Ze speaks, I note that there are two possible roads from the well. One on the right, which only the brighter souls take, and one on the left, which is reserved for the dark souls.

"The virtuous souls are taken to the upper levels of the House of Psyche, where according to their merit, they either proceed directly to the House of Moirai, where they are assigned a new fate and before being reincarnated, or they work to create more merit to gain the chance to reincarnate."

I note thoughtfully.

"And the bad souls?"

"They are taken to the lower levels of the House of Psyche, where according to their sins, they endure punishment. It takes them longer to gain merit to move up the levels and earn a new incarnation, but it is not impossible," Ze explains.

"I thought bad souls become demons," I murmur in confusion as I glance up at him.

"Some. Not all. If the messengers Correctors retrieve them before a certain amount of time, they will not become demons. Once they are touched by Omorion, they are marked for the afterlife and the chances of them becoming demons are null. Before that, however, it is very possible depending on how evil the soul is and how much anger it has collected over its lifetime.

It is not an exact science, unfortunately." He purses his lips. "We can more or less predict who is most likely to turn, and those have priority with Collectors. But there are cases where souls become corrupted when left to their own devices."

"What you mean is that as long as there will be souls, there will also be demons, no?"

His lips flatten into a thin line.

"Unfortunately. The universe relies on balance. There are the Light Primordials and the Nether Primordials, and there are the Seven. There are the Aperite Supremes, and there are the Tartarean Lords. We have our governing Houses. So do the Sons of Tenebreis. And just like that, every being has a natural mate that complements its nature," he mentions pointedly as he watches me intently.

"Does that mean your war against demons is never-ending?" I frown.

He doesn't reply for a moment before he sighs.

"It is, indeed, eternal. But that does not mean it is a never-ending conflict. Evil has been around since the dawn of time and will continue to be so. It is only when the scales of balance are tipped in favor of evil that we have to take a stance and act."

"Like now," I mention.

"Like now," he agrees. "But that is not why I have brought you here. Come. We have one more stop."

I blink in surprise.

"What do you mean..." I don't even get to finish my words as he takes my hand and flashes us someplace else.

If before I would have thought P'asala was bleak, this new place is that but times one hundred. There's a scorching heat that makes me want to shed all my clothes, including my skin. My breath comes out in labored spurts, my mouth dry as an unquenchable thirst overtakes me.

"W-w-what is t-this?" I stammer in between pants. I hunch down, my hands on my thighs as I attempt to catch my breath.

"This is Katras, the lowest level of the House of Psyche," Ze comments. One look at him, and he's absolutely fine, his back straight, his posture imposing. Of course he wouldn't be affected by whatever poison is in this air.

I'm barely in control of myself and getting worse. My vision fades slightly, and I can't even tell what's around me. There's only a thick air that presses down on me.

Ze plants himself in front of me and, placing two fingers under my chin, he tips it up so I can look into his piercing gaze. Leaning down, he comes closer to me.

"Open your mouth," he commands.

"W-what?" I whisper in confusion.

But as I open my mouth to speak, he blows cool air into me, his breath becoming my breath. Almost instantaneously, my vigor is restored and I can withstand this heavy atmosphere better.

"This is meant to be an inhospitable place. Here, damned souls suffer for their sins," he explains.

"You mean this is hell?"

"In your human terms, indeed." He nods.

I stare at him, dumbfounded. Is this his idea of a *date*? To bring me to literal hell?

FIFTY-EIGHT

My eyes stray from him to the dry and arid environment, made even more unbearable by the red, blazing sky that emits an unnatural heat. The atmosphere is thick and heavy, making one want to crawl instead of walk. And as I get a better view of a quarry nearby, filled with souls emitting a dim glow, I realize that's the purpose. They toil on their hands and knees in an attempt to achieve a task that would be easily done in normal conditions. In another gallery, a few meters over, there's another group of souls that attempt to work, only to be lashed and hit by a guardian watching from the sidelines when they fail to deliver results.

"Who are those?" I point to the guardians, the only ones moving normally, not crawling.

"Those are the Custodians. They ensure that the damned perform their tasks."

"Who are you?" an angry voice bellows from behind. We both turn and come face to face with one of those Custodians. He's dressed in a gray linen tunic that's held together at the waist by a thick belt housing a number of weapons. His hand is already on the hilt of a knife, withdrawing it and brandishing it in front of us.

Ze tilts his head to the side, a breeze blowing his long hair from his face to reveal the tattoos that mar one side of his body.

The Custodian's eyes widen, and he immediately lowers his head, his gaze on the floor.

"Forgive me, Commander. We were not expecting you," he murmurs in a subservient voice. "And this..." He slowly turns his head toward me, though he does not raise his gaze.

"This is my female, but you will not mention a word of her presence. Is that clear?"

The Custodian bows to me, bending so low, his body trembles from the effort exerted. He might be immune to the toxic atmosphere of Katras, but he is not immune to Ze's frightening tone.

"At rest, soldier," Ze intones. "This is an informal visit, and I would like it to be kept that way."

The Custodian wobbles up, though he keeps his eyes on the ground, not daring to glance at either of us.

"Of course. Whatever you need. I am at your service," he mentions, placing his open palm against his chest in another light bow.

Ze's lips curl up, no doubt satisfied with the deferential display.

"I am looking for a certain damned soul. Mayhap you could help me track him down."

The Custodian nods immediately.

"I am pleased to help you, Commander. Who is it that you are looking for? I shall help you to the best of my ability."

Ze opens his palm to reveal a small, black sphere that travels from his hand to the Custodian.

"*This* damned soul. I would also require a vial of Jì."

The Custodian falters for a moment.

"Commander..." he trails off in a tremulous voice. "You must be aware only the deities of the House of Psyche may use Jì."

Ze's expression tightens.

"I will not breathe a word of it if you do not," he mentions as he manifests a pouch in his hand. Metal rattles inside and I get a vague idea of what he might be offering the Custodian.

The man raises his gaze just enough to see the pouch, and indecision battles over his features. He swallows hard, and after a moment of deliberation, he extends his hands to receive the pouch.

"If you will follow me," he adds in a subdued voice. He swivels, leading us deeper into the hellish dimension that is Katras.

"Did you just bribe him?" I ask Ze in a whisper.

He keeps his features blank as he gives me a barely perceptible nod.

My eyes widen.

"Aren't you supposed to enforce the law, not break it?"

He purses his lips.

"It was necessary."

"Wow, the great Commander Azerius just did something illegal," I add in an amused tone.

He doesn't seem to appreciate the joke, however.

"It was the only way. I did not *break* the law. I merely circumvented it," he says, proudly pushing his chin up.

"Sure, sure. Whatever makes you feel better." I giggle.

He gives me a severe look.

"I have done it for you, human. You are welcome," he huffs.

"I don't remember asking. I don't even know why we're here, Ze."

"You shall see. It is a surprise."

"Right. I can see that. Not everyone gets a first date in *hell*. I should consider myself lucky," I add ironically—not that Ze can tell.

"Precisely." He nods thoughtfully. "Not only are you the first female I am taking on a *date*, but you are also getting an exclusive tour of hell. No one but me would have been able to arrange something like this," he says as he throws his arm over my shoulder, pulling me to his side. "I paid the Custodian a small fortune for this favor. Very few can afford that," he tells me in a *very* serious tone.

"Yep, got it, Ze. You're rich." I chuckle.

"*Very* rich," he corrects. "So you see, this is an exclusive experience only *I* could give you," he makes sure to let me know.

I nod along, amused.

He, on the other hand, is very pleased with himself, his lips curled up in a smile.

We walk behind the Custodian. Curiosity brims inside of me the more glimpses I get of this *hell*. Who exactly are we here to see? What damned soul? I would inquire more of Ze, but it doesn't seem he's very inclined to tell me.

The different galleries where souls are laboring while being lashed and caned by the Custodians are not unlike the dark tunnels I toiled in while I was at the hacienda. Except for this unbearable atmosphere, there aren't too many differences. Who said there isn't a hell on earth, too? If one took away the supernatural element, the conditions are the same.

I quietly take in the slowly shifting environment. Every quarry is worse than the other, the atmosphere seemingly even more inhospitable, which makes it harder for the souls to work, and in turn, makes the Custodians more likely to hurt them. The punishments increase, both in frequency and gruesomeness.

As we get deeper into this hellish dimension, we leave the barren land behind as we come across the entrance to a subterranean mountain.

"What's this?" I whisper as we go inside. The air becomes heavier and warmer, affecting my body and my mind. Colors mix together, my sight becoming confused the more we descend. "It's so hot," I grumble, attempting to air myself with my hand. Sweat pebbles on my forehead, dripping down my face and neck. My clothes are already damp from perspiration. The air I breathe is hot too, and I struggle to fill my lungs with it.

Damn it. I squeeze my eyes shut as I shake my head in an attempt to chase the fog away.

I hate heat. I hate anything too hot and sweaty. I especially hate hot air.

Of course Ze would bring me somewhere that has all three. And this was supposed to be a *fun* getaway.

One thing's for sure. Ze has no concept of the word fun—not that I didn't know before, but this just solidifies it.

"Easy," Ze murmurs as I sway on my feet. His arm falls to the small of my back as he keeps me upright. "Open your mouth," he says, grabbing my face with two fingers and prying my mouth open.

I'm so out of breath at this point that I don't even protest, my lips parting to allow for his cool breath to give me life. I suck in a deep breath. Then another. Soon, my body begins to regulate its temperature better and I'm no longer dying of heat. The air quality changes, too, and I'm able to breathe normally.

"Good?" he inquires.

I nod, bringing the back of my hand to wipe the sweat clinging to my skin.

"We are heading to the worst part of Katras. Very few beings can withstand this type of atmosphere," he explains. "Let me know when you start feeling hot again and I will lend you my breath."

"Now I see why people always associate hell with heat. It's *awful*." I make a disgusted face.

"Technically, it is not an association," Ze starts, putting a finger up. Here it comes—another lesson. "It sometimes happens that a soul retains fragmentary memories of the afterlife. It is rare, and those memories are never something cohesive. Feelings, impressions, that type of thing. Heat is one of them. Mortals across all realms have the same basic idea of the afterlife because of those impressions."

"Oh." I blink. "Okay. That's interesting." I nod. "I've never given much thought to my past lives. I wonder what I was." I smile at the thought. "Is there a way to remember?"

He nods.

"Jì. It is a potion that is the opposite of Letharion. But living beings cannot consume it or they will suffer great consequences. It is why it is so strictly regulated by the House of Psyche. Only authorized beings are allowed to handle it."

"What consequences?" I quip, curious.

"Do not concern yourself with that, human. You will not touch Jì."

"Not even if I'm very, very curious?" I bat my lashes at him playfully.

"No," he states unequivocally. "It will harm you, and I will not let *anything* harm you. Understood?" He takes a moment to stare me down, his intense gaze conveying his disapproval.

"Fine, fine," I mutter, rolling my eyes.

He grunts, though he watches me carefully from the corner of his eyes.

We descend lower into the ground. We stick to a narrow path, and on every side, there are galleries inside the rock that are brimming with souls that are being punished.

Their forms are humanoid, but only enough so pain can be inflicted upon them. Flesh is being cut, time and time again as it slowly mends. Organs are removed and stomped on. One individual is cut in half, its intestines pooling on the floor.

"You should look away if this messes with your human sensibilities," Ze mentions.

"I'm fine." I shake my head. And just as I'm about to ask him how much longer we have to walk, the Custodian stops in front of a gallery, the energy ball in his hand emitting a low light.

"We have arrived, Commander." He inclines his head. "Here is your vial of Jì." He hands Ze a small vial, after which he adds, "I shall give you some privacy, but please do not take too long. It will not be good for either of us if word spreads someone was allowed into the depths of Katras."

"I shall call on you when we are done." Ze nods.

The Custodian vanishes, and Ze takes my hand, leading me off the path and into the small gallery carved in rock on the right side.

The light is dim, but it's enough to make out the dark figure of a soul chained to the wall and writhing in agony.

"Is this one of your enemies?" I wager a guess as we walk closer to the wall.

"You could say so," he answers, his voice laced with anger. He takes a step forward, pouring the vial of Jì over the soul before discarding it to the ground.

Shimmery particles dissipate all around the soul, color slowly suffusing the surface of its body. And with color comes form, its features regaining their previous contour. Seconds trickle by as his past life identity is revealed. And with it comes a gasp of recognition.

"What..." I whisper, awestruck.

I cannot move. I'm suddenly thrust back into the past. My thirteen-year-old self stares at the face of her tormentor, the fear as alive now as it had been then.

"Breathe, Luce," Ze whispers from behind. "He cannot hurt you now."

"What is the meaning of this, Ze? Why..." I gulp. "Why are we here?" My eyes are wide with horror as I continue to watch Sergio's flesh meld together until he once more resembles my biggest nightmare.

Ze creeps from behind, placing himself in front of me and blocking my view of Sergio.

"We do not have to continue if you do not want. But I would like you to have a chance to exact revenge on this man."

"I don't understand..." I whisper.

"He hurt you. He enslaved you. He..." He closes his eyes as he takes a deep breath. "He died before he could suffer—truly suffer. And I aim to remedy that. If you are amenable."

"You did this for me?" I blink back tears as I stare at him, my heart beating wildly in my chest. The adrenaline is in high gear, but the fear is slowly converting into something else. Something equally terrifying and out of control, but something that feels *right*.

"Since you have told me that your tormentor perished, I

vowed I would find a way to avenge you either way. Please accept my gift," he murmurs softly, his big palm coming to rest against my cheek. His thumb brushes against my skin, and a shiver goes down my back. My eyes are attuned to his. The beat of my heart is doing a tandem march with the beat of *his* heart.

"This is..." I can barely form the words. My feelings are too wild. Too out of control. Too...ineffable. "This is the kindest thing anyone's ever done for me."

His lashes flutter, a satisfied smile slowly spreading across his face.

"I will be with you at every step. Remember. He cannot hurt you. But *I* can hurt him."

I slowly nod.

"Can I hurt him, too?"

"Do you want to?" He tilts his head to the side, an odd look descending on his face.

I lick my lips as I deliberate. My gaze flies to the wall. There's some movement and I hear the loud rattle of chains. I cannot see him, but I can feel his presence. And that is enough to make the decision for me.

How many times have I wished for a chance like this? For an opportunity to take back control?

I may have escaped the hacienda, but I've never been truly free, have I? His ghost has been hanging over my shoulders this entire time, poisoning my mind and polluting every moment of happiness. I may have survived those horrors, I may have moved on, but deep down in my subconscious, I know I remained the same scared little girl, abandoned by the only family she'd ever known and given to a sadistic monster to torture. Even while I enjoyed freedoms like never before, my mind was still trapped in that small, dark tunnel, with my fingers bleeding to the bone as I toiled as no child should toil.

In the end, no matter how much I'd like to pretend, I never *really* moved on. And it was all because in that last hour, this monster dared to die before I could look him in the face one last time and tell him that he doesn't own me—that he never did. He may have broken my body, but he never broke my spirit.

"Yes. I do," I eventually say.

Ze's lips pull up in a lopsided smile. He grabs my hand, turns it palm up, and deposits an object in it. The cold of a metal against my skin hints at his gift. My eyes move lower, perusing the small dagger. An intricate purple handle accompanied by an equally purple blade. His energy is all over it, in every atom and every pore. It curls around my hand in a tight embrace, giving me strength where before I had none.

"You made this, didn't you?" I inquire even while knowing the truth.

He nods.

My lips tremble as I dare meet his gaze.

Ze. Socially inept, endearingly arrogant Ze. And yet, with all his shortcomings, with all his inexperience with emotions and social cues, he managed to give me the most wonderful gift I have ever received.

Myself.

He gave me back myself and the opportunity to claim my past.

"Thank you," I murmur, vowing to find a way to return the favor at a later time. Regardless of the fact that he is a god—a very rich god—who cannot possibly want for anything, I will repay him.

Ze watches me for a few more moments to ensure I'm all right before he moves to the side, allowing me a full view of Sergio.

He's dressed in dirty rags that cling to his skin, stained by blood and other bodily fluids. The Jì didn't just restore his past appearance, but it also converted all the spiritual suffering into bodily suffering. His hair is the same gray-white shade I last saw it, his face wrinkled and showing the signs of his age.

Even in his sixties, he'd still gotten off on tormenting people. But there's no age cutoff for evil, is there? The desire to harm and cause pain is a ubiquitous one that withstands the test of time even when the means by which one is able to inflict it are not.

He looks pitiful. Yet I've suffered too much at his hands to have even one ounce of pity for him. All I feel is revulsion. A hate so deep, it's seeped into my bones, never letting me truly be.

But no more.

This is the last time I'll allow him to influence me, just as this is the last time I'll allow myself to think of him. It's a promise I make to myself. I've been a prisoner to this grudge for far too long.

For this moment, I'll let go. But after I'm out of here, I'll never once think of him again.

Sergio blinks as he accommodates to the light, but it's not a few seconds later that his eyes widen in realization. He recognizes me.

"*Tu...*" he grits out. "*Maldita perra,*" he spits at me, his words slurred.

"*Ya no me puedes lastimar, Señor.*"

He scrunches his nose.

"*¿Sabes donde estás?*" I ask him, deliberately addressing him informally. In the past, I would have been flogged for merely daring to meet his gaze, let alone address him with *tu.*

He looks around, his glazed eyes filled with confusion.

"*En el infierno,*" I tell him, the words filling me with great pleasure. "*Aquí no eres ningún dios. Solo un maldito pecador que va a sufrir por la eternidad.*"

He flinches, pulling back and trying to escape his chains. He lets out a pitiful cry of pain as the chains dig into his flesh. But he doesn't stop. He does everything in his power to look for an escape.

"Tsk, tsk," Ze mentions from behind. "There is no escaping. You are, indeed, trapped here for an eternity. Of course, technically you can pay for your sins with your suffering and reincarnate at some point. But I will make sure that is not the case."

"*¿Qué está pasando? ¿Quién es ese hombre? ¿Dónde estoy?*

¿Qué me han hecho?" he yells, true fear finally entering his eyes as well as the realization that he will not be able to escape.

"Why don't you tell him who you are, Ze? It might help him realize the truth of his situation." I glance at Ze.

All his life, Sergio had pretended to be a god. But how will he feel now when he finally comes face to face with one?

"My pleasure." Ze nods. Stepping forward, he wraps his hand around Sergio's neck, forcing him to look into his eyes. Trembling, Sergio can only obey. And whatever he sees there makes him so utterly terrified, he soils himself.

I wrinkle my nose in disgust.

But Ze is not done. Leaning further in, he whispers something inaudible in his ear, smiling at Sergio's blanched expression as he pulls back.

I take a step forward, curious about what Ze has to say, but a clinking sound distracts my attention. My foot must have caught on something. Glancing down, I note the empty vial of Jì Ze had disposed of. I blink slowly. I don't know what comes over me as I pick it up. I'm even more confused by my reaction to it as I stare at the translucent glass, noting a remaining drop of liquid on the rim of the vial.

Remember.

The same voice I heard before infiltrates my subconsciousness until I have no will of my own, only a sinister compulsion that echoes in my mind.

Remember.

What? What do I need to remember?

All sense flies from me as my eyes are affixed to the vial. My finger traces the rim and swipes the last drop of moisture from the glass.

Remember.

Slowly, I bring my finger to my lips, my tongue peeking out to taste the odd liquid.

Remember!

The echo becomes stronger, so strong I can barely keep my balance as I bring my hands to my temples. The sound rips through me, a whirlpool of confusion bathing me from head to toe, staining me with the knowledge of *something*. A certain remembrance I cannot name.

But just as that wave of confusion suffuses me from head to toe, in the next second, it's gone.

"He is all yours, Luce. Make me proud." Ze's voice brings me back to the present. I raise my eyes to meet his, quickly hiding the vial behind my back and letting it fall to the ground.

Ze's eyes narrow at me, scanning the surroundings as if even that small noise could not go undetected by him.

I wet my lips as I prepare a reply.

"I will." I nod, plastering a smile on my face.

Ze steps back, leaving Sergio to me.

Closing my eyes, I take a deep breath to calm myself. I palm the dagger he gifted me, feeling the coldness of the steel against my flesh.

This is it. My chance to get my precious revenge.

"You destroyed me. But not anymore. I'm putting myself back together," I declare before I throw myself forward, pushing the knife into his chest.

The advantage of already being dead is that he will not die again, but he'll feel pain. Every. Single. Time.

I remove my knife, only to bring it back against his flesh, stabbing repeatedly and closing my eyes as I listen to the music that is his cries of pain. He groans and moans, crying out and begging me to stop. But I don't. He hadn't stopped when I begged him either. I keep stabbing him until his body looks like a torn canvas, ripped to shreds, with frayed edges and bits of pieces strewn onto the ground.

My breathing becomes labored, my own body aching from the effort of my blows. I hit and hit until his throat is too raw to scream, his pain too profound to be uttered aloud.

Leaning back, I admire my handiwork. A boost of confidence surges through my veins as I see our roles reversed. No longer am I the victim. No longer am I the one in pain.

All those years of dreaming of what I would do to him have finally materialized.

But as the adrenaline wears off, I slowly realize that I'm not any more fulfilled than I was before. Sure, I got to confront my biggest enemy. But seeing him like this—knowing that this is what awaits him for the rest of time—my hate for him dims a little. Not because I feel vindicated, but because I finally see him for what he really is.

A man.

Just a man, and not the god he'd claimed to be.

A pitiful man.

He is dead, in hell.

I am alive and well.

I have won by default.

"I think I'm done," I say as I look back at Ze. He's leaning against the entrance to the gallery, one leg propped against the wall. His arms are crossed over his chest, his attention riveted on me.

"May I have my turn now?" he asks, slowly coming closer.

"Your turn?" I blink in surprise.

"You have had your revenge. Now it is my turn."

I don't get to answer as he withdraws his sword, placing his thumb at the tip and allowing the blade to nick his finger. Blood flows down onto the ridges of the blade, and with one smooth strike, he cuts Sergio in two—vertically.

I gawk in disbelief. It's the most unsettling sight I've ever seen. He can still blink and move, even cut in two. Not one second later, though, and a curdling scream erupts from both of his half mouths as he yells in pure agony.

"What did you do?"

"My blood is poisonous for most beings," Ze comments. "The Custodian will once more administer him the Letharion and he will forget this exchange. But he will never forget this pain. The torture he experienced before will not compare to the agony he will feel from now on," he explains, satisfied.

"I think that's the perfect punishment for him." I nod. "Let's get out of here now. I've had enough of him."

"Are you certain? I can think of a few more ways to make him suffer. You just say the word. I can even obliterate his soul..."

"No." I shake my head. "That would defeat the purpose. He will suffer for eternity. That is enough for me."

He inclines his head.

"I am happy if you are happy."

I raise my gaze to meet his, surprised by his words. A slow smile tips at my lips.

"I think we still have time for some *fun*," I say. "We need to celebrate after all. Do you have a pub or somewhere to grab a drink in Aperion?"

"A pub?" he repeats, confused.

"You know, an establishment that sells alcohol."

He thinks on it for a moment.

"I believe I know somewhere," he mentions. "Though I have never been myself..."

"Let's do it! I finally feel free, Ze, and it's all thanks to you. We need to celebrate this occasion."

"We do?" he asks, unsure.

I nod effusively. He gave me this perfect gift. It stands to reason I should return the favor and show him how to have *fun*.

"I have never imbibed alcohol. But I suppose for you I can make an exception..." he muses aloud.

"Yay!" I jump up and down, crashing into him. Maybe this is an odd reaction considering I'm in literal hell. But I don't think I've ever felt as free and unencumbered as I do now. The past... it's just the past. It made me into who I am today. Only the future matters now. And I aim to grasp it tightly with both hands and not let go.

Ze smiles indulgently at me.

"Yes. For you, I shall make an exception." He nods to himself as he wraps his arms around me and flashes us out of Katras.

FIFTY-NINE

R aucous noise fills my ears. I open my eyes and step away from Ze, my eyes widening as I take in the busy locale. In the middle, people are dancing to the sound of music as a live band demonstrates its prowess with instruments that look uncannily like human ones. To the back, I spot various tables already filled with people, eating and drinking their fill. I can't make out too much, but I think I recognize pies, steamed buns, and potatoes.

To the side, the most popular area of the locale is—the bar. People crowd and elbow each other to get ahead and order faster to get their drinks. There are bottles with all sorts of labels, all foreign to me.

"What's that?" I ask Ze, pointing to the huge barrel hanging from the ceiling and from which the barman pours a drink into a pint mug.

"That is Sizà mead. It is the cheapest and most common type of beverage in Aperion."

"Should I try that then?" I muse pensively.

I turn to him, my eyes widening in shock.

"What happened to you?" I point to his changed appearance.

He runs a hand over his face, threading his fingers through his hair to arrange it.

"I think you have seen what happens when I go out as Commander Azerius. My tattoos are far too recognizable, and since there is not one person in Aperion who does not bear me a grudge, it is safer if I go around as Ze."

"I see. I suppose you are right," I nod.

"Come," he says, leading me by the hand to the bar. Despite his changed look, his appearance is ever as imposing, and as his eyes narrow at the men at the bar, they immediately make space for us. Ze offers me a chair, pulling me close to the bar as he positions himself right by my side, his hand on my back. Withdrawing another pouch from his pocket, he places it on the bar table with a thud, the coins inside clinking loudly and announcing to everyone the contents inside.

The barman takes a look at the pouch, and a wide smile appears on his face.

"What can I bring you, fellas?"

Ze gives him a stare down.

"What is your most expensive drink?" he asks in a condescending tone. He might change his appearance, but he cannot change the inside. I shake my head, amused, as the barman's expression changes at Ze's supercilious countenance.

"We have a wide variety of Aperite ales and liquors as well as otherworldly drinks. The latter are the most expensive, since they are rare," the barman explains.

Ze nods thoughtfully.

"I want to try the Aperite ones," I murmur in his ear.

"Two of the most expensive Aperite ales then," he commands, handing the barman the money. He counts it, nodding at us before going to prepare the drinks.

"You know, expensive isn't always better. We could have gotten the Sizà mead," I tell him.

"Nonsense," he huffs. "I will not buy you a *cheap* drink. Who do you think I am, human?"

"Hm, the big, bad, and dangerous Commander Azerius, the God Killer whom everyone fears?" I lean in to whisper jokingly.

He nods, pleased.

"You forgot one thing," he interjects. "I am also one of the wealthiest males in the universe. I will *not* be cheap with you."

"Right, how could I have forgotten that?" I laugh.

He has an obsession with being rich, doesn't he? I wonder if he grew up without money and that's why he puts so much emphasis on it now.

"You should not. There is nothing you may want that I could not buy for you. You need only say so."

"Why, thank you, Ze. That's very nice of you."

His eyes positively sparkle at hearing the word nice, his lips curling up in a smile.

The barman slides the drinks in front of us. Ze grabs them, nodding for me to go to one of the tables in the back.

"But I like it here," I blink innocently.

His features tighten.

"I do *not*. There are too many people brushing against you," he says as his arm shoots out to block a drunken man from stumbling into me. "Too many *males*."

"But—"

"Come," he declares, somehow holding on to both glasses with one hand while dragging me away with the other. I release a small sigh as I follow him to the back where there are no empty tables—momentarily. Somehow, when people see him, they jump out of their seats and offer their table to us, an obsequious expression on their faces as they barely dare to meet his gaze.

Ze grunts. He slaps the glasses on the table before he pulls a chair for me and not so gently raises me in the air and places me on the seat.

"Now, this is good," he hums to himself.

People stare at us. Regardless of whether he has longer hair and tattoos, Ze's presence creates the same type of awe and fear in people. Their whispers are drowned by the live band, but their scathing gazes don't escape me.

"I'm very curious how this compares to Earth drinks," I mention with a smile as I pull my glass toward me. The liquid is a light amber color, similar to unfiltered ale. Before I can taste it, though, Ze gives me a warning glance as he snatches the glass from my side, taking a big gulp.

"Not poisoned," he declares.

I smile indulgently at his thoughtfulness and bring the glass to my lips, taking the first sip.

"Oh, but this is quite sweet," I exclaim in surprise. A small sip turns into a bigger one. Well, this is a type of alcohol I wouldn't mind having every once in a while.

"It is, indeed, not bad," he murmurs his appreciation, already downing half his glass.

"Thank you again for today, Ze. You have no idea how much that meant to me." I feel compelled to let him know again just how much his gift impressed me. From that first stab of a knife, a sense of freedom unlike any other had enveloped me, making me feel light and carefree for the first time...ever?

He smiles into his glass as he takes another sip.

"You are very welcome. I assume this gives me bonus points?" He raises a brow.

I roll my eyes at him. Of course he would bring that up. But not even his outrageous demands can ruin the marvelous mood I have right now.

Taking another sip of my ale, I nod.

"Yes, you can have a thousand points." I giggle. "You deserve them."

His eyes momentarily widen in disbelief before he empties his drink, slamming it on the table. Determination shines in his features as he gazes at me.

"You cannot take it back. I am in possession of a thousand points now and they are mine to use as I see fit," he declares. "One hundred are going toward my debt, which means I now have nine hundred left, which amounts to nine boons. And I will have my boons, human," he warns.

"Of course." I smile lazily. "What do you want?"

He bites his lip as he considers my question.

"I will think about it."

I nod, the same languid smile perpetually on my face now. Maybe I shouldn't have drunk the alcohol so fast and on an empty stomach. My limbs feel like jelly.

Somehow, time passes without me realizing it, and the drinks flow just as easily.

Ze grabs us second rounds, then a third and fourth.

At the fifth round, I'm close to sleeping on the table but still a happy idiot.

My arms are cushioning my head as I rest my entire upper body weight on the table, my eyes fluttering closed before I open them and remember I'm not in my bed and thus not allowed to fall asleep.

"Say, Ze," I slur my words. "Do you know what A.S.L. stands for?"

He frowns.

Placing his arms on the table, he props his head on his hands, suddenly at my eye level. The distance between us has suddenly shrunk to the point that my nose almost touches his.

Heat climbs my cheeks.

He appears unbothered by the proximity as he stares at me.

"Where have you seen that?"

"Some document in the library," I mumble a small lie.

He nods pensively.

"I do not know exactly what it stands for, but it is how Supremes sign themselves in official documents. The first letter is the House, the second letter stands for Supreme, and the third letter for their given name. But there are three Houses that start with the letter A, including Arche. As for the last letter, I could not say unless I had the document in front of me to peruse."

Damn, how is the man still so eloquent after so many drinks?

I squint to make out his features. But is it any wonder that he's immune to alcohol, too? After all, he's immune to poisons and his own blood is a poison. There's probably nothing that can hurt him.

"I see."

At least it's something. Why would a Supreme send me a letter hundreds of years ago? Maybe they could see into the future?

Before I can blink, Ze slides yet another round in front of me. My nose scrunches in disgust as I eye the foul concoction. Sloppily, I shake my head at him.

"No more."

He shrugs, downing his drink with ease.

A few noises erupt in the background, barely penetrating my close to nonexistent focus. Glancing up, I blink a couple of times as I take in Ze's appearance, convinced I'm too drunk for this.

His tattoos flicker in and out of sight, his hair growing and receding in the blink of an eye as well.

"Ze..." I murmur.

He's still drinking the ale.

"This is, indeed, a very good drink," he mentions as he sips.

I spare a glance to my right, rubbing my eyes for more clarity. Sure enough, people are staring at him, ready for attack. Another glance to my left and the same thing happens.

I gulp. Hard.

"Ze," I repeat, reaching forward and snatching the glass out of his hand. And with my lack of coordination, I end up slapping it across the floor, attracting even more attention to ourselves.

He suddenly snaps his gaze to mine, concern flickering in his eyes.

"We need to go. Dangerrrr," I mumble, waving around the room like a crazy person. I know the words to elaborate, yet somehow my mouth does not want to cooperate with me.

My words sink in and he jumps out of his seat, sending the

chair flying in the back. Purple mist dances chaotically around him. Tendrils of pure energy reach forward and strike at anyone attempting to come toward us.

"Dangerrrr," I yell, pointing behind him as someone throws a knife.

A dark tendril leaps in the air, catching the knife before sending it flying back to the person who threw it.

Ze's arm shoots out as he pulls me into his arms, his purple energy simmering around us. It engulfs me in a claiming, protective embrace as I nestle against his chest.

Turns out it's not just s'Aperiotes who frequent this establishment but also gods. Ze masterfully evades all the energy blasts before he whispers to me to hold on as he flashes us out of there.

We appear in my room, both stumbling, me because I can't stand straight and him...well, turns out he can't stand straight either. We tumble to the bed, both breathing hard. As we turn to look at one another, we burst out into laughter.

"That was..."

"I suppose I may have had one too many glasses," Ze proclaims, his words slightly slurred.

"So you can get drunk." I laugh.

"I suppose so." He sighs deeply, for the first time faced with his own shortcomings.

His appearance flashes between Ze and Azerius a few more times before he's back to normal, his tattoos marring one side of his face.

I stretch my stiff body as I pull myself higher on the bed so my head rests on the pillow. Ze follows my lead and we both make ourselves more comfortable on the bed as we try to overcome the dire effects of alcohol intoxication.

"If it makes you feel better, this is my first time getting drunk too," I tell him.

His brows shoot up in surprise.

"Your first, my first," he mumbles to himself, his cheeks reddening—though I think it's mostly due to the alcohol. Who would have thought those expensive drinks would be so potent? Certainly going by the taste, they were more like cocktails than hard liquor. I have, at times, drunk hard liquor, but I wouldn't say it's my drink of choice—certainly I've never had more than a few sips here and there. I prefer wine and cider, something I can enjoy without getting intoxicated.

That fancy ale? That's some strong stuff.

As I wiggle around, I find myself constricted by the fabric of my dress. The bodice has a corset built in that's restricting my breathing. The air is too hot, too, a flush enveloping my body. I turn from side to side as I unfasten the buttons on the back of my dress, pulling it down my body and throwing it to the floor with my feet. Since I'm wearing a shift underneath, I don't think this is too inappropriate. I'm still completely covered.

Ze glances at me in surprise.

"It's hot," I complain with a pout. "You can take your shirt off too," I add as I note the sheen of perspiration on his forehead.

He stares at me for a moment before he quickly divests himself of his shirt, throwing it to the floor next to my dress. He's now shirtless, and his half-tattooed torso is equally covered in sweat. And to my chagrin, that only serves to emphasize his muscles more as drops of sweat travel down the pebbled surface of his abdomen.

"It is hot," he agrees, his gaze on me. "*Too* hot."

I swallow.

Suddenly, it's scorching in here. I fan myself with my hand, pretending to be unbothered while staring at him from the corner of my eye. Somehow, I find it hard to reconcile the Ze I know with the one in front of me—relaxed and laid back like this. He's quite a handsome man, isn't he? He has a boyish smile on his face as he threads his hand through his hair, stray strands landing on his forehead. He inhales and exhales, his chest rising and falling with each breath. His tongue sneaks out to catch an errant drop of sweat. The room just got a hundred degrees hotter.

Goddamn. People should ask the man to model in magazines not kill gods. I'm sure he'd do just as fine in that job—at least he wouldn't be as hated. On the contrary, he'd probably have thousands of fangirls lusting after him...

I frown.

A prick of annoyance spears through me at the thought.

Maybe he's fine as he is. He doesn't need to be in any magazine.

I nod to myself. Yes. He's a good God Killer. He should do what he's best at.

We stay in silence for moments on end, our bodies near but far. Our breaths are the only echo in the room, but they're strangely in unison—not two, but one.

I turn to him, allowing myself to study him in the open. Maybe it's the alcohol that's making me more daring than before, more...comfortable.

"You should smile more often," I find myself saying, stifling a yawn.

"I should?" His long lashes flutter at me.

I nod, dragging myself next to him. Using my finger, I pull on the corner of his lips.

"There. That's better."

He catches my finger, pulling me closer until my chest meets his. His gaze lands on mine, his hot breath brushing against my lips.

I draw in a sharp breath, my heart beating wildly in my chest.

He closes his eyes, leaning forward to breathe me in.

"You infuriate me to no end," he rasps.

"W-what?"

"Why do you have to be so damn beautiful?" he asks on a ragged breath.

His eyes snap open, the purple of his irises becoming a deeper shade that threatens to engulf me whole.

"I... Ze..." I trail off, at a loss for words. "Thank you?" I force a smile, doubt churning in my gut. This is going in the wrong direction, isn't it? We're too close, too... The look in his eyes is not a normal one that a friend has for a *friend*, is it?

His hands cup my cheeks, holding me in place. Brushing his nose against my own, he grinds his teeth, as if physically in pain.

"I have never known want before. I have never *wanted* to know it. But you make me want, Luce. You make me want far too much," he whispers, his tone anguished. "Why do you have to be so tempting?"

I open my mouth to speak, but no word comes out. The beat of my heart echoes in my ears, the sound almost deafening. I stare into his eyes, willing myself to reply—tell him this isn't what I meant. That we're friends and we cannot be more— we can *never* be more. The words that would have come so easily before are now lodged in my throat, including the most important one. I'm married. I may be a widow, but I'm still married.

Tears stab at my eyes as panic overtakes me. Not at his actions, or the position we find ourselves in, but at *my* reaction. I should not be reacting at all. I should look at him and not *see* him. Yet the more I stare into those purple eyes that have come to mean so much to me, I find myself utterly speechless.

"I might be immune to all poisons in the universe. But it appears there is one thing I am not immune to," he murmurs softly. "You."

"Are you calling me a poison?" I clear my throat as I attempt a joke, yet my question comes out throaty, inviting...

"Oh, you are the most potent poison of all. And I have yet to taste you." He leans forward, his lips a razor's edge away from mine.

I blink rapidly, the moment stretching across an infinity as my being splits into two—the one before him, and the one after. Indecision cuts at me.

His breath is intoxicating, more so than any alcohol. It washes over me, imbuing me with an exhilarating but ineffable emotion. I lick my lips, still undecided about the course of my actions, for I know that if I take this step, nothing will ever be

the same. I will damn myself in a way I would have never fath-
omed. And yet, I'm tempted.

God forgive me, but I'm tempted.

Even as my husband's visage flashes before my eyes, I waver.

His lips continue their descent toward me, and at the last
moment, I half turn. His lips skim the corner of my mouth,
brushing against my cheek. The breath leaves my lungs. My
hands grip his arms, my nails digging into his flesh. A small
whimper escapes me, of rebuttal or encouragement, I don't
know.

He takes no notice of the turmoil inside of me. His lips trace
a soft line down my neck.

A shiver goes down my back.

I should pull back. Stop this madness.

But I don't. Even as the rip of material reverberates in the
room, and even as I feel him kiss his way down my chest. I just
hold on to him, drawing blood with my nails from the tension
that builds deep inside of me.

Wrapped in his embrace and with his warm lips on my skin,
there's an odd sense of peace that washes over me. One that lulls
me into comfort and safety. And as I close my eyes, letting
myself be pulled into this whirlpool of madness, I find myself
lost to a different world.

---

*The chirp of birds echoes in the stillness of the valley. Cool
drops from the waterfall splash onto the grassy banks,
hitting my skin and offering a modicum of refreshment—a break
from the scorching heat of the two suns.*

*I lie back on my elbows, tipping my chin up to bask in the
sunlight. It's a rare moment when I get some time to myself—
some freedom outside of duty.*

"Don't move. Stay like that," a raspy voice calls from behind.

*I freeze, my senses suddenly on alert just as a feeling of
unease goes down my back. He snuck up on me—again. He is the*

only being in the entire universe that I am never able to detect in advance.

Now that he's allowed me to sense him, he comes around and lies down on the ground next to me. The grass rustles against his weight and he places his head in my lap, his long black hair draping over the purple of my dress. Instinctively, I thread my fingers through his locks, enjoying the silken feel of them against my skin.

He releases a deep sigh—something akin to a purr as his chest rumbles with pleasure.

"I missed you," he says, capturing my hand and bringing it to his mouth for a kiss.

"I could not get away sooner. I'm sorry," I murmur.

He closes his eyes.

"I'm tired of hiding." He sighs wearily. "I'm tired of not being good enough for you."

"I promised you I'd find a way to break off the engagement, and I will." I purse my lips. "It's just a delicate period and..."

"When is it not a delicate period?" he demands. "Just hearing your name in conjunction with his drives me insane. The wedding of the millennium, they call it." He gives a bitter laugh.

"I cannot simply forsake my duty," I whisper.

"But you can forsake me?" He leans back, giving me a glimpse of those anguish-stricken features.

"I did not come here to fight," I say in a soft voice. "Can we not talk about this now? We have so little time as it is..."

"Why is that? Because I'm your dirty little secret. Because I'm a lowborn bastard, an abomination in the eyes of the Aperite Supremes. Because—"

"Don't," I whisper.

"You're ashamed of me," he continues.

I shake my head vehemently.

"I could never be ashamed of you. But there is my position to consider and all those souls that rely on me." I take a deep breath. "You know how I feel about you—only you. I've given you parts of

myself I've never given to anyone. I've let you see parts of me not even I knew existed..."

"That's just the thing, Azeya moyou. You belong to me, not him." He grits his teeth. "I've been patiently waiting for you, vowing I wouldn't hurt anyone in your life because you asked me to. But I am slowly dying inside. I cannot stand by and do nothing anymore—not when the urge to end him is all-consuming. Please release me from my vow so I can obliterate his soul."

"I will break the engagement off. I promised you I would. I just need to find the right time when the realm isn't in such turmoil..." My words are cut off as he grabs me by the nape, pulling me toward him until our lips are almost touching.

"If you do not release me from my vow, I shall have to break it," he whispers against my lips.

"You can't... You will get hurt if you do that and..."

"Do you care, Azeya moyou? Do you care if I get hurt?"

"How can you even ask that? Your hurt is my hurt. Always and forever," I say as I cup his cheek.

SIXTY

I wake up with a start, drenched in sweat. Glancing down at myself, I note I'm still in my shift, the material almost sheer from perspiration. As I swing my legs over the bed to head to the bathroom, a pounding headache assails me—one that nearly brings me to my knees.

Oh, damn it!

Memories of last night start flooding my mind, as well as fragments of that odd dream.

God, I drank far too much, didn't I? So much so that I... My eyes widen in disbelief as I recall being in bed with Ze and... I pat myself down. My shift is intact. I'm not naked. Nothing happened, right? I could have sworn he tore the material, but maybe that was also just a dream? Guiltily, I have to admit to myself that maybe I've been spending too much time with him and that has affected my perception of him. I care about him, of course, but our relationship can't be more—it *won't* be more. Perhaps that dream was also a reflection of that—the dilemma of being torn between two men. Being committed to one but also wanting the other...

My eyes widen, my hands gripping the wall for support as I realize I just admitted to myself that I want Ze. That...

No, no. This is impossible. We are friends. *Just* friends.

I'm married!

In the dream, too, I was engaged to someone else while dallying with another man—one that I had strong feelings for as far as I recall. The details may be fuzzy, but the emotion still echoes in my chest.

God, I'm a mess!

I hunch my shoulders in defeat as I enter the bathroom, my first stop being the sink to brush my teeth. The taste of alcohol is still in the back of my throat. In fact, as I sniff myself, I note that I'm also in dire need of a shower. The smell of alcohol is everywhere.

With a weary sigh of a person with one hell of a hangover, I lift my shift over my head and dump it in the dirty clothes basket before heading to the shower.

But as I walk across the bathroom, I catch my reflection in the mirror. I stop in my tracks as my eyes glaze over my body.

What?

I take a step closer to the mirror, tracing the smooth skin on my chest and arms. For the first time in as long as I can remember, there's no mark. Nothing except a small black spot over my right breast. I narrow my eyes at it. It's a star with fourteen sharp edges. In the middle, there's a tiny dot surrounded by one bubble on each side that contains a symbol similar to the ones I previously had on my skin.

Yet aside from that small mark on top of my breast, my skin is unblemished. There's nothing on my belly or on my thighs. Nothing at all.

"What the hell?" I mutter, utterly stupefied.

Those marks have stained my skin for so many years, I cannot even remember what I looked like without them. They were a bad memory as much as they were a core part of my identity. Because you can't have the good without the bad. You can only appreciate the good when you have the bad contrasting it.

Those marks were evidence of my horrendous past, but most of all, they were proof that I survived.

"Could it be..." I murmur to myself as I turn right and left, studying every inch of my skin. "Could it be that they've disappeared because I've finally come to terms with my past? That I've finally left the ghost of Sergio behind?" I muse aloud, my brows bunched together in consternation.

They appeared the night Sergio hurt me. Maybe they disappeared because my inner wounds have finally healed? That seems like a logical explanation.

But there's one more thing.

A.S.L.'s letter.

Dashing back to my room, I remove it from under the mattress where I hid it. My eyes quickly scan the contents again.

> *The writing on your skin—it is a promise. There is nothing evil about it, nor is it something to be afraid of. It is a vow written in blood, and in a matter of days, that vow will be fulfilled. When that happens, the mark of a new beginning will arise.*

What vow? How was it fulfilled?

And the new mark...what new beginning does it signify?

I read and reread the lines until I know them by heart. But still, I'm no closer to figuring out an answer except that whoever A.S.L. was, he or she *knew* about my marks. And against all odds, they predicted the future. But is it any wonder they did? After all, they had left a letter in a secret place hundreds of years ago, knowing it would somehow end up in my hands.

Who are you? And what are you trying to tell me?

The fact that I'm convinced that A.S.L. speaks the truth now is beside the point as I worry about this new mark and its potential meaning.

Panic swells in my breast as I pace around the room with the letter in my hand. Barely conscious of my actions, I say the name of the only person who can help me.

"Ze?" I call out. "Can you please come here? I need you," I

murmur, doing my best not to let myself be overcome by anxiety.

My limbs are weak and wobbly, my brain fogging up as I think of the worst scenarios.

I need him. Ze. I know he'll have answers.

But even as I continue calling him, he's nowhere to be found.

My eyes drop to the letter once more.

You must quit The Wishing Game.

If what A.S.L. has said so far is true, then could this be true as well? Could I be in danger if I continue in the game? Could Nikki be in danger?

I swallow hard. Confusion swirls in my brain, making me dizzy. I've never been more disoriented in my life. How do I know which is the best choice to make? Because if I quit now... I won't be able to participate again and my wish for getting Nikki back will never materialize.

But there's also the reverse. If A.S.L. is right, and so far everything they've said *has* been right, then the only way to get Nikki back is to quit.

My hands tremble as I hold the yellowed piece of paper. I stare and stare at it, truly at a crossroads.

"Where are you, Ze? I need you," I call out again, walking around my room like a zombie.

What should I do? God, what's the best decision in this case?

I inhale and exhale as I attempt to center myself in the present. I can only make a decision with the facts I have, and based on the empirical evidence at hand, there's only one right answer.

Closing my eyes, I take a deep breath.

"I wish to withdraw from The Wishing Game," I speak before I lose the courage.

"Are you sure you wish to give up?" The wraith appears before me, startling me and making me lose my balance.

"Y-yes," I stammer.

"Your decision has been noted. You are officially withdrawn from The Wishing Game. As you were part of a team, the entire team has been disqualified," she tells me in a mechanical voice. "Good day and good luck," she says before she disappears.

Shit! Thea! She wanted this, didn't she?

Damn! Did I just ruin everything for her, too?

Right at that moment, a strong pulsation erupts from the center of the mark, heat surrounding the entire area. I fall to my ass as I moan in distress. I cover the symbol with my hand, rubbing it as my breathing grows labored.

Tears fall down my cheeks as my mind explodes into a thousand little pieces until I can barely make sense of anything—of who I am or what my purpose is.

A screeching sound reverberates in the air. Belatedly, I realize that's me.

I taste the saltiness of my tears as an elusive memory knocks at the door of my subconsciousness. The feeling is there, almost as if I was supposed to know something, but I cannot put it into words.

The door to my room bursts open and Thea barges in, a worried expression on her face.

"Luce, are you all right?" she asks, her eyes widening as she spots me on the floor, naked and tear-streaked.

"I-I don't know," I reply honestly. "I think I fucked up, Thea," I add in a whisper.

"If you mean the Game, don't worry about it. I should have quit before, too." She sighs.

"You...know?"

"The wraith just paid me a visit. But I've been thinking about withdrawing for a while now. If I get caught, things will be much worse."

"You... You're not mad at me?"

She shakes her head, slowly moving toward me. She offers

me her hand and I take it, letting her pull me up. My heart is still beating loudly in my chest, my anxiety a low hum in my ears that becomes more and more distant.

"Is that why you were crying? Oh, Luce. You're too sweet." She smiles as she pats my head. But as her eyes dip lower to my chest, she observes the obvious too. "What..." she mumbles, blinking repeatedly.

"I don't know what happened. Yesterday, the marks were there. Today...it's only this." I point to the star above my breast. "But I'm not sure what it means."

"You need to talk to my mother. She might be able to help you."

My lips tremble as I gaze at her. Ze had said I shouldn't show my marks to anyone who might recognize ancient Tartareian. But what if this *isn't* ancient Tartareian? What if it's something completely different?

"Okay," I nod. "When can I see her?"

"Anytime after the ball. Everyone is busy setting up everything for tonight now."

"'Tonight..." I repeat with a frown. My eyes widen as it dawns on me that today is the day of Wyn's debut. Time passed so quickly and I've been so busy that I'm ashamed to say I... forgot.

"I was on my way to you to help you with your hair and makeup. There are certain expectations for a society ball..." Thea drones on as she explains that unmarried women are expected to dress their hair and do their makeup in a specific fashion. Even as I attempt to protest that I'm married, she shushes me, telling me it doesn't really count since I have no husband.

The statement hurts, but it's true. Nikki has been missing for a while now. But even if he *were* here, would I just go to the ball with a shadow on my arm?

The thought makes me crack a smile.

"Let's do this, then," I tell her.

She winks at me and quickly runs to bring her supplies.

Meanwhile, I shower and place the dress I'd gotten for the ball on the bed, careful not to wrinkle it. It's a beautiful mix of white and pink tulle, all tied together with a wide pink belt at the waist.

When Thea returns, she does my makeup, applying a glow foundation, some blush to my cheeks, and a dash of highlighter on my cheekbones. For my eyes, she goes for a clean and natural look, with a thin black liner, mascara, and a dot of highlighter in my inner corners and in the middle of my lower lid. Next is my hair, and she curls it before adorning it with a myriad of pink bows to match my dress. Apparently, unmarried females must aim to look innocent and young to attract the attention of a potential suitor. I refrain from telling Thea that I'm not looking for any suitor. Since this is the way people dress for such occasions, who am I to say no? When in Rome, you do as the Romans do, no?

She helps me slide into my dress before she circles around me to make sure everything is in order.

"Perfect," she declares with a smile.

"What about you? You've spent so much time on me, when are you going to get ready?" I ask as I look at the clock. It's already afternoon. The ball is supposed to start in a few hours...

She snaps her fingers and her hair is already curly, her red locks complemented by blue bows. Her dress, too, changes. She's now wearing a light blue gown with an empire waist and a light skirt. The detailing on her dress is a dark blue to match her hair accessories.

"I just need to do my makeup. But that's easy," she says, quickly grabbing a mirror and starting on her face. It takes her a few minutes to expertly do a light but beautiful look. She uses a blue liner for her eyes and a peach-red blush to accentuate her cheeks.

"I'm done," she smiles. "Why don't we go check on Wyn and we can all go to the ballroom together at eight?"

I nod, and together, we go to Wyn's room in the other wing

of the house. A cry resounds from inside the room, and we both barge inside.

Wyn is in the middle of the room with two seamstresses next to her, trying to help her put on her gown.

"I don't like it," she cries out, tears falling down her cheeks.

"Wyn?" Thea calls her name as she rushes toward her sister.

"I don't like it, Thea. I want my old dress back."

"Oh, sweetie. You know you couldn't have worn that dress anyway."

"I would have worn it," she declares staunchly between hiccups. "I don't care if everyone hated me for it, but at least *I* would have loved it."

"Wynwyn, we've already talked about this. I thought you agreed to stop pining after Aethon. He's not going to come to your ball. No one even knows where he is!"

"Can't I just do it for myself? *I* felt good in that dress. This..." she murmurs as she points to the off-white delicate gown she's wearing. It's a Regency-style dress with an empire waist and puffy sleeves. It's similar to the one Thea's wearing, but there is not one splash of color on Wyn's.

"Wyn..." Thea purses her lips.

"Is there a rule that she can't have some color on her dress?" I ask, and they both turn to stare at me.

"It is rather unusual, but I suppose it's not against the rules," Thea muses. "Why?"

"I have an idea," I say as I wink at Wyn. I know how special tonight is for her. But more than anything, it's her last time going out in society before she joins the temple. And because of that, I want her to be happy and enjoy her night to the maximum.

Picking up the seamstresses' bag, I ask for permission to go through it. Once granted, I search for an item that would fit and at last, I find a roll of dark blue ribbon. Taking it to Wyn's side, I pin some at the top of her bodice before going around her gown and layering it over the material of her dress. As it slithers around her body, it begins resembling a serpent, or if one gives it a little more thought, a blue dragon.

When I'm done with the body of the *dragon*, I fray some ribbon and add it toward the base of the skirt to simulate scales. And for the head, I use the hair accessories, removing the pins and preserving only the blue bows. Pinning them in place on her bodice, I create the effect of a side profile of a *creature*.

"What do you think?" I ask when I'm done, a little out of breath.

She turns to look at herself in the mirror, her eyes widening.

"I love it," she whispers. "Oh, Luce! I love it so much! Thank you!" She twirls in her dress, a genuine smile appearing on her face.

I give her a smile just as Thea also gives me a hug.

"Thank you," she murmurs in my ear. "You have no idea what it means for me to see Wyn so happy. She deserves the world." Leaning back, Thea watches her sister with an inscrutable expression on her face—one of pure love and so much more.

The seamstresses leave, but we remain behind to help Wyn with her hair. The time of the ball is fast approaching, and the nerves are starting to get to Wyn.

"What if no one comes?" she suddenly asks as she sips on her juice through a straw—very careful not to stain her dress.

"You know that's impossible." Thea chuckles.

"Not if Elora had anything to do with it. She may be a pest, but she has influence. She's part of the Royal Court and if she openly snubs me, others may too."

"The king cares too much about what Father thinks to make such a move. Even if Elora tried her wiles on him, I doubt he would jeopardize his connections with our family for a spoiled little girl."

"But you can't deny it's a possibility. If not the king, she could have easily told other families *not* to come..."

"You're worrying too much, Wyn. She might not even come."

"No." Wyn shakes her head. "If anything, she would come just to ruin my night. I hate her," she huffs aloud. "She's the *worst*. How can she even think Aethon could ever look at her when she's just a bully? My Aethon would never condone her behavior."

"Your Aethon?" Thea raises a brow.

Wyn, not wanting to argue, just shrugs.

"She only wants him because of his status. Why couldn't she go for Commander Azerius? He's even more exalted than Aethon, and as I hear, far richer," Wyn complains with a sigh.

My eyes flash at the mention of Ze, an uncomfortable heat accumulating in my breast.

"Because Commander Azerius is a horrible being whom no one likes," Thea adds drily.

"He's not horrible." I find myself defending him. "I like him."

Thea turns to me, her eyes narrowed.

"That makes you the only one."

"What about all those other deities you said were chasing after him?" I ask, doing my best to keep the bitterness from my voice.

"Those?" Thea laughs. "They only want him for his market value. If he paid attention to them, they would get a social boost and then they'd be able to get better matches. Behind his back, they despise him." She shrugs.

"I think you're being too harsh on him. He has his good points. But if no one gives him a chance, how can he demonstrate them?"

Thea tilts her head as she studies me.

"You've become quite the Ze defender."

My cheeks heat up.

"I just think he deserves a chance. He's really not that bad once you get to know him," I murmur, averting my gaze.

Just in time, someone knocks at the door.

"Enter," Wyn calls out.

The door opens to reveal Cer. He's wearing a fine suit in dark blue, his blazer held together at the waist with a wide black belt that houses his weapons.

"Cer!" Wyn calls out, jumping out of her seat and rushing forward to greet her brother.

Thea doesn't move, though a gentle smile appears on her face as she watches the interaction.

"You look beautiful, Wyn. I can't believe my baby sister is all grown up," he says as he hugs her carefully to not ruin her dress and hair.

"Thank you. I'm so happy you made it. Are you alone?" she asks eagerly, not even masking her interest.

"Unfortunately." He chuckles. "Who would I have with me?"

"I don't know. A date? Your friend?" Wyn bats her lashes at him.

Cer laughs as he wraps an arm around her shoulders and walks alongside her into the room.

"No female would have someone with my schedule," he jokes.

"Then maybe you should retire. You're the oldest. When are you going to give me nieces and nephews?"

"Easy now, sis. I'm not that old."

It's odd to see Cer so carefree—with a *smile* on his face. Until now, I didn't even realize the man could string together more than a couple of *very* short sentences. Yet with Wyn, it's like watching a transformed man. He's genuinely happy to see his sister, his eyes shining with affection.

"Just a bit. But it's okay. I don't hold it against you. In fact," she says in a chirpy voice, "older people are wiser, no? They are more weathered by experience," she mentions, her eyes meeting Thea's.

Thea sighs and rolls her eyes, knowing where Wyn is going with this. Only Cer is still unaware of the *true* topic at hand.

"What about your friend? I remember you saying he'd come with you," Wyn continues, blatantly fishing for information.

"You mean Aethon?" Cer blinks.

Wyn nods enthusiastically, hope blooming in her features.

"He's... He's still missing." He purses his lips. "Which is why I'll be leaving as soon as your ball is over. I'm sorry, sweetie."

"It's okay. You should help your friend." Wyn forces a smile. "But do you think..." She takes a deep breath. "Do you think he's dead?"

"All signs point to him still being alive."

A visible shudder goes through Wyn before a tremulous smile tips at her lips.

"That's good." She nods. "I hope you'll find him."

"Enough about Aethon. This is *your* night. I hope you won't forget that your first dance is mine." He winks at her.

"How would I forget it? All the other girls will die with envy." Wyn giggles.

"Will they, now?" Thea asks, her tone skeptical.

Wyn gives Thea a knowing look.

"All the girls in my class have a crush on Cer. They'll be lining up in front of him for the next dance. Just you wait and see."

"Of course. He's mister popular after all," Thea grumbles.

Cer raises a brow at her, but she simply huffs aloud as she turns her head, refusing to interact.

"Someone had to inherit all the charm," he drawls seductively.

Thea swivels, sending him death glares.

The tension becomes thick as they engage in a deadly stare contest. Wyn and I blink in confusion.

"You're overestimating yourself," Thea says pointedly, rising to her feet and plopping herself in front of him. "I bet *I* can get more dances tonight than you."

Cer regards her with amused skepticism.

"And what will you forfeit when you lose?"

"I *will not* lose."

"Erithea, you have not had one suitor since your debut three thousand years ago. What makes you think someone will suddenly pay you attention?" Cer's tone is amused, but a flicker of hurt crosses Thea's face. Though I can tell he means it in a good-humored way, this is a sore spot for Thea.

"It's only because I never *wanted* one. If I put in a little effort, all the males will swarm around me," she declares confidently, pushing her chin in the air as she challenges him with her gaze.

"The bet is on." Cer laughs. "If you get even *one* suitor, I shall give you my salary for a month."

"Seven," she counters.

"Three," he concedes. "But make it *three suitors* by the end of this evening."

"Fine. You have yourself a bet." She crosses her arms over her chest.

"And should you lose, what will I get?" Cer's lips curl up, seemingly enjoying watching her squirm.

"What do you want?" she grumbles.

"You will do the chores around my house for three months."

Her eyes widen. It's on the tip of her tongue to refuse. I can see it. But she ends up agreeing to it, though she doesn't seem particularly pleased about the terms.

"It's almost eight," I announce as I point to the clock. "We should head to the ballroom."

They all agree, and I'm happy Thea and Cer haven't resorted to violence. They must have a pretty bad case of sibling rivalry from what I've witnessed so far.

We take the stairs toward the ballroom. The sound of a live orchestra already reverberates through the house, and despite my still rather confused state of mind, I find myself giddy at the prospect of a ball—and by the looks of it, it's going to be a ball like those I've seen in the movies.

As we reach the hallway leading to the main wing of the house, an unexpected sight greets us.

Ze.

He's dressed all in black, though his belt is now a deep purple, with the sheath of his sword an identical color. His hair is brushed back, emphasizing the symbols on his face.

I slowly raise my gaze to meet his, my breath leaving my lungs.

A visceral feeling stabs at my chest. My pulse is through the roof, and I find it hard to breathe.

Our gazes are affixed to one another, his purple pupils seemingly glowing in the dimly lit hallway.

Slowly, ever so slowly, his lips stretch into a smile.

To my surprise, I find that mine do the same, returning the smile with a shy one of my own.

He puts one step in front of the other. The proximity becomes maddening, my body humming with pleasure as he stops in front of us. He offers me his arm, and I take it.

A gasp flies past my lips at the contact. The heat from his body envelops mine, making the mark above my chest pulsate with a foreign need—one that is as confusing as it is all-encompassing.

I glance up at him to find him staring at me intently, his lips half-parted.

I lick my own in response.

"You look beautiful tonight, Luce." He clears his throat, as if he's forgotten how to speak.

"You look quite dashing yourself," I manage, fighting my way against acute breathlessness.

The dress is suddenly too restrictive. Too hot. Too...

God, I cannot take my eyes off him. My blood pounds furiously in my veins. Without even realizing, I get closer to him, rubbing my shoulder against his arm—all in an effort to absorb more of his heat...of his scent.

"Ze," I whisper, wetting my lips.

His pupils grow larger.

I don't know what I meant to say—perhaps ask him to whisk me away to some place and relieve me of this ache that seems to build inside of me, a tension that's ready to snap unless I find some relief. And for some reason, I know *only* he can give me that relief.

Leaning into me, he brushes his lips against my ear.
"You are staring," he murmurs.
"W-what?" I stammer, my throat dry.
"Do not stop. I like it."

SIXTY-ONE

"I don't remember anyone inviting you tonight, Ze," Thea quips, breaking the spell.

"I invited myself." Ze shrugs, not taking his eyes off me.

"You—" She takes a deep breath as Cer grabs her hand, a warning in his gaze. "The least you could do is acknowledge Wyn. She is the one we're celebrating tonight, after all."

Ze takes one look at Wyn and nods before going back to ignoring them.

"I hate him," Thea grumbles under her breath, followed by a stern reproach from Cer.

My body trembles with relief as the fog that's taken over my mind slowly dissipates. Relief fills me to the brim. Good Lord, what was that insanity? What the hell had come over me? I'm not sure what would have happened if Thea hadn't spoken at that moment. It's almost as if my body had a mind of its own, and only one purpose—him.

I remain silent as we continue on to the ballroom.

The doors open just as we arrive, the blinding lights from the chandeliers dazzling me. The music is loud and boisterous, as is the chatter that engulfs the room. There are refreshments and small bites by the side of the room, available for everyone to help themselves. Everyone is preoccupied with socializing, and so far no one is dancing—but I assume that may be because Wyn has yet to arrive.

In line with the rest of the house, the ballroom is a combination of marble and gold, with baroque-like wall decorations. There are marble columns adorned with golden leaves at every entrance, as well as friezes depicting battle scenes on each side of the room, high up where the wall meets the ceiling.

As we stop at the entrance, Maros and Rhea come forward to greet us. As her father, Maros takes Wyn's arm, leading her into the ballroom as the butler announces their arrival.

Everyone stops what they're doing to stare at Wyn and admire her dress. Whispers abound, and I catch wind of a few remarks—mostly positive. They're praising her beauty and the way the color blue accentuates her coloring. Yet there are also the off-handed comments, and they all come from one side of the ballroom. I hold onto the sound of those bitter voices and search them with my gaze, not surprised when I spot Elora and her band of bullies present. The king is by her side too, together with a few other people whom I assume to be in the royal entourage.

As Wyn and her parents go around the room to make introductions with all people present, the butler calls out our names and invites us to proceed inside—me on Ze's arm, and Thea on Cer's.

"What happens now?" I whisper to Ze as I let my gaze roam about the room.

"Arwyn and Cerenios will open the first dance. But first, she must finish her introductions."

"Maros and Rhea are taking her to meet all the men, I see," I note drily.

Although I suppose they'll have to greet everyone eventually, it's quite obvious that her parents are vying for the eligible bachelors first, more or less pushing Wyn forward to force them to notice her.

"It is my understanding they wish to see her wed before the end of the year."

"So soon?" I blink.

He purses his lips as he nods, and I get the impression there's more to that than meets the eye.

Ze takes me to the refreshment table, straight to the dessert section, and piles a plate full of chocolates for me before thrusting it into my face.

"Eat," he commands.

"Oh, thanks," I murmur, accepting it. Did I eat today? With everything that happened, I don't remember having much. And although chocolate doesn't qualify as food—technically—it is the one thing I can never refuse.

As I take a bite of the delectable truffle confections, I turn to look for Cer and Thea. After we came inside, they somehow disappeared.

"There." Ze points to the open doors that lead into the gardens. "They are there."

I don't get to question him for reading my mind without my approval as I note the tension between Cer and Thea. He grabs Thea by the shoulders, shaking her while telling her something. His jaw is clenched tight, his body tense as his fingers dig into her bare flesh.

"What's happening?" I whisper, worried. We've barely been here for a few minutes and they're already fighting?

"Something about a bet," Ze frowns.

"What about the bet?"

He licks his lips as he slides closer to me.

"You cannot proposition a male in the middle of the ballroom, Thea," Ze says in a somber voice, and it takes me a moment to realize he's repeating what Cer is saying. "This is cheating. The bet is off."

"I didn't see her proposition a male." I blink. If she did, damn, she works fast.

"You didn't say *how*, Cer. You're just salty you're losing," Ze continues, now changing his voice to a high-pitched one to emulate Thea.

Laughter bubbles in my throat at his acting, though even more amusing is the fact that Ze doesn't realize how funny he is.

"You know, sometimes Cer acts more like a jealous boyfriend than an overprotective brother," I add jokingly.

Ze narrows his eyes at me, silently glaring at me.

My smile dies on my lips.

"Cerenios should learn to ignore her folly. She is an inconsequential female in the grand scheme of things, and his affection for her will only bring about his downfall," Ze grits out.

And that is my cue to drop the subject. I can understand that a stickler for rules like Ze would disapprove of Thea for her past mistakes, but I don't see why he'd carry such a grudge for *centuries*. He really doesn't like her. And that in turn makes any conversation that mentions her uncomfortable. He might be my friend, but Thea is my friend, too, and I don't badmouth *any* of my friends.

We remain on the sidelines as I continue to silently eat my chocolate. Ze is faithfully by my side, his hand on my shoulder as he keeps me close to him, looming over me with his imposing height.

Yet even as we keep to ourselves, it's easy to see that Ze acts more or less as a repellent to everyone in the ballroom. There's a danger zone of a couple of meters radius that no one dares to cross, just because Ze is there. The space around us is eerily empty considering the ballroom is packed. And the few people whose gazes stray to us quickly look away and pretend to busy themselves with something else.

"I hate people," Ze grumbles when a couple scurries away, careful not to breach the *danger* zone. All the while, the man warns his date *not* to look at Ze—loud enough that even I can hear him.

"I think I hate people too," I mumble, once more incensed on his behalf.

"Do you want more chocolate?" he asks when he notices my almost empty plate.

"No. I'm full," I add absentmindedly as he takes the plate from me.

He nods slowly, but he doesn't take his eyes from me.

"Would you like some ale or wine?"

I shake my head, the taste of alcohol immediately inundating my mouth.

"No. I'm good," I mutter, doing my best not to retch.

"Juice?"

I shake my head again.

"Water?" he continues.

"No, thank you."

"Hot chocolate?"

Now, that gets my attention. And not because I want some—I've had enough chocolate, thank you very much. But because Ze is being odd.

Turning to look at him, I note his brows bunched together as he studies me.

"What do you want then? Tell me and I shall get it for you."

"I don't want anything."

"You *must* want something. Tell me. Whatever it is, I will get it for you." He lays his hands on my shoulders in assurance.

"I'm serious, Ze. I don't want anything. But thank you for asking."

"Not even a cow from your world? I could get you one—just the meat this time. It might take me a bit longer to go to your world and return, but I can bring it to you in...ten minutes?"

"Ze." I blink. "What's wrong with you? Why are you suddenly bent on getting me something?"

He pauses, watching me with trepidation as he bites his lower lip.

"You do not want anything?"

"No. I told you."

He takes a deep breath before he nods, turning away from me.

"Ze. Can you tell me what brought this on?" I ask as I pull on his sleeve, willing him to face me.

He doesn't, merely staring ahead. But slowly, he signals around us with his hand, pointing to the *danger* zone. It takes me a few moments to realize what he means.

My heart is in my throat, my mouth suddenly dry.

He was trying to distract my attention from the fact that people are openly insulting and avoiding him.

Just at that moment, the orchestra changes its tune, going into a melody that resembles a waltz as Wyn and Cer slide onto the dance floor, their feet moving gracefully to the sound of the music. Far from the tense look he sported previously, Cer is gazing upon his sister with brotherly adoration.

They twirl around the middle of the dance floor for the first few minutes before other couples join in.

"Let's dance," I suddenly say, grabbing Ze's hand and pulling him toward the dance floor. Maybe this will help him take his mind off those rude assholes.

A look of pure horror crosses his face.

"Are you mad, human?" He hisses. "I do not know how to dance!"

"Neither do I. But we can follow what others are doing. Come!"

He releases a deep sigh, but he follows me.

We take our place among the many other dancers, and Ze pulls me to his chest, fitting one arm against my lower back. We move slowly to the music. We may be slightly inept, but no one's laughing—and if they were, who cares?

The heat from his body is intoxicating, speaking of safety and comfort despite the danger he poses to my senses. It's an odd dichotomy, but whenever I'm with him, I feel untouchable.

A smile pulls at my lips as I regard him affectionately, my heart as warm as his embrace. His scent infiltrates my nostrils, a combination of musk and leather and a hint of an oriental scent, spice and smoke—all making for a tantalizing combination. I breathe him in, and a deep calm settles over me. The same spell that's messed with my mind before is starting to sink its claws into me again, making me lose all willpower when it comes to this man—all ability to say no.

"See, we can do it?" I murmur, tilting my head to the side.

His pupils are dilated, his cheeks sporting the merest hint of red. His lips slowly curl up to reveal a boyish smile as he lets himself go, enjoying the moment without a care for the world, for his reputation or how people perceive him. That doesn't mean it doesn't exist, though. Unfortunately, just like before, a *danger* zone forms around us. People avoid getting too close, and the mutinous stares abound.

"Just say the word, and I will destroy them." He leans in to murmur in my ear.

"W-what?"

"If they insult you, they insult me."

"And if *you* are the one they insult?"

"I do not matter," he replies evenly.

"Why would you not matter?"

"Because I do not." He shrugs.

"You matter to me." I smile at him.

His eyes widen. He ponders my words for a moment.

"Then I matter *only* if I matter to you."

We stare at each other for moments on end, the music an insignificant pulsation in my ear as the beat of my heart—of *our* hearts—becomes deafening. So much so, I have trouble breathing, a myriad of ant-like creatures furrowing under my skin and making me infinitely restless.

"I quit the Game," I blurt out, afraid of this moment and his effect on me.

He doesn't seem surprised. If anything, his smile deepens as he nods in appreciation.

"You have made a fine decision."

"You don't want to know *why*?"

"Because you are a sensible female." He nods.

"I clearly remember you calling me sense*less*," I add drily.

"Nonsense," he scoffs. "You are merely young and inexperienced."

I raise a brow at him. I guess this is a step up from senseless and foolish.

"You are impossible." I laugh.

At that moment, the beat of the music changes, and the pairs of dancers switch partners. I glance around in confusion. Cer stops in front of us, his hand thrust forward as he invites me for a dance.

"No," Ze states vehemently, more or less shoving me behind him while glaring at Cer.

"It is just a dance, Commander," he says wryly.

"Not with *her*. Go find yourself your own female," he grits out, baring his teeth at him.

"Uhm, Ze... It's fine. It's *just* a dance."

"No," he repeats.

Cer has an amused expression on his face, silently laughing at Ze's feral one. As they are engaged in a glaring competition, I scan our surroundings, noticing that Wyn is dancing with a different man. Thea, too, has a partner for this dance.

Aha! So this is why Cer chose me to switch with. All his other choices are already taken.

"Ze, seriously. It's not a big deal."

"I said *no*, human," he mentions to me in a softer tone before turning his attention back to Cer, his voice becoming harsh and unyielding. "Stand down, Cerenios. This is an order."

Just as I think this exchange is pointless since Ze is never going to get it out of his head that I can be his friend and *also* be Cer's friend, too, both suddenly stop, their bodies tensing.

"Demons have been sighted at the South Gate," Ze mentions. "They have already overpowered the guards and are heading for the palace."

"Damn it," Cer curses.

"We need to take care of it. Now," Ze commands, to which Cer nods.

Turning to me, Ze appraises me with his gaze.

"You will be safe here. I will return once the demons have been annihilated. Should you need me in the meanwhile, simply call my name." He doesn't wait for my reply. With a glance at Cer, they both vanish out of sight.

Since I'm the only person *alone* on the dance floor, I quietly retreat to the side. But seeing that I'm now without Ze, random people swarm around me to question me about him. Despite disliking him, they sure are curious about him.

"I heard he eats a god a day. Is that true?"

"Does he even sleep?"

"Oh my, does he sleep *with* you?"

The barrage of questions keeps coming, and surprisingly, it's mostly the women who have those curiosities. Out in the open, they snub him, but secretly, they wonder what it would be like to be with someone of his notoriety.

"If you'll excuse me." I force a smile as I elbow my way through the growing crowd, doing my best to evade these hypocrites. Ze is not some zoo exhibit for their amusement, and I have no interest in telling them *anything* they might use to start some new rumor that will paint him in an even worse light. To avoid more of the same questions, I make a beeline for the double doors that lead to the inner gardens.

I take a deep breath as I fit my back to the cold wall. I suppose no matter what world you're in, people will behave the same—be they mortals or gods. There's the same hunger for gossip; the same joy at someone else's downfall.

These damn people hate Ze so openly, but they're still hungry for more information about him. Due to him being so private and closed-off, I don't think too many things are known about him other than the fact that he's scary.

And that he can kill gods, which seems to be a skill not many have.

"Enjoying the party?" a voice asks from deep within the shadows.

I raise my brows as I search for the source.

Small, graceful steps reveal a lithe woman dressed in a red gown. Her hair is in a slick bun at her nape, her makeup sultry and heavy. Her green eyes are entirely kohl-lined in black, emphasizing the color of her irises.

"Yes." I nod, mustering a pleasant smile.

I assume she's going back inside as she walks by, but she surprises me by taking a spot next to me and leaning against the wall.

"The crowd can be a crush. I've never been a fan of these events, but Arwyn looks lovely," she comments.

As I was about to put my guard up thinking she's looking for more gossip on Ze, she surprises me with her kind remark.

"She is beautiful." My lips pull into a smile. "And she looks so happy. I'm glad the ball turned out so well for her."

"It is by far one of the most successful debuts I've ever been to."

"You've been to a lot?" I blink.

She nods.

"Hundreds. But that is to be expected at my age."

She doesn't offer a number, but the implication is enough to note she's old—very old.

"This is my first one. I've only been in Aperion for a short time."

"You are human, no?" She tilts her head to the side.

"Does that bother you?"

"No, of course not. I am not a snob. I have nothing against humans or any other mortal species. We have created them, have we not? Why should we look down on our creations?"

"I've heard that not many share your view."

"They are snobs," she scoffs. "And far too arrogant for their own good. We might be eternal, but we are not invulnerable. That is something that too many of my kind tend to forget."

"I'm Luce," I offer, extending my hand.

A smile curves on her lips.

"Anami. Pleased to meet you."

"What House are you from?" I ask out of curiosity.

"House of Psyche," she answers.

"Oh, do you oversee souls after they die?"

"Some do. Not me," she replies succinctly.

It's on the tip of my tongue to question her more. Nikki is still around in his soul form, and since I quit the Game, I'm anxious to know what more I can do to get to him. The letter mentioned that he is not with the House of Psyche, but that doesn't mean they wouldn't have more information—they are the soul guardians, after all.

"Oh," I murmur.

"Someone you knew died recently," she states. It's not a question. It's an observation.

I nod.

"Your...husband," she continues.

"Yes."

A sad smile tips her lips.

"My husband died, too. Many, many years ago."

"Can't you get him back? Since you're from the House of Psyche..."

"It does not work like that, unfortunately. There are two ways in which a god can die. One is due to an injury. When that happens, their soul can be salvaged. But if they die through the second way, it is permanent. My husband died through the second way."

"What is that?"

"Execution," she deadpans, her eyes meeting mine.

I freeze, and my intuition gives me a kick in the gut.

"Once a god is executed, their soul is obliterated. And that is because the sword used to execute them, *The Infallible*, is the only weapon in existence that can *kill* a god."

The expression on her face changes. No longer does she sport a kind and inviting smile; now there's only resentment.

"I should go," I murmur as I back away.

She's faster. Her fingers curl around my arm as she pulls me to her.

"Are you not curious who I am talking about, little human?"

"I know who you're talking about," I whisper.

"You know who he is—*what* he is—and you're still by his side?" She snarls.

"It's his duty. If your husband was executed, he must have done something bad..."

"You want to know *why* Azerius killed him? Because he refused to marry the chit the Supremes commanded him to. Because he chose *me*. That is why he had to die."

"I... I'm sorry. But your gripe is with the Supremes, not with Ze. He only enforces the rules. He doesn't make them," I say as I try to escape her hold.

"And yet, you remain by his side while knowing he is a cold-blooded killer?"

"I don't understand why you're telling me this. I have nothing to do with it."

"You don't? Think better." She smirks. "I am doing you a favor, little human, because it seems the unfeeling commander has finally caught feelings. But his ability for empathy continues to be nonexistent."

"I don't—"

She cuts me off.

"Tell me you haven't wondered about the coincidence of it all. Your husband dies and you magically get an invitation to The Wishing Game. And if that wasn't enough, you suddenly get a team of the most powerful gods in existence aiding you win trial after trial. Do you think everything was by chance?"

"What are you talking about?" My lashes flutter in confusion.

"Are you not curious how you got your invite to the Game?"

"I was desperate to get my husband back and—"

She laughs. She throws her head back and laughs at me.

"If only it were that simple." She shakes her head, her tone mocking. "When I saw him save your life after you fell from that bridge, I was intrigued. It was completely antithetical to the cold, emotionless Azerius I knew. He does not help people. He *kills* them. So if he went out of his way to save you, what else was he willing to do? Had I actually stumbled upon the one weakness the great Azerius had?"

My eyes widen. Ze saved me? He was the one who...

I swallow hard, my throat dry. One by one, her words start to make sense. It *had* been a coincidence that I got the invite, and soon after, three powerful gods teamed up with me and helped me pass the first two trials.

"*You* gave me the invite?" I ask in a tremulous voice.

She nods, a smug smile on her face.

"It confirmed to me that Azerius was in deep—far too deep. He was breaking rules right and left for you. So I just watched, collecting all the evidence I needed to end him. And oh my." She laughs. "Initially, I thought about reporting him to the Supremes so he could get the same treatment he doled out to others. But I think I have a far better punishment for him. One that will finally make him understand how I, and all the other people he hurt, feel."

A shiver goes down my back.

"You're going to kill me?" I whisper in horror.

"No, no. Nothing that dramatic." She chuckles. "But I will give you a gift."

I frown.

She releases my hand and I stumble back, rubbing my aching wrist. Opening her palm, she materializes a silver mirror in front of me.

"I will gift you the truth," she says as she hands me the mirror.

"What are you talking about?" I frown.

"This mirror will answer three questions for you. Choose them wisely. But if I were you, I would be curious to know what happened on the day my husband died. Was it really... an accident?"

I stare at her in shock.

She smiles. Taking a step back, she holds my gaze as she leaves me with one last bit of information before she vanishes.

"His sword can obliterate *any* soul. Even a mortal one."

SIXTY-TWO

Her words ring in my ear, the implication too surreal to grasp. No. Ze would never do that. He's *not* like that. Yet no matter how much I try to convince myself, the doubts keep clamoring inside my mind. I clutch the silver mirror in my hands, the temptation *too* strong.

What if this is a trap? If this is a way for her to turn me against Ze? She admitted to having a grudge against him.

But that is exactly why I'm having doubts...

She told me exactly who she is and why she hates Ze. She didn't lie about that. So that begs the question...is the mirror a lie? Or is it as she said...the truth?

There's one way to find out, I suppose.

Three questions. I must choose them carefully.

I take a deep breath. Before I can second-guess my decision, I gaze down at the mirror. Anami didn't say *how* to use it, but I guess just asking the question will do.

Biting my lip, I rehearse the question in my mind once before I utter it aloud.

"Show me how Nikki got his leg injured." Although this means I will waste a question, at least I'll know better whether to trust the mirror or not since I was there.

The reflective surface of the mirror is replaced by a screen featuring a video of the past.

We're walking hand in hand on the streets of Florence when a car skids to a halt next to us. The windows are lowered to reveal three guns aimed at us. Nikki's reaction is delayed as he pulls me behind him. The bullets start flying. He pushes me to the ground, rolling with me as he blankets my body with his. One of the bullets hits the back of his knee. The car then drives away.

The image fades.

Short and to the point. It's an objective representation of the past, but one devoid of emotion and depth. It couldn't capture the way Nikki tried to calm me down even as he was bleeding and freaking out himself. It couldn't replay the kind words he whispered in my ear or the warmth of his embrace as he held on to me.

He was the one who got hurt, but I was the one comforted. How was that fair?

A sob lodges in my throat as my own memory of the event surfaces in my mind.

Bar the nuances that the mirror could not capture, everything else is accurate.

And that is my proof that the mirror works. It is not biased either. It only shows what happened, not how, or why. It's as if someone filmed the incident but omitted the script.

Now that I know it can be trusted, I need only to formulate my second question.

I close my eyes, inhaling and exhaling as I speak my next question.

"Show me what happened when Nikki died," I murmur. My voice doesn't feel like my own. Hell, my own body doesn't feel like my own.

It's almost as if I'm in a bad dream that I can't wake up from.

My limbs tremble as I hold the mirror close, silently begging it to show me something different than what Anami suggested.

Ze couldn't have possibly had anything to do with Nikki's death. He didn't know me then—he didn't know *us*. Why would a powerful god get involved with humans? More than anything, is he even allowed to harm humans? From what I remember, he can only kill with express consent from the Supremes.

I stop short as I realize how many excuses I'm making for him. Yet just entertaining the thought that he could have hurt Nikki makes me lightheaded, a vise squeezing my heart in my chest and making it bleed.

I care about him. He's my friend. He cares about me too. He's shown it numerous times.

God! Why am I even doubting him? I got to know him well over the last few months, and I don't believe he'd be capable of this. Anami was just trying to mess with my mind. The mere fact that I'm interrogating the mirror about that seems like a betrayal of trust.

Yet just as I'm about to throw the mirror away, the image shifts.

There's a fire burning in the background as two young people embrace each other on the pavement.

Me and Nikki.

The car had already exploded, one part of it hitting me in the back of my head and causing me to pass out. Even with no agency, my body is next to Nikki's, holding on to him and shielding him as best as I can. There's charred debris all around us, surrounding us like a cocoon, but one that seeks to harm not protect.

We're both bloodied. The ground around us is stained with red.

So much fucking blood.

Immediately, my arms go slack, the memories of that day too powerful. They immobilize me as tears stab at the corners of my eyes.

God, I don't even want to *see* this, for it means reliving the worst moment of my entire life.

But the image zooms out.

The glint of a sword is the next thing I make out—but it's a sword I'm familiar with. Down the middle ridge, black blood pours from its owner, dripping down the groove and onto the ground.

The image zooms out more.

There he is.

Dressed in his typical black, a contrast to the white of the sword. His eyes are as they were before—black and unfeeling. And his tattoos...they're moving somehow, shifting on his face as if they had a life of their own.

He's just standing there, his expression cold. He's staring into the distance, ignoring the people behind him. Slowly, he blinks.

In the next second, he's gone.

What...

I inhale sharply as I feel a panic attack about to sink its claws into me.

What was he doing there? Why was he at the scene of the accident?

My knees hit the hard ground. There's suddenly a dearth of air. I gasp and gasp in an attempt to fill my lungs with oxygen, but it's all in vain.

Was Anami right? Did Ze have anything to do with our accident?

Somehow, I refuse to believe this.

Come on, Luce! Think about it logically! Anami also mentioned that his sword can obliterate a soul. It's not the case with Nikki since he's been by my side all along—from the moment I woke up in the hospital. He's still with me, so Ze can't have killed him...right?

Unless... No. It cannot be. He wouldn't betray me in such a way.

With trembling hands, I turn the mirror toward me once more.

The third question. The one that can confirm or deny

everything.

"Show me the identity of the man I was with in my room on the day I arrived in Aperion."

The image changes to my room at Thea's house. The door to the bathroom opens and I come out, naked. Particles of dust materialize in front of me and my heart lurches in my chest.

My breathing intensifies just as the shimmery black smoke takes the form of a man.

A sigh of relief escapes me. It's him. Nikki. It's his ghost.

Anami lied.

I don't know if my heart could have taken it should it have *not* been my husband.

The scene continues as he caresses me, the sight odd from an outsider's point of view.

But just as I'm about to put the mirror aside, the black smoke changes again. From a mass of chaotic particles, they turn opaque, gaining life-like features.

"No," I whisper.

A fissure appears in my heart the moment I see *his* face.

His body.

His touch.

He...

The mirror falls from my hands, a sharp noise penetrating the air as the glass shatters.

It was him. With me. Touching me. *Inside* me.

My God, I think I'm going to be sick!

I stumble to my feet, numb and disoriented. I sway from side to side, using my hands to prop myself on the wall as I make my way back inside the ballroom.

The image I just saw will be forever burned on my retina.

Ze. My friend. Lying to me and touching me as I have never given him permission to.

He...

A sob racks my body as I trip over one of the refreshment tables. The blunt edge hits me in the stomach, stealing my breath from me. Tears course down my cheeks as I grasp onto the table for support, breathing hard.

Nikki was never real, was he? From the beginning, this was a giant farce.

He's dead.

My husband is dead. He's...

No!

"No!" I cry out. No one hears me, though.

A round of applause erupts in the air. I turn slowly, watching as Wyn addresses the guests, lifting her glass in the air for a toast. I can't make out what she says, though. It's all foreign at this point.

She tips the glass, taking a big sip while everyone does the same.

I wish I could drown myself in anything that might take away this grief that's tearing me from the inside out. Worse than the first time I found out Nikki was dead, this time it's not just his death I mourn but also hope.

This is the end.

I catch sight of a row of bottles and, grabbing one, I down it in one go. The alcohol burns as it travels down my throat. I choke and wheeze, but I don't give up.

Make it go away, please.

One bottle down, more to go. I grab another.

Maybe in my attempt to drown my sorrows, I'll *actually* drown. But if I do, I don't want to go to the House of Psyche. I want Ze to cut me in two with his sword too so I can join my beloved in oblivion.

Together, we were everything.

Alone, I am nothing. So to nothing I shall return.

A loud thud reverberates in the air. Gasps erupt in the crowd, as well as a sharp, grief-ridden cry. And it's not coming from me.

Bottle in hand, I push my way through the throng of people, coming to a halt as I reach the source of the noise.

Wyn is on the floor, dark blood coming out of her mouth.

Her eyes are blank, unmoving. Thea is by her side, crying out as she shakes her.

"She's dead! She can't be dead!"

Chaos ensues.

TO BE CONTINUED

For more books in the same world, check out Barbi and the Villain and House of Cryos Trilogy.